FORGOTTEN PAST

He claims he's your husband—
but you don't remember him.
You know you're his wife—
but he doesn't know you.
You can't remember ... anything.
Jacob, Jane and Beth—
how can they
build a future
on a

FORGOTTEN PAST

Relive the romance ...

by Request™

Three complete novels by your favorite authors!

About the Authors

Barbara Kaye—Popular author of over fifteen novels, Barbara's latest project is the upcoming Crystal Creek series—she's written the launch title as well as two others! Barbara lives in Oklahoma with her retired air-force-colonel husband.

Pamela Browning—This bestselling author has written more than twenty novels. Pamela loves to travel and finds inspiration for new books whenever she does. She and her husband have two children and live in South Carolina.

Nancy Martin—A well-known name in contemporary romance, Nancy has published over thirty novels, including the bestselling launch title for the Tyler series. Nancy grew up in the Allegheny foothills, and after years of travel, has settled there with her husband, two daughters and her nonstop word processor.

FORGOTTEN PAST

BARBARA KAYE
PAMELA BROWNING
NANCY MARTIN

Harlequin Books

TORONTO • NEW YORK • LONDON
AMSTERDAM • PARIS • SYDNEY • HAMBURG
STOCKHOLM • ATHENS • TOKYO • MILAN
MADRID • WARSAW • BUDAPEST • AUCKLAND

HARLEQUIN BOOKS

by Request—Forgotten Past

Copyright © 1993 by Harlequin Enterprises B.V.

ISBN 0-373-20093-5

The publisher acknowledges the copyright holders of the individual works as follows:
HOME AT LAST
Copyright © 1985 by Barbara K. Walker
UNTIL SPRING
Copyright © 1989 by Pamela Browning
BEYOND THE DREAM
Copyright © 1985 by Nancy Martin

CONTENTS

"To be able to love only once was a character flaw. Her heart should have room for more than three people— her father, her daughter... and Jim. Always Jim."

HOME AT LAST

Barbara Kaye

For Bill . . . and Bill B., Debbie,
Bob, Laura and Susie.

PROLOGUE

ALL DAY LONG Leah had grappled with the feeling that something was terribly wrong. Now, as she shifted restlessly on the living room sofa, awakening from her nap by slow degrees, the feeling returned. Heavy lidded with sleep, her eyes opened, closed, then opened again. Afternoon naps had never been part of her life, but now, as she entered the final month of her pregnancy, she found it easy to drop off almost anytime.

She lifted her arm and looked at her watch. Four-thirty. She had slept for more than an hour. Her father would have left for the bus station long ago and wouldn't have wanted to waken her. Jim would be home soon, thank goodness. Just knowing he'd be with her tonight made her feel better, because she'd missed him more than she would have imagined possible. An odd uneasiness had settled over her as she'd watched that smoke-belching bus pull away from the station the day before, and it had stayed with her ever since. She chided herself. Foolishness! They had been apart only one day and night, but it was their first separation since their marriage, and the time had passed much too slowly.

Yawning lustily, she shoved herself to a sitting position, then stood up and slipped on the low-heeled shoes she'd kicked off earlier. Her swollen stomach seemed grotesquely huge to her, for she was a slender, small-boned woman and was carrying the baby low. *I'm tired of being pregnant,* Leah thought. *I'm anxious to be a mother. Anxious for a lot of things, actually—for Jim to get home, for us to move into our own place, for the baby...* Leah was just shy of her twenty-second birthday; it was easy to be impatient for the future.

Brushing away an unruly lock of raven hair, she crossed the old-fashioned farmhouse's parlor to look out the window at the overcast March sky. The grounds, so lush and green most of the year, looked bleak and rather forlorn at the end of winter. The big white house belonged to her veterinarian father, the only home

Leah had ever known. She and Jim had stayed on after their marriage, partly because it was so convenient for Jim. And mostly because the young couple had had so much trouble finding a suitable place of their own.

Soon everything would change. Five months ago they had found the charming place in Sedona, which they were still renovating. Now it was almost finished, in plenty of time for the baby's arrival. That was the reason Jim had gone to Flagstaff—one last buying trip to purchase all the little things needed to complete the job.

Leah left the window and prowled restlessly. She paused at the wooden loom that occupied one corner of the parlor. Her half-finished tapestry beckoned to her, but she'd been too edgy all day to concentrate on it. This feeling of disquietude made no sense, and again she attributed it to Jim's absence. A small laugh escaped her lips. Good Lord, from the way she was carrying on, he might have been gone for weeks instead of one day and night.

The house was too empty and silent, and unaccountably, she felt chilled to the bone. Hugging herself and rubbing her arms briskly, she went into the kitchen to brew a cup of tea. It was as empty and quiet as the rest of the house. She called the housekeeper's name. "Tee?" There was no answer. Then Leah remembered that Tee had promised to take soup to a sick neighbor. She filled the kettle with water and set it on the stove to boil.

A car door slammed just then. Her heart leaped expectantly. Turning off the stove, she hurried out of the kitchen and into the parlor in time to see her burly father walk through the front door. "Dad! Where's . . . ?" The words died in her throat when she saw his expression. His face was ashen.

"He wasn't on the bus, Leah," her father said in a shaken voice.

Her hand flew to her throat. "He had to be! You just missed him," she said irrationally. "Let's go back."

"Jim wasn't there. I waited until the last passenger got off."

"He . . . only missed the bus. He'll be on the next one."

"The next one isn't until morning. He would have called. You know he would have called, Leah. Jim wouldn't let us just sit here and worry."

She knew what he was thinking, and it was unthinkable. "No, I—" Her lips began to quiver as panic took over. Her eyes stinging with tears, Leah did the first thing that came to mind. She rushed to the phone, reaching for it with trembling fingers. "I'll call the motel in Flagstaff. There's an explanation. There has to be."

Her father moved quickly to her side and took the receiver from her hand. "Here, let me do it." His very real concern for his daughter was evident, as was his own fear. "You sit down."

"I can't sit down! How can I sit down?" Stepping back, she watched as her father placed the call. From his end she caught the gist of it. Jim Stone had never put in an appearance at the motel where he had made a reservation. Anguish ripped Leah apart, and the tears splashed and spilled, running down her cheeks into the corners of her mouth. *I knew I should have gone with him!* She made a little sound like a choked scream. *We'll find him. I know we will. Jim can't go away now, not now, not with the baby, the house...*

But even at that moment, watching her father slowly replace the receiver in the cradle and summon up the strength to look at her, Leah knew hope was useless. They would never find him. Jim was gone. The thing they had all dreaded—sometimes privately, sometimes openly—had finally happened.

Leah clutched a nearby table for support, placing her hand on her stomach as the baby began to kick violently....

CHAPTER ONE

JACOB SURRATT was in an uncharacteristically happy frame of mind when he stepped through the starkly modern bank's smoked-glass doors. Occasionally he experienced such brief moments when he felt young and unfettered instead of old and restricted. He never knew what inspired the moments, and they never lasted long, so he had learned to enjoy them.

He glanced around the unfamiliar bank lobby, unable to recall ever using this downtown branch; usually he conducted his business at the smaller one near the clinic. This morning, however, he had attended an early breakfast meeting at a downtown hotel with some of Phoenix's civic leaders. The bank happened to be nearby, and he was short of cash.

It was early; there were few customers, so he walked directly to one of the teller windows. The smile on his face was, for Jacob, an unusually warm one.

"Good morning, sir. May I help you?" The woman who smiled back was young, not too many years out of high school, Jacob guessed, and wholesomely pretty. The nameplate beside the window informed him that she was Donna Pierce.

"Good morning, Ms Pierce. I'd like to cash a check. I assume I've come to the right place."

"You sure have if you have an account with us." She glanced at the check he pushed toward her, then back at Jacob. "Dr. Surratt?"

"That's right."

"Are you the Dr. Surratt of the Surratt-White Clinic, by any chance?"

"Yes, I am."

"My boyfriend and I drove by your new place yesterday. It's really something!" She punched Jacob's account number into the computer on her right.

"Thank you. Dr. White and I have been waiting for it for some time."

"I told Doug—he's my boyfriend—that I sure would like to see inside the place, but I wouldn't want to be sick...or visiting someone who's sick."

Jacob smiled. "We're having the grand opening Saturday night. Why don't you and your young man drop by? I must warn you, though, it's a black-tie affair."

Donna Pierce laughed lightly. "Then I guess that leaves us out. Even if Doug had a tux, I'd have a devil of a time getting him to put it on." Her bright eyes raked her customer appreciatively.

Jacob Surratt was a tall, darkly handsome man in his late thirties, impeccably groomed and dressed in an expensive gray suit. His hair was thick and dark, as were his well-shaped brows; his eyes were a smoky gray, incisive and penetrating. The lean bone structure of his face played up its angles and planes, giving him a brooding, mysterious look that many women seemed to find irresistible.

Long ago he had grown accustomed to the kind of admiring glance he was receiving from the pretty young teller. Such attention neither pleased nor displeased him, for he was by nature very reserved, not given to flirting or idle chatter. Though as a well-known internist he was readily accepted within the upper reaches of Phoenix high society, most of his socialite acquaintances admitted they didn't know him well. Jacob, they said, was just too unknowable.

Donna Pierce finally tore her eyes from her customer and returned to the computer. Jacob propped an elbow on the counter, absently studying the lobby. The bank building was impressively beautiful, full of polished marble, wood and brass, great expanses of glass. Typical of modern downtown Phoenix, it screamed of money.

His eyes moved on—and that was when he spotted the tapestry. He was aware of a quickening of his pulse. An inveterate collector, particularly of Southwestern art, Jacob occasionally could "feel" a piece, and he felt this one. Being drawn to a particular painting, a piece of sculpture, anything unique and lovingly handcrafted, was not a new experience for him, but it was always exhilarating, something impossible to explain to anyone who had never known the sensation.

He stood transfixed for a moment, almost mesmerized. Yet the emotion the tapestry inspired was not entirely pleasant. He felt...for want of a better word, "anxious" in a very personal way. Something he had never felt when looking at a piece of art. Frowning, he kept his gaze fastened on the wall.

The weaving was large, possibly eight by ten, and it dramatically dominated one wall of the main lobby. The colors the artist had chosen were earthy Southwestern hues; the design a lone saguaro cactus set against towering buff, pink and crimson buttes. A cloud-filled summer sky backlighted the whole. The tapestry seemed to capture the heart, the spirit, the very essence of Arizona. The weaver had to be a native of the state, Jacob decided, someone who felt one with his or her environment.

He stared at the tapestry until the young teller's voice snapped him out of his reverie. He turned with a start. "I'm sorry, what did you say?"

"I asked how you wanted this. Will twenties be okay?"

"Yes, that'll be fine." While she methodically counted out the bills, Jacob commented, "I was admiring that stunning tapestry over there."

"Yeah, gorgeous, isn't it? I look at it all day every day and never get tired of it. Mr. Fletcher—he's the bank president— commissioned the weaver, then had to wait months for her to finish it. It's supposed to be quite valuable, but I don't know much about that sort of thing. I just know it's nice to look at."

Jacob took the bills, counted them and reached for his wallet. "I'm looking for something exciting and dramatic to hang in the clinic's reception room. I'd been thinking of a painting, but the tapestry is so much more eye-catching. Do you happen to know the artist's name?"

The young woman frowned thoughtfully. "Funny, I can't remember it, but I think she's famous, at least in Arizona. There's a little plaque on the wall, though, and her name's on it."

"Thank you, Ms Pierce."

"Don't mention it. Have a nice day, Dr. Surratt."

"Same to you. And if you and your boyfriend change your minds about the opening, you'll be more than welcome."

Jacob's long-legged stride took him across the lobby to stand in front of the weaving. It was magnificent. The work was meant to be viewed from a distance, but up close he could study the fine detail, the superb craftsmanship of the tight, even weave, the meticulously finished edges. The weaver obviously had been practicing the craft for some time. One didn't learn to do this kind of work in a few months, or even a few years.

He had to have one like it. No, something even grander. With any luck the artist was still active. His eyes traveled to the small brass plaque hanging unobtrusively next to the tapestry.

Designs by Leah Stone
Exclusively Through
The Alexander Trent Gallery
Sedona, Arizona

Once again something stirred inside Jacob, something so fleeting it took no form. Suddenly alert, he stared at the plaque. Did one of those names have meaning for him? Leah Stone? Alexander Trent? He waited for something, anything to take hold of him, but nothing did. Perhaps it was the place. Sedona? As an art lover he had heard of the community, but he'd never been there. At least, not that he knew of. . . .

Jacob gave himself a shake and passed a hand wearily over his eyes. He often wondered if he'd been wise to call a halt to the sessions with his partner. Charles White, the psychiatric half of the Surratt-White team, seemed to think so. "We gave it our best shot, Jacob, and failed, so do your psyche a favor and drop it." Finally, trusting Charles, he had terminated the therapy, convincing himself he was only wasting valuable time—his and Charles's. Yet occasionally the longing persisted, the longing to know. . . .

Jacob reached into his breast pocket for the pen and small notepad he always carried. Jotting down the information off the plaque, he turned to leave the building, but not before pausing to study the tapestry once more.

It called to him, as ridiculous as that was; it held a fascination for him he was powerless to explain. He owned a century-old Navaho rug, one of the most valuable items in his extensive collection, yet it had never moved him the way this weaving did. Why did the piece affect him so profoundly? Why had it aroused this peculiar feeling in the pit of his stomach? Why, on a day when twenty minutes one way or another would totally wreck his schedule, was he wasting precious time gaping at this weaving?

Jacob pushed open the doors and stepped out into the bright morning sunshine. Ms Stone doubtless had many admirers; well, now she had a new one. Artists intrigued him, anyway, since they were as different from scientists as light from dark. Sometimes he sought out one who particularly captured his attention. He knew he wouldn't rest until he'd met Leah Stone.

THAT NAME HAUNTED HIM for the remainder of the day, as names often did. This one, though, was different. He had seen or heard the woman's name somewhere; he just knew it. Later, in the solitude of his own home, he picked up some magazines and rifled through them until he found what he was looking for. There it was in last month's issue of *Art News Magazine*—a four-color advertisement for the Alexander Trent Gallery in Sedona. Superimposed over a shot of the showroom was the announcement that the Trent Gallery was the exclusive representative for Leah Stone. Beneath that a quote appeared from a review in the *San Francisco Chronicle*. "Leah Stone may well be the most gifted and original American weaver currently at work."

Jacob relaxed and closed the magazine. That was where he'd seen the name. He chuckled to himself and rubbed his eyes. He was going to have to stop overreacting to names and places, to almost everything that struck a responsive chord in him. All sorts of people had trouble with names and places, not only those with amnesia.

CHAPTER TWO

LEAH PULLED THE rocking chair into the center of the porch, sat down and sipped a glass of ice tea. Late May, and already the weather was very warm, portending another scorcher of an Arizona summer. She hated to see it come, for then the house would have to be closed up and air-conditioned most of the time. She much preferred the windows open wide, the earthy outdoor aromas pouring in.

Every afternoon, weather permitting, she sat on the porch and watched for the yellow school bus to come rumbling down the road. She still found it difficult to believe Nina would soon have completed the first grade. In some ways the first six years of her daughter's life had flown by; in others, they had plodded along.

"My God, you take motherhood seriously!" Alex Trent had said once when he stopped by unexpectedly and found her waiting for the bus. Leah chuckled, recalling her friend and mentor's reaction. Yes, she took her parental responsibilities very seriously, and with good reason. She herself had been a product of a one-parent home, but although she had been motherless since the age of five, she hadn't felt in the least deprived. Whit Haskell, her father, had always given her one priceless commodity—his time. She was determined that Nina would someday say the same about her.

Leah's gaze swept her surroundings. The view in all directions was of red rock spilling into evergreen hillsides. There was nothing subtle about the landscape; it was explosive, magnificent, and had served as a background for countless television commercials and Hollywood films. Often called "Zane Grey Land" because the famous author had lived there while writing *Call of the Canyon,* it was an area of sharp contrasts and incredible beauty.

"Where do you find your inspiration?" people often asked, and Leah always answered, "On my front porch." Something of the Red Rock Country found its way into most "Designs by Leah

Stone,'' and the rug she had just completed, commissioned by a group of Michigan tourists last winter, was no exception. Small wonder so many professional artists had chosen to live in Sedona. The entire countryside—streams winding beneath cottonwoods, red-sandstone buttes thrusting out of the earth, the smell of cedar and ponderosa permeating the air—was a natural work of art.

She never tired of it. Her quaint studio-home, which had once been a one-room frontier schoolhouse, was tucked way into the cedars, blending in with the landscape. The high-pitched roof afforded Nina the luxury of a loft bedroom to call her own. Otherwise, the house consisted of one huge room, a bathroom and a small kitchen alcove beneath the loft. In another more-conventional community, Leah's house might have been an incongruous sight, but in Sedona, where million-dollar mansions coexisted with rustic cabins and vacation cottages, it fit in just right.

Leah thought she would have hated a conventional house with a manicured lawn and a busy paved street in front. She much preferred the quiet country lane that was the only access to her front gate. ''That is a miserable chassis-rattling excuse for a road, Leah,'' Alex often complained. ''I don't know how you stand living out here.''

Her inevitable reply was, ''It suits me.''

Leah had been born nearby in the Verde Valley, raised by her veterinarian father, so she was a country person at heart. As a child she had often accompanied her father as he made his rounds of the farms and ranches. Her earliest ambition had been to be a ''horse doctor,'' just like him.

In her midteens, however, the artistic side of her nature burst into full flower. At an arts-and-crafts fair she watched a Navaho woman working at a primitive loom. Fascinated, she stood there for over an hour simply watching the weaver, unable to understand the fascination but knowing it existed. That very week she purchased a small hand loom and produced a set of place mats. From that time on Leah was hooked; she wanted to weave.

When she entered college at eighteen, it was to major in textile design and weaving, not veterinary medicine. After college she continued to live with Whit in the old family home, serving as her father's receptionist, answering the phone, scheduling appointments. But mostly she practiced and perfected her craft, weaving to her heart's content.

Her life had followed this orderly, peaceful course until Jim had come along.

Leah's thoughts braked, as they always did when she dropped her guard and allowed his name to enter them. The old emptying sadness washed over her. So much time had passed, but still the hurt remained. To be able to love only once was a character flaw, she thought. A heart should have room for more than three people—Whit, Nina . . . and Jim.

Always Jim. She could go for several days without thinking about him, but eventually something would trigger the memories. Now she supposed it was the time of year, the weather. You could smell summer in the air, and it had been a summer night eight years ago when she had first seen him. Closing her eyes, she expelled a shaky breath. Unbidden images filled her mind. Eight years ago might have been yesterday.

"You can't live in the past, Leah," Alex told her over and over again. Dear Alex, the gallery owner who had given her just the push she had needed five years earlier when her professional career was beginning. In the interim she had grown so fond of him, and he quite plainly adored her. She knew their mentor-protégée relationship would quickly change to something more intimate if Alex could have his way, but for Leah such a change was unthinkable. Too much of her was tied up in love and memories of the man she had married.

Once, when Alex had been totally impatient with her, frustrated by his inability to pierce her shell, he had shouted at her. "What is the matter with you, Leah? I find it impossible to believe you can remain so devoted to a man who left you just before your child was born!"

The strained, icy silence following that exchange had alarmed Alex; such an incident hadn't been repeated. They had reached a tacit agreement: her marriage was never to be mentioned. Leah discussed Jim with no one but Whit, because her father had been there and understood. He was the only person on earth, save Leah herself, who knew what had actually happened.

Enough of this, her mind scolded. *Stop thinking about it. Stop longing for what can't be.*

At that moment she welcomed the telephone's shrill ring; normally the sound intruded on both work and solitude. Getting to her feet, she hurried into the house.

"Hello."

"Leah, I want you to get over here right away." Alex sounded elated, the way he did whenever negotiations with a wealthy buyer had gone well, or whenever he stumbled onto a particularly fine acquisition.

"What's up?"

"I'll tell you about it when you get here."

"Alex, you know I like to be home when Nina arrives."

"This is important! Call your neighbor and have her intercept Nina. A very important client is on his way here from Phoenix, and he's anxious to meet you. There's a tremendous commission in the offing."

"Can't it wait an hour or so?"

"No, it can't. The client is a busy physician, but he's taking time from his schedule to come up here for the express purpose of meeting Leah Stone. He saw the tapestry in the Phoenix bank and wants you to do something for him. I think you're going to be very excited. Please . . ."

As always Leah experienced a twinge of guilt over balking at doing something he wanted her to do. Alex was so generous with her, so enthusiastic about her career. It wouldn't hurt to expend more energy on being generous and enthusiastic in return, even when she didn't much feel that way.

She glanced down at her working clothes—jeans, T-shirt and sneakers. It wouldn't do to meet an important client dressed like that. "Give me a few minutes to change, then I'll be there."

"Thanks, Leah. We'll be waiting."

First Leah called Sandra Martin, a neighbor whose daughter, Ann, would be on the bus with Nina. Sandra was also a single parent, also an artist, a sculptor. The two women had established a satisfying friendship, each knowing the other could be counted on for last-minute baby-sitting. Sandra had been married to a domineering, stultifying businessman known to Leah only as "that bastard," and her friend's unhappy memories of her marriage had given her a bitingly humorous view of love and life. Leah had come to depend on Sandra's cynical observations and colorful language for comic relief.

Once assured that Sandra would meet the bus and take Nina to her house, Leah quickly changed into a pair of off-white slacks and a softly tailored peach blouse, then slipped on a pair of low-heeled pumps—expensive, understated clothes that were typical of the unaffected Leah. Giving her appearance a cursory glance in the mirror, she picked up her handbag, leaving the house.

A short time later she strode across the sun-dappled, tile-paved courtyard of Tlaquepaque, the unique arts-and-crafts village in Sedona, designed in a Mexican style. Her heels tapped sharply on the tiles as she passed a fountain surrounded by potted marigolds.

Leah loved Tlaquepaque, as anyone involved in the arts would. There was no hustle and bustle; no one hurried. The charming complex of galleries, shops, archways, stairs and balconies invited strolling, browsing, lounging and sitting. This afternoon, however, she had no time for such leisurely pursuits. She wanted only to get this business over and done with so she could go home. Climbing a narrow handcrafted stairway, she ducked into the serene elegance of the Alexander Trent Gallery.

The first thing that always caught her eye when she entered Alex's showroom was *Gemini,* her maiden effort as a professional weaver. It had captured Best of Show at a fair five years earlier, but more importantly, it had captured the attention of Alexander Trent, one of the judges. When he had purchased it, naturally Leah had sought him out, introduced herself and told him about other work she had done. That simple gesture had spawned an association that had been enormously profitable for them both.

Alex often declared he would never sell *Gemini,* not in a million years. Leah smiled wryly. He would when the price was right.

A well-dressed, middle-aged woman was seated at the Queen Anne reception desk. Beth Thompson, Alex's secretary, glanced up and smiled warmly. "Good afternoon, Leah. I believe he's waiting for you."

"Thanks, Beth." Leah walked through the main part of the gallery to a door at the end of a short hallway. It was open, so she entered Alex's private domain.

"Well, here I am," she announced brightly. "As ordered."

Alex was standing on the balcony, hands clasped behind him, staring down at the courtyard below. He turned and smiled, then advanced toward her. Taking her gently by the shoulders, he bent his head and kissed her lightly on the lips. "Thanks for coming, Leah."

Leah glanced around. "Hasn't the doctor arrived yet?"

"Yes, but he had to call his clinic, so he's using the other office. Sit down and let me get you something to drink. I'm sure Dr. Surratt will be with us in a minute."

"Just ice water, Alex, please." She took a seat in a comfortable armchair facing a glass-topped desk, while Alex walked to a wet bar concealed behind louvered doors. "Surratt?" she asked. "The name sounds familiar."

"The Surratt-White Clinic. I'm sure you've heard of it."

"Ah, that Surratt. Of course I've heard of it." She was impressed. In the Southwest, Surratt-White was as well-known as the Mayo Clinic. This doctor who had taken a fancy to her work must be a VIP of the first order.

She watched as Alex took ice cubes out of a small refrigerator and plopped them into a glass. He wasn't a tall man, something under six feet, but he was trim and straight and gave the impression of greater height. His wheat-colored hair now showed definite traces of silver. At forty-three, he was fifteen years Leah's senior, urbane and utterly charming, a man of flawless good taste. A quick glance around his office, at the quiet elegance of the furnishings and objets d'art he'd chosen, attested to that. "Sophisticated" was a word often associated with him. In ten more years, Leah supposed, "distinguished" would be added.

Leah knew how much she owed Alex. She'd been blessed with talent and expertise in the technical aspects of weaving, vaguely aware of her work's worth, yet totally ignorant of the business side of the art world. By the time she met Alex, Leah had begun to realize she was going to need someone knowledgeable to guide her career if she intended supporting herself and Nina. She had introduced herself to him with high hopes and plenty of doubts. That he had placed considerable monetary value on *Gemini* had thrilled her. That he had wanted an exclusive association with her had been almost too good to be true, and she had seized the opportunity without hesitation. Never for an instant had she regretted that move. She could trace the beginning of her career's rise to the day she had approached Alex.

"Here you are, dear." Alex handed the glass to her before taking a seat behind the desk.

"I suppose you know I'm about to pop with curiosity," she told him, smiling over the rim of the glass.

Alex returned her smile with one of immense satisfaction. Leah knew that smile. It meant he had just struck an advantageous bargain. For all his polish and sophistication, for all his love of art for art's sake and his professed disdain for commercialism, there was some of the horse trader in Alex.

"As I told you," he began, "Dr. Surratt has seen the tapestry in the bank, and he called to ask if I had anything else you'd done. I explained you rarely have time for speculative work anymore, because commissions keep you so busy." Alex's smile broadened. "The doctor then informed me he would pay any price for an exclusive Leah Stone design."

"Oh? I'll bet your ears really perked up at that," she said with a grin. "Does he want something for his home?"

"Eventually the tapestry he wants you to do will become part of his private collection, but for now he wants it for his clinic. Surratt-White is moving into new ultramodern quarters, and he wants something for the main reception room. Fifteen by twenty."

Leah frowned. "Fifteen by twenty? I've never attempted such a large piece, Alex, you know that. I don't even know if it's possible on a ten-foot loom."

"I'm sure you'll be able to do it," Alex said confidently. "Dr. Surratt wants something dramatic, since the physical plant itself is so dramatic. He brought two photographs with him. . . ." He reached for a manila envelope, which he handed across the desk to Leah. "I want you to have a look at them. You have to be impressed."

She opened the envelope, withdrawing the photographs. The first was an exterior shot of the clinic; it was a space-age architectural marvel, a sleekly modern glass-and-steel structure. Beautiful, she supposed, if that type of architecture appealed; her tastes ran more to renovated schoolhouses. The second photograph was of the reception room, and it was also impressive. The vaulted ceiling rose two stories high, partly supported by one intensely dramatic—and stark—stone wall.

"According to Dr. Surratt, the wall on your left is where the tapestry will hang," Alex said. "As you can see, anything smaller than fifteen by twenty would be lost."

Leah nodded. Moreover, she thought, the tapestry would be the room's focal point, the first thing anyone entering the clinic would see. For a moment she dismissed the complexities of weaving such a large piece and visualized the design. Not clearly, of course, since she didn't know what the doctor had in mind, but it would have to be a bold design done in bold colors. Nothing subtle, nothing pictorial. The excitement that always accompanied a new effort began to bubble inside her.

"Dr. Surratt mentioned that the price is inconsequential, since he fully expects the tapestry to increase in value considerably. He's right, it will. I explained how long it would take you to complete such an ambitious work, and he seemed perfectly willing to wait as long as necessary. An agreeable man, I must say. Leah, this is exciting! Do you have any idea how many people must troop through that clinic in any given week? Far more than frequent galleries and museums, I assure you."

Alex's enthusiasm was met with silence. He waited a moment, but when Leah said nothing he demanded, "Well?"

"I'm thinking. I wonder... Perhaps it could be done piecemeal, then the pieces joined together. Of course, it mustn't look that way, but I learned a lot from repairing torn rugs and tapestries. Eventually I learned to make repairs not even experts could distinguish from the original weave. Why couldn't I sew together pieces of my own weavings?"

"Working out the technicalities never worried me for an instant. I knew you could do it." Alex glanced toward the open door. "I wonder what's keeping Dr. Surratt."

"Don't you ever watch those doctor shows on television? They're always making urgent phone calls or receiving urgent phone calls. I don't see how they ever get any doctoring done."

Alex faced her. "I might as well warn you about something, Leah. Dr. Surratt has invited us to the clinic's black-tie opening in Phoenix Saturday night. Why don't you get your finery out of mothballs, and we'll make an occasion of it."

Leah slipped the photographs back into the envelope and groaned. "Oh, Alex, you know how I detest that sort of thing!"

"I know, and you know I ordinarily accede to your wishes and shield you from such affairs, but this man is an admirer of yours, obviously one who knows a thing or two about quality and art. Who knows how many dealings I might have with him in the future? I'm also a businessman, fortunately for you. Surely you can forsake your hermitlike existence for one weekend to do a favor for me and give the doctor a thrill. He's paying plenty for the honor."

"I'd really rather not. Make excuses for me if he mentions it. Nina—"

Alex waved an impatient hand. "You can't plead parental responsibility with me, darling. I know Nina can spend the weekend with your father. Loves to, in fact. Do you have any idea how often you use the child as an excuse for not going places?"

"I never use my daughter," Leah protested. "I simply would rather be at home with Nina than at one of those silly, shallow cocktail parties you're so fond of."

"I'm no more fond of them than you are, but they're a necessary part of doing business. I've acquired more clients at those 'silly, shallow' parties than I ever have sitting here in this gallery."

"You're a businessman, of course, but I prefer to let my work speak for me."

"Don't be stuffy, Leah. Clients who pay through the nose for a work of art enjoy meeting the artist."

"I'm terrible at those parties, anyway," she persisted stubbornly. "I always find myself lurking in corners, trying to fade into the woodwork."

"Actually, you're delightful in social situations. People take to you even if you don't take to them. I suspect if you'd relax you might even enjoy some of those 'silly' parties. Look, I'm going to insist you go this time. You really should see the room. A photograph only shows so much. This is an important commission, the most important of your career. For once I took the liberty of accepting the invitation for both of us, so when the doctor mentions it, please be gracious. He's making reservations for us at the Biltmore. Why don't we drop Nina off at your father's place early Saturday morning and get down to Phoenix in time to enjoy some of that luxury?"

Leah shrugged resignedly. Alex was difficult to deny. In fairness to him, she admitted he normally bent over backward to get her out of such situations. The fact that he hadn't this time could only mean the opening was important to him. "Oh, all right," she said with a sigh. "I'll tell him how delighted I am to be invited. The Biltmore, hmm? The doctor goes first-class."

"Oh, he's a first-class type, all right, no question about that. Very nice and . . . well, 'refined' is the word, I suppose. I hope you'll like him."

She wouldn't get to know the doctor well enough to like or dislike him, Leah was sure. She rarely socialized with the wealthy clients who might have welcome her into their social circles. She got just close enough to ascertain their wishes and tastes, then retreated to her studio and let Alex handle the rest. "If I was to lead a wildly exciting social life," she had once asked him seriously, "when would I weave?"

"You simply need something else," he had replied just as seriously. "Your life needs other dimensions. I do believe you'd live like a hermit if I allowed it."

Usually Leah dismissed such remarks with "You don't understand." He didn't, not really. Alex probably wouldn't have recognized the Leah Stone of earlier times, a carefree, lighthearted young woman who had lived only for the day. Time and loss had changed her, as they change everyone.

Yet the changes, as far as she was concerned, weren't particularly undesirable. Was there something basically wrong with being a loner who preferred a solitary hillside to parties and people? Apparently Alex, who thrived on socializing, thought so. He could become so exasperated with her. He accused her of wearing melancholy like a cloak, of living on memories.

Leah realized she tended to be quiet and thoughtful, less than outgoing, but to define that as melancholy was going a bit far. And if she clung to memories…well, they were her memories, and she would have been lost without them.

Alex got to his feet. "Come over here, Leah. While we're waiting for Dr. Surratt, I'd like you to see a collection of porcelain miniatures I've just acquired."

Leah stepped over to a display table behind Alex's desk. The two bent over the miniatures, so they didn't see Jacob walk quietly into the room. He opened his mouth to speak, then quickly shut it when he saw the woman standing beside Alexander Trent. She had one hand propped on the display table, the other on her hip. Her back was to him so that he couldn't see her face, but the view from behind was of a lithe body that would feel good in a man's hands. She walked a few steps down the length of the table and picked up something. The movement of her hips beneath the fabric of her slacks elicited a sharp sensation in Jacob, reminding him that his responses were still in good working order.

Could that possibly be Leah Stone? Who else would it be? Ridiculously, he was content to simply stand there and watch her for a moment. Her erect carriage, her smooth arms, her glossy hair, those shapely hips, all came under his scrutiny. She made a little half turn, and the profile of a firm breast came into view. Trent said something to her just then, and she laughed—a lovely, lilting laugh that brought a smile to Jacob's face. Anticipation welled up inside him. He could hardly wait to get a good look at her.

Leah was intently studying one of the exquisite miniatures when she got the distinct feeling she was being watched. Carefully she set down the porcelain and turned. Alex turned, as well.

"Ah, doctor, there you are. Leah and I were just discussing the tapestry. She's very excited about it."

"Wonderful. I'm sorry it took so long, but there was a minor emergency at the clinic—monetary not medical." Jacob settled his gaze on Leah Stone. Her face intrigued him; he had met many women who were more beautiful, but this was a face he would remember forever. Perhaps it was her eyes—dark, haunting, compelling eyes that had a slight downward slant. They riveted him in place. That the person whose artistry he admired so much should turn out to be such an arresting woman was unbelievable. He had been expecting someone much older. How old could Leah Stone be? Less than thirty, he'd wager.

Leah froze as she watched the tall, beautifully dressed man advancing on her, hand outstretched. She went absolutely cold for an instant, then hot, and everything inside her coiled into a tight, painful knot.

"I'm Jacob Surratt, Ms Stone, and I can't tell you how delighted I am to meet you."

That voice! A knifelike pain shot through her. The past couldn't resurrect itself without warning, she thought senselessly. For a moment the room spun in a sickening revolution. How often she had imagined this very moment, but now that it was upon her, she felt as though she was hallucinating. This couldn't actually be happening!

Though everything inside her churned with turmoil, though her heart thudded against her ribs, Leah's only outward show of emotion was a sudden draining of color, a rigidity to her stance. Her hands clenched at her sides, but to the two men in the room she looked ill rather than agitated. Feeling so much, she could say nothing. In fact, at that moment she couldn't have spoken a word if her life had depended on it.

Jim.

CHAPTER THREE

WHEN SHE DIDN'T immediately acknowledge Dr. Surratt's greeting, Alex looked at her quizzically. "Leah? Leah, is something the matter?"

Jacob's brows knitted. The woman looked ghastly. Instantly the physician in him took over; he quickly closed the space between them. "Ms Stone, are you ill?" he asked with concern.

Leah thought she was choking. "No, I—"

Alex had moved closer to her. "Leah? What's the matter?"

Dazed, disoriented, she gave a little shake of her head. "I . . . don't know . . ."

"Please, Ms Stone, sit down," Jacob said quietly. "You're very pale." Taking her gently by the arm, he led her to the armchair she'd been sitting in earlier. Too weak to protest, Leah sank into it, only dimly aware of the two men hovering solicitously over her. She pressed the palm of one hand against her stomach, and she swallowed rapidly, fighting down nausea.

"Let me get you a glass of water, Leah," Alex murmured, frowning. She had been fine a minute earlier. He knew Leah better than he'd ever known anyone, and he suspected she wasn't ill. Sensing something very complicated was going on in her head, he shifted his worried gaze to Dr. Surratt, and his frown deepened.

Jacob rubbed her hands between his. "You're trembling. Do you feel light-headed? Have you eaten today?"

Leah nodded distractedly, avoiding eye contact with him. Her mouth was bone-dry. She would have welcomed that drink of water, but she feared she'd never be able to swallow it. She was ashamed of herself for losing control, but she had reacted so suddenly that there hadn't been time for thought.

Don't be ridiculous, Leah, it isn't him! How many times in the past six years have you seen someone you thought was Jim? Dozens! Pull yourself together, take a good look at him, and you'll see he isn't Jim!

Alex didn't bother with the water. He stood at the desk, staring at Leah's bent head, and a ridiculous sense of foreboding swept over him. Something was very wrong. She had taken one look at Jacob Surratt and fallen apart. What the devil was this all about?

Jacob knelt in front of Leah, and from somewhere she mustered the courage to look at him again. He was so much thinner than Jim and looked so much older. Compared to her Jim, this man was gaunt.

But, after all, six years had passed. The eyes were the same, only sadder; the mouth was the same, only harder. Jim had smiled all the time. This man looked as though he'd never known a mirthful moment in his life. The thick dark hair she had loved to feel between her fingers was now threaded with strands of gray at the temples.

Everything was the same, only different. The differences, however, were superficial, the products of the passage of time and a changed life-style. Leah's breath escaped in short, agitated puffs. This was one time she wished she was prone to fainting. If she could simply collapse, she'd come to in a few minutes and discover this all had been nothing but a wild, cruel flight of imagination.

But he was Jim, all right. The memory of his face was emblazoned on her brain. And he didn't know her at all. Dear God, to have been spared this.

Once her father had asked, "How do you think you would react if you were suddenly to come face-to-face with him, Leah? If he's from around here, you might. You'd be a stranger to him, you know."

She had answered, "I don't know, Dad, honestly I don't. I guess I'd fall to pieces."

Which was precisely what had happened. She was in a million pieces.

"Ms Stone, are you feeling better now?"

That was definitely Jim's voice. Sometimes it seemed she remembered his voice most of all. By an act of will, Leah forced herself into some semblance of calm. "I . . . yes, I think so," she said too softly. "I'm . . . sorry."

Relieved, Jacob expelled his breath. "Well, you certainly gave me a scare. For a moment there I thought you were going to faint. I don't normally prompt such a dramatic reaction in beautiful women." No one chuckled. The attempt at levity had been feeble, and Jacob regretted it. Leah Stone was obviously in distress. "Do you feel nauseated?"

"N-no." Which wasn't entirely the truth, but Leah knew her upset stomach had no physical basis.

"Then the doctor in me insists on asking if you have a chronic medical condition. Heart trouble? High blood pressure?"

Leah stared at her hands and shook her head. "No, no."

"What about that water, Mr. Trent?"

Alex tugged thoughtfully on his chin. "I don't think Leah needs a drink of water. How about a shot of brandy?"

Jacob was emphatic. "No, I don't think brandy would be such a good idea right now."

"No, I don't want anything, thank you," Leah muttered. "I'm all right." Jacob Surratt was so close she could feel the heat emanating from his body. He wore a tangy, woodsy, masculine fragrance very different from the scent Jim had always liked, and his clothes were expensive, possibly tailor-made. He made some kind of motion with his hand, and a flash of gold from his wrist caught her eye. He still had that watch....

Tightly she clasped her hands in her lap to keep herself from reaching for him. It wasn't fair! To be so near to him and unable to touch him wasn't fair at all.

Jacob stood up. "Mr. Trent, do you have a place where Ms Stone could lie down for a few minutes?"

Leah got to her feet and discovered she was almost in Jacob's arms. Flustered, she moved away. She needed time, time to think. She was a wreck. "No, I don't want to lie down. If you'll just excuse me, I . . . I think I want to go home. It's late. My daughter—"

"Leah, Dr. Surratt has driven all the way up here to discuss the tapestry with you," Alex reminded her firmly.

"I'm sorry, I . . . can't. Not today."

"Leah, please . . ."

"No, Alex," she snapped, more harshly than she intended. "Not today."

Jacob was surprised to realize he didn't want her to leave. He wanted to get to know her better. Never had he been instantly attracted to a woman—frankly he had suspected such an attraction was impossible. Yet he had responded to her immediately. Combined with that unforgettable face and those mesmerizing eyes was an air of fragility that made him want to comfort her. He, who normally held others at arm's length, felt a tenderness for her that made no sense. The sensation was peculiar but not unpleasant.

It had been so long since he'd felt much of anything, he reflected ruefully. Concern for the patients who came to him for help, of course. And a certain proprietary pride in his clinic. Otherwise, a wearying sort of sadness he had spent six years trying to shake. It felt good to want to be near this woman, to talk to her, to want to find out what she thought about . . . everything.

Then something occurred to Jacob. Trent displayed a decidedly possessive attitude toward her, and his concern right now was evident. Did they have some sort of special relationship, or was it based purely on business? And Leah Stone had a daughter. She was married . . . or had been married, maybe. One never knew anymore.

God, she excited him in ways he didn't completely understand. He was disappointed because she wasn't feeling well, but if they didn't discuss the commission today, he would have a perfect excuse for seeing her again, provided there was no husband in the picture.

"Ms Stone, I can see you aren't feeling well, so of course we'll arrange to discuss it some other time," he said quietly.

"Doctor, I can't tell you how sorry I am—" Alex began.

"Think nothing of it, Mr. Trent. It can't be helped."

Leah's head was pounding. There was no way on earth she could do that tapestry, and Alex was going to have a fit. Just how she intended explaining all this to him was the least of her problems at the moment. She couldn't look at her friend and wouldn't look at Jim again, so she simply stammered a goodbye, made for the door and left the gallery as quickly as possible. It wasn't until she was in her car and driving away from Tlaquepaque that she allowed the first tears to fall.

ALEX PULLED TO A STOP in front of Leah's house. Pushing open the front gate, he hurried up the path and mounted the porch steps. He rapped loudly on the door, then entered without waiting for her summons. Quickly his eyes surveyed the place. No noise, no activity. Only Leah huddled on the sofa. "Where's Nina?" he asked abruptly.

"Sandra Martin invited her to stay for dinner. Or rather, I asked her to invite Nina to stay for dinner." Thank God for Sandra. No questions, just a "Sure, Leah. Give me a call when you want her home."

Leah wasn't the least bit surprised to see Alex. She had known he would be along the moment he could get free. Less than half an hour had elapsed since she'd fled the gallery.

Alex crossed the room and faced her implacably. "Dr. Surratt stayed awhile after you left, or I would have been here sooner. I think I convinced him you simply had been working long hours and had probably skipped lunch. Frankly, I don't think your health was uppermost in the good doctor's mind. Mostly he quizzed me about your private life. All right, Leah, out with it. What's going on?"

"Leave me alone, Alex, please," she said wearily.

"You've been crying."

"Yes."

"Good God, what's all this about? You took one look at that man and... What is there about Jacob Surratt that made you go to pieces?"

"I want to be left alone!"

"No dice. Not until you tell me what that man means to you. I know you like the back of my hand, Leah, and I've never seen you so rattled. Who is he?"

Leah sighed, closed her eyes and leaned her head on the back of the sofa. She had known all along that when Alex started quizzing her, she would tell him the truth. He would have sensed in an instant whether she was lying. "He's my husband," she said numbly.

Alex frowned and stared at her a moment. He had expected anything but that. "That's preposterous!" he finally said. "That man didn't know you from Eve."

"I realize that."

"You realize that? That's it?"

"Jacob Surratt is the man I knew as Jim Stone, the man I married, Nina's father. You asked me, and I told you."

Shaken to the core, Alex again simply stared at her. His sense of foreboding returned, stronger than ever. He turned on his heel and paced, hands clasped behind his back. "If Jacob Surratt is your husband, why didn't he recognize you?"

"The answer is simple. Jim Stone was an amnesiac. I married a man who knew nothing about his past. I was always aware that his memory might come back, and if it did he probably wouldn't remember me. But I loved him, and I married him, anyway."

Alex digested this. "Why haven't you ever told me before? I thought your husband was a creep who'd deserted you. I never could understand why you clung so tenaciously to his memory, why you never filed for divorce."

She stared at him blankly. "Why would I file for divorce?"

"Dammit, you might want to remarry!"

"Never. In another year he'd be declared legally dead, anyway, so what difference would it make? Alex, I don't like talking about this!"

"Well, you're going to have to talk about it. I want the whole story, and I'm not leaving until I get it."

And he wouldn't, Leah knew. Lifelessly her shoulders rose and fell. "All right. I guess I owe you that much. I put on some water to boil a while ago. Make us some coffee, will you? There's instant in the—"

"I know where it is." Alex shrugged out of his suit jacket and threw it across a nearby chair. Loosening his tie, he made for the kitchen alcove tucked into one corner of the house. Within a few minutes he was back carrying two cups. He set them on the coffee table, then took a seat beside Leah on the sofa and waited until she was ready to talk.

When she began, it was in a tired, emotionless voice. "It was summer, eight years ago. I was twenty... I had just graduated from college and was living with dad. One night we were sitting on the porch after dinner, when a pickup truck stopped in front of our house. A young man got out of the passenger side, and the truck moved on. The man had thumbed a ride, he told us. He needed a job and had heard Dad was looking for someone he could train to be a veterinarian's assistant. For some reason he thought he would like that kind of work."

Leah paused to take a sip of coffee. "He was handsome, clean-cut and personable, and he said his name was Jim Stone. I remember wondering what such a prosperous-looking man was doing combing the countryside for work, but Dad was immediately impressed with him and asked him to sit down and have coffee with us. Then Jim Stone told us more about himself.

"He wanted us to know he was a victim of amnesia. Several weeks earlier he'd woken up in a small valley hospital unable to recall his name or what he was doing in the Verde Valley—or in Arizona, for that matter. Two policemen were at the hospital with him, and they filled in a few details."

Leah sighed, struggling with her memories. Struggling, too, with her feelings for Alex. This was going to hurt him.

Alex watched her carefully; it was on the tip of his tongue to tell her to forget about the rest of her story. Obviously she was finding the recollection painful. But he was too interested, unwillingly fascinated. Silently he waited for her to continue.

"During a late-night stop at a grocery-gas station on a desolate stretch of highway, Jim had been struck on the head from behind by a person or persons unknown; his car had been stolen, too. The store owner ran outside when he heard the screech of tires in the driveway—he thought someone was leaving without paying for gas—but all he saw was Jim lying facedown near one of the pumps. He didn't witness the crime nor see the car.

"The victim had no money or identification on him; apparently everything had been in the car. He'd been wearing an expensive watch with the initials 'JS' engraved on the band, thus the name Jim Stone, the first thing that had come to mind. His clothes were casual but expensive. He remembered nothing, knew nothing of his past. He'd been doing temporary odd jobs around the valley, but he really needed permanent employment. For one thing, he had a hospital bill to pay. He wanted to know if Dad would take a chance on him."

"And Whit did?"

Leah nodded. "Dad just took a liking to Jim for some reason. I had reservations at first. We knew so little about him. I reminded dad that the man could be an ax murderer for all we knew, but Dad liked him so he put him to work.

"Jim turned out to be almost too good to be true. He seemed to have an instinct for working with animals. He got along with their owners, too, which wasn't always easy. He didn't mind the odd hours and wasn't the least bit squeamish about even the nastiest medical task. Dad gave him a room in the back of the big house, and in a few weeks it seemed he had been with us for years."

"And in all that time he hadn't remembered anything?"

"No, nothing. At first we were certain his memory would return, but weeks passed, then months, and nothing happened. The police didn't have much to go on, since they didn't know what kind of car to look for. We hoped the watch might be a lead, but though it was expensive it was also a brand name sold in many jewelry stores throughout the country. Nothing turned up in Arizona at any rate, so where did we go from there? Jim could have bought the watch years before, almost anywhere in the world. About all we could do was monitor the missing-persons bulletins and hope something turned up. Nothing did, though, and Jim finally admitted he'd lost his enthusiasm for the search. He was happy and content. Besides..." Leah faltered.

"Besides," Alex finished sagely, "he'd fallen in love."

Her lips trembled. "Yes," she said quietly. "And so had I."

It was impossible for Leah to tell Alex about falling in love with Jim. That was the most private, intimate part of her life. In retrospect, the attraction seemed to have been immediate, although in the beginning they had only been good friends. He had simply been the nice young man who worked for her father, and she had sympathized with his emotional stress, with his need to know about his past. Sometimes he had reminded her of a rewarped loom or a blank canvas, waiting for a loving hand to give it shape, form, meaning.

Together she and Jim often speculated on what kind of life he'd led before the accident. He hadn't been a laborer; she could tell that much by his hands. He must have made a good living, though, judging from the watch and his clothes. His manners were gracious, almost courtly, and his speech was educated. He hadn't grown up on the street, that was for sure. Since he didn't know how old he was, they settled on a vague thirty.

Jim was such a gentle and sensitive man. He admired her work; in the evenings he was content to sit silently and watch her weave. They often took long walks together, and she taught him to ride a horse. A country vet, she laughingly told him, needed to know how to ride a horse, because sometimes that was the only way to get to the patients.

The first time Jim kissed her, they were riding along the riverbank. She felt as though she'd never been kissed before, and in that instant she knew she wanted to stay with him forever; there wasn't any doubt in her mind. As their lovemaking progressed, he opened up a brand-new world of sensuality to her....

Leah felt a fresh supply of tears welling up then. She sat mutely for a few minutes, staggered by the memory of all she had lost. Presently Alex touched her gently on the arm, and her eyes flew to him; she had completely forgotten he was there. "Oh, I'm sorry."

"That's all right, Leah. No more."

"No, I want to tell you everything." Collecting herself, she went on. "By the time Jim had been with us six months, we were in love and talking about marriage. We discussed it with Dad, and the three of us agreed it was risky. After all, Jim's memory could return at any moment. What if there had been a wife and family in his former life? Jim argued that someone would have been looking for him in that case. We'd stayed in close touch with the police, and no one fitting his description had been reported missing. Jim's theory was, he'd been moving from one town to another, had broken all ties in the old place and not yet made any in the new. It was as good a theory as any, I suppose, and I was ready to accept almost anything.

"Then Dad came up with another problem. He had discussed Jim's condition with a physician friend and had learned something about amnesia. Jim was going through what was called a 'fugue state.' So that if his memory did return, it was entirely possible he wouldn't remember anything that had happened during the fugue period. Highly likely, in fact. Dad was worried about where that would leave me."

"Weren't you?" Alex asked sensibly.

Leah shook her head. "I was young and in love, and Jim was so sure nothing could happen to keep him from me. Anyway, in the end love won out...and Jim and I were married. By late summer I was pregnant. We decided we wanted a place of our own, and that's when we found this abandoned schoolhouse. It was farther from Dad's house and Jim's work than we had originally intended, but we fell in love with it and were determined to have it renovated before the baby came....

"I've never been as happy as I was then. I was wildly in love with my husband and could hardly wait to become a mother. My work was going well. About that time I started *Gemini.*"

Again she faltered, and Alex grew tense. He sensed she was coming to the conclusion of her incredible story. Her eyes were distant and vacant. Deliberately she picked up the coffee cup, took a sip, grimaced and set it down again. Taking a deep breath, she began to speak in a voice that, to Alex's ears, didn't sound quite like Leah's.

"A month before Nina was born, the house was almost finished, but we needed a long list of items we couldn't find in the valley. Traveling had become an ordeal for me, so Jim decided to take a bus to Flagstaff for one last buying trip. He planned to be gone a day and a night. He was carrying three hundred dollars in cash and a small suitcase. I stood at the bus depot, waving goodbye, so upset because it was our first separation. And...that was the last time I saw him until this afternoon.''

Leah's body sagged. The silence that descended was like a third presence in the room. Alex, tight-lipped, exhaled on a ragged sigh. Considering the story he'd just heard, he thought Leah had handled her confrontation with Jacob Surratt rather well. What a jolt it must have been! He was surprised she hadn't dissolved into hysterics.

No, that wasn't true. Alex couldn't imagine Leah in hysterics, ever. He turned to her, wishing he could take her in his arms, knowing it would be the worst thing he could do. She seemed bereft, beyond his reach. "Surely you tried to find him.''

"Of, of course,'' she said sadly. "I was frantic when he didn't come back. Dad and I met every bus from Flagstaff for days, which was ridiculous, but we had to do something. I kept telling myself he'd simply been delayed, but that was also ridiculous. He would have called. We telephoned the motel where he'd made reservations and was told he'd never shown up. So Dad and I drove to the bus station in Flagstaff and discovered his suitcase hadn't been claimed. His wallet was inside with the brand-new driver's license I had finally nagged him into getting. He hated carrying a wallet, so he kept his cash in a money clip, which was probably the reason there had been no identification on him when his car had been stolen.''

Leah's voice broke. She flicked at a tear with a forefinger. "I had to face it—Jim's memory had somehow returned, and he'd gone back to his former life, having forgotten me entirely. Dad and I checked with the police for months afterward, but I never really held out too much hope. I knew what had happened.''

"Didn't you circulate a photograph of him to the newspapers?''

"I didn't have a photograph, only a couple of not very good snapshots taken at a Fourth of July picnic. And, too, we didn't know what kind of life he'd gone back to. If he had a wife and family, broadcasting his face all over the place might have been a terrible embarrassment for him. Think of the dilemma—two families. Jim wouldn't have even known me. Dad and I discussed it and decided against it.''

"What . . . did you do then?'' Alex asked quietly.

"I stayed with Dad until after Nina was born. He was so worried about me, and I wasn't in the mood or condition to live alone. When I felt up to it, I finished this house and moved into it. Nina was four months old. Dad thought I ought to get rid of it entirely, but I wouldn't hear of it. Nina and this house were all I had left of Jim. Eventually I finished *Gemini,* entered it in that fair, and . . . well, the rest you know."

"Ah, Leah. . . ." Alex sighed, shaking his head. "Are you absolutely sure Surratt is your husband? A lot of time has passed, and the mind can play tricks."

"Yes, I'm sure. I remembered everything—the shape of his eyebrows, the tiny mole to the right of his mouth. But his voice most of all. Voices just don't change. The worst part was not knowing what had happened to him. I used to think . . . if I just knew he was all right, that he was well and happy, it would be better. But it isn't. Seeing him again was awful. He didn't recognize me at all, yet I wanted to throw myself into his arms. I . . ."

"Nina looks like him," Alex mused.

"Wh-what?"

"Nina. I always thought the girl looked exactly like you, but now that I know, I can see a lot of Jacob Surratt in her."

"Oh, Lord!" Leah faced Alex, her eyes earnest and pleading. "Alex, I can't do that tapestry. I simply can't! And I certainly don't intend to go to Phoenix this weekend. You understand that, don't you? I can't undertake a project that might bring me into contact with him again. He's probably married and has a family. I don't want to know anything about Dr. Jacob Surratt. I just want to be left with my memories of Jim Stone."

Alex slapped his knee and got to his feet. "Leah, as a man who loves you, I'm so tempted to forget the tapestry, but that would be dishonest of me. As the man who has guided your career, I can't let you refuse this commission. It's much too important."

"I won't do it! Make excuses for me. Say I have too much work, say I need a vacation and am going away. Say anything, I don't care, but get me out of it. I can't do it."

"Leah, darling, listen to me. I've always known what's best for your career, and I have a feeling about this tapestry, that it will lead to such grand things for you. Forget about the opening. It isn't that important, but the tapestry is. I'll act as go-between. You'll never have to see Jacob Surratt again, I promise, but don't turn down this commission. My God, more than ever I should think you would want to stay busy."

Leah put her head in her hands. Alex was right. School would be out for the summer in a few days, and Nina would want to spend most of her time at Whit's, playing with the animals and accompanying her grandfather on his rounds. This was a sacrifice Leah made for Nina, for she much preferred having her daughter with her. However, she thought it imperative that Nina acquire a deep sense of family, particularly since the child's family consisted only of a mother and a grandfather.

So summer would be a time of even greater solitude than usual. If ever she needed to stay busy it would be then, and a project like the tapestry would require months of eight-hour days, working four hours at a stretch. Usually when she was working she forgot everything else; only Nina came before the interplay of warp and weft. She supposed Dr. Surratt's weaving would actually be a blessing . . . provided she didn't have to see him.

She had to remember that Jacob Surratt was not Jim Stone. Jim was gone forever now, and she didn't even know Jacob. "All right," Leah said quietly, "but only under those circumstances. I don't care what you have to do. Tell him I'm a temperamental artist who throws tantrums if a client comes near while I'm working. Just keep him away from me, Alex."

"Oh, my dear, you can be very sure I'll do that."

Leah lifted her head and shot him a quizzical look. Alex smiled sadly. "You fell in love with him once. You might again. He...he isn't married."

"How do you know that?"

"He told me. Quite casually in conversation he mentioned he was a bachelor. And he asked if you're married. I . . . wonder if it was wise to tell you that."

Leah's eyes clouded; it seemed as though her heart weighed fifty pounds. "It doesn't matter, Alex. Dr. Surratt isn't Jim."

CHAPTER FOUR

LEAH SUPPOSED she should have invited Alex to stay for supper; ordinarily she would have. But tonight she wasn't in the mood for food and conversation. She hoped he understood. He was so good and patient with her, and he deserved more than she could give him. If she had accepted one of his many proposals of marriage two, three years ago, how would she feel now after seeing Jim again? She didn't even want to think about that.

She heated some soup and made do with that for supper, then called Sandra and waited for Nina to come home. She forced herself to be cheerful for Nina's sake, but apparently she didn't do a very good job of it. Nina immediately sensed her mother was upset.

"What's wrong, Mama?"

"Oh . . . I'm just a little sad, honey, that's all."

"Why?"

"I, ah, saw someone today, someone I used to know."

"And that made you sad? Why?"

"He's . . . changed a lot."

"Oh," Nina said, and shrugged away incomprehensible adult behavior.

Her daughter's usual bedtime routine took Leah's mind off the day's incredible events for a time, but finally it was late, Nina was asleep, and Leah was alone with her thoughts.

So often in the past she had fantasized about seeing him again, and the fantasies had taken many forms. In a favorite, she first spied him from afar. After recovering from surprise, she approached him. He stared at her in startled confusion; then recognition slowly dawned. Their reunion was so poignant.

In another, less-pleasant fantasy, a wife and children were in the picture.

Now Leah had actually seen Jim, and neither of her fantasies had materialized. He hadn't recognized, her, and he wasn't married.

He isn't married....

They had guessed his age fairly accurately eight years ago, she mused. He must be in his late thirties now, and every bit as handsome as she remembered. But so urbane, so elegant, so somber. Jim had been casual and relaxed, jovial. Leah recalled the sadness she'd seen in Jacob Surratt's eyes. What had put it there? He wasn't a man at peace with himself.

A doctor. No wonder Jim had taken so readily to his job as Whit's assistant. No wonder the fine manners, the educated speech, the expensive watch and clothing. And he was no ordinary doctor, either, but the Dr. Surratt of the famous clinic bearing his name. Leah frowned. The clinic had been open for years, originally known as merely the Surratt Clinic, probably begun by Jim's—Jacob's relatives. A prominent physician didn't simply disappear for two years. The event ought to have been headline news; in the area, at least.

Why hadn't anyone been looking for him? What had happened on that bus, or in Flagstaff, to cause his memory to return? What a jolt that must have been! Had he ever tried to find out about the two years missing from his life?

Leah sighed. So many questions, and she would never know the answers to any of them.

It had grown late. The house was completely dark, but she hadn't bothered to turn on any lights. Slowly she paced through the house, thinking of the past six years she'd spent alone, longing for what she had had with Jim, raising their daughter. They had been difficult, uncompromising years with only a few bright spots. Nina, of course, was the joy of Leah's life, and her own father had admirably tended to parenting duties above and beyond the call of duty. And there had been her work, a source of pride and satisfaction. Yet a void had remained that nothing and no one could fill.

Odd, she had sometimes experienced an eerie feeling he was near. Perhaps he had been. She often went to Phoenix for one reason or another. They might have been in the same shop or restaurant—

The ringing of the telephone startled her. It would be Alex, of course, calling to see if she was all right. Everyone should have such a friend, Leah thought as she walked to the phone beside the sofa bed. Steadying herself, she picked up the receiver, determined not to worry Alex anymore.

"Hello."

"Feeling better, Ms Stone?"

Leah's heart plummeted to her feet. "Dr. Surratt."

"Why, you recognized my voice. I'm flattered."

"It's . . . it's distinctive," was all she could think to say.

"You sound much better."

"Yes, I feel much better, thank you."

"Ms Stone . . . ah, may I call you Leah?"

"Of course."

"Leah, I took the liberty of getting your number from directory assistance. I hope you don't mind. It occurred to me that I neglected to mention the clinic's official opening Saturday night. I wondered if perhaps Mr. Trent told you about it."

"Yes . . . Alex mentioned it, but I'm afraid I won't be able to make it, Dr. Surratt." She couldn't even come up with a plausible excuse. Her mind wouldn't function properly. This was terrible! When she couldn't see him, when she only could hear his voice, he became Jim. Leah sank to the edge of the sofa.

"Oh? I'm terribly disappointed. Won't you please reconsider? I thought that would be the perfect time to discuss the tapestry."

"I'm sorry, but . . . I can't."

Jacob persisted. "Another time, perhaps? The clinic is closed on Wednesday afternoons. That's tomorrow. I normally play golf, but I can easily cancel that. I could be at your place by one o'clock."

This was unlike him. He couldn't imagine how he'd mustered up the courage—or gall—to be so persistent. A no from a woman had always meant just that; never before had he been sufficiently interested to pursue a reluctant female. But the desire to see Leah Stone again was so strong he would even risk seeming obnoxious. Until that afternoon he had never given credence to the existence of an instant bond between two people. Chemistry was one thing, but all that "across a crowded room" nonsense only existed in sentimental love songs, or so he had believed. So how else could he explain this attraction to her? "Would one o'clock be all right, Leah?"

Oh, God. What could she say? Too many tangled emotions were bundled up inside her, too many conflicts she was incapable of dealing with rationally. To have him in this house, the house the two of them had spent countless hours building, would be more than she could handle.

Suddenly something in Leah's head snapped, and her mind simply made a 180-degree turn. Her resolve never to see him again crumbled like clay. Why not invite him to the house? What if he remembered? Was it even reasonable to think he might? If seeing it jogged his memory she might have Jim back again. He had loved this funny little house so much.

But he had loved her so much, too, and seeing her hadn't brought on a flicker of recognition.

"Leah?"

Did she dare? Did she even have the right to tamper with something she didn't at all understand? Wasn't it worth the chance...? "Oh, I, well, I suppose tomorrow afternoon would be fine...Jacob. I'll wait on you for lunch if one o'clock isn't too late for you to eat." Her pulses were pounding.

She thought she heard him breathe a relieved sigh. "That sounds wonderful. I'm looking forward to it. Could you give me directions to your house?"

Leah did; then they said goodbye. When she hung up she was trembling all over.

Six years of being a single parent had made her self-reliant, she had thought. She was accustomed to making her own choices, her own decisions. She set her own hours, disciplined her time and depended on no one for support or assistance. Save for allowing Alex to handle the marketing of her work, she controlled her life.

She didn't feel in control now. Events were swirling unchecked all around her. She had just made the decision to see this doctor, her husband, again, and somewhere in the dim recesses of her mind she suspected she would want him to eventually recognize her, to remember, to love her the way he once had. If they could recapture that, she might erase the haunting sadness from Jacob Surratt's eyes.

Leah could only pray she was doing the right thing. She would never want to harm him. In a daze she stood up and took the cushions off the sofa, stacking them nearby before folding out the bed. In the dark she undressed, putting on a pair of tailored pajamas and recalling how long it had been since she'd felt the urge to wear something frilly and feminine to bed.

What she needed was a good night's sleep. She would be able to think more clearly in the morning...she hoped. "Cope" would be the watchword, although at this particular moment, Leah had never felt less able to cope with anything, least of all Jacob Surratt's bewildering appearance in her life.

AT SOME POINT during a fitful night of reenacting her marriage to Jim, something had occurred to Leah: even if Jacob recalled their life together, did she think for a minute he would prefer it to the life of a prominent, respected, sophisticated physician? Of course not, but her easygoing, private existence with Jim was what she still longed for. So what on earth had prompted her to invite Jacob here?

A sensible part of her brain reminded her that human nature being what it was, she probably would have found it impossible not to do so.

Leah climbed out of bed filled with an inner agitation that twisted her stomach into a knot. All of the instant clarification she had hoped would come with the new day didn't materialize. In a few hours Jim would be here—here! Only he wouldn't be Jim. She wondered how she was going to get through the day.

Somehow she managed her and Nina's usual early-morning routine, and the moment she had seen her daughter off on the school bus she telephoned Whit, only to be told he was out making calls and would be gone most of the day. Leah didn't leave a message for him to return the call. On second thought, she decided it might be better to talk to her father later, after she'd seen Jacob and had some clear-cut idea, she hoped, of what she was going to do—if anything.

Trying to stay busy, she vacuumed the house, dusted everything in sight, arranged and rearranged pillows and knicknacks. Still she had time on her hands. So she couldn't have been more delighted by Sandra Martin's impromptu visit shortly before eleven. The front door was open; her friend knocked twice, then peeped in. "Am I interrupting anything?"

"Not at all. I'm happy for the company. I'm just killing time until one."

Sandra stepped into the house. "What happens at one?"

"A . . . new client is coming to see me."

"Oh? That's unusual, isn't it?"

"A little," Leah admitted.

"Important commission, huh?"

"Yes, very."

Sandra strolled across the room and flopped down on the sofa, her copper-colored curls bouncing with each step. There was a pixielike quality to Sandra that Leah found adorable. She had an elfin face and a round body that the more-angular Leah sometimes envied. Sandra, however, constantly complained about her weight and was forever just on or off a diet of some sort.

Leah usually could count on her friend for a laugh or two, but this morning Sandra looked completely humorless. Leah eyed her speculatively. "Want something to drink?"

Sandra shook her head. "I've spent the morning drowning my sorrows in the coffeepot. My caffeine level must be at an all-time high."

"Something wrong?"

Sandra's mouth drooped. "You might say that. My darling ex-husband dropped by to thoroughly spoil this beautiful day."

So that was the reason for the visit. "Ah," Leah murmured sympathetically. "I'm sorry."

"I don't know why he doesn't just leave me alone!" Sandra said with an unusual degree of irritation. "That man gave me eight of the most miserable years you can imagine. When I think of the time and money I spent with my shrink just trying to get up the nerve to leave him..."

Leah remembered Sandra had once mentioned seeing a psychiatrist. At the time it hadn't made much impact on her. "I'd forgotten you were in therapy."

"I don't often talk about it. People can bore you to tears with details of their hours on the couch, and I've never been able to talk about it casually, as if it's as natural as going to the dentist. Sheer desperation sent me to see Dr. Graves, but therapy saved my life."

"The psychiatrist—you think he helped you that much?"

"She," Sandra corrected. "She helped me. Did she ever! I would never have gotten up the courage to leave that bastard if it hadn't been for Dr. Graves."

Leah was intrigued. "I've often wondered how psychotherapy works. What does the doctor do exactly?"

Sandra frowned. "Now that I think about it, she didn't seem to do much but ask questions. The object is to get you to talk, really talk, and sooner or later she'd ask the right question, and I'd open up and chatter for the rest of the fifty-minute hour. First thing I knew I was looking at myself fully and honestly for the first time in my life, and I wasn't especially thrilled by what I saw. Sounds simple, doesn't it? Well, it isn't. It's painful... and revealing."

Leah regarded her friend with new interest. Of all the people she knew, Sandra seemed the least likely candidate for therapy, but then she recalled that she'd met Sandra after the woman had undergone analysis. She crossed the room to sit on the sofa beside her friend. "What did you find out about yourself? I'm not being too nosy, am I?"

"Oh, no, I don't mind talking about it. Most people aren't really interested, though."

"I am, really."

"Well, eventually I discovered I had married a man exactly like my father, because that was the only kind of man I could relate to. Imagine that, Leah. I married at eighteen in order to get away from my father, and I walked straight into the arms of a man exactly like him! My dad wrote the book on domineering male chauvinism, and Sam might have been his disciple."

"Sam," Leah mused irrelevantly. "So that's his name."

"Samuel T. Martin," Sandra said with exaggerated hautiness. "A self-made man, blessed with endless self-esteem and the sure knowledge that he was always right and I was always wrong. Dr. Graves reminded me that no one is always wrong. I mean, even a stopped clock is right twice a day!"

Leah smiled. "True."

"Anyway, I came to realize that my ideas had just as much value as Sam's did. I wasn't being ungrateful or selfish by wanting to pursue art and live a life of my own. When I finally left, Sam couldn't believe it. I think he thought I was bluffing. When he realized I was serious, he was somewhat pissed off. He predicted all sorts of dire consequences. He knew I'd come crawling back—but now he can't stand knowing I'm doing just fine without him, thank you. I think he'd love it if Ann and I were starving. Then I had my father to contend with. He was 'mortified.' My divorce had 'disgraced' the family." Sandra paused. "Sam says he's changed." She scoffed. "That things will be different if I come back to him, but I'm too smart to fall for that."

Leah wondered. She had often detected a wistful note in Sandra's railing against her ex, and she sometimes suspected a love-hate relationship, the classic "can't live with him, can't live without him" syndrome. "You'd never go back?" she asked slyly.

"Hah! Double hah! Bound and gagged maybe, but that's the only way. I'm no fool. I'll tell you something, Leah . . ."

For the next twenty minutes or so, Leah listened while Sandra let off steam. Leah interjected a remark here and there but mostly just listened. This was a catharsis the woman seemed to need from time to time, and Leah was flattered to be entrusted with so many confidences. When Sandra finally wound down, she turned to Leah with a sheepish smile. "Sorry for the monologue, but that's something else analysis does for you—teaches you to open up. I used to be scared of my own shadow. I couldn't put together three coherent sentences if Sam was around. No more. A good shrink can work wonders, believe me." She shoved herself off the sofa. "Well, I have a date tonight. Maybe he can snap me out of this foul mood."

Leah smiled. She envied Sandra in a way. Her friend had a lot of dates and seemed to enjoy them. Which was the way it should be, she thought, all the while remembering a few disastrous dates of her own. She could enjoy a man's company only so long, until the time came for romance. Then all she could think of was Jim, the way she had felt in his arms, the way his kisses set off a series of involuntary responses that were exquisitely torturous, and she would stiffen, freeze. A few disappointed and hurt suitors had marched away from her door, never to call again. Sandra was fortunate to have developed a much healthier attitude toward man-woman relationships.

Leah walked her friend to the front gate and watched her until she disappeared from view. And she pondered what Sandra had said. She thought of Jacob Surratt and tried to imagine how he had felt when he discovered he'd lost two years of his life. If he had ever seen a psychiatrist, why hadn't it helped?

WHEN THE EXPECTED KNOCK sounded at promptly one o'clock, Leah jumped. A few seconds passed before she crossed the room to answer it. Her hand trembled as she reached for the knob. When she swung the door wide, she felt the knot in her stomach tighten.

He stood on the porch, his eyes alight and a half smile softening his somber features. "Good afternoon," Jacob said, and his eyes roamed over her in a way that made Leah catch her breath.

She would have been astonished, he thought, to know how good she looked to him. She was wearing crisp khaki slacks and a bright yellow shirt; her hair was twisted on top of her head. Foolishly, he wished he could see it tumbling down, caressing her shoulders, swinging around her face.

She looked so fresh, alive, young and vital—exactly the way he remembered her. That's what confounded him, that he'd remembered so clearly from their first meeting; that some powerful feeling grabbed hold of his senses. No one had ever made such a profound, immediate impression on him, and he was quite prepared to believe no one ever would again. He had actually been nervous while dressing this morning. Nervous as a kid. It made no sense. But then, he conceded, such things weren't supposed to make sense.

"Good afternoon," she replied in an amazingly normal voice considering what the sight of him did to her. She felt weak and disoriented. He looked beautiful, debonair even in casual slacks and a short-sleeved knit sport shirt. Not very much like Jim, who had been earthy. This man would always stand out in a crowd, no matter how much he might try to withdraw from it.

Would she actually be able to treat him like a new acquaintance? Her hand gripped the doorknob as she stood aside. "Please come in."

The woodsy, masculine scent she had noticed in Alex's office assailed her as he brushed past her into the house. "Beautiful day, isn't it?"

"Yes, lovely. You're missing a perfect day for golf."

"I don't mind in the least. There will be hundreds of perfect days for golf."

Leah closed the door. Well, that hadn't been too bad, she thought with relief. The anticipation mingled with dread subsided somewhat. She was more in control than she would have imagined possible. Sometimes her own poise surprised her.

Turning, she found herself staring at the back of his broad shoulders, his trim waist and hips, his well-remembered stance more on the left foot than the right. The shape of his derriere was as appealing as ever. Jim had had the cutest fanny. Everything about him was so damned familiar, while she was a complete stranger to him. Keeping that in mind was going to be the hardest part of the whole charade. A certain formality was called for, yet her arms ached to reach for him, to hold him to her.

She realized he was intently studying the house, not merely giving it a cursory look. Nervously she skimmed her tongue over her bottom lip. What would she do if seeing the house triggered his memory? What if he began asking questions? How much should she tell him? Perhaps she should have discussed this incredible situation with someone knowledgeable before seeing him again? But who? She waited silently while his scrutiny continued.

Jacob's eyes swept the big room that constituted virtually the entire house. It was an unusual structure, with one large picture window and high-pitched roof that added to the illusion of space. Every square inch had been ingeniously utilized; storage space existed where there seemed to be room for none. Rustic and quaint. Through artful placement of furniture and the use of area rugs, the room had been divided into three distinct sections: living room, dining room and a studio. An upright wooden loom stood in front of the big window. The machine itself was a work of art. Certainly it hadn't come off an assembly line.

Jacob's gaze moved on. A kitchen alcove was at one end of the room; a ladder rose to a loft above. One door led, he assumed, to a bathroom. Simplicity itself, yet so appealing. The house had personality, and it was perfect for Leah Stone, he thought with satisfaction. Having some preconceived and rather romantic notions about artists and their life-styles, he would have been absurdly disappointed had Leah lived in a conventional house.

"Charming place, Leah," he finally said. "Did you have it built to specification?"

Only then did Leah realize she'd been holding her breath. Silently it seeped out of her. "No. As a matter of fact, it was once a schoolhouse. We . . . renovated it ourselves."

"By 'we' I assume you mean you and your husband?"

"Yes."

"You did a good job. A schoolhouse, of all things! How on earth did you come to find it?"

"Oh, we were just looking around for something out of the ordinary and happened upon it quite by accident."

"Well, it's charming, but I believe I've already said that."

Leah couldn't give a name to what she was feeling. Neither she nor the house had jarred his memory, so nothing was likely to. Jim really was gone. Except for the wonderful good looks, she could see no traces of him in Jacob Surratt. The finality of it squeezed at her heart.

Just then Jacob made some sort of motion with his left hand, and that flash of gold again caught Leah's eye. She stared at his wrist. Surprising that an affluent man would keep the same watch all these years. "Your watch," she murmured. "It's very attractive."

Jacob glanced at it quickly, then back at her. "Thanks. I've had it some time now, almost ten years. I bought it during a trip to Hong Kong, and I wouldn't trade it for a dozen new ones."

Hong Kong, of all places! It was a good thing they hadn't wasted more time trying to trace Jim through that watch.

Jacob crossed the room to the loom in front of the window. It was bare. He appreciatively moved his hand along the polished wood. "An heirloom?" he asked.

"It will be someday, I'm sure, but actually it's only eight years old. A man in New Mexico built it, a master woodworker. You'll notice there aren't any metal screws or bolts in the frame. The workings are as tight and strong as they were the day the loom was delivered to me. Do..." She hesitated. "Do you know anything about woodworking?"

"It was my hobby before medicine claimed all my time." He turned to her with a smile. "I still love the smell of sawdust."

Leah's heart thumped. She and Jim had often speculated on his talent with wood. He had built every cabinet in the house, the fence and front gate, too. They had wondered if he had made his living that way....

"You're not working on anything right now?" Jacob asked.

"No."

"Then may I assume my tapestry will be the next work in progress?"

"Y-yes. I'll warp the loom when I've created a design for your piece." It hadn't been wise to undertake the project, Leah was certain now. She had said she would do it, and she would, but it would be difficult, knowing it was for him. The most demanding work of her career. She would want it to be special, a masterpiece. Fixing her gaze at a point somewhere above Jacob's right shoulder, she miserably pondered the impossible situation.

Jacob seemed unusually fascinated by her loom. "What prompted you to take up weaving?"

Leah told him about the weaver at the fair. "I just made up my mind right then and there. I knew that's what I wanted to do."

"At sixteen? Lucky girl. Some people never find out what they want to do. How does one get started on a tapestry, or a rug or whatever?" he asked, his eyes scanning the apparatus. "What do you do first?"

Leah snatched at the slender thread of conversation. Moving closer to him, she said, "First I draw the design, then I make a pattern draft to guide me in dressing the loom. I don't suppose that means much to you."

"Not really, no."

"The draft is to a weaver what a recipe is to a cook or a pattern is to a dressmaker. It specifies exactly how the loom should be warped in order to achieve a particular design. In pioneer days the drafts were treasured and handed down from generation to generation."

"I see," he said in a vague tone that told Leah he was interested but didn't really understand.

"The Indians did the same thing, but the drafts were in their heads. Now, as the elderly weavers pass away and with fewer and fewer young Indian women wanting to take up the ancient craft, some of the classic designs will soon be gone forever."

"I own a century-old Navaho rug."

"Really? How fortunate you are!"

"It's not in the best condition but still quite valuable." Jacob glanced at her with admiration. "It's a noble craft you've chosen to keep alive."

"Yes," she said simply, for it was true. When she worked at her loom she felt an almost mystic kinship with the Navahos, with the Scottish weavers of Hebridean tweeds, with the makers of Turkish rugs and the priceless Persians, to say nothing of the uncounted legions of pioneer women who labored over simple looms to produce enough fabric to clothe a family.

"Do you look on your work as an art or a craft?"

A question she had been asked many times. She shrugged. "Good craftmanship is vital—who wants to own sloppy work?—but the designs are all mine and set my work apart."

He grinned charmingly. "Marvelous answer, Leah."

His untouchable nearness was slowly eating away at her poise. Having him here was at once thrilling and terrible. He looked like Jim, sounded like Jim, but he wasn't Jim at all. Maybe she shouldn't ever see him again. She wanted something that no longer existed.

But he was here now, and the time would have to pass somehow. Leah gestured toward the kitchen. "Lunch is ready. I'm sure you must be starved."

He sniffed the air. "If the taste is anything like the aroma, I'm in for a treat."

"My homemade vegetable soup. I've been told a person could live happily on it and never want anything else."

And who had told her that, Jacob mused as he followed her to the table, already set for lunch. Her husband, of course. He had noted the slight twitch of her facial muscles when he'd mentioned her husband earlier. For a fleeting second there had been pain and longing in her eyes, not anger or resentment. She was still in love with him. Not surprisingly, Jacob wondered what had happened. From the information he had pried out of a reluctant Alexander Trent, he knew she'd been married, no longer was, but wasn't widowed. So that meant she was divorced. The husband must have been the one who had wanted out; otherwise, why the longing? Another woman? Hard to believe.

Only a short breakfast bar separated the dining table from the tiny kitchen. Jacob slipped into a chair at the table and watched Leah as she poured glasses of ice tea, then ladled steaming soup into bowls. She worked with economy of movement in the neat, efficiently organized kitchen. He noticed the way she reached for things without looking, and he guessed she could walk into the kitchen blindfolded and put her hand on the paprika jar. He admired organization—he himself couldn't begin work until everything was at hand and in place—but had never equated it with the creative mind. But Leah wasn't just an artist; she was also accomplished in a technical skill.

She was such a soft, fluid woman, and she excited him in a way that went beyond the obvious, the physical. Her loveliness was unstudied, almost ethereal, with an underlying current of sensuality. No, he couldn't believe a man would leave her for another woman. It was easier to imagine her marriage had fallen by the wayside for more complex reasons: a woman intent on a career and a man jealous of his wife's phenomenal success. Perhaps a clash of personalities. Almost anything was easier to believe than another woman.

"THAT WAS DELICIOUS, Leah," Jacob said after two helpings. "Isn't a good pot of soup supposed to be the proof of a cook's ability?"

Leah smiled. Lunch had been a pleasant interlude, full of talk about inconsequential things. Slowly, without being aware of it, she had been lulled into a pleasant sense of well-being. He was a thoughtful and interesting conversationalist. To her utter surprise, she discovered she had forgotten Jim Stone for a few moments, having found it amazingly easy to concentrate on the fascinating character of Jacob Surratt.

The haunting quality she had sensed the day before lurked just below the surface, giving him an air of brooding mystery. It made a woman want to plumb those dark depths. Were the two blank years of his life responsible? she wondered. Wouldn't something like that prey on one's mind constantly?

The word Alex had used to describe him, "refined," suited him to a tee. He was reserved, too. Very reserved. She couldn't imagine him opening up and spilling the story of his life. What was the story of his life? It came to her with a start that Jacob could tell her all the things she had never known about Jim.

He had a straightforward way of looking at a person that was unsettling until one got used to it, as though he could see more than the person wanted to reveal. Not an easy man to get to know well. He didn't talk about himself at all, and Leah was too concerned about saying the wrong things to ask many questions. Yet he radiated confidence, a necessity for a doctor, she supposed. "Just put yourself in my hands," his manner said, "and everything will be all right." She imagined him standing in front of an auditorium full of distinguished physicians presenting a paper, or whatever it was doctors did at those meetings. Dr. Surratt, a recognized authority in his field.

What was his field? Leah asked him, and he told her he was an internist. "Not a dramatic specialty," he added modestly. "There are those who'll tell you I'm nothing but a glorified GP."

She could tell he was interested in her as a woman, and she certainly wasn't immune to masculine appreciation. Particularly not when the handsome face across from her was the dearest on earth. She could feel the old magnetic pull between them, just as she had eight years ago; she knew she wasn't imagining it. "I must admit to being a pretty good cook," she said, returning to their earlier conversation. "Cooking is the creative side of housekeeping, it seems to me. When I'm not weaving I enjoy cooking and working in the garden, but housework..." She wrinkled her nose in disdain. "Fortunately the house requires very little care. It was designed so there would be a place for everything."

Jacob glanced around. "It's exceptionally neat, especially when you consider there's a child living here."

"Nina's neat, too. Just the two of us have lived here for a long time, so perhaps she's always sensed the need for keeping clutter to a minimum. At least she's good about keeping her clutter up there." She used her thumb to indicate the loft above their heads.

"How old is your daughter?"

"Six."

"You must have been very young when you married."

Leah's expression altered; instantly the most vulnerable part of her was alerted. *Stay away from that subject,* she warned. *Don't let him ask questions.* "Not really. My marriage...was a brief one," she said stiffly, and got to her feet in a jerky movement, gathering up their dishes. "I'll rinse these and put them in the dishwasher. It won't take but a minute."

Jacob remained at the table, staring across the room while tugging thoughtfully on his chin. Whatever her relationship with her husband had been, it had left scars. She definitely didn't like to talk about her marriage. In fact, she froze at the mention of the word. So, although he wanted to know more, although he burned with curiosity about this woman, he wouldn't ask any more questions.

HE STAYED MOST of the afternoon. He seemed loathe to leave, and Leah sensed he was starved for companionship. His reserved manner coupled with his lofty position probably made it difficult for him to form close friendships. There was a hint of entreaty in Jacob Surratt's manner that she found appealing. She imagined he would like nothing better than to relax and loosen up a bit, but simply didn't know how.

Try as she might she couldn't detect any of the easygoing Jim Stone beneath Jacob's controlled exterior. How could one man be two such different people? And how could one woman be so enormously attracted to both of them? And how, dear God, could she sit here and calmly distinguish one from the other? That was what she was doing, with greater ease than she would have dreamed possible. Without effort she could recall Jim holding his head one way, while Jacob held his another way.

Their conversation was politely friendly, befitting a meeting between two supposed strangers who were taking first hesitant steps toward getting acquainted. Most of his questions concerned her career, and he seemed especially interested in her relationship with Alex.

"How long have you been associated with the Trent Gallery?"

"Five years. When I first met Alex I'd been weaving for a number of years, but I had no clear-cut notion of where I thought my weaving would lead me. Alex took me in hand, pointed me in the right direction, and the rest, as they say, is history." She smiled slightly.

"You've enjoyed tremendous success, I understand. I guess you feel you owe it all to Trent."

"Most of it. Of course, I have to give myself a little credit, too. I'm the one who has to produce."

"He's fond of you."

"Alex? Yes, he is, and I'm fond of him. Besides being sort of my business manager, he's probably the best friend I've ever had." Leah paused before concluding, "But that's all he is." She felt compelled to add that, and the look on his face clearly told her how glad he was to hear it.

At last Jacob got around to mentioning the ostensible reason for his visit—the tapestry. Leah sketched a tentative design for him— a bold, impressionistic view of the Red Rock Country that he professed to like very much.

"This part of the state offers a lot in the way of inspiration, but if you'd prefer a desert scene . . ."

"No, I want to leave the design entirely up to you. I want you to do what you feel. I know I'll like anything you come up with."

They were sitting side by side on the sofa, deep in a discussion concerning colors, when the front door flew open and Nina burst into the room with childish exuberance.

"Mama, why weren't you waiting for me on the porch?"

Leah's eyes flew to the clock on the wall. She hadn't been aware of the passage of time, and she had vaguely expected Jacob to be gone before her daughter—his daughter—got home from school. Her heart thudded painfully as she cast a sidelong glance at Jacob, then looked at Nina's winsome face.

"I'm sorry honey. I've had company and completely forgot the time."

Nina eyed Jacob with candid curiosity. "Hi."

"Well, hello," he said with a smile.

Leah stifled a wave of panic. "Nina, I'd...I'd like you to meet Dr. Surratt. Jacob, my daughter...."

Jacob, courteously and with all the gallantry usually reserved for adults, uncurled his lanky frame and got to his feet. "It's very nice to meet you, Nina."

The child crossed the room and stood in front of him, tilting her head. "Are you a people doctor or an animal doctor like my grandpa?"

"I'm a people doctor."

"Well, I'm going to be a vet when I grow up."

"Are you? How wonderful, Nina. I hope you actually do it."

"I will. Grandpa says he'll need me."

Leah reminded herself to keep breathing, slowly, evenly. She couldn't fall apart now, though her reserve of inner strength seemed dangerously depleted. Jacob and Nina were intent on each other, so she was free to study both of them. Father and daughter. How could they not see it? To Leah's eyes, Nina was reminiscent of the tall dark man in many ways. Perhaps her eyes and mouth were more like her mother's but the rest was Jacob all over again.

Jacob stood over the girl, smiling down at her. "Nina, you look exactly like your mother."

Nina nodded solemnly. "That's what everybody says."

Leah expelled her pent-up breath. No, of course they wouldn't see it. Nina was much too young, and Jacob was seemingly too removed from them for such a thing to cross his mind. People saw what they expected to see. To Jacob, Nina's dark hair and eyes would seem to have come from her mother.

But had a third party entered the house at that moment—say Sandra—Leah feared the common genes would have been all too apparent. If Jacob Surratt became a part of her life, what kind of problems would that present? How could she even think of such a thing at this stage? She wouldn't.

The uncomfortable moment passed. Only Leah seemed to be aware of the awkwardness. Jacob sat down, and Nina shifted her attention to her mother. "Can I go to Ann's house, Mama?"

"May I go," Leah corrected.

"May I go?"

"I suppose so, but change your clothes first...and hang up that dress. It can be worn again."

"Okay." Nina scampered away and was up the ladder leading to the loft in a flash. Leah stared wistfully after her daughter's darting figure.

"She's an adorable girl, Leah."

"Thank you." She drew a few unnecessary lines on the sketch pad in her lap, thoroughly spoiling the design.

"She must be a lot of company for you."

"Yes."

"I think I'd like having children. I'm not sure I'd be a great father, though. I'm afraid I wouldn't have the slightest idea what to do with a child."

"I have news for you, not many first-time parents do. It's strictly on-the-job training. You . . . never married?"

"No. I guess there was never time. At least, that's the excuse I've always used. Actually, I suppose the problem was I never found the right person. Had I found her, I'm sure I would have found the time."

"Yes, of course," Leah said distractedly, pretending absorption in the mess she had made of her sketch. "Have you ever regretted not marrying?" The words were out before she remembered her decision to avoid the subject.

"Sometimes." Jacob paused, then said. "No, not sometimes. Often."

Leah's breath caught in her throat. It was a touching admission, and one that seemed to embarrass him. Only the greatest exercise of will prevented her from reaching out to touch him.

"Well, you've plenty of time."

"I'm galloping toward forty."

"That's not so old."

"I wonder. I'm pretty set in my ways. I wonder if I could adapt."

"Of course you could. Don't be fatalistic about it. It's important to . . . have someone to share things with. You'll find out . . . someday." Leah swallowed rapidly. Why was she saying these things? Why was she discussing marriage with him? She knew he was staring at her, and she couldn't turn to meet his gaze.

Jacob was puzzled. Here was a woman with a failed marriage behind her, one that apparently had left deep scars, yet she seemed to be encouraging him to give marriage a try, even though the very subject bothered her. Best to find something else to talk about. Nervously he cleared his throat. "Your father is a veterinarian?"

"Yes, he has a practice in the Verde Valley."

"Is that where you grew up?"

"Yes."

"So you're a country girl?"

"Through and through."

"I've often thought I might like living in the country."

He had. Jim had loved country life, and he had abhorred crowds. Leah had attributed that to the fact that he'd never quite lost his feeling of alienation from the rest of society. He had been an amnesiac, therefore "different."

She felt oddly detached from everything that was going on around her, as if she were a third person viewing the scene from afar. That she could sit and make idle small talk, exercise all the social graces when her nerves were stretched to the snapping point, astonished her. Jacob was sitting in a house he had personally renovated, on furniture they had purchased together. He filled the room with a masculine vitality she had once been so accustomed to but had since almost forgotten. When he left this afternoon his presence would be missed, just as Jim's had been six years ago. Leah glanced at his strong hands with their slender, sensitive fingers and didn't want to look away. She noticed the way his trousers fit so smoothly over muscular thighs and tried not to remember his naked legs sliding sleekly along hers....

For a moment her throat closed completely, and a warm flush crawled up her neck. He had always possessed more than his fair share of sex appeal, and they had been passionate, responsive lovers. No other man had even come close to touching her heart. During the years Jim had been gone, she had come to accept emotional emptiness as a way of life.

But inevitably there would have been other women in Jacob's life during the past six years, and she wondered what he looked for in a woman. Beauty? Sophistication? Well schooled in all the social graces? Had there been one special one? Had anyone ever broken his heart? Good Lord, if she thought about such things she would drive herself crazy!

In only a few minutes Nina was hurrying back down the ladder, dressed in shorts, halter and sneakers. She hugged her mother, favored Jacob with a little wave and bolted out the front door. The house seemed deathly quiet in her wake, and the one thing Leah couldn't cope with was silence. Abruptly she stood up. "I promised Nina I'd make spaghetti for supper. I need to start the sauce. Just make yourself comfortable...."

With apparent reluctance Jacob also got to his feet. "I really should be going. I've taken up far too much of your time as it is."

"I...didn't mind. I enjoyed it." Which wasn't entirely the truth. The pain had overshadowed the enjoyment.

"Did you, Leah? I'm glad, because so did I."

Bold, intense eyes captured hers, forcing Leah to look quickly away. If she didn't look at him she could almost forget he wasn't the stranger he was supposed to be. "I . . . ah, I'll be starting the tapestry in a few days, I imagine."

"Will I be allowed to view the work in progress?"

He was asking, in a roundabout way, if he could see her again. And of course her answer would be yes. How could she not see him again? Now that she knew where he was, she would gravitate to him, irresistibly drawn. "I have no objections to a client seeing an unfinished work," she said, although normally she did. Alex was the only interested party who was allowed to visit her while she worked.

Hearing that, Jacob fully relaxed for the first time that afternoon. From the moment he had stepped into the ridiculous, wonderful little house, throughout lunch, all the while he was making the sort of small talk he usually despised and executed so poorly, he had been planning how to see her again. The tapestry was the obvious bond . . . for now.

To Leah's consternation, he stepped closer to her. The clean male scent of him filled her nostrils, making her light-headed. Casually he took her hand and held it in both of his while saying, "You know, I've never put much stock in fate or Kismet or whatever, but . . ." He groped for words, finally settling for, "I had never been in that bank building before. Never in my entire life." His eyes begged her to understand how momentous that simple act now seemed.

Leah didn't know what to say, so she said nothing. He left quickly then, with a smile and a chaste handshake. For long moments after she had closed the door behind him, she simply stood with her forehead pressed against the cold, hard wood. It took some time for the confusing mixture of emotions inside her to run their course, then subside.

She had no idea when she would see him again, but she knew she would. When the opportunity came along she would seize it. Her life had been diverted into a new channel, and there was nothing she could do but go with the current. It was useless to try to pretend the day hadn't changed everything. For now she couldn't be bothered with wondering what she hoped would come of all this—finding Jim again or getting to know Jacob. There would be plenty of time for introspection later.

A long sigh left her lips. She was exhausted by the extremes of emotion that had assaulted her all afternoon. Honestly, she didn't know how she had gotten through it.

CHAPTER FIVE

JACOB SLID BEHIND the wheel of his Corvette, after removing his billfold from his hip pocket and tossing it onto the console between the seats. That was a habit of his that many people found idiosyncratic, but he simply disliked sitting on a wallet for any length of time.

Absently he patted the dashboard of the flashy, luxurious automobile before turning the key in the ignition. His acquaintances also found the car uncharacteristic of Jacob Surratt, and he admitted it was the one frivolous aspect of his eminently sensible life. The vehicle was totally impractical, with room for two people and nothing else, but its very impracticality was probably the reason he loved it so.

Leisurely he drove away from the picture-postcard community of Sedona, out of the deep abyss of Oak Creek Canyon, and headed south for Phoenix. For once he took the time to notice and appreciate his surroundings. Puffy pillows of cumulus cloud drifted overhead in a sky of such brilliant clarity that it hurt the eyes. The air was pure and crystalline. He rolled down the car window and sniffed deeply of it. The perpetual haze that hovered over Phoenix seemed light-years away. He was caught up in an extraordinary sensation of well-being, hardly a usual state of mind for him, and the feeling remained with him throughout the trip home.

Two hours later he turned into the driveway of his home in the swank Phoenix suburb of Scottsdale. Leaving the car in the drive, since he fully intended going to the clinic after dinner, he entered the house by way of a side veranda. The interior smelled of soap and polish, as always; all was peaceful and serene, as always, for the big house remained impervious to the trials and tribulations of the man who owned it.

He strode through the dining room and into the tiled foyer. There he was met by a tall, spare, gray-haired man—his butler.

"Good evening, sir. I hope you had a pleasant day."

"Very pleasant, thank you, Davis. Are there any messages?"

"None, sir, but George would like to know when you wish dinner served."

Jacob glanced at his watch. "Eight or thereabouts. And please tell George to keep it light. I had a substantial lunch."

"Very good."

Taking the stairs two at a time, Jacob went to his room on the second floor, stripped and stepped into swim trunks. Within moments he was back downstairs, heading for the pool at the rear of the big house. Diving in, he swam his customary daily laps with even less enthusiasm than usual. It had been years since he'd thought of swimming as recreation. Swimming and golf were his ways of staying fit; he despised jogging and calisthenics. Inside his house, in a converted attic, was an exercise room full of the latest equipment, but it was seldom used. In fact, there were many rooms in the house that were seldom used. He often wondered why he bothered keeping the place. Because it was easier to stay put, he supposed.

Swimming with precision, he performed the daily chore with the air of a man doing penance. Then he lifted himself out of the pool and went to lie facedown on a poolside lounge. The sun was warm on his back, and as he gradually relaxed, pleasant languor took hold of him. Not surprisingly, his mind strayed to Leah Stone.

He felt so drawn to her, as though he knew her better than he actually did. Not the facts of her life exactly, since he had barely scratched the surface there. What they shared was more like a communion of souls. At this Jacob chuckled derisively. That was quite a conclusion for a man who held others at arm's length.

Thinking about Leah now, he realized that his first impression was of having met her before. But realistically wouldn't she have remembered and mentioned it? She was as curious about him as he was about her; he had seen that much in some of the quizzical looks she'd cast in his direction. A plus for him. He had captured her interest, and that was half the battle.

So that first impression of a rare bond must have been nothing more than another of his overreactions. In spite of his resolve not to dwell on his memory loss, he still harbored the hope that he would someday meet someone who had known him, someone who would tell him about the lost period of his life.

He didn't know why resurrecting the past was so important to him. Wherever he had spent those missing years, whatever he had been doing couldn't possibly measure up to what he had now. Just looking around he could see it. See what? Incredible comfort, the trappings of affluence and success, an outward display of social status? All that, of course—and he was suddenly struck by his lack of interest in what he owned. If he couldn't be happy with all this, he definitely had a problem.

Yet he wasn't, not really. Most people labored a lifetime to attain only a measure of what he had. Still there were times when he would have gladly given up all of it just to find out where he'd been, what he had done during the thirty-first and thirty-second years of his life. How often he had tried to push all thoughts of those years to the back of his mind, but they relentlessly inched forward, until there were days when he thought of almost nothing else. When that happened he felt completely fragmented.

Charles had told him to give up. After fruitless months in psychotherapy with his partner, it had occurred to Jacob that he might be better off not knowing. Why possibly complicate his life? "The mind is a wondrous thing," Charles liked to say. "It can block out the unwanted." Jacob, calling upon his own knowledge of psychiatry, liked to think of the mind as a sort of cold-storage vault. Everything that had ever been put into it was still there, and would stay there until someone or something took it out.

Ah, forget it! He would concentrate instead on Leah Stone, the first woman in years who had elicited a spark of interest in him— and in Leah's case it was more like a full-fledged flame. She was lovely, artistic, intelligent. Quiet, too. Jacob had always appreciated quietness in a person. So many people talked too much and said too little. Leah listened to what was being said to her and gave some thought to her own reply. Refreshing.

If he had ever known her before he would have liked her, of that he was sure. Today he had longed to stay in that funny little house with her forever. Even the house clutched at him in some peculiar way.

Lazily he sifted through what he knew about Leah. She had been weaving professionally for five years, and Trent was her mentor, nothing more. Jacob suspected the gallery owner would have welcomed a more intimate relationship—he had gathered that much at Tlaquepaque the day before—but if it hadn't happened by now, after such a long association, it wasn't likely to. Trent wouldn't be a rival.

His potential rival—how odd to be thinking in such terms already! But it was the other man in Leah Stone's life who could be the formidable obstacle. Her marriage had been brief, yet years later she was still in love with her husband. There was the little girl, too. A child could be a problem, particularly if the girl was possessive of her mother. Jacob hadn't seen signs of that, but one never knew.

Forget that, too. He would worry about that later, if indeed it needed worrying about. Leah wasn't married anymore, and this afternoon had only whet his appetite to get closer to her. Abruptly he sat up. Damn, he shouldn't have left without making arrangements for another meeting. He might have read too much into her apparent interest in him. He knew, to his everlasting regret, that he wasn't a man who projected warmth and charm. He often found it impossible to express what he felt. She might just have been behaving courteously...then again, her apparent interest might have been genuine. What the hell— Nothing ventured...

Without giving it too much thought—for if he had, he probably would have done nothing—Jacob stood, threw a towel around his shoulders and went into the house. On the desk in his study he found the phone number he had jotted down the evening before. Dialing, he was aware of his accelerated heartbeat, of his sheer excitement as he waited to hear her voice on the other end of the line. He felt as callow as a schoolboy, and curiously, that felt wonderful!

"Hello."

"Leah?"

"Jacob?"

"Yes, I...I've been thinking. You really should see the clinic itself before you begin the tapestry. Won't you please reconsider Saturday night's opening?"

"Well, I..." Leah was hesitant about accepting eagerly when she had so adamantly refused the night before. But she wanted to go. Oh, how she wanted to go!

"Of course your friend Trent is invited, too," Jacob added hastily. "And I'd like both of you to stay at my house, not at the Biltmore. We won't have to do much more than put in an appearance at the party. I think you'll enjoy it." This was a new role for him, and he wasn't the least certain how well he was playing it.

"I...why, thank you, Jacob. I'm sure I will. I'll tell Alex in the morning."

"Are you familiar with Phoenix?"

"Yes, I went to school there."

"Anytime Saturday afternoon. I'll be home," he assured her before he gave her directions to his house.

"I'm looking forward to it."

The elation Jacob felt when he hung up was an alien sensation. Foolishly, he admitted to dangerously high expectations. A pity he had felt compelled to invite Trent along. That had just popped out, a gesture at propriety. He would have liked nothing better than to have that charming woman all to himself, but he doubted that she would have come if he'd left Trent out of the invitation.

Tugging on both ends of the towel, Jacob went upstairs to shower. He couldn't remember the last time he had looked forward to a weekend, to much of anything, for that matter. He longed for an end to the sameness of his days, an end to evenings passed without meaning or purpose to him personally. It would be wonderful if Leah Stone turned out to be the one who finally carved a niche in his life, erased the loneliness and brought peace to his mind and soul. How wonderful if she was the one who finally made him stop caring about the missing years.

JACOB NEVER DID get around to going to the clinic that evening. He ate his solitary evening meal and retired early, only to awaken in a cold sweat in the middle of the night. He had had the dream. Four years or more had passed since the last one, but tonight it had returned, unchanged. He saw a house, not clearly, and a front door. It opened. A woman stood there. He could never see her face, and the dream always ended abruptly when she appeared. The same dream, never varying.

Flinging back the covers, he went to stand at the window. His chest was heaving. Dammit, why now? Why had it come back to haunt him now, when he had finally found someone who excited him? When he longed to concentrate on someone else for a change? He passed a hand over his eyes. His amnesia had always embarrassed him, as though it was a weakness of character, although his subsequent knowledge of the subject assured him that wasn't so. For a time he had also worried about his actions during the fugue. Maybe he had done something illegal or immoral. Again, he had learned that wasn't likely.

But what of the people whose lives he had touched during those two years? No one existed in a vacuum. That bothered him most of all—the possibility that he might have left someone "out there" six years ago, someone who needed him. What if the dream was a warning, a warning not to get involved again until loose ends had been tied up?

That scared the hell out of him.

LEAH TELEPHONED ALEX the following morning. Beth informed her that he hadn't put in an appearance at the gallery, so he first learned of their upcoming visit to Phoenix when he stopped by her house that afternoon, something he usually managed to do a few times a week. He knocked twice, called her name, then came in to find Leah in the kitchen.

"Something smells good," he commented.

"Stay for supper?"

"I'd love to, but I can't. I'm due in Flagstaff for dinner. I'm meeting a marvelous new watercolorist from New Mexico. Her show in Taos drew raves."

"You're always so busy," Leah said with a smile. "I don't know how you stand all that gadding about."

"Well, I'm not going to be busy Saturday night, so let's do something. I'll take you out to dinner."

"I'm afraid we have other plans," she said slyly, then told him of Jacob's invitation.

"You what?" he exclaimed, his tone and expression registering alarm. "Leah, what on earth prompted you to do such a thing?"

Leah wasn't the least surprised by his reaction. She had anticipated it, down to the firm set of his mouth and the furrow in his brow. He would protest mightily, but he would go. "I told him we'd be there," she repeated. "He invited us, and I accepted. It was something I had to do."

His eyes narrowed questioningly. "Why did you have to do it?"

"I can't explain it, Alex, and I shouldn't have to. I want to go, that's all."

"And if I refuse to tag along?" he asked, sounding as pettish as a small boy.

Leah shot him a wry smile. "Would you?"

He regarded her levelly for a second. "No," he said finally, firmly. "No way."

Under no circumstances did he want her going alone. The situation was rife with potential disaster for more than one interested party. Leah's husband's surprise reappearance had Alex filled with dread, but he had been encouraged by her refusal to see Jacob Surratt again. Now this. Leah, it seemed to him, was asking for trouble and heartache. Surely she was aware of that. Perhaps she simply didn't care, and that in itself alarmed him.

Alex had no illusions about his place in Leah's affections; it was solid, impenetrable, exclusive—but not based on romantic love. That he had accepted. His ambitions concerning her now centered on their closeness and shared interests, their common goals. One day, he hoped, Leah would marry him, not because she was wildly in love with him, but because she wanted and needed his support and companionship. He had been willing to wait for that day.

Peculiar that he hadn't considered the possibility of another man, but he hadn't. He had been watching Leah for years, had watched men turn themselves inside out attempting to attract her. All of the attempts had been met with polite detachment, leaving Alex secure in believing he was, with the exception of her father and daughter, the most important person in her life. Until now.

It was easy to see how falsely complacent he had been, but how in God's name could he have foreseen this incredible turn of events? Jacob Surratt wasn't just any man; he was the one man she had loved. Nina's father. Handsome and eligible. And Leah had never divorced him, never remarried. Alex wasn't one to give fate much credit for anything that happened, but in this case . . .

Something had kept them free for each other. He hadn't understood why, in an age when divorce and infidelity were commonplace, Leah had remained faithful to a man she hadn't seen in six years. Now he understood. She had never quite given up hope that he would come back to her one day. Her husband may have returned in a new guise, but he had returned. Alex didn't like it one damned bit.

"What brought on this change of mind, Leah? My last instructions from you, as I recall, were to keep him away from you at all costs."

Leah smiled at him across the breakfast bar. "He came to see me yesterday, and we . . . talked."

"He was here?"

She nodded. "Most of yesterday afternoon."

"But how . . . ?"

"When he called Tuesday night he asked if he could come to see me, and I said yes."

"Why on earth did you do that?"

"Because I wanted to," she said simply.

A rush of color suffused Alex's face. "Did . . . did he meet Nina?"

Again she nodded. "But the meeting was brief. It made no impact on him. Neither did the house. He remembers nothing."

"Oh, Leah," Alex sighed wearily. "Do you have any idea what you might be letting yourself in for?"

"Honestly, no. Hundreds of possibilities have crossed my mind, but I don't know which ones are valid. I can't be bothered with all the 'ifs' and 'maybes.' I know Jacob Surratt isn't the man I married, and I know he and I might not get along the way Jim and I did. But I have to know for sure, don't I?" She waited. "Well, don't I?"

"I don't know, Leah. I swear I don't. You were so adamant about not wanting to meet with him. . . ."

"At first, yes. I was confused, frightened, still reeling from the shock of seeing him again. I didn't want to face the possibility of rejection. Jacob Surratt might not have given a fig for Leah Stone. But then he came here for lunch, and . . . I could tell he was interested in me as a woman. The spark's still there, regardless of who he is." Leah reached out to squeeze his hand. "Alex, I've missed him every day for six years. It always seemed strange that I couldn't get him out of my head, but I never could. Even lately, when I could sometimes go for days without consciously thinking of him, I've missed him. Can you blame me for... anything?"

A pall of silence descended. Leah could almost see the resignation settling on Alex, and her heart ached for him. She hoped she hadn't been too frank, yet he wouldn't have wanted her to be any other way.

"No," he said finally. "No, I suppose I can't. Apparently none of us has much control over the workings of the heart. It's you I'm thinking of. At least, I think it's you. I don't know... maybe I'm only thinking of myself. So, what time are we due at the good doctor's place Saturday?"

"Anytime in the afternoon. What about four?"

He shrugged. "Four's fine with me."

An alarming thought crossed Leah's mind. "Alex, you do realize the importance of not saying anything to Jacob that would hint at my knowing him before?"

"Damn, Leah! Do you think I'm stupid?"

"No, but something might pop out. I really don't know how to handle this, but instinct tells me to move carefully."

"Well, put your mind at ease. I'll be the soul of discretion. I guess we'll drop Nina off at your dad's?"

"No. School's out for the summer at noon tomorrow. Nina will be like a colt let out of a pen. I'll take her down then and let her run off some of that energy on the farm." A distant look came to Leah's eyes. "Besides, I need to talk to Dad. He has to know about this."

Alex didn't stay long. Leah guessed he had some emotional turmoil of his own to deal with, and she felt deeply for her dear friend at that moment. Although she had never encouraged him romantically, she imagined he had never completely given up hope. And who knew what might have happened in the future? One day she might have turned to him for solace and companionship.

Alex would cope, though, and he wouldn't let this change their professional relationship. She was sure of that. Other things would change. Perhaps it wasn't even reasonable to be so sure of that so soon, but Leah was. Lives would be altered, and all because Jacob happened to walk into that bank and spot that tapestry.

CHAPTER SIX

IT WAS MIDAFTERNOON of the following day when Leah drove through the wooden gate and up the long lane to her father's home, a large white frame farmhouse sitting in the middle of twenty fertile acres along the Verde River. At one time the Haskell property had been worked extensively, and citizens in nearby communities had gobbled up all the beans, tomatoes, corn, apples and grapes it could produce. With a two-hundred-day growing season, the produce had been plentiful. But now farming was limited to a dozen laying hens, a couple of milk goats, a few horses and a small but thriving vegetable garden. Whit Haskell's veterinary practice left him little time for other work, while Tee Santos's arthritis precluded the housekeeper doing much outside work. Farming chores were handled by two hired workers, and Whit also employed a young man to help with the clinic and kennels. Everyone resided on the premises, which meant Whit had plenty of company.

In the seat beside her mother, Nina fidgeted and squirmed with end-of-school excitement and the anticipation of a long weekend at the farm. The chief attraction for the girl, aside from her doting grandfather's shameless devotion, was the number of animals that populated the place. Dogs and cats abounded, and the queen bee among them was Bess, Whit's adored collie. Bess, now heavy in the late stages of pregnancy, ambled up to the car the moment Leah halted in front of the house. Nina leaped out to give the dog an enthusiastic hug.

"Oh, Mama, Bess is so big! She's going to have a bunch of puppies!"

Leah bent to rub Bess's head affectionately. The dog's limpid eyes closed in satisfaction. "How're you doing, girl? About ready for the whole mess to be over, I'll bet."

Nina straightened and scampered up the front steps. "Grandpa says we can have one of the puppies," she informed her mother over her shoulder. "We get first pick."

"How thoughtful of him," Leah muttered sarcastically, following her daughter. "He might have discussed it with me."

"I'll take good care of it, honest."

"Hmm. I'd like a dollar for every mother who's fallen for that one. Now don't get your heart set on it, Nina. A puppy's a big responsibility."

Leah caught the screen door before it banged behind Nina. She stepped into her father's homey living room in time to witness the enthusiastic greeting between grandfather and granddaughter. Whit's pleasantly craggy face broke into a beaming smile as his burly arms enfolded Nina in a bear hug. His head, covered with a thatch of salt-and-pepper hair, bent over the child's. "How's my best girl?"

"Fine."

"So, school's out, eh? Did you get any smarter this year?"

"Lots. Grandpa, when's Bess going to have her puppies?"

"Soon. A week maybe."

"Is she all right?"

"Bess? With me here to take care of her? Of course she's all right." His gaze swept over the top of Nina's head and fastened on Leah. "Hello, hon. What's up? You sounded kinda mysterious on the phone."

Leah cautioned her father with a frown and a slight nod in Nina's direction. Whit pursed his lips in comprehension and immediately set the girl at arm's length. "Nina, Tee's in the kitchen making chocolate-chip cookies. I'll bet if you hurry you can get one fresh out of the oven."

"Oh, boy!" Nina ran out of the room, calling the housekeeper's name.

Whit glanced at Leah with parental concern. She looked worried, or what passed for worried with Leah. She never got ruffled, which wasn't right. As far as Whit was concerned, twenty-eight was too damned young to have acquired a calm acceptance of life. That was desirable at fifty-three maybe, but not at twenty-eight. Too much inside his daughter had died when Jim disappeared. "Got something important on your mind?" he inquired quietly.

"Very."

"I thought so. Let's go out back. I was on my way to check the kennels. We'll have privacy out there."

Leah fell into step beside her father. They left the house and ambled around to the back, where the clinic for small animals and its adjacent boarding kennels were located. The moment they opened the kennel door the "guests" began barking noisy greetings. While Whit let the eager dogs out into the runs, Leah walked along the concrete path between the chain link pens, filling the water troughs. That done, her father motioned her toward his office in the clinic. Once inside, he gave her his grave attention. "Well?" he demanded.

"Dad, I've seen Jim."

Whit was halfway to the chair behind his desk. He stopped short and sucked in a startled breath. "Jim? Oh, Leah, where?"

"Right in Sedona."

"But . . . how . . . ?"

"You won't believe it. Alex called me Tuesday afternoon. He asked me to hurry over to the gallery to meet a prominent Phoenix physician who wanted me to do a tapestry for him. The physician turned out to be Jim . . . only his name is Jacob Surratt."

"Dear God! What did you do?"

"I almost passed out."

"I'm surprised you didn't."

"It was so . . . so instantaneous. I didn't have time to collect myself. I turned around, and he was just there! I thought everything inside me had exploded. Fortunately, he thought I was ill rather than stunned to my toes."

Whit's breath escaped in a whistle. He continued on to his chair and slumped into it. Leah could tell the news had stunned him, just as she had known it would. He had been unusually close to his son-in-law and had taken Jim's disappearance hard. She thought he had held out hope of finding Jim long after she had given up. Keeping her eyes fastened on her father, she pulled a chair close to his desk and sat down.

"He didn't recognize you?" Whit asked in an unsteady voice.

She shook her head. "Not at all. He didn't recognize the house, either."

"He's been to the house?"

Leah nodded.

"Has he seen Nina?"

"Yes. Oh, Dad, she's the living image of him!"

"Yeah, I figured as much. My memory's not all that good, and six years have passed, but I always thought Nina looked like Jim."

"Jacob didn't see it."

"No," Whit said thoughtfully. "I guess you wouldn't see a thing like that, not unless you expected to. Well, if this isn't something!" He felt so much for Leah at that moment. What a helluva blow it must have been, to turn and find her husband standing there! But if anyone could handle this unexpected development, Leah could. Even now, she looked calm and collected. An astonishing woman, his daughter. He had always admired her level head, and he supposed he admired her courage. Lord knows, he was awed by it half the time. But he wouldn't mind seeing her slam a door, yell, cry, something. "It must have been rough," was all he said.

"Yes, it was."

"You don't seem any the worse for wear."

"I've had a couple of days to recover from the initial shock—and I must be a glutton for punishment. Alex and I were invited to spend the weekend at Dr. Surratt's home. I accepted."

A moment passed. Leah wondered if that was really why she had wanted so desperately to talk to her father. He was the only person who knew what her relationship with Jim had been like. She wanted to confess her susceptibility to Jacob Surratt, and to seek Whit's reassurance that she had done the logical thing. She was reaching out to him for emotional comfort, just as she had as a child.

"You're going?" Whit asked with a frown.

"Yes."

"Leah, I'm not too sure.... It couldn't possibly be the same...."

"Dad, think about it. Try to see it from my viewpoint. Admittedly my first thought was to stay away, but... If you were me, would you be able to stay away from him?"

Whit pursed his lips. "No, I guess I wouldn't. Still, I can't help thinking about you, about all you've gone through."

"I'll be all right, Dad, honest."

"Yeah, probably. So... tell me about it, tell me everything."

When Leah had finished relating the details of her two meetings with Jacob, her father sighed deeply. "I wonder why it never occurred to me that Jim might have been medically trained. You could tell he was educated, and he took to this work the way a duck takes to water. The closest I came was to wonder if he had lived around animals, or maybe was a medic in the army."

"I think, after a while neither of us really tried too hard to find out about Jim's past. Not really."

"Maybe you're right. Jim got to where he didn't want to talk about it anymore, and after the two of you were married . . . well, I guess we kinda dropped it."

"But Dad, something bugs me more than anything now that I know who he is. Prominent people don't just disappear without a trace. Why wasn't anyone looking for him?"

Whit shook his head. "Damned if I know, but there's bound to be a reason. Maybe someone was, and all the signals got crossed. Tell me, Leah, how does he look? Is he okay?"

"Oh, yes, he looks marvelous. Older, of course. He's thinner than he was when we knew him, and he's quieter, more reserved than Jim was. But you'd recognize him if you saw him, especially when you heard his voice."

"I'd sure like to see him again."

"I'd like for you to. There's not much chance, but you and the farm might jog his memory."

Whit frowned. "Is that what you want?"

"I . . . I think so."

"Are you going to do anything about it, help it along by telling him something?"

"I don't know, Dad. I guess I'll just have to wait and see how the relationship develops. After all, Jacob Surratt and I have only known each other a few days. I have to keep reminding myself of that. I'm so afraid of mentioning something I'm not supposed to know." A small smile tugged at the corners of her mouth. "Jacob might be a little startled if I mentioned the scar on his hip." Instantly she sobered. "Jim had no idea where the scar had come from, but Jacob knows. He can tell me all sorts of things about Jim. Isn't that weird? I really am venturing into unknown territory. I don't have any idea what I should do."

"No, and I'm not sure anyone would. The mind's tough territory to explore."

"Something haunts Jacob," Leah said, more to herself than to Whit. "It's in his eyes. It must be those missing years."

"Well, I reckon that's understandable. If I had a couple of years gone from my life, I think they'd haunt me, too."

"Yes, I suppose so."

Whit's eyes were riveted on Leah, who had lapsed into some sort of private reverie. He studied her intently with fresh interest, for he noticed something he hadn't seen earlier: a certain radiance. An inner glow had heightened her color; her eyes sparkled with a mysterious light. Excitement bubbled just below her calm surface, and she looked the way she hadn't in a very long time—vital and alive. Whit had always thought his daughter pretty, but now she looked downright beautiful.

She was looking forward to seeing Dr. Surratt again, and Whit couldn't say for sure how he felt about that. Jim Stone had adored Leah, but what if this fancy society doctor didn't? That would kill her.

Often during the past six years he had wished his daughter would find someone else, someone who would bring a little joy into her life. He realized his values were a bit old-fashioned for the modern generation, but it just didn't seem right for a woman Leah's age to be concerned with career and motherhood and nothing else. A man could live alone without too much trouble, but a woman shouldn't. If that made him archaic, so be it.

But what would have happened if she had found someone else and then seen Jim? Whit shuddered almost visibly at the thought.

Just then Leah turned to look at her father. The radiance he had noticed intensified. "Jacob Surratt is interested in me, Dad. As a woman, I mean."

He grinned. "Oh, you know that, huh?"

"Of course. I felt the vibrations. Any woman over seventeen who doesn't recognize that look in a man's eyes is incredibly dense."

"Yeah, I figured as much. Your mother professed to be dumbfounded when I proposed to her, but I figured she always knew she could have me if she wanted me." Whit waited a moment. "How do you feel about that?"

"I don't understand, Dad."

"He has no idea you're his wife, yet he's attracted to you. Say the attraction is real, the two of you get close. Could you handle that, go on with the new and never long for the old?"

Leah thought for a moment before answering. Shrugging, she said, "I hate to keep saying this, Dad, but . . . I don't know. I honestly don't know. Something tells me I'll always want Jim back."

"Jim . . . or the life you had together?"

"The life?"

"It was a simple life, really. You both were young and hadn't known any real trouble. Except for having to grow up without a mama, you had pretty well sailed through on smooth waters, while Jim didn't even have a past.''

Leah sighed. ''You're right. It was a heavenly, carefree life, and I thought it would go on forever. Sure, I want that life back. Wouldn't you?''

''Which isn't exactly fair to Jacob Surratt, is it? He's bound to have a more intricate personality than Jim did.''

''Yes . . . he does. Much more. But I like him, too. It's complicated, isn't it?''

''If there's one thing I've learned in fifty-three years, it's that things are always complicated when you're dealing with human beings. Nothing's predictable. Maybe that's why I like working with animals. They're so simple and direct. What you see is what you get.'' Whit got to his feet. ''Let's go find out what Nina's up to. We don't want her eating so many cookies she spoils her supper. Stay for supper, hon? I think Tee's whipping up a batch of chili. Spend the night?''

''I'd love to,'' Leah said, standing up also. Tonight, more than most nights, she needed her father's companionship. ''I can go home first thing in the morning and get ready for the trip to Phoenix.''

Whit rounded the desk and put an affectionate arm around his daughter's shoulders. ''I'll be thinking of you tomorrow night.''

''I know.''

''And I'll be a basket case until I find out what happened.''

''I know that, too.''

''I wish I could tell you I'm happy you've found him again, but I don't know for sure that I am—not yet. I wish I could always protect you from trouble, but no one can do that.''

''That's true, but actually I've had precious little trouble in my life. Jim was about it. In a way, I have to be grateful.''

''Damned if life doesn't have a way of sneaking up on you when your back's turned!''

''Tell me about it!''

CHAPTER SEVEN

THE SATURDAY-AFTERNOON drive to Phoenix was anything but a joyous excursion. Leah was as edgy and nervous as a teenager getting ready for a big date; she was amazed at the butterflies in her stomach. Alex, in turn, was morose and laconic, very unlike him. Their mutual uneasiness didn't make for sparkling conversation. There were far too many clumsy silences, a first for them.

Yet underneath Leah's nervousness lay excitement and anticipation. She had hurried home from her father's house that morning to prepare for the trip, and for the first time in so long the day carried with it a sense of purpose. It had taken her an hour to get dressed, almost as long to decide what to pack, and that wasn't at all like the decisive person she normally was.

When Alex turned onto the quiet suburban street, Leah sat up straight and glanced around in confusion, as though wondering how on earth she had gotten there. Preoccupied, she couldn't remember a single detail of the journey. He braked then, turned off the street and drove through a massive wrought-iron gate, and she stared ahead of her curiously. Naturally she had expected Jacob to have a lovely home, and she wasn't disappointed. The house was a large, Spanish-style structure, built of eggshell stucco with archways and balconies and a tiled roof. Surrounding it were well-manicured grounds studded with color from neat gardens. "Gracious" was the first adjective that came to mind. A lovely, gracious home. It had probably been one of Scottsdale's finest when it had been built—some time ago, she guessed. What would a bachelor want with all this?

Which brought another question to mind: what had happened to the house during the two years Jacob had been Jim Stone? Houses like this didn't stand alone and neglected for two years. Surely whoever had taken care of it would have tried to find out where the owner was. For days her mind had been full of questions, none she dared ask.

Leah cast a surreptitious glance in Alex's direction, trying to gauge his reaction to their surroundings. Alex wasn't easily impressed, since he was accustomed to affluence himself, and he wasn't about to admit to being so now. "Very nice," was all he said.

Poor Alex, Leah mused ruefully. He was trying hard to be good about all this and failing miserably. He didn't want to be here, and he didn't want her here. Leah wished she had left him out of it altogether. But after all, Jacob had invited him, and Alex had accepted, albeit only because he didn't want her coming alone.

The car inched to a halt in front of a walled-in courtyard, apparently the main entrance. "Well, what now?" Alex asked. "Do we appear with bags in hand, or wait for lackeys to fetch them for us?"

Leah shrugged, ignoring the bite to his tone. She had never known Alex to be anything but gracious himself, and she was sure he would be now. Yet she had a feeling she was going to be under his watchful eye every step of the way. "We can always get our things later. Let's just let Jacob know we're here."

They walked through the tiled courtyard, thick with plants, flowers and vines. Leah spied a bubbling fountain nestled against a vine-covered wall; here and there stood cosy groupings of wrought-iron furniture. Such lush, green loveliness didn't just happen in Arizona, Leah knew. Somebody or several somebodies devoted countless hours to maintaining the courtyard and grounds. The entire impression was of a desert oasis.

Alex rang the doorbell. Only seconds passed before a white-coated manservant answered it. Leah told him who they were, and the man smilingly held the door wide and motioned them inside. "Dr. Surratt is expecting you," he said courteously.

They stepped into a gleaming tiled foyer, in the center of which stood a round mahogany table. On top of that was the most exquisite—and quite possibly the most gigantic—porcelain vase Leah had ever seen. It held dozens of yellow roses, grown on the premises, she assumed. Quickly she scanned their surroundings. On their left was a formal living room; on their right a dining room. Other rooms opened off a long hallway, while ahead of them a mahogany-railed stairway rose to the second floor. It was impossible to take in everything at once, but Leah sensed that Jacob's home was furnished more for comfort than anything else. In spite of its size and immaculate condition, the house looked lived in, not untouchable.

She lifted her eyes to Jacob, who was hurrying down the stairway with a welcoming smile on his face. He was dressed much the way he had been Wednesday afternoon—impeccably and casually in slacks, dark gray, and a white knit shirt. *He looks like a doctor,* she suddenly thought. *But that's ridiculous. What does a doctor look like?* Powerless to control the acceleration of her heartbeat, Leah could only breathe deeply. Would she ever see him without longing to be in his arms?

"That's all right, Davis," Jacob said, coming up behind the man. "I'll see to our guests. Please tend to their luggage."

"Very good, sir."

Jacob stepped forward, extending his hand to Alex. "Trent, it's good to see you again."

"Thank you, Doctor. I appreciate the invitation. This is quite a place you have here." Alex's voice was coolly cordial.

"Thank you. It's been in the family for a number of years, almost twenty. It's much too large for my needs, of course, and the upkeep is a constant chore, but I've never gotten around to selling."

Leah's curiosity was further peaked. A house? A family? Concrete reasons to wonder why no one had been looking for him.

Jacob turned to her, and an anticipatory gleam he couldn't suppress shone in his eyes. For two days he had been filled with excitement, convinced that some momentous event was about to occur. He had reminded himself more than once that she was coming for the opening, nothing more. She would spend one night in his house, and her watchdog Trent would be with her. Ridiculous to think anything noteworthy would come of their meeting, yet now, as he drank in the sight of her, the excitement returned, stronger than ever.

She was wearing a simple dress the color of lime sherbet, one of those straight things—he thought they were called sheaths—that skimmed her hips and stopped just below her knees. Her lustrous hair was caught at the nape with a print scarf, and tiny gold loops hung from her earlobes. For a moment he was almost mesmerized by her eyes; a man could fall into those dark eyes, he thought. Each time he saw her he was struck again by her unusual beauty, so clean and wholesome on one hand, so exotic on the other.

"Leah," he said softly, "welcome to my home. I'm so glad you're here."

"Thank you," she murmured in return. "It's lovely."

The exchange was simple and proper, yet Leah was fully aware of the sizzling current of sensuality passing between them. She couldn't have been more affected had he swept her into his arms and kissed her passionately. The sound of her own pulse hammered in her ears. Her cheeks grew very warm, and for one horrifying second she thought she was going to blush.

As much as Jacob would have liked to continue staring at her, he shook himself free from fascination, aware of the third party who was witnessing this exchange with more than casual curiosity. He could feel Trent's eyes boring through the back of his head. Rubbing his hands together in a gesture of satisfaction, he said, "Well, let me show you to your rooms. Then feel free to pass the time any way you like. We'll be leaving for the clinic around seven, returning here afterward for dinner. I hope that suits you both."

Leah and Alex assured him it did.

"This way, then...."

Leah hoped she wasn't gawking, but her head swiveled this way and that as she and Alex followed Jacob up the stairway. It was readily apparent that the house belonged to a man with eclectic tastes and a passion for collection. Evidence of that was everywhere. Some valuable paintings in ornate frames lined the stairway, each properly lighted. At the landing between the first and second floors, a stark futuristic painting was displayed on a bentwood easel beside an antique stained-glass window. A collection of dried flowers and grasses in a handwoven basket stood on the floor beneath the window, completing the display. Alex's eyes were about to pop out of his head. He would have a field day just wandering from room to room.

The house seemed to go on and on. Leah counted at least five bedrooms on the second floor. They passed one she was sure was Jacob's. It looked like him, tailored, elegantly masculine. Next to it was the one Alex was to stay in. Leah waited in the hall while the two men went inside, her interest arrested by two portraits—one of a distinguished man, the other of a regal-looking woman. She moved closer to study them.

No one had to tell her the gentleman was Jacob's father; the resemblance was unmistakable. Handsome people, both of his parents. Nina's grandparents.... If they knew about the child, would they be as foolish about her as Whit was? Leah blinked, and a lump formed in her throat. Years ago, when pregnant with Nina, she had desperately wished she could have found out something about Jim's mother and father. She didn't know why, but it had always seemed she should know more about the genes her child would inherit. Silly. Who thought about such things anymore?

There was a movement behind her. "Leah?" Jacob's voice broke through her pensive thoughts.

She turned with a start. "What? Oh, I . . . I was just admiring these portraits. Your parents?"

"Yes. They died in a boating accident while I was doing my residency." Her expression puzzled him. "Is something the matter?"

"No . . . no, nothing." She should have guessed they had died before she met Jim; parents would have frantically searched for a missing son. So who had kept the house while he was gone? Jacob was not the man with no ties they had imagined Jim to be. "Do you have brothers or sisters?"

"No, I was an only child. The last of the Surratt line, unfortunately"

There's Nina, she wanted to say.

Gently Jacob touched her elbow. "Your room is this way, at the end of the hall."

The bedroom, like everything else she had seen in the house, was tastefully furnished, a skillful blend of contemporary and antique. A king-size bed covered with a quilted terra-cotta spread dominated the room. A love seat in a coordinating print stood against one wall, and next to it was a Jacobean secretary desk. The almond-colored carpet beneath her feet was thick and plush. "It's beautiful, Jacob."

"I hope you'll be comfortable." He crossed the room and drew aside the drapes, instantly bathing the room in a lucid light. "This room has a private bath, over there." He pointed to a door on the right. "And it overlooks the pool."

Leah placed her handbag on a nearby dresser and went to stand beside him, looking down. "That's inviting."

"Did you happen to bring a suit? I forgot to suggest it."

"Yes, I did." She had packed one just in case, for she had supposed swimming pools were as common as dishwashers in Scottsdale.

"Then let's go for a swim, shall we?"

"I'd love it."

Jacob made some kind of move, to adjust the blinds or something. The only thing Leah was aware of was his nearness, his arm brushing hers, the intoxicatingly clean scent of him. If he moved even half a step closer he would feel her trembling, and what would reserved Dr. Surratt think of that? It was definitely becoming harder and harder to breathe. And she had thought Wednesday afternoon difficult! Getting through this, then tonight with any degree of poise should earn her a medal.

At that moment he took the half step she had hoped he wouldn't; his larger body seemed to hover over hers. Leah stood paralyzed, staring at the pulse point at the base of his throat. Slowly she raised her face to look at him. Her heart-stopping thought was that he was going to kiss her. If he did, she would kiss him back. And why not? She was his wife. She had every right to kiss him all she liked.

Dolt! He doesn't know that! You can't just fall into his arms. What would he think?

Jacob thought that in all his life he had never wanted to kiss anyone so badly. He might have been on an amphetamine high, because Leah had the most uncanny ability to make him feel reckless and a little impetuous—things he had never been, not even in his youth. He raised one hand, poised at her shoulder. Would she be offended by a simple kiss? Odd how little he knew about today's women.

Contrary to popular gossip around the clinic and the country club, he didn't get involved with a lot of women. For reasons he couldn't fathom, they seemed drawn to him, but he was rarely sexually involved with them. In younger days he had had frequent passionate needs. Even Jacob Surratt had lived through a period when "scoring" with girls had been the most important thing on earth. But six years ago he had emerged from his fugue state to find himself longing for something more satisfying than a casual romantic fling. Since then he had cautiously searched for something he privately suspected didn't exist. For that reason he had guarded against emotional entanglements. Solitude spared him disappointment.

Yet he wanted to become involved with this woman—emotionally, sexually and every other way. Could he possibly know that for sure in such a short time? Maybe not, but having waited so long to feel this way, he wasn't about to spoil it by asking himself pertinent questions. Wanting her felt too damned good. Wanting her felt...human. His hand touched her shoulder, and he looked down at her with undisguised hunger. "Leah..."

Briefly she closed her eyes, the better to enjoy the sensation of his touch. She opened them, and the past six years simply melted away. The look on Jacob's face reminded her of ones she had received from her young husband countless times. More guarded perhaps, but basically the same. An ache stirred deep inside her, down in the lower part of her stomach. He wanted to kiss her, and she wanted him to. It was a compulsion too real to deny. She longed to melt against him, slip her arms around his waist, rest her head on his shoulder, and she seemed to have lost all hold on reality. "Yes," she said breathlessly, dreamily.

"Do you have any idea what a shock it is for a man my age to be swept off his feet?"

His frankness was so disarming that Leah took a step backward, staring up at him in surprise. The thought of this sophisticated, urbane man being swept off his feet brought forth a giggle, effectively shattering the sweet eloquence of the moment. And for that fact she was suddenly, enormously grateful. Had Jacob actually kissed her, she feared her response would have been much too eager, anything but a "first kiss" kind of kiss. And the admiration she saw in his eyes might have diminished considerably. Damn, it was so hard to remember she barely knew him!

"The young lady's luggage, sir," a discreet masculine voice said. "Where shall I put it?"

Leah turned to see Davis standing at the threshold. He was carrying her garment bag in one hand, her overnighter in the other. Beside her, Jacob released a raspy breath. "The bag in the closet, Davis, please. And just leave the suitcase on the bed."

"Yes, sir." After following his employer's instructions, Davis quickly left the room.

Needing to put some distance between them, Leah walked to the foot of the bed and unlatched her suitcase, flipping it open and reaching for her swimsuit. "I do hope Alex thought to bring swim trunks. He probably didn't, though. I didn't mention it, and it's not the sort of thing he would think of." She chattered on. "Alex is the kind who would rather sit by a pool than dive into it."

Jacob frowned. Had he totally misread the expression on Leah's face a moment earlier? He didn't think so, but she was flustered now, charmingly so. If she was interested in him—and he had to think she was—the fact troubled her. The husband again; had to be. Ex-husband, he forcibly reminded himself. She still loved him, so showing interest in another man might seem unfaithful to her. What else would account for her skittishness where he was concerned?

So, okay, he wouldn't pounce. He wasn't sure he knew how to pounce, anyway. This was a time when he wished he was more adept at clever masculine games and come-ons. What he feared more than anything was appearing to be an insensitive clod on the make...still he knew a number of men whom he considered insensitive clods, and they seemed to do very well with women.

They wouldn't do well with Leah Stone, he thought decisively. She was different. And though they both had voids in their lives, Leah apparently wasn't as ready to let him fill hers as he was to let her fill his, so he'd move cautiously. Actually, he found her reluctance appealing; even a bit old-fashioned. But engaging nevertheless. Loyalty and fidelity weren't exactly a glut on the market these days.

Pretending nothing unusual had transpired, Jacob smiled offhandedly and made for the door. "Tell you what—I'll ask Trent if he brought trunks. If not, I'm sure I have some he can wear. Then we'll meet at poolside, the three of us. All right?"

"Yes. Yes, that's fine." Blankly Leah stared after his retreating figure. When he was out of sight she sank wearily to the edge of the bed, feeling as helpless and out of control as a lost child.

LEAH LIFTED HERSELF out of the pool and went to lie facedown on a lounge. Nearby, Jacob and Alex sat beneath an umbrella table, deep in a discussion about a new artist they both knew and admired. Leah smiled as she caught snatches of the conversation. Alex, in spite of his reservations, was enjoying himself, and Jacob seemed to be more relaxed than she had yet seen him.

She had been so aware of his eyes on her when she had first appeared at the pool. Her jade green maillot was a modest swimsuit, but it was a swimsuit. It exposed all of her gentle curves to his avid gaze. It seemed Dr. Surratt's reserve was slipping badly. He, who knew human anatomy the way she knew warp and weft, had looked at her as though he'd never seen the female form before. Even though he had stayed at the table with Alex, hadn't joined her in the pool, she had known he was watching her.

But after her first look at him she found it all but impossible to look again. He was wearing a stark white terry-cloth shirt, unbuttoned to reveal his thickly matted chest, and light blue swim trunks. She had always thought him so damned sexy in swim trunks—a lean, bronzed man. Completely desirable. Seeing him dressed that way made her aware of her own femininity, a femininity that had been held in limbo for six years.

Davis stopped at the lounge and offered her a lemonade. Thanking him, she took it and sipped slowly, idly wondering how many servants inhabited the place, halfheartedly following the men's conversation, mostly lost in a private daze. The sun induced laziness, and she closed her eyes, lulled into a half stupor by the deep resonance of Jacob's voice. Jim's voice.... Her stomach fluttered. It all might have been a dream.

Then, when she had soaked up all the sun she dared so early in the season, she pushed herself up, swung her legs off the lounge, and found her eyes fixed squarely on a pair of muscular legs. Jacob stood beside the lounge, poised on the balls of his feet. Leah took in his stance, the perfect shape of his legs, the way his bathing trunks molded to his body and blatantly outlined his masculine form. A lump formed in her throat that she had some difficulty swallowing past.

Her eyes continued upward; she was afraid she might have to sit on her hands to keep from reaching for him. He was holding something in his hand and smiling down at her. "Lotion?" he asked. "You're still very fair. You might burn."

"Thanks," she said shakily, and took the tube from him. Squirting a little circle of cream into her palm, she nervously smeared it over her shoulders and down her arms. More cream, and she covered her thighs and calves. Glancing toward the table where he'd been sitting, she saw that the other chair was vacant. "Where's Alex?"

"Inside." Jacob cocked his head toward the pool. Then, to her consternation, he dropped onto the lounge beside her and took the tube from her hand. "Here, let me do your back."

Her protest died in her throat. She tended to make too big a deal of everything regarding this man, and he would think her silly. His warm hand touched her shoulder blades, making her flinch. As it moved over her shoulders and back, rubbing gently, she felt goose bumps prickling her arms. Nervously she massaged them away, hoping he hadn't seen.

Abruptly he stopped and recapped the cream. "You're a good swimmer. Want to go in again?"

Forgetting she had been on her way inside herself, forgetting she had already had all the sun she should, she stood up. "All right. Last one in..."

They hit the water simultaneously, cleaving through it like two knives. Jacob, however, quickly outdistanced her and was treading water, waiting for her when she reached the opposite pool wall.

Surfacing, blinking away water, she crossed her arms on the concrete edge and looked at him. Slick wet hair clung to his face and neck.

"Pretty good," he said appreciatively.

"And you're awfully good. Once a lifeguard, I'll bet." She had told Jim that several times. He, of course, hadn't known if it was true.

Jacob nodded. "A long, long time ago."

She could visualize him—eighteen or nineteen years old, a tanned young man seated on the platform, pretending to be oblivious to all the admiring feminine stares. There must have been legions of dreamy-eyed teenage girls....

"And you were a Red Cross instructor, right?" he asked.

"Uh-huh. During summers when I was in college."

The pool area was very quiet; the only sound was the faint hum of the filtering system. Jacob's gaze held hers steadfastly. He saw her lashes dip under his scrutiny, and he realized he stared at her too long, too often. She laid her cheek on her folded arms. Disregarding all politeness and convention, he continued to stare at her. His hand moved beneath the water to rest at the small of her back. This need to touch her was overwhelming.

At the pressure of his fingers, Leah stiffened and raised her head, then relaxed and uncrossed her arms. While one hand gripped the pool's edge, the other reached for his solid forearm. It was true that his constant scrutiny made her nervous. Had he been a stranger she might have been offended. But there was no way he could offend her. She wanted to float right into his arms. She picked up his vibrations, and a tingling sensation shot up her legs. She closed them tightly in an effort to suppress it.

Her fingers closing round his arm encouraged Jacob to glide even closer to her. Her eyes were wide, her lips slightly parted. The look she gave him made Jacob's heart pound. *Isn't it amazing,* he thought, *that two strangers can come together like this and, with virtually no effort, establish this rapport? She feels it, too. She doesn't like it. She might even hate it, but she feels it, too.*

That knowledge sent his mind winging off on some wild, uncharted course of expectation. Beneath the water his arm encircled her waist, pulling her closer. Their thighs touched.

If he wants to kiss me now, Leah thought, *I'm going to let him. Propriety be damned.* Her hunger for him was something she could taste in her mouth.

A voice called to them from the far side of the pool. "Are you two aware of the time?" Leah and Jacob swiveled their heads to see Alex watching them with a guarded expression.

"Afraid not!" Jacob called back.

"If we're going to leave by seven, Leah might start giving some thought to getting ready."

Leah slowly expelled a controlled breath. "He's right. Not being one of you fortunate males, I can't just shower and shave and be off. It takes some time for me to put my best foot forward, especially—" she touched her drenched hair "—especially after swimming."

"Then shall we make a return trip?"

"Yes, let's."

With slow strokes, breaking the water with only a ripple, they crossed the pool. Jacob lifted himself out, then helped her. Reaching for a towel, he draped it around her shoulders, holding it there longer than necessary. His hand brushed her breast, and Leah took a clumsy step backward. "I'll see you later," she said, and feeling as unsophisticated as the woman who had married Jim Stone, she hurried into the house. She knew he watched her until she was out of sight.

Upstairs, she discovered someone had laid out an irresistible array of toiletries in the bathroom, and on the bedside stand she discovered a small carafe of wine, a wineglass, a wedge of Brie, and a peeled, sliced kiwi. She'd wager not even the Biltmore could surpass the Surratt house for hospitality.

Since she had plenty of time—Alex had seen to that, she reflected wryly—Leah treated herself to the works: luxurious bath, shampoo, manicure, pedicure. Sipping wine and nibbling fruit and cheese, she paid special attention to her makeup. Devoting undue time to the routine task of getting dressed was something new to her, but it was just what she needed. Her confidence bolstered, she was certain she could, with some effort, learn to regard Jacob as an exciting new man who had unexpectedly entered her life. She would stop longing for Jim, stop searching for him in Jacob. She was going to enjoy this. Jacob made her feel like a desirable woman, and she hadn't felt that way in a long time.

An hour later she stood in front of the full-length mirror attached to the back of the closet door. It wouldn't be enough to simply look her best; she wanted to feel her best, be at her best. Everything she had brought to wear to the opening—the simple black dress, the lacy black underwear, jewelry, fragrance—everything had been chosen with that thought in mind. The dress was a marvel of simplicity, and there was nothing like black to make her feel dressed up. Raising her arms, she clasped a single strand of perfect pearls around her neck. One more inspection in the mirror, then she picked up her small black clutch, left the bedroom and went to join the men.

Following the sound of their voices, she walked down the hallway and paused at the threshold of a paneled room that had to be the den. Floor to ceiling, book-crammed shelves lined the walls on three sides. Jacob and Alex were there, both dressed in tuxedos, both holding aperitif glasses. Since they hadn't seen her yet, she took the time to study both of them.

She had always thought Alex looked splendid in a tux, and tonight was no exception. The formal dress suited him; he was that kind of man. Often he hosted formal dinner parties in his home, and everything was done with flair—the finest china, linen, crystal, food served in proper courses with appropriate wines, ladies in long dresses and gentlemen in tuxedos. He loved that sort of thing. Leah smiled. She sometimes thought Alex would have been more at home in another era.

Then her eyes moved on to Jacob, and a shock wave jolted her. Jacob in evening dress was something to see! Tall, dark and gorgeous. He had ... presence. And savoir faire, polish and the indefinable something called class. With him dressed like that, she shouldn't find it hard to forget Jim tonight. She could count on the fingers of one hand the times she had seen Jim in anything but jeans. Once she had bought him a suit, but he never had worn it....

There you go, Leah. Stop it. She straightened, shook herself free of such thoughts and stepped into the room. "Good evening," she said brightly, and both men turned in her direction.

"Leah," Alex said, moving toward her. "Why, I don't think I've ever seen you looking lovelier."

She smiled softly. "Thanks, Alex." Almost shyly she looked over Alex's shoulder, her gaze colliding with Jacob's. She saw him swallow rapidly, then his mouth opened and quickly closed again. Apparently there were things he wanted to say but couldn't. He didn't have to; his eyes said it all. A woman is as beautiful as she feels, Leah thought, and in that one spellbound moment, she felt absolutely, ravishingly beautiful.

"Would you like a drink?" Alex inquired solicitously.

"No, thanks. There was some marvelous wine in my room. What a thoughtful gesture, Jacob."

He cleared his throat, collecting himself. "I wish I could take credit for it, but actually it was Davis's idea. He has a flair for that sort of thing."

"Then I must remember to thank Davis. Have I kept you gentlemen waiting long?"

"Not long. Alex has been enjoying some of my collection. Besides, any wait would have been worth it."

Alex took her by the arm. "Come here, Leah, I want to show you something. A signed Thomas Moran, circa 1902. Jacob has an impressive collection of Southwestern artists."

Leah smiled secretively. She noticed it was no longer "Trent" and "Doctor," and she wasn't the least surprised that the two men had taken to each other. They were birds of a feather; how could they help liking each other? She allowed Alex to lead her across the room to view the Moran.

Jacob watched them, or rather he watched Leah. Her glistening hair was wound into a sleek chignon, giving her just a hint of stylish sophistication. The dress she was wearing was simple, baring only her smooth arms and the slender taper of her shapely legs. He couldn't imagine her ever dressing in a daring or provocative manner, yet he'd wager there wouldn't be a woman at the opening who would equal her in sex appeal.

His appreciative gaze lingered on her, and anticipation welled inside him. Tonight he felt curiously removed from his customary role of prominent physician and upstanding member of the community. Tonight he felt loose and free, like a young man on a date with a lovely woman. Unfortunately—he shifted his gaze to Alex—his date was chaperoned. He wondered if he could reasonably hope for time alone with her before the evening was over.

CHAPTER EIGHT

THE OPENING turned out to be exactly the sort of affair Leah had pictured—a large cocktail party full of shine and glitter, lavish food, laughter and animated conversation. The crème of Phoenix society was there, dressed to the teeth, anxious to see and be seen. Jacob dutifully led his guests through the throng, introducing them to acquaintances; other people came forward to introduce themselves to him. Leah knew she wouldn't remember any of their names; she was too intent on observing the stir Jacob created when he entered the place. Heads turned, all right—all in his direction. She thought it odd that a man who projected aloofness drew people like a magnet, but perhaps it was that very aloofness that made him so intriguing.

He soon became separated from them, since everyone seemed to want a word with Dr. Surratt. Alex, as usual, immediately encountered someone he knew from somewhere; Leah had never been with him when he hadn't. After a few minutes of polite conversation with Alex's friend, she left the two men deep in discussion and unobtrusively backed off, helped herself to a glass of punch and found a quiet corner where she could view the proceedings with her customary lack of interest. The party's din was deafening. Were all these people really having as good a time as they appeared to be?

Brief snatches of conversation reached her. Nearby, two men were arguing the relative merits of several investment plans. A couple walked by, and she heard the woman say, "I'm surprised Peggy didn't leave town. I certainly would if that happened to me!"

Leah smiled, thinking how interesting the story behind that must be.

Three women moved past her just then, all of them elegantly dressed, all of them in their midthirties, she guessed. They stopped just a few feet from her, and though she wasn't in the least interested in their conversation, she couldn't help overhearing it. The women, she soon surmised, were close friends, married to doctors associated with the clinic and well acquainted with most of the guests. Leah tried to ignore them; possibly she would have if a name hadn't reached her ears.

"Surratt's something in a tux, isn't he?"

"Oh, I don't know. Kinda cold and forbidding, if you ask me."

"Joe says he runs a tight ship."

"Probably runs his house the same way. Can you imagine being married to someone like that?"

"He's pushing forty and hasn't ever been married, which makes you wonder about him right away."

"Well, looking at him tonight...damned good-looking, I must say."

"Too cold. Bet he makes love like a robot."

"Hell, I'll bet he could knock your socks off if he took a mind to."

The women moved on, and Leah flushed, hating the picture of the mechanical, unresponsive lover that had formed in her mind. Jim hadn't been cold, far from it, but she wondered about Jacob. She thought she had seen a side of him that was anything but.

Her gaze moved to the huge wall where her tapestry would hang. Quietly contemplating the space, she changed her mind about the design. Alex and Jacob had been right to insist she actually see the room and the wall. She decided on something bolder than she had originally envisioned, something that would draw the eye upward....

AT THAT MOMENT, across the room a door opened and a stocky, sandy-haired man of about forty walked through. Though dressed in evening clothes, he was no imposing figure. He had the uncomfortable look of a man who is someplace he doesn't want to be. He tugged at his shirt cuffs, pressed his bow tie with thumb and forefinger. He paused, and his eyes swept the room, settled for a moment on the large group surrounding Jacob, then moved on.

Dr. Charles White was late, but his arrival caused no stir. In fact, barely half a dozen people seemed to notice him at all. Of those who did, only one stepped forward to greet him—a stout, stylish matron. Extending a bejeweled hand, she beamed at the psychiatrist.

"Dr. White, how wonderful to see you again!"

Charles took her hand and searched his brain for the woman's name. To his dismay, nothing came to him. "Why, hello, there. So glad you could come."

"I wouldn't have missed it for the world. Surely you know that."

Charles's mind remained blank, but some inner sense told him he should know who the woman was. "Quite a turnout, wouldn't you say?"

The woman eyed him suspiciously. "Yes, it is." A perfectly manicured fingertip tapped the side of her mouth. "Dr. White, you don't remember me at all, do you?"

"Oh, of course I do. I—"

"Clarice Hall," the woman said with a cool smile.

"Certainly, Clarice. Wonderful to have you here." Had it been physically possible, Charles would have kicked his own fanny. Clarice was the wife of one of the clinic's chief benefactors, a local philanthropist whose donations had been more than generous. She prided herself on being a well-known local figure. People like Clarice Hall expected to be recognized. He had just committed a social faux pas of considerable magnitude, which he did far too frequently.

Damn! And it would be useless to try to make amends; the woman had seen right through him. Chagrined, he acknowledged her curt goodbye with as much aplomb as he could muster, watching her stiff, regal departure. His damaged composure was hardly helped when, a few seconds later, he saw Clarice Hall approach Jacob and distinctly heard his partner say, "Clarice, how wonderful you look!"

Shrugging away his ineptitude, Charles moved to the refreshment table to pour himself a cup of punch. Sipping it absently, he surveyed the throng, his eyes darting aimlessly about...until they fell on the slender young woman in the black dress standing apart from the crowd. They fastened on her, widened, then narrowed in a thorough inspection. Slowly he moved away from the table to stand against a wall, but his eyes never left the woman....

LEAH'S THOUGHTS were interrupted when she had the distinct feeling she was being watched. Turning abruptly, she saw a sturdy-looking man lounging against a wall several yards behind her. Apparently he'd been staring at her, and there was the strangest expression on his face. When she caught his eye without warning, he immediately straightened and looked away, flustered. For a moment he seemed to want to turn and walk away. Then he recovered and shifted his eyes back to her. A nervous smile crossed his face. Hesitantly he moved toward her, and Leah braced herself for a typical come-on, albeit not a very smooth, expert one. The look on his face was unmistakably curious. She wouldn't have been at all surprised if he had begun his overture with something as hackneyed as, "Haven't I seen you someplace . . . ?"

Curiously, she thought she might very well have said the same thing to him. His face looked vaguely familiar . . . or did it? Something made her think she had seen him before.

"Good evening," he said as he approached. "Forgive me for staring, but you seemed rather bored."

On second thought, Leah decided he just had one of those faces, ordinarily pleasant, unspectacular. He looked like dozens of people. "Do I? Well, I'm not. Actually, I was studying that wall over there." She indicated it with a wave of her hand.

The man looked at the wall, then back at her. "It's rather large, isn't it? But frankly, apart from its sheer size, I see nothing particularly fascinating about it."

Leah smiled. "No, perhaps most people wouldn't, but it holds special interest for me."

The man made a show of giving that some thought. "Now I'm wondering what would cause a lovely young woman to be so interested in a wall. I have it! You're an architect."

"Not even close. I'm a professional weaver, and Dr. Surratt has commissioned me to do a tapestry for that very wall."

The man's expression changed. "You know Jacob?" he asked in disbelief.

Leah wondered why her words had evoked that response. "Yes, I do."

"Have you known him long?"

"As a matter of fact, I only met him a few days ago." She frowned. "Why?"

The man seemed to give himself a shake. He extended his hand, and the smile returned. "Had you known Jacob long, I'm sure I would have either heard about you or met you by now. I'm Charles White, Jacob's partner."

"Oh, Dr. White." She juggled her punch cup and shook his hand. "How nice to meet you. I'm Leah Stone."

"The pleasure is mine, Leah. So . . . you met Jacob through your work?"

"Yes, he had seen one of my tapestries and contacted me."

"Interesting. Well, what do you think of our little place?"

"From what I've seen, it's impressive. And it isn't little."

"No, it isn't. But it is impressive. This clinic is unique in many ways. For one thing, our physicians work for a salary. Would you have imagined that?"

"No, I wouldn't have. But why...?" She hesitated.

"Why would a physician want to work for a salary when private practice is so lucrative? That's what you were going to ask, wasn't it?"

Leah nodded.

"Many reasons. One, the beginning salaries are generous. Two, the facilities are superb. Working here, a doctor has all the latest technology available and doesn't have the responsibility of maintaining an office, hiring and firing and all that. You'd be surprised how attractive a feature that is. Since you don't seem enormously interested in this—" he made a sweeping gesture with his arm to indicate the packed reception room "—human circus, why don't you let me show you around?"

Leah's eyes quickly scanned the room. Jacob was standing in the middle of a group of people, most of them women. She guessed it would be some time before he was free. "Why, thank you, Doctor. I'd like that."

She slipped her hand into the crook of Dr. White's elbow, and together they left the party. For the next twenty minutes or so they peered into treatment rooms and offices, X-ray centers and laboratories. Leah understood little of the psychiatrist's explanations concerning the complicated equipment. All she saw was a gleaming, modern clinic that would probably be a good place in which to find out what ailed you. Finally, at the end of a long corridor, Dr. White pushed open a double door, and they stepped into an entirely different world.

"My bailiwick," he informed her. "This is the psychiatric unit."

There was nothing clinical about this part of the building. The reception room was furnished very much like an elegant study, subdued. There was a music room, a small snack bar and a library. There were no treatment rooms, only half a dozen offices, all beautifully decorated, all with the obligatory couch, even if for appearances only. The largest and most elegant of these was set off from the others by a paneled vestibule. "My office," Charles

White said, opening an ornately carved oak door. "Please come in."

Leah stepped into a room anyone would have enjoyed occupying, decorated with thick taupe carpeting, grass-cloth-covered walls, several paintings that had been chosen more for their color scheme than for artistic value, and three enormous plants. One wall was given over to glass-front bookcases. "Lovely," she murmured. "Restful."

"It was meant to be. Patients who come to this office need to forget everyday turmoil, for fifty minutes, at least. I have sherry. Would you care for some?"

"No, thanks. The punch was enough. We'll be leaving soon, I imagine. Jacob is having dinner for us at his house."

"You're Jacob's houseguest?"

She nodded. "Alex and I are spending the night there, yes."

"Alex?"

"He owns the gallery that handles my work."

"Are you married, Leah?"

The question was abrupt, taking her by surprise. "No, I...not anymore."

Charles pursed his lips and studied her intently. Too intently, Leah thought. His manner was unusual to the point of being unnerving. She was being placed under a microscope, but with none of the usual man-woman interest. The old cliché about psychiatrists being at least as odd as their patients popped into her head; then she dismissed it. He was curious about her, but so what? Wouldn't it be only natural for Dr. White to wonder about his partner's new woman friend?

Pretending to be fascinated by the psychiatrist's large collection of books, she idly wandered toward the bookcases. "Have you actually had time to read all these?"

He chuckled. "Most of them. Parts of all of them."

"You have several books on hypnotism." Her eyes scanned the titles. "Does that sort of thing really work?"

"It can be an effective tool, yes."

"Do you use it?"

"Sometimes."

"It looks as though memory is another of your interests. Improving it, retaining it, abnormalities...." Leah turned to Dr. White. "Like amnesia?"

"Yes." He moved to stand beside her. "Fascinating subject. I once wrote a paper on amnesia, which, I'm happy to say, was published."

She wondered if Charles White knew of Jacob's condition, if that was something he would have told his partner. She had no idea how long the two men had known each other. For sure she wasn't supposed to know about the amnesia, but Dr. White was the knowledgeable person she had been wishing for. He could answer some of her questions, if she proceeded cautiously....

"I can't imagine forgetting a huge slice of your life," she commented casually. "Does a person just forget . . . everything?"

"Everything, no. Names, places, time, events—those things are forgotten. But not things like speech, manners, traffic laws, motor skills. All those things that are so heavily overlearned throughout life are normally retained."

"If you've published a paper on amnesia, you must have treated many cases."

"Many short-term cases. A few long-terms ones. My main interest is in psychological amnesia."

Leah turned abruptly. "Psychological?"

"Yes. Amnesia can be caused by illness or injury, of course, but then there's the complex world of psychological amnesia, where a patient professes to want to remember but actually doesn't. Fascinating. I've found, in most cases, that the patient's present life is so pleasant, he fears memory return will only complicate it."

Dr. White had confirmed an earlier suspicion. Once she and Jim had fallen in love, he had stopped trying to find out about his past. Could Jacob be doing the same thing? "Interesting," she murmured. "What are the chances of a patient's recalling things that happened during the fugue?"

He looked startled. "You know the name for it?"

"I, ah, once knew someone with amnesia. That's what he called it." Leah bit her lip. Dumb thing to say. It didn't jibe with all the questions she'd been asking. Oh, well. Maybe he wouldn't realize that.

"I see." The psychiatrist rubbed a forefinger across his mouth. "The chances are, frankly, poor. And the more time that passes, the poorer they become. Even good memory dims with the years."

"One more question, Doctor, and then I really should go back to the party. Alex and Jacob might be ready to leave."

"Of course. What's the question?"

"If you had a friend with amnesia, and if you knew what had happened to that friend during the period of memory loss, would you tell him what you knew?"

Charles White frowned darkly, staring at the floor a moment. Then he looked up. "No," he said decisively, "I wouldn't."

"Why not?"

"Because it would require too swift an adjustment on the amnesiac's part. And it would do nothing to restore memory, only add to the confusion. Besides . . . there's always the chance you could be dealing with psychological amnesia. By telling the patient something he or she doesn't really want to know, you might be doing irreparable harm." He emphasized the word "irreparable."

Every nerve in Leah's body seemed to tighten. Instinct had warned her against saying anything to Jacob, so in that respect she had been right. She could accept the fact that he wouldn't be able to immediately adjust to the knowledge. But psychological amnesia? She'd never heard of it. She couldn't believe that Jacob subconsciously didn't want to remember her or their brief life together. That was too much to ask of her already overburdened heart.

"Amnesia must be handled delicately," the psychiatrist went on. "Certainly it isn't something for a lay person to, er, fool around with. I'm sure you understand that." His eyes bore down on her as if to underscore the warning.

Leah nodded mutely.

"What happened to your friend?" Charles asked.

"Friend?"

"The friend with amnesia."

"Oh, I . . . I don't know," she said lamely. "He went away and I lost track of him."

LEAH RETURNED to the party to discover Jacob and Alex were indeed looking for her, both of them anxious to leave. Conversation on the way back to the Surratt house was mostly limited to offhand remarks about the party, the food, the beautiful new clinic, but Jacob seemed mildly surprised to learn that Charles White had taken the time to show Leah around.

"Charles?" he asked.

"Yes. Why?"

He shrugged. "Oh, no reason in particular. That kind of hospitality doesn't sound much like Charles, that's all."

Once they returned to the house they were immediately ushered into the dining room and treated to a superb dinner. Afterward they adjourned to the den for after-dinner drinks and more conversation.

Alex was in a wonderful mood, for this type of evening was his cup of tea—plenty of food, people and talk. Leah feigned rapt interest in everything being said, but she actually heard little of it. Her interest was centered on their host, and a vague sort of restlessness gripped her, along with disappointment. She hadn't had a moment alone with Jacob all evening. She knew no more about him than she had before, only that he seemed the antithesis of Jim Stone. Whatever she had hoped this visit would accomplish—and she wasn't at all sure what she'd expected—hadn't come about.

Her eyes wandered around the den, then collided unexpectedly with Jacob's. She thought he telegraphed his own disappointment, and her heart skipped a beat. Quickly she glanced at Alex, who, it seemed, intended talking half the night. Jacob politely returned his attention to his guest, and the minutes continued to tick by.

It was almost midnight when Alex finally got to his feet. "Well, Jacob, this has been a great evening, but I guess I'll call it a day. How about you, Leah?"

She was in the rather awkward position of having to follow him upstairs and end the day, too, or simply say something like, "In a minute, Alex. I'll see you in the morning." She chose the latter and suffered the look she received from her friend.

Jacob walked with Alex to the foot of the stairs; the two men exchanged a few more words. Once Alex had gone upstairs Jacob returned to the den. He looked at her with unrestrained pleasure. "Nice gentleman, but I thought he'd never leave."

Leah laughed lightly. "I don't think I've ever seen him in a better mood. He had a wonderful time."

"And you?"

"Yes. I did, too."

"That's good. More brandy?"

"No, thanks."

Jacob moved across the room to the liquor cabinet, where he refilled his snifter. He had tried hard throughout dinner and the postprandial session not to stare at Leah, but he had made certain observations. At some point after dinner, she had kicked off her shoes and slipped the pins out of her hair. He remembered watching her toss her head casually as the silky stuff fell in a cascade to her shoulders. A simple act that transformed her from sleek sophisticate to charming ingenue. She never looked the same twice! Taking her features one by one, Jacob supposed she wasn't more than usually attractive, but in his eyes she was distinguished from all other women, and he couldn't have explained why.

Across the room, Leah watched as he poured brandy. He was wearing his tux trousers and the starched, pleated white shirt, but his tie had been discarded, and his shirt sleeves were rolled to his elbows. A sudden self-consciousness took hold of her, and she fleetingly considered getting to her feet, saying good-night and going upstairs. But the longing to talk to him, to probe and pry into his background, was too insistent. She sat quietly, almost primly with her hands folded in her lap, waiting for him to sit down beside her.

He didn't. Instead he said, "Come with me, Leah. There's something I'd like to show you."

Interested, she got to her feet, slipped on her shoes and followed him out of the den, down a short hallway to oak double doors with etched-glass panels. "My study," he explained, opening one of the doors and standing aside for her to enter. "The one room in the house I feel is personally mine, aside from my bedroom, of course."

The study had a mellow, masculine appeal, with warm wood tones and a soothing neutral color scheme, furnished with predictable objects—a floor globe, an antique stand holding an enormous dictionary. An elaborately carved wooden desk was the focal point. At the other end of the room was a long sofa, and on the wall behind that—Leah gasped—was obviously what he had wanted to show her. The priceless Navaho rug. She moved closer to study it.

"Oh, Jacob, it's a treasure!"

"Isn't it? A shame it's not in top-notch shape."

Leah's fingers sought and found the half-dozen frayed spots and tiny holes that marred the rug's perfection. "I know of someone who can repair it for you."

"You?"

"Oh, goodness no, not me. I can repair rugs and tapestries, but not one like this. I don't have the knowledge of natural dyes needed for this kind of restoration. But there's a woman in New Mexico. I have her card. I'll get it for you."

"Thanks, I'd appreciate that," he said, seizing any means of keeping them in contact. "Here, let's sit down." The study was illuminated by one small lamp, leaving most of the room bathed in soft shadows. Leah took a seat on the sofa; then it sagged beneath his weight. "We haven't had much chance to talk, have we? And I thought this weekend would be a time for getting acquainted."

"No, we haven't, but we can remedy that right now." Leah smiled. "You never talk about yourself, do you realize that?"

"I suppose that's because there's so little to say."

"Oh, that can't be true. Everyone has a story, and I'd like to hear yours."

Her easy smile, the casual tone of her voice masked her very real eagerness. To finally learn all the things she had never known about Jim—where he'd been born, where he'd gone to school, all the mundane little details of a person's life—that was what she wanted most of all. "Just begin at the beginning," she urged. "Where were you born?"

"Right here in Phoenix. Raised here, went to school here, in another part of town. There's a shopping center where our old house used to be."

"Did you always want to be a doctor? By 'always,' I mean once you got past the astronaut or cowboy stage."

He shrugged. "I don't think there was ever a conscious decision made on my part. I simply always knew I would go into medicine. The closest I ever came to a so-called dream was thinking I'd like to be a family practitioner in a small town. It sounded romantic, I suppose."

"Why didn't you do it, then?"

"I had to take over the clinic. It was expected of me."

"Did you always do what was expected of you?"

"Always." There was no self-congratulation in his tone; rather, he seemed to be ashamed it had been so. "I never yearned to be an astronaut or a cowboy or a ballplayer, not even a fireman or a cop. Not ever. Sometimes I think there's something basically wrong with that."

In Leah's mind a picture was forming of a lonely, serious kid who had grown into an intensely private man. "Tell me about your parents," she said.

He thought a moment. "Both were intellectuals, overachievers, and they expected me to be the same."

"Were you?"

"Oh, yes. Mother thought if one was exposed to only the finest things in life, one would grow up to demand the finest. Nothing coarse or common was ever allowed in this house. It was she who collected many of the things you see, and she whet my appetite. At the dinner table we discussed music, books and art, not batting averages or local gossip. I've often thought I took up woodworking because it was such a welcome respite from . . . oh, I don't know, from all that thinking." He paused to take a sip of brandy.

"It was an insulated life, really. My privileged existence cut me off from the so-called common man, a fact brought sharply to my attention during my internship and residency. Then I was forced to deal on a daily basis with all sorts of people while they were grappling with personal catastrophes. It was an education, in some ways the most important one I received. And not long after that, I was forced to deal with my parents' deaths. I had never thought of us as a close-knit family, not like some I've seen, so I wasn't prepared for how grief stricken I was or how much I missed them."

Jacob frowned, wondering what had prompted him to put together such a string of sentences. He turned to Leah apologetically. "I'm sorry. I got rather carried away. I didn't intend to be so morose."

"I don't find it morose to talk about personal things. We all have periods in our lives when we're required to make almost superhuman adjustments."

"You, too?"

"Of course."

Jacob imagined she was thinking of the split with her husband, and he didn't want Leah thinking about her husband right now. "Anyway," he continued, "that's about it, the story of my life. My father was gone by the time I had completed my residency, so I took over the clinic. Not exactly the rocky road to the top. Almost immediately I added a psychiatric unit and brought Charles in to head it up. He bought a quarter interest in the place, and . . . there you have it."

Leah's breath caught in her throat. She knew there was more. He had to go on; he couldn't stop there. "And you've been here ever since?"

"Well, yes, except for..."

Jacob hesitated. He had never discussed the blank period in his life with anyone but Charles. For one thing, he saw it as a weakness. For another, he doubted many people would be interested, and he knew there were plenty who equated amnesia with an abnormal mind, not an abnormal memory.

Leah was so different, though. She made him want to talk. Sitting there with those fascinating eyes fixed on him, she seemed to be almost demanding he talk. Soothed by her presence, he felt a kind of loosening take place within him, and the words just popped out. "Except for eight years ago when I ... went away."

When he told her he was an amnesiac, he added, "Does that shock you?"

"Shock me?" she asked. "No, why should it?"

"It would shock some people. Most regard it as being abnormal ... and, of course, it is."

"Please tell me about it."

"Do you really want me to?"

"Of course. Really." Every muscle in Leah's body tensed. *Now,* she thought. *At last.* At last she was on the verge of learning just how Jim had come into her life.

CHAPTER NINE

JACOB SET HIS GLASS on a nearby end table, settled back against the sofa cushions and propped one ankle on the other knee. With surprising ease, he began telling her the story in a neutral voice.

"Eight years ago I was involved in a malpractice suit, brought on by a man I considered a friend. His daughter was gravely ill when she first came to the clinic, had been ill for some time. It was spinal meningitis, sometimes terribly difficult to diagnose, and immediate treatment is of paramount importance. Unfortunately, in this case treatment had been postponed. Despite all our efforts, the girl died. Her father was grief stricken, of course. He wanted someone to blame, and I was handy. So he hired one of those wordmongers, a lawyer who specializes in malpractice suits. It was the kind of thing every doctor dreads. I subsequently won in court, but the whole unfortunate mess was in the newspapers for months, and the publicity hurt the clinic for a while.

"It hurt me, too. I was amazed at how many of my friends, even some of my colleagues, thought that where there's smoke, there must be some fire. The experience left me jaded, discouraged with the practice of medicine. It came too early in my career, you see. Had I been older, more experienced, I might have brushed it aside as an occupational hazard, but I was young and idealistic, and the scandal affected me deeply."

"Yes," Leah murmured, "I can understand that."

Jacob swallowed hard and continued. "My personal life was also at a low ebb. A woman I had loved and trusted left me during the litigation. Daphne, her name was Daphne Townsend. Isn't it strange...I honestly haven't thought of her in years. I wouldn't have now, except she was part of what was wrong with me all those years ago. Daphne was a lovely socialite with all sorts of ideas about what was proper and what wasn't. My reputation had been tarnished, at least in her eyes. She couldn't take the publicity.

"I guess Daphne was the last straw. First my parents' deaths, then the lawsuit, then her disloyalty. I was hostile and depressed. Charles was worried about me and suggested a vacation, a long one. 'Others can handle your appointments,' he said. 'Just get away from it all.' I thought about it and decided the prospect was irresistible. I remember loading my car with the idea of spending the time on my houseboat at Lake Powell, but at some point I decided to hell with it. I wasn't going to the same old place to do the same old thing. Besides, Daphne and I had spent time together on the boat, so it wasn't exactly full of fond memories. I decided to just drive until I felt like stopping. I left at night. It was April and pitch-dark—it was very late. . . ."

Jacob paused, and a deep frown creased his forehead. "My mind just stops there, as if a switch had been turned off. I don't remember which direction I took out of the city. Charles tells me that's not unusual. Apparently few amnesiacs, even the ones ultimately 'cured,' ever recall the events immediately preceding loss of memory.

"The next thing I knew it was two years later. I was picking myself up off the floor of a bus bound for Flagstaff. The bus had swerved to miss an oncoming truck and some of the passengers were thrown around. I had cracked my head on the seat in front of me."

"Wh-what did you do?" Leah asked tremulously in a voice hardly above a whisper.

"I was dizzy for a few minutes, disoriented. I did have enough wits to announce I was a doctor and to ask if anyone was seriously hurt. Then I searched my pockets for a clue as to what the devil I was doing on that bus. All I could find was a money clip containing three hundred dollars, and—" he gestured with his left wrist "—I still had this watch."

Leah wanted to scream. She clasped her hands together tightly in her lap. "You must have been so frightened."

"Very . . . and bewildered, particularly when I saw the date on the newspaper lying on the seat beside me. I remember staring at that date for the longest time. It's impossible to describe the way I felt. I didn't know what else to do but get back to Phoenix as quickly as possible. I had plenty of cash on me, so the minute the bus reached Flagstaff I took a cab to the airport and caught the first flight. Charles almost dropped dead when I walked into the clinic."

"And the two years? You've never remembered anything?"

He shook his head. "Sometimes something will zap in my head, as though my mind is reaching for something and just missing it, but I've never really remembered anything."

Leah's temples began to throb. She longed to just blurt out everything, yet she wouldn't dare, not after hearing what Dr. White had had to say on the subject. "Jacob, during those two years, wasn't anyone looking for you?"

"Not for a while, I'm afraid. I had no family, and Daphne was gone. At the time I didn't feel I had many friends, apparently I didn't. Since I hadn't specified how long I intended to be gone, it was a month or more before Charles began to suspect something was amiss. He tried to find out if there had been an accident, but the one thing he didn't want to do was broadcast my disappearance so soon after the trial. Finally he convinced himself I would show up when I was good and ready."

"You mean he accepted your disappearance just like that?"

"You must remember my emotional state at the time. Charles said he frankly wouldn't have been surprised by anything I'd done."

"But what about other people, friends and colleagues?"

"Anyone who inquired was told I had taken an extended leave of absence. Apparently those who knew what I had been through believed that."

Leah was so intrigued she could almost forget what a stunning impact all this had had on her own life. "But this house, Jacob, the servants?"

"I didn't live in this house then. When my folks died, I leased it to a wealthy family from Montana. I didn't move in until I returned from . . . wherever I spent those two years."

"You must have lived somewhere," she persisted.

"I had an apartment, but I wasn't entirely satisfied with it. Since the lease was up for renewal about the time I left Phoenix, I had moved out and put everything in storage, thinking I would look for a newer, larger place when I got back."

"I'm surprised the storage company wasn't looking for you after a time," Leah said.

"To get paid, you mean? The clinic's bookkeeper has been paying my personal bills for years. As far as she knew, I had taken a leave of absence, and my furniture was in storage." He shook his head slowly. "It's so strange, Leah, how everything, every single thing conspired to help me vanish. Where on earth did I go, though?"

Oh, my dear, she thought miserably. *I wish I could help you.*
"And you never saw Daphne again?"

He smiled slightly as he looked at Leah. "Oh, yes. She came to see me after I returned to Phoenix."

"Wanting to pick up the pieces," Leah said. It wasn't a question.

"Mmm. But I wanted no part of a woman who ran at the first sign of trouble. I understand she moved to...Hawaii, I think." A lift of his shoulders conveyed his complete indifference.

"Do those two years trouble you at all now, Jacob?"

"Yes, often. I suffered terrible headaches for a long time after I came back. I think my mind was working so hard to grasp something, anything. I spent months in therapy with Charles, but...nothing. He finally suggested I give it up, and he was right. We weren't getting anywhere. You see, during those two years I had existed in what is called a 'fugue state.'"

Carelessly Leah said, "Yes, I know."

Jacob looked at her in some surprise. "You do?"

Immediately she realized her slip. Recovering quickly, she said, "Yes, I don't know how I know, but I do. I must have read it somewhere, or perhaps I saw a show on television...."

"Well, for what it's worth, my case is almost textbook. Once a person recovers from the amnesic state, events of the fugue period are forgotten. I have to accept the fact that I may never remember or may remember only bits and pieces."

Leah stared at her hands. A feeling of the most desolate emptiness swept through her once he had concluded his story. Now she knew, and nothing had changed. Jacob didn't remember, and realistically, she had to believe he never would. In some ways she had lost Jim all over again.

So how did she feel about that? She tried to confront her emotions head-on. Did it really matter whether he called himself Jacob or Jim? He was as desirable as ever. Couldn't she simply be glad he was back in her life and interested in her?

"I've depressed you." Jacob studied her pensive expression.

Her head jerked up. "Oh, no. I was just thinking what a trauma you've been through." Then she asked the question she most wanted to ask. "Do you want to remember?"

"I think so. Wouldn't you?"

"Yes, I guess I would."

"It used to be almost an obsession with me. A few weeks after I returned to Phoenix, it occurred to me that I shouldn't have left that bus station in Flagstaff so hurriedly. I should have stayed to see if a piece of luggage had gone unclaimed. That might have given me a clue, but I was so rattled at the time, I couldn't think properly. I telephoned the station, but there was nothing. So either I had no luggage with me, or..." His frown deepened.

"Or?"

"Or someone came for it. That worries me most of all, thinking I may have left some loose ends in the other life." It was on the tip of his tongue to tell her about that dream, but he thought better of it. He might already be straining the fragile beginnings of what he hoped would become a profound relationship.

Leah looked away. The suitcase Jim had taken with him on that fateful day was still in her closet, still packed. Why she had kept it she couldn't imagine. If she and Whit had left it unclaimed, Jacob might have found it and...who knew what might have happened. Damn, there were so many "mights," so many "if onlys."

Jacob drew a deep breath. "And yet, remembering might only complicate my life. There are cases on record of amnesiacs who have begun entirely new lives, learned new skills, established new relationships. Then their memories returned, and they were faced with having to choose one life or the other. You can imagine the problems."

"Yes," she said weakly. "Problems." She was recalling what Charles had said about psychological amnesia. Perhaps Jacob only thought he wanted to remember. Perhaps remembering would actually be devastating for him. The whole subject was too complex for a lay person to comprehend.

One question kept inching to the forefront of her mind, however: why hadn't Charles, with all his knowledge and interest in amnesia, been able to help Jacob more than he had? Was Jacob's case particularly complicated, stubborn—what?

"Well, wherever I was, I had been living well," Jacob went on. "I was in great physical condition. A little heavier than I like to be, but as solid as a rock. My clothes were fairly new, and I wasn't wearing a wedding ring, thank God!" At this, he looked at Leah. "Why didn't you laugh?"

"Because you didn't," she said solemnly. Jim had had a wedding ring, but once he'd gained weight it had become too tight. They had always meant to take it to a jeweler....

Jacob fell into silence, but not a troubled silence. Finally spilling all he had kept bottled up inside for so long had a disburdening effect on him. Or perhaps it was Leah who had that effect. "You know," he said after a moment or two, "I've never discussed this with another person, only Charles during therapy. Confiding in others isn't something I find easy to do. I can't for the life of me understand why I did it now."

Which wasn't all he wanted to say to her. He wanted to tell her he believed he had found a soul mate. He wanted to confess he had never felt so close to another human being in his entire life, even if that did sound absurd to his own ears. And with that confession out, he would have hoped she would have talked to him, too—told him about her husband.

But he didn't actually say any of those things, and nothing was forthcoming from Leah. She only said, "I'm glad you felt you could talk to me," and it was impossible for him to read more behind her soft, sweet expression. Right now she looked a million miles away.

Jacob longed to know if she was thinking of something else, or someone else. It was an odd sensation, this being insanely jealous of a man he had never met. Probably never would meet. Hopefully never would.

Abruptly Jacob slapped his knee and got to his feet, extending his hand. "It's late, almost one, and I've bored you long enough."

"You haven't bored me, Jacob. Far from it." Leah stood up, only to discover she was just inches from him. The lone lamp's pale light illuminated the angles and planes of his face; his eyes held her captive. For a moment they stood rooted in place. Then Jacob dropped her hand and slipped his arm around her waist, effectively holding her captive. Her breasts were crushed against the starched front of his shirt. The contact sent a thrill coursing through Leah's body, a natural, instinctive response. It had been so long, too long, and she had once known such pleasure in this man's body.

Yet for the moment her feelings weren't entirely sexual. She simply loved being close to him again. She wanted him to hold her. She wanted his warmth to enfold her.

"Leah," Jacob muttered in a low, throaty whisper. "You are such a fantastic woman."

Leah's answer to that was to slide her arms around his waist and hold him to her, letting the force of his vitality wash over her. Instead of lifting her face to receive the kiss she knew he wanted to give her, she simply laid her head on his shoulder and clung to him. Everything inside her seemed to melt. He felt so good. It was like coming out of a cold night into a warm house—a warm, familiar house. Absurdly, she wanted to cry. If he only knew how much just being close to him meant to her.

Jacob was stunned. She had walked into his arms like a lost child seeking reassurance and comfort. He didn't think anything had ever moved him so deeply. Holding her lithe body in his arms, he felt a surge of tenderness and protectiveness for her that made no sense. How did a man deal with a gentle woman like Leah? His previous experiences had been so basic and earthy, but she seemed to be asking him for something more than raw passion. He moved one hand up to cradle her head and hold it snugly against his shoulder. Alien feelings overwhelmed him. She would have to make the next move.

Leah didn't know how long they stood there with their arms entwined around each other, not moving, not speaking. Finally one of them stirred—she thought it was she—and Leah raised her face to his. Jacob lowered his head, capturing her lips with his.

It was the sweetest sort of kiss, nothing demanding or urgent, yet it triggered a series of tiny explosions in Leah. The languid warmth she had experienced in his arms became an inferno of need. It was only natural for her to draw him closer, to open her mouth beneath his, to return the kiss with the passion and abandon they had once shared so freely.

The kiss deepened, and her body settled comfortably into the niche of his hips; they fit together perfectly. It had always seemed that their bodies had been fashioned for the express purpose of melding. Leah reveled in the feel of him, for she knew every pleasurable sinew from countless acts of love. Caught up in memories of another time and place, she moved against him invitingly.

It was Jacob who broke the kiss. Leah's eyes were still closed when he lifted his head; in that instant they flew open and looked straight into his. Full of awe, they beseeched him.

"Leah?" he gasped, unable to fully believe the message her pliant response had sent him. Did she really want him to make love to her? Was it even reasonable of him to think such a thing? *Please tell me how much you want,* he silently implored her. His mouth wouldn't form the words.

The questioning, astonished look on Jacob's face brought Leah to earth with a thud. She had entirely forgotten herself, forgotten who this man really was. For a moment she had been kissing Jim, and it would have been so easy to fall into intense lovemaking, something she wanted and needed.

But this wasn't Jim! Jacob Surratt was a newcomer to her life. A sensible woman didn't fall recklessly into bed with a man she had known a grand total of five days. At least, Leah Stone didn't. Shaken, feeling as gauche as a fifteen-year-old, unable to bear the astonished expression on Jacob's face, she looked away.

"Leah?" Jacob repeated. The arms holding her so tightly fell, and he took her chin in his hand, forcing her to look at him.

"I'm . . . sorry, Jacob."

"You are?"

"I can't think what came over me."

"Can't you?" He gave her a smile of the utmost tenderness. He thought he understood her fear and reluctance. It was tied up with her marriage and the ex-husband she couldn't forget. "I'll give you a biology lesson. I want you, and you want me. We each need what the other can give. There's nothing wrong with wanting, needing. In fact, it's natural when you've gone without it—"

"I'm not love starved, if that's what you're thinking."

Jacob sighed. "Then you're very fortunate. I am."

For a man who found confiding in others difficult, his candor with her was remarkable. Leah stepped backward; her mind was in tumult. She didn't know how to handle this. "I . . . I think I'll go upstairs now. It's been a lovely evening." An inane remark if she had ever heard one.

Jacob's hand dropped to his side. "Oh, Leah, it's such a damned shame. I can't remember, and you can't forget."

She frowned. "Forget? Forget what?"

"Your husband."

"My husband?"

"He is the problem, isn't he? You still love him."

Leah couldn't have been more surprised. She thought she had successfully avoided the subject of her husband. Was she too transparent, or was Jacob too observant? "Yes. How did you know that?"

"Oh, something strange happens to your eyes every time I say the word 'husband' or ask about your marriage." Jacob chanced stepping close to her again. Again he raised his hand, this time to gently brush it along her shimmering dark tresses, finally resting it lightly on her shoulder. "Leah, I'd be a fine one to tell you to forget the past when I'm searching for a piece of my own. And I admire loyalty. Still, the present should mean something, too. I know you're not indifferent to me. The way you kissed me told me that. The most important thing should be what you and I feel right now."

"Seize the moment, you mean?"

"Would it be so terrible? There have been damned few moments I've wanted to seize."

Jacob was confessing his loneliness. She had known crushing loneliness, too, and she supposed there was nothing wrong with two people seeking solace and comfort in each other. Or there wouldn't be, except that she and this man had once come together with absolute, shining love, and tonight she wouldn't have any idea whether she was making love to Jim or Jacob.

"It's . . . too soon, Jacob," was all she could think to say. "I'd be doing it for all the wrong reasons."

"Ah . . ." he murmured sagely. A moment of silence passed. "Leah Stone, you're an anachronism, but a charming one. Please, let me say one more thing. I think I've been looking for you for a very long time. I hope someday you'll want me as much as I want you—and I don't give a damn what the reasons turn out to be."

Leah thought she was strangling. "I'll say good night now, Jacob," she said quickly, then turned and almost ran out of the room. It wasn't until she was upstairs behind a closed door that she allowed her pent-up breath to slowly escape. Jacob had her all figured out, so he thought: she was still in love with her husband, and she had traditional values, thus her reluctance about a new relationship. Right, as far as the theory went, and she would play the role of the hesitant lover until she was certain she wanted Jacob Surratt. Only Jacob, not the ghost of her lost love.

THEY WERE ALONE AGAIN for only a minute the following day. First they had a late, leisurely Sunday breakfast, then a tour of the house to take in Jacob's extensive collection of art and antiques. After that an alfresco lunch was served by the pool, and the weekend was over. Alex went upstairs to get ready to leave; Leah stood up to follow him, but Jacob detained her.

"Must you leave so soon?" he asked quietly.

"Yes. We have to stop by my dad's to pick up Nina, and I believe Alex has a dinner engagement tonight."

"Saturday, then? I can be at your house before noon."

Leah didn't have to think about her answer. He was back in her life. She couldn't stay away from him, at least not until she knew how Leah Stone and Jacob Surratt were going to mesh. "Yes," she said. "Saturday."

"Will you please think about me?"

Leah laughed lightly. "Oh, you can be very sure I'll do that, Doctor."

FOR PERHAPS THE hundredth time in the past five years, Leah blessed Alex for his considerate nature. There wasn't a thoughtless or callous bone in his body. She knew he must be itching with curiosity about developments that weekend, yet throughout the drive to the Haskell farm he asked no questions. He talked about the scenery, the weather, the Surratt home, Jacob's collection—everything but what Leah knew he wanted most to talk about.

Whit, of course, was another matter. Alive with curiosity, he skillfully arranged a few private moments with his daughter.

"How was it?" he began bluntly.

"Oh, not too bad, I guess."

"Is he . . . at all like Jim?"

"Some. Not too much."

"I'd like to see him—I think."

"I wonder if you'd be disappointed." Succinctly Leah told him as much as she wanted him to know. She spared him the details of her palpitating heart and weak knees, but otherwise covered the visit quite thoroughly.

Her father listened with interest and concern for his daughter, and after thinking it over a moment or two, gave her the best advice he could.

"Leah, I guess you're just going to have to decide if you can let go of Jim, if you're ready for an emotional involvement with another person, because that's what Jacob Surratt is—another person entirely."

"I know Dad." She heaved a sigh. "I know."

CHAPTER TEN

FROM HER VANTAGE POINT, at her loom in front of the picture window, Leah could watch Nina and Ann Martin playing in the front yard. Every once in a while she glanced up to check on them, but for the most part her attention was riveted on her work. In a burst of creative energy, she had sketched a new design and completed her pattern draft of Jacob's tapestry the night she returned from Phoenix. Now, three days later, she was well into the work itself and feeling good about it. Back and forth the weft threads went in a steady rhythm she had perfected over the years. The joy she felt as she watched the complicated design grow right before her eyes was something only another weaver would understand, just as only another artist could appreciate the loom's ability to erase day-to-day cares.

Just then her peripheral vision caught some sort of movement in the yard; Leah looked up in time to see Sandra coming through the front gate. Her friend stopped to speak to the two girls, then looked toward the window. Leah motioned her inside.

"Don't let me interrupt," Sandra said as she entered the house. "I've come to beg, borrow or steal that divine white Mexican dress of yours. I'd like to wear it tonight."

"Sure, help yourself."

"It's the only thing you own that I could possibly wear, since you're so disgustingly thin. But the dress doesn't have any shape, so I think it'll hide mine."

"I don't know why you worry so much about your figure. You're just pleasingly ... curvaceous."

"I guess that's one way of putting it."

"Big date tonight?"

"I'm going to dinner with Sam, so I want to look prosperous." Sandra chuckled.

Leah pulled the beater sharply forward to pack the weft tightly before momentarily turning her back on her work. "You're going to dinner with your ex-husband?"

"Uh-huh. He wants to discuss Ann's future," Sandra scoffed as she disappeared into Leah's walk-in closet. When she reappeared she was carrying the exquisite dress over her arm. "I don't know what brought on this attack of parental concern, but it's about time he shouldered some of the load. He never paid much attention to Ann, not even when we were married. Sam thought kids were 'women's work,' and all that garbage. Now he says we ought to establish some sort of college fund for her. I couldn't agree more. Listen, Leah, I'll guard this with my life, and I'll have it cleaned before I bring it back."

"I'm not the least worried about the dress. Why don't you take my turquoise pendant, too? It's perfect with the dress."

"Oh, I couldn't."

"Nonsense. Take it."

"I know I shouldn't," Sandra said, scurrying for Leah's jewelry box, "but I will."

"Do you want to leave Ann with me?"

"No, my mom's down from Utah for a few days. Thanks anyway."

"Are you...ah, looking forward to tonight?" Leah asked. From all accounts, Sandra's previous meetings with her former husband had been anything but pleasant.

Sandra, who was hardly ever at a loss for words, floundered for a minute. She idly caressed the turquoise pendant, then sat down in a nearby easy chair, wrinkling her nose. "I'm not sure. It's funny, but...I don't much want to fight with Sam anymore. I've proved what I needed to prove, that I wouldn't fall apart without him. Now I think I'd like us to be friends. I mean, there's Ann to consider and all. I guess what I'm trying to say is, I've turned a corner. I'm not scared anymore, and I'm no longer filled with resentment." She grinned. "Now if Sam does something horribly thoughtless, I'll just tell him to kiss off! If he doesn't like it, tough! It's nice to feel free."

"I guess so." Having never lived with a domineering personality, Leah knew she couldn't fully appreciate what Sandra had been through and had accomplished through her own indomitable spirit. "You're to be commended, not only for getting help but for sticking with it. How long did you say you were under a psychiatrist's care—two years?"

"Yeah, it takes a lot of time. A lot of time."

And Jacob had spoken of only months with his partner. How many months? After her friend left, Leah mulled over what Sandra had said, especially the remark about turning a corner. It would help if she could do that, relegate Jim to the past and regard Jacob as someone totally disconnected from any life she had known before. Whit had told her basically the same thing Sunday night.

It would be easier if Jacob would stop making those late-night phone calls. He had called Sunday night, Monday and Tuesday, too, and she was fully expecting another tonight and every night until Saturday. His calls always came after she was ready for bed, so she spoke to him, while snuggled under the covers in the darkened house. He never said anything openly suggestive—that would have been out of character—yet the sensuous quality to that familiar voice made her skin tingle and hum. Unable to see him, hearing only his voice, she was easily carried back to a time when a handsome young man had loved her passionately. Then her thoughts would turn softly erotic.

She was filled with such a desolate longing every time she hung up the phone. Desires she could name but had long since learned to subjugate surfaced to torment her, evoking dreams that were her only emotional release. She badly wanted to see Jacob again, but was it really Jacob she wanted to see?

HE ARRIVED before eleven o'clock Saturday morning. Leah had been up since dawn. Dressed in jeans, she worked first at her loom, then in the yard with Nina's "help," all the while placating her daughter, who was restless and anxious to do something. "I'm going to have company, honey. We'll have to make plans after Dr. Surratt gets here."

"That doctor who was here the other day?"

"Hmm-mmm. Did you like him . . . ?"

The child looked at her mother, then shrugged. "I guess so. Are you gonna spend all day with him?" she asked petulantly.

"I really don't know how long he'll be here, honey."

"I wanted us to do something."

"Well, let's just wait and see, okay?" Leah said cheerfully. She hadn't given any thought to what she and Jacob would do . . . or to the fact that they wouldn't be alone.

She had planned to change clothes before Jacob arrived, but the time slipped away from her. Mother and daughter had gone inside to wash up when he knocked on the door. "Come in!" Leah called from the kitchen sink, and he stepped inside the house.

To her astonishment, urbane Dr. Surratt was wearing faded jeans and a short-sleeved denim shirt. The clothes only served to heighten his aura of potent masculinity and to remind her even more of Jim.

"Good morning," he said.

"Good morning."

Jacob looked at her steadily, trying not to stare but staring nevertheless. He was coming to think of her as the most-beautiful woman he'd ever known, yet it wasn't her face that came immediately to mind, but those incredible eyes. He looked into them so long she shifted uncomfortably.

Averting his gaze, he let it wander to Nina, who was sitting on a tall stool at the breakfast bar, chin resting on her hands, regarding him with six-year-old gravity. "Well, hi," he said.

"Hi." The girl's guileless eyes fastened on him.

"How're things going? Having fun this summer?"

Nina's dark curls bobbled up and down as she nodded her head.

"That's good." Jacob cleared his throat, at a loss to understand why juvenile scrutiny should be so unsettling. He looked at Leah, his eyes asking, *What do I say now?*

Leah suppressed a smile at the exchange. Amazing how few people knew how to talk to children. In all fairness to Jacob, however, she admitted her daughter had a direct, no-nonsense scrutiny that one didn't expect from a six-year-old. *Like her father,* was Leah's next startling thought. She stepped into the awkward silence. "I didn't have any idea what you wanted to do today."

"Didn't you?"

"No, so I didn't make plans."

"Good."

Leah wiped her hands on a dish towel, needlessly swiped at the countertop. On a normal Saturday she would have been working four-hour stints at her loom, Nina running in and out, back and forth from Ann's house. Nothing Jacob would find entertaining. She should have made some plans....

Jacob wandered across the room to stand at her loom. "You've begun," he said.

"Yes." Useless to ask if he liked it; there wasn't enough of it for him to judge. Right now the tapestry existed only in Leah's mind's eye.

"This is exciting, Leah—viewing it from start to finished product. Sometime I'd like to watch you work."

"Anytime."

"This afternoon?"

"If you like."

Nina, apparently seeing a promising Saturday disintegrating before her eyes, piped up. "Let's go to the creek and have a picnic."

Leah and Jacob turned to look at her. "A picnic?" they chorused.

Nina nodded enthusiastically. "We can go to Slide Rock."

Leah explained to Jacob. "The creek is Oak Creek, and Slide Rock is . . . well, it's impossible to explain if you haven't been there." Then she remembered he had, several times. "H-have you been there?"

He shook his head. "I seem to have heard of it, but I've never actually been there."

"Then what do you say? How does a picnic sound?"

He chuckled. "It sounds fine to me. I can't even remember the last time I was on a picnic. It must have been before medical school for sure."

No, it was the Fourth of July before his disappearance. Leah had known him thirteen months; they had been married for six of them.

She wasn't doing a very good job of forgetting Jim, but she couldn't deny she was glad to see Jacob again. She was even beginning to think him more handsome than the man she married. Maybe that was ridiculous, since they were the same person, but she reminded herself that some men got better looking with each passing year. Jacob was going to age beautifully.

"A picnic it will be!" she said too eagerly. "Nina, find the hamper . . . I think it's in my closet. I'll pack a lunch."

The child scrambled off. Leah moved toward the refrigerator. "I hope you like bologna sandwiches."

"Bologna?" Jacob smiled. "The doctor in me is forced to remind you of all those nitrates, all that cholesterol. I love them! Bologna sandwiches are something else that have been sadly missing from my life for too long."

Nina reappeared. "Mama, I can't get the hamper. It's up on the top shelf."

"Let me get it for you, Nina." Jacob came to her rescue.

"You won't be able to reach it, either. You're gonna have to stand on something."

"Well, then, I have a solution. I'll put you on my shoulders, and you get it. How's that?"

Nina giggled delightedly as Jacob placed his hands under her arms and swung her up on his shoulders. Clasping him under the chin, she chortled, "Ooh, I'm up so high!"

Jacob clamped his hands firmly on her legs as he marched across the room. "Watch it. You'll have to duck when we go through the door."

Leah froze as her eyes followed father and daughter. Her mouth compressed tightly; her chest heaved in agitation. No one had yet come up with a word to express what she felt. Distractedly she opened a loaf of bread and spread slices out on the counter. *How many sandwiches could Jacob eat,* she wondered. And she supposed he preferred mustard to mayonnaise; Jim had.

She heard a light tap on the screen door; it opened to admit Sandra. She was carrying the white dress in one hand, the turquoise pendant in the other. "I just picked this up at the cleaners and wanted to get it to you before something happens to it. Sure do thank you."

"You're welcome, Sandra. Anytime."

"I'll put it in the closet. Who belongs to that fancy sports car out front?"

Just then Jacob and Nina emerged from the closet. Nina, still on his shoulders, was holding the hamper triumphantly aloft and grinning from ear to ear. "Hi, Mrs. Martin. This is Mama's friend, Jacob."

Leah cast a sidelong glance in Sandra's direction. Her friend smiled politely and said, "Hello, I'm . . ." The words died. A second or two passed; then Sandra's eyes widened considerably. Leah thought she heard the sharp intake of the woman's breath as she stood mutely, staring at the two faces, one directly above the other. Leah's breath was suspended. Had Sandra noticed a resemblance? Tremulously she forced herself to look squarely at her daughter and Jacob, but it was impossible for her to objectively judge whether Nina looked that much like her father.

Slowly Sandra turned toward Leah. With a tilt to her head and a lift of her brow, she quizzed her silently. Leah couldn't read the question being asked, and apparently Sandra realized no answers could be forthcoming at that moment. She turned back to stare at the man and the child with unabashed interest.

"Hang on, Nina," Jacob was saying. "I'm going to let you down." Relieved of his burden, he crossed the room and extended his hand. "How do you do? I'm Jacob Surratt."

Sandra shifted the pendant and shook hands. "Sandra Martin. I'm Leah's neighbor. I'm returning her dress. I . . . I'll put it in there." She hurried into the closet, hung up the dress, then closed the door behind her.

"We're going on a picnic," Nina announced.

"How nice. You have a great day for it." Sandra couldn't take her eyes off Jacob and Nina. She looked like someone who had just been dealt a severe blow to her midsection.

"Yes, very nice," Jacob agreed.

"Well—" Sandra fluttered her hands in agitation "—I guess I'd better be going." Spinning around, she faced Leah, stunned awareness in her expression. "Thanks again, Leah."

"Sure, Sandra."

"I'll be over to see you . . . soon." Emphasis was placed on the last word.

Leah sighed and returned to her sandwich making. Perhaps her overactive imagination was at work. It could well be that Sandra hadn't noticed any resemblance, but was only curious about Jacob. Well, whatever, she didn't doubt she was in for a grilling the next time she saw Sandra, so she'd just have to decide how much she wanted her friend to know.

OAK CREEK TUMBLED from a subalpine setting in the north to cactus country in the south. Near Sedona, the vast canyon the creek meandered widened to provide a summer playground for swimmers, hikers and campers. Halfway down the canyon, surrounded by woodlands of evergreen oaks, was Slide Rock, a series of shallow troughs carved into the creek's sandstone bedrock and coated with slippery blue-green algae. Six thousand gallons of water a minute gushed over Slide Rock. There a swimmer could sit down in the stream, let go and glide effortlessly along in the water. Scores of swimmers were doing just that that afternoon, Nina among them.

Leah and Jacob had staked out a spot on the bank of the creek where they could eat and keep an eye on the girl. All afternoon

Leah watched Jacob's face for some sign that the surroundings looked familiar to him, but if anything was going "zap" in his head, he was careful to keep it from her. However, he made no attempt to conceal other thoughts. Every time their eyes met, Leah received some definitely sensuous, unspoken messages. She wondered if he had any idea how attractive he was. He was a very sexy man, and the dignified doctor surprised her with each passing moment. She guessed he might be surprising himself.

Leah was right. A queer sort of elation had taken hold of Jacob. Caring for her had made him feel bold. His thoughts turned daring and venturous. Once, when she turned to find him looking at her with undisguised hunger, she asked, "What are you thinking?"

He was astonished to hear himself reply, "I was wondering if bologna might be an aphrodisiac." Her delightful response to that was to shake an admonishing finger at him.

He was pleased that the mood between them was more relaxed than before. Still she wasn't completely at ease with him, and he didn't know what to do about that. That was probably his fault. Damn the lack of warmth and charm! How he wished for some instant charisma, anything that would make her forget the past and allow him into her life.

Nina's childish voice broke into his thoughts. "Mama! Jacob! Watch!"

He turned his attention to the girl cavorting in the water and made a big show of applauding her antics, but then he turned to Leah, clearly concerned. "Isn't that dangerous for a six-year-old?"

"Not at all," she assured him. "Nina's been slipping and sliding down Slide Rock ever since she learned to swim."

"When was that?"

"When she was two." Leah raised her arm to return her daughter's wave. With the ease of a child, Nina had ingratiated herself with a group of youngsters her own age and was having a wonderful time.

"It still looks dangerous to me," Jacob said. "You're able to treat her so casually, but I have a feeling I'd be an uptight parent."

"Oh, you learn. I was pretty uptight, too, in the early days, always worrying she'd get hurt. But kids aren't nearly as fragile as you think they are."

"I'm surprised she isn't exhausted. She's been going strong ever since we got here."

"Oh, this will make for a good night's sleep, I assure you."

Leah had spread a blanket on the ground and was sitting on it, knees pulled under her chin, arms hugging her legs. Beside her, Jacob sprawled full-length, one arm propped under his head. He was lost in a kind of euphoria, all at once lethargic and exhilarating. Thoughts of the woman beside him had distracted him all week. The regulated way of life he had created for himself no longer staved off loneliness or subdued his imagination. He, who normally welcomed the steady stream of men and women who came to him with their ailments, had been impatient with too many of them the past few days. He had always felt wretched about it afterward, wishing he could explain. But what could he say? "Forgive me, I'm daydreaming about a woman." Maybe he should have. Some of them might have understood and sympathized.

Damned if he was going to ponder and agonize over every word and move. He would say whatever popped into his head, do whatever came naturally to him and hope he got through to her. He couldn't think of another course of action.

"What time does Nina go to bed?" He hadn't known he was going to ask the question until he heard the words coming out of his mouth.

"Eight-thirty, nine at the latest," she replied absently. Then her heart tripped.

"Is she a sound sleeper?"

"Like the proverbial log."

She glanced at him and found herself on the receiving end of a devastatingly and delightfully wicked smile. It was so contagious, it demanded one in return. "Wh-why?"

"Why do you think? How long do I have to wait to make the moves I've been planning all week?"

"Jacob?" She cocked her head, looking at him as though seeing him for the first time.

"I thought I made myself clear last weekend. I thought you knew what I want. Nina's a darling girl, and I'm enjoying the hell out of the first lazy day I've spent in years, but I want to be alone with you, Leah." His eyes glowed into hers. "Understand?"

She flicked a tongue across her bottom lip. "Y-yes. Don't look at me like that."

A low chuckle sounded deep in his throat. "Why not?"

"It makes me nervous."

"Because you can feel me kissing you, can't you? Here..." He reached up and touched one corner of her mouth with his forefinger, then the other corner. "And here."

She took his hand and laughed lightly, enjoying the physical pleasure of simply being close to him. Anyone looking on would have taken them for a happily married couple on a Saturday outing with their daughter. The day was peaceful, the mood tranquil. Now, this minute, it would have been so easy to squeeze the hand she was holding and say, "Jacob, I've known you before. Your name was Jim Stone, and you married me when I was hardly more than a starry-eyed girl."

She didn't dare, and that presented problems. Fear, uncertainty stirred inside her. If this new relationship continued, and she had every reason to believe it would if she allowed it, he would expect her to tell him about her marriage. What would she say?

She sighed audibly; Jacob frowned. "Why so pensive all of a sudden?"

"Oh, I was just thinking what an incredibly lovely afternoon this has been."

He didn't believe her. "No, I think you're trying to come to grips with the way I feel about you, and possibly the way you feel about me. You've been loyal to an old relationship for a long time, and it isn't easy to start an entirely new one."

"Doctor, you can't begin to imagine how perceptive you are."

"Relax and let it happen. I've waited so long for this." There was a pleading quality to his voice. Suddenly he jumped to his feet and held out his hand. "Come with me."

Leah took his hand without hesitation, allowing him to pull her to her feet. "Where are we going?"

"Just over here. Come on."

Leah cast a glance over her shoulder to check on Nina. The girl and her group of newfound friends were out of the water, seated in a circle on a boulder, playing some sort of game. Satisfied, Leah continued, clutching Jacob's hand. He was leading her away from the crowded bank up into the thick tangle of dark woods only a few feet away, and she would have been incredibly naive not to have guessed what he had in mind. "Jacob! There are coyotes and racoons and skunks, and I don't know what all in these woods!"

"They'll be more frightened of us than we are of them."

"But..."

In a moment they were obscured from the frolicking bathers below. Under the sheltering branches of a giant oak, Jacob stopped and, in a fluid motion, gathered her into the circle of his arms. "I guess we'll just have to make our own privacy," he said huskily. Bending his head, he covered her lips with his. And like the first time, her body simply melted against his, reassuring him that what he thought she had felt the other time was still there. Her arms slid up the hard wall of his chest and locked behind his neck, and she returned the kiss with the same ardor he remembered. For a week he had thought so often of her response to that first kiss. He wouldn't have thought it possible for arms to ache from emptiness, but his had. Holding her now was healing balm. One hand pressed her more securely against him.

Sweet warmth surged through Leah. She had always loved for Jim to hold her; in some ways it had been the nicest part of their intimacies. She parted her lips under his and accepted his gently probing tongue. Her hips against his felt so right and natural. A new name, a new set of circumstances, yet her feelings for this man were the same. Gradually Jim became Jacob and vice versa, until the two melded. *He belongs to me,* she thought. *He doesn't know it, but he does.*

When they broke the kiss, Jacob nuzzled his head into the smooth curve of her neck and simply held on to her tightly. Leah relished the closeness she could feel growing between them. For the time being, this would have to be enough, but somehow she would find time for them. She had to; she needed him.

Finally they stood apart, smiling at each other, he more shyly than she. "I just couldn't wait any longer," he said.

Those fascinating eyes caught and held his, and he read something in them, something that made his breath catch. He could hardly allow himself to believe it, but . . . yes, unmistakably they said, "If you want me, it's all right. I want you, too."

For Jacob it was a mind-boggling moment. He didn't know what to say. "I . . . guess we should get back to Nina," was what came out.

Leah smiled and slipped her hand into his. He didn't have to say anything; she knew. Holding his hand tightly, she led him out of the forest into the sunshine.

IT WAS LATE AFTERNOON when they returned to the house. As she opened the car door, Leah heard the telephone begin to ring. Nina bolted off her mother's lap and raced toward the house, yelling, "I'll get it!"

Jacob stared after the girl in wonder. "Wouldn't you think she'd be dead on her feet? What I wouldn't give for a tenth of that energy!"

Leah nodded. "And she'll go and go and go until she just drops. She had a wonderful time today, Jacob. I think Nina's taken a shine to you."

"Ordinarily I don't pay much attention to kids, but Nina's different. She's easy to like."

How quickly they had warmed to each other, Leah thought. She recalled all Alex's well-meant but futile attempts to get close to her daughter. Unfortunately, Alex's overtures had been designed to please Leah more than Nina, and the child had sensed it. Not that Nina disliked Alex. She simply didn't feel one way or another about him.

It had been so different with Jacob. A quick rapport had been established between father and daughter. There might be something to blood ties, after all.

She reached for the door handle, but Jacob detained her. "Leah, what about tonight?"

"Tonight?"

"Yes. Do you suppose you could get a baby-sitter or something? I'd like to..." He felt inept. What to say? *I'd like to cart you off to a motel and make love to you all night long?* Hardly poetic stuff. Hardly worthy of Leah.

It didn't matter, since he had no chance to finish the sentence. The front door flew open, and Nina raced to the car, poking her head inside the window on the passenger side. Her eyes were bright with excitement. "Mama, it was Grandpa! Bess had her puppies! He says I can come see them. Can I, Mama, please?"

"Oh, Nina, honey, they'll be too little. You won't be able to touch them. And you've had such a busy day. You need a bath, supper and bed. I know you're tired."

"No, I'm not, really. Please! I'll just look at the puppies, I won't touch. Grandpa says we can come and have supper with him and I can spend the night. Please!"

"Nina, don't beg!" Leah said sharply. "You know how I hate that." Her mind raced. She wanted to be alone with Jacob, but now that the opportunity had been unexpectedly dumped in her lap, she felt guilty. Yes, guilty about considering herself and her own needs over Nina's. Had it not been for Jacob, she knew she would have said, "No, we'll wait until morning," and been done with it.

Expectation quickened Jacob's pulse. To have a night to themselves was what he wanted, what he thought she wanted. He couldn't understand her hesitation. Had he misread her, after all? Gently he touched her on the arm. "Please, Leah. You wouldn't want Nina to miss brand-new pups, would you?"

Why not, she asked herself sensibly. *Is it so terribly wrong to want to be alone with him?* If she had sex on her mind, so what? Nina wouldn't suffer any harm, and in Jacob's arms she could find surcease from the aching loneliness of the past six years. It would be like coming home.

"Would you like to meet my father?" she asked Jacob with deceptive calm.

"I'd love it."

"All right, Nina, tell your grandfather we'll be there. We'll have to change first. And, honey, be sure you tell him I'm bringing Dr. Surratt with me." It was best, she thought, to give Whit all the warning she could. She wondered how he would receive the news.

"Oh, boy!" The girl was away in a flash.

Jacob opened the car door and got out. *Bless Nina and her grandfather,* he thought with a grin. And bless Bess and the puppies who, unlike so many offspring, had arrived at the perfect time.

LEAH TOOK A FEW MINUTES to change. Ducking into the bathroom, she put on fresh slacks and a blouse. When she emerged, she turned to a nearby mirror to tie up her hair. The clothes, Jacob noticed, were the ones she had been wearing the first time he'd seen her at Tlaquepaque. She was fiddling with her hair, but mainly he watched the movements of her breasts when she lifted both her arms. She wasn't wearing a bra, that much he knew. He raked a forefinger across his mouth as an intense longing stirred inside him. Two weeks ago he had existed in a perpetual emotional void. Now every nerve, every cell in his body was alive and attuned to her. Leah, it seemed to him, had unearthed the very taproot of his sexuality. A man unknown to him was emerging, and he wasn't a half-bad sort.

"Jacob, tie this, please."

The girlish voice brought him up short. He looked down to see Nina standing with her back to him, holding her hair off her neck.

She had changed into some sort of sunsuit, and the two straps were draped over her shoulders. He took the straps and tied them into a lopsided bow.

"That's not tight enough," the child informed him.

So he untied the straps and retied them. "How's that?"

"Fine." Nina turned and smiled. "Thanks."

"You're welcome. Always happy to come to the aid of a damsel in distress."

"What does 'damsel' mean?"

"A damsel is a fair young lady."

"What does 'distr... distr...'?"

"Distress? Well, if you're in distress, you're in trouble."

"But I'm not in trouble, am I?" she asked seriously, and Jacob laughed.

Through the mirror Leah watched them. Her heart seemed to swell to twice its normal size. What difference did it make what his name was? He belonged here, with them; she wasn't going to let anything take him from her this time.

Turning, she favored both of them with a bright smile. "Nina, did you pack your things?"

Nina nodded and pointed to a small canvas bag resting on the floor near the front door. "All right, shall we go?"

Purposely Leah directed Jacob to take the route she and Jim had always traveled to the Haskell farm. Jim had once commented that he thought he knew every pebble and bump in the road. Leah watched for any sign of recognition from Jacob, but again there was nothing.

"Beautiful country," was his only comment.

"You've never been this way before?"

"No, I fly whenever possible, and the few times I've driven north out of Phoenix I've stayed strictly to the interstate. I'm not much of a sightseer, I'm afraid, and I'm beginning to realize how much I've missed."

TWO HOURS LATER, Leah, Jacob and Whit were seated in the living room of the farmhouse, while Nina was camped in the kitchen with Tee, close to Bess and her brood. Whit's face had gone very pale when he had first "met" Jacob; now it was flushed. He kept mopping his brow, although the weather wasn't that warm, and he took countless drinks of water. Leah watched her father anxiously. She had never seen him so nonplussed. His voice was stilted, strained. Jacob seemed to notice nothing, thank God. He chatted pleasantly with the older man, and their conversation was no more awkward than any conversation between two apparent strangers.

Tee ambled in with cold beer for everyone. The housekeeper had been forewarned; Leah could tell that by the way Tee so obviously refused to look at Jacob. Only when she moved away, out of Jacob's line of vision, did she chance a full glance at him. Leah watched her covertly. Tee frowned and pressed her hand to her ample bosom, then shook her head sadly before leaving the room.

By the time supper was served, both Whit and Tee had recovered sufficiently to accept Jacob's presence. Talk flowed around the table with greater ease. Whit unfortunately called Jacob "m'boy" too often, an appellation that had suited Jim Stone perfectly but was totally inappropriate for Dr. Surratt. But Leah reminded herself that every word, every action was magnified in her mind. Jacob seemed to notice nothing but the good country food and the hospitable surroundings.

And her. Every time their eyes met, Leah felt a jolt of sensual awareness. His heart was in his eyes. The message he had been sending her all day was coming through clearer now that fulfillment was within reach. It was all so incredibly blatant and premeditated, yet she felt not the least chagrined, and all guilt had vanished.

The evening passed. Leah took a hyperactive Nina upstairs for a bath, then helped her get ready for bed. Getting the child unwound wasn't easy, but after two unnecessary trips to the bathroom and a request for a drink of water, she finally fell into a deep sleep.

Downstairs, Whit and Jacob sat engrossed in conversation, but the moment Leah appeared Jacob got to his feet. "Is she settled down?"

"Yes, thankfully."

"Want some coffee, Leah?" Whit asked.

"No, thanks. I guess we'd better be going." How casually the words came out.

Whit got to his feet, and Jacob extended his hand. "I've enjoyed it, Dr. Haskell."

The older man slapped him heartily on the back. "Whit, m'boy, Whit. Glad you could come. Hope to see you again."

"I hope so, too, Whit."

"Good night, Dad." Leah stepped forward to hug her father. She thought he held her a little tighter, a little longer than usual. When they parted, the look on Whit's face was indescribable.

CHAPTER ELEVEN

THE NIGHT AIR was dry, soft and warm. Jacob led her around to the passenger side of the car and opened the door. But before she got in, he put his arms around her waist and gently held her for a moment. Only held her, that was all, but the gesture sent her pulses leaping. Wanting to do so much, she could do nothing, so she simply stood in the comforting circle of his arms without speaking.

Jacob felt her rigidity; it was out of tune with what he had read in her eyes. He wanted to tell her it was all right, everything was fine. God knows, he was no expert on people—he doubted there was a man alive who was—but he thought he knew something of what Leah was feeling. She was attracted to him, and the attraction startled her. She was having difficulty accepting it. He had to remember what a short time they had known each other. That kind of thing might bother a woman of scruples, so he would keep it in mind. He might not have cornered the market on warmth and charm, but he did have sensitivity and compassion.

Leah, of course, was thinking none of the things Jacob imagined. She was thinking that tonight would be the end of her loneliness. Had she actually only known him two short weeks, she knew she wouldn't be taking him home tonight, but...

From that point on her thoughts became more complex. She hadn't known him only two weeks. He was as integral a part of her life as Nina was, and she couldn't deny her desires and longings. It seemed something of a dream, all at once vivid and unreal. *Tonight is mine,* she mused with satisfaction, and her feeling that all was right and natural was reinforced by the knowledge that Jacob wanted her as much as she wanted him.

He released her, and she got in the car. "Air conditioner or windows down?" he asked.

"Windows down." She needed the air.

He shut the door and walked around to the other side, his spirits soaring to unparalleled heights. Sliding behind the wheel, he placed his wallet on the console between them. Leah watched him out of the corner of her eye. She had noticed him doing that earlier in the day and had remembered Jim's dislike of carrying a wallet. At supper she had spotted Jacob discreetly removing a slice of onion from on top his salad; Jim hadn't liked onions, either. More and more the two men were becoming one in her mind. He turned the key in the ignition, the engine sprang to life, and they drove away.

In all the twenty-eight years of her life, Leah had never been party to a premeditated seduction. She and Jim had drifted gradually, unknowingly into love, and the overtures to lovemaking had progressed hesitantly, inexpertly. What she and Jacob were plunging headlong toward was neither hesitant nor inexpert. She knew exactly what kind of lover he was.

The air inside the car was charged with excitement; it was an almost tangible thing. Yet somehow during the drive back to Sedona they managed light conversation.

"Your father's a nice man."

"Yes."

"He's obviously crazy about you."

"There were just the two of us for so long, and we grew very close."

"The meal was great. Tee is a fantastic cook."

"Too fantastic, I'm afraid. I'm stuffed. When I'm eating Tee's cooking, I can never remember that you're supposed to feed only your hunger, not your taste."

"But you don't have any weight worries."

All very casual and low-key, but Leah's mind was never far from what was ahead. Outwardly she remained composed; inwardly she was shaking with an exquisite torment.

The Corvette pulled to a halt in front of her house. A soft light shone from the front window like a beacon in the night. They got out of the car. They were past the need for coy amenities, so Leah didn't go through the motions of inviting him in, nor did she pause at the front door as if to tell him good-night. She simply unlocked it, pushed it open, and he followed her into the house. Leah locked the door behind them.

Jacob could feel the blood pumping through his veins; his pulses pounded, his temples throbbed. He was aware of every move she made. His entire body seemed poised and alert, straining toward her. Once he had read or heard that one of the body's most erogenous zones was the mind, and now he believed it. All he could think of was Leah, the night . . . the long night stretching ahead of them and all the things they would do. His arousal was complete, but he would have to remember to take his time, not to rush lovemaking, to make it as perfect for her as he knew it would be for him. He wanted her to want him again and again.

Walking to the window, she pulled the drapes shut. With only a small hanging lamp on, the big room was dimly lit, as softly as if by candlelight. "Would you like some coffee, some wine, anything?"

"I don't think so. I'm going in there." He indicated the bathroom with a nod of his head.

"Sure." Leah went into the kitchen and got a drink of water. She walked out of the alcove just as Jacob emerged from the bathroom. Their gazes locked, and they smiled at each other.

He closed the space between them, raised one hand and freed her hair of its confining scarf. "I like it down," he said huskily. "It's like a lovely black cloud around your face." Sliding his fingers into the silky strands, he cupped her face, bent his head and toyed with her lips, tasting, sipping. He raised his head, and the eyes meeting hers were clouded with desire.

Without a word they moved toward the sofa. Every nerve in Leah's body was tingling, and almost before she was seated she was in his arms, wrapped around him, clinging to him as though she couldn't bear to let go. His mouth as it bound to hers was so deliciously warm, his hands arousing. The blood pumping through her veins felt like molten lava—a sensation long forgotten, exquisitely sweet. She wanted more than anything to dispense with all the preliminaries and foreplay and just make love, but he wouldn't understand that. This was their first time together as far as he was concerned, so she would have to be patient, even a little shy. She imagined Jacob would be totally put off by a woman who came on strong.

Jacob's heart was pounding so loudly he was certain she could hear it. He didn't think he possessed more than an average share of caveman tendencies, and he wasn't given to ravishment, but he had reached a fever pitch of excitement and would have liked to dispense with finesse and make love to her on the floor. However, the need to move slowly with this gentle woman was uppermost in his mind. Taking a deep breath, he tried to control his racing emotions.

"How long has it been since you necked on a living room sofa?" he asked tenderly.

"I . . . don't remember ever doing that. Did you?"

"I don't know. I must have. Something made me afraid of male parents in general. Girls' fathers always seemed so hostile."

"Possessive and protective," she corrected. "And you must remember—they knew exactly what you had on your mind."

He curved a forefinger under her chin. "I want to tell you what's on my mind right now."

"I think I know."

His expression was completely serious. "No, not that. I want you to know that I've been besotted with you since the first moment I set eyes on you, and I don't even believe in that sort of thing. Can you begin to understand how that shakes me?" Her eyelashes dipped, but he held her chin firmly. "And I flatter myself that you felt something, too, right from the start. Am I right?"

God, if he only knew! Leah opened her eyes and looked directly into his. "Yes." Her heart thumped loudly and erratically. "There are so many things. . . . Oh, Jacob, this is so difficult for me."

Because of her husband, he was sure. The man had turned out to be a greater obstacle than he'd imagined. Yet he, Jacob, had touched her in some way; she had never been indifferent to him. He had to cling to that knowledge. "Leah, I'm not asking for any breathless declarations of devotion. All I'm asking you to do is love me . . . love me tonight."

It was the easiest, most natural thing she had ever done. Warmth, real and enticing, spiraled through her. Raising her face, she first felt the texture of his cheek against hers before his lips showered nibbling kisses on her earlobe and along her jawline. His warm breath caressed her chin. By the time his searching mouth had progressed to hers, she was ravenous for the taste of him. Her lips opened, allowing his tongue freedom to mingle with hers. It was so good to have him again.

When Jacob lifted his head, his dark eyes gleamed. "I wish I could tell you how much this means to me. How much you mean to me."

"I know." Her voice was thick.

"Do you? Maybe you do. Is that the reason you turned out to be the one, the one above all others?"

Slowly he slumped back, resting on one of the sofa cushions, bringing her with him. Now she was in a position of command, and she took advantage of it. All thought of employing shy caution was abandoned. In this, he was the novice and she the expert. She knew every sensitive receptor in his body. She had learned to drive Jim almost wild with desire, and she employed the same tactics with Jacob.

First her finger made a sensitive foray through his thick dark hair. Then her fingernails skimmed over his neck, trailed down and slipped inside his collar to feel the smooth skin of his shoulders. Meeting resistance in the form of his shirt, she flicked open the first button, then another and another. Pushing the garment aside, Leah splayed her hands over the satisfying breadth of his chest. Her fingertips curled through the thick mat of chest hair, then moved to tease the flat nipples. Her lashes dipped, a sensuous smile curving her mouth. She was making love to the only man she had ever loved, and the hard, aching knot forming in the lower part of her body demanded assuagement. Her hands continued downward, jerking his shirt free of his pants, while her mouth placed a melting kiss on his.

Jacob gasped for air; he was suffocating. Never had a woman taken the time to initiate lovemaking with him by such gentle, tactile maneuvers. He was so overwhelmed by Leah that he could only respond with acquiescence. Her exploring fingers fumbled with the waistband of his jeans, then unsnapped, unzipped. She reached for him, her fingers closing around him possessively. As the ache in his loins threatened to erupt, he gripped her upper arms and held her inches away.

"I hope it's not crass to ask where the bed is—but where is the bed?"

"You're sitting on it."

It should have been awkward, Leah thought as they both stumbled to their feet to discard the sofa cushions. In a perfect love scene the bed would have been ready for them. He would have carried her to it. She would have been wearing something soft and flowing that could have been whipped off her in a second. Perfect love scenes didn't begin with the aroused participants having to first dismantle a bulky sofa bed, then undress each other with fumbling, trembling hands.

But the situation wasn't awkward at all. They both pulled out the bed, and their clothes just seemed to fall away. In only seconds they were lying side by side, bodies entwined, luxuriating in the feel of flesh against flesh. Their hands were never still—rubbing, petting, teasing, priming. For Leah it was a rediscovery, not only of his body but of the femininity held dormant so long. For Jacob it was an awakening of passions and desires he feared had wasted away from neglect.

He had envisioned guiding her, but she needed no guidance. Every touch she bestowed on him was exciting. Feverishly hot, fully aroused, enchanted with her sexual expertise, he again wanted her in a position of dominance. Lifting her effortlessly, he brought her down on top of him. Willingly she straddled his torso, sheathed him and began her slow undulations. Jacob was afraid to move; clenching his teeth, he fought for control. Above him her pink-tipped breasts were full and taut with desire, the nipples hard and puckered, enticing him beyond belief. His mouth took one—

And too quickly it was over. As the uncontrolled spasm shook him, his fingers bit into her soft flesh, and he cursed himself violently. It had been too long, he had fantasized about Leah too often, and he had been walking around all day in a mindless state of arousal. He groaned his dismay, his regret, his sense of inadequacy. How cheated she must feel.

"Oh, Leah," he choked. "I'm so damned sorry."

Leah, however, was undaunted. "Hush," she whispered. "Just relax." She had known him before, hundreds of times, and she knew what to do. His desire would return. She didn't allow him to withdraw, and she kept to her rhythmic pace until she felt him again, rigid and urgent. Every part of her came alive. She was attuned to his needs as if he was instructing her step by step. Thoughts and senses merged, so that they not so much made love as allowed it to happen. This time the union was joyous and mutual, as was the climax.

Never would Jacob have believed ecstasy could be so great that it was painful. This, then, was what he had wanted all these years and despaired of ever finding. Only Leah's tiny cry of a name at the moment of completion marred what was a perfect act of love.

THE HOUSE WAS HUSHED. Their labored breathing had slowed, and Leah lay next to him, her hand resting over his heart, blissful in the sweet aftermath. She snuggled against him, kissing his neck, murmuring, sighing contentedly. She thought they had been perfect together, and the release had brought such a feeling of warmth. It was good to feel positively sensual again.

"Leah?"

"Yes."

He took a labored breath. "Was your husband's name Jim?"

Leah's heartbeat slowed, then quickened. *I didn't! Please, God, I didn't call his name.* "Yes." She gulped.

"Do...do I remind you of him?"

"Y-yes. In some ways."

"Is that why you were attracted to me in the first place?"

"People are attracted to others for any number of reasons. You should know that," she hedged.

So that explained the instant interest. It explained her reaction to him in the gallery that first day. She hadn't been ill, she had been surprised. He reminded her of her husband, dammit! "He was your last lover?"

"He was my only lover."

That told Jacob so much about her, why she was different. There was a quality of innocence about her that made her seem vulnerable. One man in twenty-eight years. No, now two. "You called his name. Were you aware of that?"

"No. If I did, it meant nothing. A man named Jim is the only other man who ever...made me feel that way. Please, Jacob, not now. Must we spoil everything? I don't want—"

"Don't you think I have a right to know something about him? You've never told me a thing. Are you divorced?"

It took her a second or two to decide between a lie and the truth. "No," she said finally. "He just...left."

Jacob propped himself on one elbow and stared down at her incredulously. "You aren't divorced? You didn't divorce a man who left you?"

Leah huddled deeper under the covers, miserable because their sweet lovemaking had been followed by this conversation. The story she told was faltering, a mixture of half-truths. "He went away...there were reasons. I didn't divorce him...it doesn't matter. Soon he'll be declared legally dead...."

Jacob's head hit the pillow again. "This is too heavy for me. Basically, I guess, I'm a simple man."

Now Leah propped up on one elbow, looking at him earnestly. "Is it really so important to you, knowing about my marriage?"

"Not unless—" he carefully considered his next words " —unless you're using me as a substitute."

"You're not a substitute, Jacob, nor a replacement. You're you, unique. Can't you accept that?"

He digested what she'd said. "Yes, I'm sorry, but I've been so curious from the beginning. I've always known you were still in love with him."

"It doesn't matter. It has nothing to do with tonight, with right now."

"What about tomorrow?"

"It has nothing to do with tomorrow, either, nor with the day after." Leah lay down, turning her back to him. She needed to talk to someone about this; she desperately needed a set of rules to follow to get her off this tightrope she was walking. Dr. White's words had been frightening: "irreparable harm." The last thing she wanted to do was harm Jacob.

Jacob touched her on the shoulder. "Have I upset you?"

"No," she said with a sigh. "But I wish you wouldn't let my marriage bother you. I wish you would put it out of your mind."

"The man left his mark on you."

"And Daphne Townsend left her mark on you."

He smiled. "You remembered her name."

"Of course."

"I'm not still in love with Daphne."

Leah chewed on her bottom lip. "Jacob, what I'm trying to say is, when it comes to you and me, the past shouldn't interfere."

"Well, it does when you can't remember who you're making love with."

She turned and smiled at him. Her dark hair splayed, contrasting strongly with the stark whiteness of the pillowcase. Their noses were almost touching. "I knew who I was making love with."

He tilted his head and nibbled at her mouth. "Say my name."

"Jacob."

"Again."

"Jacob."

Drawing her close, he sighed deeply. "I was beginning to think I'd never find you. I've waited so long."

Leah held him tightly and squeezed her eyes shut. *Oh, my darling, you have no idea what waiting is.*

WHEN JACOB AWOKE, dawn was arriving in Red Rock Country. Beside him, Leah slept soundly, the sheet pulled up tightly under her chin, one creamy thigh exposed. His fingertips itched to glide along that satiny-smooth flesh, but he didn't want to waken her. The insomniac in him envied anyone who could sleep so soundly.

Twice during the night they had reached for each other, seeking replenishment. He had never made love before, not really. He had taken when his needs demanded it, scrupulously avoiding women who might have wanted more than he could give, but he had never made love. Not even that awful, precipitous beginning had spoiled it, thanks to Leah.

Awed, he lay still and watched her sleep. Last night he had lived out men's greatest fantasy—he had found a woman who knew exactly how to love him. The force of her passion staggered him. He, who once past adolescence had never been a so-called ladies man, had discovered the kind of love most men would die for. Jacob watched Leah a moment longer, then carefully, quietly slipped out of bed and went to the window, lifted one corner of a drape and looked outside.

A light rain had fallen during the night. The soft morning mist created a scene of ethereal beauty as the first pink rays of sunlight creeped over Gothic sandstone buttes. Jacob was experiencing an extraordinary sense of déjà vu, as if he had always known he would someday be standing naked at the window of this funny, appealing little house. That really made no sense, and he knew it.

Without warning his mind became very clear, blindingly bright; then it clouded, and shadowy images appeared. He shook his head, making the images disappear. He had experienced the dream again, and as sometimes happened, part of it stayed with him after waking. He shook his head again. Nothing was going to intrude on this perfect day, least of all his damnably unpredictable psyche. His amnesia no longer mattered, anyway. Nothing did, nothing but what he had found here. He couldn't care less about what had happened during those two years.

He turned to glance across the room at Leah, still sleeping. It bothered him that she hadn't divorced her husband, for that meant she hadn't been able to let go. Jacob wondered if he had it in him to be the one to make her forget the past. He had to face the fact—that's what he wanted. Not an affair, not an arrangement, but a total commitment. Maybe even marriage someday, who could tell? And she wasn't free. What if her husband showed up one of these days to rekindle the flame?

Yet he himself wasn't free, either, not really. What if his memory returned? The complications that could cause were endless. Was it fair to ask a woman like Leah to share a life so fragmented?

No, he wasn't going to think about those two years. They no longer mattered.

Leah stirred just then, stretched and purred, then felt the space beside her. "Jacob?" she called softly, and he was across the room in an instant, slipping between the sheets to take her in his arms. She made a little sound, part sigh, part moan, and snuggled against him.

"Shame on you," she murmured lazily. "You robbed me of the thrill of waking up beside you."

"Sorry. I was watching the sun rise."

"Have you been awake long?"

"Not long."

"What do you want to do today?"

He chuckled. "What's wrong with what we're doing right now?"

"Good heavens, you're a lusty man!"

Lusty? Was he? A far cry from his usual aloof and reserved ways. But this morning he felt lusty, and hot-blooded, virile, potent—all those hackneyed masculine adjectives. He felt like a blue-ribbon bull in the very prime of power.

Leah smiled against his chest. She licked his skin, then kissed and nipped, then teased a nipple with her tongue. "Very lusty," she murmured, "and you taste divine." Her hand began a lazy journey along the length of his lean hard torso, pausing at his hip. Gently her finger traced the pattern of the scar there. It had faded considerably after six years.

"How did you get that?"

"From a dumb-fool kid stunt. I fell out of a tree when I was sixteen. A ragged limb sliced right through my shorts."

"Ouch," she murmured, and stored away another piece of information about the man she had married.

"That wouldn't have been so bad, but the day before the stitches were to come out, I fell off my bicycle and tore it open again. It couldn't be resutured then. Clumsy kid, wasn't I?"

"Well, thank goodness you outgrew it. You're not clumsy anymore. I love the way you do...everything." Her hands continued down his thigh, between his legs, until her fingers closed around him. The combination of her nibbling mouth, her soft breasts crushed to his stomach, her fingers on the most vulnerable part of him, sent Jacob's mind reeling, stumbling. He rose and hardened in an instant.

Leah stretched full-length beneath him and accepted him eagerly. A woman could do without this for great long stretches of time, she thought, but how wonderful to make love when one's lover was the right man.

JACOB STROLLED onto the front porch where Leah was lounging and enjoying a second cup of coffee. After breakfast he had showered and shaved, using her razor, and dressed in yesterday's clothes. Bending over her, he kissed the top of her head.

Leah tilted her face to smile up at him. She was glutted with happiness. She felt as though her bones had melted. "Hmm, you smell good."

He straightened and rubbed his chin. "I didn't have any aftershave, so I used that stuff in the green bottle. What is it?"

"Skin freshener."

"That'll wake you up quick." He sat down near her. "When will Nina come home?"

"Whenever I go get her, probably tonight, so I can work all day tomorrow without interruption. Nina would stay at Dad's forever if I'd let her. And be spoiled rotten within a week, I might add."

"Will you be able to come to Phoenix next weekend?"

"I hadn't thought about it. I guess I imagined you would come here."

"There would be damned little privacy in this house if Nina was here, Leah, and I doubt you want to shuttle her off to her grandfather's every weekend. Bring her to Phoenix, and I'll turn over the entire house and all the staff to her."

Leah laughed. "And I think Dad spoils her! Oh, Jacob, I'm afraid she'd get on your nerves. You aren't used to children. Nina has an attention span of twenty minutes at best. The only thing that really keeps a six-year-old entertained is another six-year-old."

"Then bring along another six-year-old."

"Are you serious?"

"Of course."

Leah pursed her lips. "Maybe Ann," she mused. "It might be a fun change for them. They'll think they've inherited Disneyland."

"Shall we plan on it?"

Her eyes sparkled. She nodded.

"I should be getting used to having a child around, don't you think?"

She cocked her head and shot him an amused, quizzical glance.

"Aren't you thinking along those lines, too? If you aren't you should be."

"Yes, I'm thinking along those lines, too," she admitted. "Once certain things are resolved."

"Yeah, I know." Briefly his eyes clouded. "I hate long-distance romances."

"How do you know? Have you ever conducted one before?"

"No, but I want to be with you all the time. Weekends aren't enough."

She reached out her hand to him. "Oh, Jacob...but they're something!"

CHAPTER TWELVE

LEAH FULLY EXPECTED to see Sandra bright and early Monday morning, and she wasn't disappointed. It was barely nine o'clock when her friend showed up, bursting with curiosity.

"I was beginning to think that red sports car was going to become a permanent fixture in front of your house."

Leah only grinned. "Want some coffee?"

"No, thanks. He was here until eight o'clock last night."

"Been checking up on me, huh?"

"Hey, I was curious as hell. And pleased as punch, I might add. The life you've been living, without men and all, isn't healthy." A second of silence passed, then Sandra demanded, "Well?"

"Well, what?"

"Oh, Leah." Her friend sighed in exasperation. "Who was that gorgeous man who spent the weekend with you?"

"His name, as you know, is Jacob Surratt. He's a doctor. He lives in Scottsdale. I'm doing this tapestry for him." She shrugged as if to say, "That's all there is to it."

"Come off it!" Sandra glanced around. "Where's Nina?"

"Still at Dad's. I called her last night, and she can't bear to tear herself away from the puppies, so I gave her one more day. I'm going to get her tonight."

"Then we can talk. Leah, I'm not blind! When I saw that man with Nina I almost fell down. Now I know he's more than just some doctor who's commissioned you to do a tapestry. Right?"

Leah hesitated, but only for a moment. "Right. He's...Nina's father."

Sandra compressed her lips and took a deep breath. "I knew it! They do have a way of straggling back, don't they? Ex-husbands, I mean."

"It's not like that. Is the resemblance between them really that great?"

Sandra gave it some thought. "I don't know.... I always thought Nina was the living image of you, but when I saw that man... I guess I might have been expecting to see something. Maybe that's it."

"I hope so. You see, Jacob has no idea Nina's his. He thinks we only met two weeks ago."

Sandra stared at her blankly. "I don't understand," she said weakly.

"I'm not surprised."

"Leah, the only thing you ever told me about your ex is that he left you, that you didn't have any idea where he was. You seemed to hate talking about it, so I didn't pry. I figured you'd tell me anything you wanted me to know. But when I saw that man I immediately decided a straying husband had wandered back into the fold."

"Wrong."

"Do you want to tell me about it?"

Leah sighed. "I don't see why not."

She had never known Sandra to be so quiet for so long. As the story unfolded, her friend sat transfixed, never uttering a sound. At the conclusion, she slowly shook her head. "Oh, Leah...that's the damnedest thing I ever heard! Talk about a one-man woman. Don't you just itch to tell him?"

Leah frowned thoughtfully. "Sometimes. More at first than now. The weekend Alex and I went to Phoenix for the clinic's opening, I met Jacob's partner, who's a psychiatrist. He told me things about amnesia I hadn't known before. I'm not too sure I don't want to leave well enough alone."

Sandra shook her head. "I wouldn't be able to keep quiet. I just know I wouldn't.''

"Look at it this way. I've found him again, he's well, unmarried and as strongly attracted to me as when he was Jim. Wouldn't I be foolish to... complicate it?"

"Maybe. But I still wouldn't be able to keep my mouth shut."

An alarming thought occurred to Leah. "Sandra, neither Jacob nor Nina has any idea. If you're with either one of them, remember that."

"Oh, listen, when I decide to keep a secret, it's kept. What are you going to do, though? Nothing?"

Leah smiled wanly. "I guess for the time being I'll just play it by ear, take each day as it comes. We'll be seeing each other every weekend for the time being, and— Oh, that reminds me. How about letting Ann go to Phoenix with Nina and me this weekend? They can keep each other entertained, and Jacob has a house that's indescribable! I think his staff has staff. I'm sure the girls will find plenty to do."

"Sure," Sandra said without hesitation. "I was probably going to call on you for baby-sitting duty, anyway. Sam wants to take me to dinner in Flagstaff Saturday night."

"Sandra, I forgot!" Leah exclaimed, hitting her forehead with the heel of her hand. "How was your date last week?"

"Interesting. Very interesting. I haven't seen Sam so charming since our dating days. Mr. Smooth." She sighed. "Why couldn't he have used just a little of that while we were married? Everything would have been so much nicer."

"Would it? Think what you've accomplished on your own. Would you have ever done that if you had stayed married to Sam?"

Sandra's head jerked quickly. "You're right. Dammit, you're right. Even my father once admitted he was proud of me. At the time I looked around to see if he was talking to someone else!"

JACOB TELEPHONED every night that week, as well. There was some sort of physician's conference being held in Phoenix; not only was he a host, he was one of the principal speakers. He was busy, yet he found time to call every night.

Leah scrunched down under the covers that particular night, placing the receiver between her ear and the pillow. "You sound so important," she murmured.

Modestly he scoffed, "I'd be surprised if there were a dozen people in that auditorium who were actually listening to me. The rest were either half-asleep, dubious, or certain their own theories were far sounder than mine."

"Ah, go on. Such humility. I'll wager they all were thinking how extraordinarily brilliant you are."

He laughed. *He should do that more often,* Leah thought. *It makes such a nice sound.*

"Leah, darling, the only extraordinary thing about me is the way I feel about you. If I had wanted to be eloquent this afternoon, I should have presented, to the certain astonishment of my esteemed colleagues, a dissertation on the joy you've brought to my life."

"Oh, Jacob!" He could overwhelm her. It might be her husband's voice in her ears, but that wasn't Jim speaking. Jim couldn't have come up with words like that if his life had depended on it.

"Are the girls looking forward to the visit?" he asked.

"I'll say! Nina tells anyone who'll listen that we're going to Jacob's house this weekend. She says 'Jacob's house' as if it were the White House or Buckingham Palace."

"Waiting for this weekend has me feeling like a kid myself, waiting for Christmas."

"I know, Jacob. I feel the same way."

DAVIS OPENED the door wide and gave them a beaming smile. "How are you, Mrs. Stone? So nice to see you again. And these—" he held out a welcoming hand to the two wide-eyed girls standing in front of Leah "—these young ladies must be our special guests. Dr. Surratt has asked me to take extra good care of them."

Nina and Ann stood rooted in place, presenting a charming contrast, since Ann was as fair as Nina was dark. Both girls looked as though they might explode any minute from excitement. Hesitantly they preceded Leah into Jacob's house. Whispered "wows" and "gees" reached Leah's ears. Nina turned to her in astonishment. "Mama, this is bigger than school!"

Leah smiled, though she was watching Davis out of the corner of her eye. This would be the acid test, she decided. If the resemblance between Nina and Jacob was really as great as it seemed to her, surely the man would notice. But there wasn't a flicker, not a hint that he saw a thing. She relaxed somewhat. Perhaps it was true that people don't look any further than the obvious—color of the hair and eyes, shape of the mouth. Certainly in that respect Nina was enough like her mother.

Davis had everything organized. First he took Nina and Ann to the room Leah had occupied the weekend of the opening. There a tiny wren of a woman named Hilda took over. "Mrs. Stone, I'm so glad to meet you. I was on vacation the last time you were here, I believe. Now I don't want you to worry about the girls. Dr. Surratt has instructed me not to let them out of my sight, and you can be sure I'll do just that." She looked at the girls with a maternal expression. "Such lovely young things. This—" she reached out and touched the top of Nina's dark curls "—of course is your daughter. She looks so much like you. We're going to have a wonderful time, aren't we, girls?''

Nina and Ann nodded in uncertain unison.

All well and good, but Leah had some instructions of her own. ''I want you girls to have fun, but please remember this isn't a playground or an amusement park. This is someone's home, and you're to treat it as such. Understand?'' Containing their excitement for a moment, both girls nodded solemnly.

To Hilda, Leah said, ''I've brought along an emergency kit, just in case.''

The little woman frowned. ''Emergency?''

''Games, coloring books, crayons. The sort of thing you resort to when all else fails.''

Hilda smiled indulgently. ''Well, Mrs. Stone, the staff and I hope to keep the girls so busy they won't have time for coloring books and such.''

''Where's Jacob?'' Nina asked.

Davis stepped forward. ''Dr. Surratt had some work to do at the clinic, but he wanted me to telephone him the moment you arrived, which I've done. I'm sure he'll be here any moment.'' He turned to Leah. ''I'll show you to your room while Hilda gets the girls settled in.''

Leaving the room, Leah paused for one last word with Nina and Ann. ''Remember, girls, I want some shining behavior reports.''

''Please don't worry about them, ma'am,'' Hilda said, smiling fondly at her two new charges. ''It's going to be such fun having the young ones around.''

I hope she's still saying that tomorrow afternoon, Leah thought wryly as she followed Davis down the carpeted hallway. She experienced a brief moment of mortification when she saw the weekend ''arrangement''—adjoining bedrooms. She was being given the room Alex had had before. It was linked to Jacob's by a beige-tiled bathroom, quite possibly the largest bathroom she had ever seen. It was completely masculine in decor, with cocoa-colored fixtures, natural wood tones and an absence of superfluous decoration, but it was also the last word in luxury. Thick nylon carpeting that looked like fur covered the floor, and a sunken tub complete with whirlpool apparatus dominated the center of the room. It was no ordinary bath; merely thinking of sharing it with Jacob was a sensuous experience.

''Thank you, Davis,'' Leah said stiffly, overcompensating for her embarrassment with a too-correct manner. ''It's lovely.''

His expression was blank. "Yes, ma'am. If there's nothing else right now, I'll go downstairs and see if Dr. Surratt has arrived."

Once Davis was gone, Leah hung up the few garments she had brought, went into the bathroom to freshen her makeup, momentarily considered changing out of her pleated shirtwaist dress, then decided to wait and see what plans Jacob had for the afternoon.

Impatient for his arrival, she crossed the expanse of the master bath to his bedroom. She had glimpsed it briefly from the hallway, but now she indulged in the luxury of really studying it. The room reflected his personality—quietly elegant, nothing ostentatious, a wealthy man's private retreat. A king-size bed, desk and chair, a recliner and reading lamp were the main furnishings. Several books lay on a bedside table. She picked them up and perused the jackets. Very intellectual stuff. Jacob apparently read more for knowledge than pleasure, whereas Jim had devoured spy thrillers.

Leah even had the temerity to open his closet door and gaze along the neat rows of clothing. Shutting the door behind her, she had started to leave the room, feeling every inch a nosy intruder, when she heard Jacob calling to her from the other bedroom. "Leah? Darling, where are you?"

Her heart leaped exultantly. "Here!" she called back, and moved in the direction of his voice. The shortest distance to him was through the bathroom. She entered from one side, he from the other; for a moment they each stood framed in their respective doorways, simply staring at each other. Then exuberantly they raced for each other like a couple of children.

She coiled her arms around his neck as he lifted her off the floor and swung her around. "Damn, it's good to see you!" he said.

"Jacob, you're making me dizzy!" she said with a laugh.

Effortlessly he swept her up into his arms, marched out of the bathroom into his room, where he dumped her on the bed. Then he fell on top of her, a lead weight. She was the recipient of an enthusiastic kiss before he said, "I've missed you so much."

"I've missed you, too," Leah squirmed. "You weigh a ton." She tugged at the hem of her dress, which had ridden up to midthigh.

Jacob rolled off her slightly, but his hand detained hers. "Leave it where it is." He placed his palm against her stockinged flesh and rubbed sensitively. "You feel so good. What a month this week has been! I thought this moment would never come." He bent his head to kiss the pulse point at the base of her throat before searching for her mouth again.

Leah's mouth sought his as avidly. Drawing her into an ardent embrace, he kissed her again and again. His tongue explored the sweet secrets of her mouth, while his hand roamed along her thigh, pushing the dress ever higher.

"You leave me breathless," she gasped when they parted.

"For a week I've been a man with a problem," he growled, and he moved against her to prove it.

"Surely you don't . . . expect to solve it here and now!!"

Only Leah could make him feel so carefree, so lighthearted, happy and thoroughly reckless. "Hold on tight, darling," he whispered huskily, drawing her thighs around his hips. The dress was up around her waist by this time.

"Oh, Jacob, not here!"

"Why not?"

"Jacob, don't be ridiculous! There are other people. . . ." It was beginning to dawn on her what a sight they would present to anyone who happened into the room, and to her knowledge no doors had been locked.

He sat back on his haunches, his eyes glittering, and his hands began a worshipful foray along the length of her slender, shapely legs. When they reached her feet, he casually flicked away her pumps and dropped them on the floor.

"This must be the finest pair of legs in all the world," he murmured reverently, his hands inching up her rounded calves, her smooth thighs. He braced an arm on either side of her, leaned over and planted a firm, warm, moist kiss on her parted lips. Gradually he settled his full weight on her.

"Oh, Leah," he muttered, "definitely . . . a problem. . . ."

"This is indecent." It was a half protest, half laugh.

"No one's going to bother us, sweetheart."

Languorously she writhed beneath him as white-hot flame curled up from the pit of her stomach. "Couldn't you please just lock some doors? I think I could get more in the spirit of this if I wasn't scared to death that someone was going to walk in on us at any minute."

"Okay," he said hoarsely, pushing himself off her, then undoing his belt buckle and unbuttoning his trousers. "I've got to get these damned pants off, anyway. Don't move."

He went to the door leading to the hall and locked it. Leah didn't move. She merely watched him. His hair was tousled, and

with his belt hanging unfastened in the loops and his trousers unbuttoned, he was the perfect picture of aroused masculinity.
Smiling, she flicked at the top button of her dress as he moved
toward the bathroom door.

"Mama!" Nina's childish voice rent the air. It was coming from
the hall, but in only seconds, Leah was sure, her daughter would
wander into the adjoining bedroom, then no doubt into the bathroom, then into Jacob's room.

"Jacob!" Leah gasped in horror, leaping off the bed, trying to
button her dress and grope for her shoes at the same time. He
halted in his tracks and fumbled with the front of his pants. Both
worked hard to steady their frantic breathing.

"God a'mighty!" Jacob croaked.

"Mama?"

"In here, Nina!" Leah managed to say, smoothing her rumpled dress.

Nina and Ann appeared in the doorway leading to the bathroom. Both were wearing swimsuits and carrying inflated,
doughnut-shaped gadgets. The smiling girls confronted two adults
who were trying their best to look as though they had been engaged in a friendly chat. Only six-year-olds would have believed
it.

"Hilda's taking us swimming," Nina announced brightly.
"Wanna come?"

At that moment a rather frantic Hilda put in an appearance,
hustling the girls away. Over her shoulder she threw Jacob an
apologetic look. "Dr. Surratt, I'm so sorry, but they just got away
from me for a minute."

"That's quite all right, Hilda. Think nothing of it."

Hilda and the girls left, but not before Nina quickly added,
"Oh, Jacob, this is my friend, Ann." Jacob muttered something
unintelligible as the other bedroom door closed firmly behind the
trio. Leah expelled a ragged breath. Then to Jacob's astonishment, she began to giggle. Putting her hand to her mouth, she
crossed the room and slumped against him, her shoulders shaking.

"What's so damned funny?" he demanded.

"Y-you should see the look on your face!"

"Damn! What a time to interrupt a guy!"

"Well, weren't you the one wh-who needed to get used to having a child around . . . ?"

"Do you have a headache?" Leah asked seriously, sipping on her wine that evening.

"A mild one," Jacob admitted. "Nothing really."

"You're frowning, and you've been rubbing your eyes. You do that a lot."

"So I'm prone to headaches."

"Stop that, Jacob. I want to know."

They were sitting at an umbrella table beside the swimming pool, watching the sun flame and die over Camelback Mountain, enjoying a quiet, private interlude before dinner. In the distance they could see Davis driving Jacob's golf cart over the grounds. Beside him were two very happy—but surely by now—worn-out little girls who had been thoroughly catered to all afternoon. To top off their perfect day, dinner had been prepared especially for them by Jacob's cook, a robust man named George, who looked as though he had a hearty appreciation of his own cooking. At the girls' request, spaghetti had been served, but with a flair worthy of pâté de fois gras and tournedo Rossini. The trip over the grounds in the golf cart was going to be the curtain call. The moment they returned, Leah was going to get the girls off to bed. Hilda, she had noticed, wore the harried expression of a mother of five who'd just discovered the washing machine was on the blink.

"Tell me," she demanded again.

Jacob shifted in his chair and watched her. Tonight she looked ravishing; that was the only way to describe her. She was wearing some long, shimmering, emerald green thing that seemed to be a dress, but with her legs crossed he could see it was pants. The sleeves were big and floppy, the neckline draped low to hint at the valley between her breasts, and the waist was cinched with a gold belt. Her hair hung down around her shoulders, the way he liked it. It still amazed and thrilled him that this stunning woman had been attracted to him from the beginning. It was impossible to explain what she had done for his masculine ego, but he would have liked to try. He wanted to tell her she had uncovered something in him he hadn't known existed. There was so much he would like to say to her, to talk about—almost anything but his crazy, mixed-up mind.

"Let's change the subject," he suggested softly.

Leah sighed. "I suppose so, if it bothers you that much."

"Oh, Leah, it doesn't bother me." He reached across the table and took one of her hands in his. "It just doesn't seem very interesting or important anymore. Look, every once in a while, I get these. . . . It's like a flashbulb goes off in my head, and I get a headache. But it always goes away fairly quickly. That's all there is to it. I don't want to think about it."

"Please, just let me ask one more question. Have you always had these headaches?"

"At first, years ago when I came out of the fugue, I had them frequently. Then they went away. They've only come back recently. Now, let's drop it, okay?"

"Sure." Her thoughts were racing nevertheless. No doubt the headaches had returned since he'd met her. He was fighting the recollection. Damn, the solution seemed so simple to her untrained mind. Just fill in the blank spaces for him, and he could relax. But she didn't dare.

Jacob watched her. She had a very expressive face, and he could tell she was bothered by his "condition." He raised her fingertips to his lips, an action that snapped her out of her reverie. His eyes strayed over her in an almost physical caress. "Leah, it's so unimportant. The headaches used to worry me, but since I met you. . . I think what I'm trying to tell you is, I don't care anymore. I—"

A lump formed in his throat. It shouldn't be so hard to say, but in all his life he had only told one woman he loved her, and that had been a horrible mistake. This wasn't a mistake, though. Leah was so right for him. "I love you. I have since the moment I laid eyes on you in Alex's office."

"That's almost impossible, you know."

"It's true just the same."

Leah's lips trembled. "I love you, too, Jacob. Really I do." And she did. Everything she had ever felt for Jim had been transferred to Jacob, while Jacob heaped new sensations on the old with each passing minute.

He buried his face in her palm and kissed it, overcome with emotion. "I wish I could tell you what hearing that does to me. Here. . ." He placed her hand over his heart. "It's about to thud right out of my chest."

They stood simultaneously and clung to each other for a long, wordless moment. Finally Jacob stepped away from her. "Davis is coming with the girls. Let's get those two scamps in bed. The rest of the evening belongs to us. I think I'd like to take you out to dinner. It's suddenly occurred to me that we've never had an honest-to-goodness date."

THEY HAD DINNER at Trader Vic's. Jacob chose it not only for the food but for the exotic ambience, a perfect backdrop for Leah's exotic beauty. And how beautiful she did look! Before leaving the house she had changed into a swishy dress of palest apricot, with some sort of pleated furbelow at the shoulders that framed the smooth sweep of her neckline. Magically—through makeup, lighting, whatever—her cheeks had taken on the same hue as her dress. She always looked so... well, put together. He knew she wasn't a woman who spent an unusual amount of time or money on clothes, but when Leah got all dressed up, there wasn't a woman alive who could match her for style and flair.

They dined on crab Rangoon, then Indonesian lamb with peach chutney and fried rice, snow peas and water chestnuts, all washed down with a delightful chilled Chardonnay. At meal's end Leah pushed her plate slightly away from her and smiled contentedly. "It was a feast," she announced. "I'm sure I've never had a finer meal."

"I wanted it to be special."

"It's been that, all right. Very special."

"The entire day's been special. I got a real kick out of having the girls with us."

Leah chuckled. "I wonder if Davis and Hilda would say the same thing. You were really good with them."

"You sound surprised."

"You once told me you felt uptight around kids, and you looked startled out of your wits when Nina asked you to tell them a bedtime story."

"Hmm. That threw me for a while. I'm not sure anyone has ever asked me to read to them before."

"Bedtime stories are stalling tactics, don't you know that? Like drinks of water and trips to the bathroom."

"How did I do with 'The Three Little Pigs?'"

"Well... it sounded to me as if you had it confused with 'Goldilocks and the Three Bears' a time or two, but I'm not sure it wasn't more interesting that way. What difference did it make, anyway. The girls were enchanted, since they knew you had it thoroughly screwed up. They were just waiting to see how you'd extricate yourself. There's a fey side to you I haven't seen before."

He reached for her hand. "Leah, you've unearthed things in me I didn't know existed."

After leaving the restaurant, they strolled along the Fifth Avenue shops, window-shopping before returning to Jacob's house. No one was waiting up for them, and only two small lamps had been left on, one in the foyer and one in the upstairs hall. Jacob locked the front door, turned off the foyer light, and arm in arm they ascended the stairs.

When they reached the second floor, Leah said, "Let me check on the girls."

He nodded and waited for her. She was back in a minute. "Your place or mine?" he asked.

"I think I'd like being in your bed." She walked to the door to his room and stepped inside; he followed, closing and locking it behind them. Then she was in his arms, being held, petted and kissed with a desperation that staggered her. The room was very dark. Fingers of moonlight filtering through the half-closed blinds played on the wall and across the bed.

"How do you get out of this thing?" he asked, fumbling impatiently with the apricot-colored cloth.

Quickly she undid the sash and let it fall. "There's a zipper in back," she said breathlessly.

Taking her by the shoulders, he turned her, and the zipper hissed. The garment formed a peachy puddle at her feet. He kissed her on the nape, then on both shoulder blades before turning her back to him. She stood before him in a thin wispy bra and panty hose. The muscles in Jacob's stomach tightened; the swelling in his groin made his trousers uncomfortably tight. He wondered how long it would last, this instant arousal at the sight of her, clothed or unclothed. Gently he slipped his hands around her back and undid the bra, then filled his palms with her satin-smooth breasts. "You are so...beautiful. A perfect ectomorph."

Leah's legs felt like liquid, unable to support her weight. She stumbled against him. "A what?"

"Ectomorph—slender, small boned, gentle curves. You're what all the endomorphs would like to be."

"Doctor, how romantic!" she teased. Looping her arms around his neck, she nibbled at the underside of his chin. "What are you?"

"I'm an ectomorph, too."

"Take off your clothes and let me verify that."

He complied hastily, awkwardly jerking and flinging his clothes with abandon. Then he stood before her, proud and urgent, fully aroused and eager for her. She gloried in the sight. Luxuriously she ran her hands over his chest, down his sides to his waist, which was scarcely distinguishable from his lean, hard hips. "But you have such marvelous muscles."

He swallowed hard. "Ectomorphs can develop muscles."

Her hands fluttered across his shoulders, moving to his upper arms. She slipped her arms around his waist, squeezing his buttocks with both hands. "Obviously, ectomorphs have nice buns."

His hands did some exploring of their own. "Obviously." He grinned.

One of her hands came around and down between their bellies. "And this?"

"Universal to all body types," he said on a groan. Hooking his fingers into the waistband of her panty hose, he pulled downward. "One last obstacle." She wiggled her hips to facilitate the removal.

Jacob bent and with one swift motion dispensed with the bedspread, then guided her between the sheets. She reached for him as he joined her, and once again he marveled at how perfectly their bodies responded to each other. She slithered beneath him, slipping easily into the niche of his hips that seemed made just to fit her. Her legs locked around him, holding him tightly to her.

Even though a week had passed, neither of them was impatient for the consummation. They spent several long, leisurely minutes in stimulating exploration, each marvelously attuned to the other. Knowing hands performed their magic; not an inch of her escaped his lips. Jacob, caught in the throes of sexual readiness, nevertheless kept to an exquisitely torturous pace, stroking and priming until she cried out for the union. Levering himself above her, he withheld her request a moment and stared down at her, his eyes feverishly bright, his nostrils distended with desire.

"Please . . ." she whispered.

"All right, darling. Now..." He covered her body with his and filled her completely. Her arms and legs bound him like loving ropes. Jacob buried his face in the silky hollow of her shoulder, felt her soft cheek against his, her damp hair brushing his forehead. He thrust and rotated until he felt the explosion rock her, and lifting his head, he watched the ecstasy transform her face. Only when her tremors ceased and her mouth grew slack did he allow himself his own release. Certain she had been satisfied, he succumbed, and his tension broke into a shock wave of pure pleasure. Emptied and temporarily depleted, he drew her into the warm circle of his arms and, for a time, they slept.

IT WAS AFTER MIDNIGHT when they awoke. "Roll over," Leah murmured, "and I'll give you a massage."

"Sounds irresistible." Jacob rolled onto his stomach, his cheek on the pillow, and raised his arms above his head. Leah tossed the sheet away from them and knelt on the bed beside him. Tapered fingers began massaging his neck, then kneading his shoulder muscles. The ritual she performed had been perfected during her marriage and was designed to inspire and ignite, not soothe and relax.

"Feel good?" she asked after a minute or two.

Jacob's voice was muffled by his pillow. "Mmm."

"I take it that means yes."

"Mmm..."

Smiling seductively, she continued with sensitively tactile fingers, working up and down the length of him, reveling in the feel of his firm musculature. He had, it seemed to her, the perfect male physique.

"Leah?"

"Hmm?"

"Was my resemblance to your husband the reason for your peculiar reaction to me that day in the gallery?"

Her hands stopped. "Oh, God, is that what you're thinking about?"

"Was it?" he persisted.

"I... guess that was part of it."

"Do I really look that much like him?"

"I guess you do. What difference does it make?"

"None, I guess, except—" he rolled over to look at her "—except I worry that you might be making love to him through me."

Leah sat back on her heels, and her mouth compressed into a tight line of irritation. "You worry too much, Doctor. Didn't anyone ever tell you that's bad for you? Why do you find it so difficult to believe I love you, just you, nobody else?"

"I'm a walking example of chronic insecurity. Haven't you discovered that by now? I'm too crazy about you, Leah. I'm not sure I could survive if you—"

"Walked out on you? Not everybody deserts. I'm not going anywhere, not unless you persist in questioning me every time we make love. If you want to talk about something, let's talk about all your old girlfriends. We've barely touched on that subject."

"All of them?" he teased.

"There were that many?"

"No," he said seriously. "Not many. Not unless you want to go back to my wild, impetuous youth, and even that was pretty tame by today's standards."

Leah didn't really want to talk about his women friends, or even the lack of same. "All right, I'll buy that. Subject closed. Now..." Grabbing the sheet, she billowed it over their heads like a tent and crawled on top of him. The percale floated down to settle around their hips. "I guess I'm going to have to try something else, since the massage obviously didn't work."

She locked her thighs against his and began moving slowly, sensuously on top of him. He groaned. "You look like an angel, but you're a sorceress, a temptress."

Bending her head, she gently captured his bottom lip between her teeth and nibbled. "I'm trying to be," she murmured. "Lie still and let me practice."

Within seconds he had caught the pace of her relentless rhythm and begun to move with her. From the beginning he had instinctively known she was not a woman of varied sexual experience, and he believed her when she said her husband had been her only lover. Yet she inspired him to new heights of sexual prowess, so that loving Leah was the easiest thing in the world. This time when the climax came it was no earth-shattering explosion, but a wonderful sensation of joy and relief and thunderous happiness. His body was glutted with pleasure.

"Leah," he said when he was capable of speech, "if you keep this up, my reproductive organs are going to be in a bottle at Harvard Medical School."

Her response was a quiet laugh of absolute triumph.

AS SHE WAS PREPARING to leave for home the following afternoon, Jacob came into the room. "Davis and Hilda have the girls ready."

"And are counting the minutes until they see my car pull out of the driveway, I'll bet. Your staff is priceless, Jacob. This weekend they've tended to duty above and beyond the call." She snapped her suitcase shut and turned to him.

He stepped toward her, taking her loosely in his arms. "Five days is too long to be away from you."

"I know, but if we were together all the time, I'm afraid neither of us would get any work done."

His expression was intense. "I want you to do me a favor, Leah."

"Yes?" Something about the tone of his voice put her on guard.

"Think about getting a divorce."

"You dwell on that too much, Jacob."

"How else can I be sure you're ready to belong to me?"

"I belong to you."

"Then get a divorce."

"I'll . . . look into it."

"Promise?"

"Yes, I promise."

CHAPTER THIRTEEN

THE SUMMER slipped into a blissful routine. Leah and Jacob saw each other every weekend. When he came to Sedona, she made a point of driving him all over the valley, thinking he might recognize something, though whether or not he did became less and less important to her. Together they visited the impressive Indian ruins of the Tuzigoot National Monument and the picturesque and historic old mining town of Jerome. They spent a Saturday hiking Oak Creek's fantastic West Fork. Touristy things mostly, because Leah thought she had to be careful.

She couldn't risk taking him places where he might encounter someone who had known him as Jim Stone. At all costs she wanted to avoid doing him the irreparable harm Charles White had mentioned. For that reason, other than for sight-seeing, they stayed close to her house and to Whit's farm, where only her father and Tee knew the truth and were as protective of him as she was.

Jacob was never far from her thoughts. She was sure she had never been happier. For the first time in her life, Leah was being courted, wooed, and it was a heady experience. The romance was so different from the one that had developed between her and Jim. Jacob was forever bringing gifts, both for her and for Nina. He sent flowers occasionally and made those late-night phone calls that had grown increasingly erotic. He seemed to lose a lot of his inhibitions when talking on the phone.

Still, she balked at the idea of getting a divorce, and she had to examine exactly why. She didn't think it necessary, since she was convinced that the impasse could be resolved in a better way. Unfortunately, just what that "better way" was escaped her.

For one thing—and this was something she tried not to dwell on too heavily—divorce implied a rejection of her life with Jim. Foolish maybe, but that was the way she felt about it. Leah hated the idea of legally terminating a relationship that was still alive and well through Jacob.

So instead of immediately seeking a lawyer, she talked to Whit. She tried to visit her father at least once a week, and now that Bess's offspring were frisky and playful and nearing weaning age, Nina constantly badgered her mother to go to the farm. It didn't take much pleading, for Leah relished every chance to talk to Whit, her one true confidant.

"If Jacob persists in this divorce thing, I guess I'm going to have to go through with it, Dad. He sees my refusal to get one as clinging to old memories. What do you think would be involved? Won't I have to answer a lot of questions about my husband? I can't let Jacob hear any of the answers."

By now Whit knew the whole story, and he had his own ideas on the subject. "Damned if I don't think Jacob should know the truth. Sounds to me like he's worried about the past, like he might've done something awful or some such nonsense. But we know that's not so. Between us we can probably account for every single second of Jim Stone's short life." Whit shook his head. "Sure seems to me that Jacob would feel better if he knew that."

Leah chewed on her bottom lip. "That's what I think, too, Dad, but I'm no psychiatrist, and I can't forget what Dr. White said. The one thing I don't want to do is harm Jacob. I think he suffers more than he lets on."

"Well, I don't know what to tell you, but I'll send you to a fellow who might."

The fellow's name was Daniel Chapman, an attorney friend of Whit's, and most of what he told Leah she already knew. In another year, actually a few months less, she would legally be a widow. If she didn't want to wait that long she could sue for divorce on grounds of desertion. Leah winced over that one. However, Mr. Chapman went on to explain, her circumstances were a bit unusual. He would be glad to look into the case and give her a call later.

Leah left it at that for the time being. At least she could now truthfully tell Jacob she had seen a lawyer and that he was looking into it.

JACOB REGARDED Mildred Bannister across the expanse of his glass-topped desk. Hiding behind his professional mask, he appeared to be listening but wasn't. He had heard Mildred's story so many times before. She had been coming to see him at least once a month for three years or so, and according to Mildred, she was in no better health now than she had been that long-ago first day. He knew that. There wasn't anything wrong with her, not medically at least, but he couldn't seem to convince her of that.

He felt sorry for Mildred, he really did, and in some ways he could empathize with her. She didn't feel good, and she wanted help. Another prescription wouldn't help her, though. Over the years he had learned a good deal about her. She was middle-aged, had married children scattered all over the country and a successful husband who spent fifteen hours a day with his work. She had a lot of money but no real interests outside the home; unfortunately, now there was seldom anyone else at home. Pity no one had come up with a pill to cure loneliness. No one knew better than he did how rotten it could make you feel.

When the woman had finished recounting her lengthy list of ailments, Jacob gave her a sympathetic smile. "Well, Mildred, the best I can do is prescribe a mild sedative to help you with your insomnia, and there are some exercises you can do before getting out of bed every morning that might alleviate that back pain. Your X rays show no functional or structural cause for it. As for your stomach trouble . . . again, tests show nothing. We might have to chalk it up to that handy ailment called 'nerves.' I would suggest you lay off the antacids, however, and let your digestive system right itself."

The woman sighed with disdain. "Doctor, I can't believe that in this fancy clinic with all this fancy equipment, you can't find out what's wrong with me."

"I'm sorry. We don't know everything. If we can't see it or feel it or hear it, we're helpless."

"My sister-in-law's doctor just gives her Valium, and she says it works wonders for her."

"No, Mildred," Jacob said decisively. "Valium isn't the answer for you. Tell you what. There's another physician I'd like you to see."

"Oh?" The woman's eyes lit up.

"Yes. Dr. White."

It took Mildred a moment to realize who he was referring to. When she did, she bristled. "A psychiatrist? Do you think I'm crazy?"

"Why, Mildred! I'm surprised at you! Surely you know there are any number of reasons for seeing a psychiatrist. I'm merely thinking your problems might stem from a less-obvious source. Emotions, perhaps. Or from external factors beyond your control.''

She gave this some thought. ''Well, I can certainly understand how I'd be emotionally upset. Harry has no time for me, and he's not in the least sympathetic about my health problems. He says when I can tell him the name of what's wrong with me he'll start believing I'm sick. Wouldn't it do me a world of good to be able to tell Harry he's the one making me ill!''

Jacob reached for a notepad and pencil. ''I'm going to request a consultation with Dr. White for you. Will you go?''

The idea, he could tell, was taking on more appeal with each passing second. ''I certainly will, Doctor. I certainly will.''

Mildred was the day's last patient. Jacob saw her to the door, then instructed his nurse to close up shop for the day. Shutting his office door, he returned to his desk, settled into his comfortable swivel chair, propped up his feet and closed his eyes. The day had been an especially tiring one, no doubt because he had slept so poorly the night before, and the night before that.

His haunting dream was recurring with bewildering frequency. Worse, the headaches were back, the same kind he had suffered six years earlier. No longer could he pretend there was anything different about them. He had dispensed with aspirin and had begun taking a prescription medication that sometimes induced lethargy, which he hated. So far he had managed to downplay the headaches when he was with Leah, but that couldn't go on forever. She saw too much.

The past weekend in Sedona had been especially difficult for him. He thought he had successfully convinced her he had simply been working unusually long hours, until a headache all but incapacitated him. He had wasted a precious hour of their time together Saturday afternoon sleeping off the pain while she worked at her loom, and he begrudged every wasted moment.

Jacob lived for the weekends. It often seemed he was only happy and content when he was with Leah. He loved her with a mindless madness; that was the only way to describe it. She was such a quiet, addictive presence. A woman of contrasts, at once an imaginative dreamer and a serious artisan, a delightful imp and a sensuous siren. Her open passion still shook him, and he almost groaned as he thought about her.

Sometimes she came to Phoenix; more often he went to Sedona. After he had sat and watched her weave for a time, they would walk through the woods near her house or take leisurely drives through the valley. She was a great tour guide and loved the peaceful Verde. He thought he was beginning to understand why. There was something contagious about the slower pace of country life.

When Nina wasn't with her grandfather, she was with Jacob and Leah. Although the child's presence, coupled with the lack of privacy in Leah's house, were deterrents to lovemaking, Jacob never resented either. There were times when just being with Leah was enough. With her, he could relax; with her, he could be himself . . . whoever himself was.

He was a fortunate man, he knew. He had found the woman of his dreams, and both Leah's daughter and her father had accepted him into their lives with casual ease. Whit especially treated him as though he belonged, a fact for which Jacob was enormously grateful. Life was wonderful, and might be perfect if it wasn't for Leah's marital status, the damnable headaches and that god-awful dream.

Thinking of Leah's husband elicited a frown. Not even in their most private moments together had she told him about the man. The only thing Jacob knew for certain was that in some vague way he reminded her of him. Nor did she ever mention the divorce, not unless he brought it up, and then she only said some lawyer was "looking into it." Could she possibly be using the marriage as a crutch, something to lean on while deciding if she really wanted to marry a man who suffered headaches, dreams and all sorts of mental aberrations?

The headaches had no physical cause—he had made sure of that—so he had to accept that they were psychological. The past was trying to force its way into the present, and he was subconsciously refusing to let it. Why? He honestly wanted to remember, to make sure there was nothing lurking back there in the fuzzy recesses of his mind that could harm the future. He wanted to be the kind of husband Leah deserved, not some psychological freak, which was the way he saw himself half the time. He wanted to be well and whole and mentally sound.

Abruptly Jacob opened his eyes and swung his feet off the desk. He walked to the window and stood with his hands clasped behind his back. After a few minutes of staring vacantly out over the walled-in garden at the rear of the building, he paced restlessly around his office. He didn't particularly want to go home, but the office walls were closing in on him. His head was pounding, yet he didn't dare take any more medication until he was safely out from behind the wheel of a car.

This can't go on, old man, his inner voice warned.

Removing the ever-present stethoscope from around his neck, he stuffed it into the pocket of his white coat, then shrugged out of the coat and hung it up. He jerked his suit jacket off a hanger and slung it over his arm. Switching off the light, he walked through the empty waiting room into the silent corridor beyond. Automatically he turned toward the doctors' entrance at the rear of the building, then stopped suddenly. Acting on impulse, he pivoted and crossed the hall to the double doors leading to the psychiatric unit. It was as quiet and empty as the medical clinic, but at the end of the long hallway there was a light welling from under Charles's door. Striding purposefully toward it, Jacob entered the office.

Charles was standing near a bookcase. A book lay open in his hand, and reading glasses were perched on the tip of his nose. He looked up. "Ah, Jacob. Working late, I see."

"Not really. I saw my last patient a while ago. A patient I'm referring to you, by the way."

"Oh?"

Succinctly Jacob told Charles about Mildred Bannister's case. "But that's not the reason I'm here. Charles, how...how about putting me back in therapy?"

Charles frowned, regarding his partner levelly over the rim of his glasses. "What brought this on?"

"Does it matter? Can we start the sessions again?"

The psychiatrist closed the book and carefully slid it between two others in the case. He stared vacantly at the floor, not at Jacob. "I suppose that would depend on why you think you need therapy again. A lot of time has passed. I would have to guess the events of the fugue are forever buried in your subconscious."

Without being asked to, Jacob took a seat. He was never entirely at ease with his partner, though he wasn't sure why. Charles White was one of the finest psychiatrists in the country, precisely the reason Jacob had wanted him associated with the clinic. But the two men weren't personally close, a situation Jacob often attributed to his own reserved nature. That plus the fact that Charles was less outgoing probably made it impossible for the two of them to be fast friends.

However, it hadn't occurred to Jacob to go to anyone but his partner. He was socially acquainted with almost all of Phoenix's medical fraternity, several therapists among them, but he balked at going to any of them for help. Why, he wasn't sure; he wouldn't have hesitated to go to a surgeon friend if he needed an operation. This was different.

And he certainly wouldn't have considered going to one of Charles's younger associates. He did, after all, have a certain image to maintain in his own clinic. The other doctors referred to him as "the Man," though never to his face. They certainly didn't know he was aware of the nickname.

"That damned dream is back. The headaches, too," he told Charles. "I'll swear they're worse than before. Something's in there trying to get out. Can we begin again?"

"Is something personal bothering you? The woman?"

Jacob looked at Charles in surprise. "The woman?"

"Leah Stone."

"You know Leah?"

"No, but I met her once, at the opening."

"I'd only known her a few days then."

"Yes . . . I had the feeling she was someone you were going to try to get to know better."

"Is that a fact? Charles, you amaze me. I had no idea you paid that much attention to my women friends."

"You know clinic gossip. It's quickly and effectively circulated."

Jacob frowned at the suggestion that he and Leah could be topics of clinic gossip. How could they be, since they stayed strictly to themselves? So much so that his already limited social life had been placed in virtual limbo. Lately it had crossed his mind that he should take Leah out and introduce her to some of his friends and associates. Until today he had assumed no one in Phoenix outside his household even knew of their relationship. Gossip obviously had a way of getting around. "Leah isn't in the least like any other woman I've ever met," Jacob said.

"I realize that," the psychiatrist said enigmatically. "Is she your problem?"

"Leah's no 'problem,' Charles, but I want to marry her, and I'd like to make one last stab at clearing up this damned mind of mine. I think I owe it to her."

"Headaches, hmm? As I said, a lot of time has passed. The chances aren't good, Jacob. Not good at all."

"I know," he said resignedly, "but I want to try. I've got to try."

LEAH HAD JUST turned out the lights when the phone rang. Snuggling deeper beneath the covers, she reached for the receiver. "Hello, darling," she cooed seductively.

"You're going to be very surprised some night if the call isn't from me." Jacob chuckled.

"Not nearly as surprised as the caller will be."

"How are you?"

"Fine. You?"

"Pretty good."

"What's that supposed to mean? Are you having more of those headaches you keep pretending you aren't having?"

There was a pause; his husky sigh came over the line. "Why do I ever try to keep anything from you? You're a witch."

"No, just observant. I've seen you gulping those pills. You are having headaches, aren't you?"

"Yes."

"The dream, too?" she asked quietly, for by now he had told her about the dream, and she thought she could give him a pretty good interpretation of it, if only she dared.

"Sometimes."

"Why?"

"That's what I'm going to try to find out. I'm going back into therapy. Charles all but told me it wouldn't work, but I've got to try something. I can't shake the feeling there's something in my past that needs to be cleared up."

"Oh, Jacob . . ."

"It bugs the hell out of me."

"I . . . know."

"I can't for the life of me figure out why I wasn't found for two years!"

Leah wished she didn't feel so helpless. This was awful, knowing she could tell him everything he wanted to know in ten minutes, yet having to allow him to go into months and months of therapy, possibly without results.

Did he really want to know, that was the question.

Of course he does. Otherwise, why the therapy?

That's his conscious mind going into analysis. His subconscious may still block all recollection.

If only Charles White had never mentioned psychological amnesia, she thought irrationally.

"You told me remembering didn't matter," she reminded him.

"I guess I lied. It matters."

"Well, I hope therapy accomplishes what you want it to," was all she could think to say.

"Let's talk about something else, okay? How's Nina? Is she excited about summer camp?"

"Seems to be. But it's not really summer camp, more precamp. Three days at a youth camp not far from here. It's supposed to give six-year-olds a taste of being away from home, so hopefully they'll be better prepared for a week-long stay next year. I'm not worried Nina will be homesick. She spends so much time with Dad that she's not quite as tied to mama as most six-year-old kids."

"I can't tell you how I'm looking forward to this weekend. I love the little scamp, but I do want to be alone with you."

"And I with you."

They talked for their usual twenty minutes—amazing how much two quiet people could find to talk about—but Leah lay awake long after hanging up the phone. Across the room her loom stood holding Jacob's tapestry. The main body of the work was completed, as was the piece to be attached to it. Alex had stopped by the day before, pronouncing it the best work of her career. Having Jacob in her life seemed to fuel her creativity.

That wasn't all Alex had had on his mind. He could set up a one-woman show for her in a prestigious gallery in Dallas, he told her with his customary enthusiasm. Perhaps Jacob would allow her to show the tapestry before it was hung in the clinic. If it didn't prompt dozens of commissions, Alex didn't know what would. Her noticeable lack of enthusiasm sorely disappointed him, to the point where he accused her of losing interest in her career. Leah reminded him of the long hours she had been working. Did that seem to him like losing interest? Nevertheless, Alex wasn't in a particularly happy frame of mind when he left.

The thought of a one-woman show in a huge market like Dallas should have thrilled Leah, but she didn't want a separation from Jacob, not now. An odd disquiet overtook her just thinking about that, perhaps because she was remembering their last separation, six years ago. By now she was quite willing to credit any funny tricks the mind could play.

Jacob was going back into therapy, and she wasn't sure how she felt about that. In the beginning she would have been encouraged, for more than anything she had wanted him to remember being Jim Stone. That no longer seemed as important as it once had. She was happy with Jacob Surratt and thought she loved him more deeply than she had Jim. His maturity had something to do with her feelings, of course, but there was more to her change of heart than his age. Jacob was such a fascinating personality, so much more intense and interesting than Jim. Which wasn't surprising; Jim hadn't had a past to give him hang-ups.

Maybe she just feared disturbing the status quo. Things were pretty good right now. Awfully good, in fact. For the first time in years Leah was completely happy in all her roles—artist, mother, woman. And she wanted that same kind of complete happiness for Jacob, something he wasn't likely to attain until he had filled in all the blank spaces. He didn't sleep well, she knew that, and there were those headaches and that recurring dream.

Damn, it was so hard to know what to do. Watching him agonize was hard to bear when she knew all he needed to know about his past. If only she could help him....

JACOB SAT IN Charles's office, perched rather tensely on the chair facing the psychiatrist's desk. He was never comfortable here, had never become accustomed to the ritual, and he vaguely wondered if that was the reason Charles hadn't been able to help him. This time he vowed he would open up, just spill anything and everything that came to mind. He would be a cooperative patient.

"I think you're right about the Bannister woman's back problem, Jacob," Charles said. "It's psychosomatic, a bid for sympathy and attention, something she certainly isn't getting from that husband of hers."

"And medication?"

"Maybe."

"Try to find out what all she's taking, will you, Charles? I know she's been to doctors outside the clinic, so she might have prescriptions at pharmacies all over town. I doubt she levels with me. She says I always 'fuss' over her, and maybe I do, but I hate to sit idly by and watch Mildred turn into a hypochondriac."

"Of course." Charles tugged at his chin as he regarded his partner. "Shall we get started?"

"I suppose so."

"Would you like to lie down?"

"I think I'll just sit."

"However you're comfortable."

Jacob settled back into the comfortable chair, stretching his long legs in front of him. He felt every bit as foolish as he had six years ago. *I shouldn't be here,* he thought. *I should be home. I'd*

*swim a couple of laps, take a brisk shower and have Davis bring
me a drink. Read awhile, have dinner, then call Leah.*

Charles's first question was to the point. "Do you have difficulty coping with the fact that you, of all people, have amnesia?"

"Yes," he heard himself saying. "People suffer blows on the
head every day and don't get amnesia. Why me?"

"How do you know that's what caused the loss of memory?"

Jacob released a ragged breath. "I don't. I'm assuming. I
hadn't been ill."

"Does the amnesia embarrass you?"

"A little. Not as much now as it used to."

"And why is that?"

Jacob shrugged. "I don't know. Maybe it has something to do
with Leah. She accepted my murky past without a qualm."

"You've told her about it?"

"All about it."

"And she wasn't surprised, bothered, upset?"

"No, only interested."

"Did you find that odd?"

"Odd? No, I was pleased."

"Perhaps we should discuss your relationship with Leah Stone,
since she apparently is the reason you're back in therapy. How did
you meet her?"

"I walked into a downtown bank one morning about two
months ago and saw a tapestry hanging on the wall...." How
strange it now seemed to him that so much had happened because of that one seemingly insignificant act.

Talking about Leah was what Jacob did best. The words just
rolled off his tongue. When he'd finished, the psychiatrist asked
a surprising question.

"How do you feel when you're with her in that place . . . er, Sedona?"

"Feel? I'm happy . . . content. As relaxed as I ever get. Leah's
house feels like . . . home. More like home than my own ever has.
Leah's comfortable to be with. Strange, isn't it? Like with people. There are people in this town I've known for twenty years, yet
I don't really know them. But the first time I met Leah I felt as
though I'd known her all my life. I still do. We can spend hours
in each other's company without saying much of anything, like an
old married couple."

Charles cleared his throat. "Does she ever talk to you about your amnesia, try to get you to remember?"

"No. On the contrary, she's constantly telling me to forget it, that it doesn't matter. I wish I could. I wish it didn't matter, but it does."

"How does she feel about your going back into therapy?"

"She only said she hoped it accomplishes what I want it to. She's one hell of a woman, Charles."

When he left the office at the end of his hour, Jacob was surprised the time had passed so quickly. Surprised, too, that it hadn't been all that difficult to talk to his partner, although they didn't seem to have talked about much. He couldn't understand why dwelling on the present would help him remember the past, but he was reminded of what a complex science psychotherapy was. Best, he decided, to leave it to the experts. This time he was going to lick this thing!

As soon as Jacob left the office, Charles closed the folder he'd been scribbling in, settled back in his swivel chair and contemplated the opposite wall. For several days he had thought over Jacob's sudden decision to go back into therapy. He could sense an air of desperation behind his partner's determination this time, not like six years ago, when Jacob had been confused, frightened, disbelieving. Charles was faced with a new challenge.

He pondered the situation a moment longer. Then he reached for the telephone and dialed directory assistance.

"What city?" asked the operator.

"Sedona."

"May I help you . . . ?"

"Leah Stone, please. I don't know the address."

CHAPTER FOURTEEN

CHARLES WHITE'S CALL took Leah completely by surprise. The psychiatrist's voice was almost conspiratorial as he told her he wanted to talk to her, and he wanted the conversation kept confidential. Jacob wasn't to know anything about it. The matter was much too complicated to discuss over the telephone. With that in mind, Charles thought it would be better if he came to see her, rather than the other way around. He could be there at ten o'clock Friday morning.

Naturally Leah agreed, her curiosity honed to a keen edge. She gave him directions to her house and stifled the urge to quiz him over the phone.

On Friday, as she waited for Charles to arrive, fresh hope stirred inside her, although she had felt downright deceitful while talking to Jacob the night before. It didn't seem right to be keeping something from him, not even if she was doing so for his sake.

The meeting with Charles would prove to be for Jacob's good; Leah just knew it. Jacob would have seen his colleague by now and would have mentioned the role Leah had played in his life. Maybe, just maybe the psychiatrist had thought of a way she could help Jacob.

After brewing a fresh pot of coffee, Leah glanced at the clock on the wall. She had been operating at a dead run since daybreak. First there had been the last-minute flurry of activity associated with getting Nina off to camp. Then she had driven her daughter to the pick-up point, where the bus had collected the youngsters at eight-thirty sharp. Afterward she had hurried back home to wait for Dr. White. The psychiatrist had informed her he would be on a tight schedule, so she knew the visit must have some real importance. She was filled with impatience and anticipation.

Just then she heard a car door slam, front-gate hinges creaking. Footsteps crossed the porch, and a loud rap sounded on her door. Leah hurried to answer it.

"Good morning, Dr. White."

"Good morning, Leah."

"Please come in. I've just made coffee. Would you like a cup?"

"Yes, thank you." Charles stepped into the house, glancing around. "Charming place."

"Thank you." Closing the door behind her guest, Leah was again struck by a certain familiar quality about the man. He definitely reminded her of someone she knew, or at least someone she had seen somewhere. She wasn't especially good at names, but she almost never forgot a face. If she'd seen him before, where or when would come to her sooner or later.

Then Charles turned to face her, and she was astonished to see he looked ill at ease. A tremor of trepidation raced through her as she dwelled on the possibility that he had come to give her some awful news about Jacob. That thought, however, was quickly dismissed. She knew so much more about Jacob than his partner did. She knew more about Jacob than Jacob himself did.

"Cream or sugar?" she asked pleasantly.

"Just black, thanks."

"Please, sit down...." She indicated the most comfortable chair in the room. "This will only take a moment."

Once she had served coffee to the doctor, she took a seat on the sofa facing him. "You wanted to talk to me about Jacob?" she urged.

"Yes." Charles took a swallow of coffee, then set the cup and saucer on a small table at his elbow. Leah noticed he had some difficulty looking squarely at her. "I assume you know he's back in therapy."

"Of course."

"After talking to him this week, I happened to recall my first meeting with you—only meeting, now that I think about it. I remember that you specifically asked about amnesia that night."

"Y-yes."

"I also remember something about knowing or having known an amnesiac, right?"

Leah's heart fluttered erratically. "Yes, I did."

"Yet that night, the night of the opening, you said you had only known Jacob a few days."

"That's right."

"I also seem to recall a question regarding the wisdom of telling an amnesiac about events during the fugue. You even knew the proper term for it, which caught my attention right away."

"Yes." By now Leah had a pretty good idea what the doctor was getting at. The coincidence had become apparent to him. How many lay people would know two amnesiacs in a lifetime?

"Well, then," Charles went on, "I added that to my new knowledge concerning Jacob's recurring dream and headaches. Apparently they started up again about the time Jacob met you, and they've been happening frequently ever since."

"Jacob said that?" she asked, alarmed.

"Not in so many words. I'm sure he's unaware of the pattern that's developed. He considers the dream a warning of some kind." Charles paused, picked up his cup and sipped slowly. "I may be way off base on this, Leah, but it's occurred to me that you might know something about Jacob's fugue period."

She glanced at her hands, folded in her lap, then back at Charles. She couldn't think of a single reason not to tell him. In fact, she suspected she should tell him. He might be able to take the information and use it to help Jacob. "Yes," she said simply.

"Did you know Jacob during those two missing years?"

She nodded. "I...not only knew him, Doctor, I married him."

She expected some sort of surprised reaction to that, but none was forthcoming. But then she supposed psychiatrists learned to maintain a neutral expression no matter what incredible things they heard. Or perhaps Charles had guessed some of the truth before coming to see her. He only pursed his lips and grew thoughtful. "Well, Leah, why don't you tell me the whole story from the beginning."

So again she related the story of her marriage to Jim Stone. It crossed her mind that an awful lot of people had heard about it now. For six years she, her father and Tee were the only people who had known the true story, but she had since taken Alex, Sandra and Charles into her confidence. No real harm in that, she thought worriedly, provided Jacob wasn't hurt, provided no one made a careless remark.

Charles listened without interrupting, but when she had finished he said nothing for an unusually long time. Finally he cleared his throat and asked, "And Jacob gave no sign of recognition when he met you in that gallery?"

"None."

"When did he tell you about his amnesia?"

"The night I was a guest in his house. The night of the opening."

"Did he say anything specific about his earlier therapy?"

"No, only that nothing came of it, so you encouraged him to give it up."

"Not 'encouraged' exactly," Charles said quickly. "I merely suggested he might be wasting his time. He responded to therapy poorly, you see, besides which, it seemed to aggravate the headaches. I suggested they might go away if he stopped trying so hard to remember. As it turned out, I was right. At that time Jacob needed to concentrate on getting on with his life. He had a lot of catching up to do." He shifted in the chair. "And you've told him nothing, haven't hinted you knew him before?"

Leah shook her head. "When I first saw him again in Alex's office, I was too stunned to say anything, and it was apparent he didn't recognize me at all. Later some instinct warned me against saying anything. Then I met you at the opening, and after hearing what you had to say on the subject, about adding to his confusion and doing nothing to restore his memory, about psychological amnesia ... well, I wouldn't have dared say anything. The most I've done is take him to my Dad's place and around the valley."

"No recognition?"

"Not the slightest. Of course, I've been hampered in that respect. I've had to be careful and not take him anyplace where he might be recognized. Fortunately, Jacob's changed just enough in six years...." Leah moistened her lips nervously. "Dr. White, now that Jacob's back in therapy, I wondered if you've detected any change from six years ago?"

"I've only seen him once, but no, I see no change. If I had to make an educated guess, I'd say his chances of regaining his memory now aren't good. The events of the fugue are probably even more deeply buried in his subconscious than they were."

Leah leaned forward, speaking earnestly. "I want you to know I personally no longer care whether or not he remembers, but I know Jacob does. He'll be happier understanding what happened, so... Now that you have the entire story, I wanted to ask if it would be all right for me to tell him."

"No!" Charles blurted out, causing Leah to frown in confusion. The psychiatrist seemed surprised by his hasty exclamation and quickly amended, "I mean, no, not right now. I think it would be best if you gave me more time with him. I need to determine how the news would affect him."

"I realize psychiatry or psychotherapy isn't my field, Doctor, but knowing Jacob as I now do, I can't help but think he would welcome the news. Those missing years bother him so. I can interpret that dream...a house, a woman. This house and I were the most important things in Jim Stone's life. I just hate seeing Jacob suffer."

Charles stood up, clasped his hands behind his back and slowly paced, head bowed. "Yes, yes. Well ... we mustn't let ourselves be deceived by his apparent desire to learn about those years. It could very well be he's subconsciously fighting the recall."

"I can't imagine why," Leah persisted stubbornly, wanting so badly to convince the psychiatrist to let her follow her own instincts. "Jim Stone led a blissful two years of existence. He might very well have been the happiest person I ever knew. Not a single thing happened during those years in the valley that he need be ashamed of... or regret. Jacob would be enormously relieved to hear that, surely."

Charles paused in his pacing to give her a condescending look. "Well, Leah, as you've pointed out, you don't know very much about this sort of thing. Amnesia is complicated, since all sorts of factors come into play. Everything effects the mind, everything. As Jacob's therapist, I would strongly recommend not saying anything about any of this. In fact, I suggest you not discuss his amnesia with him at all."

Leah frowned. This was all so confusing, to say nothing of disappointing. Every time she had it all worked out in her own mind, she was reminded of psychological amnesia, and everything became a muddle again. "I really don't talk to Jacob about it. He's the one who brings it up, and I'm aware that it's never far from his thoughts. He wants to marry me. He's even more anxious to remember now, to—as he puts it—tie up any loose ends. I could so easily tell him there aren't any loose ends that need tying. Once he and Nina and I are back together again—"

"Nina?"

"Our daughter."

"Good Lord!" Charles muttered. "I'd forgotten that Jacob mentioned a child. Then she is his?"

"Yes. Nina's one reason I'd like Jacob to know the truth. I want to tell him she's his natural daughter, a continuance of the Surratt line. He'd be so pleased."

Why this bit of information, more than the rest, should be so unsettling to the psychiatrist, Leah didn't know, but she sensed it was. Suddenly she was more alert to Charles White's every move, his every expression. The doctor was ruffled. Odd but true.

"I repeat, Leah. You might do Jacob irreparable harm. He shouldn't be told these things until I'm sure he's ready to absorb them."

"And when will that be?"

"It's quite impossible for me to know that right now."

"Maybe never?"

"I really can't say."

"Then maybe you can answer this. Can you take this information I've given you and use it to help Jacob?"

"Perhaps."

He was being maddeningly noncommittal, but in fairness to him, she might be impinging on professional confidences. Leah knew she was impatient, wanting things that probably were impossible immediately. She had to think of Jacob and what was best for him. Her spirits sagged. "I suppose the only thing I can do is what I've been doing all along—taking Jacob around the valley and hoping something will trigger his memory. I suppose it would be better if he remembered on his own."

Charles jerked at the lapels of his jacket and went to sit down again. He picked up the coffee cup, then put it down without taking a sip. "I'm not sure that's wise. The more I think about it, the more . . ."

"Yes?" she prodded.

"It's difficult for me to say this to you, considering your relationship with Jacob, but I'm certain his welfare is your primary concern."

"Of course," she said quietly, warily.

"I'm . . . not sure it wouldn't be a good idea for you to stay away from him altogether, for a while, anyway."

Leah's eyes widened. "St-stay away from him?"

"For a while."

"Forgive me, Doctor, but I don't see the point in that."

"Think about it, Leah. The headaches, that dream—those things had left Jacob years ago. He was living at peace with himself until you came into his life, and he's known no peace since. You're the one who confuses him, although I doubt he associates the confusion with you. Yes, I'm convinced of it, and—I'm not sure how to put this delicately—your influence undermines what I'm trying to do. I have a feeling I'll discover that the headaches and the dream plague him more after he's been with you."

Leah was totally shaken. That she might inadvertently be hampering Jacob's progress, that she might even be the one causing so much of his distress, was a theory she couldn't accept. "Dr. White, if I tell Jacob I don't want to see him for a while, he won't understand. He'll be terribly hurt. I've become the one person he feels he can trust. I couldn't do that to him." *Or to myself,* she honestly admitted, though she knew it wasn't only self-concern that made her resist Charles's suggestion.

"Not even to help him?"

Leah bristled, hating the doubts the psychiatrist was putting into her head. "That's unfair, Doctor. I love Jacob and would do anything in the world for him, but I don't think staying away from him is the right thing to do."

"I realize it wouldn't be easy, but if you want to give Jacob a fair chance at restoring his memory, you should consider it."

"I . . ." She faltered. "He would expect some sort of plausible explanation, and I wouldn't know what to say."

"You could come up with something, I'm sure. Take a trip, anything to put some distance between the two of you while I'm trying to help him. Naturally I wouldn't want you to tell him the actual reason for the separation. That would only serve to make him resent therapy, in which case I wouldn't be able to help him at all."

Leah had no intention of doing what the man was suggesting. It was unthinkable! It didn't even make sense. How could stripping Jacob of something that made him happy help him? She suspected Charles of not fully understanding Jacob's sensitive nature. Perhaps Jacob found it impossible to open up fully with his partner. In that case, he probably should seek another therapist, a stranger. She wondered if he had ever considered that.

Leah focused all her powers of concentration on Charles White. In some unexplainable way the atmosphere in the room seemed to have changed. Leah had a curious feeling the psychiatrist regarded her as an adversary, which was ridiculous. They both wanted the same thing, didn't they?

As far as she was concerned, the visit had been wholly unsatisfactory. Perhaps she had been expecting too much, but not only had the psychiatrist squelched her hopes, he had told her things she didn't want to hear. Not see Jacob at all? She wouldn't. She couldn't! She quelled a brief stab of anxiety, wishing she hadn't felt compelled to tell Charles the truth.

The psychiatrist didn't stay long after that. Pleading the pressure of his schedule, he left, but not before Leah had the chance to ask him one more question. "Dr. White, eight years ago when you first suspected Jacob was missing, you tried to find him, right?''

"Of course," he said gruffly.

"What did you find out?"

"Nothing. I came up against a brick wall. The police weren't a bit of help to me, so I decided Jacob had disappeared on purpose. Why do you ask?"

She wasn't sure, except she couldn't shake the nagging wonder that a prominent man like Jacob Surratt could vanish without a trace, even given all the coincidences at the time.

"Oh, no reason. Strange, isn't it? The police weren't any help to us, either. Apparently by the time you started looking for him, Jim Stone had given up the search."

"Apparently," Charles said. "Good day, Leah."

After he'd gone Leah roamed restlessly around the house, her thoughts whirring. She was aware of a gnawing sensation inside—nothing she could name, just a disturbing feeling that something was out of kilter.

At length, however, she shook free of it. Jacob would be with her in a few hours, and there was a long, lovely weekend ahead of them. She wasn't going to give Charles's advice another thought, and she certainly wasn't going to put any distance between her and Jacob. That was the end of it! She didn't know why she made such a big deal out of everything. Right then and there she decided to get busy and get a divorce. What did the circumstances matter? Jim Stone no longer existed. All her foolish qualms about denying Jim's existence through divorce were just that—foolish.

Leah had psyched herself up into a lighthearted mood by the time she heard Jacob's car in front of the house later that afternoon. And the look on his face when she opened the door made her heart turn over, strengthening her determination to ignore the psychiatrist's advice. How could she stay away from a man whose eyes lit up like a child's on Christmas morning every time he saw her? It was asking too much of both of them. For better or worse, Jacob had become emotionally dependent on her, and she was deeply committed to him and his peace of mind. Maybe Charles didn't fully understand that.

That afternoon Jacob was as relaxed as she had ever seen him. Leah studied him carefully without seeming to. She knew he often faked high spirits for her sake, as though he feared a sullen mood would turn her off. He wasn't faking now, though. She took heart from the loosening, disburdening effect she had on him, and thought it surely had to offset his partner's claims. The psychiatrist was clutching at straws—he had to be. Possibly he was disturbed because he hadn't been able to help Jacob.

Leah could conveniently come up with any number of reasons for ignoring Charles's words.

CHAPTER FIFTEEN

JACOB WAS USUALLY TIRED on Friday nights. For that reason, whether they spent the weekend in Sedona or Phoenix, Leah never made plans for the evening. Activities were saved for Saturdays. So tonight she prepared dinner, they ate at the dining table, then he helped her clean up. Afterward she wheeled the television set out of its hiding place, and Jacob emptied his mind by watching a noisy police drama while she spent another hour at her loom. She was in the homestretch, working on the final piece of the tapestry and anxious to finish it. The noise of gunfire and screeching tires didn't bother her at all. She honestly thought she could set up her loom in front of the state capitol in downtown Phoenix and happily weave away. Temperamental, she wasn't.

Occasionally she glanced over her shoulder at Jacob stretched out on the couch, one arm thrown behind his head. His eyes were half-closed; she couldn't tell if he was watching the show or not. A contented smile crossed her face. She so loved having him with her in her odd little house. *Where he belongs,* she thought.

Her smile faded. She liked to think that, but she wondered if it was true. Being honest, she supposed Jacob more properly belonged in that big house in Scottsdale.

Leah had long since grown used to the trappings of Jacob's wealth and was no longer awed by them, but living that way seemed so burdensome to her. Leah had never been a wealthy woman; still, her father's veterinary practice had given them a comfortable living, and now her weavings commanded high prices. She could afford many of the "finer" things in life, yet she was perfectly satisfied with her renovated schoolhouse, her sensible compact car and her orderly, uncomplicated way of life.

It had crossed her mind more than once that she might have to give up this house—not just the house, but Sedona itself and the laid-back existence it represented—and she was startled to realize that bothered her a little. Startled because she honestly loved Jacob and wanted to spend the rest of her life with him. That entailed living where he chose to live. His work was in Phoenix, whereas she could weave anywhere on earth.

Putting aside her work, she got to her feet and crossed the room to look down at him. As she suspected, he was asleep, and he looked so peaceful she was loath to waken him. After placing his dangling left arm across his stomach, she carefully removed his shoes. Then she turned off the television set and rolled it back into the cabinet. She'd leave him be and sleep in Nina's bed in the loft. Sleep didn't come that easily to Jacob.

But as she passed the sofa he grabbed her hand. "Where're you going?" he asked huskily.

"Oh! I thought you were asleep."

"Nope, just dozing on and off. I was watching you watching me."

Smiling, she knelt by the sofa, placing her hands on his chest. "You looked so peaceful."

"Sorry I've been such lousy company tonight."

"You haven't been. You never are. You don't have to keep me entertained, Jacob. I don't expect you to be at your best for me all the time, and sometimes I think that's what you try to do. I won't bolt for the door if you're grouchy and out of sorts occasionally."

Jacob smiled softly. Lifting her hand to his lips, he gently kissed the fingertips one by one. "That's good to know."

"Darling, if you're too tired tonight, I can sleep in Nina's bed."

"Don't be ridiculous. I get through the week by thinking of lying next to you on Friday night."

She got to her feet and pulled him to a sitting position. "Then you take the bathroom first, and I'll make up the bed."

Once he was gone she pulled out the sofa bed and put fresh sheets on it. When he emerged and began undressing, she went into the bathroom. Undressing, she took a new champagne-colored gown off the door hook and slipped it over her head. It fell to the floor in billowing folds; the wisp of a bodice made a feeble attempt to conceal her breasts. In fact, Leah noticed as she glanced in the mirror, the gown concealed very little. It was an exquisite garment and had cost an unconscionable amount of money, but the moment she'd seen it in the boutique she had thought of Jacob and had purchased it without hesitation.

Turning off the light, she walked into the big room and found him propped up in the bed, the sheet at his waist, presenting the most blatantly appealing picture of forceful masculinity she could imagine. Pausing at the foot of the bed, she drank in the sight of him while allowing him to feast his eyes on her.

He did so greedily. The expression on his face was the very one she had envisioned when she bought the gown. Tiny pinpoints of fire leaped from his eyes, and the corners of his mouth twitched. "You don't even need makeup," he observed in awe.

"You're looking at my face?" she asked in mock astonishment. "How about this gown? This is what the well-dressed, turned-on lady is wearing this season."

"Very nice," he murmured, at a loss for anything more descriptive. The gown, he noticed, was anything but "nice." Granny gowns were "nice." Leah's gown was a sexy, alluring garment designed to arouse a man, and it was doing the job. The elemental response he felt in his groin told him that.

"I thought you'd like it," she said, glorying in the desire she saw in his eyes.

"May I assume it was purchased with me in mind?"

"Of course. You should see the tailored pajamas I used to sleep in."

"Leah, somehow I imagine you're damned sexy in tailored pajamas. Wear them for me sometime." He raised the sheet. "Come here."

Smiling seductively, she slowly walked around to her side of the bed. Sliding between the sheets, she was immediately gathered in his warm embrace. His mouth covered hers in a lingering kiss, then moved to her earlobe to suck gently. One of his hands lightly traced her body's gentle curves, now so familiar to him. He ran the back of one finger over her breast, grazing, then beneath the fabric to feel the texture of the velvety mound and the puckered tip. His finger was soon replaced by his lips.

Leah slithered along his hard length and moaned his name softly. It was an incredibly sensual experience he was giving her, completely unnecessary, for he could arouse her with a touch. From past experience, however, they knew of the exquisite pleasure awaiting them when they took their time with the preliminaries.

Finally he fumbled impatiently with her gown. "Beautiful gown," he murmured. "Pity it was destined to be worn such a short time." He quickly discarded it, and the garment fell in a heap on the floor. Sliding his tongue into the valley between her breasts, he traced a trail down her midriff to her navel, then below. The taste and scent of her skin was more intoxicating than alcohol, more stimulating than any drug ever invented. His tempting maneuvers were rewarded by a sudden arching of her hips.

"Mmm," she groaned.

He raised his head. "You like that?"

"Oh, Jacob, you're killing me!"

His heart lifted. Full and heavy with desire, he covered her body with his, thrusting for possession.

At first they made love with a quiet sort of desperation, like lovers on the eve of parting. Then he turned gentle and humble, nuzzling his face into her shoulder, moving his lips through the mass of dark hair spilling out on her pillow, kissing her breasts, declaring his limitless devotion. Jacob was a sensitive lover, for he felt things deeply. Even in the wildest throes of passion he was as concerned for her pleasure as for his own.

Each time they were together, Leah learned something new about the intimacies between a man and a woman. Jim had been carefree and uninhibited in bed, but now that she thought about it, lovemaking with him had been more of a glorious game. With Jacob it was much more profound—a heart-stopping, soul-piercing experience. They brought to each other such solace and peace. *If ever two people were meant for each other, we were,* she thought, and that didn't even seem like a cliché. Her conviction had kept her free for him all those years.

Yet tonight she clearly sensed frustration in him. Long after he was spent from the climax, he clung to her tightly as though afraid to release her. Leah held him, crooned to him and again wished for the courage to tell him there was nothing in his past that need worry him. She cursed Charles White's advice, without trusting her own instincts sufficiently to dismiss it entirely.

Finally Jacob fell asleep. For long minutes Leah lay awake beside him simply watching him sleep. In repose, he looked much younger, so much more vulnerable. Her heart filled with a mixture of emotions. Never in her life, not even during the marriage she had considered perfect, had she felt as much a sensual woman as she did when she was with Jacob. He had tapped the very wellspring of her femininity, making her feel alive. And she knew all too well how much she had done for him. No one would ever have called Jacob easygoing, but there had been some remarkable changes in him since they'd met in the gallery.

It just wasn't right to withhold from him all they had once been to each other....

Soon Leah also succumbed to sleep, only to awaken a few hours later to find Jacob had left the bed. Raising her head, she saw him standing in front of the window, one arm braced on her loom, the other on the wall. The dejected slump of his shoulders conveyed his inner turmoil.

"You had the dream again," she said. It wasn't a question.

"Yes," he said emotionlessly, not turning.

"Do you realize you always have that dream when you're with me?"

"No!" he said too quickly. "That isn't true."

It was, though. Leah sat up, pulled her knees up under the sheet and rested her head on them. Sighing, she allowed her mind to override her heart for once. Reluctantly she admitted that Charles might have known what he was talking about. Her presence was responsible for the dream's return and the headaches. Maybe she should back off and give the man's theory a chance. In the way of human beings, she had followed the part of the psychiatrist's advice that she could accept and chosen to ignore the rest.

"Darling," she said softly, "come back to bed. I'm sure everything's going to be all right."

He pivoted, moving as if each step was an effort. "You're right. I don't know why I let it bother me. As long as I have you, what the devil difference does that damned dream make?"

When he was beside her, she opened her arms and he went into them. "I'm going to lick this thing, Leah. I swear I am."

"You will. Of course you will."

Jacob fell asleep in her arms, his face nestled into the hollow of her shoulder, but sleep eluded Leah for most of the night. His torment was hers. What to do? Over and over she heard Charles White's voice saying, "Your influence undermines what I'm trying to do." Just as over and over she heard Jacob's voice saying, "As long as I have you...."

AT SOME POINT during the night Leah realized the show in Dallas might be the perfect excuse for a separation. It was the easy way out. The separation would be a short one, since they would only have to go for perhaps two weeks without seeing each other. Jacob wouldn't suspect it was a deliberate attempt to put some distance between them. Maybe she should at least test Charles's advice. The fact she didn't want to be away from Jacob shouldn't be a consideration.

Leah woke up unrefreshed, still thinking about Dallas. But she wouldn't say anything until Jacob was ready to leave Sunday, if indeed she said anything at all. Their limited time together was too important to them. When Jacob awoke, he showed no traces of last night's turmoil, so she didn't want to set him back, spoiling the weekend with talk of parting.

Over breakfast he suggested going to Tlaquepaque. He was in the mood to shop for additions to his collection, and his first visit to the arts-and-crafts village had been so hurried. That suited Leah fine, for she never tired of Tlaquepaque.

The place was filled with shoppers. Although Sedona boasted only nine thousand permanent residents, two million tourists a year found their way there, and most of those discovered Tlaquepaque sooner or later. Leah and Jacob spent the better part of the day browsing and poking through most of the forty-odd shops and galleries, and strolling through the tiled courtyards holding hands like a pair of teenagers. Jacob found an acrylic on canvas for himself, some turquoise jewelry for Leah and a kachina doll for Nina. Then, after delightedly gorging on frozen margaritas and enchiladas in a Mexican restaurant, they stopped in at the Trent Gallery to pay a call on Alex. It was during the visit that Jacob first spied *Gemini*.

"Don't tell me—a 'Design by Leah Stone,'" he said, studying Leah's maiden effort as a professional. "It's your style."

"Would you believe the first 'Design by Leah Stone,'" Alex said with a smile.

"I want it."

"Oh, Jacob," Leah protested, "it's not nearly the tapestry you're getting. In fact, looking at *Gemini* now, it seems rather amateurish. I've done much better things."

"I want it, darling. The big tapestry will hang in the clinic. I want this one for the house."

"I can do something much better for the house."

"It's not for sale." Alex's tone was decisive.

Jacob turned to him with a frown. "Not for sale?"

"No, I'm afraid not. I always told Leah I wouldn't sell it in a million years, and even though she professes not to believe that, I meant it."

Standing close to Jacob, Leah felt his body go rigid. She looked up at him. His color had heightened, and the expression on his face clearly told her he felt challenged. "Surely you'd sell it to me?" he persisted. "To Leah and me."

"Sorry, it's not for sale."

"Well, if it were for sale, how much would it cost?"

Now he was grinning, and Alex was grinning. It was obvious to Leah that the two of them were sparring and enjoying every minute of it. She watched Alex as he gave the question some serious thought. Then he quoted a figure she knew was ludicrous. "Oh, Alex, that's ridiculous," she gasped, laughing.

Her laughter, however, quickly died when she hard Jacob say, "All right, I'll write you a check."

"Are you serious, Doctor?" Alex asked in surprise.

"Completely."

Leah's mouth dropped open. "Oh, Jacob, you'll do no such thing!" Her obdurate gaze flew to Alex, who was beginning to realize just how serious Jacob was. Fun and games were over; this was real business. Leah stepped between them. "The dollar signs are in your eyes, Alex! I'm ashamed of you. You know very well that tapestry isn't worth half that."

Alex tugged on his chin. His eyes were sparkling merrily. "My dear Leah, surely you know that a work of art is worth whatever someone is willing to pay for it. Obviously, owning *Gemini* is worth a lot to Jacob."

"It is," Jacob agreed.

"Then you just made yourself a deal. It will be delivered to your house Monday." He chuckled. "No extra charge."

Leah's hand flew to her forehead. "I don't believe this!"

Her protests did no good. With the stroke of a pen in his checkbook, Jacob became the proud owner of *Gemini*, and Alex had dispatched one of the gallery employees to see that it was properly rolled and wrapped for transport.

"Never in a million years indeed!" Leah said to Alex. "You have avarice in your soul."

He only smiled. "I'm a businessman, Leah, and I'd say this has been one of my better days."

She was still fuming when she and Jacob loaded their purchases into her car. Driving away from Tlaquepaque, she said, "I can't decide which one of you I'm most furious with—Alex for charging that outlandish sum or you for being foolish enough to pay it."

"I would have paid twice that, my love."

"Why?" she demanded. "It's not nearly as valuable as the piece I'm doing now, nor nearly as valuable as anything I could do for you in the future."

"I know that."

"Then why?"

"Because I should be the one who owns it. Because I didn't want Alex having it."

His honesty took her aback. "Oh, Jacob, you're not—"

"Jealous? I don't know, maybe I am a little. But I think it's more complicated than that. I wanted it because it's a part of your early life that I don't know much about but wish I did. I've always wished I had known the young Leah." He shrugged. "I want this in my house, to look at when you're not with me. You know, when I first saw that other tapestry in the bank, it...called to me. Do you find that ridiculous? And *Gemini* did the same thing. It's something that can't be explained."

Leah gripped the steering wheel so tightly her knuckles turned white. She recalled the hours Jim had spent watching the beginnings of *Gemini*. There was so much lurking in the back of Jacob's mind, trying to get out. If she was the one preventing it...

"You know, Leah," Jacob said thoughtfully, "it's been a long time coming, this feeling. All I've ever owned I would gladly give up in return for you. The time I have to spend away from you is agony for me. I guess what it all boils down to is—you make me happy." He grinned sheepishly. "I'm not saying this well. Maybe it's because there's so much I want to say, and I don't know where to begin."

A lump formed in Leah's throat, and she reached for his hand to give it a squeeze. "You said it beautifully."

And Charles wanted her to stay away from him! How could she? To hell with the show in Dallas. To hell with the rest of the world, for that matter. She intended to savor every minute with Jacob and to present him with divorce papers the moment arrangements could be made. A separation definitely wasn't the answer, she decided in her inexpert but very human judgment.

Their weekend from that moment on was perfect. She pulled out all the stops for dinner, presenting Jacob with a meal worthy of a French master chef. Later they made slow languorous love, with just a hint of absolutely delightful wickedness about it. Leah slept soundly that night; if he had the dream again she didn't know about it, didn't want to know about it. When they parted Sunday afternoon—Leah to pick up Nina at the bus stop, and Jacob to return home—it was with the understanding that she and Nina would come to Phoenix the following Friday. When he drove away, he looked like a man in good spirits. She hoped he was.

That night Leah worked at her loom until after midnight. She told herself everything was great, just great. It wasn't until after she was in bed that the nagging fear returned, the fear that she was an obstacle between Jacob and the end to his mental distress.

nature. I knew it was with the workmen there that she had first would appear to Phoebe and following Cathy. When he went away, he took in the charter in some conflict. She would carry "That night Leah worried till her lover until after midnight. She only asked everything was great, rest great. No, wasn't could after she was so bad that Dean agree her. No record, dia... a that the was an obstacle between...

CHAPTER SIXTEEN

LEAH UNROLLED the tapestry and, with Sandra's help, hung it on two heavy wall hooks installed at ceiling height for just that purpose. By moving an armchair and the coffee table, they were able to roll the excess out on the floor. The two women moved some distance away to view the work.

"Magnificent, Leah," was Sandra's verdict. "Absolutely magnificent!"

Leah had to agree. It was definitely the best thing she had ever done. Using all shades of the red spectrum, from garnet to shell pink, with just a touch of suede gray for contrast, she had depicted rock forms that appeared to have been carved from velvet. Though some of the cliffs and buttes had edges and peaks as sharp as broken pottery, there was nothing the least harsh about the tapestry. In fact it looked strokeably soft.

"I'm very proud of it," Leah admitted. "Not even Alex can tell where the pieces were joined together."

"I'll bet you can hardly wait to show it to Jacob."

"Oh, he's seen most of it, and he's very pleased. I think it's dramatic enough. It ought to show up very well on that wall. Come on, let's have a cup of tea and you tell me what you've been up to."

The two women sat at the breakfast bar talking. Sandra was studio-bound, she declared with an air of exaggerated persecution, since she had in a weak moment promised a local gallery five new pieces within a year's time. Leah was thrilled for her, then almost choked on her tea over Sandra's next remark. "Sam's been hinting he'd like us to get married again."

"Are you serious?"

"He's definitely serious."

"Well, would you?"

Sandra was silent long enough to bring a frown to Leah's face. She couldn't help thinking of all the tales of horror she had listened to so many times before, about the terrified woman who had sought a psychiatrist's help before leaving her domineering husband.

"Would you fall down laughing if I told you I've honestly considered it? But...no," Sandra said decisively. "No, I wouldn't. It would never work. He seems to have changed—not *that* much, though. And I've definitely changed, but I don't think Sam realizes how much. I'm not the wimpy young thing he married years ago. I could never take the kind of crap I used to. My career's just beginning to take off, and it's important to me. I need time to pursue it, and in spite of what Sam says, I can't believe he'd want me taking that time. No, I'm too happy with my life the way it is now. I just can't risk it, even though—and isn't this a crock—Sam's the only man I've ever loved. Doesn't that just slay you? He's probably the most impossible person I've ever known."

Leah breathed a little sigh. "Well, I'm relieved. You're doing so well now."

"Yeah. I'm just glad Sam and I have finally called a truce. Maybe now he'll stop pestering me about it and go on and find something else, someone else. We're definitely two people who shouldn't be married to each other." Sandra took a sip of tea. "So tell me how things are going between you and Jacob. What a doll he is!"

Leah chuckled, imagining Jacob's reaction to being called a "doll." Then she sobered. "Fine, I guess. There are problems, though. He's gone back into therapy."

Sandra's brows lifted. "With the same shrink?"

"Uh-huh. This is something he did on his own."

"I keep expecting to hear you're moving to Phoenix."

"We might one of these days, when certain things are resolved."

"I'd miss you like hell. We'd have to stay in touch."

"Oh, sure." Strange, she hadn't once thought of losing Sandra as a neighbor, or of how much she would miss her friend if that happened. The two of them would often go for days, sometimes weeks without seeing each other, but it had always been comforting to know Sandra was nearby. "Poor Nina," Leah mused. "She'd be lost without Ann."

"I know. It would be hard on the girls for a while, but thank God for the resiliency of youth. And Phoenix isn't all that far away."

"I haven't moved yet, you know," Leah reminded her with a grin.

"You will. I've seen the look on Jacob's face."

Leah nodded absently, and the disquietude that had plagued her since Sunday settled over her again. It was so easy to stick to her own convictions when he was with her, but he hadn't been gone an hour Sunday before the nagging doubt started hounding her again. Did she have the right to decide Charles was wrong, that she knew what was best for Jacob?

"Something the matter?" Sandra inquired gently.

Leah's head snapped up. "Oh . . . no, it's just that— Oh, Sandra, Jacob has so many problems, and because of them, I have problems. Last week his psychiatrist came to see me, so now I'm really confused. I want to do the right thing, but I'm not sure what the right thing is. What Dr. White tells me goes strictly against my own instincts. . . ." She opened her hands in a helpless gesture.

"Yeah?" Sandra stared at her friend with concern. She had always thought Leah was one person who really had her act together. She'd never seen her so down. "Want to talk about it? Sometimes it helps. Believe me, you're looking at one who knows."

So Leah poured out everything. She was so intent on her story that she didn't notice her friend's changing expressions. First Sandra was interested, then concerned, then worried. Only when Leah had finished speaking did she venture an observation. "I swear, I think if I were you I'd just tell him. Sounds to me like that would solve most of his problems."

"I told you, Dr. White insists I say nothing, not only say nothing, but he wants me to stay away from Jacob altogether."

"So you said, and that bothers me most of all."

"Bothers you?"

Sandra nodded, then leaned forward and spoke firmly and confidentially. "You know something, Leah . . . when you first told me about Jacob, something you said didn't sit right with me—the part about Jacob's analyst encouraging him to give up therapy years ago."

"That's right."

Sandra's brow furrowed. "That doesn't make any sense. Look, I've had some experience with this sort of thing, and a good analyst simply doesn't work that way."

"I don't understand, Sandra."

"When I first went to see Dr. Graves years ago, I naturally had to hide it from Sam. He would have put a stop to it immediately. So that meant I had to hide the forty bucks an hour it was costing me, too. And after a while it got to be too much trouble and too expensive, so a couple of times I quit. But Dr. Graves kept telephoning me and sending me little notes, and I finally went back. She was right, of course. I really needed the therapy, and in the end she did wonders for me. When I finally left analysis, I thanked her for not giving up on me, and she told me no thoughtful psychiatrist would let a patient who needed help just quit without putting up a fight. That's why this guy Jacob's seeing bothers me."

Leah shrugged. "I guess Dr. White didn't think he could help Jacob."

"How could he be certain in such a short time? Psychotherapy takes years."

"I don't know, Sandra. It's all beyond me. I wish I could help Jacob, God knows, but I have to go with the experts."

Suddenly an idea came to Sandra. "Listen, Leah, I'm getting some vibrations that aren't any of my business, so I want you to do a favor for me."

Leah's eyes quizzed her with interest.

"I have an appointment with Alicia tomorrow—that's Dr. Graves. I just wanted to touch base with her and tell her about Sam and me. She likes me to call every so often. But I can do that anytime. I'd like to ask her to give my appointment to you."

"Why on earth would I want to see a psychiatrist?"

"I'm not sure, but I think you should. Get someone else's opinion on Jacob's case."

Leah laughed lightly. "I really don't think that's necessary, Sandra."

"Please!"

The unexpected fervor of her friend's voice brought Leah up sharply. Sandra tried to explain. "Look, you said it yourself—Jacob has problems, so you have problems. You've taken this White guy's word for everything, yet I have a feeling you don't really trust him, right?"

Leah didn't deny it. "I don't know why I don't, but you're right, I don't."

"Well, if Alicia Graves told me to go jump off this house, I'd do it. Will you go see her? I'll be glad to keep Nina. What can it hurt?"

Something stirred inside Leah, prompted by a variety of things. Her own uncertainty mainly, and her unfounded uneasiness about Charles White's advice. Her unfounded uneasiness about the man himself. "Sure, I'll go. As you said, what can it hurt?"

LEAH WHEELED HER CAR into the only available parking space and switched off the ignition. For several moments she sat very still, staring sightlessly through the windshield. All at once she felt foolish and wished she hadn't made this appointment. She didn't know what to say to the woman, didn't know where to begin. But she was here now, parked in front of a low-slung brick medical building, committed to spending fifty minutes and forty dollars with Dr. Alicia Graves. Sighing, she grabbed her handbag, got out of the car and entered the building.

"Dr. Graves is waiting for you, Mrs. Stone," the neat young woman at the reception desk told her, and Leah was shown into the psychiatrist's office.

The large room looked more like someone's comfortable living room than a doctor's office. It had been furnished, the artist in Leah saw, with an eye for scale and balance. A long off-white sofa stood against a wall opposite a fireplace; a collection of mismatched candlesticks glimmered on a glass-topped coffee table. Oriental stools and silk pillows coexisted in perfect harmony with Haitian prints and paper-relief wall panels. The atmosphere was cozy. It was the sort of room that encouraged one to curl up with a cup of coffee or tea and talk, talk, talk.

Leah wasn't sure what she had expected Alicia Graves to look like—a bit stern, elderly and spectacled, she guessed. Certainly not tall, slender and fortyish as this woman was, with a sleek silver-blond chignon and warm blue eyes.

"Come in and have a seat, Mrs. Stone," Dr. Graves said. "I've been waiting for you. May I get you something to drink, coffee or tea?"

"No, thank you, doctor."

"Sandra told me almost nothing over the phone, but I take it you two are friends."

Leah sat in a chair facing the doctor's desk. "Yes, we're neighbors and have become quite close. We have a great deal in common."

"I'm glad to hear she has a good friend. I grew very fond of her while she was in therapy. She's doing well, I hear."

"Oh, Sandra's fine. I'm sure you'll be seeing her before long."
Leah started to say something about Sandra and her ex-husband,
then remembered that Dr. Graves would know nothing of their
new truce. Certainly it was Sandra's place to tell her of the changed
relationship.

Dr. Graves shuffled aside some papers, then settled back in her
chair. "So, Mrs. Stone . . . it's Leah, isn't it?"

"Yes."

"So, Leah, according to Sandra you wanted to talk to me about
your husband, who is an amnesiac, is that right?"

"I'm afraid it's a little more complicated than that, Doctor."

"Are you having some trouble coping with his illness?"

"Oh, no, it's nothing like that. You see . . ." Once again Leah
related the details of her marriage to Jim Stone and her subsequent meeting with Jacob. It was a lengthy story, but Alicia Graves
listened carefully and with interest, and she interrupted only when
something Leah said wasn't clear. Once she was certain Leah had
finished her account, she leaned back in her chair and stared
thoughtfully across the room.

"And you feel sure you've accepted Jacob for who he is? You
no longer wish for Jim?"

Leah shook her head. "I don't have any trouble with that anymore, I'm certain of it. That's not why I want to tell him the truth.
Oh, of course it would be easier for me if he knew. I always feel
like I have to be on guard, not saying anything about the past or
taking him where he might be recognized. And I know he wonders why I won't tell him anything about my husband.... All that's
been going on for some time now, and I can handle it. It's for Jacob's sake that I want to tell him. And for Nina's. They deserve
knowing they belong to each other." She sighed. "But Dr. White
has been so adamant about that."

Dr. Graves frowned thoughtfully. "I realize that I don't know
Jacob as well as his own therapist does, but from what you've told
me, I see no reason he shouldn't know the truth."

Leah's heart leaped exultantly. Exactly what she had been
hoping to hear. "Really?"

"Yes, really. I can't see why it wouldn't have been wise in the
beginning, but the two of you have apparently established a mutually loving relationship, and he trusts you. Telling him about the
past won't magically restore his memory, of course, but I should
think the relief would be enormous."

"You . . . don't think he's suffering from psychological amnesia?"

Dr. Graves looked at her in mild surprise, then pursed her lips and shook her head. "No, I don't, not at all. Jacob sounds like a textbook case of retrograde amnesia, the result of a blow to the head. Now I once had an amnesia patient who had even forgotten how to tie shoes. In fact, she didn't know what shoes were. That was psychological amnesia. The poor woman wanted to forget everything, start all over again. Once I delved into her past life, I could understand why. No, Jacob's amnesia isn't psychological at all, not from what you've told me."

Leah thought it amazing how unquestioningly she could accept advice she wanted to hear. It was totally at odds with the advice she had received from Charles—she was beginning to realize just how much Jacob's partner bothered her—but her instincts, to say nothing of her heart, told her to trust Dr. Graves.

"Then you think I can just tell him, not mince words or lead up to it gradually?"

"I don't see why not. You see, Leah, it's been my experience that amnesiacs are usually a bit embarrassed by their condition. They see it as a weakness of character or some such nonsense. And almost all of them worry about their actions during the fugue, just as they worry that filling in the blank spaces will complicate their present lives. In Jacob's case, you can erase that worry in minutes. Peace of mind is priceless, you know."

"I know." Leah felt as though the weight of the world had been lifted off her shoulders. She could imagine how Jacob was going to feel.

"From the expression on your face, I have to assume that telling him is going to be a happy experience," Alicia Graves said with a smile.

"Oh, Doctor, you can't imagine how happy it's going to be!" Then she sobered. "I just wonder why Dr. White so specifically warned me not to. He even suggested I stay away from Jacob altogether, which would have hurt him deeply."

Dr. Graves wondered, too, Leah could tell, although all the psychiatrist said was, "Perhaps Dr. White doesn't fully understand the extent of Jacob's emotional commitment to you. It could very well be that Jacob doesn't open up with his therapist, given the nature of their working relationship. Frankly, I doubt it was a good idea for him to use his partner for an analyst. I'm surprised Dr. White took him on."

Leah's suspicions about Charles White were piling up in layers. "Why do you say that?"

Dr. Graves tried to explain. "You see, Leah, a unique and very close relationship develops between psychiatrist and patient...or should. They become very close...or should. The patient often comes to regard the therapist as the only caring person in the world. Two men who work together on a day-to-day basis..." She frowned and shook her head. "I don't see how that would work. And that business of terminating therapy six years ago—that's simply not sound psychotherapy. Continuity is of the utmost importance. If a patient discontinues therapy for whatever reason, and then returns for whatever reason, I have to start all over again."

Leah mulled this over. "If possible, Dr. Graves, I'd like Jacob to come to see you one of these days."

The doctor smiled. "And I'd like to see him. Do you know if he's ever undergone hypnosis?"

"I don't think so. He hasn't mentioned it, and I'm sure he would have."

Alicia Graves pursed her lips. "Peculiar. It can be so effective, provided the patient is a good subject. It certainly is a shortcut, too, for both therapist and patient. It's often used in battlefield conditions, where time is of the essence. I would always consider it with an amnesia case."

Leah hated thinking what she was thinking, that Jacob's partner had made no genuine attempt to help him, but she couldn't help it. Nothing about Charles White jibed...and hadn't from the beginning.

Just then Dr. Graves leaned forward and spoke earnestly. "Leah, I don't want you to get your hopes up too high regarding Jacob's recovery. Telling him the truth will help, but it won't be a magic cure-all. Once he's more relaxed about his past he might recall small random events, nothing in chronological sequence, but the chances of his regaining all memory of the fugue are, frankly, not good. Please understand that."

"Yes, yes, of course. You've given me such wonderful news nevertheless. I don't know how to thank you."

The hour had passed very quickly, and Dr. Graves bade her goodbye with, "Please stay in touch with me, Leah. I'll be so interested to know how things turn out with you and Jacob."

What an incredible woman she is, Leah thought as she backed out of the parking space. No wonder she was able to do so much for Sandra.

"WELL, THANK GOD!" Sandra had exclaimed when Leah collected Nina and told her friend about Alicia Graves's advice. Whit said almost exactly the same thing when she telephoned him. Now all she had to do was tell Jacob, and that certainly couldn't be done over the phone.

"Nina, pack your pajamas and toothbrush and something to wear for tomorrow. We're going to Jacob's house."

"Oh, boy!" the girl cried delightedly.

"In fact—" Leah hesitated briefly "—in fact, we'll be moving there permanently before long. What do you think of that?"

Nina stopped short and looked at her mother quizzically. "You and Jacob are getting married?"

Leah nodded. "How do you feel about that?"

"Okay, I guess."

"Only guess?"

"No, it's okay, really. I like Jacob. He's nice."

"And how do you feel about leaving this house?"

"Will we have to do that?"

"We might."

Nina gave it some thought. "I guess I don't mind much. I'll miss Ann."

"Yes, I know."

"But she could come to see me a lot, couldn't she?"

"Of course."

"Besides, she's going to be at her daddy's house some of the time. She heard her mama and daddy talking about it, and he lives in Flagstaff. She's glad about that." Nina shrugged with youthful resignation.

Leah placed her hand on her daughter's head and smiled down at her fondly. "I'm sure she is." Nina was young enough to have accepted the fact that her real father had gone away years ago, and she had never asked about him. Now she would have to know the truth about Jacob. Leah wasn't sure just how much a six-year-old would understand, but she would have to tell her. It was a crazy situation but not an unhappy one. Of course it would take Nina some time to accept Jacob as her daddy, but at least he wasn't a stranger to her.

Hurriedly Leah finished packing, and it wasn't until she had everything in the car and was locking the front door that something occurred to her. Another piece of unfinished business. She went into her closet, fumbled in the back and retrieved the small black suitcase she and Whit had claimed at the Flagstaff bus station six years ago. She had lost track of the number of times she had taken it out and stared at the contents. Well, no more. She would show it to Jacob, then in the trash it would go. Her days of living on memories were over. Come to think of it, they had been over since the day Jacob had come into her life.

CHAPTER SEVENTEEN

It was Wednesday afternoon, which meant Jacob would be on the golf course. Leah didn't bother phoning ahead, merely showed up at the front door with Nina and her luggage.

"Why, Mrs. Stone, what a delightful surprise," Davis greeted her warmly. "Is Dr. Surratt expecting you?"

"No, I'm afraid he isn't."

"He hasn't returned from the club...."

"I was sure he wouldn't have. We'll just wait, if you don't mind."

"Not at all. The doctor is going to be so pleased. Let me get Hilda."

Hilda apparently had recovered sufficiently from Nina's last visit, for she hugged the girl affectionately and immediately hustled her down to the kitchen, where she could place her order for dinner. Leah was left to pace and watch the clock until Jacob arrived home.

It was five-fifteen when he did, and he burst through the front door like a whirlwind, calling her name. When she appeared at the stairwell landing, he was up in a flash, embracing her enthusiastically, his eyes as bright as a child's.

"Sweetheart, I couldn't believe it when I saw the car! Is anything wrong?"

"Nothing's wrong. Everything's wonderful, just wonderful." Looping her arms around his neck, she nibbled on the underside of his chin. "Hmm, for a man who just came in off the golf course, you smell divine."

"I showered at the club. I only played nine holes. Too damned hot out there for more. Where's Nina?"

"In the kitchen with Hilda and George."

"May I ask to what I owe the pleasure of this unexpected visit?"

"I came to tell you a story," she said simply.

His brows knitted. "A story?"

"Mmm. Where can we talk in private?"

"Almost anywhere. What about the study?"

They descended the stairs hand in hand. "I finished the tapestry," she told him. "If I do say so myself, you have yourself a masterpiece for only the price of Alex's commission."

"Oh, no. The artist deserves her due."

"What difference does it make? We'll just put it in a joint bank account."

They had reached the study doors. Jacob opened them, almost pushed her inside, closed them and drew her into his embrace again. "You got the divorce?" he exclaimed exuberantly.

"Better than that. I...I think you'd better sit down. This story may knock you for a loop."

Jacob backed off and eyed her quizzically. She was being terribly mysterious, he thought, completely unlike Leah, who was as straightforward as they come. Crossing the room, he sat on the sofa and watched her as she followed and sat beside him. Her eyes were bright and excited. First she cupped his face in her hands and kissed him tenderly. Then she picked up one of his hands and idly played with his fingers. He was intrigued. Whatever this story was, she was having a hard time getting it out.

"Leah, I'm about to burst with curiosity!" he protested.

"Well, I...I..."

Then, to Jacob's utter confusion, she put her hand to her temple and began to cry quietly. Quickly he put his arm around her. "Sweetheart, what the devil's wrong?"

"N-nothing."

It occurred to him that he'd never seen Leah cry, never even seen her rattled, but she was good and rattled now. "Leah, what on earth—I can't stand this!"

"Oh, this is so st-stupid," she sobbed. "I've k-kept it bottled up so long and now I c-can't even get it out!"

Completely stumped, Jacob watched her cry for a few seconds. The only thing that prevented his being really alarmed was somehow knowing the tears weren't prompted by unhappiness. He shifted and fumbled for his hip pocket. "I don't suppose you have a handkerchief," he muttered, producing one and handing it to her. "Women never carry a handkerchief."

"Th-thanks." She dried her eyes, delicately blew her nose, then wadded the handkerchief into a ball and squeezed it. "Sorry."

"Are you all right?"

She nodded. "Yes, all right, really. Sorry for the outburst."

"You were going to tell me something?"

Again she nodded. Taking a deep breath, she rested her head on his shoulder and cuddled against him like a child. "It begins eight years ago, on a summer night. I had just graduated from college and was living with Dad. One night we were sitting on the front porch after dinner, and a truck stopped in front of the house. A young man got out...."

THE LATE-AFTERNOON SKIES over Phoenix were blanketed with dark clouds; jagged streaks of lightning split them open, accompanied by deafening claps of thunder. Rain fell in sheets. It was the usual sudden and violent desert thunderstorm, descending almost without warning. The thirsty earth would greedily suck up the welcome moisture, and tomorrow everything would seem as dry and dusty as ever.

Inside Jacob's study, the two occupants were scarcely aware of the storm raging over their heads. It seemed to Leah that she had spent an awful lot of time lately relating the details of her brief marriage to Jim Stone. It took an unusually long time to tell something that had actually occupied but a fraction of her life. But this time the telling was different. She wanted Jacob to know every tiny detail, everything she could remember.

"Anyway," she concluded, "I watched that bus until it was out of sight, and . . . the next time I saw you was six years later in Alex's office."

Jacob had remained as still as a statue all the while she was talking. Leah guessed he found it almost impossible to assimilate. Small wonder. She tried to put herself in his shoes at that moment, tried to imagine what was going on in his head and found she couldn't. Oddly, her mood when she finished speaking was more fearful than anything. She couldn't assess the look on his face. Shocked? Taken aback? He might even be angry that she had let him suffer so long. But surely he'd be happy, or at least he would be when it all soaked in.

A knot had formed in Jacob's throat so tightly that he could hardly breathe. While listening to Leah's incredible story he hadn't been able to completely associate it with the two of them. He might have been listening to a piece of gossip, something that had happened to someone else. Then he looked into her lovely earnest face and reality took hold. He was stunned to the point of speechlessness. To have all the fears and worries that had plagued him for years erased within moments was more than he could grasp.

A tremor raced through Leah as she watched him. Had she been wrong to blurt the whole story out? In spite of what Alicia Graves had told her, she might have been wiser to break it to him in bits and pieces. Placing her hand on his arm, she said, "Please, Jacob... say something."

"Dear God, Leah," he croaked when he could find his voice, "Why didn't you tell me this before?"

"I wanted to, from the beginning."

"Then why didn't you?"

"Charles advised me not to," she said dully. She wasn't completely sure why she had begun to despise Jacob's partner, but she had. So much of Jacob's recent turmoil, it now seemed to her, was the result of his partner's advice.

"Charles? Charles knows about this?"

Leah nodded.

"How long has he known?"

"He came to see me last Friday morning. He had telephoned earlier and asked if he could. Seems he had gotten the idea I knew something about your fugue, and of course he was right. You see, the night of the opening I had asked some questions about amnesia, and— Oh, it's all so complicated, isn't it? I wanted him to say it was all right to tell you the truth. He didn't. As a matter of fact, he suggested I ought to stay away from you altogether."

"Why would he do such a thing?"

"I don't know, Jacob. Honestly I don't." It wasn't time to tell him about her suspicions regarding his partner. Maybe she never would. They were, after all, not rooted in fact.

Jacob, not surprisingly, still looked stupefied. "I think I've always known," he said in a quiet, detached voice. "I've always had this weird feeling about us, that I'd met you before or seen you before. Naturally I thought you would have mentioned it if that was the case, so I just chalked it up to my crazy, mixed-up mind." He paused. The dawning of some incredible realization was etched on his face. "The dream... a woman, a house. It was you and the house in Sedona!"

"I have to think so, darling. In fact, I know so, and I've wanted to tell you so badly. How do you feel now?"

"Now? Well, I... I'm not sure. I guess it hasn't sunk in yet. I feel... wonderful!" he began to laugh then, a quiet chuckle at first, then a full, hearty laugh that came from deep within his chest.

"Wonderful! How else could I feel? It's over. Thank God, it's over."

Leah held him closer to her. "You're a married man, do you realize that?"

"Well, I'll be damned! I am, aren't I? That man you wouldn't divorce, the one I hated was me!"

"That's right. You were so persistent about the divorce, and I couldn't get one, couldn't reject the man I'd known and loved, the one I still love."

He locked his fingers into her hair and nuzzled his face into the silky stuff. "Oh, Leah, it's all so..."

"Incredible. I know. But nice, too, isn't it?"

"Nice? That doesn't begin to describe—"

At that moment the door to the study opened, and Nina burst into the room. "Mama, are you gonna stay in here all night? Hilda won't let me go swimming because of the storm, but she's gotta go to the grocery store and says I can go with her if it's all right with you."

Leah withdrew from Jacob's embrace. "Nina, you know you're supposed to knock!"

The girl paused. "Sorry," she said contritely, "but I've seen you and Jacob kissing before."

Beside Leah, Jacob tensed. He looked at Nina across the room, and the shock hit him, slicing through him like a steel knife. His daughter! His daughter.... Pain contorted his face even as he was filled with awe, and he took a moment to wonder if every parent experienced this feeling of chest-expanding pride. He struggled for words. "Well, scamp, aren't you even going to say hello?" The words were offhand, but his voice was choked with emotion.

Nina grinned. "Hi. Can I go to the store with Hilda?" Obediently she walked into Jacob's hug.

"May I go," Leah corrected automatically. Her own emotions were barely under control. In fact, she was dangerously close to tears again.

Jacob held Nina so long the girl looked curiously over his shoulder at her mother. "Is something wrong?" she asked.

Jacob cleared his throat and released her. "No, no, everything's just fine."

"Then can—may I go to the store with Hilda?"

"Yes, that's fine," Leah said.

Jacob's eyes followed his daughter's departing figure, and he felt a peculiar choking sensation in his throat. "You did a good job, Leah."

"Thanks."

"You had to go through the last month of the pregnancy alone. I don't know how you did what you did."

"I had to," she said simply.

"Damn, I've missed so much!"

"She's still awfully young, Jacob. You'll have years and years of watching her grow up."

"I will, won't I?" He raked his fingers through his hair. "I have a lot to learn, and I want to know everything, everything about Nina, everything you and I did together, everything we said to each other...."

"Hey, that's a tall order!" She laughed. "I can't remember everything."

"I wish I could remember just part of it."

"Is it still so important to you?"

"Not as important as it once was, but I guess I still want to remember."

"Maybe, darling, someday you will."

Jacob drew her close and held her against his thudding heart. Overcome with the knowledge that everything he hadn't been able to find was now in his grasp, he found speech impossible. So he simply held her, confident that Leah, of all people, would understand what he was going through. The room grew so quiet that the only sound was the ticking of an antique clock on a nearby table.

"Oh, Jacob," Leah whispered at last, "do you know who's going to be thrilled over all this?"

"Who?"

"Dad. The two of you got along so famously, and he missed you terribly after you went away. He still says you were the best veterinarian's assistant he ever had."

"Well, damn! I should hope so!"

Leah leaped to her feet; her eyes were as bright as diamonds. "Come upstairs with me. I have something I want to show you."

"I can't stand too many more surprises, you know."

The contents of the black suitcase were just one more startling fact of life for Jacob to come to grips with. He kept fingering the garments, staring at them. "To think you've kept it all these years."

"Dad and I claimed it, and I've gone through it dozens of times. I wonder—" she swallowed hard "—what might have happened if we had left it there for you to claim."

"I wonder," Jacob sighed, then turned to her with a small smile. "I'll never be able to accuse you of not being able to keep a secret, will I? I've said it before, and I'll say it again—I don't know how you did it. Tell me about him, darling. About Jim Stone, I mean. What was he like? How was he different from me? What was there about him that made you love him so much?"

She smiled at him with utmost tenderness. "He was a lot like you...kind, tender, a gentleman. The differences? A lot, I guess. Funny. I think I love Jim a lot more...now that he's you."

THE EVENING turned out to be a giddy, disoriented block of time. Jacob's most immediate concern was how to tell Nina. "We'll just be honest with her," Leah said. "But not tonight. Tomorrow. Let's just the two of us enjoy this happy ending tonight."

Somehow they managed to make it through dinner and Nina's bedtime with a semblance of normality, although Leah caught her daughter looking at her several times during the evening as though asking, "What's the matter with you, Mama?" Leah couldn't completely contain her excitement.

Hours later Jacob was propped up in bed watching her undress. Shedding the last of her clothes, she crawled into bed and snuggled against him. He was emotionally exhausted, she could tell, so she refrained from her usual sensuous maneuvers. Peacefully she lay beside him, happy inside, knowing he was, too. Best of all, he was free.

"I hope you sleep like a baby tonight," she whispered.

She felt him kiss her temple. "That would be a new experience for me."

"I know. More reason to hope you do."

"Why am I so tired?"

"You've been through a lot today. We both have. Just sleep, darling. If you wake up during the night, wake me up, too."

"Leah, let's go to Sedona tomorrow."

"Tomorrow is only Thursday. What about the clinic?"

"I'll go early in the morning, see if I can't juggle the appointments. For sure I'll get away as soon as I can. Strange...I've seen the house so many times, but now I want to look at it through...these new eyes."

"Sure, love. Whatever you want to do."

He drifted off within minutes—a first. Normally she fell asleep long before he did, and more often than not she awoke during the night to find him sitting up in a chair or restlessly roaming. When Leah heard his shallow, even breathing, she inched away from him, settled her head on the pillow and delighted in watching him sleep so peacefully.

This, then, was what she had wanted. They were together again, there was no need to go through a divorce, and maybe they could keep the house in Sedona. Nina might have a brother or sister before too long. Almost anything was possible now. Those awful years were over.

Surprisingly, she wasn't the least bit sleepy. There was too much to think about. She was perfectly content to lie there next to Jacob and go over in her mind, almost day by day, the time when he had been Jim Stone. She wasn't doing that in order to conjure up memories of Jim; now she had so much more than memories. But she wanted to remember for Jacob's sake. He was anxious to know everything, and he would be full of questions again tomorrow. Tonight they had barely scratched the surface.

Her mind raced over the early days when Jim had been nothing more to her than just a pleasant young man who worked for her father and occupied the back room. Then it settled on the days several weeks later, after she had known she was attracted to him, and she smiled softly against the pillow. Such happy, carefree days. Saturday afternoons had been their special times, when Jim's work week ended and they could leave the farm to follow their own pursuits. Those outings, she now thought, had been the beginning of whatever courtship had existed. Whit would give them the old pickup, and Leah always drove, because Jim didn't have a driver's license.

Usually they spent at least part of every Saturday afternoon at Green's Place, a café in the valley where they could listen to country music on the jukebox, drink a couple of beers, eat cooked-to-order burgers and catch up on local gossip. At Green's Place at that time, conversation had still been considered one of life's primary pleasures. It was always easy to find someone to "visit" with, either the regulars, or strangers who happened to stop in on their way to somewhere else....

Leah's thoughts halted, and a frown crossed her face. She had a sudden flash of recall, and she bolted straight up in bed. Glancing down to make sure she hadn't disturbed Jacob—he was dead

to the world—she put her hand to her pounding heart, and her
mouth dropped open. It couldn't be!

But it was. Dear God! Events of a long-ago day came to her as
clearly as if they had happened the day before. Green's Place.
That's where she had first seen Dr. Charles White!

CHAPTER EIGHTEEN

DAWN WAS BEGINNING to pinken the eastern sky when Jacob opened his eyes the following morning. He awoke with a strange and pleasant sensation, the sensation of having slept a deep, untroubled sleep. Then another—the sense of freedom, release from all that had plagued his life for so long. Already he felt like a different person, and who knew what today would bring, and tomorrow, the day after?

As his mind gradually cleared, he turned to Leah, fully expecting his warm lover to be ready for the lovemaking he had been too exhausted for the night before. He groped for her, only to find her side of the bed empty. His searching eyes made a slow sweep of the room and found her, dressed in a light cotton robe, huddled in his easy chair by the window. Her knees were pulled up, and her head was resting on them. She looked very tiny and very lovely; his heart turned over as he gazed at her.

"Leah, darling," he said softly, "what's with this staring out the window at dawn? That's my bit. You're usually out like a light at this hour."

She turned to look at him, but instead of seeing her winsome smile he saw an expression that didn't seem to fit Leah. "Sweetheart, what on earth's the matter?"

Leah had slept a grand total of maybe two hours, and all in fifteen-and twenty-minute increments. Her emotions had run the gamut from uncertainty to conviction to incredulity. Now she was simply angry. "I'm too damned mad to sleep."

"Mad?" He chuckled. "What on earth do you have to be mad about?"

"He never was looking for you, Jacob," she said in an indescribably cold voice. Her mouth worked as she spat out the words. "He didn't have to. I couldn't believe it at first, but now I know. He knew where you were all the time. Oh, why can't I learn to follow my own instincts? The minute I laid eyes on that man I had this peculiar feeling—"

"What are you talking about?" Jacob threw back the sheet and, oblivious of his nudity, crossed the room to kneel beside the chair. He took one of her hands in his and was astonished to discover it was trembling. She was trembling all over, and he had never seen such an expression on that gentle face. "Leah?"

"Listen to me, Jacob, and believe what I'm telling you. Eight years ago Charles White knew where you were! He's known all along."

"What? Sweetheart, come back to bed. You've been dreaming." He got her to her feet, pulled her, unresisting, with him and led her back to the bed. When he crawled between the sheets, Leah didn't follow. She knelt on top of the bed beside him, looking down at him with blazing eyes.

"I haven't been dreaming, Jacob. I've been awake this whole night, and I know what I'm talking about. Charles White couldn't find you because he wasn't looking for you. I can't imagine why, but I do know one thing—he knew where you were!"

Jacob folded his arms behind his head and studied her carefully. He knew Leah, and he knew she never went off half-cocked about anything. As unbelievable as her accusation was, it couldn't be rash; she had given it plenty of thought. "What makes you think so?"

"I remember," she said grimly. "You had been at the farm two months, maybe a little longer. Every Saturday afternoon we'd go to a joint called Green's Place. One day a stranger came in and sat at the counter. I remember it because a stranger was always noticed in Green's Place, and later he came over to our table and asked for directions to . . . someplace, I forget. Then he asked you how the fishing was nearby. You said you didn't have much time for fishing, because work kept you so busy. And he asked what kind of work you were in. I remember it just as clearly as if it had happened yesterday. That man was Charles White!"

Jacob still didn't want to believe it, and had it been anyone but Leah telling him this incredible thing he would have dismissed it as the product of a wild imagination. "Darling, that was a long time ago. Charles looks like hundreds of people."

She tossed her head impatiently. "Oh, I'm right, I know I am. There have been things from the beginning.... The first time I met him, the night of the opening, my very first thought was of having seen him before. It was just as insistent when he came to see me Friday. And there have always been questions. How could a prominent physician simply disappear for two years? That always bothered me. And why couldn't Charles, who has published a paper on amnesia, help you any more than he had?"

"Leah, do you think I haven't asked myself those questions and hundreds more?"

"No!" she said vehemently, then softened her tone. "No, not like I have, because of all your hang-ups about your amnesia. It embarrasses you a little, and you've always been afraid of what lay 'back there.' Confess it now. You've wanted to remember but have been a little bit frightened to."

He sighed. "Sure I was, and I got more confused after I met you." He reached for her with a smile. "None of that matters anymore, does it? There's nothing for me to fear."

"But plenty for you to think about. Charles was adamant about my not telling you the truth, yet when I spoke to Dr. Graves, her immediate reaction was, 'Why not?' Now does it seem reasonable to you that two people in the same profession would take absolutely opposite views?"

"Believe me, it happens all the time."

She ignored him. "So many strange things, Jacob. Strange, strange things."

"God, once you get something into your head . . . You're just not going to let this lie, are you?"

"Not a chance." Stretching out full-length beside him, she tried to relax and found she couldn't. She was full of concern, and her mind raced at runaway speed. At last she could give voice to suspicions that had been nagging at her for a long time, and there were plenty of them. "I don't think you've ever had the proper psychiatric care, Jacob. Sandra said the same thing."

"Oh? Where did you and Sandra go to medical school?"

"Be serious! Sandra said that nothing I'd told her jibed with what she knew about psychoanalysis, and she's been through therapy. Tell me . . . all the time you were seeing Charles, did you ever have the feeling that the two of you had a special relationship, that you were very close, that he was the one person in the world you could talk to?"

Jacob chuckled at the suggestion. "No, never."

"Well, you should have! Dr. Graves said so."

"This Dr. Graves has certainly made an impression on you."

Leah shot him a look of exasperation. "Then tell me something else. Did Charles ever try hypnosis?"

"No, it wasn't mentioned."

"See! Dr. Graves said she'd use it if the patient could be hypnotized. Even Charles told me it was an effective tool. Of course the reason he didn't use it with you is obvious. For some reason he didn't want Jacob Surratt to return. But once you did, he certainly didn't want you remembering the fugue. Why?"

"I don't know, Leah. I swear I don't." *But I'm damned sure going to find out,* he thought. *Later.*

"But you believe me?"

"Of course I believe you." How could he not believe that keen, sincere face? He had never seen her more impassioned.

"And you'll try to find out what it's all about?"

"I'll do what I can. The one thing I don't want is for you to worry about it, so put it out of your mind. So much heavy thinking for one morning. Take off that robe and get under the sheet with me. I want to feel you next to me. Now I realize why you always knew exactly how to love me. You did, you know."

"I know."

"Did you always know?"

"Of course not. I had to learn. I was a blushing bride. You taught me a lot of things, my love."

"Have I changed much? Am I different?"

She pretended to give it some serious thought. "Yes," she said. "You've gotten older . . . and better."

"Then come here. I haven't even properly celebrated my newfound state of connubial bliss."

Leah was unappeased, but it was dawn, and she was mentally worn-out. The mystery of Charles White could wait. Reaching out, she laced her fingers through the satisfying thickness of Jacob's hair. "It must be a shock to learn you're a husband and a father," she said somberly. "Now that you've had some time to let it sink in, are you glad?"

"I'm ecstatic," he said, and meant it.

"Sure?"

"Positive."

A soft smile curved her mouth. Shaking off the tiredness of her sleepless night, Leah discarded the robe, crawled under the sheet and shaped her body along the length of his, marveling at how perfectly attuned they were to each other's needs, how good he felt under her hands. Love was a gift, and hers, once lost, had been returned to her. Now the past really didn't matter. All that mattered was this—hungry mouths and hungry bodies clinging in a celebration of absolute devotion. No other man had ever, could ever, would ever . . .

Heat fairly radiated from their bodies, as he grew turgid and sought entrance. She melted and opened to receive him. Lovemaking had always been wonderful between them, but never as wonderful as now. Finally they had found their own happy ending, except for one minor flaw. . . .

SOMETIME LATER Jacob slipped quietly out of bed so as not to disturb Leah, who was sleeping soundly. Last night it had been impossible for him to tell her exactly how he felt. Perhaps he would think of the right words later, although with Leah words were never absolutely necessary. She knew him better than he knew himself. He was thunderstruck by the way he felt, wholesome and mentally resilient. He hated leaving her now, but she might sleep for hours yet, and there was something he had to do.

He dressed quickly and walked out into the hallway. He started for the stairway, then paused and reversed direction. The door to the room Nina was sleeping in was partly ajar; he pushed it open and moved soundlessly to the side of the bed. Staring down at the small sleeping figure who was curled into an embryonic position, he was overcome by emotion.

How quickly his life had changed. This time yesterday Nina had been a cute kid, special because she was Leah's daughter. Now she was his progeny, his link to the future. Someday this child would probably present him with a grandson or granddaughter. The thought took hold of him, and he felt absurdly like weeping.

His parents had been gone a long time; only occasionally did he think about them. Now how he wished they were there to see Nina. He would have to hunt up the old family photograph albums and show his daughter some of the people she came from.

He brushed his hand across his eyes. Lord, he was getting downright maudlin! For long moments he simply stood over the bed, staring down at her. Then, resisting the urge to bend and kiss her, he left the room as quietly as he had come.

The house was very still. He hurried down the stairs and into the kitchen for a glass of juice. There, to his surprise, he encountered Hilda in her bathrobe, brewing a pot of coffee. He had no idea the household staff rose at such an early hour.

Her employer's unexpected appearance both startled and embarrassed the little woman. "Oh, Dr. Surratt. Good heavens...." She cinched the nondescript robe more tightly round her waist, and her hands flew to her hair, which was stuffed into an unbecoming net.

"Don't mind me, Hilda. I'm just on my way to the clinic and thought I'd have a glass of juice. I'll get it."

"Oh, please, sir, let me." She hurried to the refrigerator, glancing at the kitchen clock as she did. "So early...."

"Yes, well . . . I was awake, and there are things I need to tend to," he offered by way of vague explanation. He accepted the glass of orange juice she handed him and quaffed it.

"Mrs. Stone and Nina . . . I guess they're still sleeping?"

"Yes. If Nina wakes up before her mother does, please keep an eye on her for me."

"Of course. She's a dear little girl, Doctor. I've grown very fond of her."

Jacob smiled. "That's good, Hilda, because I imagine you'll be seeing a great deal of her from now on."

There was an almost imperceptible altering of Hilda's expression. "Sir, is that something I can pass along to the rest of the staff?"

"I can't think why not. You might also tell them to get used to addressing Mrs. Stone as Mrs. Surratt."

Hilda watched the doctor leave the house by way of the back door, and she smiled a smug, satisfied smile. Oh, she could hardly wait to tell Davis and the others! Dr. Surratt's new woman friend had been the chief topic of kitchen gossip for months, and not only because of the marked changes she had wrought in their employer's personality. Mrs. Stone was a woman from his past, of that they were all sure. One had only to look at the darling child to tell that. Did Dr. Surratt honestly think they hadn't seen the resemblance?

Though now that she thought about it, Davis hadn't seen it either until she had brought it to his attention, and then he had accused her of having an overactive imagination fed by too many romance novels and soap operas.

Hilda snorted derisively. Men were such obtuse creatures, totally unobservant. Well, it was good that the doctor had decided to do what was right and marry the mother of his child. Heaven knew what kind of life that poor Mrs. Stone had been forced to lead, raising the child alone and all. Single parents had a tough time of it, and wasn't it always the woman who suffered? Knowing Dr. Surratt as she did, Hilda was surprised he hadn't done the honorable thing six years ago. But then, who could figure people when it came to affairs of the heart? Wouldn't it be interesting to know how they had happened to get together again.

This ought to shake up things in the household! Hilda snickered delightedly as she poured herself a cup of coffee. Bernice, the woman who came in twice a week to do laundry, would be there that day. *Do I have an earful for her,* Hilda thought. *This is at least as good as anything on the afternoon soaps.*

JACOB DROVE TO THE CLINIC in a mindless state, noticing only the absence of traffic at that ungodly hour. He wheeled into his private parking space, then unlocked the back door to the clinic. The building was deserted and would be for at least another half hour, which suited him perfectly.

His destination wasn't his own office or even the medical clinic, but the psychiatric unit. His master key opened every door in the place, and he used it freely, first for admittance into Records, then into Psychiatry's reception room. He didn't waste time wondering if what he was doing was ethical. He wouldn't have hesitated to pull another patient's file; certainly he was entitled to his own.

However, there didn't seem to be any records on him. Somehow that didn't surprise him at all. Locking the door behind him, Jacob walked purposefully to the office at the end of the corridor and let himself in. Charles's office, situated on the west side of the building, was dark, so he turned on the overhead light. Surveying the room, he found what he was looking for—a lone filing cabinet tucked unobtrusively into a corner behind a potted plant. He opened it, riffled through the several dozen folders he discovered and withdrew one. Then he took a seat behind Charles's desk, opened the folder and began to read. His expression at first was puzzled; then it settled into a grim cast....

SOME THIRTY MINUTES LATER Charles found him there. The light welling from beneath his door hadn't surprised him. He was forever forgetting to turn it off when he left at the end of the day. But the figure seated behind his desk prompted not only surprise but a vague rush of alarm. Charles's eyes bulged in disbelief at Jacob's temerity, so much so that he didn't waste time on pleasantness. "What the devil are you doing here?"

Jacob smiled casually. "I wanted to discuss my case with you, doctor."

"Now? Good God, Jacob, I have a full schedule this morning!" Charles took off his jacket, hung it up and shrugged into a white coat. "If there's something you want to talk to me about, we'll have to do it after office hours."

"We'll do it now."

Apparently Charles sensed something complicated was going on in Jacob's head. For a moment he stood awkwardly, looking uncomfortable. "I don't have the time," he said lamely.

"Take the time."

"I'll . . . try to work you in later."

"Now!"

Clearly agitated, Charles nevertheless mustered up an air of bravado. "Now look here, Jacob. I realize you're the head man around here, but that doesn't give you the right to barge in here and demand this and that." Then his eyes fell on the folder spread out on the desk. The bravado evaporated as his agitation increased. "What the hell are you doing?"

"Going over my case." Jacob's eyes narrowed, and in a sudden violent move he closed the folder and banged his hand on top of it. "There's not a damned thing in here, Charles! Nothing! Anyone reading this file wouldn't learn the first thing about my case. No observations, no suggestions. All jibberish. Now suppose you tell me what's going on."

Nervously Charles crossed the office to stand with his back to the desk. "It's not jibberish to me. Your case is in my head. I know how you feel about your amnesia, so I . . . thought it best not to have a written history in the clinic's files. Who knows whose hands it could fall into? I had to protect your privacy."

"Oh, bull!"

The unexpected epithet brought Charles around. "Now wait just a damned minute!"

"No, you wait just a damned minute! You knew where I was eight years ago, didn't you? You knew it all the time."

"What on earth gave you that idea?"

"The sudden recollection of a lady with a very sound memory. Leah remembered where she'd seen you before."

Charles's mouth dropped open. Caught off guard, he carelessly said, "I told that woman—"

"To stay away from me, not to tell me anything. Yes, I know. Unfortunately for you, Doctor, Leah is a thoughtful, inquisitive woman. She decided to seek a second opinion. Aren't we ethical medical men supposed to advise patients to do just that?"

Charles's face drained of color; he looked positively ashen. Jacob was reminded of the stricken look on Leah's face that day in Alex's office. Pressing his advantage, he went on. "The other psychiatrist Leah saw advised just the opposite, so she told me. Then and only then did she remember where she had seen you before. You came up to us in a café and asked directions. Then you asked about fishing...."

"Her imagination is running rampant."

"I don't think so."

Charles turned away, obviously too shaken to say anything. Every muscle in Jacob's body tensed. Until this moment he hadn't been sure, not really, and he had harbored a faint hope that Leah was mistaken. Now he knew she had remembered correctly. The downward slump of Charles's shoulders, his hands clenched at his sides, everything about his manner told Jacob that Leah was right. He didn't know when he had felt so bitterly disappointed in another human being. Sighing wearily, he said, "That was only two months or so after I'd left Phoenix, so all that time I was gone you knew exactly where I was. Admit it."

Moving as though his feet weighed pounds, Charles walked to the window to stare bleakly out at the dawning of another bright summer day. "Yes," he said dully. "I knew."

Jacob's face twisted. A long, heavy moment of silence passed while he tried to collect himself. Storming and raging, which is what he felt like doing, would accomplish nothing. He stared at Charles's dejected figure and thought, *There has to be a reason.* "Why?" he asked hoarsely. "I just don't understand. I know we've never been close friends, but I thought we had established a mutually satisfactory working partnership. Why didn't you want me back? Was it resentment or professional jealousy, or what?"

"Oh, I resented you, all right. And envied you—your looks, your social poise, even your family background. I was a poor boy who'd worked my ass off to put myself through medical school, while everything had been handed to you on a silver platter. And even though my name was right up there beside yours, I always knew who the head man was. Everybody does. And I'll even confess to enjoying being the head man during the two years you were away. But at the same time, I was grateful to you for rescuing me from oblivion and allowing my name to be associated with the clinic that had the reputation this one does. Does any of that make sense?"

"Not much."

"It doesn't make much sense to me, either. Professional jealousy had nothing to do with my decision to leave you where you were eight years ago. In spite of what you might be thinking now, I've always been scrupulously ethical where my profession is concerned."

"Yet you didn't want me back, and once I was back you didn't want me to remember anything that had happened during the fugue."

Charles didn't deny it.

Jacob ran his fingers through his hair, shaking his head. "Why, Charles? There had to be a reason. What was it?"

The psychiatrist turned from the window to look squarely at Jacob and the strangest smile crossed his face. He looked oddly relieved of a burden. "You know," he said quietly, "I'm actually glad it's over."

"Dammit, stop talking in riddles! The reason, Charles!"

"Probably the oldest known reason for a man to toss aside every scruple he ever had and plunge recklessly ahead. A woman. To be more specific, Daphne Townsend."

CHAPTER NINETEEN

JACOB SAT BACK in the chair as though reeling from the force of a blow. "Daphne?" he said incredulously.

Charles nodded. "Unbelievable?"

"It's more than unbelievable. *Daphne?*"

"I'm afraid so. Even I find it almost impossible to believe now, and looking back, if I could undo what I did, I would. At the time I was besotted, bewitched—call it whatever you like. I would have tossed you to the lions if it would have kept her with me."

Jacob rubbed his eyes tiredly and inhaled a painful breath. A mind could only absorb so much, he thought, and this was too much. He had been sorely tested during the past twenty-four hours. "Daphne Townsend, for heaven's sake! What in the hell did she have to do with it?"

"It's a long story. Do you want to hear it?"

"Oh, indeed I do, Doctor. I'll thrash it out of you if I have to."

"I . . . think I need to sit down."

Jacob shoved himself to his feet. "Take your chair. I might have to lie down."

He didn't, however. He crossed the room and sat on the sofa, propping an ankle on his knee. With engrossed interest he eyed his partner's ashen face. In a curious way he felt sorry for Charles; the man looked positively ghastly, emotionally drained. Jacob didn't prod or probe, merely waited until Charles was ready to talk.

The psychiatrist picked up a pencil and began twirling it through his fingers like a baton. "Daphne came to see me a couple of weeks after you left Phoenix. She had been in San Francisco and had returned home to the news of your acquittal. She tried to find you, but you had moved out of your apartment, so she assumed I would know where you were. I didn't, of course, and told her as much. Then she broke down, sobbed all over the place, said how sorry she was for being so wrong about you."

"Sounds like her," Jacob sneered. "Good old Daphne, as steadfast and reliable as the weather."

"Hell, I didn't know what to do, so I took her to lunch, listened to her tale of woe and tried to calm her down. I told her to come to see me anytime she felt she needed someone to talk to. She took me up on it—once a week at first, then every few days, then every day. I grew . . . fond of her."

Jacob's mouth set in a tight line. Yes, he could just picture it. Daphne was a real beauty and a charmer who could turn those baby blue eyes on you and make you feel weak in the knees. He knew, since he had succumbed to her false-hearted allure, as much as he hated admitting that. And poor Charles would have been an easy victim.

Charles cleared his throat and continued with some difficulty. "We started having dinner together, first at restaurants, eventually more often than not at my place. I knew she was using me until you got back, that she was the kind of woman who needed a man, almost any man, around. And I told myself I wasn't emotionally involved. Even after she moved in with me, I knew she'd split once you came back. I've never had a great deal of . . . success with the opposite sex, but when Daphne put her mind to it she could make me feel like the world's best. So I rationalized that I was just enjoying a brief, rare interlude with a beautiful woman, that I had my eyes wide open. But I think I always knew that wasn't entirely the truth. I was falling in love and doing my damnedest to make her do the same."

Jacob's expression was passive, though he felt uncomfortable, embarrassed. It was the hardest part of his profession, listening while people poured out their heart and soul—people would tell a doctor the most incredible things—and it was doubly hard for him to sit and listen to a respected colleague.

His thoughts suddenly went into reverse. Respected? Until today, yes, highly respected. Again, as disappointed and angry as he was, pity rose in him. He felt very sorry for any man who had the bad fortune to fall for Daphne Townsend.

Charles was frowning. "One day it dawned on me that you'd been gone a helluva long time. It started preying on my mind, so I checked with the police. At first they weren't any help, but then they found a report on an accident that had happened up near Camp Verde a couple of months earlier. The report described the victim—it could have been you—and mentioned that the man had amnesia as a result of a blow to the head. Now that hit a nerve, so

I decided to check it out on my own, very quietly. What I told you about not wanting any publicity so soon after that god-awful trial, was true. Now, dammit, Jacob, whether you believe it or not, at that point I was genuinely trying to find you."

"Okay, Charles, I believe you. Go on."

"Well, I hit a dead end. No one seemed to know where you had gone once you left the hospital, but after asking around, I found a nurse who remembered your case and was sure she'd seen you recently. She didn't know where you were living or what name you were using, but at least I knew that you, or whoever it was I was tracking, was nearby. So one Saturday I drove to Camp Verde and just started moving west, looking around, stopping in stores and the like. I don't know what I thought I might find, but the whole thing was driving me nuts by then."

He paused again to clear his throat. "Toward afternoon I got thirsty, so I stopped in at this place for a beer. And dear God, there you were—sitting at a table with a pretty, dark-haired girl, looking like you were having a great time. I swear, that's the first time I gave any thought to the deception."

"You came over to our table," Jacob prompted, unable to recall any of it but knowing it was true. Leah had remembered it correctly, almost down to the tiniest detail.

Charles nodded. "You hadn't spotted me, but the woman had. She looked at me curiously, probably because I was a stranger, before turning back to you. It occurred to me then that the amnesia thing might have been faked. Remembering your mood when you left Phoenix, I decided you might have assumed another identity just for the hell of it. It's been done before, plenty of times. But if you had been faking it, I knew I'd see some reaction if you suddenly saw me face to face. Nobody's that good an actor, and I had to know for sure. That's when I approached you."

"I didn't show any signs of recognizing you," Jacob said.

"Not the slightest, and I stayed at your table long enough to make sure. I saw the way the woman—ah, Leah, was looking at you with her heart in her eyes. Fascinating eyes. Incredible eyes."

"Yes, I know."

"You told me you were working as a veterinarian's assistant. I remember damned near choking over that one before conveniently telling myself you probably enjoyed it. I knew you'd be good at it, too. All the time I stood there at that table, I was convinced I was going to tell you who you were any minute, but somehow I never did. I walked out of that café in a trance. When I got to the car I was shaking all over. Even as I drove away, I couldn't believe I was doing what I was doing. For days I thought of nothing else. I'd go back and find you, I was sure, but then..." Charles faltered.

"Then?"

"Why not leave you alone, I rationalized. You looked happier than I'd ever seen you. You and the woman obviously were crazy about each other, and you were working at something you'd be good at, something worthwhile. Why confuse your life by giving you an identity you obviously didn't want? Oh, the mind's a wonder! It can invent all sorts of convenient reasons for implausible actions. But hell, I knew the real reason for what I'd done. I knew if you came back here, Daphne would be gone like a shot. So...I left you alone."

Jacob's face was strained and taut. "I keep remembering the look you gave me when I walked into this office that day two years later. I've never seen anyone so stunned."

"Two years," Charles mused. "Two damned years. I had almost forgotten you. Your name was hardly mentioned around the clinic anymore, and I thought Daphne was happy. She had even begun considering marriage, or at least I thought she had. Until you showed up. I dislike telling you this, but for a moment I think I could have killed you. I didn't tell Daphne you were back, but she found out within days."

"She came to see me."

"I guessed as much. She moved out right after that, to Hawaii, I think. I was shattered at first, so much so that I didn't have time to think or worry about you. But then resignation set in. The whole thing had been like a dream from the beginning, anyway. I saw Daphne for what she was then—she really was a first-class bitch, you know—and I honestly think that in time I considered her departure good riddance. She was such a demanding woman, always wanting this and that...."

Jacob had placed his head in his hands. Now he quickly looked up. "Charles, why didn't you tell me then? If Daphne was the reason..."

"I had painted myself into a corner, don't you see?" he argued fervently. "I had myself in the awkward position of not having done something when I should have, of having let so much time pass that I was bound to incur your wrath. How could I tell you I'd known where you were for two entire years? I could see all this—" he waved to encompass the Surratt-White Clinic as a whole "—going down the tube. And I damned sure couldn't risk having you remember on your own, so when you asked me to put you in therapy, I grabbed the chance. There were any number of things I could have done to help you, but I didn't want your memory to come back. You might have remembered the encounter in the café."

Dazed, Jacob could only shake his head. "You robbed me of God knows how much time with Leah," he said bitterly. "And my daughter!"

"That's been the hardest part, knowing a child is involved. I'm not without conscience, in spite of what you might think," Charles said quietly; then he slipped back into the past. "Six years! Six years had passed. I thought it was all over. Then the night of the opening I saw Leah Stone, the woman I'd seen you with in that café. Hers is a face you never forget. I just stood and stared at her, feeling like I'd been punched in the stomach. But I had to risk speaking to her, staying with her long enough to make sure she didn't recognize me. She didn't, although she looked at me strangely, as though she thought she'd seen me before.

"When I learned you had just met her, when she asked me all those questions about amnesia . . . I knew. I think I knew it was only a matter of time before the whole thing blew up in my face. I fed her every piece of misinformation I could think of, even to the point of suggesting your condition might have been psychological, that remembering would do you irreparable harm. You can scare the pants off a lay person with that kind of talk. But I was only stalling, and I think I knew it. If it's any consolation to you, I haven't had a decent night's sleep since."

"It's no consolation, Charles. Neither have I. Leah said she's suspected for some time I wasn't receiving proper psychiatric care."

Charles smiled wanly. "Your girlfriend's very astute."

"My wife."

"That's right, your wife. Will you . . . apologize to her for me? She's quite a woman. All those years! It's almost unbelievable that a woman would keep a man's memory alive all those years."

Jacob said nothing. Apologize? How could anyone apologize for Leah's six lonely years? Despair was etched in his face. A searing pain had begun at his temples, but it was different than the headaches. The headaches, he imagined, were a thing of the past, as was the dream.

"You could have interpreted that dream all along," he muttered blankly.

"Without the slightest trouble."

"You compromised every principle you swore allegiance to!"

"Don't you think I know that?"

Without another word, Jacob left Charles's office. His partner probably thought his days at Surratt-White were at an end, and admittedly, at the moment Jacob's thoughts were centered on quickly and effectively canning him!

The resultant furor could be messy, though. Staff morale was good, and Jacob wanted it to stay that way. There were a lot of considerations. Did one stupid mistake negate a career? He might just keep quiet, give Charles a chance to find a position somewhere else before asking the man to resign. Jacob wasn't a vindictive person.

And he rarely did anything hastily. He would be able to deal with this more rationally in a few days. For now he wanted to concentrate on the reality of Leah and Nina and all that was ahead for him: years and years of peace and contentment. Actually, he had hope for the future all because of Leah. She had waited. His step in the corridor was brisk and springy.

The clinic was stirring to life for the day. People were pouring through the front door, filling up the chairs in the main reception room. Jacob walked into his office and was greeted by his nurse, Mary Goodwin. "Good morning, Doctor. Isn't the heat awful?"

"Terrible."

"Yet you seem to be in unusually good spirits."

"I do? Well, I guess I am in a rather optimistic frame of mind. May I see today's appointments?"

"Only four, doctor, remember? The meeting upstairs at ten—"

"Cancel it. Everyone will be thrilled speechless, since they despise those meetings of mine. And tomorrow's appointments—see how many you can reschedule. The ones you can't, give to Stillman or Taylor. Something's come up. I won't be in the office until Monday."

"Very well. Mr. Schumann's already waiting outside."

Jacob reached for the white coat hanging on the rack. "Give me five minutes, then send him in."

TWO HOURS AFTER Jacob had gone, Leah was awakening by slow degrees. Stretching and yawning, she opened one eye and glanced at the bedside clock, then bolted straight up. Ten-fifteen! She hadn't slept this late since weekends in college.

A far-off sound reached her ears, Nina's girlish laughter. Scrambling out of bed, Leah went to the window and looked down. Nina was splashing happily in the shallow end of the pool under Hilda's watchful eye, looking as though she was having a grand time. *The child's part fish,* Leah thought as a soft smile curved her mouth. She wasn't the least bit worried about Nina's adjustment to her new life.

Leah lifted her eyes and scanned the blue summer sky. It was a beautiful day, an absolutely gorgeous day. It was good to feel free—happy to be young and alive and in love. Jacob wasn't the only one who had been burdened these past couple of months.

Turning, she made for the bathroom and a quick shower, vaguely wondering if Jacob had been able to juggle his schedule for the day. If so, when would he be home?

The shower helped her wake up. For a few minutes she emptied her mind and let the bracing needles of water pummel her skin, then turned it off, opened the door and reached for a towel—only to find a strong hand instead. It grasped hers tightly, and she found herself being helped out of the stall. Rivulets of water were streaming down her face. Brushing them aside, she opened her eyes.

Jacob stood before her, grinning. Opening his arms, he pulled her dripping body against him and held her tightly.

"Oh, I'm getting you soaked!" She laughed.

"I can change. Let's get our daughter and go home."

"Home?"

"One of our homes. We can't ever give up the house in Sedona, Leah. It means too much. We'll divide our time between here and there, maybe use the other as a weekend retreat with an eye toward retiring there someday. I know you're not a city person."

"I can be any type person I have to be as long as I have you. But I must confess, I don't want to give up the house in Sedona. Do you have any idea how many man-hours you spent on it?"

"Now my hands are itching to pick up a hammer and saw again. I think I have a new project. The first order of business will be building on a bedroom . . . with a lock on the door." His grin was mischievously salacious.

She grinned back, then shivered. "Get me a towel, darling. I'm freezing!"

Whipping one off the towel bar, he wrapped it around her and dried her thoroughly. Then he knotted it around her breasts. Since the front of his shirt was soaked, he unbuttoned it, slipped it off and used it to vigorously rub his chest. "Speaking of houses, how do you feel about this one?"

"This one? Well, it's lovely."

"Really? You really like it?"

"Jacob, it's a beautiful house. What woman wouldn't like it?"

"You know, I never thought much about this house. It was just someplace to hang my hat, but now I'm starting to think of it as a home. I want to see your jacket slung over the back of a chair. I want Nina's sneakers on the stairway and her bicycle out front. I want giggling little girls spending the night...."

Leah looked at him skeptically. "May I quote you on that in a few months?"

"Absolutely. My life has been too damned orderly for too damned long. You know, I think I'll clean out that exercise room I never use and turn it into a game room. She can have her friends over in a few years, and—" He stopped, and a look of absolute alarm crossed his face. "Leah, Nina's going to want to go out on dates someday. I can't allow that! I won't like any of the boys."

She laughed delightedly. "Well, don't waste your time now. There'll be plenty of other things to worry about in the meantime. So, what have you been doing this morning?"

"I saw Charles," he told her, suddenly sobering.

Leah stiffened. "Oh, Jacob!"

"You were right on all counts."

"He admitted it?"

"He didn't have a choice."

"If only I had followed my own instincts." She closed her eyes and expelled a heavy sigh. "If only I had told you months ago. Think what I could have spared you."

"You did what anyone would have done, sweetheart. You listened to what an expert had to say. I've been listening to him for six years."

"What are you going to do, about Charles, I mean."

"I don't know. I'll have to think about it, something I don't want to do today."

Pulling away, Leah looked at Jacob thoughtfully. "Why, you're not angry, are you?"

He shrugged. "I was, but it's wearing off. He was foolish over a woman. It happens to the best of us."

"A woman?"

"It's a long story. I'll tell you all about it later. Now, let's get dressed and get Nina. I guess we should tell her right away."

"Yes, let's." A rush of emotion overtook her, and she flung her arms around his neck. "I love you . . . so . . . much! It overwhelms me."

"It pretty well floors me, too." Bending his head, he kissed her eyes, the tip of her nose, her mouth. "And to think I never believed in fate. What else could have kept you free all these years? What else could have sent me into that bank on that splendid morning?"

"I've waited so long."

"I know you have."

"So many lonely nights," she murmured, melting against him, resting her cheek on his shoulder.

"I know it can't have been easy for you. We'll make up for them, I promise."

Smiling impishly, she raked her fingernails across his back, felt a little shiver race through him. "Can we start now? Hilda will keep Nina entertained. Do we have to go downstairs right away?"

"Not on your life." As he scooped her effortlessly into his arms, the towel gave way, exposing the body that drove him wild with desire. His eyes glittered in appreciation. "You have gorgeous breasts," he declared as he swept through the doorway with her.

"They're too small."

"Too small for what?" Gently he placed her on the rumpled bed, then stood over her, smiling as he dropped his trousers. "They fill up my hands. I'm more than satisfied, at least." As he eased himself down beside her, he showed her what he meant.

Leah sighed contentedly. "Are the doors locked?"

"Such a worrywart. Yes, they're locked. No one will bother us, sweetheart. Relax . . ."

"Oh, Jacob, are we terribly wicked and love crazed?"

"Probably. Isn't it great? You make me feel like a kid."

She smiled lovingly and reached for him. "Oh, Doctor, you're no kid, far from it. You are one gorgeous man! I'll never get enough of you, never, never."

"Well," he said as their movements began, "you can try."

CHAPTER TWENTY

LEAH EDGED ONTO the interstate and headed north. Beside her, Jacob was the picture of self-satisfaction. His legs were stretched in front of him as far as the car's confines would allow. His arms were folded across his stomach, his head resting on the back of the seat, and his mouth was set in a contented half smile.

In the back seat Nina had been unusually quiet. She had scarcely said a word since Jacob had explained—beautifully, Leah thought—the truth about their relationship. From time to time Leah glanced worriedly into the rearview mirror, but Nina was only staring out the window, apparently lost in thought. The child could look so grave at times, and when she did she looked so much like Jacob. Until this moment it hadn't occurred to Leah that Nina might not be thrilled about the turn of events. Perhaps she should have realized that the whole business might be more than her daughter could, or would, assimilate.

Suddenly Nina leaned forward, propped her arms on the back of the seats and spoke with six-year-old earnestness.

"If you're really my daddy, how come you didn't say anything before?"

Jacob straightened and shifted so that he could look at her. "Good question," he replied just as earnestly. "Well, Nina, the best way I can explain is to tell you I didn't know it myself."

That elicited a look of puzzled disbelief from the girl, prompting him to explain further. "You see, sometimes when people are sick they forget things, often for a long time, and that's what happened to me. Understand?"

"I guess so," she said weakly. "Did you forget me and Mama?"

"Unfortunately, yes."

"And now you remember us?"

"Now I know who you are, yes."

"Are we going to live with you?"

"Oh, absolutely. Or I'm going to live with the two of you, depending on the way you want to look at it. Are you happy about that, Nina?"

There was a brief pause, causing Leah and Jacob to glance at each other apprehensively. Then Nina asked, "Are you going to let me have my puppy?"

Behind the wheel Leah chuckled. "Now how's that for getting to the heart of the matter?"

Jacob nodded in wry acknowledgment. "I guess so, Nina. One puppy might be a nice addition to the family."

"Then I'm happy about it," Nina said with a delighted smile. "Let's go to Grandpa's and get Molly."

"Molly?" he asked.

"That's my puppy's name."

"You've named her already!" Jacob exclaimed in mock dismay. "Fat chance I'd have saying you couldn't have her. Well, okay, we'll get Molly. Listen though, Nina, you're going to have to take care of her. Your mother and I don't have time."

"You already sound like a daddy."

Leah grinned, looking at Jacob. "I can hardly wait to see Dad. He's going to be so pleased." Studying the road ahead of her, she grew thoughtful. "Darling, I'd really like for you to make an appointment with Dr. Graves. She said she'd like to see you."

He shook his head firmly. "I've been thinking about that, and I've changed my mind. I'm through with that nonsense, Leah. No more psychiatry for me. You can fill me in on all I need to know."

"That's not a proper attitude, and you know it, Doctor. You'll be happier if you remember on your own. I'll just bet Dr. Graves can help you, and I know you'll be comfortable with her."

"Let's drop it, darling. Okay?"

"No. Not okay."

Jacob began another protest, then threw up his hands. "I guess I can protest all I like, but I'm sure if you want me to, sooner or later I'll find myself seeing Dr. Graves."

"Good," she said smugly.

"Were you always this bossy? Did you tell me what to do before?"

"No, but you used to be more malleable." Leah grew serious. "You were going to tell me about Charles . . . something about a woman."

"Uh-huh. Daphne Townsend."

"Your old girlfriend?" Leah gasped. "The one who deserted you during the trial?"

"One and the same. When I won the case, dear Daphne apparently decided I wasn't such a bad sort, after all. She went looking for me but, of course, couldn't find me. So she went to Charles and—"

Leah grasped the situation immediately. "And he comforted her. They became . . . er, friendly, and one thing led to another."

"You got it. Except that he was always afraid she would split if I ever came back."

"Which she did?"

"Which she did."

"And you're not furious—livid?" she asked incredulously.

Jacob turned to her, his eyes compassionate and understanding. "Anger won't do any good. It messes up the judgment. Charles is only human, darling, and he did satisfy himself that I was okay, doing well, happy. Oh, I know he'll have to leave the clinic—I don't see how we could possibly work together now—but I'm not sure I want to ruin him. It's occurred to me that he could use some therapy himself. Anyway, I need to think about it, and that will take some time."

Slowly Leah relaxed. Shaking her head, she only said, "You're something else, darling. You really are."

"It's pretty hard for me to be angry at anyone or anything right now. Are you bitter?"

She thought about it. "No, not really. Charles won't be one of my favorite people, but as you said, it's pretty hard to be mad right now. Life looks awfully good to me."

They had been traveling for a little over an hour when Leah chanced to look at the gas gauge. Chagrined, she said, "Oh, oh, I should have gotten gas before leaving the city. It's not like me to forget to check the gauge."

"No problem," Jacob said. "Turn right up here at the next exit. There's a convenience store somewhere around there."

"Okay, I—" Leah glanced quickly at him. "Jacob, how did you know that?"

"What?"

"How did you know there's a convenience store down that road? We've never been that way before. I know I've never taken you east of the interstate."

"Well..." Straightening in the seat, he looked this way and that. "To tell you the truth, I don't have the slightest idea. I don't even know why I said that."

"Oh, my God!"

"Leah, stop making something out of everything. I told you, I don't know why I said that. I don't remember a store now that I think about it, but even if one's there, I could have stopped at it any number of times."

"No, you once told me you stay strictly to the interstate, and I know for sure you and I haven't been down that road together, not even when you were Jim Stone." She slowed and turned off at the next exit. "Well, I'm not going to sit here and wonder. I'm going to investigate."

It was there, exactly where Jacob had thought it would be. Leah's eyes misted with tears as she pulled in beside the gas pumps. "Oh, Jacob! Don't you see? You're relaxed and happy now, unconcerned about the past, so your memory's coming back, just like Dr. Graves said it might. Not all of it, of course. You'll probably never remember all of it, but bits and pieces."

"My amateur psychiatrist!"

"I don't need to be a psychiatrist. It's so obvious to me."

"Is it that important to you?"

"Yes! I want you to remember, not through my mind but through your own."

He looked at her with love and admiration. "We don't have any idea why I knew this store was here."

"I don't care. For sure I've never been here before. You did know it was here." Her eyes shone with joy and anticipation.

Grinning at her enthusiasm, Jacob grabbed the door handle. "The sign says pay before pumping. May I get you ladies something?"

"Can I have a Slurpee?" Nina asked.

"They might not have them, honey," Leah reminded her.

"What in the name of heaven is a Slurpee?" Jacob asked.

"It's sort of a slushy cola," Leah explained.

"Colas are bad for you."

Leah shot her daughter a smile. "There's a doctor in the house now, Nina. We may have to change some of our habits. But I want something cold to drink, too. Maybe they have juice."

"Well, let's all go in and you pick out what you want."

The gnarled, wizened man behind the cash register greeted them laconically. "What'll it be, folks?"

"My wife and daughter are going to get something to drink," Jacob said with aplomb, amazed at how easily the words came out. "And I want to fill the tank. I don't know what it'll hold, though."

"Don't matter. Pay after you fill up. The sign's supposed to discourage them that pumps and runs, but it don't always—" The man stopped in midsentence, squinting at Jacob. "Say, ain't you the fella . . . Damned if you ain't! The one that got bonged on the noggin outside some years back! Never forget a face, I don't. Good to see you lookin' fit. Heard you wuz sick a while after."

Leah gasped and leaned against the counter for support. Her heart began to race wildly.

The man had stopped when he saw the wide-eyed look on Jacob's face. Then a tiny sniffling noise arrested his attention. Puzzled, he shifted his gaze to Leah, back to Jacob. "Mister, what's wrong with your wife? Why's she cryin'?"

"How about telling me your name?"

"Jane Rhodes," she said quietly.
"People call me that."

He studied her for a long time, his eyes
appraising. "But is it your name?" he
said at last.

"It's the only name I have."

UNTIL SPRING

Pamela Browning

Prologue

1

The woman dozed west of Rawlins, Wyoming, her head lolling against the back of the seat.

She would be pretty, thought the truck driver, if only her face wasn't so thin. He jammed his foot on the accelerator. When they reached Rock Springs, maybe he'd find out what the rest of her looked like. It was hard to tell if she had much of a build underneath that tacky old coat.

She stirred and mumbled something, and then her eyes jarred open, the pupils widening as she tried to place him. There was something spacey about this chick, no doubt about it. It wasn't anything he could pin down, only a wariness or a wildness or something; he wouldn't know how to describe it. Right now she was retreating into the corner of the truck cab, almost as though she disliked him intensely. Heck, that was crazy. Females usually flocked to him; all he had to do was crook a little finger and they'd come running.

"You hungry?" he asked her, none too gently. She'd riled him by acting so standoffish.

She nodded a cautious yes, but didn't speak. Her eyes were huge in that tiny face.

"We'll pull into a truck stop outside of Rock Springs," he said.

"I don't have any money for food," she said in a faint voice.

He lifted an eyebrow in her direction. He fancied that this expression gave him a devilish look. "It don't matter," he said. "I'll feed you—if you're nice to me."

His meaning was unmistakable. He had meant it to be. He watched her, keeping one eye on the road.

"Let me out," she said. Her voice was weary, not feisty. That was too bad, because he liked feisty women.

"I can't put you out here," he said. "It's starting to snow, and there's no place for you to go."

"Stop the truck," she insisted. She drew her tattered garments tightly around her. The cat—he had forgotten about the cat—uttered a faint mew from somewhere inside the voluminous folds of the coat.

"Hey," he said in a jocular tone. "What's wrong with you and me having a little fun? Two strangers keeping each other warm for the night—it could be nice." He touched a placating hand to the knob of her knee, which was barely distinguishable under the coat.

"If you don't stop this truck immediately, I'm going to jump," she said, reaching for the door handle.

"Don't do that," he said, becoming alarmed.

"I mean it," she said. She shot him a look of pure determination.

He slowed the big rig to a stop at the side of the road. "Hey, listen, lady," he began, but before he could say anything more, she had opened the door.

It happened so fast that there wasn't anything he could do to stop her. A mixture of snow and sleet swirled inside, and the woman, no bigger than a bundle of rags, tumbled out into the darkness.

"What the—" he exclaimed, jumping down from the cab. He couldn't see much of anything in this weather, and there wasn't a sign of her. With a muttered curse he walked back along the road, but it was as if she had vanished into thin air.

It confounded him that she had proved feistier than he'd figured. He felt a grudging admiration for her spunk. He peered down the snow-covered highway embankment, trying to make out footprints or some other evidence, but didn't see anything.

He would have called her name, only he'd never asked her what it was. Finally, when ice started to form on his eyelashes, he decided to cut his losses and give up the search.

"Dumb broad," he muttered with a quickly passing regret as he walked back to the rig. He had offered her a meal and a bed, and if she was too stupid to take him up on it, she could just freeze to death out there. Serve her right, too.

2

A SNOW-COVERED LOG reared up to trip her when she started down the embankment beside the road, and when she fell, she hit her head on something hard. She rolled to the side to avoid crushing Amos, then lay stunned for a minute or two before using one of the branches on the log to help pull herself to her knees.

Amos the cat, who had somehow stayed snugly bundled inside her coat when she fell, stirred and sank his claws into her midriff. She winced, but clutched his scrawny body even closer. She was determined to hold on to him at all costs. Amos was all she had.

She waited until the obnoxious truck driver who had picked her up at a gas station near Elmo climbed back into his truck and drove away. Then she swayed light-headedly to her feet.

She should have known that the guy would be a problem; he was young and cocksure and his eyes shone with a predatory gleam. She usually rode with older, more settled types or married couples, if possible. At the time, though, she had seized upon his offer of a ride as a refuge from the frigid January gale that had roared unexpectedly out of the north.

It was so cold that her feet were numb, so cold that she couldn't feel her nose. Her right shoulder and hip ached where they had taken the brunt of the impact of her fall.

The terrain here was deceptive. Previous snowfalls had filled in the hollows, and sometimes her feet crunched through the thin surface layer of ice, so that she found herself wallowing in knee-high drifts. It was hard getting up, but she knew that she couldn't lie there, even for a minute. She had to find shelter, and soon.

She paused, trying to establish a sense of direction in the darkness. The sleet and snow were turning into a blizzard, she realized with a pang of apprehension. She saw no welcoming lights in the distance and understood bleakly that the truck driver had been right. There wasn't anybody here to help her, perhaps not for miles around.

She turned back toward the highway. Under the circumstances, it would be better to try to hitch a ride with anyone who happened along. The truck driver wouldn't be back, so intent was he on a hot meal and whatever other warmth he might find in Rock Springs.

But where was the highway? She blinked, but her eyes refused to focus in the whiteout conditions. She didn't hear any cars or trucks passing, but maybe there weren't any. Why would anyone go out on a night like this?

"We'll make it, Amos, don't you worry," she said out loud to the cat, cradling him close. He didn't answer, and his warmth felt like a deadweight in her arms. With a feeling of dread, she opened her coat to make sure he was all right. Suddenly Amos, feeling the full impact of the cold, struggled to free himself.

"Amos," she said, but he fought her restraining arms and leaped down into the snow.

"Amos!" she called frantically. She couldn't lose Amos! Where was he?

She stood uncertainly, not knowing which way he'd gone. Although she called him repeatedly, she heard no plaintive meow in reply.

Stupid animal! Why had he chosen this time and this place to wander away? Didn't he realize that she needed him? Didn't he know he was all she had?

She cast about, taking a few steps this way, a few steps that way, all the while calling his name. She headed in what she thought was the direction of the highway but soon realized that she was hopelessly lost. Her knees giving way beneath her, she sank into the snow.

It wasn't smart to rest, she knew that, but oh, how wonderful it felt. If only she were warm, sitting in front of a fireplace perhaps, or a wood stove, or beneath an electric blanket. She tried to imagine the heat spreading upward from her frozen toes to her equally frozen legs, fanning out through her body like a warm little blue flame, heating her from the inside out....

She startled herself awake, knowing that she had to get back on her feet, if she was to survive. She fought to pull herself to a standing position, but all she could manage was to push herself to her hands and knees in the snow. She wasn't wearing gloves, and her fingers ached.

"Amos?" she called, her voice barely a whisper now. "Amos?"

All she heard was the howl of the wind.

She thought she saw a flick of his ginger-colored tail out of the corner of her eye and oriented herself toward it, bowing her head in deference to the cutting wind. Slowly she crawled toward the cat, listening for his plaintive meow.

She was conscious only of her own plodding determination to propel herself through the snow. Tears froze upon her cheeks, and sleet gathered on her eyebrows, but still she pressed on.

Amos ran just ahead of her, the little imp, twitching his whiskers in that sassy way of his. Funny, but he, who had looked so bedraggled and forlorn a month ago, now sported a luxuriant coat, and he feinted and scampered playfully in the snow.

Amos, you crazy cat, I'm going to catch you now, she thought gleefully. Then she lunged for him and fell through a doorway into a place where it was blessedly warm and dry.

Chapter One

"You're not planning to go out tonight?" Rooney asked skeptically.

Duncan Tate pulled the saddle cinch tightly around old Flapjack's middle. "You bet I am," he said.

Rooney walked around the horse and stood watching Duncan as he checked the contents of his saddlebag.

"I wouldn't if I was you," Rooney said. "There's a storm brewing."

"I want to find Quixote. I've got a feeling that this is a real bummer of a winter storm." Duncan didn't add that if Rooney's ten-year-old granddaughter, the incorrigible Mary Kate, hadn't left the door to Quixote's stall open, he wouldn't feel compelled to go anywhere in this weather. He'd stay home by a crackling fire instead.

"Quixote can take care of himself. Llamas are used to the cold."

"All I need is for my prize stud to fall and break a leg, and there goes my herd."

"All *I* need is for *you* to fall and break a leg, and that leaves me to manage this llama ranch all by myself. You're our most valuable asset, Duncan, not Quixote."

Duncan ignored this and heaved himself up into the saddle. "I'm not going to take any chances with the weather, Rooney. You know me better than that. I'll just ride down valley a bit and try to get a feeling for where Quixote might be. I'd like him safe and warm in his stall on a night like this."

He urged the reluctant Flapjack out into the night, knowing that once they were free of the barn, his reliable old mount would get into the spirit of things. He was right. Flapjack headed down val-

ley, exactly as Duncan wanted him to. They'd take a look at the
far pasture, then aim toward the highway. Maybe they'd even
manage a look-see around the old mine, if the snow held back a
while longer.

No sign of Quixote in the far pasture, so they proceeded toward the highway. Duncan would give almost anything to find
Quixote tonight; with his woolly coat, the llama was well protected, but Duncan didn't like to think of him wandering around
the ranch. He was almost ridiculously attached to each member
of his llama herd, and he knew that Quixote had a tendency to be
a bit too adventurous for his own good.

During a previous escapade, this one also engineered by Mary
Kate, the llama had turned up on a neighboring spread. Somehow Quixote had managed to cross two streams and a small
mountain all by himself, and during the four days it took him to
do it, Duncan had given up all hope of ever seeing Quixote again.

A few snowflakes sifted from the sky, and then the wind picked
up some bite. Duncan reined in Flapjack before deciding to go
ahead and check out the area around the abandoned mine. If he
didn't, he knew he wouldn't sleep all night for worrying.

Before he was halfway there, he knew it had been a mistake to
go on. Sleet stung his face, and the wind began to howl like a
coyote on the prowl. Maybe that fool llama had managed to get
inside the old mine; the door had been hanging from its hinges last
time Duncan had been there, and he'd meant to have it repaired.
As long as he'd come this far, he might as well check it out.

He dismounted in front of the ledge of rock that sheltered the
mine entrance, slapped Flapjack on the flank by way of reassurance, and mentally chastised himself for not repairing the door
before this. The wind had torn it from two of its hinges so that it
hung crazily to one side, and the mine was open to the elements.
He unclipped a flashlight from his belt and trained it inside the
opening. His nostrils twitched at the familiar smell of the mine,
musty and dank and still faintly scented from Duncan's boyhood
camp fires. This had been one of his favorite camping places.

"Quixote?" he hollered as loudly as he could, thinking that the
animal could have wandered down the long curving tunnel, far
from where he stood.

His voice echoed back at him, but there was no answering
movement within. He was about to turn and head back for the
ranch when a cat, blinking warily at the bright light, detached itself from a bundle of rags on the floor.

Surprised to find a cat there, Duncan stopped and let the animal rub against his hand. It was a skinny creature, scarcely bigger than a kitten, and an ugly ginger color. Still, it had a winning way about it, butting against his hand and purring loudly.

"Guess maybe I'd better take you home with me," he said. "We could probably use another cat around the barn." Rooney would have a fit, he knew. If there was one thing they didn't need at Placid Valley Ranch, it was another cat. He started to pick up the cat, and then, from the bundle of rags came a soft moan.

It might have been the wind, but Duncan played the flashlight beam over the rags and they moved. Not much, but slightly. It was enough to make him drop the cat and spring into action.

He knew immediately that he was dealing with a serious situation. He saw a hand, white and wet, so he turned the pile of clothing over—to discover a small, pale face framed by wisps of wet blond hair that were escaping from a felt hat pulled low over the forehead.

He could see that it was a female, because no boy had ever had such fine bone structure or such long eyelashes. He knew that she was at risk from exposure to the cold. He also mistook her for a child.

Her eyes opened slowly. They were blue and void of expression. She tried to speak, but couldn't.

"Don't worry, I'll take care of you," he said gently, but at the sound of his voice, the look in her eyes turned to panic and she tried to pull away from him. It was no use, though. She was too weak.

He didn't stop to wonder why she was in the abandoned mine; all he knew was that he had to do something for her—and fast.

She was conscious; that was a good sign. From the look of the melting snow around her, she hadn't been in the mine for very long, maybe less than a half hour.

He always kept a small survival kit in his saddlebag, and he headed outside to get it.

"Please," she said in a faint voice, then coughed a deep, racking cough.

He knelt immediately. He should have let her know that he wasn't going far.

"I have to get something," he told her, stroking back the wet hair from her forehead. He realized suddenly that she had thought he was leaving and not coming back.

She managed a small nod of her head, and seeing that she understood, he swiftly went out to Flapjack, who was leaning stoically into a rip-roaring wind. When he realized the strength of the blizzard, Duncan began to have serious doubts about heading back to the ranch tonight.

The least he could do at the moment was to get Flapjack out of the wind. "Come on, fella," he said, leading the horse inside the mine. The opening was narrow but tall, and Duncan had an idea that they'd be grateful for the added warmth of Flapjack's body heat in the small space.

When he returned, he saw that the girl had tried to pull herself to a sitting position and that her hat had fallen off to reveal a mass of pale curly hair. She slouched motionless as he checked her hands for frostbite. Miraculously there was none, although they were pretty scraped up. He quickly removed her shoes, which were only a pair of old Nike running shoes, and her socks, of which there were two pairs. No frostbite on the toes, either.

"You sure picked a rotten night to go out for a stroll," he told her.

Her eyes opened, then drifted closed again. They jolted wide when he started to remove her heavy coat.

"We have to get you warm," he explained. "Water-soaked clothes against the skin can be deadly when you've been out in weather like this."

She made a little grasping motion at the edge of her coat and pulled away from him, but she was so feeble that she only slid down the wall and lay coughing on the floor of the mine.

He didn't care about her sensibilities or her protests; he only knew that she might die if hypothermia got the better of her. She already showed the signs of this dread reaction to cold. She seemed to have no judgment, no reasoning power, and had little control over her hands. She was barely surviving in a half-conscious stupor, and after collapse, the next stage of hypothermia was death. He was sure that she had no idea of the dangers.

Despite her weak cries, he stripped the coat from her body. The coat, although old, had once been a good one; it was made of pure wool. It was soaked clear through, and so were the clothes she wore underneath it: an inappropriately thin cotton shirt and a pair of blue jeans. He stripped those off, too, working methodically and scarcely paying attention to the fact that this was no girl, but a full-grown woman.

He pulled off his own coat and wrapped it around her, covering it with a thin Mylar survival blanket, which took up only a few inches of space in his saddlebag but served admirably to conserve body heat when unrolled and wrapped around a victim. Then he found a couple of heat tablets, lighted them, and melted snow in his tin cup. By the light of one of the candles in his survival kit, he dropped a bouillon cube into the hot water, keeping an eye on the girl all the while. She lay on her back on the rock floor, her chest rising and falling regularly. He was afraid that she might suddenly stop breathing or experience heart failure. Both were possibilities.

"Do you think you could drink this?" he asked gently, holding the cup to her lips. She managed a few sips, then turned her head away. He understood. She was offended that he had so unceremoniously stripped off her clothes. Didn't she understand that he had only been acting out of kindness?

He found a few oily rags in the cubbyholes near the mine entrance, and lacking anything more suitable, fashioned them into a cushion against the rocky floor.

A particularly strong gust of wind delivered a surge of snow deep into the interior of the mine, and Duncan hurried to the entrance to see if the storm was worsening. It was; visibility was zero, and he felt sure that the outside temperature had dropped. It would be foolish to try to make it home in this storm. He knew the old mine well enough to know that the temperature inside ranged in the low sixties, no matter what the weather outside, but also knew he'd better repair the door, if they were going to be there all night. He dragged it across the opening and wedged it shut with a rotting two-by-four.

When he returned to the girl, he found that she had rolled over on her side into a fetal position. Despite his coat and the survival blanket, she was still shivering.

"We have to get you warmer," he said, and he knew she understood his words because she curled herself into an even tighter ball, as though to shut him out entirely.

He started to unwrap the Mylar, but she held it fast. Losing patience, he rolled her over and dragged her out of it. The look she gave him was one of pure resentment. She must be feeling miserable, and yet she cared more about proprieties than saving her own neck. Still, her lips were blue.

As carefully as he could, he pulled her arms out of the coat, and then, looking at her naked body as briefly as possible, he wrapped his coat around the two of them and rolled them both in the Mylar blanket. Her body was so tiny that she reminded him of a bird, and he felt her heart beating wildly against his. Shivers racked her body for a long time, but finally, gradually, they stopped.

Her head rested against his shoulder; her legs warmed between his. At last she slept.

Flapjack whinnied, and Duncan spoke to him calmly. The girl didn't wake up. Outside the wind keened and whistled, and after the candle flame flickered and died, Duncan dozed off, wondering just before he did so whatever had happened to Quixote.

Chapter Two

She woke up carefully, letting the feeling flood back into each stiff limb one by one, not yet daring to move. Once she could feel her arms and legs, she was sorry. They were stiff and sore. Her throat hurt, and she stifled a cough.

She smelled his scent before she felt or heard him. It must be a throwback to caveman days, when humans depended on sense of smell much more than they do now; when in danger, she knew to rely on it again. He smelled musky and of the outdoors. It was a decidedly male smell, and her first reaction was to panic.

She forced her fear to subside because her well-honed intuition told her that he was safe. He had helped her when he found her here. She might have died if he hadn't.

His arms held her close, and his legs were wrapped around hers. Her head was cushioned from the stone floor by his shoulder. And she was naked. She closed her eyes, trying to block from her memory those few minutes when he had undressed her. It didn't work.

Was it morning? She couldn't tell. It was dark in this place. She heard a whinny and a scuffle. A horse, then. She didn't remember the horse.

She felt something furry brush against her cheek. It sank against her chest and began to purr. Amos! He was all right!

Carefully she pulled her arm free of the coat, meaning to curve it around the cat, but the Mylar survival blanket crackled and the man stirred. She felt him waking up and held her breath, hoping that he would fall asleep again. Unfortunately he didn't. Instead she felt him pushing himself to a sitting posture. He removed his legs from around hers and she lay motionless, scarcely daring to breathe as he left the shelter of the blanket and coat. She pulled the blanket tightly around her and huddled against the cat.

She heard him fumble in the dark before he struck a match. It flared and illuminated his face, which she didn't remember from last night. His cheekbones were high and pronounced, and his skin was tanned and lined. A web of fine lines fanned out from deep-set eyes. His hair was dark. He turned inquiringly toward her.

"So," he said conversationally as he lighted a candle, "you're awake."

She said nothing, but he seemed to expect nothing. He spoke a few words to the horse, which stomped its feet a few times, and then he tugged a board away from a door and pulled it open.

The glare of sun on snow made her wince.

The man surveyed the scene outside before looking back over his shoulder to address her. "Well, it looks like we'll be here for a while. I doubt that Flapjack could make it through those drifts." The storm had evidently passed, and Flapjack, she surmised, was the horse.

Her rescuer used a board to clear the snow from in front of the door and led the horse outside.

"There's a rock overhang here," he explained when he came back, stamping the snow from his boots. "It protected the entrance from the snow. It looks as though we'll have to wait for Rooney to bring the snowmobile and save us."

She only stared at him. Evidently he had decided to make her his responsibility. She wasn't sure she liked the idea, but what choice did she have? If she wanted to get out of here, she'd apparently have to depend on him. She knew that the snowstorm the night before had been a whopper.

Her eyes darted around the room, if that was what it was, looking for her clothes. She saw them hanging from a spike in the wall. She inched her way up the wall, meaning to edge toward them little by little.

His back was toward her, and she was able to make some progress before he wheeled and saw what she was doing.

"You want your clothes, do you? I'll check to see if they're dry." He reached out and tested her shirt and jeans for dampness.

He tossed everything but the coat in her direction.

"Here, I suppose you can put these on if you like. They're dry enough. The coat is still soaked."

She scrambled to collect her clothes and drew them under the blanket. She eyed him warily, wondering if he expected her to dress in front of him.

His eyes softened. "You can go around the curve in the tunnel to put those on," he said. He indicated the dark passageway beyond.

Still grasping the Mylar blanket close around her, she rose painfully to her feet. She cast a fearful look in the direction he'd indicated. A yawning black hole seemed to stretch infinitely into the rock. It smelled damp and dank.

"Go ahead. There's nothing back there. This is an old mine. The tunnel curves a bit, then splits off into passageways. Did you think you were in a cave?" His eyes invited a reply, but she merely stared at him. He seemed kind and considerate, but you never could tell. Sometimes those were the very ones who insinuated themselves into your good graces, showing their true natures only after you learned to trust them.

"Here, you can have the flashlight," he said. He took several swift steps forward, startling her so that she faltered and almost fell.

"Hey, I'm not going to hurt you, okay?" he said. The light in his eyes was warm.

She reached out a hand from under the blanket and grabbed the flashlight, then scuttled around the curve in the tunnel until she was out of his sight.

She set the flashlight on the floor, and with shaking fingers pulled on her still slightly damp jeans and shirt. There was a huge bruise on her right hip and a corresponding one on her right shoulder. She'd hit the ground harder than she'd thought when she tripped over the log.

She picked up the flashlight and inspected the tunnel. Little sparkly flecks of mineral in the rock walls glinted back at her. The passage wasn't wide, but it was about five and a half feet high, which gave her plenty of room to stand upright. The man who had rescued her would have had to crouch in here. She estimated his height at about six feet.

Amos slipped up on her and twined himself around her ankles. She bent to pick him up and rested her cheek against his warm fur.

"Don't worry," she said to him. "It'll be all right. We'll be on our way in no time." She said this only to reassure herself. Amos, she had discovered, was happy anywhere that he could nestle close to her and keep warm. He didn't care whether they reached California or not.

When she had dressed, the flashlight beam preceded her into the front of the mine. The man had put his coat back on and was boiling water in a tin cup. He spared her a glance and said, "You'd better wrap back up in that survival blanket. It'll keep the chill off. I'd give you my coat, but I want to step outside and take care of my horse. I'll also look around and see if I can find a way to get out of here. I hate to wait for Rooney if we don't have to."

He seemed to assume that she knew what he was talking about. She didn't, but his advice to wrap up in the blanket was a good idea. She wrapped herself tightly in the Mylar, leaving a hand free to push her hair out of her eyes. Her hair was matted together and could have used a good brushing. She'd carried a purse when she jumped out of the truck, but she must have lost it in the storm. It had held everything she owned in the world, which wasn't much, but had included a brush and comb. She dismissed the idea of her appearance from her mind. She wasn't trying to win any beauty contests.

"Would you like chicken or beef bouillon?" the man asked.

She blinked at him.

"For breakfast. I have chicken and beef bouillon cubes. Which would you like?"

She realized from the patient way that he spoke that he was trying to decide if there was anything wrong with her mental faculties. This gave her the impetus to croak, "Chicken, please." It definitely wouldn't do for him to think she was a mental case. What they did with people they suspected were mentally incapacitated was to call the authorities. Then someone came in a van and took you away to an institution.

"Here, you can hold this while the bouillon cube dissolves." He handed her the cup, and she cradled it in her hands. The heat was welcome.

He crouched beside her, and she wished that he'd go away. She felt uncomfortable with the way he gazed at her with such concern.

"My name's Duncan Tate. I live on a ranch near here. You were in pretty bad shape last night." He waited for her reply.

She bit her lip and looked away. He had certainly been in a good position to know exactly what shape she was in last night, right down to her bare skin. She didn't want to think about it.

"How about telling me your name? It looks like we're in for a long morning together." He smiled, and the smile tugged the wrinkles beside his eyes upward. It was a pleasant smile, full of sunshine.

But how could she tell him her name, her *real* name? She didn't even know what it was. Despair settled over her. She didn't know what to say, so she said nothing. This clearly displeased him.

"Has it occurred to you that you're being rude?" he said in an exasperated tone. He got up and walked over to the cubbyholes lining the wall. He rummaged around in one and closed his fingers over a saddlebag, from which he pulled a piece of beef jerky. He hunkered down on the floor a few feet from her and ate it, paying no attention to her.

The steam from the bouillon rose and warmed her face. She stared into the cup, blinking back tears. She felt particularly vulnerable after last night's ordeal, as though not only her hands and knees had been scraped raw, but also the emotions that she had successfully kept in check for so long. If only he hadn't asked her name! It was the one question she found difficult to handle.

During the past year she had evaded questions about where she lived and what she did, how much money she made and where she had last worked. She had cheated when she had to, lied if absolutely necessary, and run away from anything that seemed too risky. She had hardened herself against life, but she could still be undone by one simple question: "What is your name?"

When she cast a cautious sidelong glance in his direction, the man was watching her. He didn't say anything, even though their eyes locked. She found that she couldn't look away. He didn't, either. She wanted to trust him; for some reason it seemed as if she could. He had been kind to her. Her sense of self-preservation made her consider his kindness from all angles. Finally she decided that he might be of more help to her if she provided answers to his questions.

"Jane Rhodes," she said quietly. "People call me that."

He studied her for a time, his eyes appraising her hair, her face, her figure wrapped in the blanket.

"But is it your name?" he said at last.

"It's the only name I have," she replied. Her throat was so swollen that she could barely talk.

He decided that she was telling the truth. "Jane, then. That's good enough." He nodded summarily and stood up. Amos bounded over to him, and he bent absently to stroke the cat's fur.

"Is the cat yours?" he asked.

"No more than I'm his. We—we travel together," she said.

"I should find him something to eat," Duncan said.

"He can have the last of the bouillon," Jane replied. "I don't think I can drink it all, anyway."

"Okay. Before long we'll be at the ranch, and I have plenty of cat food there. What's his name?"

"Amos," she said, thinking that he might laugh at this name for a cat. Cats were supposed to be named something cute. She had chosen Amos's name from a list in a name-your-baby book at a public library where she had gone to keep warm, hiding the stray cat inside her coat so that he could be warm, too. The name Amos meant "strong and courageous," and she had given him the name to remind herself that strength and courage were qualities that she must maintain in order to survive.

"Amos. I like that," Duncan said.

Then he went outside, shoving the door into place behind him. She couldn't see it, but she could imagine the deep snow outside. She couldn't recall when she'd ever seen such a fierce storm. She sipped the hot liquid, letting it ease slowly down her throat, and it both soothed the soreness there and warmed her from within. She couldn't, at the moment, recall when she had last eaten.

That truck driver! What a jerk he had turned out to be. She'd never have ridden with him if she hadn't been so cold.

If she ever got to California—no, not *if*. *When* she got to California. She would be warm all the time in California. There were palm trees there and an ocean. The sea air would banish the cough that had plagued her since October. It had been a good idea to head for California.

Anyway, it had been time to leave Chicago. She had no desire to spend another winter there. When she had first decided to leave, her choices had been California or Florida, but the ride she got at the outset of her journey was heading west, and so California it was. She'd made good progress, catching rides with anybody who would pick her up, sleeping in bus stations or shelters for homeless people along the way. Someone had stolen her coat at the shelter in Saint Louis, but a sweet-faced social worker had found her another one in a big cardboard box in her office. It didn't fit, but that didn't matter. In California she wouldn't need a coat, anyway.

"Jane?"

She swallowed her last sip of bouillon and set the cup on the floor, where Amos could lap up the dredge.

"Jane, I hear a snowmobile. It's probably Rooney, my foreman at the ranch. He'll know that I've taken shelter here at the mine and will be looking for me." Duncan gathered up the things he had taken from the saddlebag and shoved them inside.

"We can't all ride on the snowmobile," Jane said.

He glanced at her appreciatively, and she could tell that he was relieved that she was showing some reasoning power at last.

"I'll take you back to the ranch, then return for Rooney. I want to get you into the warm house. I'm still worried about you."

"I can't stay with you there, I have to leave," Jane said quickly.

"I'm not letting you leave until I know you've come through this without any damage. I don't like the sound of that cough."

"It's just a little cough, nothing serious," she said, feeling a new one rise in her throat and trying to quell it. He only spared her a sharp look and went back to the door, where he waved at someone and shouted.

She heard him talking outside, and then an older man—she guessed his age at around sixty—entered the mine and stood looking down at her with an expression of perplexity.

"Rooney, this is Jane. Jane, Rooney," Duncan said.

"Well, Duncan, this sure ain't Quixote you've found," Rooney said, stripping off his coat and handing it to Duncan.

"No, it certainly isn't. Did that old reprobate ever show up?"

"You bet he did, only minutes after you left. Say, Duncan, can you look in on Mary Kate when you get back to the ranch? I left her watching television at my house."

"I'll bring her over to my place, so Jane here won't be alone when I come back for you," Duncan said. He wrapped Jane in Rooney's coat.

"You're giving me your coat?" Jane said incredulously to Rooney, as Duncan hustled her out into the bright daylight.

"Sure," Rooney said. "I'll be fine until Duncan gets back."

"But what about my own coat?" she said, confused. She couldn't afford to lose it; what if something happened to it?

"I'm bringing it," Duncan replied. Sure enough, the old woolen coat was rolled up under his arm. Jane relaxed then, knowing that once it was dry she could have it back.

Before she knew what was happening, Duncan had bundled her and Amos onto the snowmobile in front of him. The engine roared to life, and Duncan accelerated until their speed fairly terrified her.

The snow-covered ground disappeared swiftly beneath them. The snow was blindingly white. To one side lay the mountain, and to the other a forest of dark evergreens.

Jane, closing her eyes against the dazzle, felt the trail weave and rise and twist. The wind, exaggerated at this speed, ripped into her cheeks, and she hid her face deep in the collar of Rooney's coat. Amos, secure in her arms, dug frightened claws into the fabric. Behind her, Duncan guided the snowmobile with subtle shifts of his weight. The vibration of the machine made her queasy, and the noise grated on her nerves.

She was glad when Duncan stopped the snowmobile. They were standing in front of a two-story house that could have decorated the front of a Christmas card.

If it hadn't been for the blizzard, she could have walked here last night. She wouldn't have knocked, but maybe she could have gained entrance into the nearby barn and been able to sleep there. She could have been on her way again in the morning, before these men even knew she'd been an overnight guest.

Duncan dismounted and helped her unfold her stiff arms and legs, then held onto her arm as he escorted her up the steps to the front door.

"I can manage," she murmured, but he paid no attention. The warmth inside the house felt blissful.

"Poor thing, you look frozen," he said.

"Is it all right if I put Amos on the floor?" she asked, because the cat was struggling to jump down.

"Sure," he said.

She bent to set Amos gently on the wide wooden planking underfoot, and the little cat crouched beside her feet and cautiously sniffed the air. Jane almost fell when she started to straighten to a standing position.

Duncan grabbed her and held her firmly by both arms. His grasp was strong.

"You really aren't all right, are you?" he demanded.

"I—" she began, then her knees went weak, and she slumped against him.

He swung her into his arms with little effort and stood looking down into her face. She closed her eyes against his piercing gaze, which was delivered from a pair of eyes as dark as ebony. It felt good to succumb to his strength; she had so little of her own.

He climbed a stairway and nudged open a door with his foot. She saw pale yellow walls and white woodwork. Duncan deposited her on a bed and strode to the window, where he raised a shade partway. Jane was overcome by a fit of coughing.

She tried to struggle out of Rooney's coat, and Duncan sat down on the bed beside her, helping her remove first one arm, then the other. He was so big and she was so small by comparison that she felt like a child in his presence. Feeling like a child wasn't so bad. When you were a child, you expected someone to take care of you, or at least that was the way she imagined it. You had few responsibilities. A child had all sorts of privileges that adults don't have. It would be nice to travel back in time and be a child again, if only for a little while.

"I'm going to call the doctor," Duncan said abruptly.

"Don't," she said. "It would cost money, and I don't have any."

He took her small hands in his. Her hands were cold, and this warmed them.

"I'll pay for it. I want to," he said.

"You don't even know me," she whispered, amazed that he would take care of her, even seemed to *want* to take care of her.

"No, I don't know you," he agreed.

"Then why don't you just let me go?"

He studied her for a long moment, and she was overly conscious of how his presence filled the room, dominating it and her. She had an idea that he was used to being in charge, that she was now someone he considered his responsibility—and therefore something not to be dismissed lightly.

"I doubt that you have anywhere to go," he said.

The truth of his perception staggered her. So far she had fooled herself into preserving the fiction that she was a real person with a real place to be. "I'm on my way to California," she said defensively.

"How were you planning to get there?"

"Oh," she said vaguely, "I'll get there."

"Is your car broken down on the highway? Were you trying to get help last night? Is that how you happened to flounder across the field and find yourself in the mine?"

She waited for a few moments before answering. "No, it wasn't exactly like that," she admitted finally, avoiding his eyes.

"I noticed last night that you have two terrible bruises on your shoulder and hip. Looks like you might have been in an accident," he said.

"An accident? Well, sort of," she said. He was clearly fishing for information, but she was determined not to give anything away.

"Like I said, I'm calling the doctor. He's an old friend, and I can count on him to come to the house." *And not ask a lot of questions,* were the unspoken words between them. He seemed to sense too many things about her; his perception was frightening, in a way.

He stood up and reached into a bottom dresser drawer for a blanket, which he spread over Jane where she lay. She felt so weak that she couldn't have moved if she'd wanted to.

"I'll get Rooney's granddaughter Mary Kate to come over and stay with you until Howard Walker—he's the doctor—gets here. Mary Kate is ten, and you can baby-sit each other. She won't do anything you want her to do, and she'll be an awful nurse, but at least you won't be alone."

Jane was willing to accept Mary Kate's dubious help if that was the condition to staying here where she could recover from last night's ordeal. She sighed and closed her eyes, slipping into a half sleep where all was peaceful and quiet and, most importantly, warm.

She was vaguely aware of Duncan talking on the phone somewhere in the hall. "Yes, she's conscious, but I'm worried about her, Howard. She's all skin and bones, and her color isn't good. Yeah, if you could make it right away, I'd appreciate it. Sure, and thanks. Mary Kate Rooney will be here to let you in. Yes, *that* Mary Kate. Uh-huh. I'll see you later."

Jane opened her eyes when Duncan poked his head around the open door.

"Howard is coming as soon as he can, and Mary Kate is watching television downstairs. I'm going to go to the mine and get Rooney and see to Flapjack. Don't get up. If you want something, you can call Mary Kate. She might not come, but that's another problem. You can try her, anyway."

"Okay," she said. Her throat was hurting more and more.

Duncan seemed to have second thoughts about leaving and walked over to the bed. His look was anxious and concerned, and he pressed a hand against her forehead, leaving a cool imprint when he took it away.

"You've got a fever," he said.

"I just need a little sleep to be as good as new," she managed to say.

"I hope you're right," was all he said, and then he was gone.

Somewhere a central heating unit clicked on and off, music to her ears, and she heard the faint chatter of a television set downstairs. She slept, waking up and thinking she was dreaming when she saw pretty blue and yellow-flowered draperies at the window.

This bedroom was the one she had always wanted, she mused. *Always*, she said again, reminding herself that in her case she had only wanted a room such as this one for fifteen months, the length of time that she had existed as Jane Rhodes. Before that maybe she'd slept in such a room, been part of a family, and lived in a hometown.

She slept again, and when she woke, a gap-toothed hoyden of a girl was hanging over the bed and blowing bubble gum breath into her face.

"Want to see me blow a bubble?" the girl asked, and without waiting for approval from Jane, she inflated a bubble only inches from Jane's nose. Jane watched spellbound as the bubble grew and grew, finally collapsing with a warm puff of carbon dioxide into a raggedy pink skin that covered the girl's nose, cheeks and chin.

Unconcerned, the girl peeled the burst bubble from her face and added the scraps of pink goo to the wad of gum already in her mouth.

"Want to blow one?" she asked. "It's a relaxing thing to do. You can use my gum. I just got it broken in good."

Jane shook her head, mesmerized nevertheless by the girl's bubble-blowing prowess.

"Well, if you ever want to, you have to use Yaya Yum Bubble Gum. It's the best, and it tastes good, too. Don't buy the grape flavor, get the regular flavor. The grape makes me want to throw up." She realistically pantomimed retching, leaning over the foot of the bed.

"You must be Mary Kate," Jane said.

"Yeah, Duncan told you about me, I guess. You're Jane. I like your cat. He doesn't care much for baths, does he?"

Jane pulled herself up onto her elbows in alarm. "You didn't bathe him?"

"Yep. Sure did. Or tried to. He scratched me. I think it was Duncan's pine-scented shampoo that he didn't like. Look at my scratch." Mary Kate thrust an arm bearing an angry red welt under Jane's nose.

"Where is he?" Jane asked with more than a little trepidation.

"The cat? Oh, he fell down the laundry chute. He's okay, though. He landed on a full basket of towels and things. I dried him off with a pillowcase, and he ran into Duncan's closet. I think he's sulking."

Jane swallowed painfully and hoped that Amos would have enough sense to stay in the closet until she was able to get up to defend him, although from the looks of the scratch on Mary Kate's arm, Amos didn't need defending.

"I like animals," Mary Kate went on. "Have you ever seen a llama?"

Jane tried to think. "No, I don't think I have," she said slowly.

"They're cute. I hadn't seen one either before I came to live with my grandfather. Then I got here and there was a whole ranch of them."

"You mean this is a *llama* ranch?" Jane's head whirled. All this time she'd thought that Duncan's ranch was of the cattle variety.

"Yeah. Duncan and Grandpa raise them. Then they sell them as pack animals or pets. I hate it when they sell one, but that's how they make a living. Quixote's my favorite male, but Dearling's my favorite female. They let me name Dearling myself. She's really small for a female, so she makes a good pet. I hope they never sell *her*."

They heard a knock downstairs, and Mary Kate jumped up. "That must be Dr. Walker. I'm supposed to let him in. I won't, if you don't want me to. I *hate* doctors myself. They give shots."

"You can let him in," Jane told her, and Mary Kate ran away, her straggly black hair bouncing around her shoulders.

Howard Walker turned out to be around fifty or so. He put his medical bag on a chair beside the bed and set about examining her with sure, steady hands.

When he was through, he said, "You'll have to put ice packs on those bruises. And I'm going to bandage the cuts on your hands."

She said nothing, staring into space with her mouth clamped shut. If Howard Walker thought this was odd, he made no comment. He merely wrapped her hands in bandages, took a swab of her throat to be cultured, and wrote out a prescription.

"The prescription is for an antibiotic medicine for that throat of yours," he said, peering at her over the top of his reading glasses. "I'll give it to Duncan to have filled. Treat the bruises with ice packs, but only leave them on twenty minutes at a time. Put this ointment on the scrapes on your hands three times a day. Rest in bed until you feel better, and I'll see you in two weeks."

"Two weeks! I can't stay two weeks," she objected.

He ignored this. "I want you to eat properly. Three full meals a day, no skipping. I expect to see some roses in those cheeks next time I see you." He snapped the cap back on his pen.

"But—"

He waved the prescription in the air. "I'll give this to Duncan when I talk with him. Take care of yourself," and with that he hurried out of the room.

Jane sank back onto the pillows, pressing her fists to her hot cheeks. Two weeks! She'd planned to be in California before then. How could she stay here with Duncan all that time? He'd surely want to be rid of her.

Tears stung her eyelids. She had come so far all by herself with no help from anyone. She had made it at least halfway to California, too. She couldn't give up now.

"I'll get there yet," she whispered to herself as Amos padded into the room through the open door. When he jumped onto the bed, she made room for him in the curve of her body, taking comfort once more in his company.

"SHE'S MALNOURISHED, she almost certainly has strep throat, she has a bad case of bronchitis, and those scrapes and bruises make her look as though somebody tossed her off a tall building. Who has she been hanging around with, King Kong?"

"Howard, I don't know. I found her in the old mine last night during the storm, and for a few minutes I thought she was a goner. Is she going to be all right?"

"I'd guess that she's no older than her mid-twenties, and her powers of recuperation are probably good. She'll be fine if she gets enough to eat, and if she takes her medicine. Under no circumstances should she leave here and set out on her own. Is her name really Jane Rhodes?"

Duncan shrugged. "I doubt it," he answered.

"You'll need to get those antibiotic pills, and she must take them regularly, as prescribed. If you need me, call again." Howard clapped his hat onto his head and started out the door.

"Thanks, Howard," Duncan called after him. Howard threw him a salute and crunched across the snow to his car.

When the doctor had left, Duncan called Rooney and asked him to pick up the antibiotic for Jane when he went into town to buy groceries. Then he climbed the stairs and went into the bedroom where Jane lay sleeping.

The room was in shadow, the shades drawn against the weak winter sunlight. Duncan stood beside the bed, taking in the way her blond hair, fluffier now, spread out on the light blue pillowcases. Her cheeks might have been fine porcelain, so translucent were they, and the tiny hand resting on the blanket might have been that of a doll. Lavender shadows rimmed her lower eyelids, and her eyelashes were baby-fine, but thick. She had turned her head to the side, so that he saw her in profile. Her face was like a cameo.

He sat down on the bed beside her, wondering who she was and how she happened to be traversing the wilds of Wyoming. Despite the bedraggled hair and the quality of Little Girl Lost, she looked as though she should be gracing a drawing room in eighteenth-century England, not sheltering from a killer snowstorm in an abandoned mine.

"Jane Rhodes, who are you?" he asked softly, but she didn't answer. She didn't hear him; she was sound asleep. But even if she had heard the question, he doubted that she would have answered it. Or even could have, for that matter.

Chapter Three

Jane dreamed that night of the mine, and of lying on the floor, trying to get warm. This time the floor was not so hard, and she was much more aware of Duncan's arms encircling her. She awoke suddenly and shivered, despite Amos's comforting presence against her side.

She eased onto her stomach, her favorite sleeping position, and dozed until Duncan came into the room shortly after dawn. She came awake suddenly, immediately defensive.

"Just wanted to see if you're awake," he said, disappeared, and when he returned it was with a breakfast tray heaped with food. It held half a grapefruit, steaming hot coffee, corned beef hash with a poached egg in the middle, and toast dripping with butter.

"I don't think I can eat all of this," she said, clutching the bed covers tightly to her chest.

"Eat what you can, and I'll give the rest to Amos," he told her.

"I feel like I'm imposing," she said. She slid to a more comfortable sitting position before taking a bite of the hash. It was delicious. She relaxed slightly and told herself that there was no need to be wary here. Duncan Tate meant her no harm.

Duncan leaned against the dresser and folded his arms, watching her eat. "We don't get many visitors out this way. I'm glad to have somebody here to talk to."

"You live alone?" she asked, making an effort at conversation. He seemed to expect it.

He nodded. "Rooney and Mary Kate live in a smaller house down the road. What did you think of Mary Kate, anyway?"

"She's lively," Jane said with great diplomacy.

Duncan laughed. "I guess that's one way to put it. Actually, I think she's a terror, and so does everyone else who has ever met her. She's lived with Rooney a little over two years and every day she gets worse. Last week she came over here when I was out and decided to wash all my jeans, and she used hot water. They shrank to the point that I can't wear most of them." He laughed again.

"I'm sure she meant well," ventured Jane.

"If you can stand it, I'll have Mary Kate come over again this morning. She can refill your ice packs and get you glasses of water and stuff like that. I don't like leaving you alone, but I've got some things to do in the barn."

"Doesn't she go to school?"

"The schools are having a week's holiday—something to do with the end of the semester. She'll be over in an hour or so."

"Mary Kate told me that this is a llama ranch."

"It is. The finest in the world, we like to think."

"Are the llamas here? I mean, can I see them?"

"You'll see them when you're able to get out of bed."

"Mary Kate says they're like camels."

He grinned, but seemed pleased that she was interested. "Llamas are camelids, part of the same family as camels and vicuña and alpacas. One difference between camels and llamas is that llamas don't have a hump. They've become popular in the United States in the past few years, which is how Rooney and I happened to get into the llama business. It helps that they're lovable animals."

Llamas, Jane thought to herself. Try as she might, she couldn't pull up a corresponding picture of a llama from her memory bank. It wasn't surprising; her memory worked in strange ways. Sometimes an idea about something she'd thought she knew nothing about swam unbidden to the surface, and she would spend days wondering where it came from, or what significance it had. Other times, when a memory should have been readily retrievable, it simply wasn't there.

"So you're headed for California," Duncan said.

She stiffened involuntarily. "Yes," she said.

"Just going for a visit?"

Her mind raced. What to tell him? How *much* to tell him? She had learned to mete out only enough information to get by in any given situation, and sometimes she avoided even that.

He was smiling at her in an encouraging way, and this seemed overly familiar to her. She wished he wouldn't act so friendly, because she didn't know how to react.

"I'm planning to live there," she said finally, watching carefully to see if he accepted this. He only nodded and went on to the next question.

"Is there anyone I should call? Anyone who is expecting you?"

What should she say now? If she told him the truth, that she had no one, that she'd been living on the streets due to a bizarre run of bad luck, he might not believe that she hadn't brought all of it upon herself, or that she wasn't a mental case or—well, he might think all sorts of things that would give him good reason to boot her and Amos out into the snow. She wasn't well enough to leave yet, she knew that. She had to stay here for now if she was to survive, and survive she must.

"My girlfriend—the one I'll be living with at first—is on a—a trip. To Europe. No, there's no one to call," she said, the lie rolling glibly from her lips.

If disbelief clouded his eyes, she couldn't see it; he lowered his eyelids and seemed to be thinking.

"Where does this friend of yours live?"

"In Sausalito," she said, pulling the name of the city out of thin air.

"And you have a job lined up there, I suppose?" he asked.

"Oh, of course. I'm a librarian," she said, surprising even herself with this announcement. But library work was something she knew about after spending long hours in the library sheltering from the weather. If she had to, she could probably come up with a fairly accurate description of what a librarian did all day long.

"A librarian? Then you must enjoy reading. I'll bring some books for you."

She felt a sudden sickening wave of guilt and put down her fork. Lying had become a habit out of necessity. It was a way to protect herself, and she had become an accomplished liar. But never had she disliked herself as much as she did now, after lying to Duncan.

He glanced toward her. "Is anything wrong?" he asked when he saw the expression on her face.

There was nothing to do but lie again.

"No, it's just that I can't eat any more," she said. "It was a wonderful breakfast, though," she hastened to add. This, at least, was certainly true.

He surveyed the tray. "You did all right, considering what you've been through. Amos, do you think you could eat some of this?"

Amos stretched, got up from his place on the floor near the heat register, and followed Duncan out of the room. She heard Duncan talking to him downstairs.

So. It had started again. The deceit, the falsehoods, the scrambling to cover her tracks so that no one would learn anything of importance about her or her past. Or even her future, now that she had invented a fictitious girlfriend.

She lay back on the pillows, picturing this imaginary friend, who would, if she existed, have dark hair and blue eyes that lighted up when they shared jokes. She'd drive a small yellow car, have an office job that she took seriously and a boyfriend, whom she wanted to take seriously but couldn't because he wasn't ready to settle down. Her name would be Elizabeth, a name that Jane had always loved. She would wear a gold Egyptian ankh charm on a chain around her neck.

An ankh . . . Why had Jane thought of that? In her mind's eye she could picture it, a cross topped with a circle on a short chain, so short that the charm rested in the hollow of a woman's throat. The woman was not the pretend friend Elizabeth, but someone real and warm and dear, someone . . . *someone*. But who?

Jane squeezed her eyes shut, willing the image of a face to present itself. She saw nothing but the inside of her eyelids, a black void.

Tears forced their way between her lashes, and she beat a silent fist on the blanket. Why? *Why?* Why couldn't she remember? And where did these disconnected images come from, anyway? They intruded on her consciousness at unlikely times, empty of meaning and signifying nothing.

If only she could remember! If she could recall important things that cast light on her past, maybe she wouldn't have to start all over again. Perhaps there was someplace where she belonged, with people who would welcome her with open arms and hearts, who cared about her. Who loved her.

But of course, all of this was as much a figment of her imagination as the pretend friend named Elizabeth, or the librarian job, or any of the rest of it. The reality was that she had no one, and there was no point in avoiding it. The important thing was to get to California, and once there never to look back.

Jane sat up and swung her feet over the edge of the bed. A momentary dizziness overtook her, and she waited until it passed. In the bathroom she studied her reflection in the mirror above the sink. She looked so haggard that she scarcely recognized herself.

Everything in this bathroom was so clean and shiny. She touched an experimental fingertip to the chrome-plated faucet and quickly rubbed off the mark it left. She opened the medicine cabinet for a curious look inside and jumped when Duncan's image suddenly appeared in its mirror.

"Oh, I didn't mean to interrupt," he said.

Quickly, she closed the medicine cabinet, wishing he hadn't caught her opening it.

"I—I was wondering if you have an extra toothbrush. And a comb," she said awkwardly.

"Of course. I should have thought of that," he said. He went away for a few moments and returned with a toothbrush, a comb in a cellophane package and a hairbrush. He went away again, and Jane, waiting in the bedroom, heard him digging in a drawer in the bathroom across the hall. Soon he returned with toothpaste and other toiletries.

"There are towels on the towel rods over the tub," he told her, and then he seemed to think of something else. "Wait," he said, leaving the room. In a moment he returned bearing a pile of clothing.

"I think you might be able to find some things in here to wear," he told her. He held up a pair of jeans. "These are some of the jeans Mary Kate shrank. Maybe you can get some wear out of them. There are a couple of shirts and sweaters, all too big for you, but clean. We ought to see about getting you new clothes."

"I won't need them," Jane said with a hint of stubbornness. "I won't be here long, anyway. Only until I'm strong enough to leave."

"Dr. Walker says it will be at least two weeks," he reminded her.

Her chin shot up. "I hope to be gone before that. I can't go on being a burden to you." *And lying to you,* she thought to herself.

He rested his hands on her shoulders and looked deep into her eyes. "You're not a burden," he said quietly. "Please don't ever say that again." He removed his hands and turned quickly toward the door, as if embarrassed by his own intensity. "Enjoy your bath," he said over his shoulder, as though in afterthought.

He was so nice. Why did he treat her with such openness and trust? Perhaps he was this way with everyone, she thought, feeling a grudging admiration for him. At the same time, she felt a twinge of disdain. He wouldn't last more than a day or two on the streets.

She stopped thinking about him as soon as she stepped into the bathtub. It was a luxury to which she hadn't been accustomed. Quick washes in public rest rooms were her norm, and a cold-water shower in a crowded shelter was considered a treat. She shampooed her hair under the shower. She scrubbed her skin until it was red from the friction, and then patted herself dry with a huge white bath sheet. She had never felt so clean in her life.

When she came out of the bathroom, fresh sheets had been turned down and a note was on the pillow.

"I'll be back to see that you eat lunch," it said. It was signed, "Duncan."

There seemed no end to the man's thoughtfulness, and that only made her own deceit more unconscionable. Duncan, she thought, savoring the name. Duncan. She had never known anyone with that name before. It had a distinguished ring to it. It was different. Not like the name Jane, which was so ordinary that it was customarily used to denote anonymous people, the kind of people who didn't have a name of their own.

The simple act of bathing had exhausted her, and she fell asleep but woke up later when Mary Kate came in and jiggled the bed in a determined fashion.

"I thought you'd never wake up," was Mary Kate's impatient greeting.

"I was so tired," Jane said, pushing herself upright against the pillow.

"Duncan came in while you were sleeping. He left a sandwich for you and some soup in a thermos. Can I pour the soup into the bowl?"

"Of course," Jane said, then regretted it when Mary Kate predictably spilled soup onto the sheet. Mary Kate ran to get a damp cloth, tripping over Amos in the process. Amos scurried out of the room, clearly unwilling to tangle with her so soon after the debacles of bath and laundry chute. Jane and Mary Kate managed to mop up the soup, and Jane offered her companion half of the sandwich. Mary Kate accepted with delight.

She sat at the end of the bed, munching bologna and cheese, and firing off questions so fast that Jane's head spun. Today Mary Kate was full of questions.

"Duncan said you were in that old mine during the snowstorm. How'd you get there?"

"I walked," Jane told her.

"Far?"

"From the highway." She tried to stick to the truth; why, she didn't know. After lying to Duncan, it probably wouldn't make any difference if she fibbed to Mary Kate.

"Have you taken your antibiotic pill yet? I told Duncan I'd make sure you did."

"I took it," Jane assured her.

"Where did you come from, anyway?" Mary Kate wanted to know.

"Oh, all kinds of places," Jane said, evasively but certainly truthfully. "Say, could you hand me that glass of water?"

Mary Kate handed her the water, then settled in for more intensive interrogation.

"Where were you going? Are you planning to live there, or are you only on vacation? What kind of job do you have? Who—"

Jane thought it was long past time to interrupt this flow of questions.

"I feel really tired, Mary Kate, and my throat hurts terribly. Will you please pull down that shade? There, that's better. I think I'll sleep."

"You slept *before*," Mary Kate pointed out with a scowl, but she left the room and shut the door behind her.

Jane closed her eyes, fighting the confusion that so often enveloped her when faced with a battery of questions. There were so many questions and so few answers. It was such a helpless feeling, and you had to be careful because people's motives in asking the questions weren't always aboveboard. If you gave the wrong answers, or worse yet, if there was no answer, you could be hauled away or arrested or thrown out of wherever you were.

But Mary Kate was hardly a threat, and as for Duncan, he seemed above all to be kind and gentle. And Wyoming wasn't Chicago, where you had to be cautious about talking about yourself to strangers, or Saint Louis, where the shelter had been a nightmare, or Kansas City, where she'd had no choice but to panhandle at the bus station for money to buy food. Here the food was served regularly, and it tasted good, and no one seemed in a hurry for her to move on.

She couldn't help feeling that she didn't deserve such good fortune. And yet she had no choice but to accept it for now, at least until she regained her strength.

And then she would start her new life in California.

IN A FEW DAYS, Jane was up and about. Her bruises faded, her cough improved, and her sore throat abated. Duncan seemed happy to see her moving around the house. He would come in bearing the cold, crisp scent of the outdoors and would hang up his coat and smile at her in a way that no one had ever smiled at her before, at least within her memory. His smile brightened the days and made the cool gray and mauve shadows of winter recede into the corners of the house. For some reason that she didn't understand, it made her happy to see him smile, but she found it difficult to smile back. Usually she just looked quickly down at the floor, unsure how to respond.

Once Jane, in a fit of gratitude, tried to tell him how embarrassed she was at having to depend on him for a place to stay and for all the food that he kept pushing on her.

"Don't be silly. This is a big house, and there's plenty of room," he said easily.

When she started to feel better, Duncan invited Rooney and Mary Kate over for Sunday dinner. Duncan prepared a roast and they ate in the big dining room, where Duncan set the table with his mother's china. Jane tried to help, but she felt clumsy in the kitchen.

After they all sat down to dinner, Mary Kate entertained them with funny stories about school, and Rooney told a joke about fleas and a dog that Jane didn't understand. She laughed anyway, looking from Duncan to Mary Kate to Rooney and trying her best to fit in.

As she looked around the table at the others' smiling faces, relaxed and bright with sociability after the satisfying dinner, she knew that someday she would have friends like these in her life, people who would visit her home and relish the conversation afterward. She would figure out how to be a gracious hostess, she would learn to cook, she would—

"Jane! Jane, this is the second time I've asked you. Have you been over to see the llamas yet?" Mary Kate peered over at her, puzzled at Jane's inattentiveness.

Duncan cleared his throat. "The doctor hasn't said she could go out. It's mighty cold out there."

"I'd like to see the llamas," Jane said.

"Howard said you should stay inside for two weeks," Duncan reminded her. "It hasn't been that long yet."

She shifted uneasily in her chair. "I was thinking I could go as far as the barn. I'm feeling stronger now."

"You'd better follow Howard's instructions and wait until he gives you the go-ahead before you go traipsing around outside. Our Wyoming winters can be harsh." Thus ensued a lively discussion about the temperature, which was due to dip below zero again that night.

Jane said nothing, but since she was feeling so much better, she wondered why she couldn't leave the ranch now.

After dinner she went to her room and brushed aside the draperies to look at the llamas. She watched them with growing fascination. The llamas seemed a remarkable array of colors, sizes and shapes. They looked nothing like camels, which is what she had expected them to look like, minus the humps, of course. They sported thick woolly coats and walked with a graceful elegance.

She felt a sudden urge to get closer to them. What she could see of their gentle faces intrigued her, but since Duncan had prohibited her from going outside until the weather grew warmer, she'd have to wait. According to Rooney's weather report at the dinner table tonight, the cold spell following the blizzard seemed to have settled in to stay.

Mary Kate came into the room without knocking and stood behind Jane. "See that pale gray and white one on the far side of the herd?" she asked, hopping from one foot to the other.

"Mmm-hmm," Jane replied. She really didn't mind Mary Kate's entering without knocking; she had grown accustomed to her company over the past week. The girl seemed lonely, and so was she.

"That's Dearling, my very favorite," Mary Kate confided. "You should see her face up close. She has black rings around her eyes, so she looks just like she's wearing eyeliner."

"Why did you name her Dearling?" Jane asked.

"She's so dear, the sweetest little thing I ever saw. She follows me around better than a dog, and she never rolls in the dirt the way the other llamas do. Grandpa says that's normal llama behavior, but I think it's disgusting.''

Jane had to smile at this statement, because Mary Kate wasn't exactly the cleanest person Jane had ever met, and in her travels she'd certainly come across her share of those who simply didn't care how dirty they were.

As Mary Kate babbled on, they saw Duncan step out of the barn and call to the llamas, who turned almost in unison and made their way toward him with a dignified gait.

Jane was surprised at the way the llamas craned their long necks against Duncan's body, nuzzling at his shoulder or cheek until he petted them. She hadn't expected llamas to display such affection toward humans, but she was beginning to realize that Duncan was the kind of person who naturally inspired trust.

"Duncan knows all their names," Mary Kate said. "Every one is real special to him."

As they watched, Jane marveled at the rapport Duncan had so obviously established with the animals. Trust; a sense of affinity; the exact feelings he had inspired in her.

How did he manage it? She wanted to know, because she wanted to be able to do it. How easy it would be to attract the kind of friends she longed to meet in California if such a skill were hers. She'd never actually thought of establishing a connection with another human being as a skill. But it was—and she observed Duncan carefully during the next few days in order to learn it.

She didn't want him to know that she was doing this; it would have embarrassed her to admit that she lacked such fundamental knowledge. She studied his body language, analyzed his facial expressions, did her best to commit them to memory. She realized that she was so intent on becoming an apt student that she was mimicking his movements exactly. If he sat with his legs crossed, she sat with her legs crossed. If he leaned back in his chair at the dinner table, so did she.

If he smiled, she tried to smile, although that wasn't so easy. She didn't particularly feel like smiling.

In the first few days of her stay at the ranch, whenever Duncan came in after a day's work, Jane would be downstairs watching television in the living room. She would always jump up and make herself as inconspicuous as possible, attempting to sidle upstairs to her room without drawing attention to herself. But after she started smiling in response to him, he seemed to want to comment whenever she left the room, and finally he spoke out.

"Stay down here," Duncan said one night when she got up from the living-room couch to go to her room around eight o'clock. He had just come in from Rooney's house and was settling down in his leather chair in front of the fireplace.

"I don't want to disturb you," Jane replied, but that wasn't the real reason.

He walked over to where she stood beside the staircase and cupped his hand around her chin, turning her face toward the light. She flinched at his kindly touch, and he noticed. It worried him that human contact made her so uncomfortable.

He didn't say what he had been going to say. Instead he said only, "The last thing you would do is disturb me." He released her face and she bowed her head.

"What I mean is that you have a right to your privacy," she murmured in a low tone. Having learned long ago not to draw attention to herself, privacy seemed to her like the most precious of commodities, much too scarce to squander on strangers like herself.

"Privacy!" he snorted. "I'd call it loneliness," and when she didn't move, he took her hand and tugged her back into the circle of lamplight. He sat down in a big chair, but she stood uncertainly in front of the couch until she sank onto it at last and fixed her eyes on the television screen.

They watched the program, but even though he commented frequently on the actors or the commercials, she didn't speak. She was almost comically surprised to discover that anonymity was easier to achieve in a crowded city than in a man's living room. It was something she'd simply never thought about before.

It seemed like a long evening to her. Finally, when the late news flashed across the screen and she decided she could reasonably leave, she started to climb the staircase and he spoke again.

"Don't be so afraid to make yourself at home here," he said, his eyes very dark in the shadows of the dim living room.

She paused and turned halfway around to face him. He looked so hopeful, as though it meant a lot to him for her to like it here. For some reason this made her feel wretched.

"Thank you for everything," was all she managed to say before fleeing to her room. She had wanted to tell him that all this was new to her, that she didn't know how to make herself at home anyplace.

In her room she walked to the window, where she pulled the drapery aside and stood looking out over the ranch. Tonight it was bathed in soft moonlight glimmering on the snow. The barn was outlined in stark detail, and she saw Duncan making his way toward it. He certainly seemed to set great store by those llamas of his.

Maybe it was just that he liked all animals. He seemed to delight in Amos's antics, for instance. Yesterday he had unearthed an old Ping-Pong ball for the cat and had laughed when Amos bounded and skidded around on the kitchen floor chasing it. He had mentioned that he'd like to get another dog; his faithful companion, an Old English sheepdog, had died last year.

In fact, Duncan's propensity for animals could be the reason that he seemed to have taken a liking to her. She was like a stray; in fact, for all intents and purposes she *was* a stray. A stray human. Duncan clearly saw himself as a kind of one-person humane society, feeding and sheltering her because she had nowhere else to go and because he felt sorry for her. The more she thought about this, the colder and emptier she felt. She couldn't bear pity. Clearly she needed to reassess this situation.

She was feeling increasingly restless about her role in the household. The attention she received from these people whom she barely knew was threatening to become stifling. Their interest in her was like heat in a close room—at first it felt wonderful, but as it grew warmer and warmer, she was beginning to feel as though she couldn't breathe.

Jane had become adept at blending in, like a chameleon taking on protective coloration so that people would think that she belonged. But everything still seemed strange to her. Duncan, Rooney and Mary Kate were kind and thoughtful of her needs. They were generous to a fault.

And that was another part of the problem. She was having a hard time dealing with her deceit toward these fine, decent people who considered themselves her friends.

She wouldn't have told Duncan any falsehoods if she'd thought she had any alternatives. But to tell him that he had taken a bona fide street person into his home? Someone who'd found herself lying and stealing just to stay alive? At first she hadn't doubted that he'd throw her and Amos out if he knew her true colors.

That was then. This was now.

She was well enough to continue on her journey with or without the approval of the estimable Dr. Walker. She was ready to start a new life somewhere else under her own terms.

She counted her assets. One old coat, one set of clothes, socks and shoes, and a cat.

She realized that she'd need money to get all the way to California, but she'd spent all of her meager supply before the truck driver had picked her up near Elmo. For transportation, she had no doubt that she could catch a ride on the highway, but that would only get her so far. She'd have to eat. Sometimes strangers helped out with food, but she couldn't count on that.

There was Duncan. Maybe he'd lend her the money. But no, he didn't want her to leave. He'd be furious if she suggested it, and she couldn't tell him she was planning to go immediately. She couldn't say that she had lied from the beginning and really had nowhere to go. She certainly didn't want his pity or, more to the point, didn't want to grow accustomed to it. If Duncan thought she was a pitiable creature, it wouldn't be long before she regarded herself in that light, too. Self-pity, she knew from experience, could be deadly.

Jane was aware that Duncan often left money lying around. He liked to empty his pockets as soon as he came into the house, and he had a place where he put his wallet and loose change. It was on a table right inside the front door. There was no telling how much money he kept in his wallet, and there was usually a dollar or two in change.

She heard the door slam downstairs, and she realized that Duncan had come in from the barn. Perhaps even now he was dumping the contents of his pockets onto the little tray on the table.

She heard his footsteps on the stairs. As he always did, he went into his room at the other end of the hall and closed the door.

Jane sat on the edge of her bed, staring at the lemon-yellow walls and knowing what she had to do. Unemotionally she got up and prepared her clothes for tomorrow. She would have to leave early, before it was light. She would take only the things she had brought with her.

Except, perhaps, for the money on the downstairs table.

Chapter Four

That night Duncan couldn't sleep for thinking about Jane and her problems. She was a secretive woman, a frightened woman, and he knew that there was more to her than she wanted him to know. He longed for her to open up to him. He couldn't bear the bleak expression that he so often saw in her eyes.

There had been another woman once, his wife. He had been too busy to pay attention to the nuances of her behavior, thinking that they would eventually pass and she would be her old self once more. He'd been wrong about that. Sigrid had found someone who could be more responsive to her moods and had moved out one night a couple of years ago.

"It's not that I didn't love you," she had told him in parting. "It's just that I needed a man who could respond to me. And you never could."

The sad thing about it all was that he could have, he would have, if he'd only known how important it was to her. It wasn't that he wasn't empathetic. If anything, when faced with human problems, he always cared too much. But in the macho atmosphere in which he'd grown up, it hadn't been cool to show his feelings. With Rooney, with his father, it had embarrassed them when he tried. He learned how to cover up his caring, although he'd often managed to show people how he felt by his actions.

Then when he got married, it seemed like a whole new ball game. With his wife, he hadn't known how important it was to show how he felt, which meant that he'd really bungled their relationship. As he'd told her before she left, it wasn't that easy to open up after a lifetime of suppressing the expression of his emotions.

He'd had a couple of relationships since his divorce, and he'd worked on showing that he was the kind of understanding guy a woman would want. The relationships had never been too serious, but he felt equipped to deal with women now in a way that he had never been before, and he even felt grateful to Sigrid for making him learn something important about himself before it was too late.

Sigrid was very happy now; she had married her lover, and they were living in Albuquerque. Sigrid was expecting a baby soon.

And he, Duncan, was still alone. Since Jane had come, he hadn't felt so lonely, though. It was good to have a woman around again, even a woman who hardly spoke to him.

He'd been surprised to find that, despite the impression of Little Girl Lost, he felt desire for her as he watched her moving around his house. He chose not to act on it because he didn't want to add to whatever burdens she carried, and he suspected that they were considerable. He had never, for instance, bought that cock-and-bull story about her having a place to stay with a girlfriend in California.

Tonight she'd acted so skittish. He couldn't figure her. Her moods swung from confused to grateful to disoriented to apprehensive. Most of the time she seemed to be saying, "Please, please like me." Other times, he could swear she was recoiling from his presence.

Later that night, after Jane's light went out behind her closed bedroom door, Duncan roused himself from his solitary thoughts and went out again. He walked over to Rooney's house, something he often did late at night when he couldn't sleep. Rooney claimed to need very little sleep; he usually stayed up past midnight.

The two of them had, over the years, engaged in some productive bull sessions. The topics they covered ranged from cattle breeding to llama salesmanship, from getting along with women to rearing a ten-year-old girl. It was Duncan's belief that men could only be friends with men and women could only be friends with women. His friendship with Rooney over the years seemed to bear that out. Sigrid, his ex-wife, had certainly never been his friend.

When Duncan knocked on the door, Rooney welcomed him, offering him a cup of strong coffee, which Duncan turned down, figuring that the coffee would only keep him wider awake.

"So how's Jane?" Rooney wanted to know when they were sitting at the kitchen table finishing off the cheesecake Rooney had bought in town today. Mary Kate loved cheesecake and so did Duncan.

Duncan shrugged. "I don't know. Seems like she's recovering all right in a physical way, but I don't know what she's thinking. She's a strange woman, Rooney," he said.

Rooney lifted his eyebrows. "Ain't they all?"

"Not like her. She doesn't say much and certainly never mentions anything about herself."

"What do you expect? She might have an unsavory past, after all. You don't know where she came from. You ain't even sure where she's going."

Duncan considered this and decided there was merit in it. "That makes sense, I suppose, except that she doesn't look like somebody who could do anything wrong. She's a beautiful woman, Rooney. Have you ever noticed her eyes? And her hair? She reminds me of a Dresden figurine my grandmother used to have."

Rooney shot him a keen look. "Hey, you're not starting to feel something for her, are you?"

Duncan shifted uncomfortably in his chair before answering. "I don't know, Rooney. If anything, I'm sorry for her. She's such a sad little thing. She seldom smiles."

"She looks like a lady with a secret to me, old boy. If I was you, I wouldn't want to get too close. Never know when you might regret it."

"I thought maybe she'd open up when she started to feel better, maybe tell me why she's so all-fired eager to get to California. If that's where she's headed, that is. I see things about her that don't compute. I look at that ragged coat she was wearing when I found her and I wonder, 'How the dickens did she end up with a man's beat-up old topcoat to wear?' I've nearly worn myself out trying to figure her."

Rooney got up to pour more coffee into his cup. Before he sat down again, he clapped Duncan on the shoulder.

"You always did like a mystery, son. You'd better stick to the book variety, if you ask me. That reminds me. I picked up a few more mystery books at the library when I was in town. You want to take one home with you? Might get your mind off that little gal over there."

Duncan sighed, wishing that he hadn't confided in Rooney after all. "Yeah, Rooney, show me what you've got. I wouldn't mind reading for a while before I go to sleep," he said.

Rooney produced three well-worn paperback mystery books, Duncan chose the most promising one and took it home and to bed. All the while Duncan was reading, he couldn't stop pondering the mystery in his own house.

JANE ROSE the next morning before it was light, slipping into the jeans and shirt she'd had on when she found her way to the mine. Over those she put on the old coat, grateful that it was so warm and thick. It was bound to be cold outside.

She folded the discarded shirt of Duncan's that she used for a nightgown and left it on the bed. Carefully, feeling her way in the dark and with only the night-light from the bathroom for illumination, she pulled up the blue bedspread neatly over the bed and patted it into place. She would certainly miss this bed. It had been very comfortable.

She left the comb and brush and toiletries in the bathroom. After a moment's thought, she pocketed the toothbrush. No one else would want it, and Duncan would end up throwing it away, which seemed to her to be an awful waste of a useful object.

She tiptoed over to the heat register and picked up Amos, who, barely awake, snuggled unprotestingly inside her coat. Then, carefully and silently, she made her way downstairs.

The house was quiet, the outlines of the furniture barely discernible in the dark. Swiftly she made her way through the living room, saying goodbye to everything. *Goodbye, couch,* she said to herself as she passed it. *Goodbye, television set. Goodbye, fireplace.* It seemed silly and sentimental to say goodbye to inanimate things, but at least it gave her words to occupy her mind. She was afraid that if she thought about how much she would miss all the comforts that most people took for granted, she might not be able to leave after all.

She paused at the table beside the door. She felt around for the tray where Duncan kept his money. Her fingers closed around his wallet. He was such a trusting soul, Duncan. A person shouldn't trust other people so much.

She knew she had to survive somehow but felt terribly guilty about taking his money. She picked up the wallet, anyway. She carried it into the kitchen, where she shifted her weight first from one foot to the other in indecision. Yet what else could she do?

I'll pay it back, she thought. She set Amos down on the floor, and he immediately went to his food dish and started to eat.

She knew the location of the switch to turn on the fluorescent light over the sink, and she flipped it and waited while the light flickered and blinked on. She hadn't wanted to turn on any lights, but Duncan wouldn't be able to see this particular light from upstairs even if he got up, which she figured was unlikely at this hour.

Quickly she scrawled a note on the pad beside the telephone.

Duncan,
I needed money, so I took some out of your wallet. I'll pay you back as soon as I can.
Please think well of me,

she added after a pause. That was stupid, considering that she was actually robbing the man. She didn't like the way the last sentence read but didn't want to scratch it out, either, because then the note would look sloppy, and she didn't want him to think she was the kind of person who didn't care how a note looked to the person who received it. She signed it simply, "Jane."

She checked the money in the wallet. There were sixty dollars, so after a moment's deliberation she took fifty and left him ten. She stuffed the money into her coat pocket along with a few packages of crackers that were on the counter, and started to pick up Amos.

He pulled away from her, something he did so infrequently that it took her by surprise. He continued to eat the cat chow that Duncan had left in the dish for him.

At first she thought she would let Amos finish the last of the food, because she had no idea where their next meal would come from nor how long it would be until it materialized. Then she realized that there might not be any next meal for a long time and that she was being most unfair to Amos by taking him away from a place where he was sure to be warm and well fed. In the past week, his body had filled out and he didn't look so scrawny. His fur seemed thicker and sleeker.

"Amos, I guess this is where we come to a parting of the ways," she murmured. The thought of the lonely hours without him looming ahead of her brought a catch to her throat and tears to her eyes.

"Oh, Amos," she said, gathering the cat into her arms, and she buried her face in his ginger fur one last time. Puzzled by the unexpected display of affection, he twisted in her arms and batted an experimental paw against her cheek, seeming surprised to discover that it was wet.

Blinded by her tears, she put him down and quickly let herself out of the house before she lost her resolve. Then she set out for the highway. She knew exactly how to get there. Mary Kate had told her.

"Goodbye, llamas," she said as she passed the barn, regretting that she'd never learned anything more about them, had never, in fact, seen one up close. She spared a thought for Mary Kate, wondering if the child would miss her. Then she resolutely turned her back on Placid Valley Ranch.

She reached the highway as the sun sent up feeble fingers of light from the horizon. It was cold, but her coat kept her warm enough. Her breath preceded her in wispy clouds of mist that then trailed behind her as she walked, and as she plodded along she felt herself growing weary already. She was still weak from the strep and bronchitis, she thought. She'd soon be over that, and she had brought the half-used bottle of antibiotic pills with her. They'd continue to fight the infection.

If she were lucky, somebody would stop to pick her up soon. She gazed down the road, watching as a car barreled toward her. She stuck out her thumb and it whizzed past. Perhaps she'd have better luck next time.

She traipsed stoically through chunks of dirty snow at the edge of the highway, avoiding slippery patches of ice on the pavement. The next vehicle was a flatbed truck, and the driver didn't even notice her, much less stop to pick her up.

Jane blew on her gloveless hands to warm them, then thrust them deeper into her pockets, where Duncan's money crackled against her knuckles. She closed her hand around the bills, reassured by the security of so much cash. She walked westward, but no cars came for a long time. Finally she heard one approaching in the distance.

She turned toward it and stuck out her thumb, thinking that next time she hitchhiked in cold weather, she'd make sure she wore a pair of gloves. The Jeep Cherokee roared toward her at a blistering speed. And then it squealed to a stop.

She had barely wrenched the door open when a familiar voice growled, "Get in." It stopped her flat.

"You heard what I said," Duncan told her, barely containing his fury. He reached across the front seat and grabbed her wrist, yanking her toward him. She cried out in pain but clambered inside and watched him fearfully, wondering what he would do. Certainly he must have found out that she'd taken his money.

He slammed the vehicle into reverse and backed up, completing a turn in record time. When they were heading back to the ranch, he said coldly, "That was a fool thing to do."

Jane stared ahead, unwilling to face his anger.

"The two weeks you need for recuperating aren't up yet, and I don't take kindly to thieves. Also you left your cat."

At the mention of Amos, Jane's eyes filled with tears. She let them roll forlornly down her cheeks, hating herself for stealing and for her weakness now in front of Duncan. Duncan glanced over at her as they approached the turn onto the ranch road. He tossed a Kleenex in her direction.

"Use that Kleenex," he said more calmly. "Mop up."

Obediently she wiped her eyes, then turned toward him, wanting to explain.

"I was going to pay the money back," she said.

"We'll talk about it inside," he said gruffly.

Wordlessly she followed him into the house, where Amos ran to greet them, purring and rubbing against her ankles.

"Amos missed you," said Duncan, heavy on the irony. Uncertainly Jane picked up the cat and stood stroking him, holding him up as a shield.

"What are you going to do to me? Are you going to call the sheriff?" she asked in a tremulous voice when it seemed as though they would go on standing there and staring at each other forever.

"*Do* to you?" He shook his head as if to clear it. "What do you think? That I'm going to punish you? God, you have me pegged all wrong."

"Here," she said, yanking the money out of her pocket. "Take it back."

"It's not the money," he said, running his hand through his hair and looking more disturbed than she'd ever seen him. "It's your safety. You could easily become sick again, and as for hitchhiking, it's a dangerous thing to do!"

Something broke inside her. This man who lived such a safe and secure life—what did he know about survival? Had he ever had to live on the streets, wondering where his next meal was coming from? Had he ever tried to get a job and discovered that no one would hire him because there was no proof on paper that he existed?

"Don't tell me how to live!" she said. At her outburst Amos jumped down and ran away, and she didn't blame him.

Duncan's surprised look only spurred her on.

"I've been living from hand to mouth, scared to death because people try to hustle me and hurt me and—well, you can't possibly know about the real dangers I've faced! Hitchhiking seems tame by comparison."

"Jane, I only meant—"

"Try getting through the winter with no warm clothes! Try to find a job when you don't have a social security number! Try to find a little warmth and human kindness where none exists, and if that fails—if that fails—oh, God, why am I trying to tell you?" The money slipped unnoticed from her hand and fluttered to the floor, where it lay between them.

For a long time Duncan was quiet. The only sounds were those of her breathing and, once, a cough.

Duncan thought of Sigrid. If he had listened to her instead of brushing her off when she tried to speak to him of the matters closest to her heart, things might have been different.

"Why *are* you trying to tell me?" he inquired at last, repeating Jane's question, and his tone was so soft and gentle that she turned around, incredulous that he wasn't still angry.

He walked to her and put an arm around her shoulders. It was such a touching gesture that she felt her reserve starting to crumble. She wanted to reach out to him, to make him hold her in his arms and comfort her. He was so strong and solid; he was so nice.

"You're trying to tell me because you want to tell someone," he said, steering her to the couch and easing her down beside him. His eyes radiated goodness and goodwill, and she wasn't afraid of him. She wondered how he was able to find forgiveness in his heart after she had abused his hospitality, and she felt pained on his behalf because he had misplaced his trust in her.

"Tell me," he said, and when she looked at him she saw such sympathy and understanding that all the barriers fell away. After that, there was nothing else to do but begin her story at the beginning.

Chapter Five

Her life began—her present life, that is—one frosty November morning on the outskirts of an Illinois cornfield almost fifteen months ago.

The first thing to penetrate her consciousness was an inadvertent blow on the right leg, delivered by a muddy boot.

The first words she heard were, "What's this?"

The first object in her line of vision was a scared young boy breathing open-mouthed into her face.

"She's dead, Pop, ain't she?"

A warm hand touched her cheek, and she moaned.

"No, she's not dead. Run call an ambulance, Ollie! Quick!"

The boy's panicked footsteps crashed away through the nearby woods, and Jane became aware of tentative fingers checking her legs and arms for broken bones. When the man noticed that she was looking at him, he said, "There, now. I've sent for an ambulance. Just lie quiet, and it'll be here in a few minutes."

She was cold, so cold. And her head ached with the worst pain imaginable. The only reply she was able to make was another groan.

The ambulance took her to the Tyree Township Hospital, a small rural facility with only fifty-seven beds, and as soon as she reached the emergency room, someone asked for her identification.

"She doesn't have any," the farmer in whose field she had been found told the admitting clerk. The clerk followed the gurney right into the emergency room cubicle and stood clucking over her as the nurses swabbed the cut on the back of her head.

"Next of kin?" the clerk asked briskly, her pencil poised over the proper line on the form.

"I don't know," her rescuer said, stepping in to help when he realized that Jane wasn't able to speak.

"Honey, what's your name?" the clerk asked her, when she saw that Jane's eyes had opened.

It was a question that drew a complete blank.

"Well?"

She tried very hard to form words. "My n-name?" she managed to say.

"Yes, honey. I've got to have a name."

"Can't think," Jane mumbled. She felt as though she were wrapped in an invisible cocoon, sealed off from everyone and everything. Everything, that is, but the pain in her head.

"Well, that's okay. You just rest, and I'll be back in a few minutes," the clerk said as the punch bell on the admitting desk began to ring wildly, signifying that someone was looking for her. She disappeared through the twin swinging doors, and Jane felt a sense of relief at no longer being badgered for information that she couldn't give.

A doctor came in. "I'm Dr. Bergstrom," he said. He peered into one eye, then the other. He shook his head over her bruised cheekbone, her swollen eyelid, and then sewed up the cut on the back of her head.

"How'd all this happen, anyway?" he asked as he was stripping off his surgical gloves.

"I don't know," she answered in a small voice.

The farmer, who told her hesitantly that his name was Carlton Jones, explained to Dr. Bergstrom that he had stumbled upon her lying not far from the highway in a ditch on the edge of one of his fields, when he and his son were out looking for a lost hunting dog.

"There she was, lying there like she was dead," he said. "I thought she *was* dead. At first I figured she might have had an accident on the highway, but there was no car anywhere around."

"Do you remember anything?" Dr. Bergstrom asked her.

"No," Jane whispered. The sharp pain in her head had subsided to a dull, pounding ache. She didn't know these people or this place or about any accident. As far as she was concerned, this experience was the first thing that had ever happened to her. She didn't know who she was or where she was supposed to be, although she understood that she was expected to know these things and that these people were beginning to be annoyed that she did not.

Mr. Jones apparently knew the doctor, and the two men engaged in an intense discussion out in the hall, during which Jane heard Mr. Jones say, "But Doc, I don't know anything about her. I *sure* can't pay any hospital bill."

The doctor said wearily, "We'll go ahead and admit her to the hospital, but I have to call the police."

After that, the doctor, forcing a stiff smile, hurried back into the cubicle, and Jane was wheeled into a dingy little room with beige walls, cracked plaster on the ceiling, and nineteen-fifties-vintage venetian blinds with one slat missing. Finally, thankfully, she slept.

When she awoke, a man she'd never seen before was lounging beside her bed.

"I'm Detective Sid Reedy of the Tyree County Sheriff's Department," he said in an impersonal tone.

She blinked.

"I'm trying to find out a few things about your accident," he said.

"I don't remember," she murmured, but he hadn't heard her.

"What's that?"

"I don't remember," she said in a louder tone.

"I have to fill out a report," he said, slapping a clipboard against his knee. "Why don't you just tell me what happened?"

"All I know is I woke up and a boy was looking at me."

"Right. You were lying in a ditch between Jones's field and the highway. What I need to know is how you got there."

"I don't remember," she repeated, sounding even to her own ears like a broken record.

"Look, lady, it's late, and I'd like to get home in time for dinner just this once. So if your boyfriend pushed you out of a car or something, don't be embarrassed. I've seen and heard everything, believe me. Just let me fill out my report and I'll leave you alone." He was frowning at her now.

She squeezed her eyes tightly shut, trying to figure out if that was what had happened. But if she had a boyfriend, she couldn't picture his face; if she had been riding in a car, she couldn't recall anything about it. She forced herself to narrow her range of thoughts down to a single pinpoint somewhere inside her brain, trying to remember, to remember....

"Well?"

The sudden question interrupted her effort. A crushing feeling of helplessness descended on her. If only she could satisfy these people—the admitting clerk, the doctor, this insensitive policeman. They all demanded something that she couldn't give, and she felt so sad that it wasn't within her power to help them.

"I'm sorry," she said, on the verge of tears. "I'm really sorry."

He slapped the clipboard against his leg again, and the noise startled her.

"Okay, okay," he muttered, and he strode out of the room, slamming the door behind him.

Tears were etching shiny trails down Jane's cheeks and falling unheeded onto the pillow by the time a nurse arrived. The nurse's name tag identified her as R. Sanchez.

"Oh, did he upset you? Can I get you anything?" asked the little nurse, who appeared to be very young.

A name, she thought, staring at the nurse's name tag with longing. *Get me a name.* But she didn't say it.

Dr. Bergstrom didn't return to her room until late that night. He wore an expression of concern.

"Having any luck with your memory?" he asked.

She shook her head.

He sat down beside the bed. "Try to remember what you were doing the day of your accident. Who you might have been with, where you went," he urged quietly.

Jane tried, but there was nothing. No associations, no fragments of conversation, no faces.

"It's just—blank," she said unhappily.

"I've had the police run a missing persons check. There's no one who matches your description. No accidents have been reported along that particular stretch of highway, either. You seem to have appeared out of nowhere."

She swallowed and stared at him. "What's going to happen to me?" she ventured.

He stood up and shook his head. "I hope you're going to remember something," he said grimly before he left.

But she didn't remember anything. As far as she was concerned, she was nobody.

It was extremely frustrating not to be able to identify anything about her past life. At night when she was alone she would stare up at the stained ceiling above her hospital bed and wonder, *Who am I?* The more she tried to figure it out, the more defeated she felt. There seemed to be no clues.

Her clothing was ordinary, the kind that could have been bought in any J. C. Penney store anywhere in the United States. When a search was conducted in the area where she had been found, someone turned up a purse that might have been hers. It was handmade of a coarsely woven wool fabric, but there was nothing in it to prove that it belonged to her—no money, no personal effects, and most importantly, no identification. Someone put it in the closet along with the salvageable clothing she was wearing when Carlton Jones and his son found her. She would take it with her when she left, she supposed.

Dr. Bergstrom brought her a United States atlas, and she sat for hours poring over it, hoping that one of the town names or river names or highways might seem familiar. Because Chicago was the nearest big city, the sympathetic little nurse, whose name was Rosemary Sanchez, brought photos of some of the places there—O'Hare Airport, Lincoln Park, the Magnificent Mile, a five-story Picasso sculpture. None of them jogged her memory.

She watched television, hoping that she would see clues to her background on the local news. She didn't.

After a feature story about her plight in the local newspaper, Rosemary began to call her Jane Doe, first as a kind of joke, then more seriously. By the time she left the hospital two weeks later, it was the only name she knew. The hospital staff had grown so fond of her that they took up a collection to pay her bill, because as far as anyone knew, she had no insurance, and she certainly had no money.

A welter of good wishes accompanied her discharge. Rosemary tied helium balloons to the wheelchair that they insisted she ride to the door, and an aide settled a bouquet of flowers in her arms. Besides the handwoven purse, she carried a small donated suitcase that was too big for the meager change of clothes someone had given her.

Dr. Bergstrom had, with great difficulty, found a place for her to stay in the nearby medium-sized town of Apollonia, Illinois, where the department of social services had agreed to help her find a job. But her assigned social worker, a Miss Bird, whose task it was to pick her up at the hospital and install her at the shelter for battered women where she was to stay, turned out to be a malcontent who was miffed because she would rather have been out shopping for her trousseau.

When they got to the big converted house in Apollonia, Miss Bird all but pushed Jane out of the car and would have driven away before Jane retrieved her suitcase from the back seat if Jane had not yelped in protest. There wasn't time to grab the bouquet of flowers or Rosemary's balloons. Jane was abandoned at the curbside and left to introduce herself to the shelter's administrator, who stated with some irritation that Jane didn't really fall into the category of women that the shelter was supposed to help but would be allowed to stay anyway, since they had an opening.

Jane felt abandoned, exhausted, worried and confused. She was subject to incapacitating headaches that did not abate even with the strong pain medicine that Dr. Bergstrom had prescribed.

For two weeks Jane lived at the shelter, helping the other women care for their children when she could. The women were grateful but wary for reasons of their own. Jane made no friends.

When Jane went to the social services office for her first appointment with Miss Bird, who was supposed to help her find a job, she was curtly informed that the woman had been fired.

"Is there another social worker I should see?" Jane asked anxiously as she stood at the counter.

A harried clerk looked up from her filing.

"What?"

"Have I been assigned to another social worker?"

"I'll look it up in a minute," the woman said with a sigh.

After a short time, the clerk disappeared into a back room for fifteen minutes. When she came back, she stared at Jane as though she'd never seen her before.

"Can I help you?"

"I was waiting to see if I was assigned to another social worker," Jane reminded her.

"Oh, sure." The woman leafed through a pile of folders. "You're supposed to talk to Mrs. Engel, but she's got appointments scheduled all afternoon. You'll have to come back tomorrow."

Jane did return the next day, only to be informed that Mrs. Engel was out sick. And that day she was asked to leave the women's shelter.

"It's not that we want you to leave," the administrator of the shelter told her apologetically. "It's just that we need your room for a woman with two children, whose safety could be jeopardized if she doesn't get out of her home. Surely you understand."

"Of course," Jane said, and quietly packed her suitcase.

When she left, she had no idea where to go. She headed for the local McDonald's and sat there for four hours, nursing a blinding headache and trying to summon up the nerve to ask for a job. When she did, the manager told her that he was sorry, but he had no openings. She was terrified when she walked out. Where was she to go? What was she to do?

Thus ensued several days and nights when Jane, her head pounding, wandered the street by day and slept in the bus station by night. Finally the night manager at the bus station told her that she wasn't welcome there anymore. She would have to find somewhere else to sleep.

But where? She had no money, and she had no car. She had no identification. She didn't even have a name.

She forced herself to think optimistically and managed to land a job in a small restaurant called the Buttercup Café, slinging hamburgers behind the counter. An advance on her salary made it possible for her to rent a room in a run-down house. Jane, whose spirits had lifted, didn't mind, though. At least it was a place to sleep.

Then, perhaps because of the poor nutrition, she caught a particularly bad cold and lost her job when she couldn't work for a week. And when she didn't have enough money to pay her rent, she was politely asked to leave the boarding house.

At her wit's end, she called Mrs. Engel, the new social worker, from a pay phone and asked for an appointment.

"I can't see you until Monday," Mrs. Engel told her.

"But I'm really desperate," Jane said. By this time she was talking in a monotone. She had no energy to put into her voice. Her head had been aching steadily for several days, and the pain showed no sign of abating.

"I'm so sorry, but I have a full schedule. What time can you come on Monday?"

"I need help now," Jane said, her spirits sinking even further. This was Thursday. Monday was four days away. How would she survive until then?

"Ten o'clock Monday is the best I can do," said Mrs. Engel.

"All right," Jane replied. After she hung up the phone, she felt around in the coin return pocket in case her quarter had fallen into it, but it hadn't.

She couldn't think of anyone else who might help her. The people in the hospital in Tyree seemed far away; after all they'd already done for her, she couldn't expect more help from them. Even the nurse—the helpful one, Rosemary—wouldn't want to hear from her now. Jane was all alone.

That night Jane lingered outside a bar beneath a lamppost decorated with a Styrofoam candy cane in honor of the winter holiday season. Finally, summoning all her nerve, Jane stopped one of the patrons when he was on his way out. He bought her suitcase and the clothes in it for five dollars, squinting curiously at her in the dim light. Jane spent two dollars and sixty-nine cents on a skimpy hamburger, French fries, and a glass of milk at an all-night diner.

By the time the first angry streak of pink sunrise appeared in the eastern sky, Jane was walking along the highway outside town, hoping desperately that someone—anyone—would offer her a ride.

Finally an elderly couple with a small dog pulled over to the side of the road and beckoned her to get into their Buick. Jane didn't hesitate; she climbed right in.

"You look like you need a ride," the woman said, peering at Jane over the top of the front seat. "You going far?"

"Chicago," Jane said.

"So are we," the man told her. "Then we'll be traveling on to Milwaukee."

"We're going to visit our son in Chicago for Christmas and to our daughter's house in Milwaukee for New Year's," the woman supplied. "Are you going visiting, too?"

"No, I'm looking for a job," Jane said.

"Seems like if we're going to be riding all the way to Chicago together, we ought to be better acquainted. We're the Fosters—Betty and Herman. Our dog is Trixie. What's your name?" the woman asked.

"Jane," Jane said reluctantly. She didn't want to give her last name as "Doe." They wouldn't believe her, and her head hurt so much that she wasn't up to elaborate explanations.

"Jane what?" the woman asked.

A moving van hurtled past in the other lane, and on the side of it was emblazoned Rhodes Moving and Storage.

"Rhodes," Jane said. "Jane Rhodes."

"Well, Jane Rhodes, would you like a doughnut?" The woman reached over the top of the seat and waved a box of freshly baked doughnuts under Jane's nose.

"Thank you," Jane said gratefully and took two when the woman insisted. Trixie clambered into the back seat and licked one of the doughnuts, so Jane ended up sharing it with the dog, and afterward Trixie curled up with her head on Jane's lap, which was somehow comforting.

When they arrived in Chicago, the Fosters exchanged puzzled looks when Jane wasn't sure where she wanted to be dropped off, and finally they let her out of the car on Sheridan Road near an elevated station around the corner from where their son lived.

"Are you sure you don't want us to take you somewhere else?" Betty Foster called out the open car window, looking askance at the papers blowing around in the gutter and a few questionable characters hanging out in front of a store where all the signs in the window were printed in a foreign language.

"No, this is fine," Jane said, thanking them with a confident smile.

After the Fosters' car pulled away from the curb, Jane looked hopefully around her at the tall buildings, the traffic-clogged street and the people streaming in and out of the el station. A Salvation Army Santa stood on the pavement, energetically clanging his bell. From somewhere floated the tinny strains of a Christmas carol. Across the street were two restaurants, and the structure on the corner looked like an office building.

This was clearly a city where lots of things were going on. There were many places to work, and one of those jobs could be hers. Maybe, just maybe, she'd find the luck that had eluded her so far.

She lifted her chin and headed directly into the wind, not minding that the bite of it nearly took her breath away. She had made it to Chicago, tomorrow she would find a job, and soon everything would be all right. It was, after all, a season of hope. This New Year would be a new beginning in her new life.

THERE WAS MORE to her story, but Jane had to pause for a moment to catch her breath. The only sounds were the steady tick-tock of the clock on the mantel and the throaty rumble of Amos's purr.

"I think I'll put on the coffeepot," Duncan said. "Would you like a cup?"

She nodded, and he studied her for a moment before he stood and went into the kitchen. Amos stretched, got up, and followed Duncan.

What was Duncan thinking? she wondered. Did he believe her story, or did he think she was making it all up? It did, now that she thought of it, sound pretty fantastic. But it was true, all of it, every detail. She wished with all her heart that it wasn't.

She sighed and wiggled her right foot, which had gone to sleep. When the feeling returned, she went into the kitchen, where Duncan was refilling the sugar bowl.

"I thought I'd fix sandwiches," he said. "Neither of us has eaten, I suspect."

"I'll do it," she said.

He pressed his lips together. "All right," he said. "I guess you know where everything is."

Jane found sliced roast beef in the meat drawer of the refrigerator and piled it high on rye bread, the way she knew Duncan liked it. It was funny how many things she knew about him after living here during the past week. How he liked his coffee strong, for instance, and that he saved the daily newspaper to read at lunchtime. He also knew many things about her, as evidenced by the way he ran a bit of cold water from the faucet into her coffee, because she didn't like it either too strong or too hot.

"Aren't you going to eat?" he demanded when he saw that she had made only one sandwich.

"I'm not hungry," she murmured, setting the plate with the sandwich on it on the kitchen table at the place where he usually sat.

"Don't be silly," he said. He took another plate out of the cupboard and deposited half of his sandwich on it.

"Sit down and eat it," he directed. When she saw the stern expression on his face, she sat. She still wasn't sure that he wouldn't turn her over to the local sheriff for stealing his money.

He didn't speak before he took the first few bites of his sandwich, but after that he set the sandwich on the plate and leaned back in his chair.

"I take it things didn't work out for you when you got to Chicago," he said abruptly.

Her mouth was full of food, and she shook her head. That was an understatement.

"So you're going where?" His eyes pierced her.

Jane swallowed. The food sat like a lump somewhere in her chest, but she decided to continue the fiction she had started when she first arrived.

"California," she said. "I told you that I'm going to California. I want to start over there."

He stared out the window, apparently lost in thought. Though his face remained still and expressionless, his eyes were dark and gleamed with—what? She was reminded of a fire, damped and believed quenched, but with a glowing coal at its heart.

"What's your girlfriend's name?" he asked, shooting the question at her abruptly.

"Elizabeth," she said, lifting her chin and daring him to dispute this.

"Elizabeth *what*?"

"Elizabeth...um, Elizabeth *Maxwell*," she said, glimpsing the coffee container on the counter.

"Maxwell? Are you sure about that?" he asked, sounding dangerously skeptical.

"Well, she just got married," Jane improvised, worried that he might try to trace an Elizabeth Maxwell and not sure how common that name was. "Her name is Smith now."

"Right. Elizabeth Smith. You've already told me how you made up your own name. Do you expect me to believe this—this *bull* about an Elizabeth Maxwell Smith?"

To his amazement, she burst into tears.

He hadn't had any idea that this was imminent. Since this morning, when he'd first realized that she'd fled into the frigid Wyoming winter, he had drastically revised his assessment of her. She was deceptively frail looking, he had decided, a delicate beauty who, underneath that soft, fragile exterior resembled nothing so much as a steely trap. He hadn't expected tears.

While he was still trying to figure out how to respond, she dried her eyes on her sleeve and glared at him in defiance.

"All right," she said. "I lied. I have no girlfriend in California, no place to stay when I get there. I don't have a job and I'm not a librarian. I'm going to California, though. That much is true."

He appeared to be thinking things over, and she didn't speak again. *He's going to throw me out,* she thought in growing panic as time passed and he said nothing. *He's trying to figure out whether to have me arrested.*

"Look," she said. "I'm sorry I took the money. I knew when I did it that I shouldn't have. Just let me go now, and I won't bother you anymore."

"Go?" he said. "Are you joking?"

She swallowed the lump in her throat.

"Just let me out of here, let me go," she repeated, becoming distraught. She rushed out of the kitchen and yanked her coat from the closet near the front door, knocking over a kitchen chair in her haste.

"Keep Amos, please," she said as she struggled into her coat. "I can't give him a good home, and you can. If you'll just keep him for me, I'll send for him when I get to California, or maybe I'll send money for his food, if that's what you want—"

"Jane," he said, gripping her shoulders hard and shaking her so that the hair fell back from her face.

"Let me *go*," she said, tugging away from him so that she could place a well-aimed kick, if necessary.

"I want to help you," he said forcefully.

"I told you I want out of here," she said, grating the words, through clenched teeth.

"Didn't you hear me, you little fool? I'll help you," he repeated, and finally the words sank in.

She all but went limp. "You will?" she said unbelievingly.

He retained his grip on her. "I'll buy you a plane ticket to California," he said.

"Why?" she asked warily.

"Because you've had some bad breaks," he said, clipping the words off sharply.

"No one else ever cared enough—I mean, no one else ever wanted to help." She wrenched her shoulders out of his grasp.

"Well, I do. I'll lend you money, help you get some identification, whatever you need to start this new life you seem to want so desperately. But it'll have to be on my terms."

Jane stared at him. She might have guessed that there would be a catch. Of course he would have conditions, and she could well guess what they might be. As an attractive woman wandering the streets and traveling the highways, she had been subjected to the most disgusting and brutal suggestions. There were many ways that she could have made money, but she'd never gone in for that sort of thing. Never had the heart for it. Now Duncan was going to be like all the rest of the men who had tried to hustle her. She had been wrong to think that he was different.

"Aren't you interested in what those terms are?"

When she didn't answer, he said, "All right, then. I'll tell you. I want you to stay here until you're well. Until the weather is warmer. Until spring."

She waited, figuring that there was more to it. Finally she lifted her eyelids and saw that he was looking at her with an expression of compassion, which somehow was not what she had expected.

"And?" she said boldly. She might as well get this over with; there was bound to be more. She wanted him to come right out and say whatever else he expected.

"And?" he repeated.

"And what kind of payment do you expect for this kindness?" she said.

"Pay—" Dawning enlightenment spread across his face. To her amazement, a dark flush started at his collar and spread upward. He began to pace the floor.

"I want nothing from you, Jane. Nothing except your promise to stay here until you're well again. After that I will see you off on a plane and you'll never have to see me again. That's all, everything. I require no—*favors*," he said, underlining the word with scorn.

She stared at him. To her utter amazement, she believed him. True, he was a normal red-blooded American male. True, he had been deprived of steady female companionship ever since his wife had left. But he was apparently not looking for the kind of relationship that she had supposed.

Jane was overcome with a feeling of shame. It was only natural for her to think what she had thought; that this was a man who saw the opportunity to claim some sort of benefit from the fact that she was indebted to him. And yet she should have known— she *did* know—that Duncan Tate was a trustworthy sort and that he would do nothing to harm her.

"I'm so embarrassed," she said, dropping her face to her hands. That way she wouldn't have to look at him.

He uttered a long sigh and touched a hand to her arm.

"Don't be," he said. "I can see why you might have thought that I—that I—oh, hell, what am I trying to say?"

He waited a moment and continued. "Look—um, Jane. My intentions are honorable. It so happens that I have plenty of room here, as well as the financial resources to help you get a fresh start. It's irrelevant at the moment that you happen to be a very beautiful woman. Anyone in your circumstances would warrant my help. So what about it? Will you take me up on it, or are you so all-fired stubborn that you'll try to sneak away again?"

She lifted her head. He was, miracle of miracles, smiling at her. His good humor in the face of all she had done humbled her.

Maybe this was the chance she had prayed for, the lucky break that she had dreamed about. Was she too stupid to recognize good fortune when it stared her in the face?

There was an old-fashioned settle beside the door, and she sank onto it.

"I can't believe you mean it," she said, her eyes searching his for reassurance.

"Of course I mean it," he said. "I don't say things that I don't mean."

"I wish I hadn't taken your money. I can hardly bear to look at you when I think of it."

He stood before her, his hands linked through the loops of his jeans. "We'll never mention the money again. Okay?"

She pressed her fingers to her eyelids, fighting tears. "Okay," she said, overwhelmed by his generosity. "But I want to repay you for your kindness. I'll stay, and I'll work around the house or cook or look after Mary Kate—"

He started to laugh. "Looking after Mary Kate! Now that's a fitting punishment, if ever I heard one."

Jane lifted her hand and stared at him, wondering how he could joke. "What I'm trying to say is that I'm grateful. Maybe this is the best chance I'll ever have to get back on track. To make it."

"So you'll stay? Until spring?" He looked anxious and unsure; she didn't want him to change his mind.

"Until spring," she agreed quickly.

"Let's shake hands on it," Duncan said.

She stood up, and they shook hands solemnly, then Duncan helped her remove her coat and hung it in the closet.

"I'm overdue for an appointment in town, so I've got to leave," Duncan said. He ran upstairs, where she heard him rattling around, and he hurried out with a quick goodbye. In a minute or two she heard the roar of the Cherokee's engine, as it disappeared up the drive toward the road.

And then she saw that Duncan had left the money she'd stolen on the table near the door.

She couldn't believe that after what she'd done, he would go away on the very same day and leave her alone with not only the money she'd taken from his wallet but with all his possessions. If she'd had a mind to run, she could have stolen him blind.

Jane had no desire to run anymore. Now all she wanted was to prove herself worthy of Duncan Tate's help. She felt a sudden rush of warmth and gratitude toward him. She had lost her faith in people, but he had shown her that goodness and mercy still existed in this world.

Her guilt about what she had done to him was tremendous. But she'd have plenty of time to make it up to him. Because she was going to keep her promise.

She would stay until spring.

Chapter Six

Jane didn't know how to behave around him, and so in her confusion she turned away entirely and, for solace, withdrew into herself. She crept silently around the house when he was there; she didn't eat meals with him, but took a tray to her room. At night she heard the chatter of the television set and the hollow echoes of Duncan's boot heels as he moved about downstairs, and only came out of her room for a late snack if she was sure he wasn't in the house.

These avoidance tactics proved successful for the next few days, until finally he called her on it.

She thought he'd left the house for his office in the barn. Duncan usually came in at lunchtime, ate while he read the daily newspaper, and sometimes watched the television set, and immediately afterward she'd heard the front door slam, but he must only have opened the door for Amos, she realized later.

She was coming out of her bedroom when his solid bulk blocked the hall, so she dodged him, only to have him move right along with her.

"What's this all about?" he demanded.

"What do you mean?" she answered, her heart stepping up its beat. She was sure of his essential goodness, but no matter how much she liked him, she couldn't help being fearful of people; she had been conditioned to it on the streets.

"I mean I want to know why you're avoiding me," he said, wrinkling his forehead at her. He had a way of cocking his head to one side and waiting for her replies, and he did this now. He didn't seem angry, only perplexed, but there was something forceful in his manner too, and that alarmed her.

In her limited experience, most people who were prepared to be forceful were also inclined to be mean, and although this didn't square with what she knew of Duncan's character, her body went into its flight-for-survival mode. Her shoulders tensed, her stomach knotted, and her eyes widened.

"Come on, Jane, you know you've been staying out of my way," he said. "Ever since the day you tried to walk out of here, you've crept about trying not to run into me, and you've managed to be pretty successful at it, too."

He waited to see what she would say, and she wished that she were anywhere but here, facing Duncan Tate, having to explain her actions. Before she came here she hadn't had to answer to anyone, or if she had, it had only been under duress and to people who were uncommonly nosy about things that were none of their business, such as, "Where do you live?" or "Who was your last employer?" Her favorite defense had always been to hightail it out of there, but that wouldn't work in this instance. Duncan was too big and fast and too smart to outrun; he'd already proven it, when she'd set out on her little jaunt up the highway.

"I didn't think you'd want to see me," she murmured, focusing on the top of his right shoulder, which was on the level of her eyes. She wouldn't look at his face. His expression would only make her feel guiltier than she already felt.

"If I didn't want to see you, I wouldn't let you stay here. I'd send you over to Rooney's, or put you up in the tack room in the barn," he pointed out in a gentler tone.

"After what I did—" Jane whispered, looking stricken.

"Eaten up by guilt, are you?" he said. "Well, maybe that's all to the good. If you feel guilty about certain things, I guess you'll keep your part of our bargain."

She noticed that, true to his word, he was being careful not to mention the money she'd stolen. But her eyes involuntarily glanced up at the suggestion that she didn't intend to stay until spring.

"I'm going to do exactly what I said I would," she said defensively. "I'm not going to run away again."

He relaxed visibly and smiled. "I'm glad to hear that, but I think we need to talk about how we're going to run this household while you're here. There's got to be a better way than the way we've been doing it."

"Just tell me what to do, and I'll do it." She felt cornered; she had no desire to sit down with Duncan and discuss anything.

"I *am* telling you what to do," he said smoothly, taking her hand and pulling her along the hall, down the stairs and through the house until they stood in the kitchen.

"Where to have this discussion, that's the question," he mused out loud, finally dragging her along to the seldom-used dining room, with its eight-armed chandelier and his mother's rose-patterned china arrayed along the top of the buffet.

"This will do," he said, looking around with satisfaction. "I don't use the dining room much, but the table is a good place to sit and face each other with our concerns. Sit down, Jane. Well, don't just stand there! Sit down!"

Embarrassed, she pulled out one of the heavy chairs and sat.

"Now, the thing about this meeting is that it probably won't be the last one we have. Anytime something concerns one of us, we have the right to discuss it. Okay?" His dark eyes sparkled at her.

She seemed to have no choice but to go along with him. Certainly she had no idea what it took to live in harmony with other people in a real household, and her assumption that the best way to go about it was to stay out of everyone's way was apparently wrong, at least in Duncan's eyes.

"The thing that bothers me most is that you're here, but I never see you. You used to come down to the kitchen, help with the dishes—"

"Haven't I been helping out enough?"

Duncan sighed and looked frustrated. "Look, this isn't about helping around the house, although I appreciate the things you've done. It's about why we never see each other anymore." His eyes were direct and honest.

"Under the circumstances, I didn't want to see you," she said in a small voice, deciding that if he was going to be up-front about the way he felt, she could be forthright, too.

He studied her for a moment. "I thought you understood that all is forgiven," he said.

She looked down at the table, wishing she could crawl under it. "I guess I didn't really believe it," she said. It was the truth.

For a long time neither of them spoke, and again she didn't dare look at him.

Finally he stood up and walked around the table until he stood in front of the window, staring out. Outside the rugged landscape rose into shadowy white peaks in the distance; pines stood green-black against the mountain slopes.

"I said I didn't want anything from you, but I was wrong," he said in a low tone. He heaved a great sigh and turned around. Her eyes widened as she waited to see what he would say next.

"Don't worry," he said hastily, "it's not what you think." He walked over to her chair and stood in front of her. "What I want from you is companionship," he said quietly.

"I don't understand," Jane said, at a loss for words. She'd never suspected this side of Duncan before. She'd been so caught up in her own problems, her own attitudes, that she'd never considered him as a real person with real wants and needs.

"I don't like living alone," he said in a purely conversational tone as he sat down again.

"But Rooney—Mary Kate—" Jane stammered, at a loss to think how he could feel alone with them living right next door.

"They have their own lives," he said calmly. "Rooney is a good friend, but he's wrapped up in making his granddaughter toe the line, and rightly so, I suppose. As for Mary Kate as a companion—well, she's only a child. In my limited experience, ten-year-olds don't make especially good friends for anyone except other ten-year-olds."

"I thought you'd like your privacy," she said, regaining her composure.

"I told you one time that to me, privacy is the same as loneliness. I meant it," he said.

She sensed his emotion; it was there in his eyes for her to see. She wanted to look away, because it embarrassed her, but maybe this was the way people were supposed to make contact with each other. She managed to hold his gaze until he smiled, and this almost, but not quite, broke the tension.

"So no more hiding when I come into the house. I enjoy your company around here at night, even if it's only watching television together. And meals—why can't we eat at the same table?"

"We could," she said, feeling out of her element. Didn't he realize that she knew nothing about carrying on a one-on-one relationship with another person? She hadn't grown close to anyone since they'd found her in that ditch.

"Would it be so hard for you? Am I so difficult to be around?" He smiled at her again, this time more engagingly, and she felt the considerable pull of his magnetism.

"You're not, Duncan. I wish I could explain. You see, I don't think you understand. It's just—just—"

He watched her struggle for words and realized that she wasn't making excuses not to interact with him but was struggling to express a thought that she couldn't get a handle on. He waited patiently while she tried to articulate it and wished there was something he could do to wipe that pinched look from her face and the confusion from her eyes.

"I'm not trying to avoid talking to you right now, at this moment," Jane finally explained, her face flushing. "It's just that sometimes it's like that for me—I can't get the words out. It might have something to do with that blow on the head."

"Take your time," he told her, wishing that he knew more about amnesia and how it worked.

"Anyway, what I was trying to say is that I'm not so much afraid of you as I am about being around other people. I've learned that you're to be trusted, and Mary Kate and Rooney too, but once I get past that point I don't know how to act. I always had to be careful of other people getting too close so they wouldn't steal what money I had, or of people who had less than honorable intentions, or—well, I'm sure you get the idea. And now . . ." Her voice trailed off.

"It's okay, Jane, you don't have to talk about it if it upsets you," he said.

"I want to. Before I didn't, but now I do." She drew a deep breath, for some reason feeling free to be straight with him as she never had with any other person within her memory. Maybe it was because he had been so open with her, but for whatever reason, it was as if all her emotions, pent up for so long, burst forth.

"Don't you see that I haven't had a background of being close to anyone?" she said in a rush. "I don't remember any family. And I never made friends when I was trying to survive out on the streets. The plain truth is that I don't know how to act around you, Duncan. And it's not just you. It's everyone else, too." When she finished speaking, her eyes searched his face for understanding.

He didn't know what to say. It was, he thought, perfectly natural to assume that the people we deal with every day have the same frame of reference that we do. And yet, as in Jane's case, it wasn't always true. Often when dealing with other people we assume too much. We should make an effort to think the way they think. If he had, he might have approached her in a more gentle way.

He raked his fingers through his hair in frustration. "I'm sorry," he said. "It never crossed my mind that just being here with me might take a great effort on your part."

"How were you to know?" she said, calmer now.

He closed his eyes for a minute, and when he opened them, he saw that hers were brimming with tears.

"Is something wrong?" he asked.

She shook her head and wiped the tears away before they could spill down her cheeks.

"No. It's a relief to talk to someone. I've never been that honest before. With anyone. I've had to lie and cheat and—"

"Shh," he said comfortingly, reaching over and stilling her lips with two fingers. The bodily contact startled her, and he took his fingers away, but not before he noted that she had very soft lips.

"I'm not going to lie anymore," she said with great determination. "Ever."

He glimpsed the steel behind those blue eyes, the same toughness that had helped her to survive so many hardships. He cleared his throat. "You don't have to promise me anything else," he said uncomfortably. "You've already promised me the one thing that I wanted—for you to stay until you're well."

She shook her head. "Saying that I'm through lying wasn't a promise to *you*," she said. "I'm making a vow to myself. It's a bad habit, Duncan, and I can't build my new life, the one I'm going to have, on a foundation of untruths. One lie begets another and another. After a while you're making things up all the time, and then you hate yourself for it, and soon other people start hating you, too. There's no point in waiting to start over in California when I can begin here."

"It's really important to you, isn't it? This California business, I mean?" he asked.

"I want it more than anything. I had to have some kind of goal, otherwise I'd have stayed in the same rut forever. I couldn't live that way anymore. Amos and I deserve a better life than that. We'll make it."

"Yes, Jane, I believe you will." He stretched and stood up, looking down at her. She was beautiful but unsmiling, and tension still hardened the lines of her face. *I'd like to see her happy* was the thought that leaped into his head, but he shook it away. Happiness wasn't something he could bestow; it was something she'd have to find herself. Life and a ruined marriage had taught him that. All he could provide was a safe place where she could pull herself together, and maybe a few amenities.

"How about a bowl of ice cream? There's enough for Amos if he wants it," he suggested lightly.

"Are we through talking?" she asked.

"I hope not," he said, and then he laughed. "Was it so awful?" he asked.

"No, it made me feel better," she admitted.

For a moment Jane thought he was going to slide his arm around her shoulders, but perhaps he thought better of it, because he let her go through the door first and followed her into the kitchen.

She watched as he took the ice cream out of the freezer and began to spoon it into cut glass bowls. She felt a surge of gratitude toward him, not only for his forgiveness and for the kind manner in which he treated her, but also for the emotional release he had provided for her when she needed it.

There was more to breaking free from her past life than she had suspected, she knew now. The surface accoutrements of a new life, like an apartment and a job, were important. But she also needed to do some work on herself. Before, she hadn't known who she was or how she was supposed to act.

Now she still didn't know her identity—she might never know it.

But she knew that if there was anyone in the world after whom she wanted to model her behavior, it was Duncan.

THE NEXT DAY Duncan came in and tossed a couple of mail-order catalogs onto the couch.

"Here," he said. "You need to order some things to wear."

"I can't," she told him, shifting Amos, who was purring in her lap, to one side. "I don't have any money."

"I don't mind charging them to my accounts. You can pay me back."

"Duncan, I—"

"Only order what you absolutely need, then. You can't go on wearing my old blue jeans that don't even fit you, and you'd probably like to have a few shirts in your own size. Shoes, too. The ones you wear are pretty ragged. And you should own a decent pair of boots."

She flipped through the pages of the catalogs. A few basics wouldn't cost much, but how did she know when she'd be able to repay him?

He leaned over the couch, resting one hand on the back. "I have faith in you," he said quietly. "By letting you borrow the money, I'm saying, 'You're going to make it, kid.'"

She felt flustered, but Duncan seemed to want to take care of her; it pleased him. She decided to be gracious.

"All right," she said. "I'll order some things. Only what I need, though."

"Good," he said and went away whistling.

She ordered three blouses, a pair of gray wool slacks, sturdy outdoor boots, and, something she couldn't resist, a long warm flannel nightgown printed with tiny bluebells.

Jane spent her days looking after the house, taking long naps with Amos curled up beside her on the couch, and reading Duncan's paperback mysteries, of which he had several hundred. She was intrigued by the way the heroes and heroines of these books always triumphed. They seemed to run into none of the insurmountable problems that were posed by mysteries in real life; for instance, in her case, the puzzle of who she was. At present, she was content not to worry about that. It was enough to appreciate living in this house and to spend much of her day dreaming about her future. Her past seemed less important now that she was no longer living it.

After a couple of weeks, Jane realized with a start that she hadn't had one of her crushing headaches since she arrived on the ranch. There were even definable periods every day when she felt an emotion that she cautiously identified as happiness.

It first manifested itself as a lightness of being, which then transformed itself into joy in being alive. At first she was wary of this feeling that was so unfamiliar. She thought it was a fluke. As the days went on and it didn't go away, she learned to believe in it, much as she was learning to trust that there would always be enough food to eat and a warm place to sleep.

There are people, she thought, who have always had a place to sleep and plenty of food. Probably they've never contemplated what life would be like without these things that are so necessary. And likewise there are people who have always known this contentment, this—and she was still almost too superstitious to think the word—*happiness*. Duncan Tate was almost certainly one.

Although perhaps she was wrong about the happiness. He was unfailingly cheerful, more so every day, she thought. But was he happy? Sometimes a shadow of sadness slipped over his features when he thought she wasn't paying attention, and she wondered about it. She thought that maybe it had something to do with his former marriage. Jane had been told about that by Mary Kate, who had fallen into the habit of dropping by to visit with Jane every afternoon after the school bus dropped her off.

"I didn't know Duncan's wife very well," Mary Kate said one day as they were sitting together in Duncan's living room, cutting pictures out of magazines for one of her school projects. "But Sigrid was pretty. When she went away, Duncan left to go find her, and after he came back, he never talked about her again."

"Never said anything at all?" Jane asked curiously. She had found a gift set of bath powder and cologne in the bathroom; it must have belonged to Duncan's ex-wife. It seemed odd to think of Duncan married.

"Nope, he never mentioned Sigrid again. What food group is chocolate cake in, Jane? Do you know?"

"I'm afraid not," Jane admitted.

"Well, anyhow, Sigrid didn't come back after she left even to get the things she didn't take with her. Duncan gave me her scarves and I play dress-up with them. Do you want to play dress-up sometime?"

"Sure," Jane said, pasting a picture of a stick of butter on a notebook page.

"Sigrid was a rotten cook," Mary Kate told her. "And she didn't love the llamas like the rest of us do. So I'm glad she left, mostly. Especially because you came. You know, cutting out pictures of all this food makes me hungry. Let's make some banana pudding, Jane. Duncan loves it."

So they made banana pudding, and Duncan did love it, and that was all Jane found out about the long-departed Sigrid.

She couldn't imagine a woman lucky enough to have Duncan for a husband leaving for any reason whatsoever. And if Sigrid had stayed, chances were that Jane wouldn't be here at all. She didn't think that Sigrid, or any woman for that matter, would have allowed Duncan to take her into his home the way he had.

Sigrid's loss. Jane's gain.

IT WASN'T LONG before Jane discovered soap operas.

At first the stories seemed incomprehensible, because she didn't know the plot lines, but as she began to feel better, she didn't nap in the afternoon anymore and began to watch TV after lunch. Soon it became clear to her that daytime serials were an educational vehicle that she couldn't ignore.

Man to woman, woman to woman, man to man—all relationships were covered in detail. Table manners and other points of etiquette were demonstrated. Relationships were discussed. She was fascinated because she knew so little about such things.

To sleep with a man on the first date or the third? This was a week-long issue on *Luck of the Irish*. Skulduggery in business? An endless discussion of that very thing went on in *Thunder's Echo*. Love offered, love denied? It was the stuff of *Restless Hearts*.

Most people learned about such things over the period of a lifetime, but many of Jane's values had flown away with her real life. She had to laugh at the absurd melodrama of some of the plots on these TV shows, but nevertheless, they provided her with a way to set up a new system of values. They also allowed her to provoke interesting conversations with Duncan.

"What do I think about children moving back with their parents after they've grown?" he repeated in puzzlement, when she hit him with that question one night at dinner, after watching a segment of *Luck of the Irish* where this dilemma was featured.

"A lot of kids do that," she answered.

"I'm not one to comment since I've always lived here at Placid Valley Ranch. I'm one who never left home," he said, and then he proceeded to tell her how he had taken over the operation of the ranch after his father was thrown by a bucking horse and subsequently died.

Another time she brought up the subject of a May-December marriage, currently being considered by two characters of widely divergent ages in *Restless Hearts*. This opened a spirited discussion in which Jane came out for and Duncan remained vehemently against, saying that his father had been much older than his mother and that it hadn't always worked for the best.

It was a way to get to know each other, Jane reflected, and when Duncan, curious, asked her at lunch one day where and how, considering her loss of memory, she'd formed such strong opinions, she innocently told him that she'd been watching soap operas.

He threw back his head and laughed. "Honest? No fooling?" he said when he stopped.

She was embarrassed, but nodded.

He sobered instantly. "I'm not laughing at you," he said. "I'm pleased that you've found a way to learn about things you need to know." He knew how isolated they were out here on the ranch, but hadn't realized that Jane needed more human interaction. He supposed that he, Rooney and Mary Kate didn't contribute much to her development as a person.

He had been thinking about Jane a lot lately. After their serious talk, Duncan had figured that the pact between Jane and himself was an even exchange.

He protected her from the world; she protected him from loneliness and introspection.

Loneliness hadn't become a habit, but introspection certainly had. It was one that he would like to break, one that was as counterproductive as—well, as the lying that Jane had confessed afflicted her.

But how could he have stopped looking within himself when there wasn't any other place to look? He hadn't known the answer to that question until Jane came.

Now, instead of endlessly inspecting his own feelings, he had a distraction, and a pleasant one. Day by day she slowly lost the guarded air that made her seem slightly removed from him and took on a glow that might be the beginning of a more favorable outlook. Sometimes she hummed or sang around the house, which pleased him. His mother used to do that; he'd always considered that her low lilting voice, rising and falling with tunes she'd picked up from the radio, had made this house a home when he was a kid. After she died, there was no more music; his father had mourned her until the day he died. But now there was Jane to sing, and hearing her took him back to a happier time.

It would have been fun, he thought, to do everything for her. To give her everything. Or to shoulder her burdens for her so that she had nothing to do but lean against him. He didn't, because he knew it wouldn't work, and she would only end up resenting it.

When she went away he would surely miss her, but at the moment that didn't bear thinking about.

For now he would enjoy.

Chapter Seven

The next day Jane met the animals that Duncan prized so highly.

An unexpected warming trend sent temperatures soaring, and the sky was so blue and the sun so bright that Jane, who was feeling stronger every day, didn't want to stay indoors. She was pleased when Duncan called her on the telephone from his separate line in the barn and asked her to pay him a visit.

When Mary Kate stopped by the house on her way home from school, Jane suggested that she walk to the barn with her.

Mary Kate, acting her usual loquacious self as she skipped along, expressed delight that Jane was finally going to get a close-up look at the llamas.

"Before the snow came this winter, the female breeding llamas had their whole yard next to the barn to walk around in. Then it snowed and there were these huge drifts, but not so many on the east side of the yard, because Grandpa and Duncan built the barn so that it shelters the llamas from the weather when they're out in their pen. They shovel the snow out of the pen pretty often, so it's clear.

"Then there's the male llamas over in the stable in back of the barn. Llamas are used to cold weather, you know that? They come from some mountains called the Andes and it gets real cold there, Grandpa says. Oh, Jane, you'll finally get to meet Dearling. Aren't you excited? You should be. She's wonderful." Mary Kate gave a happy little hop so that her long ponytails bounced.

As they approached, the llamas inside the pen ambled over to the fence. One or two of them walked nervously forward, which made them look as though they were eager for this contact with humans.

"What's that noise they're making?" Jane asked, as soon as she realized that the strange sounds she was hearing came from the llamas.

"They hum. Listen, they're saying, 'Who's that lady with Mary Kate?' " She laughed and ran ahead to open the gate.

Mary Kate tugged at the gate until it opened and went inside, carelessly leaving it ajar. Once she herself was inside the pen, Jane struggled with the lock, which was so stiff that the bolt almost wouldn't slide home. When at last it was secure, she turned her attention to the llamas.

The first thing that struck her was that they all looked so different from one another. There seemed to be no one particular mold. This llama had a long neck and was tall enough to look her in the eye. That one was small, about the size of a large German shepherd. Some had ears that perked up, others' ears were slightly rounded. But all were graceful in a strangely elegant way. Jane was entranced with their looks.

Mary Kate's arms encircled the neck of the smallest llama in the pen. She rubbed her face against the curve of its neck, and the llama nuzzled her shoulder.

"This is my Dearling," she said proudly. "Isn't she beautiful?"

"She certainly is," Jane said warmly, moving cautiously closer as she spoke. Dearling didn't move, only looked slightly more alert. She seemed very tame.

"You can pet her," Mary Kate told her. "She won't bite or spit."

"Spit?" Jane asked, a little unnerved.

"Llamas spit, but hardly ever at us. They spit at each other, usually when they're having an argument over food, or over who is going to stand where or something dumb like that."

"Oh," said Jane, nevertheless preparing herself to dodge llama spittle. But Dearling was standing quietly, blinking her expressive long-lashed eyes and chewing her cud. Jane reached out and tentatively stroked the silky wool. Dearling leaned toward her at her touch, and Jane became bolder. In a few seconds, Dearling was sniffing at her clothes, and when Jane bent closer, the llama lifted her head and blew gently into Jane's face.

"Is she getting ready to spit?" Jane blurted after jumping away.

Mary Kate giggled. "No, that's what she does when she wants you to know that she likes you," she said.

Jane moved closer to Dearling and, acting out of instinct, blew gently into the llama's face.

Mary Kate laughed delightedly. "You're friends now," the girl said with great certainty.

Jane left Mary Kate with Dearling and walked around the muddy enclosure examining the other llamas. This was a pen for breeding females and their young; several young llamas huddled close to their mothers. Some of the females were roundly pregnant. All seemed boundlessly curious about her, and none were oblivious of her presence.

Duncan came out of the barn and stood watching her, a smile playing across his features. She returned his smile. Today he looked so proud of the llamas, and his stance was one of lord and master. A couple of llamas ambled toward him as if going to pay their respects.

When they reached Duncan, they nosed against his sleeve and rubbed their heads on his shoulder.

"Easy, there, Pumpkin, and stop it, Stardust," he told them affectionately. To Jane he said, "I walked out here with a corn muffin in my hand this morning, and they would have gladly relieved me of it. I guess they're looking for more goodies."

"They're beautiful," Jane said, "but I wasn't prepared for them all to look so different from one another."

"Come into my office in the barn," he said, holding the door open for her. "I'll show you some photos of llamas that we've raised."

Once inside, he opened a photo album on his desk. Jane sat on the edge of the desk and thumbed through it.

"This one has such pointed ears. And some of their necks seem shorter than others," she observed as she turned the pages.

"There are a lot of individual differences. I suppose there's no real standard of llama beauty. A pretty llama is whatever you think it is. Some people like them to be a solid color, and others prefer spots. Some think small llamas are wonderful, others like big ones."

"I didn't expect them to be so tame."

"These in the pen are females, which tend to be more affectionate than males, although sometimes I have to remind visitors that these aren't cuddly stuffed animals. They aren't really meant to be fussed over or coddled, though I have to admit that I do my share of it."

"So does Mary Kate," Jane said. She gazed out of the window at the child, who was talking to Dearling as the llama followed her around the yard.

"Ah, Mary Kate," Duncan said with a sigh of exasperation.

Jane shot him an inquiring look. "Has she done something wrong?"

"Well, not lately. Rooney and I are holding our breath, waiting until the next time. There will be a next time, I can guarantee it."

"Oh, Mary Kate's not so bad," Jane murmured in the child's defense.

"You weren't here when she let Quixote, my prize stud, out of his stall. And you weren't here when she set fire to Rooney's house. Or when she—"

"Never mind, I get the idea," Jane said wryly. She didn't need to be told about Mary Kate's affinity for trouble.

"Although I do think that the kid is behaving better since you've been around," Duncan said, eyeing her intently.

"I've tried to keep her company. She's an active little girl who seems to need a lot of attention."

"I guess you're right, and Rooney and I don't have time to give it. She's a plucky kid, and I'm fond of her, but I can't help thinking how smoothly things ran around this ranch before she came here."

"She said she's lived here for two years."

Duncan sat down on his swivel chair and toyed with a carved wooden llama paperweight.

"Mary Kate came here after her parents died in an accident. Rooney wanted her to come live with him, and she's been here ever since."

"How sad," Jane said, and meant it. She knew what it was like to be cut loose in the world with no place to go and no one to care.

"That's what Rooney thought," Duncan said. "He's always adored Mary Kate, and she was his flesh and blood, so he didn't want strangers bringing her up. I guess it's safe to say, though, that her presence here has changed his life."

"And yours," Jane said.

"And mine," Duncan agreed. "Maybe it needed changing." This he said thoughtfully, and his eyes seemed to reflect other more complicated thoughts that he didn't choose to express. Jane thought of Sigrid and wondered if Duncan still loved her.

He stood up. "You haven't met our stud males yet. Come on, they have their own stable behind the barn," he said.

They walked to an outbuilding, to which Jane had paid scant attention before because it was barely visible from the house. In front of it stood fenced pens, each separate from the others, and at the sound of Duncan's voice several llamas ambled out.

"This is Thor," he said, gesturing at a chocolate-brown llama with short-tipped ears and a heavy wool coat. "That's Paco hanging his head over the door. And this—this is Quixote."

Quixote was a majestic llama, taller than the other males, with banana ears and substantial bone structure. His coat was a golden reddish brown, and his wool was coarse with longer guard hairs.

"Is he your favorite?" Jane asked.

Duncan appeared reluctant to favor one llama over another. "He's our prize breeding stud. He came from very good stock, so he's quite valuable. And yes, maybe I am partial to him." He reached up and scratched Quixote behind the ear.

At that moment Mary Kate came around the corner of the barn.

"Jane!" she called, tramping along with Dearling following close behind.

"I guess I'd better go keep an eye on Mary Kate," Jane said.

"That's probably an excellent idea," Duncan told her. She waited for him to return to the barn with her, but he waved her away with a grin. "You go on," he said. "I have work to do in the stable."

Back in the barn, Mary Kate led Jane into the tack room. Here harnesses and saddles hung on wooden pegs on the walls, and panniers for the llamas were draped across a couple of sawhorses in the corner.

"I'm going to put a halter on Dearling," Mary Kate said as she stood on tiptoe to lift one of the halters off a high peg.

"Does Duncan let you do that?" Jane was skeptical.

"Sure," Mary Kate said. "He likes me to do it. I trained Dearling almost all by myself." She held the halter in front of the llama, and Dearling nosed into it. Mary Kate fastened the buckle on the left side before leading Dearling out of the barn. Jane tagged along behind, and the three of them headed toward the house.

"Hey," Duncan called from over near the stable. "Mary Kate, how about walking up to the road to get the mail?"

"Okay," Mary Kate said. "Will you come, Jane? It'll be fun."

"How far is it?"

"Grandpa says it's exactly a half mile from here to the mailbox," she said.

"Oh, I'd love to go for a walk," Jane said, feeling her spirits lift. It was such a beautiful day, the finest they'd seen since she'd arrived. She could clearly see the tops of the surrounding mountains. Alongside the driveway, fence posts stood in stark geometric purity against the snow of the pasture. Mary Kate led Dearling, who daintily picked her way around the remnants of snow in the rutted tracks. Once Mary Kate stopped briefly to adjust Dearling's halter, then they resumed their walk.

"Tell me about training Dearling," Jane said as they rounded a bend.

"I started last summer. Dearling's not much more than a baby, you know, and I begged Duncan to let me work with her. At first Duncan didn't want me to, but my grandpa said, 'Oh, Duncan, what could it hurt?' "

Jane smiled at this cannily accurate mimicking of Rooney's deep voice.

"Duncan said to get Dearling used to me by touching her and playing with her, but I was already doing that, so it wasn't such a big deal. She likes me, she really does!" Mary Kate looked over at Dearling and smiled.

"She's very fond of you. I can see that," Jane said.

Mary Kate beamed. "Duncan said that training a llama to like wearing the halter means adapting to the llama so it will trust you. Then, because it trusts you, the llama is ready to develop a habit, for instance, putting on a halter. So after I was sure she trusted me, I stood on the same side of Dearling every time I took out the halter, and I held it up to her face very, very patiently while I talked softly in her ear. Pretty soon Dearling got so she wasn't scared, and finally one day I just slipped the halter over her nose."

Jane wondered if training a child could be accomplished in the same way—by adapting to the child to establish trust and then encouraging the child to develop the habit of good behavior. While she was pondering this, Mary Kate dropped back to walk beside Dearling and to whisper into the llama's ear. When she returned to Jane's side she took her hand.

"Actually," Mary Kate confided, "after I got the halter on her, it wasn't all that easy to lead Dearling. It was because at first I left the halter too loose, and she didn't like it. And then she wouldn't walk—she'd sit down! That was funny, but I didn't think so then."

"What did you do?" Jane asked with an amused glance at Dearling, who seemed to sense that they were talking about her.

"Oh, I'd get behind her and push at her backside, trying to get her up on her feet, and she'd just chew her cud and look at me like I was crazy. Duncan laughed at us, but then he came into the pen and showed me how to tighten the halter so it wouldn't flap against her head. After a while Dearling was walking right alongside me. This summer I'm going to teach her to pull a cart. Then she can take us for rides. You'll like that, won't you, Jane?"

"Well, I—" she began, but suddenly stopped. She wished that she could think of an easy way to tell Mary Kate that she didn't plan to stay at Placid Valley Ranch that long. While she was casting about in her mind for something to say, Mary Kate thrust Dearling's lead into Jane's hand and ran ahead to the mailbox.

When Mary Kate came back, she resumed leading the llama and handed Jane the packet that she'd removed from the ranch mailbox.

Jane leafed through the mail and found several business-size envelopes with windows, a journal from a llama-breeding association, and a small pink envelope postmarked Albuquerque, which could easily slip out of the packet if she weren't careful. Realizing that she'd fallen behind Mary Kate and Dearling, she slid the pink envelope into the pocket of her coat and tucked the rest of the mail under her arm as she hurried to catch up.

From where she walked, she could barely see the house within its shelter of evergreen trees, but something softened inside her when she remembered that she lived in that picture-perfect house now, if only temporarily, and had her own warm bed to which she returned every night. She also had food to eat whenever she was hungry, Amos had a little plastic cat dish that Duncan had surprised them by bringing home one day, and she drank from her own favorite coffee mug on which Duncan had written her name in Magic Marker. And Duncan. She had Duncan.

Duncan to talk with, Duncan to joke with, Duncan to watch television with, and Duncan to eat meals with. At first she had felt constrained in his presence, it was true, but their relationship had become easy, even comfortable. If Jane had had a brother, she would have liked him to be just like Duncan Tate.

"This summer, maybe you can help me train Dearling to pull the cart," Mary Kate said, picking up the threads of their conversation again.

Jane decided that there was no avoiding this; she might as well confront the matter head-on. She wasn't about to participate in promoting any kind of falsehood, especially one as misleading as the one that tempted her now.

"What's wrong? Don't you want to work with me and Dearling?" Mary Kate peered upward, suddenly anxious.

"It's just that I won't be here this summer," Jane said quietly.

"Not *be* here! Why, you *have* to be here!" Mary Kate exclaimed in real dismay.

"Duncan and I agreed that I would stay at the ranch until spring," Jane told her as gently as she could.

Two red patches appeared on Mary Kate's face, one on each round cheek. Her chin jutted in defiance.

"I don't want you to leave," Mary Kate said from between tight lips.

"I never meant to stay here," Jane pointed out. "I only stayed because I was sick and couldn't leave."

"Well, I was talking to Duncan just the other day, and we talked about this summer and the llama cart and everything, and I said you could help maybe, and Duncan said he'd try to talk you into staying longer than spring. So there."

Jane didn't know how to reply to this. She knew that she had made it clear to Duncan that she would leave for California in the spring. Did he really think that she might stay longer?

Mary Kate appeared tense and fretful when they parted, but Jane waited until after dinner with Duncan that night to broach the subject of her staying until summer. True, she could have let it ride, but she had become sensitive to Mary Kate's emotional makeup, and she didn't think it was wise to raise the child's hopes. Better, she thought, for Mary Kate to know from the outset that Jane was not going to become a permanent fixture at Placid Valley Ranch.

She chose a quiet moment after dinner, when Duncan had finished watching the evening news on TV. He listened carefully while she told him all the reasons why he shouldn't lead Mary Kate to think that she, Jane, was planning to stay at Placid Valley Ranch beyond the time that they had agreed upon.

Duncan, who was sitting in his big leather chair near the fireplace, stared at the floor in front of the hearth for a long time after Jane finished talking.

"I suppose I was wrong," he said slowly. "I didn't realize that Mary Kate would take it for granted that you really would stay through the summer. Maybe I encouraged her to think that there was a possibility, but I thought she knew that it was just conjecture.''

"She takes everything literally, and she doesn't understand conjecture,'' Jane told him. "Mary Kate is a child who has experienced enough rejection in her life. I wouldn't want her to think that I'm rejecting her, too.''

Duncan smiled at her. "You've become attached to her, haven't you?''

"Well—''

"I watched you walking up the drive today with Mary Kate holding your hand. You looked as though you belonged together.''

Jane jumped up, suddenly feeling agitated. She stood staring into the fire, trying to sort out her feelings. She *had* tried to build a relationship with the girl, mostly because she felt sorry for her.

But to be more honest about it, perhaps the reason that she had grown close to Mary Kate in the short time that she'd been here was that she herself craved closeness. She had Amos, but he wasn't a human being. He couldn't talk to her. But Mary Kate did, and Mary Kate had made her feel welcome here, even needed. She had never identified within herself that desire to feel important to someone before; it came as a surprise to her that the urge existed at all.

"Mary Kate needs the gentleness of a woman,'' Duncan said. "It's good that you're here for her.''

Jane whirled and looked at him, and then found that she couldn't look at him because his gaze was so penetrating. She turned away again and opened the glass door over the face of the mantel clock. The key lay beside it, and for the next few seconds she wound the clock. It was just busywork, but something to do with her hands seemed important at this point.

When she had closed the glass cover again, Duncan said, "You're welcome to stay at Placid Valley Ranch as long as you like, Jane. I thought you knew that.''

Because she didn't know what else to do, Jane sat down on the edge of the raised hearth, the fire warming her back. Across the room, Amos lay curled up on the couch, the tip of his tail trailing across his nose.

"I'm only planning to stay until spring,'' she said.

"I know that was our original agreement,'' Duncan said. "But if you want to change it, we can always renegotiate.''

"No," she said. "You're so kind to me. But I want to be free to set out on a life of my own. To have a home of my own. To make friends. I want meaningful work that will allow me to be independent. I'm not ungrateful, but now I'm at the point where I can see an end to my quest, and I want to get on with it."

"You really know what you want, don't you?" he said. His eyes were somber now.

She nodded.

"The last time I saw such determination was when my wife left," he said reflectively.

"You haven't ever spoken of her before," Jane said. She wouldn't have known about Duncan's former marriage if Mary Kate hadn't told her.

"She found someone else, and she left me a couple of years ago. By the time she'd made up her mind to go, there wasn't anything I could do or say to make her change her mind."

"Do you ever see her anymore?"

"No, she lives in Albuquerque with her new husband. We keep in touch, but—" He shrugged.

The mention of Albuquerque reminded Jane of the pink envelope that had arrived in today's mail. She jumped up and went to the closet, where she rummaged in her coat pocket and produced the envelope. Silently she handed it to Duncan.

He slit the envelope with a brass letter opener and read the contents quickly. When he had finished, he tossed the pink paper onto a nearby table.

"Well, what do you know," he said heavily. "It's from Sigrid. She's had a baby girl."

He looked so sad that Jane sat down on the ottoman in front of his chair. She regarded him with a frown.

"Duncan, is everything all right? With you, I mean."

He lifted his shoulders and let them fall. "I thought it was. I figured I had handled the situation with my wife—I mean my ex-wife—pretty well. I was over it. But now I get this birth announcement from her and I feel like going and burying my head in the sand. Explain *that*." His face, usually so handsome, suddenly seemed to have developed lines where none were before.

Jane felt at a loss for words. Behind her the fire crackled and spat glowing sparks up the chimney, and outside the wind had picked up. She felt as though she'd like to melt into a small invisible blur rather than talk about this. She had had so little experience with events that normally occurred in people's lives that she had no store of wisdom from which to draw at the moment. Yet she suspected that she was the only person in Duncan's life with whom he could discuss the things closest to his heart.

"I can't explain why you feel the way you do, Duncan," Jane said after she had groped within herself to find the right words. "I can only tell you that it seems to me that you're fortunate to have been married once. It must be wonderful to find someone you want to spend the rest of your life with, and even if it doesn't work out, at least you have something. For a while."

"You're right, Jane. It was a good marriage, a strong marriage, for a time. And when it failed . . ."

"When it failed, it couldn't have been entirely your fault," she pointed out.

He focused his eyes on her. "Once I thought it was. I've tempered that judgment, because I see now that we both were at fault. I wasn't sensitive enough to her emotions, or at least I could find no way to let her know that I was, and she was wrong, because she didn't try hard enough to make me understand how important it was for her to know that I cared. And I cared, Jane. I really did."

"I know you did, Duncan," she said softly.

"This birth announcement underlines the truth that Sigrid and I can't do it over again. It's too late for that."

Jane rested her hand on top of his. "Sigrid thinks enough of you to share her news about the baby. You should both congratulate yourselves on managing to split up without hard feelings."

"In a way I wish she hadn't sent the announcement. It makes me see that she's been going forward with her life while mine has stood still. She has a husband and child, and I have—well, I have a herd of llamas and a ranch foreman. Oh, and don't forget Mary Kate." He gave a snort, which was probably meant to be a laugh but fell short of the mark.

Jane was relieved that Duncan was trying to make light of his situation.

"You've forgotten Amos and me. We're here," she said before she thought.

His eyes suddenly went bleak. "But only until spring," he said.

Duncan continued to look at her, and all at once the room seemed too hot, the fire too bright, his expression too needy.

Overhead the mantel clock's tinny gong struck the hour, and Amos stirred.

Elaborately casual, Jane stood up. "I guess I'll turn in," she said.

"It's early," Duncan pointed out.

Jane faked a yawn. "That walk to the mailbox must have tired me out," she said. It was a lame excuse, but at this point anything would be. Duncan looked as though he was ready to pour out his soul to her, and she wanted to avoid that at any cost. Suddenly she knew that any kind of intimacy was more than she could handle.

He said nothing, only watched her as she fled; never had the staircase seemed as long as it did on this night. When she reached her room, she discovered that her heart was pounding out of all proportion to the physical effort involved in running up one flight of stairs.

Almost immediately she heard his footsteps mounting the stairs, and she went to her door and listened for the sound of his door latch. She didn't hear it, and presently he walked past her room on his way out of the house. That wasn't so unusual; he often went over to Rooney's place in the evening.

It took all her willpower not to open her bedroom door and speak to him as he passed, although she realized with a start after she heard the front door slam that she had no idea what she would have said.

Chapter Eight

The next day Duncan woke up, looked at himself in the mirror, and said to his reflection, "You fool." After that he cut himself shaving and had to look all over for his styptic pencil, which he never found.

He was a fool for pouring his feelings out to Jane last night, when it obviously made her so uncomfortable. And he was twice a fool because he'd been entertaining the thought that Jane would stay past spring. That particular season, which he had long considered a time for beginnings and renewal, would this year be a time of ending. He found that he didn't relish the idea of her leaving.

He had grown accustomed to Jane at breakfast, to Jane humming as she dusted the furniture, to Jane folding the clothes fresh from the dryer and looking over her shoulder to greet him when he came in during the day. He had grown accustomed to *Jane*. Or whoever she was. That her name wasn't really Jane did not matter to him. What mattered was that he had grown to care about her. Her story touched him; he couldn't imagine not having a past.

His past was with him constantly. He had grown up here on the ranch, helping his father and Rooney with what was essentially a cattle operation in those days. His mother had been a delicate, gentle woman not unlike Jane. They sometimes visited his maternal grandparents in Moscow, Idaho, where his grandfather was a professor at the University of Idaho. His grandparents and his mother always seemed slightly startled that she had married a rancher who was many years her senior and that she now lived on an isolated ranch in Wyoming.

Duncan was an only child, and there was never any doubt that he was going to take over the ranch when he grew up. His mother, fragile until the end, had died of complications from the flu when he was thirteen. Duncan had vivid memories of the events leading to her death, which was why he was so insistent that Jane take care of herself.

Then ten years ago, when he was only twenty-two, his father had died. From then on, Duncan had relied on Rooney's help and advice in running the ranch, and when Duncan decided after much thought and study to convert from cattle to a llama-breeding operation, Rooney had encouraged him to ease into this new livestock management program. They both needed a challenge, and llamas could provide it.

Their venturesome endeavor proved worthwhile. No longer regarded as novelties for zoos and animal parks, llamas had recently come into their own in the United States as pack animals and wool producers. Last year he and Rooney had sold their best breeding female at auction for $80,000. The sale was a triumph for Placid Valley Ranch, and it validated Duncan's decision to become a llama breeder.

He couldn't imagine what it was like for Jane, who faced the monumental task of recreating herself after losing her memory. What would it be like to have no memory of your heritage and no guidance from the past? How would you know who you were, much less what you wanted to do with your life?

It was good, he supposed, that Jane had set goals for herself. But why California? Why so far away? Why couldn't she stay here?

Silly questions. After all, there was no work for her here. There were no apartments such as the one Jane would like to have, and as for friends, well, he and Rooney and Mary Kate were just about it. In town she might meet people, but Durkee, Wyoming, was thirty miles away and consisted of little more than a post office, a gas station and a convenience store where, in a shed out back, the owner sold junk as a sideline. Duncan hardly thought that the town of Durkee was enough to keep Jane here.

After giving up the search for the styptic pencil, he went downstairs, surprised at how late it was. Jane sat at the kitchen table leafing through his mother's cookbook. She had been trying to learn to cook, with mixed results.

"Good morning," she said brightly. Her hair held the color of the sunlight streaming through the kitchen window; the fine strands shimmered like gold.

"Good morning," he returned. The place where he had cut himself shaving still smarted.

They heard footsteps on the back stairs that were followed by Mary Kate's sharp knock. "Duncan," she called. "I've brought the Sunday paper."

This was a Sunday morning ritual in which Duncan had long participated with Mary Kate; she walked to the road and retrieved the Sunday newspaper from the box beside the mailbox, and in return, Duncan read her the comics. This ritual persisted, even though at the age of ten Mary Kate was able to read the funnies to herself. Now she peered through one of the windowpanes in the back door, and he hastened to let her in.

"Are you ready for me to read the comics to you, Mary Kate?" Duncan asked.

"As soon as I pet Amos," Mary Kate said, dropping her coat onto the kitchen floor and darting into the living room in pursuit of the cat.

"Come back and pick up this coat," Duncan ordered. "And hang it in the closet."

Mary Kate, having caught Amos, walked slowly back to the kitchen, scratching him under the chin. The cat closed his eyes in obvious bliss.

"Amos likes me," Mary Kate bragged. "The other day he let me rub his stomach and didn't even move. He didn't used to let me do that." She set him down gently on the floor and picked up her coat without complaint.

"Mary Kate, why don't you stay and have French toast with Duncan and me?" suggested Jane. "I'll make it while Duncan reads you the comics."

"You're making French toast?" asked Duncan.

"I found this recipe for Orange Blossom French Toast, and we have all the ingredients. I think I'd like to try it."

"Oh, good," Mary Kate said, grinning from ear to ear.

"We'll be in the living room," Duncan said, leaving Jane to her recipe.

It all seemed so domestic to Duncan, with Mary Kate sitting close on the couch as he read, Amos purring on the rug at their feet, and delicious aromas floating in from the kitchen.

He tried to recall ever having this cozy feeling on a Sunday morning when Sigrid was here, but all he remembered from those days was Sigrid's discontent at being cooped up here on the ranch with only Rooney and himself for company, Mary Kate having arrived shortly before Sigrid departed. And when Sigrid had cooked, it had been done grudgingly. Unfortunately, his ex-wife had never taken to life at Placid Valley Ranch.

He read to Mary Kate with one ear cocked toward the kitchen, where Jane hummed as she went about her tasks; he loved the way she hummed as she worked. Duncan looked up between comic strips, catching a glimpse of an ankle as she temporarily moved out of view, appreciating the way her hair curled against her cheek, and was rewarded for his vigilance by her glance in his direction and a fleeting half smile before she turned toward the stove again.

"The French toast is ready," Jane called finally, and he and Mary Kate sat down with Jane at the kitchen table to eat hot French toast made from a recipe that Duncan recalled from when his mother was still alive. It almost seemed like the old days to Duncan, like the time when he lived here with both parents, to be pouring steaming orange syrup out of the gravy boat with the spout that he had chipped when he was about Mary Kate's age, to be joking and teasing and laughing with Mary Kate and with Jane, who kept urging French toast on him until he asked her if she expected to feed the whole French army. Jane laughed at this, her cheeks slightly flushed with happiness, and Duncan thought, *Why, Jane likes this kind of atmosphere, too.*

After Mary Kate went home, Duncan lighted a fire in the fireplace, then he and Jane spread out the sections of the newspaper on the floor and took turns reading them, passing the most interesting items back and forth with a comment or two. Jane brought the coffeepot into the living room, and Duncan remarked that she made wonderful coffee. Jane replied offhandedly that it was one thing she had learned to do at her short-lived job in the restaurant in Apollonia.

Finally, when the newspaper was neatly piled to one side of the couch, Duncan poked at the fire and, because he was curious, said, "You never talk about your life before you came here. You've never told me how you managed to get along in Chicago."

Jane, sitting on the floor, leaned back against the couch and clasped her hands around one knee. "It doesn't seem like entertaining conversation," she said.

"I suppose you would like to forget about that period of your life," he suggested.

She stared into the fire. "No, not forget, exactly. I'm still trying to come to grips with what happened to me. Maybe talking about it would help. I keep having flashbacks to the hard times, especially to the period when I was in Chicago. It didn't turn out the way I expected, that's for sure." Briefly she looked unsure of herself, like the Little Girl Lost she'd been when he found her.

"What do you mean?" he asked.

"When I arrived in Chicago, I tried to get a job right away, but it's hard to get a job when you have no past," she said.

"What happened?"

"Well, when I went to fill out the job applications, they asked for a social security number. I didn't have one, which posed a problem."

"Didn't you tell your prospective employers about your situation?"

"I was always afraid that if I told anyone I was an amnesia victim, they'd think I wasn't a good risk, so usually I left the space for the social security number blank. If an employer asked me about it, I'd say I'd left my social security card at home and didn't remember the number. Usually that would work for a few weeks or months."

"You could have applied for a social security card," Duncan pointed out.

"I did. The people at the Social Security Administration told me I had to have a birth certificate in order to get a social security number, but of course I didn't have a birth certificate. At that time I was still having severe headaches, and I couldn't pull myself together enough to decide what to do next."

"Poor Jane," Duncan said sympathetically.

"Poor *somebody*," Jane agreed. "I know I have a name as well as a birth certificate somewhere, and probably I have a social security number, too. But there seems to be no way to find out who I am."

"There must be people who knew you before your accident, who were your neighbors, co-workers, something. They must be worried sick about you."

"As far as I know, no one ever came forward to say I was missing. You'd think someone would, wouldn't you?" she said wistfully. Her eyes seemed large and dark, mirroring her sadness. Duncan's heart went out to her.

"Someone like you, someone so beautiful—yes, it does seem as though someone would have cared about you and looked for you," he replied softly.

"Do you really think I'm beautiful?" she asked unexpectedly.

The question took him by surprise, but he didn't have to hesitate. "Yes, I do, Jane. Very beautiful," he said.

She seemed satisfied with his answer. "Beauty isn't a quality that I identify with myself," she explained. "I was so busy trying to survive that I didn't care what I looked like, as long as I was neat and clean. Oh, that reminds me of something I've been meaning to mention. I found a portable sewing machine in my closet, Duncan. Would you mind if I used it to make myself some clothes? Somehow I think I can figure out how to sew."

"Of course," he said.

"There's material, too. I wonder if—"

"Take anything you need," he said. "The machine was Sigrid's, and the fabric was hers, too. She didn't want to take it when she left."

"If you want to ask her again if she wants her sewing machine, I won't mind," Jane said. She hadn't known it was his former wife's; she'd surmised that it had belonged to his mother.

"Nonsense. Sigrid hardly used it, and she won't want it now."

"Thanks. Duncan. I think I'll go upstairs and look through the patterns. She must have been about my size."

"No. Sigrid was heavier," Duncan said; somehow he felt uncomfortable comparing the two women.

"Well, anyway, I guess I'll go upstairs."

"Please don't," Duncan said.

"What?"

"I said, please don't go. This is my only day off. If you go, I'll have to spend another Sunday alone. I enjoy your company." There was a cajoling tone to his voice; he'd never used it before.

Jane, who had risen to her feet, sat down on the couch. "Duncan, I think we should talk about this," she said slowly.

"Is it worth calling one of our meetings?" he asked with a grin.

"Meetings— Oh, I'm not sure. Maybe." She looked confused.

"Well, what's bothering you?" he asked.

"You know what I mean. You're getting too attached—I mean, I'm getting too attached—oh, I don't know." She bit her lip in chagrin.

"You think it will be harder when you leave if we become close now," Duncan supplied.

"Yes, I suppose that's it," she said unhappily.

In the fireplace, flames crawled upward until they consumed another log. The heat made Jane's face glow, and Duncan wished that he'd initiated this discussion sooner. In it he saw a replay of her insistence that Mary Kate not get any ideas about Jane's staying past spring. He stared at her, at a loss as to how to impress upon her how much he wanted her to reconsider.

Jane had blossomed, losing that wan, debilitated look that she'd had at first, and the ample food had filled out that slight frame of hers. The delicate shadows under her cheekbones had disappeared. When she had asked him if he thought she was beautiful, he had felt like shouting out his answer, because not only was she beautiful, but she had imbued this house with that beauty, and for that he was grateful. He had never realized how drab and dull his life had been before she arrived.

He liked everything about her; the way she cared for that little cat of hers, her interest in the llamas, her responsible shepherding of Mary Kate, her thoughtful ways. She didn't deserve the buffeting that life had meted out to her, and he wanted to make it up to her.

He wanted—but what difference did it make what he wanted? At night he often thought of her lying alone in her bed. In his fantasies she came to him, looking soft and ethereal, and he imagined reaching up to her and pulling her down to him, imagined being absorbed into her.

"I suppose we could become too attached to each other," he said with all due gravity, but his thoughts refused to run in this groove and instead leaped around inside his head bearing images that he had only dared to dream. Jane in his bed, Jane stepping naked from the shower and reaching for a towel, her shape outlined by the light from his bedroom, Jane everywhere.

The real Jane wrinkled her forehead, unaware of the way he had pictured her. *What a pity that she will never know,* he thought, and before he knew it, moving as if in a dream, he had taken her chin in his hand, turned her face toward his, and kissed her on the lips.

"Duncan!" she said when he released her. Her eyes widened and darkened; he sensed how much he had shocked her.

"I couldn't help it," he said truthfully.

She looked rattled. "It's just—just—"

"Just what?"

"That I've never thought of you in that way. Never."

"How do you think of me?"

She ran a hand through her hair and looked off into space somewhere over his left shoulder.

"As—as someone who has been more than kind to me. As someone who is easy to be around. Easy to respect. Oh, Duncan, I don't know," she said in obvious dismay.

Quickly he masked the disappointment in his eyes. She didn't reciprocate his feelings. She had no inkling of how he felt. He found her innocence very moving, although at the same time he was annoyed by it.

"Forgive me, Jane," he said, knowing how abject he sounded. That was genuine, too, as real as his feelings for her.

"This changes things," she said with certainty. She looked perturbed in a way that he had never seen her.

Duncan, you idiot, now you're three times a fool, he told himself. Aloud he said, "It needn't change anything. It was a whim, a mark of affection, and no more than that."

"I'm reading too much into a simple kiss. Is that what you're trying to say?" Her troubled eyes rested on him, seeking reassurance.

"Yes, perhaps. It was a mistake, and it won't happen again." He sounded stiff and formal even to himself. No telling what she thought.

She sighed heavily and leaned back on the couch, massaging her elbows through an old sweater of his that was a favorite of hers. She closed her eyes and seemed to be deep in thought.

He was angry with himself. He'd muddled their relationship, that was for sure. In the past few weeks he had allayed her basic mistrust with both words and actions, and then, with one misguided kiss, he had destroyed what they had. He couldn't allow himself to show his bitter disappointment that she didn't reciprocate his feelings; he made himself adopt an air of icy detachment.

"I think it's time I went to my office in the barn," he said. He got up and took his coat out of the closet.

Jane was up immediately.

"Duncan, I'm not angry. Only confused," she said. She looked so lovely standing there with the winter sunlight from the window slanting across her face.

"Confused," he repeated.

"I've had a lot to deal with where men were concerned," she told him. "All of them weren't as nice as you."

He paused in the act of shoving his Stetson onto his head.

"Which means what?" he asked, the ice starting to melt.

"That as far as I know, I've never had the chance to develop a normal relationship with a man. That I've never even wanted to."

"And do you want to now?" he demanded.

Her eyes searched his.

"Maybe," she said, her voice a mere whisper.

He shook his head. All this was almost too much to fathom. He was accustomed to being straightforward and up-front with his relationships. He didn't know about all this hemming and hawing and trying to figure out the meaning of the many nuances that could be felt when a man and a woman were getting to know each other.

But he wanted to learn, and most of all he didn't care to repeat past mistakes.

"Like I said, I'm going to the barn. I'll be back in time for dinner."

"Shall I roast the chicken as we planned?"

"Sure," he said, able to give her an easy smile.

She handed him his muffler because he had forgotten it in his haste, and he felt her eyes on his back as he made tracks toward the barn. Whatever had happened back there, it was a surprise to him that he felt pretty good about it, when all was said and done. Except that he didn't know what his next step should be, or if there would even be a next step.

AFTER DUNCAN LEFT, Jane went upstairs and sorted in a desultory way through the fabric that Sigrid had not taken with her. It was hard to think about sewing now that the situation with Duncan had taken this new and disturbing twist, although he had reassured her about it. *A simple mark of affection,* that was what he had called his kiss. She decided that she could accept this explanation. After all, he had asked for nothing more.

She sat with neatly folded packets of fabric in her lap, reviewing her experiences with men, or at least all the experiences she could recall.

There'd been a lecherous fry cook in one of the restaurants where she'd waitressed for three weeks; he'd been more than twice her age and claimed to have arthritis, but he was certainly agile enough when it came to pinning her up against the shelves in the pantry. Fortunately, she'd been fired before things went too far. Then there was the calculating owner of a laundromat where she'd been employed to make change and sell detergent powder. He was married and the father of two little girls, but that didn't stop him from asking her out.

A man who worked at an employment agency had promised her a pleasant office job if she'd move in with him, and a teenage newspaper vendor had once blurted that he had a crush on her. And a wino in a shelter had forced his attentions on her, until she was rescued by a minister who was there to provide chaplaincy services.

She might say that her experiences with men had been less than satisfying; or, being honest with herself, that they'd mostly been terrifying. It wasn't easy to trust men after what she'd been through.

She reminded herself of a few standouts: the concerned and kindly Dr. Bergstrom, who had treated her after she was found in the ditch, a thoughtful shelter attendant who had let her stay in the building to use his phone to look for work during the day, when homeless people were expected to vacate the premises, and, of course, Duncan.

Duncan. She liked him so much. If she were ever to fall in love with someone, she'd like it to be with someone like him.

In a sense, Jane was curious. She knew her experience with men had been mostly limited to the deadbeats, the down-and-outers, the immoral and the lechers. This was not a fair cross section of American men. It was reassuring that someone of Duncan's caliber thought she was beautiful, liked her, and was physically attracted to her.

Duncan had always made it clear that he recognized her as a real person, someone unique. When he kissed her, he was reaffirming that sense of herself that she had long hoped to develop. Also, and this surprised her, she had liked kissing him. She hadn't pulled away. But she knew that what she felt wasn't love.

Though she had had little experience as far as she knew, she understood what went on in a physical relationship between men and women. She had heard plenty of talk about it; there were all those affairs on the daytime dramas, and when she'd lived on the streets, she had even seen frantic, shadowed real-life couplings. That kind of thing seemed ugly and shameful. She had never had any doubt that love was the ingredient that made sex worthwhile.

But to make love—ah, that was an experience that she had begun to anticipate with pleasure. To lie in a man's arms, to be cherished and adored so much that he wanted to be that close to you and you to him; it seemed like a wondrous way to express affection.

When she thought about it, she couldn't imagine the act of intercourse taking place without love. It was a value left over from her past life, her other life, the one she'd had before she became Jane Rhodes. That and other values kept popping up out of nowhere, often confounding her. How did she know that love made what went on between men and women special? If she had experienced it in her past life, it was one of the things that she longed to remember.

Her attitude toward love caused her to wonder if she had ever been in love, just as her knowledge of fabrics and sewing inspired the question, *Did I lead a very domestic sort of life? The kind where I often sewed, say, for my children?* Had there been a man to love, children for whom she sewed little overalls and pajamas, dancing costumes and dresses?

Duncan's kiss had shown her that she was ready to learn more about herself, including satisfying her curiosity about a real relationship with a man, present as well as past. She'd meant it when she'd told him that she thought he was lucky to have been married once.

She stood up, tossed the fabric onto the floor, and went to the window where she could see the barn. She half wanted to march over there and confide her feelings to Duncan, because he was the only person she had to talk to.

Only this was something she couldn't discuss with Duncan.

She sighed and picked up a large piece of blue wool. She loved the way it felt between her fingers, and she idly inspected the warp and woof of the fabric. Warp and woof? How did she know those terms? The warp was the thread that ran lengthwise in the loom, and the woof was the name for the threads that crossed the warp.

She sank onto the edge of the bed, overcome by this glimpse of knowledge. She hadn't known that she knew anything about fabric or how it was made; the information had merely arrived unbidden out of that vast black store hidden somewhere within her brain.

What else did she know that she couldn't call to mind? Would she ever remember all of it, or even most? In the future, what important snippets of her past would drift into her consciousness from time to time, perplexing and confusing her? How would she deal with them when they did?

And what if she developed a relationship with a man, and then one day the memory of a husband and children surfaced? What on earth would she do then? Who would come first—her old family or her new relationship?

How would she deal with something like that?

Chapter Nine

Any concerns about getting too close to Duncan were squelched by the distance he effectively put between them during the ensuing week. He spent long hours in the barn, barely talked to her at meals, and either rode into Durkee or went over to Rooney's every night. She watched television and waited for his tread on the back porch in the evenings. Most of the time she was already asleep when he came home.

She missed the easy rapport that had developed between them, but at least she had Mary Kate for company. Mary Kate continued to drop by every day after school.

One day Mary Kate arrived at her usual time, and Jane hurried to let her in.

"Hi, Jane," Mary Kate said breezily as she dumped her book bag on the couch. "Let's go over and talk to the llamas today."

Without too much regret, Jane turned off the TV set.

"Okay," she said, slipping on her coat. "Maybe you can explain more about their ear movements to me." This was something that they had only briefly touched upon on their other visits to the llamas, and Mary Kate was pleased to oblige Jane's request.

"Grandpa says that the Indians in Peru called the llamas their silent brothers," Mary Kate said importantly as they shoved their hands deep into their pockets for warmth and headed toward the barn. "That's silly, I think, because everyone knows that llamas hum, and that isn't what I call silent. Anyway, they communicate in other ways. Duncan calls it body language."

"Give me an example of llama body language," Jane suggested as they reached the pen and Mary Kate unlatched the gate.

Jane went through and left Mary Kate to put the latch back on. Dearling knew Jane now, and she was always friendly to her.

"Well, see how Crystal's ears are laid back? That means she feels unhappy or maybe threatened. And see how Dearling's ears are perked forward? She's interested in you. Sometimes when I want to get the llamas to do something, I just put my hands up to my ears like this, and I move them the way a llama would in order to say something." Mary Kate put her hands up into the sides of her head and wiggled them at Dearling in llama fashion. Dearling pointed her ears even farther forward. Jane could have sworn that the llama was smiling.

"I don't know what you said in llama ear language, Mary Kate, but Dearling must like it," Jane told her as she stroked Dearling's silky head.

Mary Kate giggled. She hugged Dearling around the neck. "Come on into the barn, Jane. Let's say hello to Flapjack and the other horses."

Dearling followed them as they left the pen, and once again Jane let Mary Kate fasten the latch after them. It was only by chance that she glanced back to observe that the gate was swinging free.

"Mary Kate," she said. "You've left the latch undone."

"Oh, will you fasten it, Jane?" Mary Kate said carelessly.

About this, Jane was prepared to be firm. "*You* do it," she said. "You know that Duncan and your grandfather think gates and latches are very important." She, as well as Mary Kate, knew the results of her irresponsibility on past occasions.

Reluctantly Mary Kate turned and went to the gate, latching it carefully this time, so that the llamas were secure in their pen. Jane double-checked the bolt to make sure that Mary Kate had done the job right this time. She could well imagine Duncan's fury if his breeding females were somehow to escape.

In the barn, the horses were in their stalls. Flapjack swung his head around with interest when they approached him.

"Good old Flapjack," Mary Kate said. She went to a sack hanging from a nail on the wall and produced a carrot. "Here," she said to Jane, "you can feed this to him."

Jane held the carrot on the flat of her palm and Flapjack gobbled it down. He was a beautiful animal. His coat was shiny and black, and he had a white star on his forehead. She stroked his nose; it was like rubbing warm velvet.

Mary Kate led her from stall to stall, reeling off the names of the horses.

"Here's Rabbit, my grandfather's horse. And this is Nellie Mae. Grandpa rides her sometimes. Here's Diggory; Sigrid used to ride him. This is Jericho, my pony, but I'm getting too big for him. Grandpa says he'll have to get me a bigger horse this summer."

"Why don't you just ride Nellie Mae? Or Diggory?"

"Well, I tried to ride Nellie Mae one time and she tried to scrape me off on a fence post. And Diggory's getting kind of old. I want a pretty little mare, maybe a roan. Do you like roans?"

"I don't know much about horses," Jane admitted.

"Well, this summer when I get my mare, you and me can ride together. You could start out on Diggory. He's real gentle."

Jane stopped stroking Diggory's smooth flank and turned toward Mary Kate. "But I told you I wasn't going to be here this summer," she said patiently.

Much to her surprise, Mary Kate's face flushed red, except for a white line around her mouth. "I won't let you leave," she said in quiet fury. "I won't."

The child was suffering, Jane could see that. And yet Jane wouldn't, couldn't change her mind.

"Mary Kate, please try to understand. I—"

Mary Kate's blue eyes flashed and she stomped her foot. "You're not leaving here, Jane, you're not!"

"But—"

"You're staying! Forever and ever! I'll hate you if you go away!" And with that Mary Kate wheeled and ran out of the barn, slamming the door behind her so hard that the rafters shook and Nellie Mae let out a startled whinny.

The tantrum had happened so quickly and so fast that it momentarily stunned Jane. She waited for a moment, thinking that a repentant Mary Kate might return as quickly as the angry Mary Kate had slammed out. But the young girl didn't come back, and after a minute or so, Jane looked around and saw Dearling calmly chewing her cud in a corner.

Jane sighed. "Come along, Dearling," she said, putting her arm around the little llama's neck, and an acquiescent Dearling followed Jane as though she was used to doing this every day of her life. When they reached the females' pen, Jane unlatched the gate and shooed Dearling inside, taking care to make sure it was securely fastened when she closed it.

She looked around in vain for Mary Kate. Well, she had probably run home and was sulking. In any case, Jane didn't feel like discussing her departure again. The child refused to understand that it was inevitable.

Jane felt heavyhearted and sad, wishing she could do something to help Mary Kate, but the more she thought about it after she got back to Duncan's house, the more sensible it seemed to leave well enough alone. Dispiritedly Jane pushed aside Mary Kate's book bag, which lay forgotten on the couch, and resumed hemming a skirt she had made for herself.

After a while, she heard Rooney's pickup truck start up over by the barn and hoped, for the child's sake, that he had decided to take her to town with him; she knew he was going because he had stopped by earlier to ask if she and Duncan needed anything from the grocery store.

Jane tied off her thread and went into the kitchen to check on the pot roast. In a few minutes, she saw Rooney walking purposefully up the freshly shoveled path to the back door.

She met him there. "I thought you went to town," she said with some surprise.

Rooney's eyebrows were knitted in the middle of his forehead. "I was going to," he said. "Then I heard Duncan take my truck. Do you know where he went?"

"Duncan? I don't think he went anywhere, because he told me he was going to be looking over the account books in the barn until supper."

"But I heard it start up and thought he must have decided to run an errand."

"I don't think so," Jane said.

"Well, tell Mary Kate she can ride into town with me when Duncan gets back with my truck," Rooney said.

"Mary Kate's not here," Jane replied, her heart turning over.

"Not here? She always stops by after school." He looked rattled.

"She did, but when we were over in the barn, we had a—a slight disagreement, and I assumed she went home," Jane told him. Her forehead wrinkled in a frown. Where could Mary Kate be?

"She's not at the house," Rooney said flatly.

The thought occurred to them at the same time.

"The truck!" both exclaimed.

"She couldn't drive your pickup truck," Jane said, shaking her head in denial.

"The keys were in it—maybe she could. I'm going over to the barn to see if Duncan is there," Rooney said, sprinting away.

"I'm coming, too!" Jane called after him and followed, pulling on her coat as she ran.

Duncan was bent over paperwork in his office, and glanced up in surprise as Rooney and Jane burst through the door.

"Mary Kate's gone, and so is the truck!" Rooney shouted.

The three of them ran outside and stood for a moment scanning the ranch. Llamas in their pen looked up in interest. The darkness of a lowering sky hinted at snow in the offing, and there was no sign of Mary Kate. The pickup truck was nowhere in sight.

"Where could she go?" Jane wondered aloud as they all clambered into Duncan's Cherokee.

"To the highway," Rooney said grimly as a few flakes of snow began to waft out of the sky.

"She wouldn't," Jane said with certainty.

"You don't know Mary Kate the way we do," Duncan said in an ominous tone.

Duncan drove as fast as he could in the frozen rutted tracks of the driveway. It wasn't easy driving, and Jane doubted that a child could handle a truck under these conditions. Jane realized that none of them knew what to expect. What had ever possessed her to take Rooney's truck?

Jane recalled the anger Mary Kate had shown when she was acting out her frustration at Jane's certain departure; maybe the youngster had deliberately decided to misbehave in a really big way in order to get everyone's attention.

"There! That's the truck," Rooney said, sitting forward in his seat and squinting ahead through the downy swirls of snow.

Jane saw that the pickup truck had pitched headlong into a high snowdrift, denting the snow with its bumper. Clouds of vapor unfurled from the exhaust pipe, and the engine was still running. Loud country music blared from the truck's radio.

Duncan leaped from the Cherokee and wrenched open the door on the driver's side in an instant. Out tumbled Mary Kate.

"Grandpa!" exclaimed Mary Kate, throwing herself into her grandfather's arms.

Duncan reached inside the pickup and turned off the ignition key, silencing both engine and radio. It was suddenly very quiet.

"You scared us," Jane said, shattering the stillness with her shaking voice.

Mary Kate blinked at her. "I didn't mean to. I only wanted to drive the truck."

"We'll talk about it when we get home," her grandfather said, and they could tell from the tone of his voice that he was furious. The air was filled with frosty clouds of vapor from their breath.

"Is the truck okay? I didn't mean to hurt it, but it slid off the road," Mary Kate said, once they were in the Cherokee.

"It looks like there's no great harm done. You were lucky, young lady. Exactly where did you think you were going?" Duncan inquired, glancing briefly over his shoulder as he backed and turned.

"To the mailbox. I thought that if it was a half mile to the mailbox and back and I drove at one mile an hour, it should take me an hour to get home. I drove real, real slow."

"Well, 'real, real slow' or not, it was a stupid thing to do, and I'm going to reckon with you when we get back to the house," Rooney said.

Mary Kate looked momentarily chastened, then said, "I had to scrunch the seat way forward to reach the pedals, and I sure wish I knew how to get the emergency brake off."

"You mean you drove all the way up here with the emergency brake on?" Duncan asked in disbelief.

"I guess so," Mary Kate said with a shrug.

"Where'd you learn to drive, anyway?" Duncan asked.

"By watching you and Grandpa."

"Well, next time watch how we release the emergency brake before we shift into gear. Just in case you decide to go for any more little outings around the neighborhood."

"She ain't going on any more little outings," Rooney grunted. "I can promise you that."

Duncan let out Mary Kate and Rooney in front of their house and parked the Cherokee at the barn. When he and Jane had returned to the house, Duncan said, "I thought Mary Kate spent her afternoons with you these days."

Jane heaved a giant sigh. "She usually does, but today we had a disagreement. In a way, I suppose that it's my fault that she took the truck."

"Don't be silly. Mary Kate's always doing something she shouldn't do. You know that."

"I think she does these things when she wants more attention and isn't getting it. Like this afternoon." Quickly Jane related how Mary Kate had insisted that Jane mustn't leave the ranch, and how she had firmly told her young friend that her departure was inevitable.

"Rooney tries to cope the best way he can," Duncan said. "It's hard being mother, father, sister and brother all rolled up into one. Mary Kate will certainly miss you when you're gone. She models herself after you, and, as a matter of fact, ever since you arrived here, her behavior has improved."

"I can't take credit for that," Jane objected.

"Of course you can. You're good with her, you know. She listens to you."

"I'm company for her," Jane said.

"No, it's more than that."

Jane thought about it. He was right. She discovered that she felt good about making a difference in Mary Kate's life, even for so short a time. She was pleased that Duncan had noticed it.

"Mary Kate is a sweet child. All she needs is love and attention," Jane said.

"So do we all," Duncan said reflectively. Then, as though he realized he had said too much, he stood up and went to the door, giving her one long last look before going out and closing the door softly behind him.

She stared at the door, wishing he had stayed. They had just shared more of themselves than they had in days. She heard the rumble of the Cherokee's motor as Duncan left, and went up to bed before he came home.

While she was lying there in the dark, she realized that their conversation had not been about Mary Kate as much as it had been about themselves.

MARY KATE'S PUNISHMENT for driving her grandfather's pickup truck turned out to be a restriction to their house every afternoon for a week and a strict prohibition on any contact with Dearling. This hit her harder than any of them anticipated.

Jane, who stopped by the Rooneys' the next day to drop off some cookies that she had baked, happened to arrive when Mary Kate was throwing a tantrum.

"But Dearling won't know what happened to me if she doesn't see me for a whole week," Mary Kate was raging when Jane stepped inside the door.

"I didn't know what happened to you, either, when you disappeared with my truck," Rooney pointed out.

"It's not fair, it's not fair," the young girl sobbed as she ran off to her room.

"Thanks, Jane, for the cookies. I'm sorry Mary Kate's in such a state," Rooney said apologetically.

Jane had to speak loudly to be heard over Mary Kate's crying. "You're welcome, and tell Mary Kate I said hello," she told Rooney, but Jane found the child's sobs heart-wrenching. She knew that Rooney felt that he had to punish Mary Kate for such a serious offense, but she wished he had chosen some way other than prohibiting his granddaughter from seeing Dearling. The llama seemed to be a stabilizing influence on Mary Kate, and she knew that to the child herself, this must be the cruelest punishment that Rooney had ever devised.

Jane went to the barn every day to get Dearling and to talk to her the way Mary Kate did, but knew that as far as the llama was concerned, she wasn't a good substitute. She always had the feeling that Dearling was looking over her shoulder, expecting to see Mary Kate come bouncing around the corner of the barn any minute.

It was a slow week, and when Mary Kate was finally released from her restriction, Jane didn't have the heart to say no when Mary Kate, showing her old exuberance, appeared on the back doorstep, begging her to come over to the barn for a reunion with Dearling.

Dearling seemed thrilled to see Mary Kate again, butting her in a playful fashion and blowing gently into her face. Mary Kate laughed delightedly.

"She didn't forget me, did she, Jane?" she said, her arms locked around Dearling's neck.

"No, Mary Kate, it would be pretty hard to forget someone like you," Jane said with a smile.

When clouds blocked out the sun and it became too cold to stay outdoors, Mary Kate, in a lively mood, insisted that they go into the barn, but not just to see the horses.

"Does Duncan let you play in there?" Jane asked doubtfully.

"Sure. Let's play hide-and-seek."

"Well . . ."

"Come on, Jane, don't be a stick-in-the-mud. I'll be It and you hide." Mary Kate turned her back, hid her eyes against the side of the barn, and began to count loudly by fives.

"Wait a minute," said Jane. "What am I supposed to do?" She wanted to honor Mary Kate's request; it seemed the least she could do after Mary Kate's long confinement, and the child was obviously lonely for playmates.

Mary Kate stopped counting and wheeled around. "Haven't you played hide-and-seek before?" she asked incredulously.

"I don't think so," Jane said. All this made her feel exceedingly incompetent.

"I'm It. I count all the way to one hundred by fives, and when I'm through counting, you're supposed to be hidden. Then I try to find you." Mary Kate crooked an arm over her eyes and started counting again.

Jane looked around her frantically, trying to figure out where to hide. Duncan's horse hung his head over the door to his stall and whinnied. A couple of barn cats, half tame, jumped down from a barrel and ran into the shadows.

Jane, still not completely comfortable around the horses, decided to avoid their quarters as hiding places. Mary Kate had already counted all the way to seventy before Jane finally let herself quietly into the tack room and concealed herself behind the sawhorses where the llamas' panniers were stored.

"Ready or not, here I come," Mary Kate cried, and Jane could hear her slamming doors and growing progressively closer in her search.

When she found her, Mary Kate pounced. "There you are! Now it's your turn to be It!"

So Jane hid her eyes and counted, and afterward she found Mary Kate behind some old clothes hanging in a cubbyhole beside Duncan's office door. The game went on for almost half an hour, much to the interest of Flapjack and the other horses.

They were both tiring of hide-and-seek when Jane found Mary Kate in what appeared to be a storage closet that was seldom used; the door was behind a heap of tractor parts. When Jane opened the door unawares, suddenly Mary Kate reached out, caught her by the wrist, and pulled Jane down into a pile of something soft and warm.

Jane sputtered and pulled herself to a sitting position. Whatever it was, the stuff was full of dust, and she began to sneeze.

"What *is* this, anyway?" Jane asked when she had her sneezing under control. She picked up a handful of it and rubbed it between her fingers.

"It's llama wool," Mary Kate replied, taking a clump of it and lobbing it at Jane. Jane tossed a fistful back, and soon they were exchanging volleys of it, until Jane began to sneeze again.

Finally they pulled themselves to their feet, and Jane brushed the wool off her clothes. It was feathery light to the touch; she held it up so that she could see it better. The fibers were long and ranged in color from white to every imaginable shade of brown and gray.

"It's beautiful," Jane said, reaching down for another handful. Something about the fibers seemed to awaken a tactile sense that she'd never known she had. Suddenly she longed to feel the pull of it between her fingers as she twisted and drew it out into yarn.

Confused by this thought, she stood there staring down at the wool. A tiny blip of memory sparked her consciousness. It reminded her of the time when she had been sorting Sigrid's fabric and had realized that she knew the meaning of the terms warp and woof.

"Jane? Jane! Come on over to our house, I want to make some hot chocolate. Grandpa said it was okay as long as I use hot water from the tap and instant cocoa. Jane? Don't you want some hot chocolate? You can bring a bag of that wool, if you want. Duncan wouldn't mind."

Jane followed, her mind cluttered with newfound information that seemed to unwind from a dark place inside her head. In order to spin wool, she would need a spinning wheel. She had used one before. She knew it. And as for the wool from the llamas, it seemed softer than sheep's wool. She had no idea how she came by this information; she just *knew*, that was all.

Wool, spinning wheels, warp and woof. What did they all mean? What relation did they have to her past life? All she knew was that she wanted to encourage more such knowledge to unfold from her subconscious. Maybe it was the key to the person she had once been.

That night she asked Duncan about the wool in the closet.

"Oh, we've been collecting llama wool as long as we've had llamas, which means that there's many years' accumulation of it. Most of it is in bags, but Mary Kate got in there one day and opened several of them, leaving the wool strewn about. You're welcome to all of it, if you like."

"I need a spinning wheel, Duncan," she said.

"A spinning wheel?" he said with some surprise.

"So I can spin the wool into yarn. Don't ask me how I know how to do it. I just do."

Duncan regarded her with a smile and more interest than he'd shown in a week. "A spinning wheel, huh? Well, what do you know."

"Do you have any idea where I can get one? Are there any catalogs around where I might be able to order it?"

"I'll see about it," was all Duncan would say, but she noticed that when he came back from the barn later that night, he walked around suppressing a sly smile.

Duncan left the ranch before she woke up the next morning and didn't leave a note to let her know when he'd be back. She ate a solitary breakfast, but by the time she was loading her dishes into the dishwasher, she heard the Cherokee coming down the driveway.

She stood at the door and watched wide-eyed as Duncan opened the back doors of the Cherokee and unloaded a very old spinning wheel.

"Where did you get it?" Jane asked, wearing a big smile as he brought it in and set it down in front of the fireplace.

"Friend of mine in Durkee has a little junk shop. I recalled seeing this in there one day and wondering who in the world used spinning wheels anymore. Now I know." There was laughter in his eyes.

Jane tentatively approached the spinning wheel. It was dusty, but the drive cord was taut and no parts were missing.

"Are you sure you know what to do with this thing?" Duncan asked skeptically.

"Yes, oh yes," she said happily. "I just don't know how to thank you."

"I guess none of those characters on the soap operas you've watched have ever been given a spinning wheel, right?" He was laughing at her now, and in a new spirit of fun, she chased him out of the house, returning to gaze at the spinning wheel for a long moment before she went to get the llama wool that she had spent last night laboriously picking and cleaning in preparation for the day when she would spin it into yarn.

It felt strange but familiar to sit at the old wheel and begin the rhythm of twisting and drawing out the wool as she pedaled with her foot. She worked tentatively at first; then, as yarn coiled on the bobbin, she became more confident. By the time Duncan appeared for dinner, she had spun a skein of lovely brown yarn.

After that she spun every day, feeling more at ease with the spinning process as time went on. *I wish I had a skein winder,* she thought to herself, then wondered, *How do I even know what a skein winder is?* But she *did* know that a skein winder could be attached to the spinning wheel for the purpose of skeining up the wool she was spinning. It was just another example of random memory, and it frustrated her with its hint of her unknown past.

Later that week as she sat spinning, Duncan, who had started staying home in the evening hours, said, "You look so contented when you work at that."

She smiled at him. "I feel good when I'm spinning. I don't know how it figures into the life I once lived, but I'm sure it was a skill that was important to me. Here, Duncan, hold your hands up. I want to wind this yarn around them."

Duncan complied, his eyes never leaving her face as she swayed from side to side, wrapping the wool around his outstretched hands.

"You know," she said, "I don't think that going to California is going to be enough. I think I want something more, something else."

"Such as what?" Duncan asked in surprise.

She divested his hands of the wool and wrapped the skein carefully in tissue paper. She took her time in answering. "I don't think I can start a new life until I know who I was. Who I *am*."

"You said that no one could find out anything about you after they found you in the ditch," he reminded her. "They checked police reports, missing person reports, newspaper accounts, everything. Didn't they?"

"Yes, but at the time I had to leave the search up to others, because I was too ill to work on it myself. Now that I'm feeling stronger, I'd like to attempt to figure out where I came from, where I lived, what I did for a living." Her face became dreamy. "I try to see myself in a house somewhere, sitting at a desk balancing a checkbook, perhaps, or walking my dog. Do you suppose I had a dog? And if I did, where would he be now? I've got to find out my true identity, Duncan." She wrapped her arms around her knees and rested her chin on top of them.

"Why is this so important all of a sudden?"

"I keep learning things about myself, suddenly realizing that I know how to use a spinning wheel, for instance. I've come to hope that eventually I might remember who I am, but what if that happens when I'm in the middle of a new life? What if I were suddenly to regain my memory and realize that I've got a husband and a couple of kids someplace? Wouldn't I have to go back to them?''

"I don't know," Duncan said, as though this was a new thought.

"You've always understood before," Jane said urgently. "Don't you see why I need to know?"

For the first time since she'd known him, Duncan seemed unnerved.

"Well?" she prodded gently, wanting his blessing and needing his help.

"I suppose you're right," he said, but his features had become strained and taut, and a muscle in his eyelid twitched.

"Help me," she said in a pleading voice. "You will, won't you?"

He turned to her, and for a brief moment bewilderment flickered in his eyes. He overcame it quickly. "If that's what you really want," he said slowly.

"I think it is," Jane said. "I know it is."

"Then that's what we'll do," Duncan said, but he looked less than enthusiastic.

"What's wrong? Don't you like the idea?"

"In some ways," he said.

"What does that mean?"

He shrugged, and his eyes burned into hers. "You might not like what you find," he said.

She stared at him, then managed a smile. "I'll have to take my chances, I guess."

"Why not leave well enough alone, Jane?"

She thought about it and said, "I'm more afraid of not knowing who I am than of knowing."

"They say that what you don't know can't hurt you," Duncan offered.

"What you don't know certainly can hurt you, especially if it rears its ugly head at an inopportune time," Jane retorted. She softened her tone when he drew his lips into a tight line, and continued, "Anyway, I'd love to find out that I have a family—mother, father, brothers and sisters. I feel so—so alone in the world," she said with an embarrassed half laugh.

"You have us," he said, encompassing the ranch with a gesture. "You have me, Mary Kate and Rooney."

She was glad he considered her part of their close-knit little group, and her heart warmed to him. "Mary Kate and Rooney—

I don't know them as well as I know you," she said slowly. "But you—you've been wonderful to me, Duncan. My own brother couldn't have been more decent."

"On that, I think I'll call it quits for the evening. Good night, Jane," he said gruffly. He stood up, put on his coat and headed toward Rooney's.

She had said something wrong. But what? That she wanted to find out who she really was? Or was it her comment that he had been as kind to her as a brother would have been? She had meant it only as a compliment.

Anyway, why wouldn't he be pleased that she thought of him as a brother? They were both really alone in the world. She had no known relatives, and he had none living. Was it only that he had trouble thinking of her as a sister? Did he think that she was being overly familiar in even suggesting that they had a brother-sister kind of relationship? Or was it only that he had never considered how comforting it would be to have siblings that he could depend on when he needed someone?

Okay, so she wouldn't say anything like that again. She felt that she had overstepped her bounds, or failed him in some indefinable way, or—oh, what was the use?

Feeling vaguely troubled and unsure of her ground, she gathered her skeins of yarn and went upstairs to bed.

Chapter Ten

A brother. She thought of him as a brother, for Pete's sake. It was not an auspicious sign.

What would it take to show her that he cared for her in a way that was anything but brotherly? How could he get that point across without scaring her half to death?

Her emotions were still raw; she admitted that she was wary of men. Still, he thought she had learned to trust him. No, he *knew* it. So it must be something else that made her hold back.

He studied himself in the mirror the next morning while shaving. Was he physically attractive enough to appeal to her? He'd never had any complaints in that department before, but his face was more weathered now than it had been when he was in his twenties, and there were deep lines around his eyes. He had all his own teeth, and his hair wasn't receding yet. No beer belly; the work around the ranch kept him in shape.

He tried parting his hair on the other side, but he didn't think the change made any appreciable difference in his looks, so he parted it again the way he always had. He swished mouthwash around his mouth, just in case. No sense in taking chances.

When he went downstairs, she smiled at him while she was taking eggs out of the carton, and, acting as normally as he could, he found a package of bacon in the refrigerator and stuck it into the microwave so that the slices would separate more easily.

"Good morning, Duncan," Jane said serenely.

"Morning," he replied as he laid the bacon slices in a pan and shoved it back into the microwave oven to cook.

They sat down at the table when the eggs were ready, and Jane asked, "How am I doing on the eggs?"

"Just the way I like them," he told her, and it was true, too. "How am I doing on the bacon?"

She munched on a piece, holding it daintily between thumb and forefinger. "Exactly crisp enough," she said.

They went on eating, and Duncan wondered if this spirit of co-operation between them was the problem. Was it possible to be too compatible? It might be better if they didn't get along so well. Still, he couldn't imagine having a squabble with Jane. They always talked everything out, which was the way it was supposed to be— but it certainly hadn't been that way with Sigrid.

"I've been thinking," Jane said carefully before they got up from the breakfast table, "about going back to Illinois. To talk to the people who found me." She watched him, waiting for his reaction.

This was mainly one of dismay, although he didn't want her to know that. "Have you been thinking about this long?" he asked.

"The idea seemed to be in my head when I woke up this morning," she admitted with a little laugh. "It's become a possibility since I've found out that I might be able to sell my llama yarn."

"How did you find that out?"

"I was looking through one of those magazines you get from the llama breeding association, and I found an article about llama owners who sell and use the wool for knitting, crocheting and weaving. In the classifieds there was an ad placed by a woman who wants to buy yarn, so I phoned her. She wants to see samples. I'll have my own income if she buys some." Jane's eyes were shining.

"You mean you'd use the money you make to pay for a trip back to Illinois?"

"Yes," Jane said. "I'll pay you back what I owe you, don't worry. I can travel cheaply and—"

"Forget about the money. What about our bargain? You promised you'd stay until the cold weather's over," he said gruffly.

"I'm well now, and I'd only be gone a week or two. I'll come back, Duncan. I promised you I'd stay."

He couldn't share her pleasure in this idea; he didn't want her to go. He was still concerned about her health, and for reasons that he recognized as purely selfish, he didn't want her to leave the ranch. Such a journey would remove her from his sphere of influence.

"Duncan?"

He hurriedly drank the last of his coffee. "You can do whatever you want, I suppose," he said and fled the house, feeling her reproachful gaze on his back.

He was ashamed of himself for being unfeeling, but he needed time to get used to the idea of her leaving, even briefly. And he didn't want to talk about it with her. Thinking about it was hard enough.

Then he came up with the idea that Jane might be able to find out the things she needed to know about her past without ever leaving the ranch. He didn't mention this to her. In fact, he spoke to her very little during the next few days. He was aware that she was waiting for him to mention her proposed trip, but he didn't. If she was making plans to go, he didn't want to know.

Behind the scenes, calling from the barn where she couldn't hear, he spent the next few days telephoning. He called the sheriff's department that had handled the investigation of Jane's case in Tyree County, Illinois, and was told that the investigating officer was long departed from the department. A new man answered the phone, and to Duncan's surprise, the fellow told him that he had stumbled upon this unsolved case during his first week there and had been curious about it ever since.

"It's like this," said the detective, a guy named Bill Schmidt. "A woman appears in a ditch near one of the locals' cornfields, and nobody knows where she came from. Afterward, nobody knows where she went, either. I mean, I can't figure it, you know what I'm saying?"

"I know," Duncan assured him. "As it happens, she's here with me. What we still don't know is where she came from. Are there any leads?"

"Leads? You got to be kidding. The case isn't closed, but it might as well be. We're overworked and underpaid around this place, you know? We don't have time to work on old cases."

"What if I brought her to Tyree, so she could see the records of her case?"

"There's not much to see, although she's welcome to go through our file. The guy who investigated told some of the fellows around here that he figured that her boyfriend got mad at her and dumped her out of the car. Or something like that."

"Something like that," Duncan repeated. Various scenarios flashed through his mind, and inwardly he shuddered.

"You could talk to Jones, the farmer who found her. He has a kid who was with him that day. Practically fell over her where she was lying in the ditch, I hear. It's not something you'd forget easily, you know what I mean?''

Duncan hung up, wondering if he had made any progress. He decided that he had at least made a contact with someone who was chatty enough to convey whatever information he knew, and at least this Schmidt fellow sounded interested and energetic. That was something.

He placed his next call to the administrator of Tyree Hospital, who was polite but could not provide any information at all.

"No, Mr. Tate, as far as we know there were no identifying labels in her clothing. She had no identification whatsoever. I'm sorry we can't help you," she said.

Discouraged by this dead end, Duncan hung up the phone when the conversation was over, shrugged into his coat, left his warm office and trudged toward the house, which was lighted from within by the lamps Jane always turned on in the evening. He recalled all too well what it was like to come home to an empty house. He had done that every evening since Sigrid left, until Jane came.

A chill wind nipped at his cheeks. The night was clear, and in the pen beside the barn, the llamas shuffled and hummed to one another. The pungent scent of wood smoke drifted toward him, and he realized that Jane had lighted a fire in the fireplace. It was good to be going home to Jane.

Under the shelter of the porch, welcoming light beamed from the windows, casting a mellow glow over the snow. As he drew closer he could see Jane's blond head bent over her spinning wheel, and he smiled to himself. She had taken to that thing and made it her own, and he was pleased that she had shown this new interest. New interest? It must be an old interest, otherwise she wouldn't know how to do it. He wished he understood more about how her memory worked. Or didn't work.

And if her memory did improve, where would that leave him? Especially if there were, as she had pointed out, a husband and children somewhere, anxiously awaiting the return of a wife and mother. The thought of Jane as someone else's wife was like a wound to the heart.

He had fallen for her, and she thought of him as a brother. Someday she would pick herself up and move away, and that would signal the end of warm welcomes in his house, the end of companionable evenings sitting beside her as she spun, the end of the connectedness that he had begun to feel for another human being.

He supposed Jane never thought of that. She was too all-fired eager to start a new life in California, of all places.

Well, let her go if she wanted. He wouldn't stop her. He would even help her, if that was what it took to keep her happy; he had given his word about that when he was persuading her to stay until spring.

It hadn't been hard to be kind to her when she needed kindness, nor had he had a hard time forgiving her for stealing from him, and he hadn't found it difficult to bear with her in those early days, when she still didn't trust him. No, with Jane everything was easy, including falling head over heels in love with her.

The hard part was going to be saying goodbye.

HE THOUGHT ABOUT IT for a long time before he reluctantly told her about calling the Tyree County sheriff's department and the Tyree hospital. The main reason that he wanted to tell her was that she seemed determined to find out about her past, and he didn't want her to discover later that he had been there first, without telling her.

The opportunity to divulge this information came at dinner one night when she told him with quiet pride that she had sold her entire store of llama yarn to a hand knitter in Vermont.

"I didn't make a lot of money, but it's a start," she said. "As soon as I can afford it, I'm going back to Illinois and try to retrace the path that led to that ditch in Carlton Jones's field."

Duncan felt his mouth go dry, but could no longer keep from telling her what he knew. "Jane, I have news," he said.

She stopped chewing and swallowed. She gave him a questioning look.

"I called the Tyree sheriff's department the other day. I talked to the detective on the case, Bill Schmidt was his name. He's not the officer you talked with after they found you. He's a new guy who took over after the other one left. Anyway, he says he'll let you look at the records if you want to."

"Look at the records?"

"The report of the detective who came to your hospital room."

"Detective Sid Reedy," Jane said slowly. "I remember that day."

"If you'd like to talk to this Schmidt, why don't you call him up? Maybe he could send you a copy of their records. And you could phone Carlton Jones tonight, if you'd like."

"I want to go there, Duncan. To see if standing in that ditch outside Tyree brings back memories of anything that happened to me. To ride along the highway and try to figure out why I was there and where I was going." Her gaze was steady.

"Are you sure, Jane, that this is what you want to do?"

"Absolutely sure."

Duncan decided from the set of her chin that Jane was going to go on the trip whether he liked the idea or not. He heaved a big sigh. "Well, if you're so set on going, I'll lend you the money," he said. "It'll take a while to make enough money from selling your wool, and you should probably go as soon as possible, so your tracks won't get any colder than they already are." He surprised himself by offering this; he still didn't want her to leave.

"I've already imposed on you too much," she said.

"You'll pay me back," he pointed out. "How do you plan to get there, anyway?"

"By bus, I guess. It's probably the least expensive way to go. There must be a Greyhound leaving from Rock Springs."

"I think you should fly. A bus trip would be so tiring, and you're still recuperating," he said, watching her closely. She had suddenly gone thoughtful.

"Is anything wrong?" he asked.

"I'm scared, Duncan," she said. She turned wide eyes upon him, and he saw the panic in them.

"You said you wanted to go!"

"You have to admit that taking off by myself on a search like this is pretty intimidating," she said.

He considered this. True, she had seemingly come into her own here at Placid Valley Ranch, but then again, this was a place where she felt comfortable. The world had not treated her well the last time she'd been out in it on her own, and the things that had happened to her were hard for her to forget.

"I could go with you, I suppose," he said after a while. He hardly dared to hope that she would agree to this. But he was rewarded by a leap of interest.

"You could? Really?" She seemed dazed by his offer.

"If you want me to," he said.

"It's another imposition," she said slowly.

He regarded it as an opportunity, but he didn't say that. "I'd rather fly than take the bus. Will you call the airlines and make the reservations, or shall I?" he asked, expecting an argument or at least a long discussion, but she surprised him.

"I will," she said, smiling the brilliant smile that always made his heart turn over, and went to do it right away.

"YOU AND JANE are going to do *what*?" Rooney asked, when Duncan told him that they would be leaving.

"Search for her past," Duncan said.

Rooney scratched his head. "What for?" he inquired.

"She's afraid she left some loose ends that might need tying up," Duncan told him.

Rooney considered this. "Well, she might have. You never can tell," he agreed after a while.

"So we're going to fly to Chicago, rent a car and head for southern Illinois."

"One question for you, Duncan," Rooney said. "Why the hell do you care?"

"Hey, you know I like to read mysteries. Why not try to solve one?" Duncan managed a crooked grin, but he was well aware that he couldn't admit how much he cared for Jane even to Rooney, who was his closest friend.

"I sure hope you won't be gone long. Jane either. Mary Kate is going to miss her like crazy."

"You and Mary Kate will have to hold down the fort around here, Rooney. You think you two can manage it without Mary Kate demolishing the whole place?"

"Jeez, Duncan, I don't know. Just to make sure, why don't you take Mary Kate with you?"

Duncan laughed. "I don't have anything against southern Illinois, that's why. Anyway, she's been behaving herself pretty well since she drove your pickup into that snowbank, hasn't she?"

"Yeah, but the truck ain't never going to be the same. She burned up the emergency brake, you know."

"It could have been a lot worse."

"A lot of things could be worse. Which brings us back to our original subject. Why don't Jane leave well enough alone?"

"Because she can't, Rooney. And if she can't, I can't, either." With that, Duncan jammed his hat on top of his head and walked out of Rooney's house into the cold night air. Let Rooney make anything he wanted out of that statement. Being in love with a woman who had no intention of staying with him was hard enough; not talking about it was even harder. Maybe Rooney would get the hint and understand how it was between them.

"BUT I THOUGHT you were staying until spring!" Mary Kate cried accusingly.

"I am, Mary Kate. In fact, I should be back before then," Jane said.

Mary Kate tossed the wool she had been carding for Jane onto the floor and jumped up from her seat at the kitchen table. "I want to go with you," she said.

"That's impossible, you know. You have to go to school."

"I hate school. I hate everything," Mary Kate said.

"That's not true—you love Dearling," Jane reminded her.

Mary Kate stuck out her bottom lip. "Uh-huh, I love Dearling," she agreed. Her expression darkened. "You said you were going to teach me to spin."

"I can show you how to spin with a simple drop spindle before I go," Jane said soothingly. "And I'm hoping you'll take care of Amos for me while I'm gone."

Mary Kate considered this. "He does like me," she conceded. Then she frowned again. "Do you have to go, Jane? Absolutely have to?"

"Yes, Mary Kate, I do. It's really important to me to find out my real name and where I came from. I've decided that I can't go on with my life until I know."

"Why?"

"Because I keep remembering fragments of it, and I'm curious about them."

"Why?"

"You would be, too, wouldn't you? Think how you would feel if you didn't know where you came from or where you belonged."

"Why?"

Jane was growing impatient. "Stop playing this silly 'Why?' game with me, Mary Kate. I'm trying to talk to you the way I'd talk to another adult."

This seemed to sober Mary Kate. "You are?"

"Sure. You're my friend. I'll miss you when I'm in Illinois, you know."

"You'll miss me? Really?"

"Really. And I'll bring you a present."

"A present!"

"What would you like?"

Mary Kate considered this. "A frilly dress. With ruffles and petticoats and sleeves that you can see through."

"A frilly dress?" Jane was stunned. Mary Kate wasn't the type for party dresses.

"Yeah. A pink one."

"Well, okay," Jane said dubiously.

"Something nice, Jane. Really nice," urged Mary Kate.

Jane smiled. A soft shade of pink would brighten Mary Kate's sallow complexion.

She bent to hug Mary Kate. "I'll buy you the nicest, pinkest, frilliest dress I can find," Jane promised.

DUNCAN AND JANE left the ranch a week later and flew into Chicago in early afternoon. They rented a car and left the city, Jane staring with conflicting emotions at the buildings looming against the city's skyline. Behind them jets soared up and out of O'Hare Airport, and Jane couldn't help but recall all the times she used to wish she was on one of them and headed for California.

"You're awfully quiet. Is everything okay?" Duncan asked anxiously.

"Not really," Jane was able to tell him.

"You look tired," he said.

Jane pulled down the car's visor and checked her reflection in the mirror. Her face was pale, and there were deep circles under her eyes. She had hardly slept at all last night. She shoved the visor up again and tried to smile through her fear that somehow the city might swallow her up again, if she wasn't careful.

"Seeing Chicago again makes me feel like I've been socked in the stomach," she said.

"Was living here that bad?"

"I couldn't keep a job, I was constantly trying to find a place to keep warm, and I mostly lived in shelters for the homeless. One time some men came in a police wagon and started rounding up people on the streets, and we heard later that they'd been taken to a mental hospital. I thought they'd get me next, and I hid in the basement of an abandoned building with some other street peo-

ple until I was sure the threat had passed. Yes, it was that bad."
She hunched herself into the corner of the seat.

"Didn't you go to the authorities and explain what had happened to you? That somebody was supposed to help you get on your feet and find a job?" he asked incredulously.

"Sure, but no one seemed especially interested. I don't think anybody believed me. The prevailing attitude was that I was a lot better off than a welfare mother with children, so I was left to fend for myself. I was still having headaches when I lived here, and it made holding a job difficult."

"You don't seem to be having headaches now," Duncan observed.

"It's really odd, but I don't think I've had a headache since I fell and hit my head in the snowstorm the night you found me in the mine," she said. They were on an interstate now, driving past neat subdivisions. Traffic moved faster, and she sat up and looked around. Now that they were away from oppressive tall buildings and ugly warehouses, she felt better.

"And your cough is almost gone, too," Duncan said, trying to cheer her.

"The antibiotic medicine did wonders. I thought I'd need a warm climate to shake it," she told him.

"Is that why you decided to go to California?" he asked. He was curious as to why she had chosen that particular state for her new start.

"There was another reason, too. All the time I spent in the library trying to keep warm, I used to read a lot. One of the magazines I read outlined a training program they have there. I thought I could learn to use a computer, so I could get a good job someplace."

He sent her a sharp look. "Is that what you still want?"

"Maybe. Oh, I don't know. It all depends on what we find out on this trip. Perhaps I have marketable skills and I just don't know it." She stared out the window at a passing blue van. It was a Ford Econoline, and it somehow seemed familiar. She shook the feeling off because there was nothing she could tie it into; there was no van like it at the ranch.

The flat land stretched out white and frozen on both sides of the road. They were in the country now, and the roads were straight with few intersections between the towns. Duncan held their speed at a steady fifty-five miles per hour, and the dotted line in the middle of the road hypnotized her so that all she wanted to do was

NO RISK, NO OBLIGATION TO BUY...NOW OR EVER!

GUARANTEED

PLAY "ROLL A DOUBLE" AND GET AS MANY AS FIVE FREE GIFTS!

HERE'S HOW TO PLAY:

1. Peel off label from front cover. Place it in space provided at right. With a coin, carefully scratch off the silver dice. This makes you eligible to receive two or more free books, and possibly another gift, depending on what is revealed beneath the scratch-off area.

2. Send back this card and you'll receive brand-new Harlequin Superromance® novels. These books have a cover price of $3.50 each, but they are yours to keep absolutely free.

3. There's no catch. You're under no obligation to buy anything. We charge nothing – ZERO – for your first shipment. And you don't have to make any minimum number of purchases – not even one!

4. The fact is thousands of readers enjoy receiving books by mail from the Harlequin Reader Service® before they're available in stores. They like the convenience of home delivery and they love our discount prices!

5. We hope that after receiving your free books you'll want to remain a subscriber. But the choice is yours – to continue or cancel, anytime at all! So why not take us up on our invitation, with no risk of any kind. You'll be glad you did!

NOT ACTUAL SIZE

You'll look like a million dollars when you wear this lovely necklace! Its cobra-link chain is a generous 18" long, and the multi-faceted Austrian crystal sparkles like a diamond!

"ROLL A DOUBLE!"

PLACE LABEL HERE

SCRATCH HERE

SEE CLAIM CHART BELOW

334 CIH AKXH
(C-H-SR-08/93)

YES! I have placed my label from the front cover into the space provided above and scratched off the silver dice. Please rush me the free books and gift that I am entitled to. I understand that I am under no obligation to purchase any books, as explained on the back and on the opposite page.

NAME _____

ADDRESS _____ APT. _____

CITY _____ PROVINCE _____ POSTAL CODE _____

CLAIM CHART

 4 FREE BOOKS PLUS FREE CRYSTAL PENDANT NECKLACE

 3 FREE BOOKS

 2 FREE BOOKS

CLAIM NO.37-829

THE HARLEQUIN READER SERVICE®: HERE'S HOW IT WORKS

Accepting free books puts you under no obligation to buy anything. You may keep the books and gift and return the shipping statement marked "cancel." If you do not cancel, about a month later we will send you 4 additional novels, and bill you just $2.96 each plus 25¢ delivery and GST*. That's the complete price, and – compared to cover prices of $3.50 each – quite a bargain! You may cancel at any time, but if you choose to continue, every month we'll send you 4 more books, which you may either purchase at the discount price...or return at our expense and cancel your subscription.

*Terms and prices subject to change without notice.
Canadian residents will be charged applicable provincial taxes and GST.

0195619199-L2A5X3-BR01

HARLEQUIN READER SERVICE
PO BOX 609
FORT ERIE ON L2A 9Z9

MAIL ▷ POSTE

Canada Post Corporation / Société canadienne des postes

Postage paid   Port payé
if mailed in Canada   si posté au Canada

Business   Réponse
Reply   d'affaires

0195619199   01

let her head loll back against the seat. They played the radio to break the monotony, but soon it became part of it, droning on and on about commodity prices or community happenings that had nothing to do with them. They were travelers in a strange land, part of the landscape but curiously detached.

It was growing dark when they reached the outskirts of Springfield. Duncan pulled the car off the interstate and into the parking lot of a large chain motel. Jane waited while he went inside and registered them in two different rooms.

When he came out, he seemed to be thinking about something else, and she had to ask him their room numbers twice. The rooms were on an inside hall, and Jane trailed behind him, lugging the suitcase she had borrowed. He offered to carry it for her, but she refused. Duncan shook his head, as if to say that it was her own business if she didn't want his help, which made her feel as though she had fallen short of some mark that she hadn't even known was there.

He unlocked the door of her room for her and handed her the key.

"Let's eat dinner later at the restaurant across the street," he suggested. "Say, at seven o'clock?" His eyes in the light from the lamp on the wall seemed overly anxious.

She smiled and he seemed to relax. "I don't have a watch," she reminded him. "I won't know when it's time."

"I'll call you on the phone," he promised. He shifted awkwardly back and forth; Jane thought about asking him if the unfamiliar shoes he wore hurt his feet. At home he always wore boots. Suddenly feeling shy with him, she didn't ask him about the shoes.

"I'll see you later," she said instead, and went inside. She heard his room door open and close next door.

Jane set her suitcase on the luggage stand and looked around. The window faced the parking lot, where she could see their rental car. She closed the sheer draperies, but not the heavy light-blocking ones, and moved restlessly around the motel room, examining it. She opened a door, thinking it was a closet, and found its twin shut and latched. The second door must open on Duncan's room. She closed the door on her side very carefully so that he wouldn't hear.

After that, an inspection of the dresser drawers turned up a folder full of stationery; she hated the dresser with its plastic top, but the little plastic glasses in their wrappings of cellophane on the tray there amused her. She tested the double bed, which after the comfortable one at Duncan's ranch seemed hard, and the rust-colored carpet was ugly.

She'd grown accustomed to the welcome of a lived-in room full of lemon-polished furniture and scented with the fragrance of wholesome food cooking in the kitchen. *You've gotten awfully particular,* she chided herself. A few months ago she would have counted herself lucky to be in a room such as this for only a few hours. Here there was all the heat she could want, there were clean sheets, and no one was around to tell her to move on.

But she had changed since she arrived at Placid Valley Ranch. What had once seemed like enough—a warm place to live, plenty of food—was not adequate for her needs now. She had to have more. She had to know who she was.

She lay down on the bed to rest, and before she knew it she was asleep. She didn't wake up until Duncan called her on the phone.

"Hi, beautiful," he said. "Are you ready to go to dinner?"

"I fell asleep," she admitted, thinking that "Hi, beautiful" didn't sound like the kind of thing Duncan would say.

He laughed, and she didn't let him in on her puzzlement.

"I'll be knocking on your door in ten minutes or so," he told her.

When she hung up the phone, it was a few seconds before she could move. All at once Duncan was acting differently. Had he been this way on the ranch? She didn't think so.

There he had always been helpful and forthright; she could usually tell what he was thinking. As soon as they'd checked into the motel, he'd changed. It was as though he was trying to figure out how to act in these circumstances, as though he were trying to impress her.

But why?

She was used to his habits, used to the way he acted around her, used to *Duncan.* She didn't want anything between them to change.

What was she thinking? That Duncan was interested in her in a way that she couldn't accept?

No, that was ridiculous. They'd covered that ground the time that he'd kissed her.

If anything was wrong, it must be her imagination.

Chapter Eleven

She and Duncan had never been anywhere together except on the
plane today, and she realized that she was as nervous about it as a
girl on her first date. Which was an unfortunate comparison, she
told herself. This wasn't a date. This was just Duncan.

When he rapped twice, she opened the door to her room. He'd
had his hair cut before they left Wyoming, and while it usually
grew slightly down over his ears, now it didn't. His ears looked
pink and shiny, as though he'd scrubbed thoroughly for this outing, and she wanted to smile at the idea. Instead she only stepped
into the hallway to join him.

When he took off his coat in the restaurant, she saw that he had
put on a suit. She'd never seen him wearing a suit before, but he
looked wonderful in it. She couldn't recall ever thinking that
Duncan was handsome, but now she realized with a start that there
was no man in the restaurant who was better looking.

The waiter came to take their order. Duncan ordered a steak,
and when Jane hesitated and said that she didn't know what she
wanted, he ordered the same thing for her. She was glad, because
she found that she couldn't think about the choices on the menu
with him sitting across from her, looking as though he was hanging on her every word. This was another difference from the way
things were at the ranch.

What to talk to him about? She cast about for something, anything. She didn't understand why it should be so hard to think of
a topic; talk had always seemed to flow easily between them.

She knew that Duncan was having an equally hard time trying
to start a conversation. But this was small solace when her tongue
seemed to have turned to lead, and her brain was too mushy to

think. She had an idea that they were both thankful when the waiter brought their salads.

Every word Duncan said seemed pulled from him; it was unnatural, unreal. Jane wished that she had made this journey alone, and then was glad she hadn't. She was grateful for his presence and most of all for his help. His help... Maybe they could talk about tomorrow.

"Do you think I should bother to go to the hospital when we get to Tyree?" she asked.

He latched onto her question as though it were a lifeline. "I think the first stop should be the sheriff's department. Then you can decide if it's worthwhile to go see this Carlton Jones and his son, or whether you want to drop by the hospital."

A shadow passed across her face. "I know all the nurses and doctors at the hospital would be glad to see me. I was a favorite. Yet I'm reluctant to go there." She finished the last of her salad and sat back.

"Why?" Duncan wanted to know.

She shook her head. "Why should I deserve any more of their attention?"

"They'll be happy to see that you survived," Duncan said. "There's a lot to be said for that. It wasn't easy."

"No, it wasn't," Jane said, recalling all the times she'd been evicted and the close call when she might have been shipped off to the mental hospital; when you were on the streets, if anyone suspected you of acting irrationally, they'd get suspicious. Sometimes it was hard not to act irrationally when your head had been aching for a solid week and you'd gone without a decent meal for that long, too.

"It's not easy for you to think about those days, is it?" Duncan observed with a sharp look after the main course arrived.

"I suppose not," Jane responded. "After all, I don't feel that far removed from that time in my life."

Duncan stopped eating and held her gaze with his own. He reached over and covered her hand where it rested in her lap. "Those days are over," he said firmly. "Believe it."

Embarrassed by the steadiness of his gaze, she lowered her eyelids. They finished eating in silence.

After dinner, Duncan surprised her. "Let's go into the lounge," he said.

Through an archway framed by wrought iron scrollwork Jane saw a bar where people were sitting and drinking, and from farther inside came the sounds of a live band.

"I don't know," she said doubtfully, but Duncan overcame her objections when he took her hand and led her inside.

In the small cocktail lounge they were seated at a table about the size of one of the big dinner plates at the ranch, and Jane commented on this. Duncan laughed. She hadn't thought that what she said was all that funny but was pleased that Duncan thought so. Maybe she'd think of something else to make him laugh. She couldn't stand the way either of them was acting tonight.

They ordered drinks, but Jane didn't know what to order and took Duncan's word for it that she would like a whiskey sour on the rocks. When it arrived at their table, she sipped it and made a face.

"It tastes like rotten lemonade," she said, and he smiled but didn't laugh.

"Why don't we dance?" he suggested. He started to get up, but her hand on his arm stopped him.

"I'm not sure I know how," she said, eyeing other couples on the dance floor. One man was whirling his partner around and around in wide circles; as Jane watched, he dipped her so that her long hair touched the floor.

"All you have to do is follow me," Duncan said as though that settled everything, and before she knew it they were standing on the edge of the dance floor facing each other. Jane's knees felt a bit unsteady, but she thought it was because of the alcohol in her drink. She put her left hand on his shoulder, the way the other women on the floor did with their partners, and discovered to her consternation when he took her right hand in his that her palm was sweaty. If he noticed, he didn't react.

The beat was slow and rhythmic, and the tune was not something that she recognized. It was good music for dancing, however, and as she loosened up, she found that she was stepping on Duncan's toes less and less. He wasn't a spectacular dancer, like the man who was showing off on the opposite side of the floor, but after a while their feet began to move in predictable patterns.

He looked down at her. "See, I told you it would be easy," he said, his eyes glinting with pleasure. He pulled her slightly closer, and she stiffened again, but when she learned that it was easier to follow him when he held her like that, she relaxed.

He smelled of fresh pine scent, and she remembered that Mary Kate had told her that he used a pine-scented shampoo. She smiled at the memory. That had been on the first day that she'd arrived at the ranch, when Mary Kate had given Amos a bath with that shampoo.

Duncan chose that moment to lean away from her. His expression was puzzled. "Something funny?" he asked.

"Just remembering something Mary Kate said," she told him, and he replied, "Let's not worry about Mary Kate while we're on this trip." After that he pulled her so close that his chin rested against the top of her head and her body was pressed against the length of his.

The colored lights over the bandstand glowed bewitchingly. She and Duncan let the other dancers flow around them and moved their feet only slightly, and Duncan held her closer and closer until she was full of the scent and the feel of him in her arms. For that was where he was, in her arms, and the sensation was so new and so overwhelming that she chose not to say anything until she could get a handle on the way she felt about it.

On the occasions when the music stopped playing, they didn't sit down but waited for it to start up again. Before they'd got up to dance, while she was watching the other couples on the dance floor, Jane hadn't realized that dancing was anything more than a refined type of exercise. She hadn't been prepared for the way the music made her feel, or for her reaction to being so close to Duncan.

It was confusing. She had already decided—in fact, she thought that they had decided together—that their feelings for each other weren't sexual. And yet this was definitely a sexual stirring. Sexual electricity, even.

When she'd lived in Chicago, there had been buildings that she passed every day; she had gotten used to the look of them. And then for some reason, maybe when she was riding a bus or walking down a street she seldom used, she'd look up at a building that had seemed so familiar before and wouldn't recognize it from the new angle. Away from the ranch she was seeing, feeling, experiencing Duncan from a different perspective.

They had forgotten about their unfinished drinks on the table, and when the band took a break, they came back to find that the ice had melted. Duncan took one taste of his whiskey and soda and made a face.

"I'll order more drinks," he said.

Suddenly she didn't want to dance anymore, didn't want to sit across from him at this tiny table and make small talk. Fill-in words weren't enough, *she* wasn't enough. She wasn't up to any further posing or posturing for his sake or hers.

"I—I think I'm ready to go back to my room," she said quickly. "It's been a long day." She could think of no other way to put an end to whatever was going on between them.

For a moment he looked as though he was going to object, but then Duncan apparently decided to play along and to ask no questions. He paid the check without comment, although she knew that he was watching her. She turned away, unwilling to explain herself.

Duncan had driven the car across the highway to the restaurant in case it started to snow, and neither of them spoke as they drove back to the motel. She turned slightly to look at him, admiring his strong profile. He didn't speak; maybe he felt as constrained as she did.

At the door to her room, Jane turned to face him and forced herself to smile.

"Thanks, Duncan. It was a lovely dinner," she said. She had to restrain herself from the impulse to reach out and touch his cheek with her fingertips.

He smiled, too, but the smile didn't reach his eyes.

"I'll see you in the morning," he said. "We'd better get an early start."

"Right," she said. Her heart started to pound, and she knew that if she didn't go inside her room right away, he would bend his head and kiss her.

"Good night," she murmured quickly, and closed the door, leaving him standing there.

At that moment she was sure that Duncan recognized the highly charged emotional tension that was developing between them, and that in some way he was even responsible for making it happen.

She slept fitfully between the chill sheets of her bed, jolted awake several times during the night by unfamiliar noises. People talking in the corridor, doors opening and closing, the moan of the plumbing pipes—all of this made her uneasy. She felt so alone in her sterile motel room. She knew that it would be unseemly for Duncan to sleep in the same room with her, but all the same she missed the familiar sounds that accompanied him. At the ranch she could hear him running the water in the morning as he shaved, knew the familiar *thwump!* that his closet door made when he closed it just before coming downstairs in the morning.

She was lonely, she realized. Lonely for Duncan. Lying on her stomach, clutching the stiff motel pillow, she finally slept.

BREAKFAST THE NEXT DAY was hurried because they wanted to get on the road. Fresh snow had fallen in the night, and ice had left hoary patterns on the car's windshield. Duncan scraped the ice and snow away, and soon they were headed south toward Tyree.

Sometimes they didn't see a car for miles on the rural roads; the only things that accompanied them on their journey were wires swinging from pole to pole in front of fields white with snow. Duncan seemed worried, withdrawn. Jane tried to engage him in conversation several times, but after she realized that he wasn't responding in anything but monosyllables, she gave up. She wished he would be his old self again. If anyone had the right to be anxious and upset this morning, she did. After all, she was facing the prospect of finding out who she really was, and she could only imagine the impact that the discovery would have on her goals and her dreams.

Jane kept consulting the map on the seat between them. Forty miles to Tyree, then thirty, then twenty.

As they approached the town, Jane's throat went dry and she tried to remember the passing scenery. That billboard—did she recall seeing it on the day of her accident? That house in the middle of that field—was the yellow brick familiar? But nothing seemed like anything she'd seen before.

Once they were there, Duncan drove directly to the sheriff's department and they went inside to meet Detective Schmidt, the man who had replaced the other detective on Jane's case.

Schmidt, a wiry fellow with a good-natured grin, ushered them into the boxy room that served as his office and invited them to sit down.

"So you came back to find out if anybody knows who you are, is that right?" he asked.

"I'm hoping that someone will remember something that will help me find my identity," Jane said.

"Everybody familiar with this case seems to think that you were pushed out of a car onto the highway that runs past Carlton Jones's farm. You had a head injury. I tend to think that you were driven to Tyree and dumped by somebody passing through. Do you remember anything at all about the events preceding your appearance in that ditch?'' asked Schmidt.

Jane shook her head helplessly. "No," she said quietly. "Nothing."

Schmidt studied her intently for a moment. "Well, that makes it tough, you know what I mean? Now, as far as Tyree goes, this was kind of a big case. The papers around here published your picture and told the story of how you were found. Seems like someone from these parts would have come forward at the time if they knew you."

"There was no one," Jane said. "No one."

Schmidt shoved a folder across the desk. "This is what you came to see," he said. "Everything we have on 'Jane Doe' is in there. Do you go by any other name?"

"I use the name Jane Rhodes, but I know it's not my real name," Jane said. She leafed through the information in her file. It seemed sparse, and she tried to cover her feelings of disappointment. She had been hoping for more.

"You said you've never closed the investigation," Duncan said.

"That's right. 'Course, we didn't get very far. No clues. Mighty strange, you know what I mean?"

"Where do you think we should start looking for clues?" Jane asked.

"Talk to Carlton Jones and his teenage son, see if they remember anything. We asked them the usual—you know, like did they recall any strangers in the area that day, that sort of thing. They didn't have a clue. I hear that the kid was pretty upset, he thought you were dead when they found you. He might be glad to see that you're very much alive."

"Do you think she's in any danger?" Duncan asked, looking up from Jane's file. "It says here that they thought at the time that her head wound might have been caused by a blunt instrument. Is there any chance that somebody might come after her now, if she starts asking around?"

Schmidt considered this. "I can't say," he said after a while. "Maybe, maybe not. Seems like if somebody wanted to hurt her, they would have done it before. She was a patient in the local hospital, she worked in Apollonia, she was there for anybody to find." He eyed Jane. "Anyone ever make any threats? Bother you in any way?"

Jane thought about the men who had tried to abuse her, the person who had stolen her coat in Saint Louis. Those weren't deliberately calculated actions, though; they had happened on the spur of the moment.

"No," she said.

"All I can say is, report anything that worries you, but we think you're safe," Schmidt told them.

They stood up to leave, and Schmidt said, "Good luck with your search. We'll be in touch with your number at the ranch in Wyoming if we find out anything more, but frankly, we don't have the manpower to do the kind of painstaking work you're going to be doing."

"Can you suggest a place to stay around here?" Duncan asked as they were about to walk out the door.

Schmidt chuckled. "There are only two, but I'd recommend the Prairie Rose Motel. Turn right at the light and go two blocks. And good luck with your search."

They checked into the last two rooms available at the small Prairie Rose and went out again to a nearby Western Steer steak house for a quick dinner. In the foyer of the restaurant Jane used the phone to call Carlton Jones. He seemed pleased to hear from her, to know that she was in good health, and he readily invited them to the farm after dinner.

Jane sat forward in her seat as they drove to the farm, peering out at the dark fields on either side of the car.

"Do you recognize any of this?" Duncan asked.

She shook her head. "It's so dark," she said. She strained to see something, anything that would give her her bearings. "Slow down, Duncan, I think that's the sign Mr. Jones told me to look for," she said at last.

The sign said Jonesdale Farms, and the road led to a brown-shingled house surrounded by trees. The path to the door was shoveled clear of snow, and when they knocked, Carlton Jones welcomed them with an expansive smile.

"Come in, come in," he said, rubbing his hands together.

Jane stood awkwardly on the mat before the front door.

"Let me take your coats," he said. He spirited their coats into an adjoining room and hurried back. They sat in his living room and Carl, as he asked them to call him, wanted to be told Jane's history since she left Tyree. She obliged, skipping over the worst parts.

"The reason we're here, Carl, is that I'm hoping you might know something more about how I happened to be in that ditch," she told him earnestly.

"I wish I did," he said with a doleful shake of his head. "But I told the sheriff's men everything I knew. First thing I knew was when I found you there."

"You don't recall a car, or perhaps an odd noise, or anything at all the night before?" Duncan asked.

Carl thought for a moment, then shook his head again. "I looked for tire tracks or something at the side of the road, but I didn't see any. I wish I could help you, but, well, I don't know anything more."

Duncan stood up. "Then I guess we won't waste any more of your time," he said.

"Please don't go," Carl said. "I've made coffee, and Ollie and I baked a cake. Imagine that," he said with a chortle, "I baked a cake! My wife died a few years back, and I've had to learn to take care of Ollie and me almost from scratch, but I'd never thought I'd be baking cakes."

Thinking that Carl might be offended if they left, Jane restrained Duncan with a look of resignation. They both sat down again, and Carl disappeared into the back of the house.

"I thought you wanted to leave," Duncan said under his breath.

"Well, I do, but he's so *nice*," Jane whispered back.

"Careful, Ollie, don't drop it," they heard Carl say in the kitchen just before Ollie appeared, his tongue between his teeth in concentration, as he balanced plates of cake in his hands.

"Ollie, you remember me, don't you?" Jane asked. She attempted to put the boy at ease with a smile.

"Sure," Ollie said. "You're the lady we found."

Carl returned with coffee for the adults and a glass of milk for Ollie. He sat down and Jane decided to keep pursuing information, any information that might help her.

"Do you remember anything at all unusual about that day?" she asked Ollie gently.

He swallowed a mouthful of chocolate cake and shook his head. "It was early in the day yet," he said. "We'd only just got up, Pop and me."

"So I must have been left in the ditch the night before," prompted Jane.

"Yeah, I remember old Jiggers—that's one of our dogs—was missing. We went out early to look for him."

"It took us a while to find him, too. The ambulance blowing its siren ran him off when it came to get you," Carl said with a twinkle.

"We didn't ever find him, Pop. He came home all by himself," Ollie said.

Carl and Ollie got into an interminable discussion about what time Jiggers had loped up to the back porch after his jaunt in the woods.

Jane had nearly finished eating her slice of cake before she could slip into the discussion and ask, "How about the night before? Do you recall any strange cars or lights or anything?"

Carl started to shake his head, but Ollie said, "Yeah, I do remember something! I was out looking for Jiggers—sorry, Dad, I know I was supposed to be in bed, but I was worried about Jiggers and went out after you were asleep. Anyway, I was out looking for him, and I was trying to stay out of the woods, 'cause it's scary in there in the dark. And I was on the other side of the field from where we found you. I saw this van going real slow up by the road."

"Ollie! How come you never told anybody from the sheriff's department about the van?" Carl wanted to know.

Ollie's face flushed and he looked down at his shoes. "I forgot. And even if I'd remembered, Pop, I probably wouldn't have said anything. You told me not to go out by myself after dark."

Carl looked exasperated, but Jane smiled warmly at the boy. "Do you recall what color it was? What make? If it had an Illinois license tag?"

Ollie thought, but shook his head. "I shined my flashlight on it, but it was so dark that it was hard to tell," he said. "The taillights lit up the back of it a little. It was blue, I think. Or green. No, I think it was blue, because my friend's father was looking at a blue van to buy, and we went with him just a few days before. But he didn't buy it, so I know it wasn't him."

"Did anyone get out of the van?"

"I didn't see anyone. Only a van driving real slow. Then it speeded up and went fast."

"How about the license tag?" Duncan asked.

"I was too far away to read it," Ollie said.

Repeated questioning of Ollie turned up no further information, but Jane thought that the van might be a good lead. After Carl told her how to get to the exact spot where she'd been left all those months ago, they thanked both Joneses and left.

It was too dark and cold to examine the ditch near the cornfield that night, so they reluctantly headed back toward the Prairie Rose.

"A blue van—does that mean anything to you?" Duncan asked.

Jane shook her head, but then a picture of a blue van unexpectedly flashed into her mind. They had seen a blue Ford Econoline van on the road yesterday as they were driving out of Chicago, and she had noticed it, had studied it carefully, had even wondered why she was paying so much attention to it.

"Duncan," she said with a kind of darting excitement.

"What is it?" he asked, glancing quickly over at her.

"A blue van. I remember something about a blue van."

"What?" he asked, sounding alarmed.

She squeezed her eyes closed and tried to think. The only thing that appeared was the image of the blue van she had seen riding along next to them on the highway yesterday. She willed the image to disappear, to clear her mind for something else to come through, but it refused to go. A blue van, a blue van...something about a blue van hovered on the edge of her consciousness, waiting to be recognized.

"The Coke spilled," she said suddenly.

Duncan braked the car. They were coming into the outskirts of Tyree now, and a bright sign from a local hamburger joint cast a fleeting glow across his face.

"What Coke?" he asked.

"A can of Coke was sitting in one those consoles that fits over the engine compartment in a van. It got knocked over and spilled all over the carpet, and I was angry and wanted to clean it up." She didn't know where the words were coming from, and suddenly her mind went blank.

"*What* are you talking about?" Duncan said frantically. He pulled into the Prairie Rose parking lot and switched off the engine.

She turned to him, feeling as though she had accomplished a major breakthrough.

"I don't know, Duncan, I can't understand what it means, but I *remember*! I *remember*, Duncan!"

He looked startled, but when he saw that she was serious, that she really had remembered something about her past life, he opened his arms and she fell into them.

All Jane could do was say over and over, "I remember, I remember," and soon she was sobbing the words as though her heart would break.

Chapter Twelve

Jane didn't want to be alone. She couldn't be alone. She had to talk, and Duncan was happy to oblige her by listening.

It was much too cold to stay in the car, so he bundled her up the walkway to the motel, making sure she didn't slip on one of the many ice patches.

"It's so strange," she said, heedless of his hurry to get her inside where it was warm. "I have a clear memory of a big van, and it was blue just like Ollie saw, and I know I was sitting in it and the Coca-Cola went all over the floor, and I was angry because it was making a big mess and—"

"Shh," he cautioned as they approached the door of her room. "Someone nearby may be trying to sleep."

She lowered her voice. "So I looked around for something to blot up the Coke, and that's where the whole scene stops."

Duncan unlocked the door of her room for her, and she put a hand on his arm. Her eyes were enormous, and they pleaded with him.

"Don't go," she said. "Please come in."

If he were to be invited into her room at all, he would have preferred the invitation to be couched in romantic terms, but if this was all she could offer at the moment, he wouldn't refuse. They stepped inside her room, and Jane shivered, even though she still wore her heavy coat.

Jane seemed tense, restless, as though she couldn't be still. "It's too cool in here," she said, resetting the controls on the heater built into the wall. After that she seemed not to know what to do with herself. She stared at Duncan for a moment, as though she wasn't quite sure what he was doing there.

"I'd better hang up our coats," she said, and he saw that she had calmed down, but not much. He wondered if he should be concerned about her mental state.

Wordlessly he slipped out of his coat, and she took both his coat and hers and hung them together in the alcove that passed for a closet at the Prairie Rose Motel.

His gaze wandered to the bed, which was an ordinary double bed, but it seemed so large. So welcoming. He looked around for somewhere else to sit. There was only one chair, a stiff plastic-covered armchair, so he sat down on the edge of it. The room was small and intimate; the light from the dim bulb didn't reveal the sparseness or coldness of the standard motel furniture.

Jane returned and hesitated before sitting down on the edge of the bed. Duncan thought it best to return the conversation to her memory of the van.

"You were saying that the Coke spilled," he prodded gently. "Who spilled it?"

Her knuckles bleached white with the force of her grip on the edges of the mattress. She leaned forward in concentration. "I—I can't picture another person," she said finally. "And yet it doesn't seem as though I was alone."

"Were you sitting on one of the front seats in the van? And if so, which one?"

"It seems like I was to the right of the spilled Coke, so I'd be in the passenger side, wouldn't I?" she asked tentatively.

"I suppose so," he said. He felt sorry for her. She seemed fragile and tiny, and the Little Girl Lost quality that had made him want to protect her in the beginning had returned. He wanted nothing so much as to take her into his arms and comfort her, to tell her that everything was going to turn out fine.

To his surprise, she stood up and started pacing the floor. She looked so pretty in the clothes she had made out of Sigrid's discarded fabric; her figure was petite and yet rounded in all the right places. There was certainly nothing wrong with his own memory. Anytime he chose, he could summon to mind a sharp picture of the way she had looked when he stripped off her wet clothes in the old mine and discovered that she was not a girl, but a woman.

Jane stopped pacing in front of him, deep in thought. "I'm sure I was in a van shortly before I was found in the field—it definitely rings a bell. The fact that Ollie saw one late the night before I was found is an important coincidence, don't you think?" she asked. Her eyes were anxious.

"Yes, I do," he said, although it was easier at the moment to think about the unintentionally alluring way she moved than about the blue van.

"And Detective Schmidt might be able to trace such a van," she said. She reached for the telephone. "I'm going to call him."

His hand reached out and stopped her. "It's much too late for phone calls," he reminded her.

"What time is it?"

"It's after ten o'clock. He could be sleeping. Besides, we don't know his home number."

Jane pressed her hand to her temple for a moment and closed her eyes. When she opened them, it was with a rueful laugh. "I forgot about time. I'm so intensely involved in this thing that I don't think about anything else."

"We'll call him in the morning," Duncan said, rising to his feet.

"In the morning," she agreed. She seemed to deflate at the idea that this had to be put off until then, and he could sense her disappointment.

She went to get his coat, and he turned away so that if his longing showed on his face, she wouldn't see it. He would have given almost anything to stay the night with her.

"I'll see you tomorrow," he said more gruffly than he intended, then let himself out of her room. He could have sworn that she said his name as the door closed, and he stood outside listening, in case she spoke again or opened the door, but she didn't.

He let himself into his own room and took in the sight of the tightly made bed with distaste. It was a king-size bed with a mattress that he was sure would be too hard. He wouldn't have chosen a room with such a large bed on his own, but it had been assigned to him by the desk clerk. The size of it would only remind him of how alone he was. He briefly contemplated sleeping on the pull-out sofa that occupied the far wall, then discarded the idea. Those things usually had flimsy mattresses unsuited to his big frame.

As he took his clothes out of the suitcase, he wondered how much longer he and Jane could go on like this. More to the point, he didn't know how much longer *he* could go on like this. This brother-and-sister malarkey was a charade.

He was head over heels in love with her and sure that she wasn't aware of the depth of his feelings. But last night when they had danced, he had been convinced that she had been aroused by their sexual chemistry as much as he had. Dancing with her had been sweet torture, knowing as he did that he could take things no further until she gave him some sort of sign that she was ready. He was honor-bound to be nothing more than her protector until then.

He threw himself across the bed, thumbing through the paperback mystery he'd brought along to read. He couldn't get interested in it, though, because the real-life mystery of Jane Rhodes was so much more absorbing.

He tossed the book to one side and linked his hands behind his head, thinking.

What was Jane's connection to a blue van? And did she really remember spilling a Coke in one? Was it merely wishful thinking on her part? Or perhaps only part of a dream she'd had? He didn't know what to think.

He tried to figure out if he knew how amnesia victims went about regaining their memories. He'd once seen a segment on television's *60 Minutes* about a man who had been missing after an accident where he'd bumped his head, had disappeared from his former life and been absent from home for twenty years or so. After this period of building a new life for himself, he'd been inadvertently hit over the head by the boom on a sailboat, and when he'd regained consciousness he remembered who he was and where he was supposed to be. He'd gone home to discover that he'd been declared dead, his wife had remarried and raised a couple of kids with her new husband.

He turned out the light, rolled over on his side, and tried unsuccessfully to go to sleep. His mind was too active; he kept thinking about Jane in a blue van, Jane in her blue slacks, Jane and her blue eyes. Finally he gave up and turned on the light again. There was no use trying to sleep when he felt so wide awake.

He dressed and went down to the lobby where there was a small display of magazines. In his present frame of mind, he wanted something that wasn't too stimulating, so he bought a newspaper.

He was no sooner back inside his room than he heard a light knock on his door. To his surprise, Jane's voice called, "Duncan! Duncan?" It held a frantic note, and he flung the door open wide to find her standing there in an old flannel robe of his and looking pinched and white.

"Is something wrong?"

Much to his amazement, she hurtled into his room and all but fell into his arms. He steadied her with one hand, closing the door with the other.

"I thought you had left. I came over to knock on the door and you didn't answer and I was afraid you had gone," she said all in one breath. Her eyes were dark with alarm.

"Left?" he exclaimed incredulously.

"Gone home. To the ranch." She clutched his arm tightly.

"I would never do that," he said in gentle surprise. He saw her pulse beating in a pale blue vein at her temple, and realized that she really was frightened.

"But you weren't here," she said in bewilderment, and he slid his arm around her shoulders, to discover that she was trembling as though she was very cold.

"I went downstairs to buy a newspaper," he explained. He pointed to the paper on the table.

"I don't know what's wrong with me," Jane said, her teeth chattering. She managed to calm herself slightly. "I know you wouldn't go off and leave me here alone, it's a completely irrational fear, but it's all I could think of when you were gone," she said, attempting a smile.

"Shh, it's all right," Duncan said as—against his better judgment—he pulled her close. He felt her heart beating beneath the thin robe; the beat slowed as he stroked her hair. He could only imagine the terror in her heart; he had never been alone in the world as she had. That kind of experience was sure to leave its mark, and even though she had come so far since the night he had found her in the mine, she still had a long way to go before she felt totally secure.

Slowly his hand found its way under her long hair and settled on her neck. His touch seemed to have a calming effect on her. She heaved a great shuddering sigh and moved closer, resting her head upon his chest. And that was when *his* heart started to beat louder.

It was a moment of great tenderness between them, and Duncan cautioned himself not to ruin it. He wondered why she had come across the hall to knock on his door while he was downstairs.

Presently Jane lifted her head and asked unsteadily, "Would you mind if I had a glass of water?"

He pulled himself away, though he hated to do it, and went to the sink where he ran water into a glass. She followed him, taking the cup from him after he'd filled it and holding it between both hands as she drank the way a child might.

"Thanks," she said after taking several big gulps. She looked somewhat revived and put the cup back on the edge of the sink. When she turned around again, he saw that the front of her robe gapped slightly, and he averted his eyes.

"Why did you come over to see me?" he asked.

"I remembered something else. When I was in the van—when the Coke spilled—I was worried about some things in the back. Whatever they were, they belonged to me, and I have a vague memory of hoping that nothing happened to them."

"What kind of things?" Duncan said. He was interested, but she was very beautiful, very intense, and he kept thinking of how soft and warm she had felt when he comforted her in his arms.

"Oh—personal belongings. And something else." She wrinkled her forehead in concentration.

"I wish I could help," he said, feeling helpless in the face of her obvious anguish at not being able to recall what she needed to know.

She pulled herself out of her thoughts and focused startled eyes on his face. "You wouldn't have had to get involved in any of this," she said. "You are helping. You *have* helped."

"Not as much as I'd like," he said.

"I can never repay you enough," she said, her voice low and troubled.

"When you get a job—" he began, deliberately misunderstanding.

"I don't mean the money," she returned quickly. "I was talking about the moral support. Being there. It means a lot."

Duncan knew that Jane was sincere, but they seemed to be dragging this conversation out between them. He tried to think of some way to ease her exit. It wasn't what he wanted to do, but he thought she'd better leave before he said or did something stupid.

"I'd better go," she said with that uncanny faculty she had of reading his mind.

He started for the door, but then she raised anxious eyes to his and said in a low tone, "But I'd rather stay."

"Stay?" he inquired.

"Just—to not be alone," she replied. In her eyes he read the message, *Don't get the wrong idea.*

His mind ran off on a couple of tangents. She wanted to stay— but didn't want it to go too far. She was lonely. She was afraid, for some irrational reason that was the result of her background, that he would somehow disappear. She was struggling with a memory that was foggy and unreliable.

In other words, she wanted to spend the night with him, but wasn't looking for anything more than comfort.

Duncan wavered, one part of him wanting to put her out of temptation's way by gently telling her that she should go back to her own room. The other part of him was more human: he didn't relish being alone, either.

"Never mind," Jane said resolutely, correctly reading his uncertainty for what it was. She turned, but he reached out and caught her shoulder. She spun around, her quickness taking him by surprise.

"I overstepped my bounds," she said stiffly. "I'm sorry."

"No," he said, desperate that she understand.

"I'm going," she said, twisting so that he had to capture her in his arms to make her stay.

Her face was no more than five inches from his as he held her there, and he could have kissed her if he'd wanted to. Instead he chose to hold her eyes with his for a long moment, and the communication delivered almost as much impact as something more forceful.

"I want you to stay," he said. "I'm lonely, too."

"Please, I—"

"Nothing will happen that you don't want to happen," he said firmly. "You can sleep on the couch. It makes into a bed."

She only looked at him, and slowly he released her from the circle of his arms. She was breathing hard, as though she'd just run a couple of miles, but so was he. In order to regain control of his emotions, he walked over to the couch and opened it out. It was already made up with sheets and a blanket, so he took a pillow from the other bed and tossed it onto the thin mattress.

When Jane saw that he was serious about her sleeping there she hesitated for a moment, but then she walked around the end of the couch and crawled under the covers without taking off her robe.

Duncan got into bed—the big bed that seemed even lonelier now that she was only a few feet away—and switched off the light.

"Good night," he said softly into the darkness.

She shifted slightly, and he heard the springs creak beneath her.

"Good night," she answered, and when, after half an hour or so of staring into the darkness he levered himself up on his elbows to see if she was awake, she didn't move. She was already asleep.

JANE WOKE UP before Duncan the next morning and lay quietly, trying to determine exactly where she was. The draperies with the splashy print, the thin mattress, the king-size bed and the nightstand attached to the wall on the other side of the room... It took her a few moments to recall that she was in the Prairie Rose Motel in Tyree, Illinois.

And Duncan was asleep in the bed across the room.

She might have a faulty memory, but she certainly remembered the events leading up to her being there in this sleeper sofa in the same motel room with him. He must think she was crazy. First going all to pieces when she remembered the blue van and the Coke spilling in it, and then rushing over here like a wild woman last night and practically accusing him of running off and leaving her. Her behavior embarrassed her.

She heard a noisy group of guests tramping down the hall and slid upward against the back cushion of the couch so that she could sneak a look at the sleeping Duncan.

He lay on his side, his hands pillowing his cheek. He didn't look much different now from the way he did when he was awake. More peaceful, maybe, but that wasn't saying much because Duncan was one of the most peaceable men she'd ever known. Not that she had known many men, but she doubted that most dealt with the other people in their lives the way Duncan did, accepting them as they were and going out of his way to help them, if that was what they needed. She liked that about him.

He stirred in his sleep, and she quickly slid out of bed. She didn't want him to open his eyes to find her inspecting his face so closely. She groped in the pocket of her robe for the key to her room; it was still there. Carefully she unlatched the chain lock and slipped out, closing the door silently behind her.

A man stepped into the hall from the room next door. He was carrying a newspaper and a suitcase, and seemed taken aback when he saw her standing there in her robe with her hair mussed. Then he smiled conspiratorially, and Jane flushed deeply as she realized what he must be thinking. With shaking hands she unlocked her own door and closed it securely behind her.

She had the satisfaction of knowing that what their neighbor was thinking wasn't true, then realized that it might have been true if Duncan were another kind of guy. He could have taken advantage of her in the state of mind she'd experienced last night. What if he *did* want more? Was she prepared to give it?

Shaken by her own thoughts, she went into the bathroom and ran the shower until the water was warm enough to get in. She adjusted the flow of the shower nozzle, her body slowly coming to life. As the soapsuds slid down her neck, into the crevice between her breasts and past the cleft between her legs, it was easy enough to think about the way she'd felt when she and Duncan had danced. The attraction between them that night had definitely been physical.

She was rinsing off the last of the soap when the phone rang. Wrapping a towel around herself as she walked, she hurried to answer it.

"Jane," Duncan said. "I was worried when you weren't here when I woke up. Are you all right?"

"Oh," she said, "sure. I came back to my room to take a shower. I didn't want to wake you."

"It's time to get up, anyway. Let's meet for breakfast. Say, in half an hour or so? We can try the coffee shop attached to the motel."

"Okay," she agreed, and they hung up.

He had said nothing about last night. She knew from experience that he probably wouldn't. He would go out of his way to avoid embarrassing her.

She dried herself on the big towel and studied her assets in the mirror. She was small-boned and delicate, and her skin tone looked alabaster pale in the harsh overhead light. Legs: slender. Hips: could be narrower. Breasts: small but well proportioned to the rest of her. All in all, she wasn't bad. Duncan thought she was beautiful. Was she? She certainly couldn't compare with any of the women on the soap operas she'd watched, but didn't think she was impossibly ugly, either. *Beautiful*. A bountiful word, and one that she was pleased to have applied to her by someone like Duncan Tate. She dressed quickly.

When she met Duncan in the motel coffee shop, it was business as usual.

"Since it's still too early to call Detective Schmidt, I want to ride out to Carlton Jones's field and see if it jolts my memory," Jane told Duncan as they finished eating breakfast. "I'd like to see it early in the morning, which is the same time of day that I was found there."

His eyes searched her face. "Are you sure you really want to go?" he asked.

"I *have* to," she told him, and he nodded slowly in silent acceptance.

After Duncan paid the check, they climbed into the rental car and headed out of town. Duncan drove competently, sure of the way to the field where the Joneses had stumbled across her so many months ago. Jane stared out the window, trying with all her might to remember something, anything about this place.

Snow glistened on either side of the blacktop highway, and as they left behind the town of Tyree, they drove past widely scattered houses with smoke curling from the chimneys. Not many people lived on this highway, Jane observed as she studied the landscape. No wonder there weren't any witnesses to what had happened the night she was left in the ditch.

Duncan slowed the car as they passed the Jonesdale Farm sign. Carl had told them that the place where Jane had been found was about a mile down the highway, just south of a small red billboard. Sure enough, there was the billboard, and as Duncan pulled the car off the road, Jane stared at the billboard long and hard, hoping that its message would mean something to her.

"Anything look familiar?" Duncan asked, reaching over and squeezing her hand.

She shook her head, not trusting herself to speak. Coming here was something she felt that she had to do, and yet it was shaping up into an emotional ordeal. Here was the place where she had effectively left her identity behind; here was the place where Jane Rhodes, aka Jane Doe, had come to be. She was surprised to feel a great revulsion for this field and the ditch beside it. She didn't want to get out of the car.

"Jane?" Duncan was saying in a tone of concern.

She bit down hard on her bottom lip to keep it from quivering.

"Jane," Duncan said more forcefully, and she heard a great roaring in her ears, as though she were losing consciousness. She saw spots whirling before her eyes, and thought, *I shouldn't have come here.* Then Duncan's voice pulled her back to reality.

"Are you all right?" he asked anxiously. He was still holding her hand.

She threw him a panicked look. "I—I'm not sure," she said finally.

"Want to leave? We don't have to do this," he said.

She stared at the ditch, its contours rounded by drifts of snow, and let her gaze roam the field beyond. A small straggly wood stood to one side of the field, and the leafless branches of the trees rattled in the wind.

"I want to get out of the car," she said unsteadily.

Duncan hesitated, then squeezed her hand again. "All right," he said finally, slid out of the car and came around to open the door for her.

They walked to the edge of the ditch and stood there. The wind was blowing briskly, twitching the ends of Duncan's scarf. Jane dropped his hand and walked slowly along the edge of the ditch, willing her mind to stillness in readiness for some sort of impression to form. Her boots crunched in the snow, the sound echoing eerily back at them from the woods on the other side of the field. When she had walked about twenty feet, she stopped and peered down into the gentle white contours of the ditch.

Was it here that she had lain in the night, bloody and unconscious? Or had she been conscious part of the time, trying to scratch her way up the steep sides of the ditch? She tried to home in on a memory of that night. Surely she must remember it; how could she go through an experience such as that one and not remember it? She clenched her hands into fists in frustration.

"Well?" Duncan said.

She turned to face him, a bleak smile on her face. "I can't recall anything about this place. I might never have been here before. Funny, isn't it?" Her words shattered the stillness surrounding them.

He shook his head and walked over to her. He touched the sleeve of her coat. "No, it's not funny. It's sad."

She wasn't ready to be comforted yet; somehow she wanted to experience this place for a little longer. And she wanted to be alone.

"I'm going to walk over toward the wood. Maybe something will occur to me," she said.

He understood that she didn't want him to walk with her.

"I'll go back to the car," he told her.

He dug his hands deep into his pockets and walked quickly toward the highway, his head bent against the wind. He could only imagine how hard this was for her. He stopped once and turned, watching her as she picked her way in the direction of the wood, a small forlorn figure in a coat that was too big. His heart went out to her; he would have made everything all right for her if he could have, but he couldn't. No one could.

Jane stopped at the edge of the wood and looked back across the field. Of course, snow wouldn't have been on the ground at the time of year when she had been found; it had been autumn. She must have been cold, lying there in the ditch. Why couldn't she remember?

She brushed the snow off a fallen log and sat down on it, hunching her shoulders against the cold. She thought about the aftermath of being found in the ditch; kind Dr. Bergstrom, that friendly little nurse. What was her name? Rosemary. Rosemary Sanchez. Rosemary had been so helpful in looking for clues to Jane's previous life, but nothing had helped, just as nothing was helping now.

She sat on the log until her nose began to grow numb, then stood up. It was no use, she thought in despair. She didn't remember anything at all. She might have been standing in this field for the first time in her life.

When Jane trudged up to the car, Duncan was waiting, leaning against the fender with his arms crossed.

"It didn't work," she said broodingly.

He uncrossed his arms and put them around her, folding her against his chest. His heart beat reassuringly beneath his coat.

"Let's get into the car where it's warm," he said.

He started the car in silence, and when they were headed back toward town, he turned to her and asked, "Now what?" He was surprised to see that she was silently crying, her small hands clasped and held to her mouth, her shoulders shaking.

He pulled the car onto the shoulder of the road, nearly getting annihilated by a tractor-trailer rig in the process. When the car had bumped to a stop, he left the engine on and drew her into his arms.

"I can't help it," she cried, weeping against his shoulder. "I want to know who I really am. And I don't know if I'll ever find out."

"Shh," he said soothingly, stroking her hair away from her face. "It doesn't matter. It doesn't matter."

She swallowed and pulled slightly away. "Of course it matters," she said. "That's the whole point of this search."

"What I mean is that you'll still be the same to me, even if I never know your real name. Why, even if I found out that your name was Mehitabel or Wilhelmina or Esmeralda—"

"Esmeralda!" she exclaimed, wiping her eyes.

"—or whatever, I'd still feel the same way about you. I'd want to—"

She lifted stricken eyes to his, and placed a gentle fingertip over his lips. "Please," she said. "Don't talk about—about feelings."

He shook off her hand. "Why not?" he demanded. "I want you to know that I do have feelings for you, that I do care about you."

"You shouldn't care too much," she said brokenly.

Duncan stared at her for a long moment. Jane self-consciously resettled herself on her side of the seat. Figuring that he'd be better off not to say anything at all, he threw the car into gear and pulled back onto the highway.

Considering their uncertain future together, he couldn't say she was wrong.

But it was possible that she wasn't right, either.

And as far as caring too much went, he'd been doing that all along, hadn't he? And now when he'd finally found the knack of talking about the way he felt, she didn't want to hear about it.

At that moment he would have agreed with Rooney. Women were strange creatures.

Chapter Thirteen

Later, over lunch, Duncan said, "Do you still want to talk to Schmidt?"

Jane, who hadn't been able to summon up much appetite, stirred the vegetables at the bottom of the bowl of soup she'd ordered and thought about it. Since her visit to Carl Jones's field, she'd had an urge to do something else this afternoon, and figured it might be a good idea to follow her urges.

"I think it's important to check on blue vans—for instance, we need to know if there were any traffic tickets given on that night to a van like Ollie saw. Or if anyone in this county owns one like it. Or—well, Detective Schmidt will know how to check it out. But what I really want to do is pay a visit to the hospital. I want to see Rosemary Sanchez again."

"Then I'll call Schmidt. Unless you'd rather do it yourself later."

"If I go to the hospital now, I might not be able to get to Schmidt until tomorrow. I think it would be best to explore every area we can in Tyree as soon as possible and then, if our search isn't productive, I'll feel free to move on to someplace else. Although where, I don't know."

"Perhaps Rosemary or that doctor who treated you will know something," Duncan said, mostly to be encouraging. This elicited a more hopeful look from Jane, and on that note they parted, he to pay a personal visit to Detective Schmidt, she to return to the hospital where she had been treated and released into her new and ultimately unhappy life.

The hospital was an easy walk from the Prairie Rose, so Jane set out at a fast clip. She was surprised at how alone she felt as she made her way down the street past the city park and the grocery store. Lately she'd begun to think of Duncan and herself as a team, a partnership. A twosome. She shook her shoulders, trying to rid herself of that feeling. If she was to survive on her own later, she couldn't keep thinking that way.

The low red brick building that was Tyree Township Hospital hunkered behind a parking lot full of cars. She slowed her steps as she walked up the curved driveway to the main entrance and went inside. Funny, she didn't remember this part of the hospital. She had been taken to Emergency when she was admitted, and her life here had been lived on the ward and in its environs.

She approached the receptionist on duty behind the wide desk, hoping for a sign of recognition. When she realized that the receptionist was a new one whom she didn't know, she asked if Dr. Bergstrom was in the hospital.

"Sorry, but Dr. Bergstrom is out of town and won't be back for two weeks. Can someone else help you?" The receptionist regarded her with an expression that said, "Haven't I seen you somewhere before?"

Jane didn't feel like taking time to explain who she was and what she was doing.

"Um, no thanks," was all she said, and when the woman was distracted by a ringing telephone, Jane followed the directional arrows on the wall until she arrived in Wing A, the place where she had first come to think of herself as Jane Doe.

"Rosemary?" she said softly when she stood in front of the nurse's station.

Rosemary Sanchez, the little nurse who had been so kind to her, looked up from a patient's chart. For a moment she stared as if confronted by a ghost. Then her face flushed with pleasure.

"Jane!" she exclaimed. In a matter of seconds, Rosemary had rushed around the desk to administer a quick hug. It felt good to be welcomed so warmly, but Jane had a sensation of not being able to get her bearings. She clung to Rosemary for a minute, then took a deep, shaky breath and laughed self-consciously.

Rosemary patted her arm. "I'm about to take my break," she said to Jane as another nurse, someone Jane didn't recognize, arrived behind the desk. "Come with me into the solarium," Rosemary suggested with an encouraging smile. She entwined her arm through Jane's and propelled her along the corridor.

The solarium was a big round room with windows looking out over what Jane recalled was a garden in warmer months. Now the fountain was dry and the narrow paths were bordered by piles of snow. Still, the scene reminded Jane of a winter wonderland; icicles in the bare-branched trees had melted and formed stalagmites of ice on the snowy ground. They sat down on a small sofa, and Rosemary squeezed her arm and said, "Tell me all about yourself. Did you manage to get a job? Did you find out who you are?"

For a moment Jane contemplated telling her the truth, but she couldn't bear to destroy the warm light in Rosemary's eyes. She was struck with the realization that when she needed help, Rosemary might have been her friend. No, she corrected herself, Rosemary *definitely* would have been her friend, but she, Jane, had been too sick and too wrapped up in her own problems to realize that then.

"Things didn't work out in Apollonia," Jane managed to say smoothly. "I moved to Chicago. Lately I've been staying in Wyoming, and I hope to live in California before long. I still don't know my real name."

"You poor thing!" Rosemary said, her eyes widening in dismay.

"That's why I'm visiting Tyree. I was hoping that you might remember something about me, anything at all. I'm trying to get some ideas about where I came from, or where I was going when I landed in that ditch," and she went on to relate Ollie's new information about the blue van.

Rosemary pursed her lips in thought. "I don't know anything about a blue van in connection with you, Jane. I mean, I don't know much about cars. And as for anything else—well, I'm sorry, but I draw a blank."

"Was there anything I mentioned while I was here, or that I seemed to be interested in, or something that didn't seem important at the time that might make a difference now?" she asked.

"I'm sorry, but I don't think so. It was so long ago," Rosemary said helplessly.

Jane felt as though she had reached an impasse. "If you think of anything about me that seemed the least bit unusual, will you let me know?" She told Rosemary that she was staying at the Prairie Rose, and gave her one of Duncan's cards with the Wyoming address in case she needed to reach them after they'd left town.

When Jane made it clear that she had to leave, Rosemary said, "I'll walk you to the lobby. I feel so awful that I haven't been able to help."

Jane smiled at her. "You were a big help when I was a patient here, and that's what counted then," she assured her.

They reached the front door of the hospital, and when Jane turned to say goodbye to Rosemary, she saw that her forehead was knotted in thought.

"There was just one thing," Rosemary said slowly.

"Yes?"

"That purse you carried," she said.

"Purse?"

"It was handmade, like something you might buy at a crafts show. I noticed it because I have an aunt who used to have an old loom at her house. It belonged to my grandmother, and Aunt Frances knew how to use it. I still have a blanket she wove. Your purse reminded me of that handwoven blanket. The same kind of pattern."

"I don't have the purse anymore," Jane said. Still, she remembered it well. The handbag had been large and rectangular and had been woven of variegated shades of dark wool with a wide fringe at the bottom. Even though it had grown old and worn, Jane had kept it until the night of the snowstorm; she must have lost it in her flight from the truck driver. There was no telling where it was now.

Rosemary's face fell. "Well, it's not much of a clue, I guess. But you did want to know if there was anything about you at all that was different, and that purse was the only thing. I know we looked inside it when we were trying to figure out who you were, but it was empty. There wasn't even a label on it, which is another reason that I thought it was probably handmade."

Jane bade Rosemary goodbye, and as she slowly walked back toward the Prairie Rose, she tried to figure out if the purse was a real clue. She'd lived with the purse until she lost it, never thinking that it might signify something important about her past life. It had been old and out of style, and the reason that she'd kept it had been that it was so big that she could carry many of her belongings in it when moving from place to place.

Duncan arrived at the Prairie Rose shortly after Jane, and he looked hopeful.

"Schmidt's going to use his resources to try to uncover any irregularities involving a blue van around the time that you were found," Duncan said. "He says that even though whole cases have pivoted on information like that, then again it might not mean a thing.''

"What should we do now?'' Jane asked.

He touched her shoulder. She looked drained. "Let's see if we can turn up any information about that blue van ourselves,'' he suggested.

They spent the rest of the day riding from one service station to another both in Tyree and Apollonia, asking questions about a blue van. Several people told them that they had let too much time pass before looking for such a van, and others gave them a quick brush-off. When they returned to the Prairie Rose that evening, both Jane and Duncan felt discouraged.

Jane was quiet over their dinner of Salisbury steak, mashed potatoes and lime Jello in the Prairie Rose's coffee shop, and Duncan tried to lift her spirits.

"It must have made you feel good when Rosemary Sanchez was so happy to see you,'' he prompted.

"Yes, but...'' She bit her lip.

"But what?''

"I couldn't help but think what a difference it would have meant in my life from the time I left the hospital until the time you found me, if I had felt free to go to her for help. I mean, I knew she liked me, but I thought it was a professional interest.''

"It probably was, but she would surely have helped you when you were down-and-out if she could have. Don't you think so?''

"I didn't at the time. I was sick, you see, and—well, the lone-liness was awful. I was sure that no one in the world cared about me.''

"I can imagine,'' he said evenly.

Her eyes searched his face. "Can you imagine it? Really?'' she asked softly.

"Oh, yes. I've been lonely. Not the way you have, of course, because I've always had a home and enough to eat. But—well, it wasn't easy for me after Sigrid left. And before I married her I didn't have anyone except Rooney, and the ranch is so isolated that I didn't often have visitors.''

"You and Rooney are such good friends,'' Jane said.

"Yes, and once I thought that the only true friendship existed between man and man or between woman and woman. I didn't know it was possible for men and women to be friends.''

"And now?''

"You've shown me that it's possible for men and women to develop close bonds, something that I couldn't have imagined before. What we have feels like a real friendship to me, Jane. I have to thank you for that." His eyes were clear and steady upon her face.

Jane didn't know what to say. She looked down at her plate, embarrassed. But she found his words singularly beautiful.

"Have I said something wrong?" he asked quietly.

She shook her head. The tears in her eyes had begun to blur her vision.

"What's the matter, Jane?" he said.

"You give me all the credit for our friendship, when you should be the one," she said in a quavering voice.

"Me?"

She blinked the tears away and lifted her head. He was regarding her with all the care and concern that she had grown to expect in his dealings with her. There was no doubt in her mind that she could count upon Duncan's help, no matter what the situation. She had angered him, lied to him, borrowed and even stolen from him, and yet he had always treated her in the same fair-minded way.

She had known, for instance, that she couldn't really count on Rosemary Sanchez when the chips were down. Rosemary might have cared, but not enough to do anything about the circumstances in which Jane found herself—on the streets, out of a job, and down to her last dime. On the other hand, when Duncan cared, he cared with his whole heart. Thinking about it, she realized in that solemn moment that Duncan Tate was her best friend in the world.

"You see people as basically good, Duncan. You saw me that way, too, even though I was—well, maybe acting up the way Mary Kate does, except that my actions grew out of the wish to survive in a hostile world. You were almost too good to be true, and I couldn't quite believe that you were real. I had to test it."

"I cared about you from the beginning," Duncan told her.

"When you cared, it was with all your heart. Not halfway."

He looked stunned, then his features softened. "You say it so well, Jane. I can't improve on it. I still care with all my heart. More than you know."

She was overcome with a great certainty that whatever had gone wrong in her life, it was about to be corrected.

"I do know," she said with growing wonder. "I think I've always known."

"You've always known that I love you?" he said in surprise.

She stared with astonishment into his dark eyes, his endearing face. "Yes," she said. "Yes."

THERE WAS NO WAY that either of them could finish eating dinner. In fact, they were oblivious to everyone and everything except each other, and as they left the restaurant, Duncan barely remembered to pay the check.

They stood outside on the sidewalk, shivering in the chill.

"What now?" Jane asked. "I'm not sure I know how to act."

"Where can we go? I wish we were back at the ranch," Duncan said.

She smiled at him, knowing how he felt. "I'm sorry about the—the inappropriateness of our surroundings. It's definitely my fault," she commented.

He laughed but immediately became serious. A man stopped his car in the street and hurried to the newspaper-vending machine outside the coffee shop; he took a newspaper from inside it and released the door with a loud clang. Duncan lowered his voice so that the other man wouldn't hear. "I would very much like to kiss you," he said. "But not here."

"Not here," she agreed, and smiled again. It seemed that she couldn't stop smiling.

Above the vintage neon sign of the coffee shop, the sky was velvety dark and slitted with stars. Duncan found Jane's hand at the exact moment she reached for his. An air of expectancy hung between them almost as tangibly as their frosty breath.

"Do you want to go for a drive?" he offered.

"Let's walk," she suggested impulsively. "There's a park down the street; I passed it on my way to the hospital today."

They headed down the main street of Tyree. Not much traffic was out, and with the exception of a few passing cars, they were alone.

It seemed to Jane that she could feel the warmth of Duncan, even though a wide space separated them. Perhaps he felt it, too, because he put his arm around her and pulled her close.

"We fit together walking," he said with satisfaction.

She laughed. The notes of her laughter sparkled in the clear cold air.

"It's important to fit together walking," he assured her seriously, and she laughed again, which seemed to please him. When she looked up at him, her face was alive with happiness.

Around them the park was peaceful and serene under its snowy blanket; the snow shimmered like crystals in the light of the street lamps. But his eyes were all for her. "How lovely you look," he murmured.

They stopped walking, and slowly her hand went up to touch his cheek. It was warm to her touch, and she laid the flat of her palm along it, soaking up his warmth. But that was what she had always done, soak up his warmth. Now she knew that it had been something more, perhaps from the very beginning.

"Duncan," she began, overwhelmed by the force of her feelings for him.

"Shh," was all he said. "Don't talk." And then he took her into his arms, drew her close and brought his lips down to hers.

His lips were sweet and demanding, and Jane ached with the knowledge that she had been missing this during all the past weeks. She touched her fingertips to the strong line of his jaw, felt the smooth texture of his skin, the rough abrasion of his beard. All of it so familiar and yet so new, and she wanted to memorize everything about him, to hold him in her heart forever and ever.

He pulled her closer, unwilling to allow even a small space to widen between them. "You needed time," he said. "I knew that."

"But you were my best friend! Do people often fall in love with their best friends?"

"I don't know, but they should," he said, smiling down at her.

"I wasn't ready to be in love with anyone before," Jane said. "It still seems odd to have found the other half of myself before I've even found my real *self*. Maybe I'm not ready for this."

"Well, if you're not, is it all right if I go on being your best friend?" Duncan asked lightly, and she looked up to find that he was grinning at her in good humor.

She took heart from this and pulled slightly away. "We should talk about this," she said gravely. The last thing she wanted to do at the moment was talk, but she knew it was necessary. And she knew that although Duncan might not agree with her, at least he would listen.

"You're serious, aren't you?"

"Very," she said. "I'm having problems coming to grips with knowing that what I feel for you is love. I had your role in my life all figured out; you were my friend. And now—"

"And now that notion is shot all to blazes, right?"

"Right. And it puts everything—living at the ranch, conducting this search—in a new perspective for me."

"Which affects me," he said.

Full of doubts, she lifted her face to his. "I suppose it's asking a lot to expect you to be patient. But—" She made a little gesture of helplessness with her hands, finding her thoughts hard to put into words, as she had so often since her accident.

He waited patiently. She finally got a grasp on the idea she was trying to get across, but that still didn't make it any easier to say the words.

"It's just that I don't feel right about—about—" Jane stammered.

"About making love when you don't know if you're free," Duncan said in a low voice.

She glanced up at him. "Yes," she replied.

He sighed and she glimpsed a trace of sadness in his eyes. "I knew you felt that way before we started out. The possibility of a hubby and a couple of kids waiting somewhere for you to come home and put on the coffeepot is the reason you wanted to learn your true identity. So this isn't exactly news," he said with grim irony.

She realized that she was shivering. "We'd better go back to the Prairie Rose and tackle this. It's getting colder out here," she said.

He kept his arm around her shoulders as they walked past tattered remnants of snowdrifts in the park, and she thought, *Maybe I should throw caution to the wind and let our love take its natural course.* It would be so much easier to do that; she wanted to lie in his arms all night, to make love with him and to wake up where she would be the object of his first smile in the morning.

They had reached the motel, and he held the door open for her. They traipsed through the lobby under the bored eyes of the desk clerk, and when they reached their hall, Duncan pulled out his key. Jane dug deep into her pocket and found hers, too.

"So I guess it's separate rooms, right?" he said.

She offered him a shaky smile, painfully aware of her own strong need to be with him. But she knew that it would be harder to leave a lover than a friend if she found out that she was indeed part of another compelling life somewhere without him.

"Duncan," she began, feeling her uncertainty like a sharp pain in her heart. If only she could get all of it over with and be free of the weight of her forgotten past!

"I understand," he said heavily. He took her key from her and started to insert it into the keyhole in her door, but her hand stayed his.

"No," she said. "Is it possible—I mean, do you think—?"

"You mean, can we sleep together the way we did last night?" His eyes burned into her.

She caught her lower lip between her teeth and, her eyes never leaving his face, she nodded, once, twice. She remained perfectly still.

He closed his eyes and pulled her close to him. Could he occupy the same room with her all night and not touch her? And if he touched her, if he needed her warmth and softness, could they restrain themselves from the ultimate act?

It was a chance they would have to take. He wanted to be with her for now and for always, and he would respect her decision in this matter as much as he respected Jane herself.

"Whatever you want," was all he said.

She pulled slightly away, and, her eyes never leaving his face, took his key from his hand. Then she led him across the hall to his own room and unlocked the door.

THEY OPENED OUT the couch bed, looked at each other over its expanse of white sheets and blue blanket, then without a word folded it back up again.

Jane went with him to the big bed, and he walked around to one side while she stood on the other. She felt confused; overlaying her very real desire for him was a kind of constriction. It pinned her down, made her motionless. She didn't know how to go about this.

Duncan made it easy for her. He came around to her side of the bed and kissed her gently on the cheek. "Come to bed," he said softly, easing her down beside him and turning off the light.

They lay in the dark, both of them unwilling to move. Through the thin walls they could hear the occupants of the room next door moving about, conducting their bathroom ablutions, talking.

Duncan turned over and punched his pillow; Jane lay stiffly, staring up at the ceiling and thinking that this had been a mistake. Duncan muttered something, but she couldn't make out the words.

Time passed. It might have been minutes, it might have been hours; she had no idea how long it had been since they got into this bed together. She counted sheep, she named all the colors of the rainbow, she named all the cast members of *Luck of the Irish*. Still she did not sleep.

"Duncan?" she asked, her voice sounding higher and more timid than usual.

"I can't stand this," he observed abruptly, reaching out and yanking the chain that turned on the bedside lamp. The room was filled with light, and Jane pushed herself up on one elbow.

"I'd better leave," she said. "This isn't going to work. I can't sleep, you can't sleep, and it wasn't a very good idea. It's my fault."

"Don't be so quick to take the blame," Duncan said. "I agreed to the arrangement."

"I should have known better," she said, making as if to get up, but he reached for her and pulled her to him. She let herself be drawn toward him, resting against his chest.

"That's better," he said comfortably. The sounds from next door quieted, and Jane sighed. It was so pleasant to be close to Duncan this way, she thought, nestling into the warm curve of his body.

"I think what was wrong was that we were both trying too hard not to touch each other," Duncan said. "We both want to, but we're afraid that one thing will lead to another and that we wouldn't be able to stop."

"Exactly," said Jane, drawing the word out to its full length and growing drowsier as she said it.

"So let's not try too hard. I promise that nothing is going to happen until you want it to," he went on.

She shifted in his arms, intending to tell him to turn out the light, but suddenly they heard the rhythmic squeak of bedsprings from the room next door. Her eyes flew open.

Duncan groaned. So did someone on the other side of the wall, in a slightly different tone.

"Oh no, not that," Duncan said in disgust.

Jane started to laugh. She muffled her laughter against Duncan's chest, and the hair on his chest tickled her nose. Soon he was laughing, too, and they couldn't stop, no matter how hard they tried.

Finally the sounds next door subsided—and so did their laughter.

Jane ventured a look at Duncan. His face was red, but his eyes were bright.

"Duncan, I love you," she said.

"And I love you. Now can we please get some sleep?" he demanded.

"Turn out the light," she said, and when he did she swiveled her head and kissed him.

That night she slept fitfully, her back against his, bracing herself against him the way she would against a strong, solid tree trunk.

Chapter Fourteen

Waking up the next morning with Duncan beside her should have been heartening. Jane should have felt supported and strengthened by their declaration of love, but in truth all it did was worry her. If her past life required it, how would she find the strength to leave him? She loved him, and she should have been happy. Instead she lay beside him in the gray morning light, not merely listening to his breathing but feeling him breathe. That was the difference between friendship and love—with friendship, you merely listened. With love, you felt.

She didn't want to feel this love, not on this particular morning when she was so tired and worn out by the uncertainty of her life. She would have liked to be free of it, relieved of the doubt, fear and vulnerability. Instead she must get up and smile at Duncan, be the receptacle for the caring and compassion that he heaped upon her, unable for the sake of their love to express her negative thoughts. This morning all she could feel was the awesome responsibility of love.

After breakfast she sat on the bed in the motel room while Duncan called Detective Schmidt and learned that he had been able to uncover no news about a blue van in relation to Jane's appearance in the ditch.

"Ollie Jones seems to be the only person around town who saw a blue van that night," Schmidt offered in an apologetic tone.

"But *I* remember a blue van, too!" Jane said when Duncan related the conversation to her. "Doesn't that count for something?" She was so disappointed; she had been sure that the blue van was an important clue.

Duncan shook his head. "I guess not, Jane. I'm sorry." They both knew that her brief memory of the blue van meant nothing unless Jane somehow managed to recall something more about it.

Jane nibbled on a thumbnail and stared into space. A blue van. What did it have to do with anything, anyway? What did it mean? Who had been in the van with her? She reached into the far recesses of memory and came up with—zip—zilch—nothing.

Duncan interrupted her thoughts. "Well, Jane," he said. "It looks like we're stymied. What do you want to do now?"

"I'm packed," Jane said abruptly. "Let's leave Tyree."

"Is that what you really want to do?"

"Why not?" she replied, her tone sharp.

He wavered for a moment, not sure if leaving was a good idea. Jane seemed very much on edge this morning, but, considering the circumstances, he supposed that this wasn't surprising. "I guess there's no reason to stay," he admitted. "It's just that I was hoping we'd learn more while we were here." He made his voice relax, hoping that it would calm her.

"So was I," Jane said. She had begun to take on the air that he recognized as her stubborn look, the one where she got a mulish glint in her eyes like Quixote when he got his dander up. If she hadn't been so strung out this morning, he would have taken her in his arms and attempted to kiss the mood away.

Later, he promised himself as he gathered up his shaving gear and tucked it into a corner of his suitcase. *Later.*

"Let me get that," Duncan was quick to say when they stepped outside the motel carrying their luggage, but as usual, Jane refused his help, marching ahead of him across the icy parking lot with an air of determination.

From where he stood, he spotted the slick patch of ice, and cried out at almost the same time as she stepped on it. And then, heart in mouth, he watched helplessly as her feet flew out from under her and she lost her balance, landing on her back.

Heedless of his own safety on the icy asphalt, Duncan set off at a run and reached her in a matter of seconds, his pulse pounding in his ears. He thought he would never forget his fear as he stared down at her motionless body.

Jane, he thought, and bent swiftly to touch her, to wipe the spot of dirt from her pale cheek, praying that she was not hurt.

A man who had seen her fall rushed across the street.

"Everything okay?" he asked anxiously.

Jane forced herself up on her elbows. She felt nothing; her whole body was numb. And then feeling began to seep into her limbs, bringing with it a huge buzzing that filled her ears, and she couldn't hear what anyone in the small gathering crowd was saying. She had eyes only for Duncan, whose stricken face expressed all the love and caring that she knew he felt. Her head—how it hurt!—but she had to let Duncan know that she was all right, and so she tried to speak, tried to get the words out, but none would come.

"She's had the wind knocked out of her," she heard someone say, and with that she realized that the buzzing in her ears was receding. Her elbow ached; she'd have a big bruise there, she knew.

Duncan's hand was supporting the back of her neck, brushing her cheek, and when at last she could speak, she said with more confidence than she felt, "I'm okay. Really. I'm fine," and warmed to the relief in Duncan's eyes.

"Can you get up?" he asked, and she surprised him by sitting up and taking hold of his arm, hanging on to it as someone gave her a boost from the back.

"I'm all right," she repeated, and the man who had run across the street left, and the woman who had stopped her car nearby got back into it and drove away, spewing plumes of exhaust in her wake.

They were alone in the parking lot, Duncan's arm encircling her waist. She leaned on him for a moment, glad to have him for a protector.

"Do you want to check back into the motel? You may be sore later," Duncan said. He was still concerned; she had a kind of glazed look about her.

"I'm ready to leave Tyree," she said, summoning the strength to speak firmly. "I may have a bruise or two, but there's no serious damage. Honestly," she added when she saw how disbelieving he looked.

Reluctantly and at her own urging, Duncan settled Jane carefully in the passenger seat of the car. She leaned her head back against the headrest while Duncan was stowing their suitcases in the trunk. What an awful fall it had been! She had hit the back of her head on the pavement. She was sure that the fall wouldn't have happened had it not been for her ragged nerves and too little sleep, and knew she was lucky that she hadn't been hurt more seriously.

Duncan shot her a worried look when he slid in behind the steering wheel.

She smiled weakly. "Duncan, don't look at me like that," she chided. "If I wasn't feeling ready to travel, I'd tell you."

"You still seem a little dazed," he said.

"You would, too, if you'd fallen as hard as I did. Besides, I think I bit my tongue," she said, but didn't mention the headache that was burgeoning right behind her eyes. She couldn't recall having headaches since she'd arrived at the ranch, and hoped that the fall hadn't precipitated their return.

To set Duncan's mind at ease, she tried to carry on a conversation as they left behind the outskirts of Tyree.

"I wonder if we really accomplished anything here," she said softly as Duncan accelerated to a comfortable fifty-five miles an hour on the open highway.

"It was a start," he told her, and she was pleased that he seemed willing to forget the fall she'd just taken in the parking lot.

Her head didn't stop hurting all day. If anything, the pain was aggravated by their many stops as they related Jane's story and left Duncan's business card in several gas stations and convenience stores. Jane surreptitiously took two aspirin, but they afforded little relief. She refrained from mentioning the pain in her head to Duncan, knowing that it would only worry him. Instead, she tried to concentrate on their task.

Surprisingly, the people to whom they spoke had often heard about Jane and knew of her initial search for her identity during the time when she was a patient in the hospital in Tyree, but they were able to shed no light on the mysterious circumstances of her appearance in Carlton Jones's ditch.

Sometimes when they'd had a chance to study Duncan's business card for a moment, they expressed more interest in the llamas than they did in Jane.

"I'd better talk to Rooney about hauling a bunch of llamas to southern Illinois," Duncan joked after they'd left a store where the woman behind the counter had become overly enthusiastic about llamas, but had paid scant attention to Jane and her plight. "I bet we could sell quite a few around here."

"You haven't phoned him since we left the ranch, have you?" Jane asked.

"No, and I'd better. I'll call tonight," he said.

That night found them staying in a motel in a small town not far from the Indiana state line, and after dinner, during which they each unsuccessfully tried to bolster the other's hopes, Duncan called Rooney.

Jane, still fighting her headache, tugged at his sleeve. "Don't forget to ask about Mary Kate," she urged in a whisper.

Duncan surprised her by asking after Mary Kate as soon as Rooney answered the phone, and as he listened to Rooney's reply, his expression immediately become more serious. "She did?" he asked sharply. "Are they all right?"

Sensing something amiss, Jane sat up straight. It sounded as though Mary Kate was in trouble again.

"Well, it doesn't surprise me that Dearling stayed around. She's a tame one. Yeah, it's a good thing none of them wandered over by the highway. Okay, I'll call you again soon. Right. Goodbye, Rooney."

"What has Mary Kate done?" Jane asked with a certain sense of foreboding.

Duncan looked angry. "She left the gate open on the pen beside the barn and the breeding females got out. Fortunately, Rooney's managed to round all of them up. That Mary Kate! Why can't she behave herself?"

"She can't help it," Jane sighed. "Anyway, the latch on the gate isn't particularly reliable."

"It's reliable enough when the rest of us use it. Mary Kate is the only one who seems to have trouble with it," Duncan said angrily.

Jane tried to soothe him. "Mary Kate might be in need of attention right now. With both of us gone, Rooney is busy running the ranch. Mary Kate didn't want me to leave in the first place, and now she's probably very lonely."

"Lonely or not, she has no business letting my llamas out. Above and beyond what could happen to them, her carelessness could have cost us thousands of dollars. Many of my breeding females are pregnant, and their offspring are potentially worth quite a lot of money. Mary Kate had better thank her lucky stars that nothing happened to those llamas."

"I'm sorry, Duncan. I'm glad they're all right."

"So am I. Rooney says he's going to devise a severe punishment for Mary Kate."

Jane's heart sank. In her mind she pictured Mary Kate's defiant face the last time Rooney had imposed punishment by restricting her contact with her beloved Dearling. She knew that it was only right that Mary Kate face the consequences of her irresponsible action, but nevertheless her heart ached for the child.

Both Jane and Duncan were exhausted by their busy day, and the troubles at Placid Valley Ranch weighed heavily upon both of them. The bruises she had suffered in her fall kept Jane from falling asleep until late, and when she woke up, she still had a nagging headache.

Although neither of them had slept well, they struck out early that morning, determined to pay a visit to a newspaper in nearby Terre Haute that had published a story about Jane when she had still been a patient at Tyree Township Hospital. Jane thought that the sympathetic reporter who had written the story might be interested in writing a follow-up, and they both thought that any publicity would aid their search.

They had stopped for gas in a Terre Haute suburb and Jane got out of the car to stretch her arms and arch her stiff back. As she was about to get back in, she was almost blinded by the glint of bright sun on the chrome bumper of a car in front of theirs. At first she held up her hand to shield her eyes, but she felt such a sharp pain in her head that she decided to look for a water fountain so that she could take two more aspirin.

Her head swam, and even the cold outdoor air didn't clear it. She headed toward the gas station where Duncan was studying the snack vending machines, but found herself turned around going the other way. The pain throbbed inside her head, and she couldn't see where she was going. She heard a shout and felt the breeze from the passing of a car too near, but she was confused and didn't know which way to go and turned around again, looking for Duncan.

"Lady, get out of the way!" somebody yelled. She dug her fists into her eyes because they hurt so much, and when she took her hands away, there was a pink dress in a store window, and she wanted to buy it for Mary Kate. Then she crashed headlong into a solid object and rebounded. She heard herself sobbing, and the next thing she knew, a woman was holding a cool cloth to her forehead and saying, "There, there, you'll be all right. Just a little dizzy spell, wasn't it, dear?"

Jane swallowed and felt someone squeeze her hand. She pushed aside the cloth on her forehead to see Duncan looking pale and worried. She summoned the strength to smile at him.

"Jane, you scared me half to death," he said.

"What happened?" she asked, bewildered. She had never seen this woman before, and as for the plaid couch on which she was lying and the room where she found herself—well, nothing gave her a clue. Where was she, anyway?

"This nice lady, Mrs.—"

"Alice Beasley," the woman supplied as she returned with a hot cup of tea.

"Mrs. Beasley was in the window of her shop, arranging the merchandise, when you came reeling across the street in front of a car, and when a bicycle on the sidewalk almost hit you, she opened the door and brought you inside," Duncan explained.

"I couldn't see," Jane said, remembering how the reflection of the bright sun on the chrome had affected her.

"I knew something was wrong," Alice Beasley said with great certainty.

"My headache's gone," Jane said in a tone of amazement.

"You never said you had a headache," Duncan said accusingly.

"I didn't want to worry you," she said.

"You should have seen a doctor after that fall. I knew it," he said.

"Don't be angry, Duncan. I feel better now. I know it sounds silly, but I'm fine." Indeed, she felt a resurgence of energy, and the cloud of depression that had hung over her that morning seemed to have disappeared.

"Now listen to me, Jane. If you've started having those headaches again, you must see a doctor," Duncan said.

"I know a good one. Dr. McKelvey. He's been my doctor for over thirty years. I'll call and make an appointment with him, if you like," Mrs. Beasley volunteered.

"Yes, that sounds like a good idea," Duncan agreed.

"No," said Jane.

"Jane—"

"I'll just drink this tea and we'll be on our way. And that pink organdy dress in your window—what size is it?"

"A girl's size twelve, dear. But should you be thinking about that? Shouldn't you see how you feel in half an hour or so?" Mrs. Beasley's face wrinkled into a maze of concern.

Jane surprised them both by swinging her feet off the couch. She felt more energetic than she had in days. Weeks, even. She wasn't sure just what had happened to her, but there was no doubt in her mind that it had been beneficial.

"I want to see that dress," she said firmly.

Duncan and Mrs. Beasley exchanged looks. Finally, as though she were humoring an invalid, the reluctant Mrs. Beasley said, "Well, I'll take the dress out of the window, dear, but if I were you, I'd rest."

Jane paid no attention. Instead she followed Mrs. Beasley to the window and stood entranced as the store owner divested the mannequin of the pink dress.

"Wouldn't that be perfect for Mary Kate?" she asked Duncan.

Duncan, who wasn't sure that Jane was entirely well, eyed the dress doubtfully. It had large puffed sleeves, a satin sash, and dainty white lace edging above the hem. He couldn't for the life of him imagine such an exquisite dress on a child whose knees seemed to be permanently skinned, whose hair hung in limp clumps, and whose fingernails were more often than not rimmed with dirt. Anyway, did someone as careless as Mary Kate deserve such a fine present? As exasperated as he was with her irresponsible behavior, he didn't think so.

"You've got to be kidding," he said. He stood close to Jane in case she became dizzy again, although he had to admit that she looked perfectly healthy. In fact she looked wonderful. He couldn't imagine what had come over her.

Jane was enthusing over the dress. With its delicately embroidered bodice and its petal-pink petticoat sewn of the finest batiste, it was even lovelier than she had thought, and it looked close to Mary Kate's size. What else had Mary Kate said? Oh, yes. The dress was required to have transparent sleeves. These, made of organdy, would fit the bill.

Jane turned to Duncan. She was pleased that she could move her head without feeling that awful dull ache behind her eyes. "Duncan, you don't understand. Mary Kate asked me to bring her a pretty pink dress, and I promised I would. It may be a little too big for her, but with a few tucks here and there I could make it fit," she said.

"This dress was handmade by one of our consignees," Mrs. Beasley told them. "In fact, all of the things in my shop are handmade. Do you do crafts as well as sew?"

"I'm a weaver," Jane said without thinking, then was astonished at the words that had come out of her mouth. Duncan stared at her, unable to move.

She looked at him, still stunned and scarcely believing what she had said. She was a weaver! Not merely a spinner of yarn, but someone who wove it into cloth!

The edge of a memory fluttered somewhere on the outskirts of her mind, and she tried to draw it toward her. But no matter how hard she tried, she couldn't grasp it. It kept eluding her.

"Well, dear," Mrs. Beasley went on in a conversational tone, unaware of the astonished but silent byplay that was going on between Jane and Duncan, "since you're a weaver, you really ought to stop by Shanti Village while you're here. If you feel up to it, of course. I notice from your car license tags that you two are from out of state. Well, I always tell visitors to go to Shanti Village. It's kind of an attraction around here. They have all these crafts people who live and work there, and sometimes you can go right into their houses and watch them work."

"Shanti Village," Jane said. Suddenly a flash of memory, no longer than a second or two, flared in her head. It was of a smiling, deep-voiced, deep-breasted woman who wore a gold Egyptian ankh charm on a chain around her neck, whose laugh was not only frequent but loud, who worked at a loom while her baby slept in a rush basket on the floor beside her. *Moonglow*, Jane thought. *That woman's name was Moonglow. And we used to ride together in a blue van when we went grocery shopping.*

"Yes, I'd be happy to give you directions to Shanti Village, if you'd like. Now, how about the dress? Would you like me to wrap it up for your little friend?" asked Mrs. Beasley.

"Yes," Jane whispered, the way she uttered the word drawing sharp looks.

"Maybe you'd better lie down in the back room again," Alice Beasley said solicitously.

"I—I'm fine. And I do want the dress. Only—only could you tell me how to reach Shanti Village? Here, I'll pay you for the dress, and you can wrap it and we'll pick it up later." Jane fumbled with her purse.

"I'll pay for it," Duncan said, whipping cash out of his wallet, while Jane turned toward the window and stared out at the street, as though she had seen a ghost.

"Shanti Village is about thirty miles north of here on the highway. You'll see a sign on the side of the road right after the railroad tracks," Mrs. Beasley said, clearly confused.

The words were no sooner out of her mouth than Jane was out the door, walking at a fast pace.

Fortunately, the street was miraculously devoid of traffic. Duncan managed a few disjointed words of thanks to Mrs. Beasley, then sprinted after Jane, his long legs barely keeping up with her shorter ones as she clipped smartly along to their car, parked across the street at the gas station.

"What was that all about?" Duncan asked, trying to get a good look at her face.

"Shanti Village. I've *been* there, Duncan! I know a woman who lives there. She's a weaver, like I am. And this street—it seems so familiar!" She kept walking, apparently propelled by the strength of her own convictions.

Duncan was amazed at this revelation. "Jane, what is this all about? Are you sure you're feeling okay?"

"I haven't had a loom since I first became Jane Doe, and maybe if I had, I wouldn't have known what to do with it. But I know now. I used to spend my days at a loom, working in a rhythm, a certain rhythm that was as natural to me as the ebb and flow of the tides is to the sea. How could I not have known that about myself? And I'm certain that I must know other people at Shanti Village besides Moonglow. I *know* it! Oh, Duncan, don't you see? It's coming back to me, something's making me remember!" Her eyes sparkled up at him.

"Moonglow? Is that a person?" he asked, feeling at a loss to cope with all of this information at once.

Jane got into the car and pressed her hands to her cheeks. "Duncan, she's a friend of mine, and she lives in Shanti Village. I'm feeling chills run through me, just thinking about seeing her again. She's somebody I knew, Duncan! Don't you see what a breakthrough this is?"

Duncan pulled her hands down from her face and kissed her. He couldn't help smiling back at her, she looked so happy. And he was happy, too. It didn't matter how or why she remembered. All that mattered was that she remembered. He could only hope that at last they were on the right track.

He started the car and pulled onto the highway.

"What brought all of this on, anyway?" he asked.

"I don't know, it's like a—like a light suddenly went on in my head, illuminating all the dark corners. I must have lived at Shanti Village, Duncan, don't you see? Because I remember my loom! It was set up in the same room as Moonglow's, we used to talk about the patterns we were weaving and I would spin the wool that we both used, because she used to hate to spin, but I was good at it, and—oh, Duncan, that handbag I had! The one that Rosemary Sanchez mentioned? I made that, and I must have made dozens like it! I sewed little labels in them and sold them."

"Why wasn't there a label in the one you had? Didn't Rosemary tell you that there was no identification in it?"

"I remember that handbag and why I had it! It was a reject, one that wasn't good enough to sell, and I kept it for myself. That's why there wasn't a label in it! Those labels were expensive, and I didn't use them on things I made for myself."

"What about this—this *Moonglow*? How did you meet her?"

"I don't know. I only remember that I liked her a lot. And she was having some kind of trouble, some difficulty and—and because of that I moved in with her. What was it—what was wrong?" Jane racked her brain for some sense of Moonglow's trouble, but she couldn't think of it.

Finally she gave up and focused on her friend, whose face she could see clearly in her mind. "Moonglow has long dark hair, and there's a baby, too. A tiny blond baby who sleeps nearby while Moonglow works at her loom. We knew each other well, so well that we used to go shopping for food together in my blue van. *My* blue van, Duncan! The blue van is mine!" She clasped her hands together to keep them from trembling and watched the road unfurl in front of them. But it was different from all the other roads she had followed—this one led to Shanti Village and to Moonglow. And it led to her past; she knew it.

"Who was with you when the Coke spilled all over the floor of the van?" Duncan asked.

Jane frowned and bit her lip. "I don't know," she said. "I can't remember that, just like I can't remember my own name. But Moonglow will know. Surely she will, won't she?"

Duncan curved an arm around her shoulders. "I certainly hope so," he said quietly.

Jane stared out the window, willing the memories to surface, trying to recall her name, trying to figure out why she had been in a blue van when Coke had been spilled, but when she thought about it, all she got was a strong feeling of anger and foreboding, of something amiss. It was akin to the emotion she had felt when she had revisited Carlton Jones's field and tried to remember the events of the night when someone had dumped her into the ditch. But this time she refused to despair. She would find some answers soon.

Before long, they crossed railroad tracks and came upon a fancifully lettered sign that pointed in the direction of Shanti Village. They set off on a narrow road that passed several farms and then curved through a patch of woods. And when they came out of the woods, Shanti Village lay before them.

It consisted of a neat clump of houses gathered around a large central hall, and at the end of the street was a gaily painted building with a sign designating it the Shanti General Store. Two children pulled another on a bright red sled in the distance, and several people hurried along the sidewalk. Jane scanned their faces to see if she knew them. If she did, she didn't recognize them, nor did anyone recognize her.

Duncan pulled the car to a stop in front of the store. "Want me to go in with you?" he offered. He wasn't sure that it was a good idea to get their hopes up about this place or about Jane's sudden memories of this Moonglow person, whoever she was. Jane's memory might very well turn out to be unreliable. She had, after all, been acting strangely.

"I'll just run inside and see if anyone knows Moonglow," Jane said, and he winked reassuringly, hoping for her sake as well as his that this was a real lead.

Jane went inside the store, which was deserted except for a man sitting behind a counter watching a game show on a small television set.

Jane barely glanced at the batik wall hangings, the hand-quilted bedspreads, and the woven blankets draped over a stair rail.

"I'm looking for someone named Moonglow," she said to the man.

He cast her a brief look. "You a friend of hers?" he asked.

She nodded, her throat feeling dry. She felt a need to explain but didn't want to waste the time. She wanted to find Moonglow now, right away.

"Third house on the left. The yellow one," he said, returning his attention to the TV set.

Duncan, waiting outside, drummed his fingers impatiently on the back of the seat. He couldn't help the sensation that things were moving too fast. All this talk of someone named Moonglow and Shanti Village—where would it lead?

All at once he recalled the story of the man who had lost his memory due to a blow on the head and regained it only after a second head injury many years later. He was struck with the certainty that Jane's recent fall was a factor in the sudden return of her memory now.

"Any luck?" he asked when she slid back into the car.

Jane felt jittery and on edge. "The man inside says that Moonglow's in the third house on the left," she said tersely.

"Hey, are you sure you want to do this?" Duncan asked.

"I'm scared," she admitted. "What if she doesn't know me? What if it's the wrong Moonglow?"

"How many people named Moonglow have you known in your life?" Duncan grinned as he started the engine, and with that Jane relaxed slightly. He *did* have a point.

When Duncan drove up in front of the yellow house, she hesitated.

"Would you mind coming with me this time?' she asked him.

"Of course not," he assured her, and they walked up the path to the house together.

Jane took in every detail about the place: the window boxes that must have held flowers in the spring and summer, the green shutters and white trim, the uncurtained windows hung with small stained glass sun catchers. If Moonglow had been her friend, wouldn't she remember this place?

And then she did remember. The house hadn't always been painted yellow. Once the clapboards had been white. But the porch floor had always been painted dark green, just as it was now. And—

Duncan rapped sharply on the door.

"Come in!" called a voice, a familiar husky voice. Moonglow's voice.

"Should we?" asked Duncan, and Jane found that her legs felt rubbery and she was clinging tightly to his hand.

"I said, come in!" the voice said more impatiently, "I'm changing a diaper."

"She's a trusting soul, letting in people she can't even see," Duncan muttered as Jane reached out a trembling hand and turned the doorknob. He was nervous, too, although he never would have admitted it.

Inside, the sweet fragrance of sandalwood incense hung in the air, and it was overlaid with the aroma of freshly baked gingerbread. *Gingerbread—it's one of Moonglow's specialties,* thought Jane. A complacent white cat jumped off the windowsill and proceeded to wash her face under a loom in the corner, and the word *Lotus* appeared unbidden in Jane's mind. It was the cat's name.

"Lotus?" Jane said tentatively. The cat stopped washing, the tip of her pink tongue protruding from her mouth, and Jane smiled. She and Moonglow had always laughed at Lotus when they caught her with her tongue hanging out.

"Be with you in a minute!" Moonglow called from somewhere down the hall, and Jane knew that she would be standing at the old dresser that they had converted into a dressing table for Moonglow's baby. Somehow it heartened Jane to think that she hadn't been gone long enough for the baby to be toilet trained yet.

Then she heard brisk footsteps on the hardwood floor, and Moonglow Everlight, the familiar gold ankh at her throat, stood at the entrance to the room.

They stared at each other. Moonglow's face drained of all color. Jane didn't know what to say, could have said nothing, even if she'd tried.

And then Moonglow gasped, "Celeste! Oh, Celeste! You've come back!" Bangle bracelets jangling, long brown hair afloat, Moonglow hurtled headlong into Jane's arms.

Chapter Fifteen

Celeste. Jane's real name is Celeste, Duncan thought as he watched the two women embrace. And then he thought, I would have never pegged her as a Celeste.

"Where have you been all this time? Do you know how hard I've tried to get in touch with you? Why didn't you call or write or something? I've been frantic!"

Jane, still in shock over finding someone who actually seemed to know her, gently disengaged herself. Suddenly she found herself in the position of having to explain, and she knew that it wouldn't be easy. There were still so many blank spaces.

"I think we need to talk," she said, and Moonglow, after a curious glance at Duncan, drew them over to a couch where they all sat down and, in sudden embarrassment, kept looking from one to the other.

Jane was the first to pull herself together. She introduced Duncan, and then she began to relate her story. At first Moonglow was incredulous, but as the story progressed, she had to dab at her eyes with a tissue more than once.

"I can't believe that someone could get so lost," she kept saying, even though Jane and Duncan assured her that it had really happened exactly as Jane had said.

"So," Jane said, finishing up her story, "I'm here to find out about my life. I don't know if I have a family, or children, and only today did I figure out that I was a weaver. Please tell me everything you know about me."

Moonglow reached out and gave Jane an impulsive hug. "I just can't believe that you're sitting here beside me after so long," she said apologetically. "And you are my best friend and I know a lot about you, so it's going to take a long time to tell you everything."

"Please," Duncan said. "Tell us."

So Moonglow told them that Jane's real name was Celeste Norton, and that she and Moonglow had both been weavers in this small community of craftsmen before Jane disappeared.

"You had a disagreement over policy with the community leaders," Moonglow said. "They wanted to turn this place into a tourist attraction in the summer months, with an amusement park for children, a petting zoo, and even a miniature train that would circle the village and feature cowboys and Indians jumping out of the woods. We both felt that the prime purpose of Shanti Village was to give artists a place to create, not to provide fun for tourists. The people who were in favor of this amusement park concept argued that it would bring more people to the village and thus provide more customers for our crafts, but you said you didn't want them turning this place into a circus."

"I didn't like that man—what was his name? He had a beard and I used to joke that he looked like a pirate," Jane said, recalling him with a shudder. He had tried to make her life miserable here, she recalled. She had led the group that opposed him.

"His name was Fenton Murdock, and I'm happy to say that we voted him out of the village council shortly after you left," Moonglow told her. "In fact, he and most of his followers left. He's driving a cab in Newark these days, I hear."

Both she and Jane laughed, and Jane's heart warmed to Moonglow's familiar, throaty laughter.

"Anyway, Fenton used to assign you to work extra hours in the village co-op's store, and when you objected and told him that serving those additional hours meant you had less time to spend at your loom, he called you a troublemaker. You were outraged and appeared before the village council, calling for equitable scheduling. That made Fenton really mad, and when some of those handbags you used to make disappeared from the store and turned up in a boutique in Urbana, Illinois, you suspected that he had stolen them and passed them off as his own, pocketing money that should have been yours."

"I *remember*," Jane said excitedly. "One of the boutique's owners called here and asked to speak to the person who made those big woven handbags, and when I called her back I realized what had happened. The man she described as the creator of them was Fenton Murdock!"

"You and Fenton had a big row, and you said you couldn't work here anymore. You said you knew of a colony of weavers in Ohio where you could work in peace and where there was a ready market for your work. So that very night—you wouldn't even wait until morning—you sat here and took your loom apart, and you packed it and everything you owned into the back of that blue van of yours, and you rode away, promising to let me know where I could reach you. And that was the last I saw of you." Moonglow's eyes brimmed with tears again.

"A loom! That's what was in the back of my blue van, Duncan! I was so worried about it that night, the night the Coke spilled!"

"The Coke spilled?" Moonglow looked confused.

Quickly Jane told her about the brief memory of Coke spilling on the carpet of her van, and how she recalled trying to clean it up and being worried about the things stowed in back.

"Of course I would have been worried about my loom," she said. "It was my livelihood, the way I made my living. I was afraid that if something happened to it, I wouldn't be able to support myself."

"Can you remember when I left here?" Jane asked Moonglow.

Moonglow thought a moment. "It would have been in November of that year," she said.

"I was found in the ditch on November 3," Jane told her.

"I was so worried because November 10 came and went without a word from you. Sun-One was three months old on that date, and you promised to call because it was her three months' birthday."

"Sun-One," breathed Jane. "The baby. May I see her?"

Together the two of them tiptoed into the small nursery. It had, Jane realized, once been her own room. But her twin bed had been pushed into a corner and was piled with pillows like a couch, and Sun-One's crib was where the bed used to be. And asleep in the crib was Sun-One, sucking her thumb.

When they were back in the living room, Jane clutched Duncan's hand excitedly. "The nursery used to be my room, Duncan. I remembered it! And Sun-One—she's beautiful, Moonglow. I helped deliver her, didn't I? You wanted a home birth, and I was the one who went to get the midwife."

"In a pouring rain," Moonglow agreed, finishing her sentence with that laugh of hers. "And you coached my breathing."

"It was why I moved in here, wasn't it? Your husband ran away with another woman, and you needed someone to help you pay expenses because you were going to have a baby. And I moved here from—" Jane faltered and couldn't remember any more from that.

"From one of the studio apartments over the general store. There was a waiting list for them, and we both thought it would be a good idea for you to live with me, because it would make the studio available for someone else. As you said, I needed the help, and you were going to help me bring up the baby. You always loved babies, Celeste."

Jane grew suddenly quiet. "I can't get used to being called Celeste," she said.

"It's the only name I've ever known for you," Moonglow told her. "I remember when you came here, fresh out of a dead-end office job, so eager to make a living with your weaving, which is the thing you love to do most."

"Me? In an office job?" Jane could manage only a vague recollection of a huge office furnished with row after row of gray metal desks, and glaring fluorescent lights overhead, and people who spent their lunch hours comparing their bowling scores. She had never fitted in.

"Yes, and there was nothing to hold you there, no relatives except that old aunt of yours, who practically turned you out of her house when you told her that all those old newspapers piled up inside were a fire hazard and that she ought to get rid of them."

"Aunt Hildegarde," Jane said, calling to mind a sparrowlike woman who had insisted that Jane come to live with her after her parents died, and then had proceeded to make Jane's life miserable with her irrational outbursts.

"You got a letter from her doctor after you left here. I opened it, because when I saw the doctor's name on the return address, I thought it might have something to do with your disappearance. She died in a nursing home. I didn't know how to let you know," Moonglow said.

Jane was silent for a moment, wishing that she could have done something to help her aunt.

"I'm sorry," Moonglow said softly.

Jane shook her head. "It's okay," she said with a sigh. For so long she'd wondered if she had any family, and it was a deep disappointment to know that Aunt Hildegarde was gone, even though the two of them had never liked each other much.

"Look at me, forgetting my manners. I've just baked fresh gingerbread," Moonglow said. "You'll have some, won't you?"

It wasn't an offer that Duncan was about to turn down, so they trooped into the kitchen and sat down around a round oak table, eating as they pieced together Jane's story.

"What I can't figure out," Duncan said, "is how Jane got into Carlton Jones's field."

"I think she was somehow abducted on the road," Moonglow hypothesized. "Somebody hit her on the head and left her for dead."

"But then where is her van? It's hard to hide a big blue van, you know," Duncan said.

Jane tried in vain to remember driving away from Shanti Village in the van, tried to recall if she had stopped anywhere along the way. It was no use. She couldn't remember anything about the trip.

"If I was going to Ohio, I was a long way from there when they found me outside Tyree, Illinois," she reminded them.

"Whoever kidnapped you headed in that direction," Moonglow offered.

"If only I could *remember*," Jane said. Her memory loss was even more frustrating now that she could recall so many other things. She wondered if she would ever find out exactly what had happened in the time between the moment she left Shanti Village and the morning that Carlton and Ollie Jones found her in the ditch.

One thing she did know after talking with Moonglow. She was not now nor had she ever been married.

"You almost got engaged once," Moonglow filled her in. "It was to a man who worked in that office with you. Only he didn't have any appreciation of your weaving, and you finally decided that you couldn't spend your life with someone who admitted that the highlight of his year was watching the Super Bowl on TV. That was one of the reasons you sought us out at Shanti Village."

Jane glanced at Duncan; he had gone limp with relief. She smiled at him, and he rewarded her with a wide grin. He reached over beneath the table and squeezed her hand.

Moonglow wouldn't hear of their going out for dinner; instead she prepared a vegetarian meal in a wok, and even though Duncan had misgivings about eating it, he managed to down two full plates. Afterwards, still hungry, he tried to recall if there was a steak house on the highway back into town.

And later Jane played with Sun-One, marveling over all the words she could say, and Sun-One, now a bouncing twenty months old, brought all of her favorite toys out of the closet and laid them one by one in Jane's lap until Jane was almost hidden under a heap of rubber duckies and fluffy stuffed animals. Duncan thought how lovely Jane looked with her face pressed against the baby's silky hair, the tiny clutching fingers wrapped around her thumb.

At that moment he was supremely thankful that Jane had no husband and children to whom she must return because he, he wanted to be the one to give her children. He could imagine it—little replicas of Jane and himself leading llamas around the ranch. That reminded him that he was supposed to call Rooney. He asked Moonglow if he could use her telephone.

His conversation with Rooney left him worried; Rooney sounded overwhelmed by dealing with the problems of running the ranch as well as holding the headstrong Mary Kate in check. It was, he knew, time to go home. He made reservations for the next day on a flight to Cheyenne.

Jane and Moonglow parted tearfully after Jane promised to write and to call, leaving the Placid Valley Ranch address in case Moonglow needed to reach her.

"I'll be there until spring," Jane promised Moonglow.

And beyond, Duncan thought to himself, imagining Jane in summer, with her hair bound back by a yellow ribbon, riding along beside him on Diggory, the horse that he had decided should be hers. He tried to catch Jane's eye, but she was handing Sun-One back to her mother and didn't see. He couldn't wait until they could be alone.

Duncan found a hotel in Terre Haute where he checked them into the best room in the house and, still hungry after his experimental foray into vegetarianism, ordered a steak from room service. He ordered one for Jane, too, thinking to celebrate the end of their search. But when they sat at the table across from each other, the candle that the waiter had lighted with such a flourish casting a golden glow on their faces, she appeared distant, thoughtful. *She seems,* he thought with a certain amount of disbelief, *like someone I don't know very well.*

The thought, once it wormed its way into his consciousness, wouldn't go away. Maybe it was because today he had seen Jane in a place that was totally different from the surroundings—his ranch—where he had first come to know her. Shanti Village was a rarefied kind of environment, a place for artsy-craftsy people, the kind of people with whom he had never associated. In fact, all that talk about Fenton Murdock and selling handbags to boutiques seemed to have little to do with the Jane Rhodes he knew.

The *Celeste Norton* whom he knew, he corrected himself. Only he didn't think he would ever be able to call her by that name. To him she would always be Jane. Dear, sweet, wonderful Jane. He smiled at her across the table, a little light-headed from the champagne he had ordered. But she wasn't smiling. Now she was talking animatedly about the day's events, hardly noticing his own silence.

"After all this time, it's amazing to find the place where I belong. It felt so right sitting there in Moonglow's house, playing with her baby," she said, alight with excitement.

Duncan stopped in midchew and forced himself to swallow. This was a development for which he wasn't prepared. "You don't have any urge to return to Shanti Village, do you?" he asked, the words catching in his throat.

"I don't know," she said. "It's all so new."

The faraway light came back to her eyes, her mind clearly drifting elsewhere. All her tension seemed to be vibrating at a new and higher frequency; her sensibilities were focused on Shanti Village, he could tell. He hadn't realized that the place had had such a strong attraction for her.

Suddenly Duncan couldn't eat any more. "You're coming back to the ranch with me tomorrow, aren't you?" he said.

The air fell deadly quiet, and it seemed like an eternity until her eyes lifted to his.

"I don't know," she said again.

He set down his fork and pushed back his chair from the table. He missed the barn, his usual refuge when things weren't going right, and he felt as though he might be sick.

He went to the window and stared out. They had left the draperies open, and the lights of the town twinkled up at him. Car headlights crawled along the length of the bridge across the river. His own reflection stared back at him, and he blinked.

Jane's reflection slid into place behind him on the darkened window. She wore a bleak expression, and for once he was tired of it. Tired of always putting her first, tired of constantly thinking of her well-being, tired of the pressure they had both been under for days, even weeks. What about his needs? He loved her. He loved her!

"Duncan," she said, touching his arm.

If they had been at the ranch, he would probably have slammed out of the house and walked over to the barn to cool off. But they weren't at the ranch; they were having a late supper in some hotel room in Terre Haute, Indiana, with a table set with gleaming silver and a rose in a silver bud vase, and a candle flickering mellow light over all of it. A *candle* for Pete's sake, and it was supposed to be romantic, but it wasn't! That made him angry.

"Damn," he swore softly under his breath.

"Duncan, I just don't *know*," Jane said brokenly.

"Well," he said, "just when will you 'know'?"

She responded to the unexpected sarcasm in his tone by drawing back as though he had struck her, and uncertainty flickered in her eyes.

"What I mean is, now we've found out all the information you wanted, whether you have a home and a family, who you are, where you lived, even right down to old Aunt Hildegarde, and you don't *know*? What else is there to find out, Jane?"

"I—"

"Let me answer that," he said, turning around to face her. He took in the eyes widened in surprise and hurt, the fingernails bitten to the quick, and hardened his heart. He had waited long enough; what he wanted now was commitment.

"I'll tell you what there is to find out," he went on. "Just one thing. And that is if you love me or not."

He watched her as color suffused her face. The hurt in her eyes almost broke his resolve, because he hated to see her hurt. He worked to control his emotions.

"Of course I love you, Duncan, but it's all so hard to deal with. Finding out that I have a real name, that I apparently had a satisfying life at Shanti Village, that I'm fully capable of earning my own living as a weaver—it's a shock." She stopped when she saw the vein pulsing at his temple, then drew a deep breath and went on.

"And the ranch—of course I'm grateful to you for letting me stay there and helping me get on my feet, for believing in me when no one else did. Just because I've found out who I am and where I once lived doesn't mean that the quest is all over for me. I'm still searching. Trying to figure out where I fit in. If I go back to the ranch with you now, you'll be on my mind every second, I'll live only for you. How will I know who *I* am? I'd always wonder if I could have made it here on my own. If my previous life was the one I should have chosen." Her chest heaved, and her hands were clenched into tight little fists at her sides.

"I never dreamed that you might want to stay here," he responded, unnerved by her words.

Her voice fell into a gentler cadence. "Would you rather I pretended that everything is okay? That would be as bad as lying, and you know how I feel about doing any more of that."

For once Duncan wished that she'd never developed her penchant for telling the truth. Lies could be so much simpler—for a while, at least.

"Duncan?" she said, waiting for him to speak.

Duncan's anger subsided suddenly. He saw her point. He ran a hand through his hair and sighed. The anger had been replaced by an ache in the vicinity of his heart.

"I was going to make love to you tonight," he said. "It wouldn't be such a good idea, would it?" He risked a look at her agonized face.

She looked as though she might cry, and he hoped she wouldn't. His jaw clenched in resistance. If she cried, he'd want to comfort her, and that would lead to something more, and all at once he yearned to feel her cool hand against the back of his neck, her soft lips against his.

Although he stood motionless and, he liked to think, stolidly, she reached up and put her arms around him. He forced himself to think of something else, anything else, anything but her small body pressed against his.

But then she pulled his head down, his arms involuntarily circled her and tightened so that she drew even closer, and as she found his lips with hers, his detachment dissolved entirely.

She began to unbutton his shirt, and for a moment his hand stayed hers, but she brushed him away impatiently and kept unbuttoning. He kissed her more deeply, a long, passionate kiss, and by the time it was over he was completely undressed and she was feathering her fingers across his back, something that always excited him.

Somehow he managed to get her clothes off, she was telling him over and over that she loved him, and they fell back onto the bed.

They had shared a bed before, but never like this, throwing back the bed covers, tangling in them, expressing all their pent-up passion. Her ardor surprised him, and he was amazed at the way she abandoned herself to pleasurable sensation. He touched her breast, reverently at first, then cupping it to his mouth so that she moaned and then sighed his name. And when he lifted his head she was smiling at him, a smile full of love. Then he knew that it was real, that she really did love him, and that he loved her more than he had even admitted to himself.

If he had thought she would have said yes, he would have asked her to marry him there and then. For that was what he wanted, to live with her forever at Placid Valley Ranch, and there was no doubt in his mind that it was meant to be. But he had done all he could to help her; if she wasn't sure what she wanted now, perhaps she would never know. And, as she had once said about his relationship with his wife, it was better to have had something than nothing; now they would have this night.

The light from the bedside lamp was shining full into his eyes, and she reached over to turn it out, the vulnerable slender white underside of her arm brushing his face for a brief moment. When it was dark he tumbled her over and slid his thigh between the gentle softness of hers.

As his eyes adjusted to the glow from the candle on the table, she seemed to float beneath him, light and buoyant, and then he was part of her, being absorbed into her body, knowing her, *knowing*.

Now it didn't matter if there were things that she still didn't know, that there were uncertainties, because for all time he would know, would know *this*. And for the moment, it was all he wanted.

HE DROVE HER to Shanti Village the next morning. She sat close beside him, her face pale and drawn, her lips swollen from their lovemaking the night before.

"I'll call you," she promised as they stood on Moonglow's doorstep beside her suitcase.

"I wish you'd come with me," he told her.

She tried to smile. "I know," she answered, and bent to lift the suitcase.

"I'll stop by Mrs. Beasley's store and pick up the dress to take to Mary Kate," he told her, wanting to postpone his leave-taking as long as he could.

"Thank you, Duncan. For everything," she added. She wished she knew what else to say.

"It's all right." Icicles were melting off the roof overhang. One fell and broke with a tinkle on the porch railing. He tried to make a joke. "This place is a far cry from California, wouldn't you say?"

"Yes," she said. "I guess it is."

"You'd better go in," he said. He didn't know whether to kiss her out here or not.

She nodded, then put the suitcase down again. "Oh, Duncan," she said, and went into his arms.

As he tried to memorize the way she felt in his embrace, he remembered the first time he had held her. It had been the night he found her in the mine, and she'd lain naked in his arms all night long. Like last night, except that on that first night she had slept. Last night neither of them had slept much. There had been other things to do.

"I won't say goodbye," she said. "It seems so final."

"All right. Give Moonglow my regards."

"I will. Tell Rooney hello, and tell Mary Kate—" Here her voice broke. She swallowed and began again. "Tell Mary Kate I love her," she finished.

Duncan nodded, backed down the steps, then turned swiftly and walked to the car. He drove away without looking at her, and when he summoned the strength to glance into his rearview mirror, the porch was empty.

He stopped to pick up the dress for Mary Kate, evading the questions of the kindhearted Alice Beasley. He hand-carried the package all the way home but didn't give it to Mary Kate. That was something for Jane to do.

If she came home. *No,* he corrected himself. *When* she came home.

Chapter Sixteen

Jane and Moonglow moved Jane's old bed into Moonglow's room, and Jane settled into the household routine. Up early in the morning, breakfast with Moonglow and the baby, scheduling time on Moonglow's loom so that they each had a turn. She took to wearing loose jumpers over tights and high-topped shoes, the way Moonglow did. She bundled up her bright hair in a snood. When she looked in the mirror, she seemed to have become someone else, someone she didn't know very well.

It was a life that Jane—Moonglow called her Celeste, but somehow she still thought of herself as Jane—that Jane remembered, but it didn't seem quite real to her. It was as though this was a movie she had seen and liked a long time ago, not a real life.

And if some mornings she woke up and expected to see the yellow walls and flowered draperies of her room at Placid Valley Ranch, well, maybe that, too, was a movie she had seen once. With a real-life hero who had rushed to her rescue, who had treated her with unfailing kindness and consideration, and who loved her. Now that she was caught up in life at Shanti Village, her life at Placid Valley Ranch sometimes seemed more like a dream than a movie.

She wove an afghan and sent it to Duncan, thinking that it would warm him on cold nights when he sat reading in his chair by the fire. He called and thanked her for it, but communication between them was stiff and awkward. They had many such conversations, and Duncan was always terse; he seldom told her anything that was happening at the ranch. She always hung up the phone feeling sad and missing the warmth and happiness she had felt when they were together.

"Why don't you go back to him?" Moonglow asked once when they were having one of their frequent heart-to-heart talks.

"Because I don't have a real sense of who I am yet," Jane said, staring at the floor.

"If you love each other, you should be together," Moonglow said firmly.

"If only it were so simple," sighed Jane. "You see, when I came into Duncan's care I was lost and angry and defiant, and he let me know that he cared about me, so all I wanted to do was to be like him. It worked for me then. But now I've learned that I had a life before that, and I want to live it for a while. Then I'll know if I can go back to the ranch and pick up where I left off."

"What about California?" Moonglow asked.

"Going to California was a dream I had. Maybe it wasn't realistic, although it kept me going through the hard times. Oh, I don't know. All I want right now is to live here and do my work, and I'm so grateful to you for letting me stay."

"Nonsense," Moonglow said as she swung Sun-One onto her lap. "This is your home, too."

Many of the people who lived in Shanti Village before the Fenton Murdock faction came into power had moved away and were now moving back; Jane quickly reacquainted herself with the ones she knew, and they were eager to accept her once more. They held potluck suppers every Tuesday and Thursday night, afterward lingering for long talks over coffee, during which the villagers engaged in mutual support of their endeavors. A warm, convivial feeling enveloped the place, and Jane's work went well. She began to produce handbags for the boutique market and learned to weave new patterns, as well. She was happy enough.

But she missed Duncan. All she had to do was hear his voice on the phone and it would send her into a blue funk for days. She would think about the way he laughed with her over lunch at the ranch, the way she could tell by the set of his shoulders when he came in from the barn how tired he was, about how he looked with Mary Kate settled into the crook of his arm as he read her the Sunday comics with Amos purring in snatches at their feet. And she would wonder if he missed anything at all about her—her attempts to cook the same foods that his mother used to make, the hum of her spinning wheel as they kept each other company in the living room on those long winter evenings, the way they had made love that last night in Terre Haute.

The lovemaking had exceeded her expectations. She hoped it had lived up to his. And now that she had had a sample of it, her body ached with wanting him.

As if all that wasn't enough, during her third week there she received an incoherent phone call from Mary Kate, who had found her telephone number scribbled on a notepad in Duncan's house.

When the phone rang, Jane picked it up and immediately heard someone sobbing on the other end. It only took her a few seconds to realize that this was a long-distance call and that Mary Kate was the caller.

"Mary Kate? Mary Kate, now listen to me. Calm down, honey. Calm down and tell me what's wrong," she said. The sound of the child's crying made her frantic. She didn't know if something had happened to Amos, or Duncan, to Rooney or Mary Kate herself.

"J-J-Jane," was all Mary Kate could say, and this made Jane even more worried.

"Mary Kate, honey, can't you tell me what's wrong?"

Mary Kate struggled to contain her crying, and after a moment, she hiccuped a few times. "D-Dearling," she managed to stammer at last. "They s-sold her."

Jane felt only shock. *"What?"* she gasped, incredulous.

"They sold her. My Dearling. She's gone!" Mary Kate began to sob again.

Jane tried to get a grip on the situation. Dearling sold! But Duncan wouldn't do such a thing to Mary Kate. He'd been angry about her letting the breeding females escape, but he wouldn't have done this.

"Tell me about it," Jane said apprehensively, not really wanting to hear. She still couldn't believe it.

"G-Grandpa did it. He sold her. He's punishing me. But I miss her so much! Dearling won't be happy anywhere else," Mary Kate said all in a rush.

"Oh, Mary Kate, I'm so sorry," Jane said. A deadening depression began to seep through her; she felt helpless to do anything to make Mary Kate feel better.

"You are not! If you were sorry you'd come back here. You promised! You *promised*! And then you didn't come back and didn't come back, and now you're never coming back!" She began to cry again, tears of anger and despair and frustration, feelings that Jane recognized because they were all too familiar.

Mary Kate was right. She *had* promised. In the aftermath of discovering her lost identity, her promise to the girl had dimmed in importance. She felt sick with guilt.

"Look, Mary Kate, may I please speak to Duncan?"

"He's not here," Mary Kate said coldly, then slammed down the receiver.

Moonglow happened to walk through at that moment, leading Sun-One by the hand. "Bad phone call?" she asked with interest as Jane slowly set the receiver on its cradle.

"Very bad phone call," Jane agreed. Trying to think, she sat down on the floor and leaned her head against the wall.

"Problems, I gather," Moonglow said, dashing down the hall to retrieve Sun-One as she toddled away.

"Sit down here, Moonglow, and help me figure this thing out," Jane said, patting the bare hardwood floor beside her. So Moonglow brought Sun-One and set her down to play nearby while Jane outlined the situation.

"If I were you I'd get myself back to Wyoming," Moonglow said when Jane had finished.

"If I go back, I won't want to leave," Jane said.

"So what's wrong with that?" Moonglow asked, rolling her eyes and getting up to chase after Sun-One again.

"I'm just starting back to work, and I do like it here, and—"

"And you've been mooning after Duncan Tate ever since he dropped you on my doorstep. Now I ask you, does it really make sense to stay here when you're head over heels in love with the man?"

"I didn't know it was that obvious," Jane said ruefully.

"You can't talk to him on the telephone without going all fluttery, and afterward you're no fun to be around, believe me. And he's obviously crazy about you. Go for it, kid. As a woman alone, I can tell you that it's no picnic. If Duncan Tate was in love with me, I'd snap him up so fast it would make your head spin."

Jane digested this, then thought about Mary Kate again. "I can't believe they sold Dearling," she said under her breath.

"Sold what?" Moonglow said.

"Dearling. Mary Kate's pet llama. I just can't believe it. Oh, I've got to talk to Duncan and find out his version of the story."

She picked up the phone and dialed Duncan's phone number in the barn, which, according to her calculation, was where he would be at this hour. No one answered.

"I'll call him at the house later," she said.

But when she tried to reach him just before her bedtime, the phone rang and rang, and she finally decided that Duncan was out. She called the Rooneys' house, and Mary Kate answered. She sounded as though her nose was stopped up.

"Mary Kate," Jane began.

"I *don't* want to talk to anyone," Mary Kate said before slamming down the phone.

"Poor Mary Kate," Jane said brokenly.

"She sounds like a real pain to me," Moonglow observed.

"You don't understand. Mary Kate's had a hard life. She needs lots of love and nurturing and—oh, if only I were there," Jane said, burying her face in her hands.

"Then why don't you go?" Moonglow urged.

"It's not exactly around the block, you know," Jane said.

"I know, but you could fly out of Indianapolis and be there in a few hours."

"I'll sleep on it," Jane said, pulling the bed covers up over her head.

She didn't sleep well that night. When Moonglow made Cream of Wheat with cinnamon and brown sugar for breakfast, she hardly ate any.

"Look, this is ridiculous. Why don't you try calling Duncan again?" Moonglow suggested a few hours later when she saw Jane sitting motionless, staring at her idle loom.

"I did," Jane admitted. "Twice. And I called Rooney's house and the office in the barn. There's no answer there, either."

"Bruce Hodges is driving into Indianapolis this morning to pick up supplies. Want me to call him and see if he'll give you a ride to the airport?"

"I'm not ready to leave."

"Get ready, then. Look, you love Duncan. You love these other people. It doesn't make any sense for you to be here if they're having trouble. You belong with them."

"You're right," Jane said, lifting her eyes. "They helped me when I needed it."

"Exactly," Moonglow replied. "That's what it's all about, isn't it? Letting your lives spill into each other, taking from someone else's cup when yours isn't full enough."

"I was going to California because I intended to find a life for myself and people who would love and care about me. But I found all that at Placid Valley Ranch, didn't I?" Jane stood up.

"Shall I call Bruce Hodges?" Moonglow offered again.

"Please. And where did you store my suitcase, Moonglow?"

Moonglow looked as though she would have jumped up and clapped if she hadn't had a baby in her lap. "It's in the closet in Sun-One's room," she called as Jane rushed down the hall.

Jane packed in record time. She hung the loose jumper borrowed from Moonglow in the closet and put on her gray slacks, along with one of Duncan's favorite sweaters. When she looked into the mirror, her first impression was that she looked like her old Jane self, not the new Celeste self she had become since moving back to Shanti Village. She was discovering that she preferred her old Jane self, the self she had become at Placid Valley Ranch.

"Goodbye, dear friend," Moonglow said, hugging her before she left.

"I'll see you again soon," Jane promised, kissing Sun-One on her dimpled cheek.

"I doubt it," Moonglow said, laughing through her tears. "I expect you'll stay a while once you get there."

"Come see me if I do?" Jane asked.

"Maybe. Does that Duncan of yours have a brother?" Moonglow asked hopefully.

"No, there's only Rooney," she said.

Moonglow made a face. "I'm not interested in a man who would sell a kid's *pet*," she sniffed.

At the airport, Jane discovered that air traffic was backed up due to weather problems in the west, but she added her name to a waiting list for flying standby to Cheyenne and spent her time nervously pacing up and down the concourse by the gate from which the plane would depart. She hoped she would get a seat on it; if she didn't, she would wait here until another flight left.

She had no idea what she would say to Duncan when she saw him. She had no idea what he would say to *her*. She thought up imaginary conversations in her head. Instead of the usual platitudes like, "How have you been?" and "I'm fine, thanks," they would get right down to the central issues.

"I was stupid," she would say, looking him right in the eye. "We had something special going, and I didn't realize how good it was until I didn't have it anymore."

"I forgive you," he'd say. "And besides, it was really out of character for me to get angry that last night in the hotel in Terre Haute. It's you who should forgive me."

Then they would fall into each other's arms, never to be separated again.

At least that was the way she pictured it, the way it would happen on *Restless Hearts*. But by this time she knew that real life hardly ever followed the approved script.

Finally, when the tension of waiting became almost unbearable, she sat down in a seat near the gate and forced herself to read a newspaper that someone had thrown down beside her. Moonglow didn't get a newspaper at Shanti Village; with no television set, either, Jane had often felt cut off from the world while she was there.

She read the front page first, then tried to read the comics. Nothing held her interest, until she spotted a headline in a story across the bottom of a page of state and local news. She bent over the newspaper, scarcely believing what she was reading.

Van in Pond Is Clue in Jane Doe Case

An irrigation pond on the property of Tyree farmer Elwood Merck yielded valuable information in Tyree's mysterious "Jane Doe" case, according to Detective Bill Schmidt of the Tyree County, Illinois, Sheriff's Department.

"Mr. Merck was draining his pond in preparation for the growing season, and at the bottom of it was a blue Ford Econoline van registered to Ms. Celeste Norton, who is known to this community as 'Jane Doe,'" Schmidt said.

The Jane Doe cited by Schmidt captured Tyree's interest seventeen months ago, when a young woman bearing no identification was found lying in a ditch on the farm of Carlton Jones. She was suffering from a head wound, Schmidt said.

The van found in Merck's pond contained a handgun that was traced to a convicted murderer, Harry Milton Furgott, Jr. Furgott is presently serving time in the Indiana State Prison.

Schmidt says that Furgott has admitted to abducting Ms. Norton near Indianapolis seventeen months ago.

"Apparently Harry Furgott had just broken out of jail on that date, and he saw Ms. Norton's van at a service station, where she was filling it with gas. When she went inside to pay for the gas, he hid in the van, and when she reentered the van, he held her at gunpoint and forced her to drive to Illinois," said Schmidt.

Schmidt says that Furgott told authorities that Ms. Norton became angry when he spilled a can of Coca-Cola in her van, and he struck her on the head with the butt of the gun. He panicked when he thought she was dead and tossed her out of the van into a ditch.

"After that, he was in an agitated state and drove around Tyree and its environs trying to figure out what to do. The night was exceptionally dark, and he wandered off the main roads, becoming lost and by accident driving Ms. Norton's blue van into Mr. Merck's pond. He had to swim for his life, but managed to hitchhike out of the area after walking to the highway," Schmidt said.

Furgott was recaptured two weeks later near Des Moines, Iowa, and returned to the Indiana State Prison.

Schmidt added that Furgott will probably be charged with kidnapping and assault with intent to kill.

JANE LET THE NEWSPAPER drop to her lap. She felt a rage of murderous proportions. After all this time of not knowing what had happened to her, now she knew. She could dredge up no actual memory of Harry Furgott or his act, but the knowledge of it, sharp and corrosive as acid, hit her hard. She allowed herself to feel anger, to feel hate, to feel disgust for someone who would hurt another human being. For he had done more than hurt her physically; he had robbed her of her past, left her with no present, and jeopardized her future.

The drone of the public address system speaker directly over her head jarred her out of her thoughts.

"Passenger Jane Rhodes report to Gate Two, passenger Jane Rhodes report to Gate Two," the voice said, and Jane, feeling slightly nauseated, stood up. At the last minute, she scooped up the fallen newspaper and stuffed it into her purse. She would want to read the article again.

"You may board Flight 832 to Cheyenne," the ticket agent told her, and she hurried through the jetway to the plane.

As she sat in her seat waiting for the plane to take off, her mind flowed with replays of her life since she encountered Harry Furgott on that fall day seventeen months ago. The hospital, kind Dr. Bergstrom, and that awful social worker who had been supposed to help her. The shelter for battered women, and her job in the little restaurant in Apollonia. Her bewilderment at being forced out onto the street, and the bus stations and shelters where she had slept. Finding Amos and hiding him in the recesses of her coat in the Chicago library, where she had so often gone to keep warm. Losing her coat in Saint Louis, and the truck driver who had given her a ride in Wyoming. She was overcome with the unfairness of it all. But finally she'd found Duncan. Oh, how happy she would be to see him again!

But what about this man, this Harry Furgott, who had virtually stolen seventeen months of her life? He had certainly wronged her. She was amazed to discover that she felt no malice toward him. The huge surge of anger that had hit her after reading the article was gone. Even when she looked deep inside herself, she could dredge up none of the earlier rage.

Harry Furgott would surely be brought to justice for his crime. And she—she had a future again. She had no intention of jeopardizing it by hanging on to her anger. It was best to let it go; she already had.

The flight to Cheyenne seemed mercifully short, and Jane was surprised when the captain of the plane spoke to them over the plane's public address system and told them that they were landing just ahead of a powerful snowstorm that was sweeping out of the west. She edged forward in her seat to look out the window as they descended. The sky was the color of lead.

Her heart sank. She knew all too well from personal experience how severe a Wyoming snowstorm could be. By the time she had claimed her luggage, no one was leaving the airport. Visibility was near zero.

Gazing out the airport window at the blowing snow, Jane told herself stoically that at least it looked as though it would be a long time until spring. Duncan wouldn't insist that she leave until then; that had been their bargain, and he was a man for keeping his word.

At first she held out hope of being able to contact Duncan at Placid Valley Ranch, but long before nightfall it became apparent that this was impossible. No vehicles were leaving or arriving at the airport. She soon learned that all hotel rooms in the area were booked by delayed passengers, which meant that she spent the night arranged across several hard plastic seats in the airport. She slept better than she'd expected, but then there had been many a night in her past, the past she was so eager to forget, when she'd found worse accommodation. If it hadn't been for the snores of the woman on the row of seats beside hers, she would have had a good night's sleep.

In the morning she tried calling the ranch again, but there was still no answer from any of the three telephones.

When someone told her that the roads would soon be clear enough for buses to get through, she elbowed her way to a counter and managed to buy a ticket for a long-distance bus that was bound for Rock Springs on I-80. Perhaps she could talk the driver into letting her off near Durkee.

The bus was crowded, but in spite of the storm, or perhaps because of it, a holiday atmosphere prevailed, and someone offered her a chicken leg from his sack lunch, which kept her from being too hungry. Two lanes of the interstate highway had been cleared of snow, and although their progress was slow, it gave Jane time to watch out the window for wildlife. Her seatmate, an elderly man, pointed out rabbit tracks at the side of the road, and twice they saw deer turning tail and leaping away over the snowbanks.

Even though he was reluctant to do it, the bus driver let her off at an interstate highway rest stop not far from Durkee, and Jane plowed through the snowdrifts to reach a pay phone. It alarmed her when there was still no answer at Placid Valley Ranch.

"Duncan Tate?" said the caretaker at the rest stop, when she asked him if he knew how she could get to the ranch. "I know him. Happens my sister went to elementary school with Duncan. You want to go out to the ranch?"

Jane assured him that she did, and he rubbed his chin and allowed as how he could take her there when he got off his shift in an hour or so, if she didn't mind riding in his pickup truck with the heating system on the blink.

Jane said no, that wouldn't bother her at all, and for the next hour she huddled against the tile wall in the women's rest room, turning the hand dryer on from time to time for warmth from the heated air.

They set out from the rest stop at a crawl, and Jane thought they would never reach the Placid Valley exit. They kept passing abandoned cars, dark hulks barely visible beneath the snow. Her anxiety grew; it worried her more and more that no one had ever answered the ranch phones.

The highway past the ranch entrance had been plowed, and they were able to increase their speed. The heater in the pickup kept switching on and off with a thump, and Jane frequently blew on her hands for warmth, eliciting profusely apologetic looks from the man who was giving her the ride.

When they finally reached Placid Valley Ranch, Jane was pleased to see that although the mailbox at the entrance of the driveway was mounded with snow, the driveway had been plowed. She got out of the truck, pulling her suitcase after her.

"If you want me to drive you down to the house, I will," said the man, peering anxiously out the crack in his side window at Jane, who was hopping from one foot to the other trying to keep warm. But the pickup's engine had developed an ominous knock, so Jane waved him off and, carrying her suitcase, began to trudge resolutely toward the house.

In the distance the mountains shadowed blue-tinged billows of snow, and the roof of the barn peeked over the trees. It seemed so long since she'd walked this road, so long since she'd seen Duncan! Her heart began to beat faster at the prospect. She wondered if he would welcome her with a kiss, or if the love he had felt for her had changed. She didn't think it would have died, not so soon, but she knew very well that it could somehow have taken a different shape, could have cooled into a feeling more akin to friendship. For friends were what they had been before they became lovers. Best friends. And she knew that friendship was not all she wanted now.

When she was halfway there, she set down her suitcase on the packed snow and rubbed her aching hands together. A puff of smoke from Duncan's chimney wended its way lazily up through the trees, and she took heart. Someone was home, someone was here; despite the unanswered phones, nothing could be wrong if there was a fire in the fireplace.

At the front gate she abandoned the suitcase and ran, mindful of icy spots after her last fall, to the front door of Duncan's house. She knocked, quietly at first, then more loudly. *Duncan,* she said to herself. *Finally I'm going to see Duncan.*

He opened the door. He was wearing his old flannel shirt, a familiar one with a frayed collar. And he wore his boots, so that he seemed even taller than she remembered. He stared down at her, nonplussed. He shook his head slightly as though he couldn't believe she was really there.

"It's me," she said quietly, all the meaningful things she had planned to say scattering to the four winds. "I'm home."

He didn't say anything, only opened the door wider and engulfed her in his arms. And then she was laughing, he was smiling and she was sobbing, and Amos came and twined himself around their ankles, purring so loudly that Jane wiped her eyes and bent to pick him up.

"I'm beginning to enjoy snowstorms. They usually bring you," Duncan said, wrapping his arms around her. Amos was crushed between them, but he seemed not to mind.

"Oh, Duncan, they found my blue van," she told him as he drew her inside where it was warm, and then she told him about the newspaper story that named Harry Furgott as her assailant.

"Schmidt called a couple of days ago, and I tried to call and tell you about it, but our phones have been intermittently out of order because of the storm, and I gave up trying to dial long-distance," Duncan told her.

"That explains why I couldn't reach you," she said as they sat down together in front of the fire.

"Why didn't you wait to come when it would be easier to travel?" he asked, holding tightly to her hands, as though he expected her to disappear if he didn't.

"I hadn't heard about the storm when I left for the airport in Indianapolis. All I knew was that I had to get here. I was worried, Duncan, because of a phone call I got from Mary Kate," and she related how Mary Kate had called and told her that Dearling had been sold.

Duncan's eyes became solemn. "I would have stopped Rooney if I could have," he said. "By the time I knew about his selling Dearling, he had already clinched the deal. Dearling's new owner is a fellow over in Scottsbluff, Nebraska. He wrote and said he suddenly had a hankering to have a llama for a pet, and Rooney called him up and told him he had a nice, tame, trainable llama available. They agreed upon a price over the phone, and the guy showed up right away and hauled Dearling away in a van."

"Mary Kate is heartbroken," Jane said.

"I know, and there's not a thing I can do about it. Rooney is punishing her for letting the llamas out of their pen."

"But such a cruel punishment! Dearling was everything to Mary Kate," Jane said.

"I agree. It's a shame. I'd personally give my right arm to get Dearling back, but there's no way. Anyway, I couldn't have overruled Rooney's decision. He was disciplining Mary Kate."

"Mary Kate needs love and attention, not harsh punishments," Jane said with conviction.

"I agree with you, and even Rooney admits that he was wrong. He'd like to get Dearling back as much as anyone, if only to improve Mary Kate's disposition.'' Duncan said. He paused and studied her carefully. "Is Mary Kate the only reason you came back?" he asked.

Jane stopped scratching Amos's chin. "No," she said. "No, it's not. I missed you, Duncan. Terribly."

She was gratified when he enclosed her in his arms. She inhaled his familiar pine scent and closed her eyes as he stroked her hair. They sat like that for a long time, and then he stood up, gently took her by the hand and led her upstairs to his bedroom.

"We'll move your things in here, okay?" Duncan said, murmuring against her temple.

She pulled away. "I've just thought of something, Duncan. I left my suitcase out by the gate!"

He laughed, a low rumble deep in his throat. Then he unbuttoned the top buttons of her sweater and impatiently pulled it over her head.

"We'll get it later, my love," he said. "Much later."

Then he took her to bed.

Chapter Seventeen

The next morning when Jane was passing by her old room, she noticed a large box on the bed, topped with a big pink bow. Curious and wondering if it was for her, she investigated, only to discover from the sales slip tucked under the bow that the package was from Alice Beasley's shop near Terre Haute.

No doubt the package was the dress that Duncan had picked up to bring back to Mary Kate. Jane had assumed that he had already given it to her.

"Duncan," she called when he passed the door of the room. "I thought you'd already given this to Mary Kate."

He stopped, leaned against the door and looked down at the floor. "Well, I didn't," he said sheepishly after a moment or two. "I thought it would be best if you did. When you came back."

"How did you know I would?" she asked in surprise.

"I didn't. But I was hoping," he said. He crossed the floor and kissed the top of her head.

She turned and circled her arms around his torso. How well they fitted! She was still glorying in their physical proximity when he said, "Look out the window. You're going to have a chance to give Mary Kate the present right away."

Outside, Mary Kate was working her way along the tamped-down snow path from Rooney's house. Only this wasn't a bright-eyed, exuberant Mary Kate. It was a Mary Kate on whose sagging shoulders the world had settled.

"Oh, she looks so unhappy," Jane said, going to the window so that she could wave if Mary Kate looked up. But Mary Kate didn't. She kept her head down, and dragged her feet when she walked.

Jane ran downstairs and met Mary Kate at the back door. When she threw the door open, she said, "Surprise!" and a startled Mary Kate's mouth fell wide open.

"You came back," Mary Kate said flatly.

"Yes, and I've been wanting to see you," Jane said, overjoyed to see her young friend again.

"Well, you didn't come over."

Mary Kate's cool welcome deflated Jane only momentarily. She was determined to make the child feel loved. With so much love in her heart now, there was plenty left for Mary Kate.

"I would have stopped over at your house in a few minutes, but you've beaten me to it. Come in, Mary Kate, you're so cold, you look as blue as a Smurf."

"I think I'll go home," Mary Kate said, still resisting her overtures.

"But Mary Kate—"

"You're here, but you might not stay. And then I'll be all by myself again. Without Dearling. Or you," she said pointedly, her face shut against the world.

Jane refused to assign importance or credibility to this statement. "I'm going to bake something special for Duncan's lunch," she said. "It's gingerbread. A good friend of mine, the one I was visiting in Indiana, gave me her recipe. I was counting on you to help."

"Gingerbread?" Mary Kate asked. Jane detected a note of interest.

"Yes, and it'll be the best you ever tasted, I promise. Hurry inside, Mary Kate, or you'll freeze out there."

Mary Kate reluctantly came inside and tossed her coat over a kitchen chair.

"The coat goes in the closet," Jane pointed out as she busied herself finding pans, measuring cups and flour sifter. She watched out of the corner of her eye as Mary Kate grudgingly carried her coat to the closet and hung it lopsided on a hanger.

"I made an F on my geography test yesterday," Mary Kate announced as though it was something to brag about. "What do you think about that?"

Jane saw the challenge but rose to it. "I think it's awful. You should have studied.'

"Ha! I don't care about dumb old Africa or dumb old Asia. I don't care about my dumb old teacher, either. He says he's going to have to ask Grandpa to come in for a conference." Mary Kate energetically greased the cake pan, dropping a wad of Crisco on the floor in the process.

Jane quietly cleaned up the Crisco with a paper towel, then washed her hands again. "Well," she said while drying her hands, "maybe that's what you want."

Mary Kate slanted a grudgingly respectful look in her direction. "Maybe," she said.

"All right, now we have to sift the flour. Would you like to do the honors?" Jane asked, and Mary Kate nodded. She managed the chore without spilling much, and Jane began to measure out the other ingredients.

"I don't think Grandpa has ever gone to a parent-teacher conference," Mary Kate volunteered as she swung on a cabinet door.

"Why not?"

"Never had to, I guess. Maybe he'll have to now. He'll have to go get the teacher out of the teachers' lounge, I'll bet. That's where he stays all the time."

Jane privately thought that if she had a student like Mary Kate in any classroom where she was in charge, she'd probably take up permanent residence in the teachers' lounge, but thought it might be better to change the subject.

She handed the bowl with the batter in it to Mary Kate and said, "How about stirring that for me? Seventy-five stirs, and try to keep the batter in the bowl," she cautioned before running upstairs to get the present.

When she returned, Mary Kate was counting, "Sixty-one, sixty-two, sixty-three," and Jane let her count all the way to seventy-five before she produced the beautifully wrapped package from behind her back. Mary Kate was so surprised to see it that she almost dropped the bowl.

"Wow! Is that for *me*?" she gasped. Jane deftly removed the bowl of batter from Mary Kate's hands before slipping the box into them.

Mary Kate's eyes were as wide as saucers as she unceremoniously tore the ribbon and paper off the box.

"Oh!" she exclaimed as the dress spilled from the box in a flutter of pink organdy. "It's my pink dress!" She held it up and danced a madcap dance from one end of the kitchen to the other.

"Do you like it?" Jane asked anxiously. Mentally she was running up darts in the bodice and shortening the skirt to fit Mary Kate.

"Do I! It's the most beautiful dress in the world, Jane. The *very* most beautiful. It has sleeves you can see through and everything."

"I'll have to alter it to fit you," Jane said, holding the dress up to Mary Kate's bony shoulders.

"That's okay. You're a good sewer. When can you do it?"

"After we put the gingerbread in the oven," Jane said.

"I'll go show Amos my dress," Mary Kate said, and ran to rout Amos from his napping place on the living-room couch.

Duncan came downstairs and watched Mary Kate as she twisted and turned in front of the mirror beside the front door. "I take it from the squeals I heard as I was coming downstairs that Mary Kate likes the dress," he said.

"She loves it," Jane said as she tucked the pan of gingerbread into the oven. "I'm so glad I bought it for her. It only needs a few alterations here and there to fit her perfectly."

"I was thinking," Duncan told her, planting a kiss on her cheek. "Since the loom you owned is presumably waterlogged after spending a year and a half under water inside your blue van, we'll have to get another loom for you. Why don't you order it?"

"I will. And do you know that I received three more orders for my llama wool from hand knitters back East? Not only that, Moonglow says she wants to try it. If I get some of the fiber artists at Shanti Village interested in llama wool, that's a good, steady market."

"Duncan, look at my dress," Mary Kate demanded as she twirled by.

"Mmm. You'll look like a fairy-tale princess in it, no doubt about it. Would you mind telling me where you're going to wear such a gorgeous outfit?"

"For my birthday party next month. Grandpa said I could have one. *If* he doesn't change his mind," she said with a frown.

"Tell you what, Mary Kate. If he changes his mind, you come to see me. Jane and I will change it right back again," Duncan told her. He had already extracted the admission from Rooney that he wished he could get Dearling back but could think of no way to do it.

"Let's go upstairs and get started fitting that dress," Jane suggested, and as she ushered Mary Kate out of the kitchen, she turned and mouthed silently to Duncan, "Ask Rooney when Mary Kate's birthday is." She knew he understood when he answered with a wink.

"I WANT TO DO something really special for Mary Kate's birthday," Jane told Duncan that night as they were lying in bed.

He traced idle circles on her shoulder. "Like what?" he asked sleepily, his chest vibrating as he spoke.

"Like doing something with the llamas. The other kids will love it."

"Like doing *what* with the llamas?" Duncan asked, slightly more awake now.

"Oh, maybe a pack trip. And didn't Mary Kate say something about llamas pulling a cart? Couldn't we give the kids rides or something?"

Duncan hooted. "Her birthday is only a few weeks away, sweetheart. On April 25, in fact. And we still have snowstorms here at that time of the year. Why, I remember last year when—"

"Snowstorms? In April?"

"This is Wyoming, Jane. Not Chicago. Why, Chicago's weather can be *tropical* compared to Wyoming's. So I don't think we should plan a pack trip, and as for pulling a cart, Mary Kate was going to train Dearling to do it. But Dearling, unfortunately, is gone."

Jane sighed. "She misses Dearling terribly. I walked out to the barn to get more llama wool out of the closet today, and do you know what I found in there? Mary Kate, sobbing her heart out. I don't see how Rooney could have been so heartless."

"He thought he was doing the right thing at the time. He'd like to atone for his mistake, which is why I think he'll agree to have this big birthday party for Mary Kate. He wants to make it up to her."

"Nothing can ever make up for the loss of Dearling," Jane said with great certainty. "Nothing. Not even a party."

"You're right, of course. Now don't you think it's time to go to sleep?"

She thought about her own feeling of loss when she was separated from him; but they had come together again in the end, and she was glad. She reached out to him, marveling at the tautness of his muscles, the warmth of his skin.

"Of course I think it's time to go to sleep," she said as he responded to her touch. "But not just yet."

JANE SET UP HER NEW LOOM in the bedroom that had once been hers, and she began to weave llama wool into blankets. Llama wool was less elastic than sheep's wool, and she experimented with mixing in ten percent sheep's wool as she spun her yarn. She was pleased with the results, and after providing samples, Moonglow asked her to send more. She also sent a check representing the proceeds from the sale of Jane's creations in the boutique in Urbana and at the Shanti General Store.

Jane put away the check, biding her time before mentioning it to Duncan. Once it would have paid her way to California, but now she wasn't sure what the future held. Her dream of a new life there seemed unnecessary at this point; it had served her well when she needed it, but now she knew that she had no desire to enroll in a computer training program. She was well able to provide for herself through her spinning and weaving. She had proven it.

But what about the future? Duncan had said nothing about his expectations, and she didn't want to bring it up. She was happy. So was he. Right now it suited their purpose to live one day at a time, enjoying their new relationship.

It was Jane who answered the telephone when Dearling's new owner called. She was tying up the treadling sequence on her new loom one day when the trill of the phone interrupted her, and she didn't want to answer it. But Duncan and Rooney had both gone into town, and Mary Kate was at school, so there was no one else. She rushed to pick up the phone and was out of breath when she answered.

"No, Duncan Tate isn't here right now," she said, pushing Amos away when he tried to play with the phone cord. "May I take a message?"

When she started to write down what the man was saying, she realized with a jolt that she was talking to Dearling's new owner.

"Like I say, the llama looks like she's ailing. Nothing major, you know, but I thought I'd call."

"Is she eating? Drinking?" Jane asked in alarm.

"I can't say. I travel a lot, and I got her for my boy. He's kind of lost interest in her. She stays in the barn and well, he's an average boy. Interested in baseball and girls. The llama's a novelty, but he doesn't pay much attention to it."

"I'll ask Duncan to call you," she told the man, and hung up feeling dismayed.

When she told Duncan about the call, he appeared concerned. After phoning the man and talking with him, he seemed even more so.

"It doesn't sound good," he told Jane. "In fact, it sounds like the worst way to treat a llama. Llamas are herd animals, and they like to have others around. I suggested that he get another llama to keep Dearling company, but he scoffed at that. He said that he wasn't about to go out and buy another one when his son didn't pay attention to the one he already had."

"Dearling was such a tame llama, used to a lot of petting. She's probably pining away from lack of love."

"I gave him some suggestions. All I can do is call at the end of the week and see how Dearling is doing," Duncan said on a note of apprehension.

They waited out the week, but didn't mention Dearling's troubles to Mary Kate, who would have been even more heartbroken to know that Dearling's new owners didn't appreciate her. When Duncan came in from the barn that weekend after calling to check on Dearling, his lips were set in a grim line.

"It's worse," he said. "In fact, he wants to get rid of Dearling, he said."

"You mean sell her?" Jane asked.

"I guess so. He says he's got money tied up in her that could be used for better things."

Jane put aside the wool she was carding and went to kneel beside Duncan's chair. "Duncan," she said quietly, "I want to buy her."

"Buy her? Are you serious?"

"Definitely. Because I want to give her to Mary Kate."

"Well, I suppose I could give him a refund," Duncan said slowly.

"I don't mean that. *I* want to pay for her. With my own money. I have money, Duncan, enough to buy Dearling. It's from selling my wool and my shawls and handbags and blankets and—well, once I would have used it to start a new life in California. But now I know that the best thing I could do with it is to buy Dearling back as a birthday present for Mary Kate."

He saw that she meant it, and cupped her chin in his hand. Her eyes, a deep, dark blue, gazed back at him with a candidness that he knew he could trust. His heart spilled over with happiness.

"I'll call him and tell him that's what you want. If it really is," he said.

She let the vision of palm trees and aquamarine swimming pools, of computer classes and friends who sported deep suntans, slip away forever. That dream had never been real to her, had only been a stopgap solution. And it had never offered the safety, security and love that she had found here at Placid Valley Ranch.

"It's really what I want," she said, and reached up to kiss him lingeringly on the lips.

THE TWENTY-SIX FIFTH-GRADERS, members of Mary Kate's class at the Placid River Elementary School, milled around the kitchen, dining room and living room of Rooney's small bungalow.

"Now who wants to play Pin-the-Tail-on-the-Donkey?" Rooney shouted into the melee. No one paid the slightest attention to him.

Nine or ten children watched the cartoon video he had rented for them. Three were having a popcorn fight. Another was energetically grinding kernels into the carpet, and one boy was sound asleep under the kitchen table. Five were stuffing cake and ice cream into their mouths and occasionally someone else's. Mary Kate, wearing a pointed gilt cardboard hat, was arm-wrestling the class bully.

"Nice party," Jane said as she poured Kool-Aid into glasses.

"Nice party, my eye," Rooney grumbled. "When I was a kid, we all sat around the dining-room table and kept quiet until the birthday kid opened his presents. Then we all went home."

"But I bet you didn't have half as much fun," Jane observed.

Rooney grinned. "You're probably right," he said.

"I wonder where Duncan is," Jane said, tilting the blind at the window so she could see up the driveway.

"I don't know, but I wish he'd get here pretty quick, so we can clear these kids out of here soon," Rooney said, before rushing to pry apart two boys who were rolling on the rug and trying to poke out each other's eyes with their fingers.

Jane had gone to assist Rooney when she heard the rumble of Duncan's truck rolling across the cattle guard at the end of Rooney's driveway. The truck pulled a small trailer, and Duncan parked so that the trailer was directly in front of Rooney's front door.

She signaled to Duncan with an Okay sign and went into the living room.

"Mary Kate," she said over the din, "there's a package for you outside."

Mary Kate brushed her bangs out of her eyes and trod across the cake crumbs to the door. Her eyes widened when she saw the pickup and trailer.

She sent Jane a puzzled look.

"Go ahead," Jane urged gently, and by this time several of Mary Kate's classmates had gathered to watch.

Mary Kate pushed open the front door. Suddenly shy, she hung back when Duncan, smiling broadly, held out his hand.

"Come open this trailer door for me, Mary Kate. It seems to be stuck."

"*You* open it," Mary Kate said in a choked voice. "I can't."

Behind Jane, Rooney snorted. "Seems to me you're pretty good at opening gates and doors and that kind of thing. Seems to me you know how to *leave* them open, too," but he said it in a joking tone.

Mary Kate said, "Oh, Grandpa, hush."

"What's in the trailer, Mary Kate?" asked the boy whom she'd beaten at arm wrestling. A girl said, "Just wait and see," and soon everyone was clamoring to know what surprise was waiting for Mary Kate.

She walked slowly up the ramp to the trailer door and fumbled with the latch. Then it sprang free and the door swung open. Finally there appeared a dazed Dearling, who, appearing somewhat startled by the watching crowd, lurched into Mary Kate's arms.

"Dearling! Oh, it's my Dearling!" Mary Kate cried, and the little llama nuzzled her cheeks, seemingly puzzled by the salty tears that now flowed freely down Mary Kate's face.

"She's a birthday present from Jane," Rooney said, pointing to the huge red ribbon around Dearling's neck.

As the group of awed children gathered around Mary Kate, Duncan slid an arm around Jane's slender shoulders and drew her apart from the group. The snow on the ground was thawing into mud, but he walked her over to the fence behind Rooney's house, where they stood looking out over the pastures and at the mountains beyond.

"That was a good idea you had, buying Dearling back," he told her.

"Dearling's all right, isn't she?" Jane asked anxiously. "I mean, she's not sick or anything, is she?"

"I expect she'll make a full recovery. She was suffering from a broken heart, and that, in this case, is easily mended."

Jane leaned on the fence and inhaled a deep breath. "I smell spring on its way," she said, resting her head against Duncan's shoulder.

The sun was bright and golden, chasing the tail end of winter, and on the snow-covered mountain ridges, dark rivulets heralded the thaw. Soon the pastures and the mountainsides would burgeon with the gentle greens and yellows and pinks of spring.

There was something so optimistic about spring, Jane thought. No matter what went before, no matter how cold the winter or how many snowstorms it brought, you could count on spring coming along to make everything fresh and new. And after spring, summer, that golden flowering time when life seemed infinitely precious and beautiful.

"It was just this kind of day I used to dread," Duncan said, gazing down at her. "I thought you would leave in the spring."

"I'm not leaving, Duncan. Ever. Not in spring, summer, winter or fall."

"Of course you're not. You're going to marry me," he said comfortably, fitting her into the curve of his arm.

"Soon," she agreed.

"And we'll raise children," he said.

"And llamas—"

"And we'll live happily ever after, Jane Doe. You're home at last."

Mary Kate called them back to the party, and from where they stood they could see that the pink sash of her organdy dress was trailing in the mud. They looked at each other and laughed.

Then, hand in hand, they walked back through the melting snow toward a future as new as spring, as bountiful as summer, and bright with the radiance of the rest of their lives.

"What do you remember about the facts of life?"

"Wh-what?" She was surprised to find herself blushing.

"I'm just curious," he said, trying to pretend that the question was a perfectly natural one for a husband to ask his wife.

BEYOND THE DREAM

Nancy Martin

CHAPTER ONE

THERE WERE TWO kinds of men, Beth knew; those who were on the make and those who looked at women with only a passing interest. The tall man who got on the hospital elevator ahead of her, the one who turned around and immediately looked her square in the eyes, was the safe kind. He was probably married or engaged or recently widowed and therefore not interested. But the sight of Beth must have caught him off guard. His clear, grayish-green gaze met hers and didn't waver and his face went oddly still.

Beth turned and reached for the panel of buttons. She had to juggle her armload of books to do it, and the one on the top slid precariously, teetering at the edge of the pile, threatening to fall. She lunged forward to trap it against the wall, and barely managed to keep her balance. She watched as the book slipped anyway and landed at the man's feet.

The noise startled him out of his thoughts.

"Oh, really, I'm sorry," Beth exclaimed immediately, feeling foolish. "Would you mind? It didn't hit your foot, did it?"

He had already bent to pick it up. "Not quite."

She forced a laugh. "Somebody told me that books make great conversation starters. Do you suppose—?"

"That this is what they had in mind?" He smiled at Beth, a gentle, natural smile that held no hint of sexual come-on. "Hitting me with it is a more direct approach—"

"Than an intellectual remark designed to wow you with my brilliance?" Beth asked, delighted that they could finish each other's sentences like playful spouses. "You mean I really didn't have to read all this stuff?"

He was extremely tall, she realized when he straightened to his full height beside her. His hair was dark and probably too long, but it was straight and combed close to his head, so the length didn't matter. His face was handsome, she thought, though not conventionally so. His brows were level across deeply set grayish-green eyes, and his nose wasn't quite straight—probably broken a long time ago. His mouth was also straight, like those painted of serious-minded Quaker gentlemen in early American works of art—very thoughtful without losing a subtle sensitivity. It was an ascetic face, solemn featured but vividly alight with the glimmer of intelligence in his eyes. He was dressed in what Beth had come to call "expensive casual." He seemed like a man who could afford very good clothes, but his aged navy flannel jacket and well-tailored trousers appeared to be familiar and comfortable, and that was more likely why he wore them.

Beth realized that she had studied him pretty thoroughly, and she quickly reached again for the panel and the fifth-floor button. As the doors began to close, a hospital orderly ducked into the elevator and punched another button. He didn't glance at Beth, who was suddenly a little glad that she wasn't alone with the tall man who had such wise eyes.

The elevator door hummed closed, and the three were alone together. The orderly ignored Beth and the stranger, who had used the same few seconds of interruption to take in Beth's appearance more carefully. His gaze traveled swiftly across her features, resting just fractionally on the quivering smile that Beth pasted on her mouth, before traveling just as measuringly down her throat, past the too-short candy striper's uniform to the slim length of her bare legs and comfortable flat-heeled sandals.

He must have remembered himself then, for his gaze snapped up to hers once more, and he made some inner decision about the way her face and sleek blond hair contrasted with the cheap hospital outfit. He said bluntly, "You're a little old to be reading textbooks and wearing that uniform, aren't you?"

"Thanks," said Beth tartly, smiling still in spite of the rush of shyness that threatened to make her blush. "Do I look more like the gray lady age bracket? Before I'm thirty?"

He gave her a smile also, a self-deprecating one that grew, the longer he studied her face. "I'm sorry," he said. His voice was low and drawling, not a Southern "y'all" drawl, just a honey-tinged mellowing of syllables learned in some civilized place like maybe Virginia. He explained, "I've been a hermit for the past two years, and my polite small talk wasn't so hot before that. Are these really textbooks you're delivering?"

He took a look at the book still in his hand.

"Not textbooks, and I'm not delivering," Beth said promptly, and as the elevator ground to a halt at the second floor, she balanced the large stack of books one-handed to reach for the one he had. "Not to patients, anyway. They're mine. Mine to read, that is, not to own. I'm returning them, in fact. I've been reading a lot lately."

"So I see," he responded with another smile at the huge stack of evidence in her arms. He passed the book, but Beth couldn't grasp it, and he put out his other hand to help steady her load. "Can I give you a hand? I haven't carried a girl's books since high school."

"Oh, I can manage, honestly. I'm just heading up to Dr. Westham, and his office is right off the— Oh, rats! Yes, oh dear, take these off the top before I really—"

The orderly had pressed the third-floor button, and as the elevator opened again he thrust past Beth to hurry out onto the hospital floor. He bumped her load of books, and they balanced dangerously in Beth's arms.

The tall man took a quick pace forward and caught half her load before they all fell to the floor. He hefted them in his own arm, but one slim paperbound volume slipped. He caught it neatly in one palm, noticed the title and stared at it in surprise. "Heavens," he murmured then, sounding truly prayerful. "You read this?"

Beth took a peek over his arm at the cover, checking. "Yep. I read them all. Some were better than others. *Bitten,* that's a play, not a book, really."

"Yes," he said quietly, turning it over in his hand to look at the back cover, though there was nothing printed there. He kept his head bent, and Beth couldn't see his expression. "Did you like this one?" he asked. "Better than the others, or not?"

Beth shifted her load and pressed the button again with her left hand. "I suppose it was fine. Very famous, I'm told. Pulitzer Prize and all that."

He lifted his head and smiled into her eyes, a disquieting kind of amusement flickering on his lips. "You're not answering. Did you like it?"

Beth popped her eyes comically and tried to shrug. "It was over my head, to tell you the truth. All about some poor fellow who'd been bitten by a rabid dog—or at least a dog they thought was rabid. And his very young life passes before his eyes, including a girlfriend or two and his old grandfather who told dirty jokes, but he could get away with it because he was an old coot and very old men seem to be able to get away with that kind of . . . Yes, to answer you, I liked it. But I'm not sure why. It was funny, though. Awful-sounding when I tell it, but it was funny. Sad-funny.''

He nodded in acceptance of that response and tucked the book under the others he had taken from her. "Good enough. You'll make a critic one day." He looked straight into her face then and said, "You're the Jane Doe, aren't you?"

Beth froze in consternation. The elevator started upward again, and her stomach lurched.

"I've heard about you in the newspapers."

That sinking feeling assailed her, an awful sickness in her stomach. "You—you're not a reporter, are you?"

She was thankful that at least he didn't manufacture a laugh and say, "Oh, my, no!" But after noting Beth's expression, he took a step backward. He moved away, as if putting the distance between them might help allay her obvious fear, and said simply, "No."

Beth knew he wasn't lying. Stiffly, she said, "I don't like reporters very much."

He nodded. "I'm sure. You've been through quite—"

"Don't say 'ordeal,' okay? I'm sick of the word."

He smiled again, his interest sharp upon her. Perhaps Beth's spirit had shown through for an instant, and he was faintly surprised by the fire she demonstrated. Without a shade of indulgence, he asked, "What do you call it?"

Beth shrugged, tipping her head to one side. He looked safe enough, and she couldn't seem to stop her honest answer. "It's life, that's all. For me, it is. Waking up and finding I had no past and no name was just starting a new life, that's all."

The elevator doors parted, and he held them open. "You don't use any of those clichés about being reborn, I notice."

"No," said Beth. "That's what reporters say, isn't it?"

"Yes," he said with an amused, but commiserating wince. "Does it bother you?"

"It bothers me that my life's not my own," Beth said promptly, lifting her chin. "People think they've got to help me, and that's frustrating. Somebody tried to hurt me, I'm told, and I got a broken head for it, but I'm not a helpless baby. I just don't know who I am, that's all."

"You were badly hurt, though. That man—"

"I'm better now," Beth said firmly.

"But you're still in this hospital."

"Tell me about it!" Beth snapped, and then she laughed ruefully. "I'm sick to death of this place, but I haven't got a home to go to, and the police probably wouldn't let me leave if I did." She was feeling especially bitter today, so she added vehemently, "I'm a prisoner, pure and simple."

The bustle of the fifth-floor nurses' station was just the same as ever. Beth hesitated before stepping out onto the floor. Lamely, she said, "Look, I don't mean to sound bitter. Everyone here has been wonderful. I'm just—well, three months of living in this place makes me a little crazy sometimes."

"You're entitled, I think."

Beth smiled with him. "Thanks. Nice talking with you. Are you visiting someone? Or are you a doctor? Insurance guy? You're not a drug salesman."

"I'm visiting," he said. "Let me help with the books. Where are you headed?"

"I'm all right, honestly. You don't have to. Load me up and I'll let you go on your way. Thanks. I hope whoever you're visiting is okay."

"I think," he said quietly, "that she'll be just fine."

CHAPTER TWO

AT THE TIME, the incident in the hospital elevator did not affect Beth. It had been a pleasant encounter with a personable stranger, one that she enjoyed reviewing in her mind during the next few days of her captivity as Beth Doe.

John Doe was universally acknowledged as an anonymous name for an anonymous person. Jane Doe was just as bad, just as boring, just as meaningless. She had been at Johns Hopkins for several weeks before they allowed her to choose a nicer name, and she had lain on her bed in the ward and thought for several days before coming to a decision. Beth. That was it: Beth. She didn't know why she chose it exactly, but it sounded familiar, so she kept it.

Nothing else was familiar, certainly. She remembered nothing. She knew only what the doctors and the endless stream of policemen had told her, and later the bits of gossip from the nurses, none of which was pleasant.

She'd been beaten, she was told. Perhaps tortured also, though thankfully she remembered none of it and could treat the whole story as if it had happened to someone she didn't know. Her right arm had been broken, and her skull had been repeatedly struck against some asphalt surface. Despite the fact that she'd been found dressed in little more than a slip and a torn blouse, with a wedding ring and a shredded pair of panty hose, she had not been raped as all the other women had.

And she had escaped. None of the others had gotten away from the man that the media—particularly the supermarket tabloids—were now calling the Strip-Mine Murderer. He had struck at least six times, abducting women from in and around art galleries in New York City and taking them to remote sections of Pennsylvania to dispose of their bodies in abandoned coal-mining excavations. Somewhere in between he performed cruelties so sadistic that the police refused to release the details.

Beth had been found near a strip mine three months ago and had been taken by Life Flight helicopter to Johns Hopkins where doctors could tend her and the FBI had easy access.

She was the only witness, the only survivor, the only woman who had seen the man and lived. And Beth couldn't remember him.

Either her brain had been injured or the trauma had been so great that she had lost all her memory of her past. The amnesia—frequently and therefore inaccurately depicted on television soap operas—was rare, but that hadn't made any difference. The cops were angry with her inability to help them with their case.

Amnesia, Beth had learned, could be caused by two factors. The first, physical damage to the brain, meant that some or all memory was lost forever. Such brain damage could also cause all manner of related problems, ranging from loss of sense of smell or taste to actual paralysis of limbs, depending upon which part of the brain was affected. Beth showed no signs of other brain damage besides her inability to remember her past, thank heaven, but such symptoms could possibly show up later. The second cause of amnesia, her doctors explained, was emotional shock. Because of a traumatic experience, the subconscious mind might shut off the memory in order to protect the victim from remembering horrible events. The patient would only forget certain segments of his or her life, not everything entirely. That, they reasoned, was probably Beth's case since her general memory seemed fine—she could take care of herself and had retained the basic skills of reading, writing, and recognition of the world and how it worked. If hysteria caused her memory loss, her probable chances for recalling all of her past were relatively good.

If brain damage and emotional trauma *combined* to render Beth a blank slate, however, there was no telling when or how much she might ever remember about herself or what had happened to her. The doctors did not make any predictions, and Beth privately thought their unwillingness to make a formal judgment was a bad sign.

At first the authorities, mostly the FBI, had been patient with her, trying to coax some small clue from Beth's subconscious almost as soon as the doctors brought her out of the coma. Now that she was stronger and no longer frightened, however, the police were increasingly rude and disgusted with her. Beth reacted to their frustration with growing infuriation herself. She wanted to get out. Three months was too long to be cooped up in any situation, let alone one as charged with tension as this.

Oddly enough, however, no one had stepped forward to claim her.

Beth found it difficult to put her yearning into words, but one particularly miserable afternoon she tried to explain to Dr. Westham how she felt. The doctor had become fond of her, and he listened patiently, sympathetically as she talked, then ranted, and finally cried. Had she been abandoned by her past? Why didn't anyone care enough for her to come rescue her now? The nurses, her only friends it seemed, all had family or husbands or boyfriends to go home to every night, people to whom they belonged. Why didn't Beth have *anyone?* She was capable of giving a great deal, she knew. She longed for people who were *hers,* people she could rely upon and love.

But, though the New York papers were full of her story for weeks, and even the television networks had reported the story nationwide, no one came to Johns Hopkins to identify Beth Doe. Not for three months.

Then Beth's life was given back to her.

Dr. Westham broke the news gently. Someone had come to the hospital claiming to be her husband. Dr. Westham, chief of psychiatric medicine at Johns Hopkins, told her a little about her playwright husband, and, before she could panic or even rejoice at finding her chance to have someone of her own, someone she could really love, Westham took Beth along to meet the man. For the first time since her delivery into his care, the doctor held her hand.

Even before she was led into Westham's office, Beth knew who it was going to be.

Westham laid his hand on the knob and pushed the door open. The FBI man was there, and so was the detective from New York. Both were smoking, heads bent over the smudged pages of a manila folder as they sat on the cushions of the leather sofa. Above them, the mounted heads of a bighorn sheep and two mule deer stared glassy-eyed at the unfolding scene.

And *he* was there too, leaning against the wall by the window. The late-afternoon sun was slanting over his shoulder, and the glare obscured his face for a split second as Westham pushed open the door and let Beth through. He straightened then, and his head came up with a snap. He was even taller than Beth remembered, and he wore ordinary blue jeans and the same navy blazer over an unbleached cotton sweater—not at all what Beth imagined a renowned playwright might wear on an occasion such as this. Her first impression had been that he was too lean, but she saw now that he was just fit, with the whippy kind of power of a lanky younger man.

Beth hesitated a step inside the door.

The blackness in her head sometimes frightened her, but once in a while she experienced the sensation of diving deeper and deeper into a dark pool, swimming down and down to a tiny speck of light that beckoned. Was this man's face going to appear out of that tiny spot of light?

His expression was blank, yet not without the power, the kind of magnetism that Beth remembered from their few moments together in the elevator. And his gaze was disconcertingly direct—not warm, nor hostile, but as if he had submitted to this public reunion unwillingly. Yes, Beth could understand that! She'd submitted to a few indignities herself in recent weeks! Her heart suddenly hurt in her chest with a great panging thump. Sometimes hope felt like that. Sometimes her desire to know who she was became a pain just like this one.

"Do you know this man?" Westham asked with that annoying mildness—that damned casual tone he used to hide the fact that something important might be happening.

Beth didn't answer. She couldn't.

His expression must have mirrored her own. Anticipation and dismay sparkled simultaneously in his eyes. His face had slackened momentarily, drained of strength perhaps, but he had taken a quick, fortifying breath. He had prepared himself for something awful, Beth could see. He was very still, and then a kind of inner check valve must have closed, for he controlled his face as if unaccustomed and unwilling to share his emotions with strangers. He had his hands shoved sullenly into the front pockets of his jeans.

When Beth took an uncertain step toward him, though, he pulled his hands out very slowly, as if someone had drawn a weapon and was holding him at gunpoint. He didn't speak.

Beth found her voice first. "That was a rotten trick you pulled the other day."

"The elevator? Yes," he said. "But you didn't know me."

Beth gritted her teeth, trying not to sound accusatory. "You could have told me who you were. Who I am."

He tried to smile and shook his head. "I didn't think it was a good idea to spring it on you just then. I thought you'd need some help with this."

Beth didn't argue his point. Not yet, anyway. Sounding deceptively remote, she said, "Dr. Westham told me a little about you. He says your name is Sam."

He nodded slowly, carefully. "And you're Elizabeth. Elizabeth Sheridan."

Beth eyed him uncertainly, trying hard not to deal with the jumble of emotions that warred inside her. Dr. Westham had been right. This was hard, and yet there was a wonderful, exciting feeling, a sudden lifting of her heart. Struggling to sound normal, Beth asked in an infuriatingly small voice, "Am I really your wife?"

He steeled himself then. He got a visible grip on his own inner turmoil and came slowly, very slowly the rest of the way across to her. Beth didn't move, and he paused, hovering above her for an instant. The planes of his face were harsh, but a kind of compassion glimmered in his gray-green eyes. Beth didn't breathe.

Cautiously then, Sam Sheridan murmured, "Yes, Elizabeth," and he put his arms around her.

In his embrace, Beth lifted her hands uncertainly. Then instinct took over and she slid them up under the satinlike lining of his jacket to touch his back. He was muscled under that sweater, and not from the kind of work that writers do. The feel of him surprised Beth. He pulled her close, drawing her slender body into his bigger, stronger frame until they were locked in a hug that shut out the world. Beth closed her eyes and breathed the light scent that clung to his hair, his sweater—the smell of sunbaked grass and open fields. She wanted to breathe great gulps of that scent, but her chest was locked with emotion. Finally—she had *someone* who belonged to her! She found her own embrace tightening in response to him, holding fast to this tall, strong stranger until her heart quit its swift craziness and steadied once more.

He loosened her first, gently moving one hand up her back until he found the delicate nape of her neck. He eased her away from his body a few centimeters and tipped her face up to his. His eyes searched hers for only an instant before moving on to absorb the rest of her face, as if memorizing what he found there. When he could manage it, he asked simply, "Are you okay?"

Close to tears or laughter, she wasn't sure which, Beth smiled and rocked against his body out of instinct. "Yes, I'm fine."

Though he must have seen the still-apparent stitch marks that showed through the blond fuzz growing in behind her ears, Sam passed his hand down through her freshly washed flaxen hair, down her neck and along the curve of her shoulder and back. The caress was over too soon. He did not turn Beth loose, but cradled her in his arms before him. His hands had found her ribs, and his fingers lay neatly in each groove, as if he knew just where to hold her. Beth could feel the firm support of his thumbs just under her breasts, and the sensations did not feel strange. He felt her body relax, and he smiled a little. "I think we're supposed to be happy now."

He had read her thoughts. Laugh or cry? Believe or not? Beth tried another smile. "It—it's a jolt, though."

They smiled into each other's eyes then, having passed out of the first stage of discomfort and into a fleeting moment of curiosity. Beth took a long time deciding what she saw in his steady gaze. He had been afraid. In fact, she suspected that he had dreaded this meeting and was now relieved to discover that she wasn't weeping or carrying on like a victimized idiot.

Marcus, the man from the FBI, got up from the sofa and faced the two of them with an air of impatience. "Can we get on with this?"

Sam Sheridan turned on the FBI agent without letting Beth go. She could feel the muscles suddenly tauten within him, and she automatically pulled her hands away, standing stiffly as his fingers bit into her shoulders. Over her head, he said coldly, "Surely you've done enough already, Marcus."

"We haven't done a thing." Marcus dropped his still-smoldering cigarette in the ashtray. He crushed it with careful precision before looking up into Sam's face. "The stuff you brought isn't proof enough, in my book."

"Gentlemen," Dr. Westham intervened before the hostility grew, "I thought you had finished this discussion, or I wouldn't have brought Beth here. You've had several days to discuss the matter of identification."

"I'd like to see some dental records or fingerprints or something more conclusive before we allow Jane Doe to go off to heaven-knows-where with this character."

"I'm satisfied," said Dr. Westham firmly. He was a big, fatherly sort of man with a florid face, a neatly trimmed beard and a pursed little mouth set in a perpetually stern expression. He had become Beth's friend and confidant during her recovery, a man with whom Beth felt the bond of friendship, not just the doctor-patient relationship. He came quickly to Beth's defense, saying, "I've seen her birth certificate and a marriage license, and you've found in our talks that he knows more about Beth than any of us, Mr. Marcus."

"Those documents are easily forged," snapped Marcus. "I don't trust you, Sheridan."

"For God's sake," Sam said roughly. "We've been through this a hundred times! My face has been on every magazine in the country in the last ten years. Do you think I could get away with kidnapping your only witness?"

Marcus narrowed his eyes and slid one hand into his trouser pocket, feigning a casual air. "Are you hoping to get a few more magazine covers out of this affair, Sheridan? I hear you haven't written a play in two years."

"Publicity isn't going to change my literary career," Sam said coldly. He loosened Beth and spun her behind him, as if to protect her from the FBI man, but was unconscious of the power of his own strength on her body. He hurt her arm, which he continued to grip, and Beth was abruptly—fleetingly—afraid of him. No one had ever handled her so roughly in the hospital, and it felt strange.

She brushed the momentary fear aside, though, as Sam went on, saying, "I thought I made my aversion to the press perfectly clear. The more secrecy, the happier I am."

"That in itself makes me suspicious," Marcus muttered.

Dr. Westham crossed the room to take the seat of command behind his walnut desk. "If my opinion matters at all at this point, gentlemen, I must say that I agree with Mr. Sheridan. Beth needs no more publicity. In fact, anonymity from now on may be very good medicine."

"Come on, doctor!" Marcus said, throwing out one arm in exasperation. "If this character was a parolee from Sing Sing, you'd let the girl go. You've been pushing to get her out of this joint for weeks."

"She's well enough to go," Westham said calmly. "And she needs a change of scenery. She's beginning to wear thin under your interrogation sessions."

"Exactly," Sam said, joining forces with the doctor. "She's had enough. She's been traumatized and you go on tormenting her for no purpose."

Marcus exploded, "We're trying to catch whoever did this to her and half a dozen or more young women who haven't survived! There's a murderer running around loose, Sheridan. You seem to have forgotten that detail! And this woman is our only link with that maniac!"

"You haven't gotten very far with her, have you?"

"We're making headway," Marcus said stubbornly, flushing.

"She hasn't remembered one iota of information," Sam said, voice rising. "The doctor tells me that her memory may be permanently—"

"If her brain—"

Westham cut off the FBI agent's shout. "Gentlemen, there's no use arguing. Beth may regain her memory if her brain was un-injured. If her amnesia is a result of her emotional trauma, then the chances of recovery are better. But the longer she goes with-out remembering her past, the more unlikely it becomes that she will ever—"

"We've heard this before, doc," snapped Marcus. "If her brains got scrambled because of her head injury, then we're sunk. But if she's just got hysterical amnesia, we have a chance. I can't take the risk of letting her run off with this guy! I've got an in-vestigation to run, and this lady is our only witness. She's the only woman who saw this maniac and lived to tell about it."

"Gentlemen," Dr. Westham cut in sternly, "I would never have allowed my patient to be present if I had realized this discussion was going to deal with Beth's condition and prognosis."

"Face it, Marcus," Sam said coldly, "you aren't any closer to catching the man who hurt my wife than you were when the whole thing got started!"

Beth watched Sam in wonder. The man who had held her so sweetly moments before was now full of barely suppressed fury. She wanted to twist out of his hurting grip, but was suddenly afraid of his reaction. She realized with a start that she was actually afraid of Sam, for he was the first person she thought might be capable of hurting her. She held her breath and battled with her own thoughts. She *wanted* to have someone in her life. She didn't want to face any more days of being alone in the world. Sam was hers, if she wanted him enough. She must try not to be afraid.

Byers, the burly New York detective, was on his feet by then, dropping his cigarette into a foam cup. He glared at Sam. "What you're trying to say, Sheridan, is that you intend to keep your wife away from us from now on?"

"Yes," Sam said. "For the next few months, she won't be out of my sight, and we're going to stay as far from the rest of the world as we can get."

"She must get away," added Dr. Westham. "She'll be much healthier if she has some time alone. Let her go to Wyoming with him."

Sam swung on the FBI agent again. "Maybe when she's had a chance to get her bearings again, she'll be more use to you, Marcus. Like this, she's not helping you or herself."

"You're damned protective of your little wife suddenly," Marcus sneered, leaning both fists on the edge of Westham's desk and bending closer to cross-examine. "Where have you been for the last three months, Sheridan? Looking for her? Or writing the great American novel someplace? How come you didn't come knocking at the hospital door until now?"

Sam leveled a lethal look at the FBI agent. "I don't owe you any explanations. If you're going to hold my wife here, Marcus, I suggest you charge her with a crime. You can't restrain her any longer."

"This is crazy!" Byers objected anxiously. "We haven't got any real reason to believe he even knows this woman! He's practically kidnapping her!"

"Yeah," said Marcus. "Where's the girl's brother we heard so much about? You promised we'd get a shot at him, too."

"Did I say that?" Sam asked mildly. "He's at home. Somebody has to look after the ranch while I'm down here wasting my time with you. Why don't you let us go home and you smart guys can get back to your job—whatever that is."

"Isn't it convenient," sneered Marcus, "that she hasn't got any more family than that? No parents, no aunts or uncles, nothing. Just a brother who can't leave the farm."

"Believe what you like, Marcus," Sam said. "Just don't expect us to wait around here for weeks while you start another of your incredibly slow investigations. We're going whether you like it or not."

"Jeez," Byers exclaimed. "You can't do this! You can't take her away from us."

The scene had been played before Beth as if she was an impartial audience. Until that moment, she had been an observer, silently soaking in all kinds of impressions. Not only the words affected her, but the expressions and tones of voice. Sam's body, braced in front of her protectively, passed a multitude of information to her. He didn't like the police. In fact, he might even have a real hatred of Marcus, the FBI agent. He had an anger inside that none of the others could sense, she was sure. He was hurting her and didn't seem to realize. She had to do something.

"Look," she said suddenly, coming out from behind Sam and pretending that the policeman's words had stung her into reacting. "Nobody is taking me anywhere. I can go wherever I choose whenever I like."

Marcus pointed a reprimanding finger at her. "We're trying to help you, sweetheart."

"And I've tried to help you," Beth said staunchly, controlling the quiver in her voice. "Give me a chance now, will you? I'm not going to drop off the edge of the earth. I can pick up a phone if I remember something, can't I?"

"Are you sure about this?" Marcus demanded. "Are you sure this guy is your husband? If he isn't, just what are you getting into, lady?"

Beth sent a swift, uncertain glance up at Sam. The police were right. This man was a stranger. He might even be the man who had inflicted his worst on her three months ago, though Beth immediately dismissed the thought. Impossible. She sensed he was gentle—certainly he couldn't have meant to hurt her a moment ago—and he was her husband. She knew it! There was an electricity between them!

Here was the opportunity she'd been praying for. It was her chance to become a person, to step out of her role of patient, victim and nameless woman. Now she had a past and a husband to share a future with. She could get out of this dreadful hospital and get away from the constant badgering of Marcus and his collection of investigators. She looked at Sam and felt her heart lift again. There was something in the air between them, something good and familiar. Perhaps this was what real trust felt like.

Yes, when Sam Sheridan held her eyes so firmly, so determinedly with his own, Beth sensed a tug of familiarity. Surely the small stirring of recognition in the back of her dark mind was the best sensation she had experienced since coming out of her coma three months before. His ascetic face held an elusive quality that the police could not have seen. There shone a kind of gentleness from Sam's light eyes, a sensitivity in the way he mastered his mouth into a straight line once more. When his anger melted away, he looked at Beth with a kind of confidence in her, with respect. Yes, that was it. Respect. No one at this hospital or from the police had respected her. She had been a patient, a thing to be poked or prodded or taken care of. This man was looking at her as if she had the power to make a decision for herself.

Beth turned back to Marcus, lifting her chin a fraction higher. "I think I'd like to go home now."

There was shouting, of course, and Marcus threw a tantrum, but Beth was not to be shaken. She smiled tremulously at Sam, and he took her hand snugly in his. From then on, the afternoon continued to be just as volatile. The press was summoned, then sent away at Sam's insistence. The police stood around in corridors looking disgusted and exasperated. And then there were hordes of doctors to be seen one last time before Beth could be discharged. Dr. Westham saw that all of the paperwork was dealt with as expeditiously as possible. It was a whirlwind.

Foremost in Beth's mind was hope. She had a chance now to be like everyone else in the world. She had hated being different, being alone. Everyone else seemed to have a network of friends and family, but Beth had absolutely no one. Now she wanted to get away, to put the hospital behind her and make her life again with Sam. She wouldn't be afraid of him. She was not going to be frightened by his strength. He was someone she could belong to.

Finally, Dr. Westham took them both into his office alone and outlined Beth's prognosis.

"Take it as slowly as you can," he had told them. "Beth, don't push yourself. You must absorb your past slowly. Too many facts are going to overwhelm you and set back your recovery. Be patient, and you may regain some parts of your memory. I do think you will regain some of it, my dear. The fact that you chose a new name for yourself that is remarkably close to your real name has given me cause to rejoice. Just don't rush yourself. And Sam, don't expect miracles. She probably will never be the same as before.

With that message ringing in their ears, they were finally taken to the airport by Dr. Westham's graduate assistant, a young man who chatted happily with Sam about Wyoming for most of the trip. Beth was quiet, suddenly nervous. She'd been safe in the hospital, though she had hated it there. Dr. Westham's final words had shaken her confidence.

What had she gotten herself into now? Sam glanced out the window of the car, and Beth covertly peeked at his profile. She bit her lower lip gently. After all, he was a stranger, and now she had deposited herself completely into his care. She longed to ask a question or two, just to get her bearings. Why hadn't Sam come sooner? Where were they going? Who else would she be meeting?

But Dr. Westham had warned her, warned them both, and Beth told herself that his advice was probably the best. Don't push for too many answers too soon. Each member of the family had been through the trauma in various ways and was going to have difficulty coping with Beth's return, just as she was. She should be careful and not expect to take up her old life in a matter of days, or even weeks.

Still, this sudden departure was disconcerting. Beth was secretly dismayed by leaving the security of the hospital, and she was almost afraid to inquire about her past now that it was a reality. She wondered how Sam felt about her disappearance. Surely his outward calm was a manufactured one. In fact, he seemed oddly willing to pretend that she'd never been out of his life.

Beth swallowed nervously and clasped her hands in her lap. Time would tell, she supposed.

At the airport, Sam took her hand as they walked into the terminal, as if Beth were a child known for wandering off in crowds. She didn't resent the unspoken message, but rather liked the constant physical contact he kept with her. She was alone with him for the first time, and Beth was nervous—both about this stranger who had suddenly appeared in her life and about the new freedom abruptly thrust upon her. She hadn't set foot from Johns Hopkins except in the company of a doctor, and she was startled by the frantic bustle at the airport. When Sam bought first-class tickets for Denver with a connecting flight to Casper, Wyoming, Beth stood closely at his elbow, clutching her plastic bag of belongings to her chest.

Her blond hair, always straight as fresh-cut pine planks, fell neatly across her cheek as Beth bent her head, and she was glad of it. She could hide her feelings from Sam. He was observant, and she didn't want him to see her distress.

When the transaction was complete and he was tucking his credit card back into his wallet, though, Sam turned to her and asked, "Feeling brave?"

Beth looked up and tried to smile. "Sure, I guess so."

Sam took some bills and folded them in half before handing them to her. "You're looking like a refugee with that plastic bag. Why don't you run into that shop and get yourself a carry-on suitcase? Do you need some clothes or anything? The plane doesn't leave for an hour. You might as well spend the time in there."

Beth had packed her meager supply of clothing into a pathetic plastic sack emblazoned with the name of the hospital. Yes, she must look like someone on the lam from the psych ward. Trying to be funny, she asked, "Do I like to shop?"

He pulled a comic face, looking pained. "Very much, I'm sorry to say. Here."

Beth took the money, but couldn't stop the next question. "What are you going to do?"

He met her eyes, and she could see that he was suddenly sorry for taking her independence for granted. Gently, he said, "I'm not going anywhere without you. I've got to call Connor, though. It'll just take a minute."

"Connor?" Beth repeated.

The surprise flickered in and out of his grayish eyes. "I thought Westham had told you more about us. Connor—he's your brother. He's waiting to hear from me."

Beth looked down at the cash in her hand. A twenty-dollar bill was on top, quite a few more beneath.

"I promise," said Sam, giving her a gentle push toward the shop with his hand lightly laid on the curve of her lower back. "I'll be right back. You look tired, and I don't want you to have to run from one end of this airport to the other, no matter how healthy you feel. Go on. I'll be along as quickly as I can."

Beth nodded, head down. He was standing very close, but he took another half pace toward her and touched her face. With one forefinger, Sam brushed a stray wisp of Beth's blond hair away from her cheek. His fingertip touched the crest of her cheekbone, and Beth desperately wished she could bring herself to look up into his eyes. They were so expressive, and she longed to see what his thoughts were just then.

He said, "Don't be afraid."

Instead of looking up, Beth bit her lip and murmured, "Thank you, Sam. You're very kind."

The effect of his name, spoken for the first time between just the two of them, was instantaneous. He dropped his hand and didn't move. "Listen," he said slowly, "I will try to be kind to you...."

He had been about to say her name, Beth knew. She risked a look up at his face and waited, taut with uncertainty. He couldn't say it.

"I'm sorry," he said at last, explosively, looking away and raking one hand through his hair. "I don't—you aren't Elizabeth, anymore, are you?"

Calmly, more calmly than she felt, Beth said, "I'm not the way I used to be, I suppose. You don't have to call me that if it makes you so uncomfortable."

"I'm not—" He began to deny the fact, but stopped.

"You don't have to call me Elizabeth," she said quickly to fill the pause. "I noticed that you've almost avoided it from the time we met. It's—I understand, Sam. If it's easier, you could call me Beth. That's the name I've been using at the hospital."

"Beth," he repeated, testing the sound. He scanned her face once more. Trying some humor, he said in a rush, "Yes, that's nice. Thank you. It suits that princess-of-the-realm face and those sexy sloe-eyes of yours. Elizabeth hated nicknames."

Beth was silent. He was talking about Elizabeth in the past tense. She could feel her smile disintegrate on her face, and her stomach turned over in a great lurch. Sam's real feelings had slipped past his steady, controlled demeanor and had caught Beth unawares. Perhaps he didn't like this new version of his wife.

Sam must have remembered himself then, for he looked startled and said hastily, "God, I didn't mean that."

"It's okay," Beth said just as fast, quickly turning her back so that passersby couldn't see her face.

"Beth," he began, as he laid a suddenly awkward hand on her shoulder, "I'm sorry. It slipped out. I didn't mean—"

"It's okay," she insisted, her voice sounding stronger than she felt. He wasn't ready to accept her as his wife. Not yet, and maybe not at all. She wasn't Elizabeth to him, she was a stranger. Beth brushed her hair back from her face, but kept her fingertips pressed to her temples for an instant. She said, "Maybe it's better this way. This approach, I mean."

"What approach?"

She swallowed and avoided his gaze a little longer. "Acknowledging we don't know each other yet. It might work better than making believe we love each other as husband and wife."

"If you're worried about—" Sam hesitated. He took her arm again, finding the crook of her elbow with his firm, yet gentle hand, then plunged into the topic that must have come immediately to his mind. "Look, if you're afraid to sleep with me, Beth, it's only natural. I won't lust after you, I promise. Don't be afraid of me, all right? You weren't before. Don't start now."

Beth knew she blushed, and she rubbed her forehead to hide her eyes. When she slid her shaking hand down her cheek to her throat, she could feel her own pulse pounding. Of course the idea had crossed her mind! Here she was suddenly married to a man! His hand was riding steadily on her arm, a touch so electric that Beth had to give herself a mental command not to shake him off. Certainly she must have slept with him, made love with him in the past, for the mere pressure of his hand on her arm spoke a message that was instinctive between men and women. But Beth could not remember making love with this man. He could remember, undoubtedly, for he touched her with the sureness of familiarity. Did he expect to renew the intimacies of their marriage so promptly? She liked Sam, of course, but Beth didn't feel capable of lovemaking at this point. He was a stranger, after all!

"Believe me," Sam said heavily, catching the drift of her thoughts with no trouble at all. "Sex couldn't be further from my mind at the moment. That's not a promise that I won't be chasing you around the barnyard in a week's time, mind you, but right now we both need time to get reacquainted. I'm just as nervous about what's ahead of us as you are."

Beth smiled weakly and found that she was beginning to tremble with the release of tension. She said, "That's a relief. I thought I was the only one with a tempest in my tummy."

Sam shook his head, amusement returning. "Westham was right. This isn't going to be easy. Just be yourself, all right? Don't try to be Elizabeth, please. Beth will do just fine."

She smiled genuinely. "Thank you."

"Go buy some clothes now," he said, letting her go. "I'll be right back. That's a promise, too."

Beth nodded again and wished desperately that he'd give her another pat—just a quick touch to steady her again. She needed to know more. She needed some kind of confirmation, she supposed, some sign that he really cared for her. She wanted him to touch her again.

But he didn't. Sam turned away and set off walking up the concourse toward the bank of telephones. He didn't look back. Beth watched him go off at a casual, long-legged stroll, his shoulders military-straight, his hands slid comfortably into his jeans pockets. He looked like a midwestern farmer inspecting his fields at sunset—in no hurry but with a purpose. Struggling to control her sudden surge of panic, Beth hugged her bag to her chest and tried not to call out after him. Adrift in the huge, noisy terminal without a familiar face in sight, she watched Sam's straight back and smooth dark hair until he was swallowed by the crowd.

He'd be right back, though. He had promised.

CHAPTER THREE

WHEN BETH WOKE from a long, dreamless night of fitful sleep it was morning. And for the worst half minute of her life she was afraid it was all happening again. She didn't know who or where she was.

She was curled on the bed, shoeless, but still dressed in her skirt and blouse and wrapped in Sam's jacket. Sam. Oh, yes. He'd brought her here very late after a long, confusing jumble of connecting airplane flights and a jouncing truck ride. He'd shown her the room, and she'd been too exhausted to undress, so she'd fallen across the coverlet and gone immediately into deepest sleep without another thought for him.

Beth sat up on one elbow, taking a sharp breath when her stiff muscles protested. She was alone. The double bed was plenty big enough for two, but Sam had chosen to sleep elsewhere, it seemed. Pushing her thick straight hair back from her face, Beth took a more careful look around her. The bedroom was square, with a low ceiling. Two windows had been hung with white ruffled muslin curtains, tied back with a calico ribbon that matched the pretty, but not effeminate patchwork coverlet. An overstuffed chair with a checked slipcover sat in one corner, a thick afghan thrown over the back and Beth's new suitcase on the cushion.

The curtains hadn't been drawn, and no one had bothered to pull the shades. The September sunshine was beaming through the window with an intensity that didn't match any of the meager light that had penetrated the smog-fogged windows at Johns Hopkins. This was morning with a vengeance.

Beth stretched cautiously and crawled to a sitting position. Several hours on an airplane and a few more in a truck had taken their toll on her recently pampered body. She swung her long legs over the edge of the bed and got up, dancing quickly when her bare feet met the cool smoothness of the oak floor. Laughing at herself, she skipped to the chair and unzipped her new suitcase. Ah, socks right on top. And here was her hospital bathrobe, though she wasn't quite brave enough to face a strange man over breakfast in that! She hopped on one foot and then the other to slip on her woolly socks.

She remembered that the bathroom was connected, and slipped in to take a wary peek at her reflection. No change. Same too-straight ash-blond hair with slightly darker roots showing, same thickly lashed blue eyes. Same mouth. Except . . . the smile had a bit more life to it this morning. Yes, definitely more life. Beth grinned in delight. She was out of the hospital!

A few minutes later, she let herself out into the living room. When she and Sam had arrived so late the night before, she'd been too tired to absorb much of anything. She had remembered this room, though, for it was huge and octagonal. The walls were covered with roughly hewn planks, a rustic effect made more dramatic by a collection of antiquated farm implements that, in Beth's foggy state of mind, had looked more like medieval devices for enforcing chastity than tools. Now she saw that the antiques were cleverly displayed for a quaint, yet artistic look. Had she done it herself?

Just viewing the belongings that must have been hers once gave Beth the familiar pang of longing again. She wanted very much to regain her memory! Dr. Westham had not made any promises, but he had suggested that her mind might be jogged by a familiar setting. Beth looked carefully around her and hoped she might get a flash from her past.

Sam had said something about the house being a hunting camp before they had "made some changes," and Beth could see that the original small room had been expanded by the addition of this two-story octagon that served as parlor, dining room, kitchen and office. A huge stone fireplace commanded one whole wall, though by now the fire had gone out and the September breeze was zooming down the chimney as if Santa Claus was about to make his entrance. The ceiling high above showed the roof's riblike structure, which was broken only by two bubble-top skylights. A wrought-iron spiral staircase curled upward to a balcony that overlooked the larger room, and Beth could see stacks of bookshelves lined there, library-style.

Furniture was minimal and a little worn out. Two lumpy-cushioned sofas faced each other by the hearth, and a paper-cluttered roll-top desk and swivel chair stood along the wall by the front door. A Formica counter separated a state-of-the-art kitchen from the area where a long trestle table showed evidence of a late-night powwow—a coffee pot, a sugar bowl, two mugs and an overflowing ashtray. Someone had been smoking. The smell hung in the air.

At the opposite end of the great room was an open archway leading onto a sunporch. Beth took several automatic steps in that direction and discovered that the sunny room served as a study, for it was crowded with more books, stacks of magazines and comfortable furniture in addition to an empty desk with a typewriter.

And Sam was sound asleep on the couch under the windows, his hair tousled, his nose buried in the cushion and a wedding-ring quilt thrown over his long legs.

Shyly, Beth backed up several paces.

"Elizabeth!"

Beth gasped and spun around to face the man who'd come in behind her.

He was slight and not as tall as Sam. He was blond, Beth saw, and probably about twenty-six. His clever face held a too-thin nose, a sensually bowing mouth and china-blue eyes that were wide and turbulent. He couldn't quite smile for the shock, and his features were pinched with conflicting emotions. "Sis!"

Connor, Beth thought, as he flew across to her. He lunged and grabbed her up in a huge hug. She held him mechanically, but Con hugged her hard, breathing as if he'd run a mile, and rocked her in his arms. His voice was strangled. "Oh, Elizabeth!"

This was hard, Beth thought fleetingly. He wanted a joyous reaction, and she wasn't able to manufacture one. With Sam, there had been a spark of delight, a wonderful moment when their eyes locked and the past didn't matter. With Sam, there had been recognition of some kind. But this was different. Beth tried to smile as she patted his back. "Hi."

Con held her away from his body to look at her face. He squished his own features up in anguish and hugged her once again, more swiftly and lightly this time. "Oh, Sis, we were so upset. Are you okay? Is it really you? We missed you so much! I can't believe you're just walking back into our lives, not after what we've been through!"

"I'm okay," Beth said weakly. "It's a surprise to see you here."

"I came last night after you'd gone to bed. I'm so glad you're back!"

When she looked up into the young man's face, she found that his blue eyes were full of tears. An awful tightness seized her chest, and Beth tried another smile. "Thank you, Connor."

"Call me Con. You always have." He smiled then, and his grip on her arms lessened fractionally. His face was full of light and quick to change with his inner thoughts. His blond hair was thick but curly, unlike Beth's, and it had been styled fashionably, a contrast to Sam's no-nonsense and slightly too-long haircut. Con was handsome in the popular, television pretty-boy way, and Beth wondered if he made use of his looks with girls. He smelled of cigarettes and too-sweet after-shave lotion.

He certainly had charm enough, for he collected himself and said in an ingenuous rush, "I'm here to help, all right? I want you to remember everything, and I'll be your coach, okay? We were playmates practically from the cradle, and nobody knows you as well as I do, I promise. Not even Sam. I'm the one who knows all your secrets! Right, Sam?"

Beth wriggled her way out of Con's embracing hands and spun around again in time to see Sam slowly emerging from the sunroom, one hand sleepily raking his dark hair back in a classic it's-too-early-in-the-morning scratch.

He stooped under the archway and met Beth's eyes with his own. Click. There it was again, that glorious moment of recognition. Sam's face was motionless, but the sleepy haze evaporated from his eyes instantly. The morning sunlight streamed down from the skylights above, creating a glowing patch of gold around them on the oak floor, a circle of light that included just the two of them in its warmth. Beth's heart and respiration went out of control, so she took a deep breath and held it. She thought Sam did the same, so she smiled and felt her mouth quiver.

"Good grief," said Con. "You didn't actually sleep out there, did you? On the sunporch?"

Of course, he had. Sam was still wearing his jeans from the day before, though he'd stripped off his sweater and stood before them in his rumpled button-down shirt and sock feet. Sometime during the night Beth had again forgotten how tall Sam was. The vaulted ceiling of the great room suited him, she could see. He needed space around him. He was probably just as happy sleeping on the airy sunporch as in the tiny bedroom with its simple double bed.

"What an idiot!" Con exclaimed. "Her first night back and you hide out there like a nervous bridegroom! Honest, Sis, there were times I'd come out to stay with you two, and Sam here would practically push me out the door so you and he could get back to playing all sorts of erotic games that just—"

"Easy," Sam warned.

"Yes," agreed Beth with a sliver of a laugh. She turned to Con and said too brightly, "I'm not used to all this attention, Con. I've been sleeping on a mental ward, you know."

Con's eyes widened in genuine surprise. "No kidding? Man, you must be ready for some peace and quiet!"

Sam came the rest of the way into the room. "If that's an offer, Connor, we'll take you up on it. Why don't you go away and fix some breakfast? Beth only had a snack on the plane and is probably hungry."

"Great," said Con without animosity. With a grin for Beth, he went on happily, "You used to love blueberry pancakes, Sis. We had a contest one summer, and I beat you—I ate fourteen and you had twelve! I don't suppose you remember that?"

"No," Beth said, smiling. "I think I'll play it safe and not challenge you this morning."

"You'll have to get into training," Con agreed, teasing her. He caught Beth's chin roughly in his hand and pulled her face up to his. He gave her a hard kiss on the cheek, one that almost hurt. "I'll go see how our supply of blueberries is, okay? Coffee and bacon, too?"

"All right," Beth agreed, shaken by all the brotherly attention. She took an unconscious pace away from him when he released her.

Con pointed a finger at her nose. "You take your coffee with cream. Did you know that?"

"No, I—"

"And you like your bacon extra crispy. Remember that?"

Sam to the rescue. His arm came smoothly around Beth from behind in an embrace that was deliciously natural. "Let's not start cross-examining yet. Give her some time to get used to that face of yours, Con. It sometimes gives me a jolt in the mornings."

Con thumbed his nose cheerfully at Sam and headed for the kitchen, snatching the coffeepot off the table with a long-armed swipe.

"Easy now," Sam murmured in Beth's ear when Con was out of earshot.

Beth remained in the circle of Sam's arm, liking the sensation of his radiating body heat. "I'm okay," she said, though her voice quavered.

"You're looking like the inquisition has started again. He's just pleased to see you," Sam explained kindly.

Resenting his gentle tone suddenly, Beth said, "I am not a frightened rabbit, you know."

He grinned abruptly and let his arm fall away from her. "Yes, I know. You're much too lovely for that. You took my breath away a moment ago."

Beth blushed again, feeling foolish at the compliment rather than pleased this time. Was he patronizing? She avoided his gaze. "You're protecting me."

"I won't, if that will make you happy. I remember what you said when I first saw you at the hospital."

She peeked up, curious. "In the elevator?"

"Yes. You said you hated people helping you all the time."

"It's still true."

"No doubt. Just take it easy where Connor's concerned. If he's going to shove your past down your throat, I'll send him away, all right?"

Beth lifted her head and found Sam's eyes steady on hers. She smiled at his ready concern. What a fool she'd been to feel afraid of him yesterday! "Actually, I think I'm ready to hear a little about my past. I'd like to find out who I am."

Sam let out a low, perhaps uneasy breath, but he made light of his reaction. He shrugged. "You're the best judge. When you've soaked up enough, take a break, all right? Remember what Westham said. Take it slow."

"I'm tougher than Dr. Westham thought."

Sam smiled, amused, and before he could stop himself, he quoted, "'Seek thy brother with a tale that must be heard howe'er it sicken.'"

Beth looked blank. "What?"

"Sorry," Sam said with a self-effacing grin. "Euripides' *Electra*. Go ahead and talk to Con, if you like. He'll tell you anything you want to hear and some you don't, I'm sure. I feel no compulsion to do it."

"No?" Beth asked curiously, too quickly.

Playacting again, Sam lifted his hand in a pose and quoted again, " 'Enough of tales—I have wept for these things once already.' Also Euripides, but I forget which play. Maybe *Helen*. Forgive me, it's a bad habit. It saves me from thinking up my own words. I'm not as tough as you are in this situation. Talk to Con."

Beth had a suspicion, and it was being confirmed before her eyes. Sam didn't want to talk about their mutual past. The details of their marriage and his feelings about what had gone on before were not subjects he wanted to discuss. Not yet, and perhaps not at all. Come to think of it, practically everything Beth knew about Elizabeth Sheridan had come from Dr. Westham. Sam hadn't offered much information at all. Perhaps the marital picture hadn't been quite as rosy as Con painted.

Sam said, "How about some breakfast? If you'd rather skip the blueberry stuff, I'm sure there's oatmeal or just plain toast."

Beth followed him into the kitchen, still wondering. Another bit of evidence pointed to the fact that Sam's emotions were mixed. He rarely touched his wife. Beth could count on her fingers how many times he had inadvertently laid his hands on her. He was treating her cautiously, and where Beth was relieved that she wasn't going to be forced into bed with him immediately, she wouldn't mind a small caress now and then. And not even a kiss? Heavens, even some of the hospital staff had given her goodbye kisses! Sam hadn't given her one. Not one.

She'd heard the nurses talk, of course. They all had men with whom they shared all sorts of intimacy. Beth had listened to their talk—mostly silly joking that was full of innuendo rather than confession, but it had affected Beth. Happy people had lovers, she realized. She felt a need within herself, a need to have someone for her own.

She eyed Sam's back thoughtfully. She'd like a kiss, darn it! He was, after all, a terrific specimen of manly good looks. It wasn't just his slim, neat head of hair and the gentle-bear impassiveness in his expression. Walking behind him, Beth studied Sam's body.

His hips were narrow, and his jeans rode tantalizingly low—enough to show the supple curve of muscle at his lower back through the well-aged material of his shirt. And his long back was so nicely encased by that shirt that the contours of bone and muscle were obvious to the observing eye. His back was soldier-straight, and the firm curves of his shoulders and tight-fitting shirt-sleeves told Beth that Sam undoubtedly did most of the farm work himself. He didn't develop a body like that sitting at a typewriter. No, Beth thought. She wouldn't turn down a kiss.

Sam went straight to the cupboard and counted out three coffee mugs, then took them to the sideboard where the pot was just beginning to percolate.

"Sit down, Sis," Con suggested, puttering at the refrigerator. "We'll trade places for once. You're a great cook, y'know. I've sat on that stool a hundred times while you whipped up some great meals. Today I'll be the chef. Sam, what do you want to eat?"

Sam was looking out the window at a thermometer placed conveniently there. Then he glanced up at the nearly cloudless sky. "Eggs," he said to Con. "I'll skip lunch and finish the top hay field today."

Con pretended to shudder. "That means baling soon. Gawd!"

Sam was unsympathetic. He patted Con's shoulder as he went by. "Relax. You can spend the day with Beth, if you behave yourself. Call me when breakfast's ready. I'm going to change."

Sam left them alone then, and Beth moved to lend a hand preparing the meal. Con began to talk.

BETH SPENT almost the entire day in Connor's company, in fact. After breakfast Sam went out to work, and Con talked while Beth listened. Her head felt as if it was full of angry bees, for all the information she absorbed. Connor ignored Sam's words of warning and chattered endlessly, chain-smoking as he talked.

He told Beth about their family, how their mother had died when they were both teenagers, and how their father, a physician, had battled with cancer for many years before passing away just five years ago. Con explained these facts without emotion. For him, the wounds had healed.

He told Beth about incidentals, then, like what games they had played as they were growing up, and about their trips out West with their father on hunting expeditions. They had gone canoeing in Wyoming, their father's home state, and Elizabeth had grown to love their vacations there so much that she had apparently determined to settle there after graduation from the Sloane Artist's Academy.

He told her about her work, her spinning and weaving, and the surprisingly good living she had made out of it. He even took her upstairs to her studio to show her how she had spent her days. He demonstrated how the loom and the spinning wheel worked, but Beth was not very interested, and Con let the subject drop. They sat together for a while in the studio, and Con reminisced some more.

Connor also told Beth about her dislikes in food and clothing and people. He described her prom dates and a few of her unsuccessful liaisons with fellow art students. But when Beth had asked Con about Sam, he clammed up.

"Oh," he said doubtfully, his smile turning sly as he exhaled his cigarette smoke, "you'll have to talk that over with him, won't you? You never told me much about your marriage, Sis."

Beth had nervously clasped her hands together, momentarily sorry she had betrayed Sam by asking someone else for such intimate information. "He's a bit—well, reticent, Con."

"That's Sam, all right!" Con agreed with a grin, flicking his cigarette in the general direction of an ashtray. "It used to amaze me that he was such an acclaimed writer. The man doesn't speak unless it's absolutely necessary. I suppose economy of language is his theory."

"I suppose," Beth murmured doubtfully.

"Don't worry about his silences, Sis. He's not a brooder, honestly."

"It didn't really worry me, it just—"

"I know. Sometimes I wonder what he's thinking, too." Con sighed and shrugged, looking amused. Conspiratorially, he leaned closer and said, "He's smart, Sis. He's an iron fist in a velvet glove. It took years before I figured out that Sammy could make me do almost anything he wanted. It's not that he's bossy, it's his—well, his presence that commands, isn't it?"

Beth became flustered then, for she hadn't meant to talk behind Sam's back.

Con saw her quick glance away, and he became expansive once more. He patted her on the back. "I wouldn't worry, Sis. You and

Sam were in love, and it's just going to take a little time to get that kind of feeling back. You just be affectionate, and he'll come around, I'm sure.''

Beth hoped Con was right, but she felt guilty for having extracted information from him about Sam. She changed the subject and didn't speak of Sam again.

Con kept their supper warm until Sam came in from working that night, and the three of them were tired enough from their own exertions during the day that the conversation was minimal. Beth longed to spend some time with Sam that evening, but he remained quiet, and Connor was forever flitting around offering more coffee or suggesting a game of Scrabble or a walk down to the lane. Sam accepted Elizabeth's homecoming, but he wasn't celebrating the way Con was.

Beth was enthusiastic about learning from Con. She asked him questions and listened eagerly to what he had to say. Sam, however, seemed less than happy about the growing relationship between brother and sister. Beth caught him watching her that evening, and she wondered about the concerned expression she'd seen in his eyes. Was Sam afraid of the answers she was getting? Or had she misread his carefully controlled face? Shortly after that, Sam went outside to walk in the darkness, and Beth dismissed the thought from her mind. She turned back to Con, anxious to hear more about herself.

THE FOLLOWING DAY was much like the first. Beth spent her waking hours mostly in Con's company, while Sam went off to work.

She thought she was adjusting rather well—until her third night in the brass bed.

Beth wasn't sure, but perhaps it was the past-probing conversations with Con that triggered her bad dreams again. She had experienced a frightening, nonsensical nightmare for her first few weeks in the hospital, and after a night or two in her own home, it began to recur. She hated it, for it made no sense and signified a weakness Beth didn't like to admit. Though her doctors insisted the dream was a healthy sign—evidence that her brain didn't shut down completely when she was asleep—Beth intensely disliked the clammy, heart-slamming feeling of waking up in a cold sweat with her mind full of scary images.

More than any other part of her recovery, she hated the nightmare.

By her third night, she was afraid to close her eyes and relax for fear the dream would wake her. Just like her early days in the hospital, she was afraid to go to sleep.

She sat propped against the pillows and tried to read. Outside, the weather had begun to change, and the sound of brisk wind and the occasional spray of rainwater on the roof did its best to lull Beth into relaxation. Still, it was past midnight when her body insisted, and she finally dozed off with the lights on and the magazine still leaning against her upraised knees.

The dream always began the same way. A cat. Not even a big cat, just a plain yellow striped cat with malevolent eyes that brightened when the cat opened its mouth. Its teeth were neat and very sharp, and as the mouth grew wider and wider, the sound began: a cry turned to a shriek and finally became a scream like tires on an oil-slicked roadway. Beth sat up in bed and clapped her hands over her ears, struggling with her own impulses to yell and fight and get away. The roadway became a street then, crowded with people who paid no attention.

She leaped out of the bedclothes before she could think, and the magazine went flying. It hit the brass bedpost and then fell to the floor with a thunk that startled her anew. Beth flattened herself against the bedroom wall, arms tight around her head and her heart fairly pounding against her ribs. *Don't scream. Don't cry out and wake the others.* She panted, terrified, and then reality swam into perspective.

She was safe. She was home and safe.

Thunder grumbled in the sky, just far enough away to sound threatening. No way she was going to sleep tonight. No way. Still not thinking straight, Beth hurried to the door and threw it open. She charged out into the great room by instinct.

Sam looked up from the couch on the sunporch.

Beth froze in the middle of the oak floor as if she'd been caught in a prison break.

"What's up?" Sam asked immediately, though he didn't move from the couch.

Beth wrapped her arms around her body, more to quiet her racing heart than to modestly conceal her flannel nightie from his startled eyes. She tried to swallow, but couldn't. She squeaked, "Me, I guess."

Sam's smile appeared. "Stupid question. Sorry. I should have asked what's wrong. I've never witnessed a better example of someone who's seen a ghost. You're white."

Beth tried to smile back, and she took a few mechanical steps toward the sunporch, rubbing her cheeks ruefully with her palms to restore her color. "Do I look scared? I must."

Sam shifted on the couch, not getting to his feet, but just getting into a better position to study her face. "The storm isn't very noisy yet. What? A mouse in the bathroom?"

A nervous laugh escaped her throat. "I wish there was. It'd give me something real to think about."

Sam tipped his head, puzzled.

"Don't mind me," Beth assured him, coming to a halt in the archway. "I'm not making any sense to myself, either."

"Bad dream," Sam guessed, not making it a question.

She nodded quickly and hugged herself. She managed to swallow finally. "Lord, I hate those!"

"Do you have them often?"

"I—I thought I was finished with them," she said, putting her shoulder against the wall to lean there in what amounted to a cringe. "I had them for a while in the hospital."

"Now they're back," Sam observed. "I saw your light last night. You should have come out if you were scared."

"I didn't realize you were awake. It's late!"

Sam rolled his eyes in amusement. "I'm always awake. Come here and sit. We might as well be insomniacs together."

Yes, it was obvious he had staked out the couch for a long night of wakefulness. He had a half-finished bottle of beer within easy reach, a depleted bowl of popcorn tucked under his elbow, a book, a stack of magazines close at hand and a quilt to ward off the night chill. He had kicked his shoes off and cast them haphazardly under the coffee table.

Beth remembered that she was dressed only in her nightgown. It was made of soft flannel and could hardly be described as revealing, but it was short and showed a fair length of her long, bare legs. If she went back to her room for her bathrobe, she'd only have shown Sam the rear view of her thighs, and that was worse than just scooting over to the couch and diving under the quilt there. That was the route she chose, though her walk wasn't quite as smooth as she'd planned, for she ended up having to step over Sam's relaxed leg and caught her toe on his trousers, so she landed awkwardly on the other end of the couch with a generous flash of thigh and found that she was blushing.

Sam was unperturbed. He even tugged the quilt into place around her knees as he asked, "So why are your dreams starting again, do you suppose? Have you called Dr. Westham about it?"

Beth shook her head, unnecessarily adjusting the quilt. "I was hoping they'd go away in a day or two. I don't want to bother him yet."

"You don't want to admit defeat," Sam suggested in a loaded tone. "Do you?"

Beth looked up and saw that he was eyeing her with gentle amusement. She felt herself turn pink again and ducked her head to hide it. "I don't like to lose any fight, I suppose. I'd like to lick this on my own."

Sam nodded, but didn't pass judgment. He asked again, "How come they're starting?"

"I don't know," Beth said in quick exasperation at herself. "It could be anything, couldn't it? Stress, most likely, though that's a word I've come to despise!"

"Uh-oh," murmured Sam, looking pained. "Coming here was supposed to cut down on the stress."

"It has," Beth assured him quickly. "It will, I mean. I've been—it's just—oh, I don't know. I'm feeling stupid about it."

"About what?"

His grayish eyes were steady, his expression calm. If Sam was annoyed with her, it didn't show. Comfortably settled against the opposite arm of the couch, he appeared relaxed, not disgusted with her admission of weakness. He had one leg lazily stretched to the floor, and the other propped casually against the back of the couch. He'd been looking at a magazine. No, Beth saw, it was a catalog, and he laid it down between them to devote his full attention to her.

Beth felt some of the tension leave her body, and was faintly surprised to find that she'd been tense in the first place. She needed to talk, she realized, and hadn't felt right with Con. This was better.

Sam pressed again, "What's up, Beth?"

She smiled sheepishly. "The last thing you want to hear is me sniveling."

He laughed outright, his eyes slight. "Sniveling? You? I can't imagine."

"All right, I tend to bottle it up, but the temptation to let it all out is there. Psychiatrists encourage it, as a matter of fact, and I used to come out of those sessions just hating myself for carrying on like a twit."

"Go ahead. Carry on. Is it me?"

"You? No, of course not. We've barely spoken, have we?" The words were out before she could stop them. Beth looked startled, for she hadn't meant to say such a thing.

Sam turned his head and looked sidelong at her.

"Oh," said Beth. "That didn't come out right."

"But . . . ?"

"Honestly, I didn't mean that the way it sounded. Don't be angry."

"Never angry," said Sam. "Not with you."

She smiled shakily. "You're very nice. No, you couldn't have a thing to do with my nightmares."

Sam said simply, "Then it's Connor."

Beth put her face into her hands and rubbed, as if trying to massage some sense into her head. "It can't be, can it? He's been wonderful, honestly. We've talked for hours."

"Too much, maybe."

"No, I don't think so. I liked it."

"Past tense," Sam noted.

"Lord, you're quick!" Beth exclaimed on a laugh. "Even Dr. Westham didn't pick up on my slips of the tongue so fast."

"Language is my trade, don't forget," Sam said with a half smile. "It used to be, anyway. What's changed? You've heard enough about yourself for a while?"

Beth shook her head. "I don't know. I think Con's getting tired of talking about me so much. I—well, the emphasis of our conversations seems to have shifted, you could say."

Sam was silent, but his eyes sharpened. He waited for an explanation this time.

Beth looked away, her fingers playing idly on the quilt as it lay across her legs. She said, "We—today he asked a lot of questions about what happened to me. The crime, I mean. What I remembered about—you know, what was done to me before I woke up from the coma.''

The gray in Sam's gaze changed imperceptibly then, becoming flinty, and there appeared a kind of angry stiffness around his mouth. "He asked you about—"

"The murderer, yes," Beth said too quickly. "What did you call it? 'The tale that sickens'? Look, I don't remember a blessed thing about it, and that's the truth, Sam. Con—he—well, he wanted to know little things, not the morbid stuff, thank heavens, and I just—it's very difficult after all the police and the FBI trying so hard to pry some tiny little fact out of my thick head when I couldn't even find a simple—"

"Easy," said Sam, soothing.

He had heard her voice turn high and sharp. Beth hugged the quilt to her breast to stop herself.

The thunder rumbled again, closer this time. Beth looked up at the skylight, flinching from the sound at the same time.

Sam reached across the space and took her wrist in his hand. "Con's upset you with talk about what happened before."

Beth squeezed her eyes shut, hoping she wasn't going to humiliate herself and cry. Not now! She'd held up just fine until this very moment! Sam's hand was gentle on her arm, but irresistible at the same time. He didn't pull her, but just steadied her with the strength of his hand. Why break down at this moment when the pressure was off and nobody was hassling? The old Elizabeth Sheridan had become a presence almost, a presence that created tension. She nodded fast, her hair dancing around her shoulders with the nervous gesture. "Maybe so."

"Okay," said Sam. "I'll send him home in the morning."

Beth jerked her eyes to his. "Oh, Sam, you can't. You'll hurt his feelings and I—"

It thundered again, very loud overhead. The panes in the sunporch windows trembled. Beth jumped.

Sam pulled slowly, gently, to draw Beth across the couch into the space between his knees. It was a natural and easy folding of one body to another, and Beth obeyed in spite of the absurd tightness in her chest. She wasn't going to cry. At least, she hoped not!

Sam was rock steady. He pulled her into his body. In a second, Beth was turned and nestled safely against him, her back braced against his chest, her hips between his relaxed thighs. Sam wrapped one arm around her body, holding her snugly, comfortingly, against him. His voice was deliberately gentle. "Nonsense. Con's overstayed his welcome already. I'm famous for tossing out relatives. Didn't he tell you?"

Beth laughed and tried to relax back against Sam. She laid her hand along the ridge of his arm for lack of a better place to put it. She was glad he couldn't see her face. It was easier talking this way. "Yes, as a matter of fact, he told me you order him around."

Sam must have smiled. "So one more chapter in that book won't make a difference. He goes tomorrow."

"What if that doesn't cure my nightmares?" Beth asked lightly, managing to control the timbre of her voice.

"Think positively," Sam suggested.

He brought his head close to hers, and when Beth unconsciously tilted back to him, she could feel the sandy stubble of his day's growth of beard against her cheek. She could smell the freshly washed scent of his hair; he had ducked into the shower before supper. Cautiously, she eased her shoulders the rest of the way into his chest, slowly relaxing in his comforting embrace. It felt good. She moved her head just slightly and laid her cheek more securely against his, then smiled and closed her eyes.

The rain started then, pelting so hard against the windows that it sounded like pebbles hurled against the glass. Beth didn't mind the noise, not in Sam's arms. She could feel his pulse in his wrist, and when the thunder sounded again, she didn't shiver. This was home, not the brass bed in the other room or the spacious kitchen with its complicated array of expert's utensils. Sam's arms, that was it.

He lifted his head to hear the storm and murmured, " 'Thunder, that deep and dreadful organ pipe.' You're not frightened now."

"No," said Beth. "Storms don't bother me. Not too much, anyway. It's my own head that's got the turmoil in it. Have you got a quote for nightmares?"

"Only Lady Macbeth," said Sam with a half laugh. "And she's depressing."

"Try one," Beth challenged, tipping her head back and smiling. "Something suitable for a stormy night."

"'What is the night?'" Sam asked, jostling Beth to make himself more comfortable beneath her. "No, no, that won't do. How about 'Light thickens'—that's one of my favorites. Can't you see light thickening?"

"Yes," Beth mused. "At twilight."

"'Light thickens and the crow takes wing to the rooky wood; Good things of day begin to droop and drowse, while night's black agents to their preys do rouse.'"

"You're wonderful!" Beth exclaimed. "How can you remember all those lines and pull them out of your head so neatly?"

"I can't sleep," Sam said promptly. "I'm worse than you. I read all night, and it sticks, I suppose."

"I'll try it," she said. "Find me something good to read, will you? I might as well be improving my mind."

"Certainly nothing else needs improving," Sam said blandly.

Beth was struck silent by that remark and turned her head so she might see his expression.

But Sam held her snugly, not allowing her to turn in his arms. "Steady now," he said, sounding amused. "I'm not lusting after you. Not quite yet, honestly. You're charming as you are, Beth, and you don't need to improve your mind. It's quite nice as it is."

Beth curled up her legs to get cosy once again. "Was I this way before? Has my personality changed?"

Sam didn't answer right away, though the sounds of the storm around them filled the silence for a time. Finally he hugged her lightly and Beth wasn't sure if he pressed a kiss to her head in a tangle of her hair just behind her ear. He might have, but then he said, "Let's leave dissecting the past to Connor, all right? I'm definitely more interested in the future."

CHAPTER FOUR

WHEN BETH WOKE in the morning, she was still cradled in Sam's arms, and he was breathing rhythmically into her hair, sound asleep. She awakened with a lazy smile on her mouth, and when she realized where she was and with whom, she began to grin even more broadly.

One of them had finally fallen asleep first, and Beth dimly remembered that it must have been herself. Rather than waking her, Sam had also succumbed to his body's inclination while cuddled with her on the couch. He was undoubtedly going to be stiff, and if he had any circulation in his left leg, Beth was going to be astonished. Her own body was draped over his, her head turned into his shoulder and her left arm falling naturally along the line of his long, warm thigh. The quilt had been kicked aside—or maybe he had lifted it away during the night, so that Beth's bare, slender legs were completely displayed by the morning light. The thought that Sam must have appraised the slim muscle of her calves and the lithe length of her curving thighs at first brought a heat to Beth's cheeks. Her nightgown had tangled and twisted so that one hip was almost completely bare.

The more she considered the situation, though, the more Beth liked it. No, she wouldn't mind Sam admiring her body. And Con had suggested that she play the loving wife and give him time to respond.

But how much time was it going to take? Was Sam going to stop pretending she was his kid sister—a weak girl who needed his protection? She was married to him, after all!

Deliberately, Beth smoothed her hand up along his thigh, as a waking wife might unconsciously caress her husband.

Sam woke with a start. His arm tightened under her breasts, his thigh muscle bunched and he shifted her weight very quickly off his other leg. "Beth," he said, as if identifying her in his own mind.

She pretended to wake and whispered, "Yes."

He moved again, but more slowly, drawing her to sit up with him on the couch. He sucked in a breath of pain.

"You're stiff," Beth said immediately. "Oh, I'm sorry."

She turned at the same moment he did, and they were suddenly face to face and only three inches apart. Beth blinked and became very still. So did Sam.

The inclination was there, Beth could see. He could have kissed her. He could have eased back into the cushion and taken her with him, his arms around her shoulders so that they toppled back together. They might have been entwined together in two painless seconds. His eyes quickly scanned the curve of her mouth, the morning-pale color of her soft cheeks and the sensual tumble of her sun-bright hair. His hand, in fact, stole gently up the nape of her neck, his fingers melting through her silky hair with appreciative slowness. Then his eyes met hers, and Beth wasn't sure what he saw there.

He let her go with a self-mocking half smile. "Good morning. I guess we got to sleep after all."

"Yes," Beth agreed, swallowing her disappointment. "I'm sorry. Have I crippled you for life?"

"No," he said, and laughed as they sat up properly and parted. "But you're going to embarrass Connor if he comes out and sees you like this."

He stretched out one hand and passed a quick caress up Beth's thigh.

She shivered at the touch, not from a chill, but from her own inner surge of timeless attraction. So there *was* some chemistry there! She pushed off from the couch before he saw her silly reaction and got to her feet, as unsteadily as a colt. "I'll go get dressed then. Can you walk? Shall I give you a hand? A crutch?"

Sam laughed again. His drawl was suddenly thick and languid. "Run along. I'm fine. Unless you hang around and tantalize me with those legs of yours." He shot a look up at her, one that sparkled with warmth. "I'm going to toss Connor out of here so we won't have to worry about him anymore."

Beth smiled back at him, suddenly very happy the night had turned out the way it had.

WHEN CON GOT THE NEWS, he accepted it with good grace. He didn't mind being thrown out, Beth realized. He probably had his own life to get on with. He did, however, enjoy teasing Sam about the circumstances of his leavetaking.

"I can't believe you're tossing me out," he said, standing by his car as he finished his cigarette.

Sam dumped Con's suitcase into the back seat and straightened. "Believe it. Beth's had enough of you, and I can only take small doses of your charming company before it begins to—"

"All right, all right!" Con laughed, cutting him off.

"Come back soon, will you?" Beth asked anxiously. "I feel terrible that Sam's making you go."

"It's okay," Con said with a smile for her. He tossed his spent cigarette away and glanced up at Sam briefly. "That only means he can handle things on his own, I guess."

Sam didn't answer, but his eyes touched Con's, and a message sparked between them.

"I don't need to be handled by anyone," Beth countered quickly, sensing a sudden tension in the air. "I promise to be a good girl."

"And you, Sam?" Con asked. "Will you be good also?"

"Of course," Sam said smoothly. "Goodbye, Connor."

So Con left, and Beth was secretly glad to see him go. It was not that she hadn't enjoyed his company. She had loved hearing about her past from him. But talking with Con had somehow rekindled the anxiety Beth had experienced while staying in the hospital. Each time the police or FBI had questioned her, she'd felt almost sick. Rehashing the past with Con had created that same scary feeling in Beth, but she felt guilty making the connection. She was glad that Con left under orders from Sam.

Besides, Beth realized, she wanted to spend her time with Sam. Just Sam. He was intriguing and gentle and sometimes surprising, and Beth wanted to concentrate on him alone. Connor had filled a hole, perhaps, but Beth had known all along that Sam was the one with whom she felt comfortable sharing herself. She belonged with Sam, and she didn't want to be diverted from him just now.

She had many questions to ask Sam, but the timing hadn't seemed right with Con around. Perhaps now she could concentrate on rejuvenating her marriage.

Sam wasn't entirely cooperative, however. When Connor had been gone only a few hours, he moved his work clothes and a pair of boots from the hall closet into the room Connor had vacated. Beth realized that he meant to sleep in there from now on. During the afternoon, she planned her counterattack. She was determined to get her life back to normalcy.

The farm, Beth discovered, was actually a kind of ranch. There were no chickens, no piglets, no animals around the house at all, except a big collie-shepherd dog that hung around the barn and went loping off behind Sam's tractor every morning. Beth heard about the cattle from Con and Sam, but she had never seen them, for they were out to graze in a pasture some distance from the house.

"I have to go up and check on them tomorrow," Sam told her when they were together drying the supper dishes. "Will you mind being alone for a few hours?"

"Can't I go along?"

Sam smiled at her askance. "I'm not taking the truck."

"I can walk!"

"I'm taking one of the horses," Sam explained. "And I don't think you ought to risk getting thrown off in your condition."

"My condition," Beth muttered, dropping a pair of forks into the drawer with ill-disguised annoyance. "My head's not an eggshell, you know."

"Close enough," Sam countered, putting an end to the argument. Then he relented. "All right, if you're feeling brave enough, you can come with me tonight and we'll catch the horses."

"If I'm brave?" Beth demanded in mock outrage, as she ripped off the towel she had tucked into her trouser waistband to serve as an apron. "Is that a challenge, mister?"

Sam gave up on the dishes also, tossing his own dishtowel onto the counter. "Okay, kid. Go get a sweater, and I'll meet you by the barn in two minutes."

Beth obeyed, glad she was going to get some fresh air as well as a new experience. She'd been cooped up too long at the hospital not to enjoy some time outdoors. When she met Sam in the yard, he had a halter and a length of yellow nylon rope slung over his shoulder, as well as a tin pan of oats in hand.

"What's this for?" Beth asked, taking the pan from him. "Bait?"

"Exactly," Sam said, and he whistled for the dog. "Come on, Thiz!"

"Thiz?" Beth objected, laughing. "What a terrible name for a dog. Poor thing."

Sam laughed and set off away from the house, walking backward to see her face until Beth caught up. "What would you rather she be called?"

"Something regal, I guess. Regina or Ginger. Where'd you get Thiz?"

"Short for Thisby," Sam explained, watching for her reaction with a grin. "Even better, right? Actually, it's a character from a play. *Midsummer Night's Dream*. Watch where you step, all right? There are bound to be holes from the gophers."

They walked in silence, strolling through the failing light along the rail fence that ran up into the orchard. Before the hill got too steep, Sam helped Beth climb over the rails and then vaulted easily after her. They tramped through the pasture, cutting diagonally through the ankle-high grass toward a distant gate. Sam pointed out a field above them, and for the first time Beth saw the cattle, though they were too far away to really discern clearly. Brown bodies and white faces were all she could make out in the evening light. On another faraway hillside, she spotted a cluster of white stones, laid symmetrically.

"It's a cemetery," Sam explained, "dating from the pioneer days. It's too far to walk, though, and the road's not good enough for the truck. And I'm sure there are rattlesnakes."

Suddenly a rabbit bolted out of the grass in front of them and dashed for the fence. Thiz's head shot up and she took off like a lightning bolt.

Anxiously, Beth cried out, "Oh, don't!"

"Don't worry," said Sam, watching the dog gallop after the skipping rabbit. "Thiz never catches anything."

But the rabbit dodged one way and the dog made a lucky cut and kept gaining. Beth clapped her hand over her mouth in dismay, but her cry escaped anyway.

"Thiz!" Sam shouted, before the collie lunged for the kill.

"Sam, please!" Beth begged, catching his arm.

"Thiz!" Sam bellowed.

The dog faltered in stride: the rabbit leaped high, landed in a thicket of grass and dove out of sight. Thiz barked once and glanced at Sam, then checked her pace and made a wide arc to return to her master. She snuffled along the ground, hackles high, but then approached Sam, tail wagging.

Beth let out a long breath of relief.

"Steady there," said Sam, putting his arm across Beth's shoulders. He pulled her against his body, and they walked a few paces like that. Finally Sam said gently, "It was just a rabbit."

"Rabbits are people, too," Beth shot back, trying to joke her way out of a vulnerable spot. "That dog is well fed and doesn't need a snack. Poor bunny."

"Remind me to send you to town when we start cutting meat this November."

"Cutting—?" Beth began. Then she gave Sam a startled, wide-eyed look. "You don't mean that you actually kill the cows? Yourself?"

"Just one," Sam explained, with a grin at her squeamishness. "Beth, where do you suppose your dinner comes from? One steer lasts us just about all winter, and the rest go to market."

Beth shuddered under his arm. "Oh, dear. Yes, please send me to town when you do it. I'll stay away until it's neatly packaged for the freezer."

Sam nodded in agreement, popped the latch up on the gate and let it swing open before them. Then he reached for the pan. "Stay here and let me catch them. You seem a little fainthearted today, I'm afraid, no matter how tough you talk."

"Telling me I can't is the surest way to make me try," Beth said tartly, and she slipped through the gate with him.

There were three horses standing with heads lowered just a furlong or so down a short hillside, and at Sam and Beth's approach, all three heads came up and looked. One horse was white with gray dapples across its haunches and two were brownish, Beth saw. All three looked noble and elegant until she got closer, and then she realized that they were enormous beasts. Sam shook the oats into the tin pan and couldn't help but note Beth's reaction to the horses. The noise was like magic to them. They came thundering—well, Beth called it thundering, but Sam later claimed none of them even broke into a trot as they pressed toward the feed pan.

Beth ducked behind Sam and cowered there as the three horses arrived and shouldered one another out of the way to get at the food he offered. They stretched their long noses into the pan and greedily snatched mouthfuls of the proffered grain.

"They're very gentle," Sam told her, noticing her uneasiness, and keeping his body between her and the curious animals. "This is Jigs and Tonto, and here's Calico. You'll like her best, when your head isn't quite so fragile. Hello, Jigger."

The biggest of them all was one of the brown ones, with a white splash down his nose and a nick out of one of his ears. His eyes were roguishly concealed by a forelock of long, tangled mane, and his tail swished ferociously as he swiftly gobbled up his share of the oats. Neatly, Sam slipped the halter over his head. When the pan was empty, Sam handed it around to Beth and proceeded to buckle up the halter.

"There," said Sam, giving Jigs a slap on his muscled neck. "How about a night in the barn?"

"Sam," Beth called nervously.

The other two horses weren't convinced that the pan was empty, and they were nosing close to Beth, giving her leg a nudge, and then snuffling noisily at her hand. She backed up quickly, but the huge animals bore down on her with even greater determination. She stumbled over a thick tuft of grass and cried out again, "Sam!"

"Drop the pan," he commanded, taking half a second to snap the nylon line onto Jigs's halter. Then he came after her, shoving the gray's rump out of his way and giving Calico a slap on her withers. With the now docile Jigs tagging behind him, Sam arrived at Beth's side and took her hand, laughing. "You shouldn't be scared, but I know how you feel. They look pretty big to me too, but they're big babies."

"Emphasis on the word big," Beth said bitterly.

"I suppose you don't want to ride back? I could boost you up. It'd be like the pony ride at a carnival."

"Forget it," Beth said, glancing up at Jigs's back as if it were Mount McKinley. "I think I'll stay home tomorrow and start my reading program. You can go off and admire cows all you like."

"All right," Sam agreed with a complacent grin, reaching to the ground for the pan.

He handed it to her and put his arm naturally around Beth's shoulders again, leading her through the darkening light over the uneven terrain. Jigs followed behind, his long legs swishing in the grass and his breath puffing like a noisy engine as he sniffed the grass or Sam's back pocket. The other two horses followed at a careless distance, unwilling to be left in the field without their companion. After a few steps, Sam asked curiously, "What's your reading program?"

"Books," said Beth, tucking the feed pan under her arm. "I might as well exercise my brain, don't you think? I started reading in the hospital. Dr. Westham brought me things."

"Like what?"

Beth glanced up at his profile. "Popular stuff, mostly. Paperbacks. And a few books that were supposed to be food for thought. And your play."

Sam glanced down and met her eyes. "Westham gave you that on purpose, you know."

Beth kept walking, enjoying the feel of Sam's body next to hers. It was a rare occurrence—his holding her this way. She didn't want it to end too soon. She said, "I figured that, yes. He wanted to see if I could recognize it, I suppose. He was always pulling sneaky tricks like that! I liked the play, though."

Sam's laugh was rich. "You weren't so sure when you didn't know who I was!"

Blushing gracefully, Beth admitted, "Maybe not. But I've thought about it some more since then. *Bitten* isn't about you, is it? The hero, Fuller, he isn't like you."

"No," said Sam, getting serious finally. "He's a character, not a person."

"But he must be a reflection of your thoughts," Beth pressed cautiously. "A means through which you convey your feelings to an audience."

Sam let her go so he could bring the horse through the gate and shut it. He didn't notice Beth's disappointment at being turned loose. Working, he said, "You're sounding like a textbook, Miss Beth."

She laughed, feeling pleased. "I did read that in a book, as a matter of fact! I wish I could remember the quote and surprise you with your own habit!"

His amused look was both laughing and sharp, packing the power of a laser. "Are you going to start making changes in my personality already, wife?"

"No!" Beth claimed quickly, surprised that he could suggest such a thing. She stopped in midstride and faced him. If she'd been a different sort of woman she'd have hurried into his arms. But Beth knew instinctively that Sam didn't want her touching him very much. Unsure how to convince him, she said uncertainly, "Heavens, no."

"That's the common understanding about married life," Sam said, dropping the latch into place once they were all through the gate. He turned to Beth, leading Jigs behind him once more. "As soon as a man takes a wife, she starts working on his bad habits."

"It's not a bad habit!" Beth was flustered. "It—I mean—I thought we were supposed to complement each other, that's all. Two people have to bend and mold to fit together, don't they? I just thought I ought to experiment with the things you enjoy."

Sam was still standing in one spot, winding the rope around his hand in a loop, his head bent as he listened to her. He glanced up, though, and studied her face thoughtfully. He said, "You *are* different, you know. You're not Elizabeth."

Beth thrust her free hand down into the pocket of her trousers. "Is that good or bad?"

Sam smiled out of reflex, not amusement. "I don't know yet. We'll see, won't we? Come along. It'll be dark in five minutes."

Beth started walking, keeping pace with Sam as he strode across the pasture. She had blundered into tender territory, and Sam was annoyed, she knew. She wasn't sure which of them was more uncomfortable talking about the old Elizabeth. Still, sometimes Beth thought she'd go crazy not knowing about herself. Tentatively, she began, "Sam . . ."

"No," he said patiently, "I'm not angry."

"I didn't think you were," Beth said firmly, groping for the truth. "I just—"

"You're different, that's all," he said, unwilling to clarify his observation just yet. Inadequately, he added, "Different from the way things used to be."

"Con told me a little about how things used to be," Beth said. She had to clear her throat before she could continue, for a nervous bubble prevented her from sounding normal.

"About us?" Sam demanded shortly, not looking at Beth as they walked.

"No. I didn't ask him. Not much, anyway. I thought—I think that's between you and me."

He sighed, sounding annoyed. Or maybe resigned.

Beth tried to laugh and make light of the situation. "It's going to happen sooner or later. We've got to talk about what happened before I ended up in the hospital. I want to know, and you can't pretend I just dropped into your life for the first time a week ago."

"No," said Sam. "I guess not."

"I can't help being curious," Beth said. "You can't blame me for that."

Sam was silent. They gained the opposite fence, and he jammed the gate latch up hard.

"Sam," Beth pleaded, coming to a halt.

He heard her frightened tone and turned. His face was set, but not angry.

"Talk to me," Beth said quietly, watching his eyes with trepidation. "I can't resent what happened in our marriage before. It isn't real to me. What matters is—well, what's between us now."

Abruptly, Sam said, "I don't want to lie to you, Beth."

She swallowed hard and nodded. "I realize that. You don't want to talk about the past because it's going to hurt my feelings, right?"

He took a breath and held it, not answering.

"I know," she said, translating the silence easily. Beth looked away and placed the feed pan on the top rail of the fence, steadying it with both hands. She couldn't look at him. "I—I also realize that you don't love me. Not the way we're supposed to love each other. If you did, you'd be treating me differently, I can tell. You're a sensitive person, and I just know that you'd treat someone you cared for a great deal in a much different way than you're behaving with me now."

"I haven't—"

"You've been very nice," Beth went on swiftly, before he could deny or explain. "You're a gentle man with a kind heart and—and a deep—oh, God—a deep sexuality that you're keeping hidden from me in the way strangers behave toward one another, so I know you must feel—"

"Beth," he said, stopping her harshly.

She put her hand on her face and prayed she wasn't going to cry.

"I don't want to hurt you," he said. "Not while you're feeling this way—this vulnerable. You're still recovering. You think you're stronger than you really are. When you're ready to assimilate—"

"Damn it," Beth snapped. "I want to know now! I've been sleeping alone at night with nothing but dreams that scare the hell out of me, and now I want to understand what's happened! I already heard all the gruesome stuff about that—that crazy man, but now I want to know about us! Why didn't you come looking for me? Why was I waiting so long to be found?"

"Because," Sam said quietly, "I didn't know you were gone."

Beth looked at him and blinked. "What?"

He held her eyes. "You left. We had a lot of reasons at the time, but you took your work and went to New York to sell some of it."

"But—"

"We weren't speaking," Sam said bluntly, watching her face for some sign that she'd burst into weak woman's tears. "We had no reason to call each other, and it wasn't until nearly two months had passed before I realized you weren't where you said you were staying. By that time, the first publicity from the hospital had blown over, and out here I don't get many newspapers anyway. I had no idea you'd been hurt. I thought you were on the road peddling your weaving to little galleries or something."

"I see," Beth murmured, thinking rapidly, putting the pieces together in her own mind.

"I'm not ready to talk about most of this," Sam continued, his voice rough. "It's been a shock for me, too, Beth. Just a week ago I heard what happened to my wife, and believe me, it's not easy to accept what he did to you."

"I don't remember it," Beth said quickly.

"That doesn't matter!" Sam ground out. "Right now I feel guilt and anger, but I can tell that it hasn't really hit me yet. Beth, there's a bomb ticking between you and me, and I'm just trying to hold off the inevitable explosion a little longer."

"A bomb," Beth repeated. "Our marriage, your feelings—"

"Yes, all of it." Sam put up his hand and raked his hair back in a gesture of surrender. "I can't think sensibly about everything that's happened. Not yet, anyway."

"You need time more than I do, perhaps."

"Maybe so," he said steadily. "Silence can't hurt us right now. Talking too much might."

Beth picked up the feed pan. Darkness had closed in around them, and the only sounds were the hush of the night breeze in the grass and the noisy grinding of horses' teeth as they snatched the grass and ate it. She felt cold suddenly, and longed to go to Sam and feel the weight of his arm around her, the warmth of his lean frame next to hers.

"I'm sorry," Sam said.

Beth looked at him, though in the poor light she could not see the expression in his eyes. If there was only a way to explain to him how alone she felt sometimes! Beth needed someone now, so she wouldn't feel afraid. Somehow she knew Sam wouldn't want to hear that! Gently, she said, "Sam, I wish I could use words as well as you do. I wish I could explain to you that my life is really pretty simple right now."

"Simple?" he asked, startled.

She gave a weak laugh. "Yes. I haven't got a past. I don't remember what issues broke us apart several months ago, and I don't have any memory at all of the horrible—oh, well, I might as well call it an ordeal since everyone else does. I don't remember it! It doesn't matter to me!"

"It matters to me," Sam said, sounding deadly.

"You mustn't feel angry or guilty. If I suffered, it's okay now—"

"No," Sam interrupted fiercely. "It isn't okay. I can see your eyes, Beth. You've been changed by what's happened to you. You're a different woman, not the woman I fell in love with, and not the woman I was—hell, I was almost glad to see you leave me later on when the marriage disintegrated. You're somebody new, and I can't imagine what he did to you that—"

Beth went to him. She laid her hand on his arm to stop his voice. She felt Sam shudder once under her fingertips, as though her touch sent a charge of electricity through to his soul. They touched so rarely that the slightest contact seemed extraordinary. She gave him an instant to collect his reasoning, and then looked up into his face. Her own mouth was trembling, but her eyes were bravely dry as she asked, "Are you feeling the worst because you weren't there to stop what happened?"

Sam's eyes were filled with smoke and the embers of fire. He threw Jigs's line into the grass, then reached and touched her face with his hand, slipping his palm along the line of her delicate jaw until he cupped her cheek and tipped her face to his. His thoughts were confused, Beth could see. He was struggling with many concepts, and took a long breath before he spoke. His voice was barely a murmur. "Beth, I don't want you to be hurt again. Not now. Not by me."

She smiled. At least, she tried to smile. "I won't be hurt, Sam. I can take care of myself."

Sam was silent, thinking. He looked into her face and felt her smooth cheek beneath his hand. He met her eyes.

"I wonder," he said oddly, "if perhaps you're right."

He kissed her then, a cursory brushing of his lips against the cool skin of her temple. Beth closed her eyes to savor the sensation, the lovely wonderful sensation.

Sam hesitated. The breeze around them gusted suddenly, just enough to enclose the two of them in a solitude made more intimate by their silence. Sam moved, this time as if entranced. He kissed her cheek very softly and then again. His mouth was warm. His hand was sure on her face as he tipped her chin higher. Beth took an uneven breath, and on her still-parted lips, Sam came to press a gentle, melting kiss. It was tentative and almost uncertain, and therefore erotic. Perhaps he had meant to console or comfort her, but the moment changed and the kiss with it. Sam took possession of Beth's mouth, his lips seeking to make the contact perfect.

By instinct Beth put her hands flat against his chest, not to push him away but to feel his pulse and test the contour of his body. He was taut with hard-worked muscle and yet he felt relaxed, as if this kiss was the culmination of the last few tension-filled days. His lips tasted both sweet and salty, though those fleeting sensations were soon replaced by a headier, more satisfying flavor. Desire washed over Beth like warm oil flowing from a jar of sensual pleasures. He had been her rescuer and then her friend.

He smelled of the shower and sunshine and faintly of horses, though Beth also inhaled the more elusive scent she had come to associate with the night spent sleeping in his arms. She slipped her hands higher, and at that signal Sam deepened the kiss as if he had been holding back. He wound his other arm around her body and pulled her into him, easing Beth familiarly into the firmness of his body. He moved her head, first this way and then that, seeking the right melding point. His mouth moved also, offering the gentle warmth of his lips and finally delving into her mouth with his tongue. He was experimenting, appraising, savoring, and Beth found herself responding to his curiosity, his delicious sexual question. Time evaporated, and she gave herself to the pleasure of being in Sam's arms and of thrilling to his masculinity.

Just then one of the horses snorted, and reality rushed back into Beth's mind.

Sam broke the kiss and didn't move for a split second. Tense again under Beth's hands, he let her slide away and avoided her gaze. "God, I'm sorry. I didn't mean for this to start."

"This?" Beth repeated, unsure of what he meant. She kept one hand on his chest, though she lightened her touch.

Sam kept his head down. His hands were not gentle on her upper arms, as if holding her off. "Being attracted to you is making everything more difficult."

"Why?" Beth asked, a laugh starting down her throat. "Because I left you months ago? Sam, that was another woman. I'm here now, and I don't mind being attracted to my husband."

Sam laughed ruefully, almost self-mockingly. He looked at Beth, his hands gentle once more, then shook his head. "Oh, Beth," he said, looking bitter and amused at the same time. "If I made love to you now, you'd hate me later. I can't explain, though I wish to hell I could. Let it ride, please? Let's be sure you understand everything before I turn my instincts loose."

Beth smiled and decided to obey him. She was afraid to push Sam sometimes. He was always very controlled, but she felt that he held a lot of emotion inside, emotion that could turn frightening if he chose to release it.

She stood back, and he gathered up the horse's reins once more to lead him through the gate to the corral. Beth followed thoughtfully. She was puzzled, but elated at the same time. He didn't want to make love to her. He was fighting a tug of marital sexuality, too. That was nice to know. At least he found her attractive. That was also nice to know.

CHAPTER FIVE

THERE WERE CATS in the barn. Beth realized it too late, and there she was, cowering like an idiot on the fender of the parked truck because a scrawny little black-and-white tom came slinking out from under the tractor to rub along Sam's trouser legs.

"Can you find the light switch?" Sam asked, already leading Jigs into the straw-strewn stall to the left of the barn door. "Just over your right shoulder. See?"

Beth got a grip on her hysteria and gasped something affirmative. She swiped at the switch and escaped out into the cool night air before she really made a fool of herself. Sam was none the wiser. She slowed down and caught her balance on the gas pump just outside the door, breathing hard.

"Beth?" Sam called curiously.

She didn't answer. To explain her silly nightmare to him would only make Sam feel more protective. He believed he had failed her once, and he hadn't left her side since Connor went away. He was shielding her, she knew, and Beth didn't like it. She could take care of herself.

She looked through the open barn door warily, ready to jump aside if the cat came out. The light was on, and the interior of the barn glowed gold from the single bulb. Beth could see Sam's lean silhouette, tall and spare, as he worked to bed down the horse. Rakes and farm implements hung on the wall behind him, and she noticed a sleek bicycle suspended on a pair of pegs.

When Sam came into the doorway and looked out into the darkness, Beth spoke first. "It's a nice night."

After a beat, Sam said, "I thought you ran away from me."

Beth forced a laugh. "Of course not. I just came out to breathe the air. It's a big change from the hospital. Is that your bike?"

Sam glanced at it over his shoulder. "Yes," he said, not hearing the falseness in her voice. "I haven't had it out in two weeks. Are you going to stay out here? Or do you want to call it a night?"

Beth pulled her hair back off the top of her forehead with one hand, trying to be casual. "I think I'll go back to the house."

"I'll be along in a minute. Can you find the lights? If there's— what's wrong?"

The cat was back, sliding craftily between Sam's legs and wickedly eyeing Beth with suspicion and distaste.

"Beth? What's—?"

"I'm okay," she gasped, already running for the house with her hair streaming out behind.

Sam must have dodged back into the barn to switch off the lights, but he caught up with her before she made it into the kitchen. He grabbed the screen door in one hand and held it wide. "Beth, what is it?"

"Nothing, nothing." Beth flew into the kitchen and jammed on the light, casting a fast, instinctive look around the floor for more insidious cats. "I just—I got cold and I didn't—I just—"

"Easy," said Sam, staying a few feet away but holding out both hands as if to steady a fractious colt. "I won't hurt you. I'm sorry I had to tell you all those things out there. If you want to call Dr. Westham, we'll do it right now. Just calm down."

"Dr. Westham?" Beth repeated stupidly, pushing her hair away from her face with a shaking hand. She knew her eyes must have looked round with fear, but she couldn't stop herself from staring at Sam. He looked frightened by her panicked behavior. "You're sorry...? Oh. Oh, Sam, no, it's not that. Honestly, it's my own silly imagination, that's all. It was that cat."

"The cat?" he echoed, disbelieving.

"I don't know why I have this..." Beth shook her head, trying to collect herself. She hadn't meant to admit it to him, but the truth came out before she could contain it. She smiled ruefully and avoided Sam's eyes, nervously combing her hair with her fingers. "I'm scared of the cat, I guess. It's part of my dream, you see."

"Your nightmare?" he asked, calming down once he realized he was not to blame for her bizarre change of mood. He came across to her in three strides. "You dream about cats?"

"Not lots of cats. Just one." Beth leaned back against the counter and folded her arms tightly, comfortingly, across the front of her sweater. "It's yellow and has creepy eyes and a huge mouth that keeps opening up. And it screams. It's awful!"

Sam hesitantly touched the shoulders of her sweater and gradually firmed his grasp until he felt her body shudder beneath his hands. He absorbed the tremor. Instead of quick reassurances, he asked solemnly, "Is it the same dream every time?"

Beth nodded. "Every night. There's a road too, and then a street that's jammed with people who don't pay any attention."

"Did you tell Dr. Westham about it?"

Again, she nodded. "He says it's probably very significant, but neither of us has the faintest idea what it means." She cast a half-hearted smile up at Sam. "How are you at dream analysis?"

Seeing her smile, he seemed to realize that he was holding her again, so he let Beth go with a gentle push and said, "A rank amateur, I'm afraid. Look, why don't you go run a very hot bath, and I'll pour you a glass of wine or something. We'll get you really sleepy and you won't dream at all tonight. How does that sound?"

Beth lifted her eyes to his, unsure about what he was suggesting. "A hot bath?"

"For yourself," Sam corrected her impression firmly. "I meant what I said outside. You're just going to have to accept my reasoning for the time being."

Beth smiled. He was serious about not making love to her, she could see. She didn't know why, but it mattered to him. "All right. I trust your judgment. I trust you. I don't suppose there's any bubble bath?"

Sam shoved the sleeves of his bulky sweater up to his elbows again, showing the lean muscle of his forearms once more. He reached for the refrigerator handle and pulled it open. "Have a look around. There might be something left from the good old days."

Laughing at that, Beth went along to the bathroom, stripping off her sweater as she walked. She sat on the edge of the claw-footed tub, pushing aside the modern shower curtains, and turned on the bathwater. When the temperature suited her, she put the stopper in the drain and straightened up to have a look in the medicine cabinet. Yes! There was a tube of bath oil. Upon checking, though, Beth found its scent too sweet for her taste. No wonder it hadn't been used. Perhaps she'd received it as a gift.

Beth decided to forego it and reached for one of the fluffy bath towels. With that thing over her shoulder, she let herself into the bedroom to take off her clothes.

Sam tapped lightly at the bedroom door a minute later. "Beth?"

"In here," she called over the sound of rushing water, in the act of wrapping the towel around her otherwise naked body.

He didn't think, of course. He pushed through the door to the bedroom, assuming she was safely in the tub, and was instead halted in his tracks just as Beth clasped the ends of the towel to her breasts. She looked up into the mirror and met Sam's startled eyes there.

He didn't move.

"Oh, you brought the wine," Beth said when the rush of water running had become the only sound between them. She demurely secured the towel around her and turned around, smiling. "Thank you. I was just about to go soak."

"You're tanned," Sam said.

Beth drove a pin into her hair to hold it up off her neck, and then she practically had to pry the glass from Sam's hand. It was a tall, fluted one with a healthy splash of white wine in it. "Yes," said Beth, knowing full well that she was teasing him shamelessly. Even before a single swallow of the wine, she was feeling intoxicated. "You can still see the bathing suit marks after three months. See?"

Sam did look as Beth turned and dropped the towel lower off her shoulder blade to show him the curve of her back. She knew her body was slim enough and almost as toned as his. He couldn't help but look.

Sam had the composure to smile at himself. Then he coughed lightly and said in an exaggerated, self-mocking version of his own Southern drawl, "I am at a loss for words."

Beth laughed and passed by him, conscious that barefooted she hardly came as high as his chin, though she was a tall woman. Sam moved mechanically aside to let her into the bathroom, his hand on the doorknob. Beth paused in the doorway and lifted her glass as if to toast him. "Thank you, sir. If my husband heard you say that, I wonder what he'd think?"

Sam didn't respond, so when Beth was safely on the other side of the door, she ripped off her towel and passed it back out to him through the still-cracked door, laughing lightly.

Sam took the towel and groaned. He closed the door and a moment later called, "You're making my life miserable, you know!"

Pleased, Beth countered, "I'm glad!"

She shut off the water then and prepared for a long, relaxing soak in the tub. She sipped her wine, found it crisp and dry, and lay back, resting her hand on the porcelain rim of the old-fashioned bathtub.

As she lay there, Beth's mind began to organize the facts. Sam was worried about their past, she knew. He wasn't in love with her, and since Beth had spent her first few days aching for a tiny sign of real love from him, she wasn't surprised when he had confirmed her guess. She was disappointed, yes, but not surprised. Perhaps he cared for her, but a passionate love did not exist anymore. Sam couldn't know how badly Beth needed someone now to fill her inner void. Sometimes she had thought the loneliness would swallow her into a cold darkness.

Apparently Sam's relationship with his wife Elizabeth, though once healthy, had deteriorated in the time before she left for New York. Whatever had happened before Elizabeth left had made him feel that physical love now would be a terrible mistake.

Beth caught herself. She was still referring to the old Elizabeth as if she was a different person. It happened a lot. Unconsciously, Beth had begun to think of herself as someone different from the wife Sam had once married.

Well, what did it matter? If Beth couldn't remember the past, was it relevant any longer? Wasn't it water under the bridge now? Why not start anew? Perhaps there was a way to salvage this marriage, she reasoned, smiling to herself. Sam didn't seem opposed to the idea, not really. He had been gentle with her and certainly friendly. He was just adamant that they take their time getting reacquainted. Why not start fresh?

Of course, she was ambivalent. The old Elizabeth was her only real link to Sam, after all.

It was worth a try, though. The night they had slept together on the couch had told Beth many things, though Sam hardly touched her. It was the way he touched her, the way he sheltered her in his arms and allowed her to fall asleep, though he must have been uncomfortable himself. He was a man with the potential for deep sensitivity, no matter how he had joked her out of being afraid for that silly rabbit in the field by macho talk about butchering cattle.

Beth reached for another towel and climbed out of the tub feeling renewed, not sleepy. She dried herself and slipped back into the bedroom.

It would be foolish to try teasing him into a sexual relationship. That wasn't what Beth wanted, anyway. She suspected that physical intimacy might be nice with Sam—his impulsive and gently experimental kiss in the field had been proof enough. But Beth knew she wasn't ready to charge into a full-blown seduction. Making love, if it ever came to that, was going to require some careful thinking on her part before the moment of truth. Beth knew what a physical relationship meant, but she didn't remember the feeling that went along with the actions. Perhaps with Sam she would one day rediscover those feelings. One day they might both be ready to try.

Though she liked Sam and was learning to respect him for many things, Beth was also going to have to learn to love him before she could share the physical aspects of marriage with him. Smiling at her dreamy-eyed reflection in the mirror while she brushed her straight hair out of its pins, Beth admitted that she was already well on her way to falling back into love with him. So far, the man had proven himself to be a Prince Charming beyond her wildest fantasies.

She dressed herself in her nightgown and donned her terry bathrobe also. She was going to have to be subtle, she realized. Sam might toss her out the door if she came slinking to him like a Mata Hari on the make. No, some finesse was definitely in order.

Sam was tinkering with a portable radio that had been parked on one of the sunporch windowsills. He had moved it to the desk and was checking through the stations when Beth arrived carrying her empty glass. He glanced up, then automatically down her slender legs and back up, still turning the dial on the static-producing radio.

"Baseball game?" Beth asked lightly, aware that he had enjoyed his brief inspection of her bare legs.

Sam grinned and went back to concentrating on the dial. "I wish. That's one of the most serious drawbacks to living out here. No decent baseball. The bottle's on the chair."

Beth found the newly opened bottle of wine and refilled her glass. "Are you a baseball fan? Really?"

"Sure. Red-blooded American boy all the way."

"Your favorite team?"

"Ah," sighed Sam, sitting back on his heels, "I'm afraid that was dictated by geography. I'm an Orioles fan."

Beth perched on the edge of the couch, wineglass clasped between her hands. "Really? I thought you'd be from Virginia."

"My accent? I thought I had dropped that. My father's family's from Maryland. They're still there. Gentlemen farmers. My mother's people come from Charleston, though. Very Southern. We'll make the trip to see them all when you're feeling better."

He had found some music he liked. Beth wasn't good at guessing what kind, but from the haunting horn and the casual improvised sound of background instruments, she figured it was jazz, the sophisticated kind.

Sam got lazily to his feet and stretched, his long, sinewy arms reaching over his head until his spine made a satisfying little crack and he let out a breath. Sock-footed, he paced to the nearest window with the lithe grace he tended to conceal when he was thinking of it. He moved evenly, as if his body was a well-honed piece of machinery he preferred to keep under cover until it was really needed. Beth had watched him pitch bales of straw that morning, lifting the whole things by the twine that bound them and tossing them easily down out of the barn's second story to the stall below. He had worked smoothly, with a minimum of effort and no complaints at all.

He unlatched the window and lifted the sash three inches, enough to let the evening breeze waft over the sill.

"Fresh air, wine, a hot bath," said Beth. "I ought to be asleep already."

"If only Connor were here. A game of his brand of Scrabble, and you'd be out like a light."

Beth watched Sam as he switched on the brass floor lamp by the opposite end of the couch and then put out the light that blazed from the ceiling. He had brought along his habitual bottle of beer, and it sat sweating condensation into a well-established ring on the battered coffee table. He liked this small room better than any other in the house, she decided. It suited his purposes and wasn't spectacularly beautiful like the living room. There were squat shelves, haphazardly packed with books, built underneath all of the windows. The furniture was comfortable but had not been purchased to match, and his typewriter, an expensive but old IBM electric model, sat as a silent reminder, rather like those fat little Buddha statues with such blissful expressions that people are forced to pause and reflect each time one comes into sight. Beth wondered if he ever used the typewriter. What had Marcus said? He hadn't written a play in two years.

There had to be a place to start, so out of the blue, Beth asked, "Do you like my brother Con?"

Sam wasn't surprised by the question, but he remained standing above her, and the light shone upward on his face, obscuring the clarity of his eyes momentarily. He said, "Do you?"

"Yes," Beth answered. "He's got a good heart, I think, no matter what his faults. Yes, I like him. He's endearing, though I realize I'm speaking from a woman's point of view. Notice I'm not saying 'I asked you first .'"

"I noticed," said Sam, sounding amused. He came out from behind the lamp and sauntered into the center of the sun porch. "You're not like him, Beth."

"No? We're both blondes." She put her hand to her hair, slipping her fingers into the flaxen length. "But I lighten mine, right? The roots are giving me away pretty badly."

Sam wisely didn't respond directly to that. He came around the table and reached for his beer. "It's lovely. I want to touch it all the time."

Beth blinked, startled by his admission. She hid her surprise by taking a sip of wine.

"Do I like Connor?" Sam asked rhetorically before he took a long swallow from the bottle. He had his back to Beth once more, as he looked out the tall, black windows into the night. He answered, "Yes and no. He's got courage, I'll give him that. He's braver than I am."

Curious, Beth tipped her head. "What d'you mean?"

"You'll see it soon enough, I suppose," Sam said, and he moved around the table and came to the couch. "'Conscience does make cowards of us all.' He's a policeman, did he tell you?"

"You mentioned it."

"Right," said Sam, easing himself into the cushions of the couch, a safe four feet from Beth. "Connor's okay, I suppose."

"I'd have thought his—well, his pettiness might annoy you."

"I don't annoy very easily," Sam said, and he smiled at her.

Beth laughed. "Remember, you shouldn't challenge me like that! I'm liable to start testing your patience just to prove you wrong."

"You do plenty of testing," Sam observed lightly, taking another draught of his beer.

"Sorry," Beth said, not denying anything. He seemed to like her blunt acceptance of certain truths, and Beth intended to keep his respect on that account. There was no sense pretending they didn't each understand what the other was talking about. "Does it bother you? That I want to know things?"

"It scares the hell out of me sometimes," Sam said frankly, relaxing even more comfortably into the cushions and parking one leg up on the couch. "But I don't blame you a bit. If I were in your shoes, I'd be crazy to know what's going on. You're very accepting, Beth. Very—well, giving seems an inadequate word, and generous doesn't fit exactly. You're thinking about the rest of us, aren't you? And it's not because Dr. Westham told you to take it easy on Connor and me."

He was right, perhaps. She was worried about the old Elizabeth and the new Beth, but she didn't want to alienate anybody else in the process of discovering her own personality. Trying to sound jesting, she asked, "Is that good or bad?"

"Different," Sam said, watching her face again without smiling. "Just different."

Beth moved and set her glass on the table. She'd had enough to drink, she decided. A couple of compliments from him, and her head was light. Carefully, she said, "I feel different sometimes."

Sam waited. He didn't move, but somehow his attention sharpened.

Beth smiled at herself, though she wondered if now was the time to tell Sam about her anxieties—her two selves. Unwillingly, she said, "I was just thinking in the bathtub that I don't feel like Elizabeth Sheridan yet. I still feel like Beth Doe, and I wonder if that's ever going to go away, if I'll ever be Elizabeth again."

"Beth Doe is a nice person," Sam suggested. "It wouldn't be such a bad thing to live the rest of your life as Beth."

She met his eyes and wondered. He had loved Elizabeth once. Longing to ask him to elaborate and tell her about their life together, Beth looked away again and quickly shook her head to dispel the inner wish. She clasped her hands and sighed.

"There's more," Sam guessed.

"It's silly."

"Tell me."

She sat back on the couch, but didn't look at Sam. As if speaking to the darkened windows around them, Beth said, "I feel like a stranger, Sam. I feel as if I don't belong. I hope to heaven that sensation goes away. I've been trying to fit myself into Elizabeth's place, but I don't quite make it. Con tried to help. He took me—you're going to be angry, I can tell from the way he acted when he took me up there, but Con showed me the studio upstairs."

Again, Sam was silent.

"It's a pretty room," Beth said quickly, trying to put into words her feelings when she had seen the studio with Connor that afternoon. "All that light, and that huge music system, and the looms are so, well, dramatic in a kind of spidery way. He showed me around, and I went back up there by myself just to sit. It didn't— Sam, it didn't *feel* like that was my place, and I must have spent hours and hours up there working—"

Sam put out his hand, laying it palm up on the back of the couch between them.

Beth obeyed his silent request and put her own hand in his. His fingers closed firmly around hers, steadying her. The gold of her wedding ring sparked once from the lamplight. Beth smiled and added more collectedly, "I know it's silly to worry about it already, but I wondered if I'm ever going to be able to do that again. Weaving, I mean. Honestly, I don't understand how—" She shot a quick guilty look at Sam and said, "I don't see what's so pretty about the things I was making. Darn it, some of them are downright ugly!"

Sam laughed. He threw back his head and laughed heartily.

"What?" Beth demanded, her smile appearing. "What's so funny?"

"Nothing," Sam said, still chuckling. He pulled Beth toward him, adding. "We're in perfect agreement, Beth. Some of those woolly things baffled me completely!"

Beth crawled comfortably into his embrace, smiling. "The one that looks like a fuzzy mammoth? With that crazy horn thing sticking out? Whatever did I have in mind when I made that? My artistic philosophy must have been rather unique."

Sam wound both arms around her, but didn't draw Beth against his chest as he had done the previous night when the thunder rolled high above the rooftop. He kept her body next to his, but turned so that they could see each other's expressions. This was new, and wonderfully exhilarating for Beth. He linked his fingers and rested them on the point of Beth's hip as if it were a desk and he an attentive schoolboy. "The too-obvious quote, I'm afraid, is 'There are more things in heaven and earth than are dreamt of in your philosophy.' No, I haven't any theory about Elizabeth's art. She—you were in a class excluding the rest of the world."

"Dr. Westham said Elizabeth was successful at what she did."

"Certainly," Sam agreed, falling into the easy practice of referring to the old Elizabeth as a separate person. "She was an acclaimed artist. She made as much money as I did, and I was supposed to be theater's gift from God at one time. Her weaving was a standard by which others were measured, I'm told. She made a good living at it, and that's rare."

"We have some money?" Beth asked. "Enough to pay the hospital, I hope?"

"We're okay," Sam said smoothly. "There's a good accountant in New York who sends me my allowance. He says we'll float for years."

Beth tipped a smile up at him. "Writing plays must have been lucrative."

Sam shrugged. "Not millions, I'm afraid."

"Am I allowed," Beth asked slowly, her eyes on his, "to know why you don't do it anymore?"

Sam moved, bringing one of his hands up to touch the blunt ends of her hair. He caressed Beth there and seemed not to notice that she arched imperceptibly to his hand, like a pet wanting to be fondled. Quietly, he said, "I still do it. Writing, I mean. But not for anyone to read."

"Ohh."

"Don't worry," Sam said, filling his hand with her hair. "I may snap out of this one day and stop pretending I'm the man from American Gothic with my pitchfork in one hand and my farm to keep me busy."

"The theater life must have been glamorous," Beth observed.

He laughed. "Mine? Hardly. I waited on tables in New York and swept out theaters from the time I was eighteen. Glamorous wasn't even in my vocabulary!"

"So what happened?" Beth asked, truly intrigued by his story. "How did you become such a success? Dumb luck?"

"You read *Bitten*," Sam challenged, giving her hair a tug. "Didn't that demonstrate my genuine wit? My surreal compassion for the human condition? My dissatisfaction and unfailing depiction of man's love affair with womankind?"

"Whom are you quoting now? Reviewers?"

Sam laughed. "You're delightful!"

"Just smarter than you first thought I was," Beth said immodestly. "Tell me the rest, please."

"Nothing to tell. I went to college, but when I got out, I didn't feel capable of competing in the real world. I ended up in theaters—New York, finally. And I developed a kind of network of talented people. We collaborated."

"No," said Beth, knowing she was right. "*Bitten* was your work, not somebody else's."

"I was influenced by many people."

"Aren't we all? Take it from me, the one who can only absorb from everyone else's past experiences! But *Bitten* was, well, too vivid to be the work of many people. It has this—I guess it was a feeling that Fuller's voice told the story, no matter what the other characters said. I bet reviewers called it 'powerful.'"

"Yes," said Sam, with a grin. "And also 'haunting,' 'exhilarating' and the ever-popular 'poignant.'"

"It was all of those things. I'd like to read some others. May I? There's one you won another award for, right?"

"*Lions in a Cage* and *Christian Boys*—that's about three boys and the priest who's their father figure. I like *Seduca*, too, mostly because there's stuff in it I don't completely understand myself, and I enjoy hearing someone else read the parts. It was almost poetry, not dialogue."

"I'd like to read them all," Beth said. "I'd like to see them performed, too. Are they still produced?"

"Some places," Sam said, and he began to tell her—in his casual and therefore humble way—about the theaters that called him occasionally for guidance or insight and invitations to come for rehearsals or performances.

They talked like that for another hour, though Beth was not once aware of time. She only knew that she was soaking up Sam's life, learning his past and understanding his personality a little better with each passing moment.

He had met some very famous people along the continuum of his life, she found, though at the time they were nobodies just like Sam. Like them, he had risen within the highly competitive, often criticized, and rarely praised world of dramatic theater. He directed a little, he had acted when he needed the money, and all the while he read voraciously and wrote with just as much burning energy. He had been prolific in the beginning, writing furiously. Some of his early work, he admitted, was explosive.

Then, with growing insight, he had slowed down and begun to create more complex, more challenging works. *Bitten* was the greatest commercial success, and he had even directed that himself.

After a time, Beth began to become aware of how Sam was telling his tales, not just the words. He was willing to talk, but he shared no enthusiasm with her. His eyes were steady, he reached now and then for his beer and unconsciously touched Beth's hair or her shoulder from time to time, but he displayed no energy for the subject. He had no fire inside, not the kind Beth expected he might still be carrying for his work. Though he would not stoop to using the cliché, Beth realized that he had closed the book on that part of his life.

After a while, Beth felt brave enough to ask him about it. "What are you writing now? The things you don't let other people read?"

Sam shrugged. "Notes, mostly. I can't help it. I trained myself to use the language to create characters and conflicts, so I can't stop entirely. I do a lot of thinking. Perhaps one of these days I'll put it all on the desk and see what it's become. Maybe it's a novel by now. *War and Peace Revisited* in four volumes."

"I haven't seen you write," Beth pointed out. "Do you sneak in here and tap away on the typewriter in the dead of night?"

He shook his head, smiling, his eyes alive with awareness for her. "I'm busy with other things. The farm. You."

"Don't let me interfere," Beth said quickly, laying her hand on his chest. "I can take—"

"—care of yourself," finished Sam, laughing. "I know, I know. Look, it's been a hectic time for all of us, even Connor. Give me a few days, and we'll be firmly into our rut again."

"What is your rut?" Beth asked, smiling. "What do you do all day, Mr. Sheridan?"

"Work," said Sam, turning over his hands so she could see the roughened surface of his palms. "I spend a lot of time taking care of this farm, though it's technically a low-maintenance kind of ranch."

"And the bicycle you keep stashed in the barn?"

"Oh," said Sam, his grin turning guilty. "That's for fun. I ride every day."

"Where? Up and down the lane?"

"No, no. I ride for two hours. At least I try to. Then on the weekends, I do a century. This summer I started—"

"A century?" Beth asked, stopping him.

He smiled. "One hundred miles. It's a race. I started joining them this summer."

"Wait. You pedal a bike for a hundred miles?"

"Sure. You want to try?"

"Heavens!"

"You could do it," Sam insisted. He dropped his hand to her thigh and tugged at her bathrobe until the fabric pulled open and away from her leg. "Look at this. You didn't get that kind of muscle from walking the hospital halls."

Beth braced the ball of her bare foot on the coffee table and looked down at her own thigh and arched calf with new interest.

"Forgive me for noticing," he said with a grin, touching her thigh by laying his hand flat on the curving length, "but you've got terrific legs for just about any form of exercise. I remember when I first saw those legs, I thought, 'She looks as though she must have been a real jock in high school—or worse yet, a cheerleader.' C'mon, let's see these muscles ripple."

"Muscles, hmm? I never really thought about exercise much," Beth said doubtfully. "I went jogging with one of the residents one day and I hated it. So boring!"

"But could you keep up with him?"

"Oh, yes," Beth said, and began to laugh. "I could see he was getting embarrassed, so I faked a stitch in my side and begged off. He never asked me again. I figured he decided I was unattractive enough without beating the socks off him at his own sport so we never—"

"Unattractive?" Sam repeated, incredulous.

"My hair is so straight, and the roots are growing out—"

Sam hooted a laugh. "My dear Beth, you're stunning! With that face? A perfectly snooty Yankee nose that clashes with those blue bedroom eyes of yours? Not to mention the most breathtaking pair of legs since—"

"Enough!" Beth giggled, pushing his hand away from her thigh. He moved as far as her knee, but kept his fingertips resting there, as if enjoying the warmth of her bare skin. She nestled back into the curve of his other arm contentedly. "You're going to fill my head with nonsense."

"Better nonsense than bad dreams. Mind you, it's pleasant talking with a woman who apparently has no idea of what she can do to a man simply by holding a bath towel to her breasts! You're so lovely. I can't stop watching you."

"It's the same for me," Beth said with a smile, though she couldn't quite meet his eyes. "We must have had good chemistry once. You're very nice to look at, too."

Struck silent, Sam petted her hair again, watching the blond strands slip through his fingers. His expression wasn't unhappy. It wasn't anything. He was thinking, weighing the situation in his mind. He sighed finally, and murmured, "Oh, Beth."

She touched his chest through his sweater, running the backs of her fingers up and down in an aimless caress. "I know. You don't want to talk about us—our prehistoric time together. You can't expect me not to be tantalized by the situation, though. What have we done together? We must have had fights and unpleasant times, but did we—Con said—"

"Erotic games," Sam supplied. "I heard him."

"Well, that sets the wheels of my mind turning!"

Sam's hand was still on her hair, his other very light suddenly on her knee. In a moment he was going to pull away, she thought. He said distantly, "Mine, too."

They sat together in silence for a time, not listening to the breeze or feeling the presence of the lamp or the rest of the room. Beth was acutely conscious of Sam's body and her own. Wherever he touched her—the casual weight of his arm across her shoulders and the feathery way his fingertips felt through her hair and on the back of her neck, the smoothness of his palm just above her kneecap and the way the pinpricks of his nails brushed the sensitive flesh on the inside of her knee—all those points of contact seemed to burn with static. He caressed her so infrequently that this kind of embrace was wonderfully exciting. Her heart had begun to trip along, sending Beth's warming blood in a race to her now light head.

Sam must have known her physical response was starting. He took his hand from her knee very slowly and smoothed the terrycloth of her robe, up past the knotted belt to the modestly drawn lapels of the garment. Gently, he touched two fingers to her skin, a spot just below her collarbone, and then moved the robe aside, just a little, then a little more. Her chest was bared just enough to see its quick rise and fall, evidence that Beth's breathing was just as erratic as her heartbeat.

Under her own hand, Beth could feel that Sam's respiration had not increased. If anything, it was even more slow and measured than before. She took a deep breath and tried to steady herself. "Sam," she said, her voice becoming maddeningly soft, "when you kissed me outside—did you—was it because you felt sorry for having told me how bad things were between us before?"

"Did I kiss you out of guilt?" he asked, his mouth curving finally, though just at the corners.

"It started that way, I know," Beth murmured, unable to look into his face. Instinctively, though, she slipped her fingers higher and touched the bare skin at his throat, where summer sunshine had tanned his skin, and a few tiny curls of hair teased her fingertips. "You started to kiss me to comfort me, I think."

"Yes," he said honestly.

"But it didn't—I felt as if it was something else then."

"Y-yes," he said, very slowly.

"Sam," Beth murmured, lifting her eyes to his. "Would you—? Could—"

He touched her hand instinctively, caressing it. Her ring winked between his fingers once again, and he said, "Don't make me kiss you, Beth. It's wrong, honestly."

"Maybe to you it seems—"

"It's wrong," Sam repeated.

Beth was silent. She met his eyes though, and knew that her own gaze was full of indecision.

Sam responded, of course. He hesitated at first. Then his touch on the back of her neck changed to a grasp. He pulled, sliding his other hand down the curve of Beth's waist and around her back, saying with regret in his softly whispered words, "It's very wrong, and you're going to hate me for it."

But he kissed her anyway. Sam gathered her against him, waiting until Beth slid her arms up and around his shoulders before he pulled and brought her breasts softly against his chest. Then his mouth found hers. His lips were gentle and exploratory, first touching hers lightly, then withdrawing just a centimeter. He gave up the pretense of restraint and took her mouth completely, draining Beth of her common sense with the first rush of heat.

It was a carnal kiss, a kiss between strangers, perhaps, but one that communicated an inevitable sensuality. Sam softly mouthed Beth's lips, seeking and appraising. He tilted her head to his satisfaction, then with a skillful, circular motion, eased her lips apart and tasted deeply of her. His tongue swiped once across her lush lower lip and retreated. She felt the gentle tug of his teeth next and then a more leisurely exploring with his tongue of hers. She slipped both hands to his face, holding her palms to the prickly surface of his cheeks, as if to keep him with her, to hold his mouth to hers. Very slowly, Sam lay back on the arm cushion, drawing Beth's body with him.

Atop him, Beth was shy suddenly. She might have broken the kiss, but Sam held her mouth firmly, insistently now, to his own. Presently, his other arm tightened around her back, pressing her to fit more intimately with his frame. Then he relaxed and smoothed his hand down the hollow of her back, down caressingly over the roundness of her bottom, until he met the lithe slimness of her thigh. Instinct told her she should loosen her legs and straddle him, but she could not. Perhaps he sensed her misgivings, her hesitation, for he merely steadied her suddenly trembling thigh and caressed her gently.

He took his mouth from hers, but pressed an open-mouthed kiss to her throat and another to the sensitive spot just below her earlobe. Beth heard her own breath catch and quiver, and she was afraid to open her eyes. She was afraid of what she might see in Sam's expression. Did he want her? Yes, the message was clear.

"I want to make love to you," Sam murmured, his voice barely a whisper in her ear. He nipped with erotic gentleness at her throat and said, "I said I wouldn't lust after you, and I've thought about very little else since I said it."

"Sam," Beth said quietly, testing the sound of his name in this new, passion-softened voice she didn't recognize.

"You're lovely," he said, caressing her back lightly through her robe. "I can't help wanting to have you like this."

Beth blinked and opened her eyes at the exact moment Sam pulled away. Their gazes met uncertainly. "I think," Beth whispered, "that I want you, too."

"Beth, you trust me too much," Sam said roughly, a pain in his gray-green eyes. He turned her whole body so that her weight was no longer resting on him alone. With her arms still looped around his neck, and her supple legs entwined with his own, Sam eased her down into the comfort of the couch.

"How can I trust too much?"

"You can. You're beautiful and vulnerable, and the trust in your eyes gives me a feeling of power that sometimes makes me afraid. I don't want to do anything bad."

"No, Sam, nothing you would do to me could be bad."

"You don't know me well enough. You don't understand what I can do to you yet. Here I am protecting you from the rest of the world, and suddenly I'm the biggest threat to your happiness."

Beth smiled, feeling warm again inside. She touched his face once more. "You're not making sense."

"Maybe not yet." Sam smoothed her hair back from her temples and pressed a soft, final sort of kiss on her temple. "Can you sleep now? Like this? If I carry you to bed right now, I'd do something foolish."

"Do you want me to go?"

"No," said Sam, sounding tired. "Forgive me, but I want to hold you."

CHAPTER SIX

SOMETHING WAS WRONG, and Beth knew it. She could sense it. She *knew* things were more complicated than Sam was telling her.

But Beth did not wonder. She deliberately ignored the signs of deeper trouble and hoped that Sam would overcome whatever demons were haunting him. She did not want to know.

The best she could do, she decided, was to try very, very hard to be his wife, to please him, to settle into her home as firmly as if she'd never left it. She needed time to collect herself and to regain not only her memory but her mind. The swift repartee of conversation with Sam had proven to Beth that she still wasn't thinking like an adult. She was still too concerned by what was happening to her to think clearly. The one idea that kept erupting in her brain was that Sam—and Connor, too, when he'd been with them—took great care to think things through before they spoke to her. It was as if—and Beth was trying hard not to imagine why—they were watching their words in order to prevent inconvenient slips of the tongue. Perhaps they were sparing her feelings. Or perhaps something else was in the wind.

It was just a perception she had, one she tried to ignore.

Beth woke the next morning on the bed and alone. Sam must have brought her to the bedroom after all and gone to sleep somewhere else. As she slowly awakened, with bright shafts of morning sunlight beaming around her, Beth began to plan. She wanted to find the fastest way to get her life back to normal. It made her feel good to make mental lists, and she found herself smiling.

She was interrupted when Sam entered the bathroom from the other side and ran water hard and fast into the sink. He splashed and blew, then shut off the faucet, and Beth heard the towel rack rattle. A moment later he pushed cautiously on the door to the bedroom, towel in his hands as he dried his face. He peeked around the door, trying to be soundless. His hair was damp around his forehead and his eyelashes sparkled with water, too.

Beth blinked and smiled and sat up lazily. "Hello. Did you sleep?"

"Enough," he replied, giving up trying to be quiet once he saw that she was awake. Sam rested his shoulder against the door-jamb, and finished drying his face. Beth realized that he wasn't wearing a shirt. He'd come to her with a bare chest, in his work jeans and wool socks. He looked naked to her, oddly enough. Beth was rendered momentarily speechless by the sight, but Sam smiled a little and either pretended he didn't understand her silence or honestly didn't believe she could be mesmerized by the play of sunlight across his shoulders and chest. Certainly pretending last night never happened, he asked only, "Breakfast?"

"Y-yes," said Beth, swinging her legs over the edge of the bed, but staying where she was. She felt shy. An idea struck her and she tipped her head, looking at him sideways. "How about if *I* make it?"

Sam laughed at her hopeful expression, but refused. "I've got work to do this morning before it rains. I'll do breakfast. If you want, you can try dinner, okay?"

"You think I can't make a three-minute egg?"

Sam wasn't going to be dragged into a contest of wills. "On the chance it might take three hours the first time you try kitchen duty, I take care of the eggs today. We'll let you practice for a while, all right?"

Beth agreed and stayed on the bed to watch as Sam flipped the towel over his shoulder and sauntered out through her room toward the kitchen. She watched his fluid walk, the way his lean back curved down into his jeans, and the easy way he raked his hair back with his fingers as he moved away from her. Sam looked at ease, she decided. Perhaps he was becoming accustomed to having her around now.

They had a quick breakfast together, for Sam was obviously feeling geared up to start the farm work. Or perhaps he just wanted to put some distance between them. Beth wasn't sure. When he had gone, she washed the dishes, got dressed and then found herself sitting on the sun porch wondering what to do next.

Enough aimlessness, she decided. It was time to start puttering around, getting settled in. For the first time in ages, she was alone and ready to try something new.

She made a beeline for the kitchen and the recipe box, a wooden container whimsically made to look like a miniature cottage with shutters painted on it and a handle in the shape of a chimney. Connor said she liked to cook. Today she'd try.

Beth slid onto the kitchen stool, put the box on the counter and began to sort through the typed index cards that were haphazardly arranged inside. Whether Sam had made use of the recipe cards and stuffed them back into the box so carelessly, or if she herself had worked from such a chaotic arrangement, Beth couldn't guess. She spent some time stacking all the vegetable casseroles, the meat dishes, the salad recipes, and the vast collection of cookie cards into separate piles. Thus organized, she set about reading through all the recipes, looking for a great meal to impress Sam for dinner.

After several trips to the refrigerator and the pantry closet to see what supplies were on hand, Beth settled upon something called Fast and Easy Chicken, Peas and Carrot Mixup and—in a burst of self-confidence—chocolate mousse. If she had time, there would be baking soda biscuits, too. Happily, she found an apron, assembled all her ingredients, made herself a pitcher of iced tea and set to work, preparing to enjoy herself.

What a mistake!

By early afternoon Beth decided that the chicken dish was going to be neither fast nor particularly easy. The Peas and Carrot Mixup had been aptly named, and as the afternoon wore on she was feeling less and less like tackling chocolate mousse. At two o'clock she threw out the first batch of peas and carrots, having thawed the carrots and then overcooked them into a soggy mass. At three o'clock she dumped the iced tea down the drain and opened a bottle of beer for herself, hoping to steady her nerves. No sign of Sam, thank heaven, but a build-up of storm clouds on the horizon promised that he'd be home soon.

At three-thirty some thunder startled Beth out of her concentration and she burned her finger on the side of the saucepan—she hadn't the faintest idea what a "double boiler" was, so she'd decided to make do with a saucepan to melt the chocolate squares. She yelped, stuck her finger in her mouth and fumed. Had Connor told her the truth? Surely she could never have enjoyed cooking!

She glared out the kitchen window, feeling angry. The clouds were definitely building, turning the horizon a leaden gray. The kitchen curtains were blowing from the increasing breeze. She shoved the window closed. Another storm was definitely on its way.

Beth decided to abandon her cooking long enough to close all the open windows in the house before the rain started. There wasn't much time, she was sure. She ran like a rabbit from room to room. Finally she hurried onto the sun porch and slammed the last of the windows down just as the rain started to spit through the screens.

When she skidded back into the kitchen, the chocolate was smoking.

"Damnation!" Beth snatched the pan off the burner and threw it into the sink. The pan hissed angrily, just another sound added to the cacophony of cooking noises: the jingle of the saucepan lid as the peas furiously boiled; the gurgle of filthy dishes soaking in the sink under a dripping tap; and the simmer of chicken juices from inside the oven, the kind of sound she imagined might come from a creature in a dark and disgusting swamp. None of the noises was especially familiar or comforting. In exasperation, Beth groaned and exclaimed aloud, "I'm ready to give up!"

The thunder answered her, grumbling ominously.

Beth glared up at the ceiling. "My feelings exactly!"

The timer on the stove began to buzz, and Beth dove for a pot holder and yanked open the oven door. The chicken looked worse than it had twenty minutes ago. It was turning a kind of gray color. What had she done wrong?

Just then the peas boiled over. A smelly, smoky steam billowed up from the burner.

Beth swore for real, slammed the oven door closed and grabbed for the pan handle. The roiling steam burned her all over again, and she cried out and dropped the pan with a clatter. Peas foamed out from under the lid, struck the burner and began to blacken. More smoke. What a stink!

"*Damn* it!"

Beth's emotions boiled over too. Out of impulse, she picked up her empty beer bottle—not thinking—and hurled it straight against the doorjamb, where it smashed and shattered into a thousand satisfying pieces.

Ten seconds later, Sam opened the door from the outside, his face a picture of wonderment.

They stared at each other for a long, noisy moment in which Beth could not breathe or think or speak. She moved back from Sam until her spine was pressed firmly against the counter. She felt guilty and absurdly juvenile, like a kid caught defacing the school yard walls.

Sam waited, one hand on the door, making sure she wasn't going to throw something else. Then—cautiously—he came into the kitchen. He left the door standing wide open behind him so that the storm blew in, sending a spattering of misty rainwater along the kitchen tiles. Keeping a wary eye on Beth, Sam paced to the window, his boots crunching on the broken glass. He lifted the window sash. Almost immediately, a cross ventilation between the door and window started clearing out the smoke.

With one more silent, speculative gaze through the smoke at Beth, his eyebrows suitably raised, Sam bent and picked up a shard of her broken bottle. Straightening, turning the glass over in his hand, he said very dryly, "Beth, darling, I think you're finally developing a temper. Congratulations."

Beth let out a long, tense breath. She felt her eyes grow round as silver dollars, for she was amazed at herself. Why had she thrown the bottle? She couldn't remember ever experiencing such anger! She said slowly, "I— I can't believe I did that."

Sam dropped the bottle fragment into the sink and crouched down to pluck up the rest of the big pieces. They chinked together in his palm. He glanced up at her, and finally there was a smile at the corner of his mouth. "Lost your patience all of a sudden?"

"Hours ago," Beth said weakly. She put one shaking hand to her forehead, feeling a desperate need to hold back the turmoil of emotions that threatened to break through at any second. Her own voice sounded ragged. "Honestly, I don't know what came over me."

Sam got back to his feet and carefully dumped the pieces into the sink. He shut off the stove switches next, saying over his shoulder, "Actually, I think it's the best sign yet."

"Sign?" Beth repeated, still numb.

"Of your improving health. You've kept yourself on a very even keel up until now. That can't be very natural." He turned to face her. "You've been like an automaton. Nothing changes your emotions. You don't react."

Immediately Beth argued, "I react!"

"Yes," Sam agreed, though unwillingly. He took two steps to her, moving slowly, cautiously. Then he put out one hand and cupped her arm as if to steady her. His voice was gentle. "But always cautiously. Ever since I first saw you at the hospital, you've been thawing little by little. At first you were childlike. Now you're starting to show a wider spectrum of emotions. You're growing up, if that makes any sense."

Still confused by her own display of uncharacteristic anger, Beth asked, "Is that bad?"

Sam didn't laugh at her, but took both her arms under his hands comfortingly, and drew her closer. He was a little wet from the rain, but his body heat felt as warm as ever. He answered, "Of course not. Maybe it's easier for you not to have yo-yo emotions like the rest of us, but it's not good for you. You've been keeping enough bottled up inside as it is. I think this is a breakthrough."

Frowning, Beth blurted out, "I don't like it, acting like Joan Crawford."

He did laugh then, really amused. "Joan Crawford? You're anything but. It amazes me what you remember sometimes!"

"I didn't mean to throw the bottle at *you*." Beth looked up into his face, thankful that he was trying to tease her out of her stunned state. Feeling guilty, she added, "I didn't know you were there, honestly."

"That's a relief," Sam said with a grin. He let her go and moved away once the tense moment was past. Easily, he said, "If I hadn't stopped on the porch to take off my slicker, I'd be nursing a headache for sure, wouldn't I, Miss Crawford?"

"I won't do it again." Irritated at herself, Beth added in a mutter, "There are a lot of things I won't do again."

Sam followed her glance around the kitchen, where the shambles of her many false starts on dinner were obvious. Amused, Sam let out a low whistle. "What tornado hit this place, anyway?"

"Hurricane Beth. Oh, honestly, Sam, I couldn't cook if both our lives depended on it. There's so much to *know*! What's a double boiler? Why is this chicken looking so horrible? I must have done something wrong, but I can't—''

"It looks like you made a valiant effort," Sam intervened gently, surveying the mess with yet another of his gentle smiles. "Why on earth did you start so early?"

"Early? I—I don't know. I wasn't sure how long everything would take."

"You mean you've been playing at this all day?"

"*Playing!* It was hard work!"

Sam laughed at her outrage. "All right, all right. I can see that. You can remember Joan Crawford but not how long it takes to boil—what *is* this stuff, anyway?" He picked up the pan that moments ago had held gurgling, hissing vegetables, and placed the mess in the sink. "Maybe you tried too hard. Why don't you start with easy things before you start the Julia Child routine? Nobody ever said you had to be a terrific cook."

"Connor did," Beth shot back, still bristling.

Sam hesitated, a quick freezing of his whole body that lasted just three seconds. With his back to her, he said, "Well, that was then. This is now. You don't have to be anything that doesn't feel right."

Beth grunted in annoyance. "This fiasco certainly felt wrong from the time I opened the recipe box!"

"Well, no wonder." Sam picked up the roof lid to the recipe file. "This box was a Christmas gift from my niece. My sister's daughter made out all those cards—so you wouldn't recognize any of those recipe things."

"Really?" Beth asked in surprise. Happiness bloomed within her once again. Maybe she didn't have to feel foolish about her feelings after all.

His back to her, he replaced the lid and put the box back on the shelf where it had been. "Of course. Don't agonize over it. Those silly recipes were probably my sister's and my mother's, and they're not at all what I eat now. Hell, I hate peas and my mother knows it. I bet that package in the freezer was three years old."

Beth laughed weakly. "I wondered why it was stuck down there underneath everything! Why did you keep the package if you hate them?"

"I hate cleaning out freezers even worse than I hate peas. Brother, you really incinerated something here! What is this?"

Sam looked as if he had every intention of starting to clean up the dishes in the sink and the monumental disaster that was burned on the top of the stove. Feeling happy suddenly, Beth crossed to him and patted the small of his back. "Who knows? Who cares? Don't start cleaning up my mess, all right? I feel like a worm already. This will be my punishment for nearly cracking your skull. Wouldn't it be something if we both had broken heads? Go get something dry on, will you? Your jeans are soaked, Sam! Go on. Get dressed again and I'll tackle this job. You're not hungry, are you?"

Sam grinned and moved away from her hand. "Starved, in fact. Give me a minute to change, and I'll show you how to make popcorn."

He left then, striding out through the house to the bedrooms. Beth, smiling to herself, tackled the kitchen with a lightening heart. Sam had been proud of her, she thought. He'd been pleased that she was recovering. A little bit of praise acted like raindrops on a sun-parched garden. She was eager for more.

When Sam returned, showered and freshly dressed in a shapeless sweatshirt and a clean pair of shorts, he made the promised bowl of popcorn and a stack of ham and cheese sandwiches that rivaled the Tower of Pisa. The rainstorm had lessened by that time, so they ate on the porch steps, sitting side by side, thigh to thigh, watching the rain. Afterward, Sam said he wanted to go tinker with his bicycle in the barn, and he promised to run off any cats if Beth would come along and talk with him as he worked. She agreed, and they dashed through the diminishing rain to the open barn door.

With Beth perched on a bale of hay, Sam lifted his bicycle down off its pegs and began to adjust the fine spokes of the front wheel. Talking with Beth over his shoulder, he spun the tire, watching carefully, then used a small tool to tighten the wheel here and there. The rain had stopped, so when he'd finished with the tuning job, he rode the bicycle once around the yard, fiddling with the gears and testing his work. He pedaled the bike with slow, easy revolutions, his legs looking long and lean and very strong. Sam didn't look silly on a bicycle, Beth decided, just fit and surprisingly graceful. He balanced one hand on the handlebars while the other played through the gears. Seeing Sam at play made Beth smile. She hugged herself, for the afternoon had turned chilly after the storm, and watched him fondly. Sam's face was grave, as always, even when he was riding a bike. What was it going to take to make him happy? Truly happy for longer than a few seconds?

He guided the bicycle back to Beth and swung his leg over it. "Want to try?"

"Me?" Beth looked surprised. "Do I ride a bike?"

Sam rolled his eyes and laughed. "Everybody rides a bike, for crying out loud! Come on." He reached for her elbow and pulled Beth around to one side of the bicycle. "Here."

"My legs are shorter than yours. It won't—"

"Just get on," Sam said with another impatient laugh in his voice. "Your legs are plenty long enough. Here, put your hands up here if it feels uncomfortable."

He helped her onto the tall seat, and Beth gripped the handlebars where he showed her so that her body was not in the low, racy crouch that Sam had used, but sitting straighter. She slid her feet into the pedals, seeking the toe grips with the tips of her shoes. Awkwardly, she pushed off and started to pedal. The bike wobbled once, and she cut around a puddle.

"Wait," Sam said, just behind her. "Let me show you the gears before—"

But Beth started to laugh.

It felt glorious. It felt perfect. She *knew* the gears! She knew instinctively.

She settled down into the crouch, her hands resting on the proper grips, her body low, her legs extended—perhaps too much, but not uncomfortably so. She picked up speed and used her weight to steer the fine machine. The bike obeyed her slightest movement. Laughing at Sam's immediate shout of concern, Beth applied herself to pedaling until she had the bike up to speed. She flew through the farm gate and out onto the loose stones of the road. She kept the front tire exactly in the center of the packed down truck tracks and let her body take over.

It was natural. The cool wind in her face, eyes half squinted, the pain-pleasure of stretching muscles down the length of her calves, the warmth of working muscle in her thighs. Rhythm. Speed. Exhilaration. This was home.

She hit the highway and kept going, head down, her hair flying. After the dust-mustiness of the barn, she breathed the oxygen-rich thunderstorm air, sucking the loamy scent of rain and freshened earth into her lungs with an instinctive inner rhythm. Her heart had accelerated to pounding, but Beth had found a kind of physical threshold for herself and stayed there, her body working fluidly, perfectly—neither tiring nor losing momentum. She pedaled and pedaled, the distance flying past her in a blurred green-brown landscape. Too focused on the sensations within herself to notice her surroundings, she rode along the highway with her heart in her throat, joy ready to burst from her. She loved this. This was right and good. It was a place she'd been before.

She pedaled for a mile, maybe two, but seemingly without effort. With the bike adjusted to Sam's height, she knew she wasn't getting the maximum benefit from her muscles, but still it felt terrific.

Sam. He'd be worried. With a grin, Beth applied the brakes, downshifted and turned the bike around. She pedaled back to the farm, sprinting hard for half a mile on the smooth pavement until she spotted the turnoff. She eased back on her speed and cruised onto the road to the farm. In seconds she could see the gate. There was Sam, one hand on the topmost rail to keep himself from running out to her.

"How do you feel?" he demanded anxiously, seeing Beth's expression before she stopped.

Beth stuck her leg out and caught her balance on the ground. With the too-tall bike tilted sideways, she stopped and smiled brilliantly up at him. "Oh, Sam, it was wonderful!"

He wasn't smiling, just looking shaken. His face was slack, his eyes sharply scanning hers. "I can see that. You—you looked great, Beth."

"I *felt* great! I can do this, Sam! It was like—I don't know—it felt *right* somehow!" Beth was excited, her words tumbling out almost too fast to be understood. "I've done this before, haven't I? It's so different from what I've felt before! I—it's like—I *recognized* it somehow! Sam, do you think . . . ? Could I be . . . ? Is it . . . ?"

Sam grabbed the handlebars. His gaze locked with hers, quick and searching in a new intentness. Odd-voiced, he said, "You're remembering, aren't you?"

Beth let out her breath in a whoosh. Eyes wide, she put out her hand to him, reaching, asking for his help. Suddenly Beth wasn't sure she should be happy anymore. She had remembered something! "I—I think so. Oh, Sam!"

He caught her in a hug before she could go on. With the bike between them, Sam held her as snugly as he could. His shoulder was tense under her cheek, but he said, "It's okay. Don't be scared."

"I am scared," Beth said, wrapping her arms around Sam's neck. She tried to laugh. "I'm suddenly afraid to remember my past. Isn't that crazy?"

"No, not crazy."

"It's what I want, I think. I thought I wanted my memory back."

Sam didn't answer. His heart, though, beating just below Beth's ear, was racing in a rhythm just as fast as her own.

She continued, her words stumbling. "Everybody's been trying to help me regain my memory. I thought I wanted to remember who I was. I should be happy. I was happy when I was out on the bike. Now it's like—oh, gosh. I really *am* another person, aren't I?"

"What?" Sam jumped, his body taut as steel wire.

"I mean—I'm not just Beth anymore, am I? I'm Elizabeth, too. Sam!" Beth hugged him as if he was the only anchor left in her life. Her voice cracked and filled with anguish. "Sam, it feels weird being two people all of a sudden!"

Sam was silent, stroking her hair, trying to get a grip on his own thoughts, it seemed. His voice, also strained, whispered softly, "It's okay."

"There *is* another part of me," Beth explained, hardly thinking out her words before she said them. "I feel like there's a trapdoor or something in my head, and I just—I just started to fall through it. I got back through it, though—back to me—to Beth—again, but Elizabeth is there...I know she is, now! I could feel the other person when I was riding the bike."

"Easy," Sam said, pleading gently. "Don't get upset."

Beth hugged him as hard as she could. "It's a good kind of upset, Sam. It's scary, but it's good, I can feel it."

Even as she said the words, Beth felt the pinprickly feeling behind her eyes—the signal of tears threatening. Emotions, she thought, were queer things. The good and the bad muddled together somehow. It was a new realization for Beth, but she knew that it was something Sam already understood.

"Don't be scared," he said again, and he kissed her hair.

Somehow, Beth had the feeling that it had been Sam who was the more frightened.

CHAPTER SEVEN

SAM TOOK HER to a town that evening. They went shopping for a bicycle.

"You'd better have a bike of your own," he said as the truck puttered along the highway through the after-storm fog. "If you enjoy it as much as this, we might as well ride together."

"Didn't I have a bike of my own before?" Beth asked, sticking her hand out the window as they drove so that the cool wind rushed through her fingers. She had brushed her hair and put on a pretty heather-blue sweater, and she felt happy.

Sam, too, had recovered from the afternoon's revelations. He said easily, "Sure. Every kid has a bike, right?"

"What happened to it?"

"What?"

Beth laughed at him. "My bike, silly. You're getting as absentminded as I am. What happened to it?"

"I am not absentminded. I just--you know, Beth, it's very difficult to do all the remembering for two people!"

She glanced across at Sam. "What's so difficult? All I asked was—"

"I know what you asked."

"Okay," she said doggedly, "did you sell it or something?"

He was gripping the steering wheel as if it was a lifeline and his tone was annoyed. "Sell what?"

"My bike, Sam! Gosh, but you're scatterbrained tonight! Did you sell my old bike?"

"Why should you care now? All right, yes!" Sam exploded with exasperation. "I sold it! End of subject, all right?"

The testiness with which he spoke did shut up a much puzzled Beth for a moment. In the resulting silence, Sam rolled down his window so that he could adjust the side mirror. With the wind ruffling his dark hair, he asked abruptly, with fresh cheer, "What kind do you want this time?"

"What kind of what?"

"Now who's absentminded?" he asked with a laugh that sounded forced. "What kind of bike are you going to choose for yourself this time?"

"Kind? Heavens, I don't know anything about fancy bikes that—" Beth stopped, then interrupted herself decisively, "Yes, I do know. I want a red one."

Sam grinned across at her. "You're getting cocky now, aren't you?"

"Why do you say that?"

"Picking a favorite color like that. When you bought those few clothes at the airport you didn't have any opinions about colors and how things ought to look. If I hadn't come along, you'd have bought everything in beige. You are showing some progress, Beth."

She put her hand to her sweater. The vividness of the color had prompted her to choose to wear it today, Beth realized. Sheepishly, she asked, "Am I looking better?"

He had seen her automatic gesture and was kind. "From when I saw you in the elevator, yes."

She wrinkled her nose and glanced across at him. "I must have looked dreadful."

"Your clothes?" Kindly, he admitted, "You were not exactly a fashion plate. You always look good now. But we'll order you some more things to wear, if you like. Brighter things."

"Yes, please! Could we?"

"I get magazines and mail-order catalogs by the truckload. We'll order whatever you want. Anything but sequins."

Beth laughed. "I'm not the sequin type, I don't think."

"Not in this setting, no." Sam sent her a grin. "But I bet that you'd look pretty showy if you put your mind to it."

Settling comfortably in her seat, Beth smiled ahead at the highway. Sam was not the sort of man to heap on the compliments, so she'd take whatever he'd give. Happily she said, "I'm glad, I guess. If I was mousy before, I definitely want to change."

"You were never mousy," Sam chided. He rested his elbow on the open window and seemed to be enjoying her good mood. "But it's amazing how much self-confidence one smashed bottle can give."

By seven in the evening, they arrived in a crossroads kind of community, complete with an old cattle yard near the train depot. On such a Friday night, even small-town shops stayed open, so Sam found his way to a sporting goods store on a back alley. The front window was crowded with camping equipment and a pyramid of bug repellent cans. There were three lovely wooden canoes in the showroom, arranged like works of art in a gallery. Racks of running shorts, warmup jackets and nylon swimsuits were arranged along one wall. In the back of the store were the bikes, all sleek imported machines.

A clerk appeared from behind a curtain that divided the showroom from the employees' work area, wiping his hands in a greasy rag as he approached. "Hi, folks. Can I help you tonight?"

Sam fell into conversation with the young man, and while the two of them talked technicalities, Beth wandered through the bicycles, running her fingertips along a leather seat here or tape-wrapped handlebars there. Each bike looked the same as the next, at first, the way all the horses in the pasture initially had to Beth when she saw them. But gradually the horses had become three distinct personalities, and Beth soon began to see small differences in the bicycles, too.

"She wants a red one," Sam said with amusement, raising his voice so that Beth could hear. He signaled for her to come back to him.

"Red?" The clerk asked rhetorically, eyeing Beth's figure with the air of a French couturier sizing up a model—detached and scientific. "I think we've got something in red that'll fit this little lady. We carry only the best bikes, so you're gonna be pleased, I'm sure. Except when it comes to paying for it," he warned. "We don't sell cheap machines, you know."

"That's all right," Sam said placidly. Then he stood back to relinquish command of the shopping expedition.

They searched through the displayed machines, and the clerk soon chose a slim Motobecane with a burnished red finish, spanking new tires and sparkling chrome. It was practically weightless, Beth discovered, for the clerk asked her to pick it up. He also asked her to get aboard, and he got out his tape measure. He wanted to be sure the bike fit her body perfectly.

Beth sat on the seat, her bottom slipping instinctively, it seemed, into the groove of the saddle. The clerk crouched below her, and grasped her knee. He was businesslike. "Now stretch," he commanded. "There. Good."

His hand felt impersonal, yet firm on her knee. Beth obeyed his command and held still while he measured. Then he slid his hand higher, positioning her thigh so that she extended her muscles. Beth smiled to herself. How could one man's hand feel so different from another's?

She glance up at Sam.

He stood observing with one hand thrust down into the pocket of his jeans, seemingly entranced by the sight of the young man handling the curve of her thigh through her khaki-colored slacks.

"Nice extension," the clerk noted. "Very nice. Okay, bend here. Good."

Beth obeyed him, rotating the pedal once while he measured and adjusted. He slid his hand up the outside of her thigh until he was almost clasping her bottom. Beth didn't shift away from his touch, but she suddenly felt awkward with another man's hand on her. She closed her eyes and tried to pretend that nothing was happening. Then—foolishly—Beth began to imagine that it was Sam who was touching her. Would his hand feel so impersonal? No, Beth decided that Sam would handle her quite differently. Unconsciously, she began to smile at her thoughts.

"A little more," the clerk said, and he steadied her again, on her buttock this time.

Sam cleared his throat meaningfully, and the moment broke.

The clerk looked at Sam, then snatched his hand away, and Beth opened her eyes hurriedly. Sam was all but glowering at the clerk, who was suddenly nervous enough to start chattering about the bike, giving vital statistics and naming famous international bicyclists who were using that particular model. Beth didn't listen. She knew Sam wasn't listening either. He was actually flushed!

When Beth looked up and caught him frowning, Sam jerked his attention from the clerk, and tried to collect himself. He managed a weak smile for Beth, but ended up looking guilty and a little embarrassed, and definitely stubborn. With inner glee, Beth realized that Sam was jealous!

Then, as the clerk nervously talked on, Sam must have realized how foolish the moment had become. He also read something in

Beth's expression, for his gaze warmed on hers. It was a communicative look that passed between them, a look that left Beth's cheeks tingling with a blush of pleasure. Whatever had been on Sam's mind, it certainly had something to do with her thighs!

He winked at her then, his smile growing. While Beth watched, Sam allowed himself one long appreciative look down her body, his eyebrows eloquently lifted to show her that he approved of her long, slim legs.

Still pink-cheeked when the measuring was done, Beth slid off the bike when she was told. Sam caught her hand to steady her, and Beth impulsively slipped her arm around his waist. She smiled up at him, and Sam responded by moving his hand up into her hair and giving it a fond tug.

If the clerk noticed their behavior he might have thought that they were newlyweds, but he was too busy chattering, having been caught inadvertently fondling the wife of a jealous man. Still anxious, he promised to have the machine ready in an hour and ushered them out the door.

Beth found that she was just as excited by Sam's attentiveness as she was about getting her new bike. She hugged his hand in both of hers and hoped that he wouldn't let her go as soon as they got outside.

Sam, playing the indulgent parent, decided they had better celebrate the new bicycle. Still holding her hand, he took Beth across the street to a restaurant with no name except a neon sign that read Eat outside. A few tables were full of middle-aged, casually dressed men and women, some smoking after-dinner cigarettes, some with their chairs tipped back comfortably. A few cowboy hats were in evidence, Beth noted, as Sam threaded his way through the murmuring crowd. No one spoke to them. Sam's hand was proprietorily firm around hers anyway as he led her toward the back of the restaurant.

They found a booth, one with well-used red leatherette cushions and a gray marbleized tabletop, which showed a cigarette burn on one corner. Sam helped Beth in and then slid into the opposite seat against the wall. He plucked plastic-coated menus out from behind the sugar dispenser and handed one across to her. Beth took it and pulled, but Sam didn't let go, teasing her, until she met his eyes and smiled at him. Satisfied, he let her have the menu and settled back to read his. Beth was so pleased by his increasing attention that she couldn't concentrate on the printed pages. If she didn't know him better, she'd say he was almost flirting!

Perhaps just seeing another man touch her had thrown a switch in Sam's head. He was suddenly quite possessive of his wife. Perhaps a caveman just needed to see another Neanderthal clubbing his mate before he decided he wanted to keep her after all. Men were always making peculiar decisions about women, she decided. And Beth didn't mind at all in this case. She hid her smile behind her menu.

Reading down through the list of selections, Sam said, "I'm starved all over again. You?"

"A little," Beth admitted. She looked at him shyly over the rim of her menu, still smiling. "Now that I think of it, as long as we don't have to cook or do dishes, I'm famished. Think they'd give us a few orders to go? To last a few days?"

Sam laughed at her and said he doubted it, and then a gum-cracking waitress arrived to take their orders.

Because Beth couldn't decide quickly enough, Sam ordered hamburgers and home fries for both of them, a beer for himself and a milkshake for Beth. As an afterthought, he added a side dish of onion rings for them to share. Beth laughed at him, for he was unwilling to give up the menu too quickly. He enjoyed eating, after all, she thought.

"I guess I'd better get my cooking skills back," she said when the waitress had gone. "You're too thin, I think."

"I'd better stay that way if I'm going to keep up with you on your new bike," he said with a grin, changing the subject. "You're a speedster."

"Am I?" Beth asked, eager to cash in on Sam's newfound policy change on flirtation. So far, he had not been one to turn a woman's head with sweet talk.

"Fishing for compliments?" Sam asked, seeing through her, immediately. His green-gray eyes were sparkling as he watched her face.

"How am I going to get any compliments if I don't fish?" Beth demanded lightly. "I have only one person in the entire world to communicate with now, and with my usual luck I've landed a man who talks to his horses more than he does to me!"

Startled, Sam blinked. "What do you mean?"

Beth waved her hand in careless dismissal. "I shouldn't complain. I used to be in a crowded hospital, that's all. Everybody used to make a fuss over me, so I'm spoiled. Now I'm out here in No Man's Land and there's no one to talk to but you—and you're doing your Gary Cooper imitation all the time."

Without taking offense, Sam gave her a real Gary Cooper-ish stoic look and drawled, "Yup."

Beth laughed at his playacting. "See what I mean?"

"I don't talk to you enough? All right. I'm just afraid of saying the wrong thing, to tell you the truth."

"You can't say the wrong thing. I'm not going to go crazy, you know."

With a sudden grin, Sam asked, "Do you know how close I came to getting my head broken open by a flying bottle today?"

"I'll never live that down, will I?"

"Probably not," Sam agreed with a laugh. "All right, I'll talk more with you, Beth, if it's going to help. How do you know about Gary Cooper?"

Beth laughed in astonishment. "What? How did we get around to him as a topic of conversation?"

Sam shrugged his shoulders guilelessly. "We've got to start somewhere. I'm curious, that's all. You remember some very obscure things sometimes, and the rest of your mind is blank. How do you know about Joan Crawford and Gary Cooper and not know things like—"

"Like how to melt chocolate in a double boiler when I must have done it a hundred times?"

"Exactly."

The waitress arrived with their drinks, and Beth accepted her milkshake with a half-hearted smile at the woman. She began to peel the paper from the plastic straw and said pensively, "I don't know why I remember some things and not others. It's a weird feeling. Dr. Westham said that my brain might be damaged in some places, but perfectly healthy in others. The other theory is that my amnesia is hysterical. I *want* to remember some parts of my life, but my subconscious is suppressing the things that I don't want to recall."

Wonderingly, Sam shook his head. "It's phenomenal."

Beth's smile was quick and half apologetic. "I like to think my problem is brain damage, not hysteria. Otherwise, why would I want to suppress my life with you? It couldn't have been—was it bad, Sam? Our life together? Why would I want to forget it?"

"I can't imagine," Sam said calmly. Then he drank off the top of his beer and said, "But you are beginning to remember certain things, aren't you? Today, when you got off the bike, I could see a new—I don't know exactly, but you looked different, as if you'd discovered something important."

"I had. The bike felt so totally—so perfect, I guess. I just *knew* I'd been there before." She smiled curiously. "Did I really look different?"

He laughed and sat back, toying with his glass of beer and watching her. "Fishing again. Yes, for a moment I thought you had remembered everything. I thought you knew exactly who you were."

"How did I look different?" she pressed, determined to get a nice word out of him. She put her elbows on the table and tried not to look too coquettish.

"Not different different." Sam grinned. Then he relented and said, "All right, yes, you looked beautiful. You're very nice to look at, Beth. All the time. I spend half my time gawking at you like a teenager, and don't pretend you don't notice. There was a different excitement about you today, that's all. You had an animation in your face I hadn't seen before."

"There you go again. I'm an automaton, am I?"

"That's too strong a word," Sam said promptly. "I'm sorry I used it before. You're just—" He thought for a moment and said, "Sometimes you just look as if you've retreated into yourself. You don't respond as quickly or with as much life as . . ."

"As I used to? As Elizabeth used to?"

Sam didn't answer that. He said only, "You just need more life in you, I think. I'm not a doctor, Beth. I don't know what's best for you. I should be giving you more, I suppose, and I'm not."

Trying to stay light, Beth said, "You're just afraid I'm going to go crazy like I did today. You don't have to treat me like an invalid, you know. I'm pretty tough, honest."

"Tougher than I am," Sam agreed with a smile. He reached for his pocket and changed the subject abruptly. "How about some music? Let's see what songs you can remember, all right?"

There was a jukebox in the corner, just a few steps away, and it didn't take any coaxing to get Beth out of her seat and hanging over the bright lights of the machine. Sam, with an uncharacteristic burst of foolishness, found a bunch of quarters in his pocket and fed them all into the jukebox. Beth chose a few songs, mostly Beatles oldies, but she laughed at Sam's choices, which included a song about a teeny weeny bikini and something sung by squeaky-voiced chipmunks.

What was nicest of all was the casual way Sam slung his arm around her shoulders, his hand resting lightly on her collarbone as he talked to her. When he wasn't pointing at the numbers of the jukebox, his fingertips grazed the top of Beth's breast through her sweater. If he had moved an inch lower, he might have felt her nipple, which was suddenly taut and erect under his seemingly unconscious touch. Feeling light-headed with her own bravery, Beth slipped her hand into the back pocket of Sam's jeans, the way she'd seen a young girl do at the hospital. Underneath her palm, she could feel the smooth contour of his buttocks. Sam didn't move away, but didn't seem totally unaware of her touch either. Beth smiled with him, but felt her throat go very dry. In this public place they could touch and fondle each other with so much more ease than in their own kitchen! It didn't make sense, and yet Beth didn't care. It felt great to stand next to him, to feel his arm, his hand, his bottom. In a moment he made her laugh again. His next choice was a song sung by a growly-voiced man who wanted a woman with a wiggle in her walk because, he sang, that's what made the world go 'round.

They were still laughing over the machine when their food arrived. Beth wished they could sit on the same side of the table together, but Sam passed her down into her own seat once more and sat across from her. Separated, Beth felt absurdly shy with him again, but she tried to mask that feeling.

They ate, still in good spirits. Beth teased Sam about his appetite, and he responded quickly by deriding her cooking abilities. They laughed warmly and enjoyed themselves. Beth was delighted to find that Sam could shed his serious nature in favor of his sense of humor from time to time. She finally felt that he had let down his guard with her.

In spite of their late-afternoon popcorn and sandwiches, Sam polished off Beth's milkshake for her when they'd cleaned their plates, and then he went to the counter to pay the bill. Beth lingered by the doorway, watching Sam with a smile as the waitress tried futilely to flirt with him. Sam didn't notice, it seemed. He pocketed his change, returned to the table to leave a tip and came to the door, taking Beth's elbow with familiar ease.

"All set?"

"Sure."

Sam pressed through the door and steered Beth out onto the sidewalk. They hesitated there in a pool of artificial light, for evening had fallen. Above Beth's head, Eat flashed.

From several yards away, a man's voice hailed them. "Sam! Sam Sheridan?"

Sam spun around, as if he'd been shot instead of spoken to.

The man, a lean but bow-legged stranger in dusty jeans and a denim jacket advanced on them, one hand in his pocket, the other fingering a toothpick at the corner of his lip. He had a black cowboy hat on his head, set back on the crown. He was young, but his face was craggy, and his neck was tanned from working outdoors. He exuded an almost sexual kind of confidence men use when confronting their equals. He was squinting at Sam, grinning. "It is, isn't it?"

"Oh," Sam said, sounding disconcerted. "Delaney, right?"

The man extended his hand and shook Sam's heartily. "Yeah, that's it. Ralph Delaney. We met at the spring auction and you came back with us for coffee. I thought I recognized you even gussied up for town."

"Hello," said Sam, who was looking perfectly ordinary to Beth in his jeans and sweater and his Harris tweed jacket slung over his shoulder. To the man who was making friendly overtures, he said, "You bought some sheep, I think?"

"And nearly ruined my reputation as a cattleman," Delaney agreed with a sudden grin. He looked directly at Beth. "I see you've got a friend with you this time."

"Uh, yes," Sam said. "Beth, Ralph and I met several months ago. He has some property north of us."

Beth smiled and stuck out her hand. "Hi. Glad to meet you."

The rancher shook her hand awkwardly, like a man not accustomed to shaking hands with women. He was a small-town Lothario, apparently. He bobbed his head and tipped his hat and gave a funny little bow, as if going through all the possible gestures a man ought to politely give a lady. He studied her intently as though deciding how attached Beth might be to Sam and calculating his own chances with her. He smiled. "Nice to meet you, miss. In town to do some shopping?"

"Yes. We're buying a bike."

"Oh," said Delaney, glancing up at Sam with a friendly frown. "I figured you folks'd do your shopping in Two Forks. This is kind of out of your way, isn't it, Sam?"

Sam took a step backward to escape the irritating flash of neon light. Strangely—for Beth felt it rather than saw it, so she couldn't be sure—Sam's manner changed. Abruptly he was the famous playwright from New York, a superior man greeting a lesser individual. He held his head stiffly, as if aloof. In a cool voice that didn't sound a bit normal, he explained, "We drove over here to look for a place that carries imported bicycles. The good ones are hard to come by sometimes."

Beth glanced up at Sam uncertainly, puzzled by his condescending tone. Was he jealous of this character, too?

"I see," agreed Delaney, eyeing Sam warily now, also. He tried to be friendly again, though, asking, "How'd those calves turn out for you? Gettin' up to weight?"

"Yes," Sam said, and—unwillingly—he answered the other rancher's questions about his cattle.

Beth listened, not to their conversation, but to Sam's inflections and choice of words. Either he didn't like Mr. Delaney, or he wanted to terminate the conversation as quickly as possible. Wondering why, she glanced across the street at the sporting goods shop and noticed that the clerk had already snapped off the lights in the front window. So that was it. Sam wanted to pick up the bike before the store closed for the night. Beth slipped her hand into Sam's and squeezed gently to give him a signal.

"Well, we'd better get along," Sam said half a second later, as he gripped Beth's hand tightly. His voice sounded falsely cheerful. "Good to see you again, Ralph."

"Sure," Ralph Delaney said. "Maybe you'd like to pay us a visit again one of these days? You know where to find us."

"Right," Sam answered, already pulling Beth off the sidewalk and out into the street. "G'night."

If Beth hadn't been watching for oncoming traffic, Sam might have walked directly into the path of a passing pickup truck. Beth yanked on his hand, and the truck whizzed by with just eighteen inches to spare. The driver stuck his head out the window and shouted something back at them, shaking his head.

"Jeez!" Sam said under his breath, startled by the truck.

Beth laughed at him, trotting across the street to keep up with his long strides. "What's the matter with you, anyway? You acted like that poor man had a contagious disease."

"Did I?" Sam asked, disbelieving. He loosened his crushing grip, but didn't quite let go. Regaining the companionable tone of voice he'd used in the restaurant, he teased, "You must have imagined it. Something else is wrong with your head now!" With his other hand, Sam whisked Beth's straight hair back from her cheek. He smiled down at her. "Ready for your bike?"

"Yes," said Beth, returning his smile warmly. Never before had she felt so close—so attuned to Sam. She hoped they weren't interrupted by any more Ralph Delaneys for the rest of the night. She just wanted to be alone with Sam again. Swinging his hand a little, she dismissed the last few minutes of his odd behavior from her mind, and decided to tease him back. "Do you think I ought to ride it home? Or don't you want to be left behind?"

Sam smacked her on the bottom, and Beth scooted through the shop door, laughing.

He paid for the bike, and the clerk helped him put it into the back of the truck. After the machine had been strapped down, Beth lovingly covered it with a tarp, taking care that it wouldn't flap loose during the drive home. Sam helped her into the truck and then went around his side and got in behind the wheel.

He slammed his door shut and said, "Well? Do you like it?"

Beth sighed contentedly, settling back. "I love it!"

"Pleased with it?" he asked as he stuck the keys into the ignition. "You're sure that's the one you want?"

"Of course!" She looked at him in surprise. "Are you having second thoughts?"

Sam smiled a little and rested his forearm on the steering wheel. "About the bike? No. The temperature's dropping, isn't it? Are you cold?"

Beth couldn't see the expression on his face. The distant light from the street didn't quite reach into the cab of the truck, so Sam's eyes were in shadow. There was a quality in his voice, though, that caused Beth to hesitate. He didn't want to be thanked, she knew. Oddly, though, she knew he wanted something.

By instinct, she said softly, "Yes. I'm a little chilled." and she slid across the seat to him.

"Better?" Sam asked with a smile in his voice as he reached for the ignition.

So he had felt a new intimacy growing between them, too.

They rode the whole way home, or at least half an hour's worth, in silence. At first it seemed a silence full of anticipation. Gradually, however, the wonderful tension of their evening began to fade. Though Sam did not speak, Beth knew that he was drawing away from her. The closer they got to home, the more he seemed to retreat physically from her body.

But Beth remained determinedly nestled into Sam's side, with one of her legs curled up under the other so that her thigh was snug against his harder muscled leg. Each time the truck bounced, Beth's whole body lurched into his, though the contact was not a shock, but rather an absorbing of the energy.

Beth didn't dare turn her head to study Sam's face as it was illuminated by the dashboard lights. It wasn't that she was afraid of what she'd see. She knew what would show in his expression. He would smooth his face and pretend he hadn't been thinking what he'd been thinking. She'd seen him do it fifty times a day.

Why did he have to be so damned cautious with her? Why couldn't he just act natural when he admired her legs or made some casual reference to how nice she looked? At home Sam wouldn't dream of winking at her, and yet he'd done exactly that at the bicycle shop. Was he still worried about her reaction to his growing sexual interest? Beth reasoned that they weren't going to get any closer if Sam was always pulling back out of concern for her well-being.

Suddenly Beth didn't want to go home. Once they were alone in their own house, Sam would back off and pretend he had never smacked her in fun or rested his hand just above her breast. He'd keep his distance, as he'd done before. The evening was almost over. Cinderella's carriage would soon be a pumpkin again.

Casually, Beth dropped her fingertips onto Sam's thigh. Through his jeans, she could feel no tensing of muscle, but no careful relaxation either. It was as if Sam deliberately suppressed his response to her. Thoughtfully, experimentally, Beth traced her forefinger down to his kneecap. It felt good to sit near him this way. It was almost going to hurt to be separated from him when they got home again. Beth wanted to prolong their happy evening together.

Perhaps—for a few more minutes—Sam wanted to sustain the intimacy of this time, also. As if the wispy pressure of Beth's fingertips on his knee had prompted him, Sam broke the stillness.

"Beth," he said, sounding cautious, "what do you remember about the facts of life?"

CHAPTER EIGHT

BETH'S HEART LEAPED. "Wh-what?"

"The facts of life," Sam repeated. "The birds and the bees. Sex, I suppose. The—"

Beth let out a sputtering sort of laugh and snatched her hand from his knee. She covered her smile and couldn't stop herself from glancing up at Sam's profile. The lights from the dashboard illuminated the almost stark planes of his face, and Beth belatedly tried to swallow her laugh. Sam was being serious. She jerked her gaze back to the highway in front of them. "I—I know what you meant."

"I'm just curious," Sam said, trying to pretend that the question was perfectly natural. "You remember the strangest things, that's all. Joan Crawford and bicycles. I just wondered what you remembered about . . ."

Beth fixed her eyes on the highway and determinedly did not giggle, though the temptation was incredible. Finishing his sentence, she said, "Erotic games."

"No," Sam said, sounding uncomfortable. "Just—physical intimacy, I guess. I wondered what you remember, if anything."

Beth was surprised to find herself blushing, and she was glad Sam couldn't see her. He'd back off if he thought he was upsetting her. Now it seemed that Sam's attitudes really were changing! To be blunt was the best way to answer, she decided, and she said, "I know what goes where, if that's what you mean. You don't have to explain the logistics to me."

He smiled grimly at that. "That's a relief."

Beth linked her hands in her lap. Getting braver, she added, "But I didn't remember all about bicycling until I was actually on the bike, you know."

Sam started to say something, then reconsidered his response and ended up clearing his throat instead.

Tentatively, Beth peeked up at him and asked, "Sam, are you leading up to something?"

"No," Sam said promptly.

"Sure?"

"I just wondered, that's all. I'm trying to find out what kinds of things you do remember and what you don't. Naturally, I wondered if—uh—well—"

"Naturally," Beth agreed, turning her gaze back to the columns of light created by the truck's headlights. "Sam?"

"Yes?"

Beth stretched her legs comfortably and tried to sound casual. "Should I be afraid of sex?"

"Afraid?" Sam was startled. "Of course not. I didn't mean to frighten you by asking. I just—"

"You're being very cagey," Beth interrupted gently. Her gambit was working. For once she was getting some feelings out of Sam, instead of pouring out her soul to him. She said, "I'm beginning to wonder if there's something I should know. Have you got some perversities?"

He laughed shortly, as if embarrassed. "Where did you learn about perversities?"

"I was in the mental ward, remember? With a dozen cops hanging around me day and night who wanted to know all about a rapist-murderer."

"Oh, God," Sam sighed. "You must have gotten quite an education."

"Actually, I got my best information from the television, not the cops or other patients. Do you know what goes on during those afternoon drama programs? Very hot stuff," Beth said cheerily. "I learned a few things, all right, but there's probably something you can still teach me about eroticism."

"Beth . . ." he protested, cautious again.

After his voice died out, Beth waited an eternity and finally had to prompt him. "I'm listening," she said.

But Sam just sighed once more, apparently giving up.

This subject was too fascinating not to finish properly, so Beth plunged ahead. "Sam, I really wish you'd stop being so darned careful with me all the time. I'm *nervous* about the facts of life, as you so quaintly called it, but I can't understand why you're so uptight about it. Unless there's something you're not telling me. Or maybe you just don't find me very attractive!"

"Of course I do," he said immediately.

"Do you?"

"Yes. You're beautiful," Sam insisted, rising to the bait. "And you turn me on at the strangest times, believe me. Tonight when that guy had his hands all over your legs I wanted to—to—"

"To what? Have sex with me?"

He must have winced, because his voice was tense next when he said, "It wouldn't be sex, Beth."

"Why not? Oh—" Beth said, catching on. "There's a better word?"

"For people who are married, yes. For people like you and me, yes."

"Making love," Beth said quietly. The fun of teasing him left her like a whoosh of cold air putting out a candle. Her pleasant evening—her Cinderella night of romance—had suddenly turned to reality. Until now, she could pretend that Sam had happily taken his wife to town to buy her a love present. Absently, without thinking, she said, "I see."

"What do you see?"

She might as well say it and get everything out in the open. Beth swallowed and said tersely, "That we're not going to make love, because we're not *in* love."

"Lord, Beth," Sam breathed, sounding agonized. "Don't make me feel like such a louse!"

Beth looked up at him in surprise. "Do you feel like a louse?"

"Yes, dammit. Look, you know that I care for you very much. I do, honestly, but you've got to understand!"

"Understand what?"

Explosively, he said, "That we're just not ready yet."

"So there's hope?" Beth asked, with a flicker of malice. "We *may* fall back into love?"

Sam was clenching his teeth, obviously feeling very uncomfortable. The truck had gained the entrance to the farm by that time, so he concentrated fiercely on negotiating the gate, which was wide enough for a Sherman tank, let alone a small pickup. Still, Sam pretended to need all his attention for driving.

He pulled the truck slowly—very slowly—under the light at the door of the barn, but didn't shut off the engine. Then he set the emergency brake, sat very still, both hands on the steering wheel, and asked quietly, "Is that what you'd like?"

"To fall in love with you?" Beth didn't touch him, though she wanted to. She wanted to hold him, to slip her arms around Sam's neck and whisper the words in his ear. But some instinct told her that it would be more effective just to tell him bluntly.

So she said simply, "I have already."

Of course, absolute silence is not what a woman wants to hear at such a climactic moment. The nerve-racking rumble of the engine made Sam's lack of response even more obvious. When a full thirty seconds had passed, Beth reached forward with irritation, fumbled with the keys and finally shut off the truck herself.

In the resulting deathly stillness she sat back and folded her arms. Tartly, she said, "I think the prince is supposed to kiss the frog now and we'll live happily ever after."

Sam didn't laugh, didn't move. "You're not a frog."

"And you're certainly no prince, are you?"

"I'm sorry," Sam said, still not moving his hands from the steering wheel. "I wish I could think of the right thing to say."

"No quote for the occasion?"

Sam must have heard the tension quaver in her voice by then. As if common courtesy finally took command in his brain, he turned toward her, his voice gentle. "No quote," he murmured, reaching for her wrist. "I like your idea better."

He had every intention of kissing her, but for the first time Beth resisted him. He had her wrist in one hand, and he slipped his other hand around the back of her neck, caressing her bare skin underneath the curtain of her hair. He paused then, waiting like a courtly gentleman for Beth to turn toward him, to offer herself to his kiss.

But she stubbornly didn't move.

Sam tugged at her hand, coaxing.

Beth deliberately disengaged herself and slid across the seat to the passenger door. She said, "You don't have to kiss me if you don't want to."

"Beth!" Sam objected in frustration.

She let herself out into the chill of the night and closed the door behind her without slamming it. At the back of the truck, she started to untie the tarp.

Sam piled out of the other side and slammed the door. With the barn light shining above them, he faced her over the bed of the truck. "Beth, I didn't mean to make you angry."

"I am not angry." She yanked the cord, and the tarp flapped noisily free.

"I've insulted you, then. I'm sorry. I wish I could say the right things to you, but I won't lie—oh, brother!" He ran his hand through his hair and started again, "I don't like being dishonest with you, so—"

"Never mind, then. Will you help me with this damn thing, please? I can't get the bike out myself."

"I'd rather—"

She cut him off, threatening, "I'll do it by myself if you won't help!"

"All right," Sam said swiftly, giving in. He vaulted over the rim of the truck bed and clambered in beside the bicycle. As he started to loosen the bungee cords, he said, "Beth, I want you to trust me—to keep on trusting me, so I won't tell you anything that's—"

"Just drop it, all right? I never said you had to love me back. I can't help the way I feel, Sam. You've been very nice to me. Sweet even. How do you expect a girl *not* to fall in love with you when you act the way you do? And this touch-me-not attitude of yours just makes me want to touch you all the more. So don't—"

"I never said you couldn't touch me."

"But you jump like a mountain goat every time I do."

"I do not!"

"Oh, God!" Beth exclaimed, wheeling away from the truck in frustration. "This is such a stupid argument!"

"Don't go storming off like a wounded female!"

Beth spun around and glared up at Sam. "I *am* a wounded female! *You* put the silly bicycle in the barn! I'm going inside where I won't be in your way."

"Beth, you do not—Beth!"

But she started walking and didn't look back.

Sam uttered a heartfelt oath and gave up on the bicycle. Beth heard him jump down from the truck, but she didn't stop. He came charging after her, catching up when she got as far as the porch.

"The door's locked," she said crossly. "I don't have any keys."

"It's never locked. Forget the door," Sam said, catching her by the shoulders. "Wait a minute."

Beth threw off his hands and spun on him. Her eyes were narrow, their color cold. "Don't touch me, please. I feel like I'm asking too much when you touch me."

Sam stared. *"What?"*

The light was bad, and Beth couldn't see his face exactly, but that didn't stop her. The words burst angrily from inside her. "You're so damned stingy when it comes to simple things like hugs and—and little pats and things! I think you've already used up your quota today, so don't—"

"I touch you constantly!"

"You do not!" she cried. "I can count exactly how many times you've ever laid a hand on me! You always hesitate before you do it—like you're deciding if the particular situation is suitable for a—a hug or even a kiss once in a while. Except for a very few times—like that first morning when I got here and Connor was—was pushing me and you came up from behind and just held me until I felt better. Except for a few times like that, you've got to *think* before you do it!" Beth turned and walked to the porch railing. To the night, she said coldly, "I will not beg for attention from you, Sam!"

Mystified, he demanded, "Beg for—?"

"You heard me. Don't pretend you don't understand."

"I pay attention to you constantly. When I'm here, I mean. There's still a farm to run, and I can't always be—"

This was getting too scary for Beth. Baiting Sam with teases had been one thing, but risking her own temper and teetering on the edge of some kind of outburst was another. Still, she was determined to make her point without giving up this time. Beth cut him off, but her voice cracked. "You just don't pay the kind of attention to me that—that a wife expects from a husband."

Sam stopped, and his hands fell to his sides. Perhaps trying to disarm her, he said lightly, "What do you know about husbands and wives? What you learned from television soap operas?"

Beth heard his tone. *"Don't* patronize me, Sam!" she snapped nastily. "Save your condescending superiority for Mr. Delaney and the FBI. You know perfectly well what I mean!"

He gave a quick unamused laugh. "Do *you* know what you mean?"

Beth seethed, grinding her teeth and clenching her hands at the same time. She felt like she was holding a California earthquake at bay all by herself, and she couldn't hold on much longer. Something made her go ahead, though. She said, "Yes, I do. I like it when you're natural with me. And when you're not being natural, I can feel the wall you put up around yourself. It—it's a wall that's very strong when we're here in this house alone together. But tonight . . . in town when you—when we—"

"Look—" he began.

"If you're going to go back to being standoffish, you can't blame me for wondering why!" Beth was half shouting now, and her body was trembling so that she had to hug her arms to contain herself. "I'm not stupid, you know. A simple explanation would satisfy me, so don't worry about hurting my feelings. Just don't play games with me, dammit!"

Mildly, he said, "You can really get angry after all, can't you?"

Beth could have turned around and kicked him. Or slapped him. Or even punched him right in the home fries. He was absolutely thickheaded to not *listen* when she was telling him about her deepest concerns. Frustration and anger welled up inside her, but she was helpless to release them. She should have clobbered him.

As it was, however, she burst into tears.

"Oh, God," said Sam, really shaken.

Humiliated, she put her face into her hands and didn't turn around. "Go away."

"Beth—"

"D-don't *touch* me," she commanded before his hands made contact with her again. Hunching her shoulders, she warned, "Just d-don't."

"You've been very good up until now, Beth. Don't spoil your record. Come on. Don't cry." Annoyed, he added, "Please."

Gritting her teeth to hold back the threatening deluge, Beth managed to say, "If you don't like crying, you're going to have to go away and leave me alone for a while. I can't just shut my feelings off the way you seem to be able to."

He sighed. "You were right. This has been a very stupid argument—but this is an even more stupid way to end it."

"Ooh, you make me angry!" Beth smacked her hand against the porch railing.

"Come inside and we'll talk about this."

Stubbornly, she snapped, "I've already talked. If *you* want to talk, do it right here. I'm sick of talking. I talk all the time." Beth gave a hard, hiccupping kind of sob and dashed the tears from her face with a swift gesture. She added, "I think it's your turn for once!"

Deadly silence. Finally, Sam asked from behind her. "Do you want me to lie to you?"

Beth squeezed her eyes shut. "No."

"Then I can only tell you again what you should already know."

Sam came forward a pace and laid his hands on her shoulders. If Beth winced and tried to escape, he didn't notice. His grip was hard, almost hurting, as if he wanted to press the weeping out of her for good. Abruptly, he said, "I'll explain as clearly as I can, if it will help. Look, Beth, I care for you, and you know it. How could I not? But I'm not storybook in love with you right now because our past is *nothing* like our present, is it?"

Beth didn't answer.

Sam continued slowly, "I said from the beginning that I wouldn't force myself on you in any kind of sexual or emotional way. And I've been making an honest effort to keep my hands off you so I wouldn't scare you into the stratosphere by bringing back bad memories. You have a right to be scared. Beth, the last man who touched you—touched you the way a man touches a woman—was a crazy, murdering sadist. Don't you think that's going to affect things between us if we ever end up in bed together?"

She didn't move, didn't speak, but listened, her head turned slightly, her light hair falling straight across her cheek so that he couldn't see her face shining with stupid emotional tears. So Sam had been afraid, too. He'd been afraid of getting close to her in case she associated his advances with the man who had put her into the hospital.

Getting no response, Sam said, "Beth, I don't want to frighten you and God knows I don't want to hurt you. But if you're going to push me like this—"

"I'm not pushing you," she interrupted stiffly.

"Tonight at the bicycle shop when you—"

"*I* didn't do anything at the bicycle shop. I acted just the way I've always acted. Whatever happened took place in your own head."

Shortly, Sam released a breath. "Maybe so." He loosened his grip on her shoulders, but was not quite gentle yet. "Maybe being around you is finally getting to be too much of a temptation for me."

Beth whispered, "I'm not asking you to make love to me, Sam. I only wanted to understand why you've stayed so far away."

"It isn't because I'm not attracted to you." He slipped his fingertips up into her hair and played with it for a moment. "I just don't want to make things worse for you, Beth."

"What could be worse than being held at arm's length by the one person I want to share everything with?"

Something snapped inside him, for Sam gave up trying to explain. Roughly, he twisted his hand in her hair, jerking her head back until he could see her face. It was painful, but Beth didn't cry out. Meeting her gaze with his own, he said, "*This* could be worse. I can hurt you, Beth."

She saw the straight, unyielding planes of Sam's face, his serious mouth drawn into a tight line, and the warning glimmer of light behind his green-gray eyes. His expression was set like a mask. For a split second, Beth felt a tweak of fear inside herself. It pinched her in a spot just below her heart and froze her breath in her lungs very briefly. It was a queer feeling, for it sent a shiver of adrenaline racing through her system. She was afraid of Sam—just a little. He was strong, a fact she'd forgotten since that time in Dr. Westham's office. The promise of violence crackled in the air.

Without meeting his eyes, she whispered, "I—I don't think you could hurt me."

"Yes," said Sam, with the menace in his low voice very clear now. "I want you in every possible way a man could have a woman, and at least one of those ways could—"

"Physically I can't be hurt," Beth said swiftly.

Sam tightened his hold in her hair until Beth gasped and spun around completely to face him. Holding her hard, he demanded, "You can't?"

"Not for long," Beth said, keeping herself very still in spite of the way Sam held her head upright. She was more frightened now but tried to sound calm. "I've proven my strength, haven't I, Sam? Whoever beat my head and did all those other things to me—he tried to hurt me, didn't he? And I'm fine now. Nobody can hurt my body for long."

Sam put his other hand on Beth's hip, turning her just a fraction away from him—far enough that he could touch her freely. He found the curve of her waist, and smoothed his hand upward. It wasn't a caress, but something he intended to be unpleasant. "And emotionally, Beth? Can I hurt you emotionally?"

"M-maybe so," Beth replied, though her words were still barely a whisper. She suppressed a shiver as Sam touched her. He held her hair, tipping her face to his, but with his other hand he inched up along her sweater so slowly that he might have been counting her ribs beneath. Beth held still, barely breathing.

He found her breast and didn't hesitate. In the next second his thumb had found the nub of her nipple, and over it he made a slow circle and then another. Beth shuddered deep inside herself, and then her mind went deliciously blank. It wasn't unpleasant at all. Inside, her breast seemed to tingle with yearning. Her nipple turned hard under Sam's thumb; she was powerless to stop her own response.

Quietly, he said, "If I hurt your body for just a few minutes, what's that going to do to the muddle in your head, Beth?"

She met his eyes uncertainly. "What do you mean?"

"Is something going to snap in your mind?"

"Are you afraid I'm going to remember that other man?"

"If I make love to you? Yes." Sam smoothed his hand across her sweater and found her other nipple easily. He squeezed it between his fingers, all the while never taking his smoky eyes from hers. "Are you going to remember sex with him when you're with me?"

"I n-never had sex with him."

"But you could have come close."

"I don't know," Beth said, her throat jerking as she swallowed nervously, "I don't know what he did to me."

With his other hand, Sam found a better grip in Beth's hair, fondling it before he grasped the back of her head in an inescapable hold. He glanced up at the sky and mused coldly, "It was probably a night a lot like this, wasn't it? Not chilly yet. Not raining yet. A night with a storm in the air."

Mesmerized by his voice and the not-too-gentle handling of her breasts, Beth said stubbornly, "I don't know."

Sam bent closer and touched his lips to her temple. His mouth was warm, but demanding. With his lips against her cheek, he murmured, "I wonder if he kissed you?"

Beth closed her eyes, for her heart was skittering out of control and Sam was sure to see her warring emotions. She was determined to keep her cool, to show him that she couldn't be hurt by him. Unconsciously, she slipped her hands higher on his shoulders.

On her cheeks, Sam was tasting her tears, she knew. Then, swiftly, he found her mouth with his, and parted her lips at once, startling her. It was a hot kiss. His tongue sought its way inside before Beth could respond. Sam was rough, exploring boldly what he'd never tasted before. He ran his tongue along her teeth, under her tongue, around the warmth of her mouth so thoroughly that Beth could only cling to his shoulders and let him have his way.

Sam fumbled at the bottom of her sweater and tugged out the tail of her shirt. With her clothing loose, he invaded once more and found her breasts underneath. Pushing the brassiere out of his way, he covered her bare breast, his fingers feeling cool against her flesh until he pinched her nipple again. Beth didn't gasp. She wasn't frightened anymore, though some other emotion was sending her body into a rushing kind of high. She moaned very softly, sounding like a stranger to herself.

"He must have touched you here," Sam was saying, keeping his head close to hers and speaking right into her ear. His breath was quick against her throat. "He must have felt how soft you are. I wonder if your nipples did this for him?"

Sam withdrew his hand and then deliberately began to peel her sweater off. Beth felt the air strike the bare skin of her throat like a splash of cold water. A moment later Sam backed her into the porch railing and pinned her there with his thighs. He began to unfasten the buttons on her shirt. Beth held still to make the job easier, but even then she heard some buttons snap and scatter on the wooden floor. He was impatient. Beth, too, felt instinct take over. Though Sam was too excited to notice, Beth started to pull at his sweater also. By the time he had stripped her of her shirt and was irascibly pulling her bra over her head, Beth had successfully divested Sam of his sweater, too.

Barebreasted, she shivered in the night breeze. Her flesh popped out in goose bumps, but Beth didn't care. She didn't cover herself or try to pull Sam against her for warmth, but let him hold her at arm's length and gaze at her naked breasts. At the fiery expression in his eyes, she wasn't afraid. She felt happiness and pride that he found her desirable.

She didn't smile, though. Sam wanted this to be an experiment, it seemed. He was going to play this erotic game until she remembered the past and pulled away, or until he was satisfied that she was going to respond to him alone, not to the bizarre episode of three months past. She held still and let him play his fingers across her breasts. Then he stepped closer and smoothed his hands down her bare back, finding her throat with his lips. He pressed openmouthed kisses there, and, letting out a pent-up groan, pulled her close.

Sounding distant and dull-voiced with desire, Sam continued to mutter to himself, "I wonder if he thought you were beautiful? If he liked the way your back felt—strong, but smooth as porcelain? I wonder if he kissed your breasts?"

Sam pressed her into the railing and trailed his mouth down her chest. His breath was hot against her skin, and Beth let out an odd little sigh when Sam kissed her breast. He took the nipple in his mouth and rolled it with his tongue, not biting, but sucking her deliciously. Beth felt her legs weaken and sat back against the rail. She ran her fingers into Sam's hair, holding his head so that the hot contact was not broken. Letting her head loll back, she felt her hair brush down her shoulder blades. A moment later, Sam caught that hair in his hand again and pulled downward so that her body arched to meet his kisses. Beth might have been floating weightless on a warm ocean, for all she knew. Delight washed over her like sunshine.

He groaned against her skin, running his nose around one nipple and then the other. He didn't notice that Beth succeeded in unbuttoning his shirt. He didn't notice when she eased the fabric from his shoulders. Indeed, he found her throat with his mouth and bit lightly at the slender tendons there. "Beth," he whispered, "do you suppose he took your clothes off or made you do it? Did he tie your hands? Did he make you touch him? Did you feel how ready he was?''

Beth slipped her hands down Sam's bared chest, down his belly, down to his jeans. As bold as he, she cupped her fingers around the already rigid proof that the game had gone too far to call back. When Sam pressed eagerly into her hand, Beth smiled and said softly, "I feel how ready you are."

Then Sam unsnapped her slacks and slid his hand palm down inside. His fingers met the feminine curve beneath, and Beth struggled to contain her unconscious cry. This was new and scary, for her own body was responding with tiny explosions of carnal pleasure. Her blood was roaring in her ears so much that she could hardly hear Sam's voice. She felt his hand, though, insistently making his way lower.

Time to end the game. He was going over the edge of reality, and Beth put a stop to it. She lifted both her hands to his face, stroking his hair back gently. She found his lips with hers and kissed him lightly, once, twice, three times. She melted her mouth across his, coaxing the return of his gentleness. She touched his face, caressed his temples, then aligned her body with his and pulled Sam close to her.

She wrapped both arms around his shoulders and hugged him like a child to her breasts. Softly, she whispered, "I don't remember what he did to me. I only want to remember you, Sam. Make love to me any way you like, but don't play a role. You are, aren't you? Let's be you and me for the first time, please?''

Sam heard her. He hugged her for a moment, so hard that her ribs hurt with the pressure. He buried his face against her hair and tried to steady his breathing, regaining his wits. She thought he said her name, prayerfully soft. Then he bent and effortlessly picked her up in his arms. He kissed her mouth, gentle this time, though his eyes did not smile when their lips parted. Sam hesitated, and it was obvious to Beth that he was teetering on the edge of an unspoken question. The brief moment of decision stretched, during which she felt her heart take a despairing plunge, but she touched Sam's cheek and tried to smile at him. Her lips trembled like autumn leaves on the brink of falling.

From the darkness, a soundless breeze caressed the couple then, a cooling sign from beyond their own consciences. It carried the heady scent of storm-soaked pines, which sharpened human senses. Whatever message that breeze spoke to Sam, he reacted as if the words had been given aloud. *It was all right*. He could have her and not be guilty of wrong-doing. The time had come. Beth trusted him too much to be afraid.

Sam kissed her mouth once more and then turned toward the house. He shouldered the door open, carrying Beth inside, and strode through the kitchen without stopping, past the darkened furniture of the great room. Blue shafts of moonbeams slanted down from the skylights, eerily illuminating the room. By that light, Beth tried to see Sam's expression, but it was impossible. He went straight across to the bedroom door and pressed through. At the bedside, he set Beth on her feet.

"Beth—" he began, gathering her body to his own.

"Don't say anything," Beth interrupted quietly, as she slipped her arms around his neck and pressed her cheek to his in the darkness. "You'll just talk yourself out of this."

"Not now," he said with a half laugh that belied his tension. "If our lives depended on it now, I couldn't talk myself out of making love to you."

CHAPTER NINE

TENDER, SEARING and uninhibited. With rapture in her heart, Beth absorbed every beautiful sensation: tensile strength and contained power; an urgent quest for relief, and yet a mellow savoring of each new discovery; seething one moment and pliantly surrendering the next; an anguished cry followed by an echoing groan of sated male instincts; and finally a glow—a pensive time in which two souls mingled in tenderness and newfound contentment.

Making love with Sam had been slow, for he had thrown aside all attempts at self-control and had teased and taunted Beth far from her shyest inclinations to a sensual plane in which she did not recognize herself. She envisioned her body in a sensual vortex, heard her own breathless voice calling his name, pleading for release while urging him to greater abandon, too. Finally the rhythmic struggle cast her into a blissful abyss in which she clung to Sam and savored the pulsing moments of complete union. Beth had wept, for at last she had found her place, her home, herself. She had needed a base from which to blossom, a footing for her growing persona. She found a peace in Sam's arms, the power of another's strength to support her.

She could be her own person now, she knew. From Sam she had learned the value of being Beth. She wasn't going to seek the old Elizabeth anymore. She liked herself as Beth.

She slept in the curve of his body, secure in the belief that she was also snuggled deeply into his heart. Whether he could say the words or not, Beth knew that Sam loved her. It would just take him some time to realize that she wasn't Elizabeth anymore. He hadn't loved Elizabeth. At least not anymore. He did love Beth, though. She knew it. How could he make love with such passion, without reservation, and not love her?

He woke her with kisses before daybreak. They made love again, gently, without words, and when it was finished, the rays of sunshine lay warmly on the bed.

When Sam rolled over and started to sit up, Beth moaned in protest and locked her arms around his waist from behind. She pulled him back down into the warm sheets. "Don't go yet, please. I feel like this is a dream."

His voice was husky with sleep, wonderfully deep, yet soft. "You don't want to wake up yet?"

"No, not yet."

Sam turned and took Beth in his arms. He murmured, "No more nightmares?"

"No, no. I had a beautiful dream instead." Beth slid her hands up his arms, enjoying the warmth his skin radiated. She met Sam's eyes, then, feeling shy, yet compelled to tell him about the emotion she was feeling. Words seemed inadequate, though, so she whispered only, "A wonderful dream. I don't want to wake up at all. I think this is heaven."

Smiling at her, Sam kissed her tender mouth very lightly and quoted, " 'What angel wakes me from my flowery bed?' "

Beth smiled with him and closed her eyes, floating, it seemed, on a cloud very distant from reality. Heaven, yes.

Sam traced the shape of her features with his lips, reciting, " 'I pray thee, gentle mortal, speak again. Mine ear is much enamored of thy voice.' " He gave a funny growl and added lecherously, misquoting the rest of the lines from the same play to suit himself, "So is mine eye enthralled to thy shape!"

Smiling, adoring every tiny caress as much as the delicious presence of Sam's body aligned with hers, Beth felt the words come up from within the darkness of her soul. Without thinking, she said, " 'Thy fair virtue's force perforce doth move me On the first view, to say, to swear, I love thee!' "

The words were out and suddenly so startling that Beth's eyes flew open and she tensed in Sam's arms. She stared at him in surprise, astonished by what she had said.

"Beth!" Sam gasped, waking fast and equally amazed. "You just—do you—that was—"

"I quoted something!"

"*Midsummer Night's Dream*. I gave you the lead-in, and you knew the rest!"

She clutched him then, her nails digging heedlessly into Sam's shoulders. "Why? How? I hardly—"

"You did it!" Sam crowed delightedly. "You're really remembering, aren't you? A real literary quote, and a relatively obscure one at that! What a student you must have been!"

"Gosh, that's scary," she breathed, glad that Sam was holding her so snugly. "It's a funny feeling, you know. Like somebody else really is living in part of me. Oh, Sam."

"Steady, my angel," he said, cuddling her, petting her gently. "You're just gradually waking up from a very long dream, that's all. Don't be worried, all right?"

Beth began to relax at once. She supposed this was a sensation she was going to have to get accustomed to. Now and then her brain was going to expel a tiny clue to her past, but there was apparently no telling when or how the bits of information would come. Thoughtfully, she said, "I'm not worried. Not really. It's odd, though. So far, the things that I do remember are things I certainly don't expect. I didn't expect to be able to quote things from a play."

"You shouldn't be surprised. You're quite articulate. I think you're more literary than you expected, yes." He stroked her hair and said, "Don't let it worry you, all right? Let it come a little at a time, and we'll try to enjoy everything that's new."

Beth beamed at him and felt her heart expand with love. He was a gentle man with a steady wisdom she truly appreciated. How she loved him now! She closed her eyes once more and pulled him close to her again, sighing contentedly.

"You're not still sleepy?" he asked in a murmur, gathering her underneath him once more. "Are you going to spend all day in bed?"

Beth didn't open her eyes, but grinned whimsically. "With you?"

Softly, and with a smile in his eyes, Sam said, "I could be convinced."

Beth looped her arms around his neck and opened her eyes sleepily, her mouth curving. "What would it take? A promise of erotic games beyond imagination?"

"No," said Sam, his smile fading abruptly. His grayish eyes were solemn so quickly that it almost hurt Beth inside to see the light die out. He continued, "I think we'll avoid those for a while, all right? Please?"

Quick to respond to his change of mood, Beth stroked his hair with her fingertips and said seriously, "We played one last night, didn't we? You were—"

"We don't need to talk about it," Sam said swiftly, ducking his head to avoid her gaze. He played his nose in her hair and added, "Let's just forget last night. I shouldn't have acted that way."

"No," Beth whispered, hugging him close. "I won't forget it yet. Sam, I know you meant to test my memory, and now I understand that you stayed away from me for my own good. Do you know now that my knowledge of that—that attack is completely gone? That I don't remember any of it?"

"Yes," Sam murmured, holding her very tightly. "And I'm glad, Beth. Stay with me. I won't hurt you."

"You can't hurt me," she corrected with a returning smile.

Sam didn't answer, but he stroked her side and kissed her temples.

Beth trailed her fingertips up the back of his neck and played with his hair for a moment. She felt lazy and satisfied, and hardly inclined to leave the bed for the next several hours. She was content. It was time to put aside the unpleasant moments of last night and look to the future. Beth touched her lips to Sam's ear and asked softly, "It's Saturday, isn't it?"

Sam came up on one elbow, not sure he had heard her whispered change of topics correctly. "What?"

"It's Saturday, right?" She smiled winsomely at him. "You don't have to do any work, do you?"

Sam's eyes regained their sparkle, and he grinned curiously. "Are you insatiable, Mrs. Sheridan?"

She blushed, of course, and had to brazen it out. "For food, yes! I'm hungry after all those erotic things you showed me last night. Does my husband's pampering extend to breakfast in bed?"

Sam laughed, cuffed her bottom and sat up. "I'm spoiling you, aren't I? Enjoy it, my girl. Pretty soon we're going to reverse roles and you're going to pretend I'm a very demanding sultan."

Beth waved her hand airily to dismiss him. "Until then, I'll cash in on my good luck. Go peel me a grape, Abdul."

Sam threw his pillow at her and reached for his jeans.

Happily, Beth propped the pillows together and sat up in bed, watching while Sam snapped his jeans and sauntered out into the house. She admired his walk with glowing eyes and a quirky smile on her lips. He was quite a specimen of the male animal, she decided. Very nice to look at, and even more wonderful to touch. And this morning he was a little shy. So was Beth, she admitted, for they were new lovers now. With Sam suddenly yards away, Beth felt foolishly nervous. She wished he'd hurry up and come back, and considered calling him to the bedside for another kiss. But Sam had disappeared into the kitchen, and Beth heard him start to make coffee.

While the coffeepot gurgled, he returned with a fat stack of magazines and catalogs. He threw them on the bed and ordered her to start looking through them.

"Find some sexy nightgowns," he commanded playfully. "I'm partial to blondes in slinky black ones."

Beth reached for the catalogs, but looked up in surprise. "Really, Sam? Black lace?"

"Sure. What man doesn't like black lace?" He was smiling as he bent over Beth's reclining figure and tugged the sheet away from her breasts. He licked her there and laughed when she squealed and blushed bright red. Straightening, he added lightly, "Red lace and pink lace and blue lace. Anything that I can see through. Find some other things to wear, if you like, too. Skirts or shirts or pants. Whatever you want. You must need some clothes."

"Anything I want?" she inquired, and she sent a veiled and devilish look upward at him. "As long as you can see through them?"

Turning to go, Sam smiled ruefully. "Right."

He brought breakfast back to bed and shucked his jeans before climbing in with her again. Together, they ate toast and drank coffee and looked through the collection of catalogs. Some of them had rested on Sam's desk for months and were out of date, so Beth quickly sorted them and threw the really old ones over the side of the bed. Sam made a few suggestions, while munching his breakfast, pointing out a sweater he liked and then—with his morning shyness slowly evaporating—a sexy nightgown with doves appliqued over each breast.

Not too long after they started, though Sam got bored with looking at women's clothing, so he picked up some magazines and began glancing idly through them. While Beth leafed through Talbot's latest mail-order glossy, turning down the corners of certain pages and mentally making decisions about her new wardrobe, Sam read through an outdated issue of *Cycler's Highway* and an even older one of *Bike News*.

The morning went slowly, and that suited Beth just fine. Sam didn't look the least bit inclined to get out of bed, either. It was good to be side by side this way, a marital intimacy they had both needed. At last, however, Beth closed the last catalog and bravely inveigled her way into his arms, pushing aside his magazine. Sam laughed at her and they cuddled for a while, talking, making plans for the day, and now and then kissing tentatively, with the odd sort of shyness that had overtaken them now that they had blundered their way to a new plane of life together.

In time they decided to ride their bikes to Two Forks, to get a few groceries to supplement the vast supply in the freezer. Beth hopped out of bed with enthusiasm for the excursion. She showered and put on her khaki slacks again, reminding herself as she dressed to order some clothes suitable for bicycling. She joined Sam in the barn where he was tinkering with the bikes.

Sam handed over a biker's helmet and told her in his best parental tone that she had to wear it or there would be no cycling. He helped her put on her helmet and, while fastening the straps, took a moment to press a brief but very warm kiss on her mouth. Delighted, Beth wrapped her arms around him and turned the kiss into a steamy embrace that Sam had to break by tickling her into giggles.

Looking very handsome, Sam sat astride his bicycle, pulling on his fingerless biker's gloves and fastening them across the backs of his hands. Beth was conscious that he was watching her with an appreciative half grin on his mouth as she swung one long leg over her bike. He didn't say a word, but his gaze was full of admiration. They looked at each other then, read each other's thoughts and laughed. Beth was blushing, she realized, with pleasure. Young love—what a silly thing!

In a short while they were on the road, pedaling side by side and enjoying the warm sunshine. Sam challenged Beth to keep up with him, so they had a race up one very long hill. At the top of the incline, Sam eased up and glanced back. He was surprised to see Beth right behind him.

"You made it!"

"Of course I made it," she shot back, trying not to sound out of breath as she pedaled. "What do you think I am, anyway?"

"The woman who ought to be exhausted after last night," Sam said, laughing. "Okay, Beth, let's see how tough you really are. Ready? We'll start training for the Tour de France. Think you can catch me?"

Beth beat him over the crest of the hill and started down without hesitating. Over her shoulder, she called in a phony French accent, "Do you think *you* can catch *me*, Jean-Paul?"

The race was on, and Sam later had to admit that he had to work at keeping up to Beth's pace. She rode until her legs ached and her lungs hurt, but it was a wonderfully exhilarating kind of pain. With Sam riding hard on her tail, she cruised into Two Forks, the clear winner and happy to flaunt her victory.

Sam complained that he had suffered an excruciating cramp, but Beth wouldn't let him make any excuses. Laughing with her, Sam showed the way to the bank, and cashed a check at the drive-in window. Then they rode sedately down the street to a small grocery store.

Sam dismounted and gave a short exclamation. "I don't believe it."

"What?" Beth asked, easing her bike to a stop beside him.

"I forgot to bring the locks for the bikes." He yanked the Velcro loose from the back of his right hand glove and pulled it off. Combing his hair back with his fingers, he looked around, saying, "One of us ought to stay out here with them. I'd hate to lose that machine of yours before it's broken in."

Getting off her bike, Beth said, "I don't mind. You go do the shopping. I'd be no good at that stuff, anyway. I'll stay out here in the sunshine and work on my tan."

"Good," Sam agreed, fastening his gloves together and laying them over the seat of his bike. "I'll just be a few minutes."

Beth took off her helmet and shook her hair loose while Sam went into the grocery store to do what little marketing he had decided to do. Lounging against her bike with her face upturned to the sun, Beth thought about their morning together and the easy camaraderie that seemed to be growing between them. This was the life she had most wanted while she had been hospitalized, she decided, the kind of happy life she had envied of the nurses and hospital staff. She had longed to be a part of someone else, not alone in the world. Being with Sam was perfect. She smiled. She didn't feel like a stranger, different from everyone else anymore. Beth Sheridan was a person.

Sam came striding out of the store a few minutes later, but halted on the sidewalk. He looked sharply up the street in one direction and then the other.

"What's up?" Beth asked, surprised at his abrupt manner.

Sam was frowning. He came down to the bikes with a small grocery bag under his arm and something annoying obviously on his mind. He snapped, "I don't believe it."

"What?"

"Bill—the store manager. He's a friend of mine. He says the Feds are around asking questions."

"The Feds?" Beth asked, still puzzled.

Sam rapidly packed the groceries into the saddlebags on his bike. "The FBI. They're here."

Beth bolted upright and looked up and down the street as Sam had done. No sign of anyone but an older man in overalls hanging around the door of the hardware store. There were a few cars and some trucks parked along the street, but no one else in sight. Still, Beth shivered, thinking that from some concealed place someone was watching them. Without thinking, she began to scan the second-story windows of the buildings around them. Her voice went high. "What are they doing here, Sam?"

He buckled the saddlebag and straightened, reaching for his gloves. There was an angry cleft between his brows and a glitter of annoyance in his eyes. "They're checking up on us, no doubt. Dammit!"

"Checking up—? Why? Do they think I'm doing something wrong?"

"They probably think that *I'm* doing something wrong," Sam said, yanking on his left glove. He turned then, and when he saw Beth's expression, his own changed abruptly. He reached apologetically for her arm with his still-bare hand. "Don't let it upset you, Beth. I'm just blowing off steam."

"I—I'm not upset," Beth said uncertainly, glad that he had grasped her arm so firmly. She turned her face up to Sam and scanned his eyes. "Should I be?"

"No, of course not," he said gently. Making a visible effort to contain his temper, he explained, "I'm just disgusted because they obviously don't trust me to take care of you properly."

"Why—why haven't they come out to the house if they want to see me?"

Sam let her go and shrugged, reaching for his bike. "Who knows? Let's get out of here, all right? Are you rested enough to ride back home?"

"Of course," Beth said, trying to summon a plucky smile. "Aren't you?"

He got on his bike and grinned at her. "Get aboard, wench. I'm going to tire you out so you'll have to take a nap when you get home."

"A nap?" Beth asked suspiciously as she tucked her hair behind her ears and began to refasten her helmet strap.

"Well," said Sam, looking deceptively innocent, "at least some time in bed. Ready?"

Laughing, Beth hopped onto her bike and quickly pulled it in a tight circle before pedaling hard to catch up with Sam. They sailed around the corner side by side, Sam pedaling one handed while he tightened the Velcro on his right glove. Legs revolving effortlessly, they rode slowly up the street.

Together they paused at the next intersection, then proceeded when the light turned green. Both noticed immediately, however, when a car pulled smoothly out from a parking space and began to follow them.

Sam swung over to the side of the street to let the car pass, and Beth slipped behind him to cling tightly to his tail. The car did not overtake them, however, but stayed a few yards behind and showed no signs of going away. Sam glanced once over his shoulder at the car, then again.

Beth looked back, too. The car was a green sedan, nothing extraordinary. She looked again and noted the white federal license plate on the front of the car. It was the FBI, no doubt. In a wavering voice, Beth called, "Sam . . ."

He dropped back to ride beside her and gave Beth a cheerful grin. "I think we've got company."

"Why?" she asked nervously.

"Don't look back," Sam advised, sounding casual. "We're the innocent ones, remember? Just keep going. If they want to stop and talk, they'll ask politely, I'm sure."

Beth forced herself not to look over her shoulder at the car that stayed so carefully behind them. She had unconsciously picked up her speed, though. She said, "Sam, I don't like this."

"Me neither," Sam replied lightly. "Shall we have some fun?"

Beth looked across at him. "What do you mean?"

He jerked his head at an upcoming side street. "At the next corner. You take a right, and I'll go left. We'll see which one of us they really want to chat with, all right?"

"It's me they want," Beth said, her voice really quavering this time. The last thing she wanted to do was start answering horrible questions all over again!

"Don't be so sure," Sam said with confidence. "Maybe I've finally made the Ten Most Wanted list. Or do they just want to look at your legs? Let's find out. Take a right. Ready?"

"Ready," Beth said breathlessly.

"Don't be scared if they stop you. Just do your Princess Beth routine, okay?"

"My *what?*"

Sam laughed, but didn't answer. He veered off to the left, cutting down the side street, and Beth made a right turn and kept pedaling. She cruised half a block before she was brave enough to look back. The car was gone. The FBI had followed Sam.

Beth gulped. She was suddenly afraid. She knew the FBI very well indeed and knew what questions to expect from them. But why would they want Sam this time? She cut her bike through the next alley and began to double back. She didn't want Sam to get into trouble alone. She wanted to be with him. Her breathing was coming in gasps, but not from exertion. She was afraid for Sam. Foolishly, heart-poundingly afraid.

She couldn't find him. Where had he gone? Had they taken him away?

Beth raced through two intersections, hung a left and cruised a less-traveled block in search of Sam or the green car with the federal license plate. No sign. She cut diagonally across the next cross street and flew two blocks. Still nothing. With her heart in her throat, Beth zoomed back into the main street and pedaled to the intersection where they had parted. She took Sam's path this time and tried to guess where he might have led the FBI agents.

There he was—calmly resting by the curb with his bike propped easily against his thigh as he adjusted his glove.

Beth squeezed her brakes and came to a shuddering halt beside him. "Sam! What happened?"

He glanced up. "Oh, there you are."

Even Sam's studied, innocent tone of voice could not divert Beth from seeing immediately the fire in his eyes. He avoided her gaze at once, pretending to fuss with his glove, but Beth had noticed. He was angry. Angry and something else. Not afraid, Beth was sure, but something. Again, she asked, "What happened?"

Sam tried to grin. "Nothing much. They stopped me."

Beth was still breathless. "And?"

Shrugging, Sam answered, "Nothing too earth-shattering. Marcus asked after you. Remember him? I hope you don't mind that I didn't exactly invite him or his sidekick to the house for dinner."

"No. What—did they—? Is everything okay?"

"Sure," Sam said, swinging his leg over his bike once more. "Nothing to worry about. They were just expressing their concern for you, I think. Ready to hit the road again?"

Beth longed to be taken in Sam's arms for a hug just then. She needed some physical confirmation of his casual dismissal of the incident. Beth was afraid that something had happened between Sam and the FBI that he was going to keep to himself. She had been afraid for him—though there was no logical reason for her to feel that way, she reasoned, now that the moments were past. But she wanted to be in his arms, just to know that everything was indeed all right.

Sam, however, was pushing off and turning his bike for home. He didn't look back at her or wait for Beth to catch up. He wanted to put some distance between them, perhaps. Puzzled and disappointed, Beth pedaled in his wake, uncertain about how to assimilate what had just happened. Sam, it seemed, was not willing to talk.

There were still barriers between them, Beth realized. There was still something preying on Sam's mind.

Beth rode quietly behind him until Sam made the effort to tease her out of her silence. Once out on the road, they sprinted and played tag with each other. Beth's anxious mood faded after a few miles, and she began to enjoy herself again. It was easy to forget unpleasant things, she was discovering. She could simply deny them, and they went away. So she tucked the FBI incident into a mental file where she dumped a lot of things she didn't want to think about. It was a childish practice, she knew, but it worked. In a few minutes, she was enjoying herself again.

In fact, they overshot the farm gate and rode several miles on the northbound road before Sam suggested they turn around. "We'll be in sight of Delaney's farm soon," he told Beth. "And we don't want to get stuck having afternoon tea with them, or something."

"Why not?" Beth asked. "I'd like to start meeting people and visiting some of our old friends, Sam."

"No," he said. "I intend to spend a great deal of time alone with you for a while."

Beth knew what he meant and sent him a wry look. "Until the novelty wears off, right?"

He grinned. "Or until we run out of games to play. How about one last race? To the gate. Think you can beat me this time?"

"Easily. Up till now I've been toying with you. Ready, Mr. Sheridan?"

"Ready, Mrs. Sheridan—hey! Wait for me!"

They arrived at the gate at the same time, and both were puffing hard when they wheeled their bikes into the barn. They took a few minutes to wipe the road dust from their machines, and then Beth helped Sam hang them from their pegs. With groceries, helmet and gloves in hand, they started for the house.

The phone was ringing in the kitchen. Beth heard it before they arrived on the porch.

"Run," she urged Sam, taking the equipment from his hands. "You can get there in time, can't you?"

But Sam didn't hurry. "Let it go," he said in his lazy drawl. "Whoever it is will call back if they really want to get through."

Beth glanced up at him. "You really like this hermit life, don't you?"

"What?" he asked with a surprised laugh.

"You heard me. You're a hermit. You like staying away from the rest of the world, don't you?"

Sam pushed the door open and let Beth go through first. The phone had indeed stopped ringing, which Sam noted with a quick, significant glance at the wall unit. He set the groceries on the counter and shrugged. "I guess I do. No excuses. I like being alone out here. Fewer complications." He smiled at her anew. "And fewer distractions."

Beth leaned her hip against the counter nearby and put the helmet down. Casually, she inquired, "Is that supposed to mean something?"

He laughed. "You're getting positively coy, Beth! It was a compliment, you idiot. I don't want to be distracted from you."

He took her hands, peeling the gloves out of her grasp before lifting her fingers to give them quick kisses. His eyes were alight. "Even sweating and dirty, you're a sight to behold."

Beth smiled shyly at him. How quickly he could turn into the attentive lover! In town, he couldn't get away from her fast enough. His changeable manners were the most exasperating part about Sam. One minute he couldn't seem to get enough of her, and the next he was still afraid to show her what was going on in his head. Still, Beth couldn't resist moving to stand with her slim body pressed to him. She touched her fingertips to his face, smiling. "You're not a bad sight, yourself, Jean Paul. You're pretty good out there on your bike. I especially like your shorts. Nice legs, for a Frenchman."

He was laughing. "Not half as splendid as yours. You've got an especially nice bottom, Beth. You have no idea how terrific it looks on a bicycle seat. And a nice back, nice arms, nice hands, nice—everything."

He turned her hands over in his, and looked at her palms. Without thinking, he said, "Look, you don't even have any blisters. How did you manage that?"

"Blisters? Why should I?"

Sam's interest sharpened. "You've got calluses in the right places. See? I've still got to wear gloves or the handlebars cause terrible blisters. Look at you."

Beth withdrew her somewhat dirty hands from his and pretended smugness. "Just more proof of my superiority, dear husband. I don't even sweat, did you notice? Well, not much. While *you* look like a slightly drowned cowboy. I don't suppose I could talk you into taking a shower?"

Sam remained leaning against the counter, watching with a grin as Beth haughtily made her exit. Then, coming after her, he asked, "A shower? Sounds good to me. Shall we see what other superior parts of your anatomy come to light?"

CHAPTER TEN

BUT LIFE WASN'T PERFECT. At least not for Sam.

On their second night together in their shared bed, he woke, apparently from a nightmare.

He convulsed out of a deep sleep and sat up so quickly that Beth too, was startled to consciousness. She put her hand out and touched his bare back, finding it slick and cold to her touch. And Sam was trembling.

Beth struggled up in the bedclothes, reaching groggily for him. "Sam? What's wrong?"

He had his face in his hands, as if to shut out the images that must have been rioting in his head. He didn't answer. Beth put her arms around him instinctively, still half asleep. Her voice was whispery. "Are you okay? Awake now? What happened?"

He collected himself, and tried to laugh, though his breathing was uneven. "A dream, I guess. It's okay. Go back to sleep."

"I'm awake already," Beth murmured, and she gently smoothed his hair back from his temples. She put her cheek against his sweating shoulder. "Want to tell me about it?"

"Hell, no," Sam muttered. Then he gave a bitter sort of laugh and added, "We're a pair, aren't we?"

"You've had dreams before?" Beth asked, knowing she was right. "That's why you stay up so late, isn't it? You're as bad as I am!"

"Probably worse. Don't worry, all right?" Sam asked, and finally turned and reached for her, gathering Beth against his chest in a hug. With her safely against him, he sighed over her head and said without thinking, "Darling Beth, what have I done to you?"

Smiling, Beth hugged him back, her palms flat against the muscles of his back. "I can stand to lose a few minutes of sleep, you know. I'm glad you told me about your bad dreams. We really are a pair, aren't we? Have you had them long?"

"A couple of years."

"*Years?*" Beth demanded, startled. "Heavens. Maybe you ought to talk to Dr. Westham about them. He's really very good, Sam."

Sam grunted derisively. "I'd rather stay up all night. Go back to sleep, all right? Come on, lie down." He eased her head back into the pillow and tucked the bedclothes around her body once again, kissing her forehead and then her nose. "Don't mind me," he murmured.

"You're not going to get up, are you?" Beth caught at his shoulders to prevent him. "Sam, don't. Stay with me. Please!"

He had been about to get out of the bed, Beth knew. Unwillingly, he relented and lay down with her again, holding Beth loosely in his arms until she fell asleep once more. He kissed her hair and caressed the underside of her breast with his thumb, but he didn't speak. Even as sleepy darkness overcame her once more, Beth knew that Sam was going to stay awake. He wasn't going to let himself sleep.

FOR SEVERAL DAYS they lived like newlyweds, content to be out of each other's sight for only an hour or two at a time. Mostly, they just enjoyed being together, not necessarily talking. They became companions.

Sam continued to work around the farm, and Beth even went along the day he took a neighbor's borrowed baler up to a high field to bale the sun-dried hay. She stood on the back of the tractor behind him, clinging to his waist and wearing an old Stetson hat they'd dug out of a closet. They shared a picnic lunch in a stand of pine trees, after which Sam took a snooze while Beth simply watched contentedly. Finally, when she couldn't stand it any longer, she wisped a clover across his nose until he woke and pulled her down with him to kiss her. Later, they left breadcrumbs for the birds and went back to work.

Connor called every few days, and Beth enjoyed chatting with her brother. He promised to come visit again soon, if only Sam would let him. Then Sam got on the phone, pretending gruffness at first. The conversations between the two men were always long, and Sam rarely answered more than "yes" or "no" to Connor's questions, which led Beth to believe that Connor wanted to know what kind of progress Beth was making.

They rode their bikes together every day for two hours, a time that Beth enjoyed immensely. She loved the freedom of sailing along the highway with Sam just behind her, cracking jokes about her abilities or making clever, complimentary remarks about how pretty she looked. Sam laughed more frequently when they were riding. He seemed to loosen those inner restraints that were so evident when they were in the house together. He looked younger when he was biking. Happier.

In the evenings they read, consuming books and magazines seemingly without effort, and then talking about what they'd read until the wee hours of the night. Beth studied Shakespeare, memorizing lines she knew she could later use to make Sam laugh.

Then each night—inevitably—a casual touch would change the mood, and they'd been in each other's arms. They made love every night and sometimes in the mornings, like new lovers.

Beth hoped that the rest of their lives was going to be just as full of joy.

On the following Friday, however, Sam let Beth walk down to the mailbox alone to get the day's mail. She dawdled, and when she returned and handed over the mail to Sam in the kitchen, he told her that a theater group in San Francisco had called while she was out.

"Oh?" she asked, alert at once in spite of Sam's nonchalance. "What did they want?"

Sam flipped through the envelopes that she had brought back from the mailbox. Head bent, he said, "They want me to come see their production of *Bitten*. The dress rehearsal is tomorrow and the first performance is on Sunday night—a benefit."

"Tomorrow?" Beth asked in a small voice.

He lifted his head at that and smiled at Beth, his gray-green eyes steady with understanding. "Do you want me to skip it? I will, if you like."

A choice. He was giving her a choice! Beth blinked in confusion at the enormity of the decision. He had been asked to go away for a few days, and he was letting her make the decision! Beth said cautiously, "Would you really? Skip it, I mean?"

He shrugged and glanced back down to study the electricity bill. "Sure. But it's just a couple of days. I'd be back by Monday night. Connor's been pining to come for a weekend, so you wouldn't be alone. But if you'd like me to stay here, I will, of course."

His tone, his casual air and his unwillingness to meet her eyes put Beth on her guard. After a moment, she asked, "Do you have to go?"

"No," he said simply. Sam leaned against the opposite counter and did meet her gaze then, devoting his full attention to their discussion. Carefully, he explained, "I'd be doing somebody a favor—a man I knew in New York who's running this California theater now. Some big name who was supposed to appear cancelled at the last moment, so he asked me to come to promote the play, since they're raising money—as usual. But I don't have to go, Beth."

Beth swallowed with difficulty and couldn't bring herself to look at Sam for a moment. She ran her fingernails along the edge of the counter. "I—I don't suppose you'd consider taking me along?"

"No, I wouldn't consider that," he said gently, but with absolute authority. "I remember how you looked in the airport when we came here—like you were about to be dragged before a firing squad. I won't put you through that kind of—"

"Don't say 'ordeal,'" Beth commanded darkly, glancing up.

He smiled. "Okay, I won't. But I meant it. It took you a lot of days to get over that trip, Beth. It's too soon for you to go anywhere again yet." He paused and toyed with the envelope in his hand, as if studying it. More slowly, he said, "I'd like to take you somewhere this winter, though. Maybe to a beach when the temperature here is twenty below."

Beth looked up hopefully. The idea of a honeymoonlike vacation sounded magical to her. "Really? Just you and me, Sam?"

"You don't think I'd take Connor along, do you?" he asked on a laugh, seeing her face. "I intend to buy you a selection of revealing bathing suits, but I want to see you in them by myself. We'll have to find a deserted beach, that's all. This California trip has to be me alone, in the meantime. Think of it as being good for us."

"*Good* for us?"

"Sure." Sam came across to her and wound his arm around her waist. With a grin, he pulled Beth against his hip and smiled down at her. "Think of how much fun we'll have welcoming me home."

Beth sent him a pouting glare, though on the inside she was melting like caramel. Sam only had to touch her to make her brain go blank. She rested her hands on his chest, automatically playing with the buttons on his flannel shirt. "I suppose I have to give you permission to go. If I don't, you'll think I'm being a baby."

"I think you're anything but a baby," Sam murmured, dipping closer to nuzzle her throat.

He knew exactly how to cause the shudder of pleasure that always caught Beth off guard. She eased her head back, exposing her throat and laughing weakly. She did not try to escape the caress that Sam inched down to her collarbone.

"Well?" he asked softly, with his nose tracing sensual, persuasive paths up and down the most sensitive parts of her neck. "Shall I call Connor? Should I go to San Francisco or stay here?"

It was a tough decision. By letting him go, would she draw Sam closer, she wondered? Was a short absence going to make his heart grow fonder? Or was the separation too painful for Beth to bear? In his arms, eyes half closed with the pleasure his lips evoked, she nearly asked him to forego his trip. She couldn't stand even a few days without him. And yet, he clearly wanted to go. For her, it seemed a no-win proposition.

Feigning exasperation, Beth shoved him gently away. "Oh, go call Connor! If you keep this up, I won't allow you to go anywhere. You'll be my prisoner of love forever. This is your last chance for escape."

Sam tousled Beth's hair, already releasing her from his embrace. "I don't want to escape—just a weekend away to make you appreciate me all the more."

"You're impossible!"

"No," he disagreed, amused. "But I'm working on irresistible."

He did phone Connor then, who apparently agreed to come and spend the weekend with Beth, though he complained that he had to break a very hot date to comply.

Sam spent some more time at the telephone, making plane reservations and hotel arrangements. Beth listened to his voice, feeling miserable inside. He hadn't tricked her, exactly, but she felt as if he was abandoning her. Just when their relationship was becoming truly wonderful, Sam wanted to dash away for days to help raise money for a stupid theater!

While Sam was busy making plans, Beth realized that she was hungry, so with plenty of noise that didn't make her feel the least bit better, she set about making a big salad for them to share. As she cut up some leftover ham and bits of cheese to sprinkle over the vegetables, she felt her resentment grow. It wasn't fair that he could come and go as he pleased while she was trapped here, with Connor and his incessant questions. She threw the paring knife into the sink with a clatter. She was just going to have to prove to Sam that she was much stronger now than she had been when he'd first brought her home. The next time, he'd be sure to take her along.

Sam must have sensed her mood—he certainly heard her slamming things around the kitchen, for when he got off the phone and Beth put a plate of salad in front of him, he glanced up at her with a sparkle in his gaze.

"Hey," he said, catching her hand and pulling her to his side once more. "Do you realize that you just made your first solo meal, Julia Child? You *are* getting better, aren't you?"

That he noticed her efforts filled Beth with childish pleasure. She gave up her snit of temper and sat down with him for lunch. Sam enjoyed the food and tried to charm her even more. Listening, laughing with him, Beth knew that she was going to miss him intensely.

Connor arrived in a whirl of dust the following morning, just fifteen minutes before Sam had to leave for his drive to the airport. Connor marched straight into the house as if he owned it, shouting his hellos.

The morning had been hectic. Beth gave Connor a quick kiss and dashed for the bedroom with an umbrella that she was sure Sam was going to need. Of course Sam laughed at her concern for his welfare, but he didn't argue with her and accepted the umbrella peacefully. Whether he had put off packing to the last minute to avoid a teary morning, Beth couldn't be sure, but Sam was stuffing clothes into a suitcase without much care for their condition. He paused only when Connor came into the bedroom calling good-mornings. While the men talked, Beth repacked the suitcase with care.

Sam gave Connor several directions concerning the farm and the running of the household.

"And don't let Beth ride her bike until I get back," Sam said, bringing his shaving gear from the bathroom. "And if—"

"Wait a minute!" Beth objected in outrage, halting in the act of folding a pair of twill trousers. "Why can't I ride by myself?"

"You can't," Sam said flatly, giving her a stern look. In his button-down shirt and tie he appeared even more authoritative than usual, and he made the most of his advantage by drawing himself to his full height to look down at Beth with a no-nonsense gaze. He said, "I am forbidding you to ride while I'm gone. End of discussion."

"It is *not* the end of the discussion!" Beth cried. "For heaven's sake, I've certainly proved that I can ride—"

"I'm not doubting your abilities," Sam explained, elbowing her gently out of the way so he could squash his shaving kit into a corner of the suitcase. He straightened and turned on her. "I just don't want you out on the road by yourself in case some of our friendly federal agents come along and decide they want to cross-examine you again."

Letting out her breath, Beth said, "Oh."

Sam continued to press his point. "You're doing just fine without their interference, and I don't want you to be upset by a lot of questions, without me around."

Of course Beth had forgotten the FBI hovering in town. She had purposely put it out of her mind like everything else she didn't want to think about. Why was she becoming so fuddle-headed all over again? Reminded of the FBI, she sat down on the bed and gave in. "All right."

"Federal agents?" Connor asked curiously from the overstuffed chair where he was enjoying a cup of coffee. "What have I missed lately, Sam? You didn't mention any feds."

Sam was annoyed with the subject and wasn't inclined to elaborate. He observed Beth's reaction for a moment and then said shortly, "The FBI has been lurking, that's all. There are a couple of agents still assigned to Beth's case, apparently. I don't want her to be harassed, Connor. You think you can keep them away from her?"

"Sure," her brother answered with confidence. "I'll keep a close watch on you, Sis."

Beth managed a halfhearted smile at him, but she was conscious that Sam had studied Connor's relaxed frame for a long moment before he turned away and started to zip the suitcase closed. Sam didn't continue the topic, but lifted the case upright and announced, "That's it, I guess."

"Got your wallet?" Connor asked lightly. "Your razor? A supply of clean socks?"

"Connor," Sam said firmly, "why don't you carry this out to the truck for me? Be a good boy and clear out for a minute."

With a sly grin, Connor agreed. He got lazily to his feet and grabbed the handles of the suitcase. "Sure," he said, with a heavy-lidded smile down at Beth. "I can see that things are back to normal marriagewise around here. Take all the time you want, Sammy."

Sam held back a retort and waited until Connor had gone out into the house with the suitcase before he turned back to Beth. He put his hands into his trouser pockets and didn't touch her. "Well? Think you can manage? There's a steak in the refrigerator for to-night, and tomorrow Con make make dinner out of that piece of—"

"We've already gone over the menu," Beth reminded him, determined not to cry. She sat very still on the edge of the bed and didn't raise her head. "I think Connor and I can cope without you for a couple of days, Sam," she said tartly.

"Hmm," he murmured, coming to stand over her. "That's not exactly what I wanted to hear."

Beth didn't dare look up at him. There was a lump in her throat the size of a peach, she was sure. She knotted her hands in her lap to keep them from shaking and said, "Isn't it? Don't you want us to be okay?"

"I want you to miss me terribly," he said quietly, putting out a finger to caress her hair. "I want you to tell me to hurry back."

Beth gritted her teeth. Her voice squeaked. "H-hurry back."

"Beth . . ." he began patiently.

"I'm not going to cry."

"Good. I don't want you to cry. I'd like to kiss you, though, so—"

"If you kiss me, I'll cry for sure, and I don't want—"

"We're going to have to risk it," Sam said with a gentle laugh quivering in his voice, "because I can't go away without a kiss from you. Come on. You'll be fine without me. You were fine without me all those weeks in the hospital."

"No, I wasn't," Beth said tensely. "I was awful without you. I was scared and lonely and stupid and now—"

"You said you weren't going to cry."

"Well, I was wrong, dammit!"

Sam crouched down on one knee in front of her and took Beth's hands in his, and the whole scene just made things worse for Beth, who was crying for real by that time. He dried her cheek with his fingertips and said, "Don't cry. Your nose will turn pink. You're stronger than this, Beth, I know you are. You aren't as dependent on me as you think. Kiss me."

Beth gulped and flung her arms around his neck and squeezed until her arms ached. "I wish you weren't going!"

"This is your big chance to prove how tough you are," Sam said gently. "So don't start talking like that. Am I going to get my kiss or not?"

With her eyes squished shut to hold back more tears, Beth said, "I'm still deciding."

Sam laughed and kissed her hard on the side of her head. Then he pried her loose and took a proper kiss from her lips. His own mouth turned insistent, and in a moment they were clasped in a warm embrace that spoke more than words. Sam broke the kiss gently and then looked deeply into her eyes.

The look between them was charged with many messages. Beth felt her heart rend into the silence that only three little words could fill.

But Sam didn't say them. Finally, he dropped another kiss on her lips and said, "Goodbye. I'll be back on Monday."

She stayed on the bed as he got up and ran a quick caress down the back of her head. Then, he went out through the house and Beth stayed behind. When he had gone into the kitchen, she whispered, "I love you, Sam."

The truck started and Connor called something funny. Beth listened to the diminishing roar of the truck's engine, and then Sam was gone.

It took her a few minutes to regroup. But Beth soon tottered weakly into the bathroom, washed her face, put on some lipstick and felt good enough to face Connor again. The house was too empty to stay in alone, so she went outside looking for her brother.

Connor was pleasant enough company, she supposed, as they spent the first morning together. He was clever and funny, and he tried very hard to make her feel better about Sam's departure. They made some lunch and took a walk. Thisby, Sam's dog, accompanied them, sticking close to Beth and ignoring Con.

Because Beth was feeling less than talkative, Con told her about his girlfriend, Darcy, who expected him to spend far too much money entertaining her. Con complained about her expensive tastes, making Beth laugh with an imitation of her breathy way of talking. He batted his eyes and called her "honey" until Beth had a pretty good idea of what kind of girl this Darcy was. Connor, however, seemed genuinely enamored of the young lady, despite his complaining. Beth suspected that Darcy was crazy about Con, too, and would do a great deal to "tie him down" if she could get away with it. It was going to be fun to see how that romance turned out.

"Romance?" Connor hooted. "There's no romance between Darcy and me, dear sister. There's lust, maybe, but no romance. Why, the girl thinks candles are for use during a power failure. No, I don't think it's going to turn out right at all."

"Are you a romantic, Con?"

He smiled loftily and threw a twig for the dog to chase. Thisby ignored him, so Connor gave up trying to tempt her and said, "I have my moments, I admit. Why?"

Beth shook her head ruefully. "You ought to give lessons, I think. Romance does not come easily to a man, does it?"

"Oho," Connor said, eyeing her sidelong. "Things aren't as cozy as they seem at the Sheridan household?"

"Oh, things are cozy, all right," Beth said, swishing her shoes through the grass as they walked. "Just not very—oh, I don't know. Not very satisfying, sometimes."

"Sex?" Connor asked bluntly.

"No, no. no!" Beth blushed and hurried to say, "I'm talking about romance, I guess. I shouldn't be talking to you about it at all."

"Why not? Listen, we all need to get stuff off our chests now and then. What's wrong? The sex is great but he doesn't respect you in the morning?"

Beth laughed nervously, feeling uneasy about discussing her marriage with anyone, including her own brother. She shook her head again, trying to rid herself of the inward dilemma. "There's nothing really wrong. Nothing I can put my finger on, I mean. I think a lot happened between Sam and Elizabeth before that—"

"Elizabeth?" Connor asked abruptly.

"Oh," Beth said, hearing his startled tone. "I think of myself as Beth now, Con. And the person I was before is Elizabeth." She explained her little theory simply and smiled at Connor as she spoke, but he had his head averted, so she continued, "I think Sam has a lot of grudges against Elizabeth, or something. He hasn't been quite able to let go of the past yet. Could he—I wonder if he's holding the past against me sometimes?"

"I see," Connor said. He took her hand and helped Beth to clamber over the fence. When she was safely on the other side, Connor said carefully, "The past was pretty complicated between you two, I think, Beth. I didn't understand the situation completely, but I think you and Sam were..."

"Yes, Sam explained," Beth interrupted kindly, to spare Connor the discomfort of giving her bad news. "He told me that we were separated when—at the time of the attack. I think we must have been ready to get a divorce, to tell you the truth, Con. It's just a feeling I've got—the fact that nothing here belongs to me, my bike and all my clothing gone. Sam didn't go into the issues, though."

"He doesn't want to rake up old arguments, I'm sure. Listen," Connor suggested when he had climbed over the fence himself and stood beside her. "I wouldn't worry about your marriage, Sis. Sam seems content to me, and I'm sure you'd know if something was really wrong—like a love triangle of some kind that—"

"I don't think Sam is into adultery," Beth said firmly, turning away to walk.

"No," Connor said from behind her. "I was thinking of you. Maybe there was another man in your life."

Beth stopped and turned. She stared at Connor. "What?"

Connor shrugged it off. "Could be, right? I mean, if Sam's got a grudge against you for something, the best possible choice would be another guy. Maybe you were having an affair."

Aghast, Beth could hardly speak for an instant. She found her tongue in a rush. "Connor, no! I couldn't—I would never hurt Sam like that!"

"*You* wouldn't," Connor said, watching her face. "But before. Elizabeth might have."

Beth found a rock and sat down quickly on it, as if all her strength had been drained away. She hadn't imagined such a possibility. Surely she couldn't have found a man more desirable than Sam! Could she? She said angrily, "I don't believe it."

Connor lounged above her, unconcernedly taking his cigarettes out of his pocket. "Who knows? Sam isn't talking, and you can't remember. I could be wrong. It doesn't matter now anyway, does it?"

Beth rubbed her hand over her eyes and murmured, "Oh, I hope not, Con. I would hate myself if I'd done something horrible! I couldn't have done something so cruel to Sam."

"Well," Con said agreeably, putting an unlit cigarette between his lips, "let's think about it for a while." He crouched beside her and patted Beth's knee. "See if you can recall the circumstances. Have you had any flashes of memory since you've been here?"

"Just about bicycling," Beth said dully, her brain still whirling with the possibility of having cheated on her husband. It was too awful! Was this why Sam had kept such a tight rein on his emotions? Had she hurt him so badly that he was afraid to love her again?

Connor was ready to move the discussion ahead. He struck a match, puffed some smoke and asked purposefully, "How about people? Any faces look familiar? Or places?"

"N-no."

"What things do you feel comfortable doing?" Connor asked, tossing the match into the grass. "Cooking?"

"Not at all," Beth said with an unhappy shake of her head. Thisby arrived at her side and poked her slim collie's nose into Beth's lap for some petting.

"Walking? Reading?"

"Well, sometimes reading," Beth said. She absently scratched the dog's head and started to think with Con. Perhaps she could remember something that would explain the present circumstances with Sam. Any kind of memory might help. She frowned, considering Connor's questions. "I've been looking through some books that Sam has. Some of them I've read before, but others I haven't. And all of Sam's plays are new to me, too, though I must have read them. That seems strange. If I've read some books and remember them, why haven't I remembered his plays?"

The question was a valid one, one that had bothered Beth a great deal before she thrust it into her let's-not-worry-about-that-today file. Connor brushed the question aside, though. "Forget that for a moment. What else have you found that's familiar? Certain television shows?"

"We don't watch any."

"How about the newspapers? Some people in the news?"

Beth lifted her shoulders helplessly. "I remember some things, but not everything. I—I'm not very up-to-date."

Connor continued to press. He was patient and encouraged Beth to talk. After a while, he made her get up and walk with him some more as they discussed the past and the present. Beth noticed that Connor's police training was in evidence. He began to sound just like the FBI agents who had questioned her in the hospital. At first they had been patient, asking apparently random questions and eventually homing in on certain areas. When Beth's memory had proved to be so lacking, they had become angry with her. Connor was doggedly cheerful, though he chain-smoked at an even faster pace than usual. He asked many questions and let Beth talk all she liked.

They went inside after a while, and as they prepared dinner Connor decided they ought to backtrack. He began to ask her about her hospital experiences—when had she awakened, with whom had she first talked, how had she felt, what had she been wearing. At first Beth did not realize in what direction Connor was leading her. All she could think about was Sam.

It became obvious as the hours went on, though, that Connor was interested in the crime and what had happened to her at the hands of another man. He wanted to know everything she knew about the man who had attacked her.

"Maybe your breakup with Sam had something to do with this guy who hurt you," Connor suggested over dinner.

Beth, by that time, was unable to eat at all. She wasn't hungry, and her stomach was rolling with unpleasant emotions. She sipped from her glass of wine and tried to concentrate on everything Connor said. She blinked unhappily at her brother. "You don't think—you don't suppose I really *knew* the man who...?"

"Oh, I'm not suggesting that your lover—if you had one—was the man who hurt you. Of course not." Connor took a healthy bite of his steak and chewed it thoughtfully. He swallowed and added, "But anything's possible, right?"

Beth felt sick. In the space of a few hours, Connor had raked up all the horrible things that she had managed to sweep out of sight since she'd come home with Sam. Connor prodded and probed, looking, she assumed, for some small moment of recognition from her. But Beth just got more and more depressed as the evening wore on. She longed for Sam, wishing that he'd come walking through the door any minute to put a stop to Connor's endless questions.

At last Connor saw that she was distraught, and he apologized. "I'm sorry, Sis. This was supposed to be a nice weekend for us, and I'm dragging you through all this bad stuff. Let me do the dishes. Why don't you go up to your studio and do some work?"

She didn't tell Connor that she hadn't set foot in her studio since the week before, but a little solitude sounded wonderful just then. Yes, she would go hide in the studio and let Connor clean up the kitchen. She needed some time alone to think over the possibilities.

Beth climbed the steps into the spacious room that had once been her weaving studio. She closed the door and sat down on the stool by the spinning wheel to think. Could she have had another man in her life? Surely not. Sam seemed to fill her every minute now! How could she ever have wanted to get away from him?

And all Connor's talk about the man who had attacked her was especially unpleasant. He had pressed her about her dream, the yawning, yowling cat. Beth shivered. Without Sam beside her, she was sure to dream about it again tonight. The prospect was unnerving, and Beth wished she had poured herself another glass of wine. Without thinking about her actions, she began to tinker with the wheel in front of her, just as Connor had shown her. Keeping her hands busy might very well help her get all these disruptive thoughts out of her head. She wanted to push them under her mental rug, but tonight she felt too tired, too upset.

Beth put her foot on the treadle and watched the wheel go around. Then she tried to remember what Connor had showed her. At first she was awkward. The woollen thread she spun was lumpy and thick in places, and so thin in others that it would snap. Then with growing rhythm, Beth caught on and worked without really concentrating. How could she possibly have enjoyed such mindless work before, she wondered, her fingers aching from pulling on the wool thread.

Her head went round and round with questions as she maneuvered the treadle and the wool, trying to remember her mother's techniques that Con had demonstrated. Had Sam kept her at arm's length because he resented what she had done in the past? Or had he told her the truth and kept his distance so that he wouldn't remind her of the sadistic attack of three months ago? And even today when he'd had the chance, Sam couldn't tell her that he loved her. Even with the inherent timing of a playwright, he had missed the perfect opportunity to say the words. Why? Did some part of Sam hate her?

Beth had tangled the wool around the spindle and was trying to get it undone, conscious that she was barely holding tears of frustration at bay. She cut her finger then, but stifled a cry of pain, not wanting Connor to come up and find her so upset and on the verge of tears. She sucked her sore finger and then looked blankly at her hands.

She had blisters.

Blisters from the wool. Her hands were callused enough to make cycling painless, but spinning, where she must have spent hours every day, had rubbed her fingers raw. Beth stared at her aching hands in surprise.

From below, Beth heard the telephone ring. The sound startled her out of her thoughts, though Beth could not tear her eyes from the blisters on her hands.

Too much was happening. She couldn't think.

A moment later, she heard Connor's voice as he spoke into the telephone. He sounded cheerful, though Beth couldn't hear the words he spoke. Then he put down the phone and walked across the wooden floor below, his footsteps echoing. He called to her up the stairs.

"Beth? Can you come to the phone? It's Sam."

Beth flew to the door and wrenched it open. She clattered down the steps and hesitated before Connor, who was smiling at her. She said, "Oh, Con. Do you mind . . . ? Could I talk with Sam—?"

"In private?" Con asked with an indulgent grin. "Sure. I was just going out to check on the horses, anyway. Tell him I'm being very conscientious, all right? Go ahead."

Thanking him breathlessly, Beth dashed into the kitchen and snatched up the receiver from the counter. "Sam?"

Beth clutched the telephone to her ear with both hands. She closed her eyes to savor the sound of his voice. "Oh, I'm so glad you called."

Sam must have smiled, for he said gently, "You haven't been out of my thoughts for two minutes. Are you okay? Connor treating you right?"

Beth hesitated, for Connor had just arrived in the kitchen and was pulling on his sweater to go out. She said uncertainly, "Yes, I suppose so."

"What does that mean?" Sam asked sharply.

"Nothing, nothing. I—"

"Is he still there? Hanging over your shoulder?"

"Yes."

"Well, tell him to leave, dammit. I don't want this to turn into a conversational triangle. Beth—"

Connor waved and let himself out the door. Beth turned back to the phone and said quickly, "He's gone now. Oh, Sam, are you all right? Your plane wasn't late or—"

"Of course I'm all right. You? You sound—not good."

Beth laughed unsteadily. "Not good? I'm awful, in fact. I feel like you've been gone for weeks. Sam, I can't seem to function without you!"

"I wish that were true," Sam said surprisingly. "Darling Beth, listen to me. When I saw you in the hospital elevator, you were bright and self-reliant and determined to get well on your own. Somehow since then I've turned you into a—well, I've weakened you somehow, and that makes me sick. Don't, *don't* do this to yourself. You're just fine."

"No, I'm not," Beth said stubbornly. She hadn't been prepared for a lecture, and she responded to it with childish annoyance, complaining, "Connor and I—we discussed the murder and the rape—the near-rape, and all the possible ways I could have escaped that man who—"

Sam swore softly, but lamentably. "Why has he dredged that up again, for God's sake?"

Beth sighed, trying to calm herself. Why *had* she and Con spent the whole day talking about an event that didn't matter anymore? She put her face into her hand and longed for Sam's presence, his calming, steady hands and firm kisses that took her to a sensual place that was ever so much nicer than the rest of the world. The long-distance line crackled faintly with static, making Sam seem even farther away. Beth said weakly, "I don't know. I don't understand anything anymore."

"You will," Sam said. "Sooner than you think."

Beth summoned a laugh and said, "I hope so. Blast you, Sam Sheridan, come *home!*"

He laughed with her, sounding relieved. "That's my Beth. Darling, I love you."

The words were out so easily that Beth wasn't sure she had heard correctly. She stood stupidly still, staring at the refrigerator while his voice seemed to echo in her head.

"Beth?"

"I—I heard you."

"Did you?" he asked, sounding urgent suddenly. "Beth, I mean it. I love you very much. I miss you probably more than you're missing me."

Beth laughed uncertainly. Her hands were shaking so much that she had to grip the receiver with all her strength. "I can't believe you're telling me this now, of all times!"

"It's far too late," Sam agreed. "Do you understand me, though? It's taken me until now to decide, fool that I am. Beth, I want you forever, all right? I'm going to do everything I can to make sure that happens. Can you stand Connor until I get back?"

Confused by his sudden urgency, Beth said, "I—I think so."

"Give him your Princess Beth look. You know, the one that shuts me up every time, like you're thinking I need a swift kick in the pants."

"You do, sometimes. Like right now!"

"My usual good timing," Sam said. "Look, I've got to go."

Desperately, Beth said, "I wish I was with you!"

"When I come back, we'll get everything straightened out, all right? In the meantime, promise me you'll remember that I love you very much, Beth. More than anything. Whatever we discover about ourselves, that's got to be the most important thing. Will you promise?"

"Of course," Beth said quietly, puzzled. "Yes, I promise."

Sam didn't speak for a moment. They listened to each other's silence for a time. Then, abruptly, he said, "I'll see you on Monday."

"Yes."

He hung up then, leaving Beth listening to a dial tone.

She stared at the telephone, unseeing. His voice, his urgent words, his tense silences—all clues to Beth, who had ignored such warnings in the past.

Something was wrong. She couldn't deny it any longer.

CHAPTER ELEVEN

SHE HAD BEEN incredibly stupid. The facts fell into place as soon
as she replaced the telephone receiver, like a child's puzzle that had
been thrown into the air and magically—incredibly—had fallen to
earth in just the right formation. Sam had told her, though without words. And Beth realized how utterly, disgustingly, dim-
wittedly stupid she had been.

And that made her angry.

She told Connor that she had a headache, and without waiting
for his response she went to her bedroom. She did not sleep,
however, but sat on the bed and thought, with her hands clenched
so tightly that her nails bit painfully into her palms. She thought
about everything that had happened since she met Sam in the
hospital elevator. What she realized at first stunned her, but it
didn't take long before she was consumed by an icy fury.

She knew it all without a doubt.

The blisters on her fingertips had been the proof that tipped the
scales. Why did her hand blister from the wool? If she had truly
been a spinner and weaver, she would have had calluses on her
hands in the right places. As it was, her hands were hardened from
bicycle handlebars, *not* from spinning. Sam had said he had sold
Elizabeth's bicycle, but Beth knew now that he had lied. Elizabeth had never owned a bike, Beth decided. And tonight, Sam's
voice—urgent now and raw with yet more unspoken messages—
had told her the truth. The facts came up and hit her so hard in the
face that Beth could not even cry. She *knew* that she was not who
Sam had pretended she was.

Her name was not Elizabeth Sheridan.

She was not Sam Sheridan's wife, and she had no place in his
home. She had been a prefect stranger to him the day they had
met.

Beth did not feel confused or frightened. She was finished being stupid. She was angry. She began by opening every drawer in the room and emptying the contents completely. No signs of feminine touches here. All of Sam's clothes were haphazardly organized inside, but not one thing that could have belonged to his wife. Not a photograph, not a note, not a forgotten handkerchief or pair of socks. Nothing. She searched under the bed. No signs that might have been left by a wife.

She looked in the bathroom, trying to be quiet so that she did not arouse Connor's suspicions. She took the tube of bath oil out of the cabinet and stared at it. She had never liked the fragrance. It was too sweet. But Elizabeth had liked it, Beth knew. For some reason, Sam had never thrown it away. He had been careless.

When she was sure Connor had gone to bed and was asleep, Beth crept out into the sitting room. She stood in front of the desk, the cluttered roll-top that undoubtedly contained every scrap of paper even connected with Sam's life. Sam, who had tonight told her urgently that he loved her. Tonight, when a thousand empty miles lay between them, he had said the words she had longed to hear from him. Why had he chosen to bare his soul when they were apart made perfect sense now. He had always kept his distance. Sam had put up barriers between them for fear he might let the truth slip out. He had been afraid Beth would discover their real relationship.

Beth turned on the desk lamp without emotion. Until now she had turned off her ability to think. Now she turned off her emotions. She methodically began riffling through the drawers. Bills of sale, income tax forms, insurance papers. Beth leafed through those with hands that were shaking not from anxiety, but from newfound rage.

There. Elizabeth Sheridan, named Sam's beneficiary on an insurance policy five years old.

So Elizabeth had existed. She had been Sam's wife at one time.

Beth continued her search. She found more papers and a few books. At the bottom of one drawer, carefully wrapped in tissue and packed in a box, was a leatherbound copy of *Bitten*. Beth found that she was chewing her lips to hold back the sounds that leaped to her throat when she saw the inscription.

"Sam, *'We are such stuff as dreams are made of.'* With love, Elizabeth."

There was a photograph tucked inside the first page. It was too bright, as if the sun had been beating down around her.

She had been blond, with a curving mouth and dark, dark eyes that glinted unexpectedly with the sunlight. Her face was narrow, with sharply cut cheekbones and brows that arched catlike to give her an expression of cryptic amusement. She had eyed the camera askance, as if teasing the photographer from where she sat on the porch steps. And below her, on the next step down, was Sam. He had turned to look up at his wife so that only the back of his head showed to the camera. His hand, however, lay on her thigh. Beth wondered only briefly what his expression might have been. Had he smiled up at his wife adoringly?

Beth closed the book coolly and packed it in its box. It might have been her heart that she wrapped and replaced in the drawer. She had seen enough. She turned out the lamp, needing nothing else. Elizabeth had lived. But *she* wasn't Elizabeth.

She went to the bedroom and sat on the floor for an hour, half sick and almost hoping she could vomit. She wanted to be rid of everything inside her. She wanted to be empty again.

Beth fell asleep there, exhausted. Her nightmare did not return, in fact she did not dream at all.

She woke on the freezing floor, having slept a few short hours. The morning was cold and still half-dark, but Beth was not deterred. She pulled a sweater over her head and found a bicycling anorak of Sam's. Then, she spread some peanut butter on two slices of bread and wrapped them in foil. Without waking Connor, she let herself out of the house. In the barn, she lifted down her bicycle and walked it to the gate through a swirling fog.

Once on the road, Beth's mind began to function again. She wanted to punish her body to make herself think. How she had gone so long without using her brain was incredible. It was time to regain her wits and take control of her life. As the sun came up and began to burn off the fog, the facts began to fall into place. She had been very stupid. Ever since she had come to Sam's house, she had allowed him to think for her. He was right. She had allowed herself to become dependent. She hated herself for becoming a weak, silly female so eager for love that she was blind to what was going on around her.

There had been many signs, and Beth had ignored them.

Sam's words—or lack of them—told the story. He had never come out and admitted things straightforwardly. He said things like "Be yourself." And "Don't try to be someone you're not." And "I like you as Beth. Forget about Elizabeth." Sam had readily joined her in pretending that she was a totally new person. At first she had thought he was just relieved that they were not going to begin their marriage where it had left off. But actually, Sam had been unable to pretend that she was his wife. He had preferred to start their relationship as Sam and Beth, not Sam and Elizabeth Sheridan.

The real proof was in Beth's head. She had never felt comfortable as Elizabeth Sheridan. She had known from the beginning that Elizabeth's soul was not inside her somewhere.

She pedaled her bicycle to the north through the fog, hardly noticing the chill in the air. In time, she came upon another farm. The mailbox had been hit by some vehicle and leaned precariously to one side. In sloppy hand-painted red letters, it read Delaney.

It was Mrs. Delaney who opened the door. She was still in her housecoat, but didn't look frightened or surprised to find a guest on her doorstep.

"Good morning," Beth said firmly. Though she wasn't sure how to introduce herself now, she heard her voice sounding strong. "I'm sorry to disturb you so early. I'm a neighbor, staying with Sam Sheridan—down the road a bit. Is Mr. Delaney at home, by any chance?"

The woman said that he was, and directed Beth to one of the outbuildings.

Beth found Ralph Delaney wearing an oilskin apron and holding a long and hideous butchering knife in his hand. Beth had heard the expression "butcher knife" before, but had never actually seen the genuine article. It was huge and curving, and she stopped dead in her tracks when her eyes fell on it.

Ralph Delaney saw her dismay at once and laid the knife aside. He came out of the building and kindly stood with her in the gray morning light.

"Yes," he told her when she asked. "I knew Sam's wife a little. Met her in Two Forks a few times. She was a good girl. Nice girl. Very pretty. Like you, miss. I was glad to see you with him last week. I don't know Sam very well, but it isn't natural for a man so young to hide himself away from the world the way he's done.''

"No," Beth agreed. "It isn't."

"He ought to get over what happened by now. He needs to get married again," Delaney said cheerfully. "You'll do him some good, I think."

"Thank you," said Beth, "but I don't think I'll be staying too much longer. Thanks for helping me."

"Did I help?" Delaney asked with a disconcerted grin. "What did I do? I thought you wanted some answers."

Beth started away from him and waved. "You gave me enough, thanks. I won't take up more of your time, sir. Good morning."

Mrs. Delaney had stayed on the porch and watched as Beth crossed their drive and approached her bicycle. She lifted her hand and waved as Beth swung her leg over and settled into the seat. Beth waved back mechanically. Mrs. Delaney must have known Elizabeth and was curious about this other woman who had suddenly appeared at the Sheridan farm.

Beth wondered how many people in the area had known about Elizabeth and puzzled about who Beth was. No wonder Sam had kept her isolated at the farm. He had taken her shopping for a bicycle at a town half an hour's drive away so that he could avoid anyone who might have known Elizabeth and would question him about Beth. The day he had finally taken her to Two Forks, he had pretended to forget the bicycle locks so she would have to stay outside with the bikes instead of going into the store with him. Sam had not wanted Beth to guess that she wasn't Elizabeth.

Why had Sam created this elaborate hoax? Why had he pretended to be her husband and brought her here, so far from the rest of the world? He had cut her off from the hospital and made her totally dependent upon him alone. He had even duped the FBI into thinking she was Elizabeth Sheridan!

Or had he?

Had the FBI believed him when he came to claim his wife? Or had the FBI been a part of the plot? When Sam and Beth had been bicycling in Two Forks and the FBI car began to follow them, why had Sam suggested they go separate ways to see whom the car would follow? He had wanted to be alone with the agents, perhaps. Or maybe he was afraid they had finally caught up with his scheme and didn't want Beth to hear any accusations before they could be proven.

Why? *Why?* Why was Sam pretending?

Beth squeezed the brakes on her bicycle and stopped at the roadside. Suddenly, the image of Ralph Delaney's butchering knife came to her mind. Standing in the middle of the highway, she felt a cold shiver overtake her, seizing each part of her body until she was shuddering with fear. Terrible, unreasonable fear. She couldn't control herself. She was shaking and crying out, clapping her hands over her mouth to stifle her instinctive sounds of agony. The question hit her like a lightning bolt.

Who had been the man who had kidnapped her? Who had beaten her, tied her up in the trunk of a car and taken her to a deserted mine site and tortured her with knives and ropes until she had lost consciousness? Who had thrown freezing water in her face until she came to life and fought and screamed and kicked with the strength of a madwoman? Who had been afraid of discovery and had tried to escape, dragging her stillbound body along the road, battering her head against the asphalt until the rope snapped and allowed her to roll free? Who had run away before he could kill her like all the other women he had brutally murdered?

The images came upon her in a rush like a summer thunderstorm, quick and violent. She could see herself. It had happened to her. She could feel the ice water on her face, feel the bite of nylon twine around her wrists, the warmth of her own blood on her throat.

Beth dropped her bicycle with a clatter and ran. She ran to the side of the highway, holding her head, holding her thoughts inside. It couldn't have been Sam. No, surely not.

Not Sam. He wasn't capable of crazy sadism. He wasn't capable of murder. Not Sam, who had tried to frighten her with a menacing seduction and failed miserably, then made eloquent love to her. And last night, when he had told her how much he loved her, he had known she would discover the truth. He'd been afraid.

What had he said? "Remember that I love you. Whatever we discover about ourselves, that's got to be the most important thing."

Beth left the bicycle on the highway and started to run. She ran until she stumbled over a cluster of rocks, and then captured her runaway imagination. Steadying herself, she walked, talking aloud nonsensically. The man who assaulted her was not here, not now. She had to think. She had to calm herself.

She hiked up through the pines until she struck a grassy pasture, then walked along the fence, still breathing hard although the exercise was not exhausting. She came to a corner of the field, climbed the fence and walked higher, as if by putting some distance between herself and the bike she might clear the emotions out of her mind and leave only cold truth. She wanted to be able to think clearly. She walked.

She climbed another fence and found herself standing on the edge of a neatly mowed field. No, not a field at all. There were white marble stones here, laid in two precise lines. It was the cemetery.

She had seen it from the house once and had remarked upon it. Sam had said, "It's a cemetery dating from the pioneer days. It's too far to walk, though, and the road's not good enough for the truck. And I'm sure there are rattlesnakes."

He had wanted her to stay away.

The grass was tended, though. Someone had taken care of this place. There were no rattlesnakes, Beth knew. She walked through the stones, reading the inscriptions carved on old, crumbling stones.

Caleb MacAllister, 1898, doctor, poet, husband and father; Sojourn MacAllister, 1894, dearly loved, sorely missed; Francis Westham, 1903; Hilary MacAllister Westham, loving wife and mother; Caleb Connors; Meredith Westham Connors; Dr. Connor MacAllister; and then Caleb Westham, 1957.

The last one: Elizabeth Westham Sheridan.

Beth sat down at the headstone and read it again and again. The date of the death was two years old. "Elizabeth Westham Sheridan . . . May flights of angels sing thee to thy rest."

Connor and Elizabeth, brother and sister. Their name was Westham. Dr. Westham, a physician from a long line of doctors. Sam must have come along sometime and been welcomed into a family that respected poets. Sam and Elizabeth Sheridan. A close family, a family with roots in the past. A family that worked together, loved each other, respected one another. A *family*.

That left Beth at square one. She did not know who she was.

CHAPTER TWELVE

THERE WAS NO sense crying. Beth felt drained and exhausted. There was no sorrow within her. She did not pity herself. She found that she was still angry, though—furious that she had been fooled. Tipping her face up to the cloud-concealed sun, she wished that its meager rays would beat some logic into her mind. She needed to think, to plan. Beth was damned if she was going to go walking back into the house and pretend to Connor that she didn't know exactly where she stood.

How did Connor fit into things, anyway? The question unnerved Beth, and she sat up suddenly. Instinctively, she knew that she was in danger. She felt sick again, for fear tasted sour in her mouth. Whoever had tried to murder her once could certainly try again. And he had the advantage. He knew her face, but she didn't know his. Could it have been Connor? Beth shivered but did not push the thought aside. She was not going to ignore any possibilities anymore.

Beth wrapped her arms around her knees and sat with her back against Elizabeth Sheridan's headstone. She would not go back to the house, not with Connor there. Yet setting off on her own without preparation seemed an equally foolish plan. She could always go back to the Delaneys', she supposed, and as the sun rose higher in the sky, Beth began to consider that option more seriously. At night the temperature was going to drop close to freezing, and Sam's anorak was not going to provide enough protection. With no money, she wasn't going to get far.

And with no memory, she was at an even greater disadvantage. She was going to have to make up for that by being brave. Brave and smart and cool.

Beth got up and cautiously worked her way down through the pines until she reached the pasture fence. She could see the house from there, just a quarter of a mile away. Connor's car was gone.

He had found her missing, she supposed, and the bike gone, too. Of course he would have panicked and gone looking for her. It would only take him an hour at the most to find her bicycle abandoned on the highway. Beth sat down among the trees to wait. She remembered her sandwich and pulled it from the oversized pocket of the anorak. She ate her makeshift meal without really tasting it and watched the house from a safe distance.

In the early afternoon Connor returned. Beth eased herself back into the shadows of the trees and watched. He had her bike in the trunk of his car, and the collie dog sniffed at it as Con lifted the bike to the ground. He ran to the house without looking up into the hills where Beth watched from her hiding place. He was hurrying, no doubt, to telephone his accomplice, Sam.

Beth stayed in the trees and waited. She could be patient.

In a few minutes Connor came back outdoors and stood for a long time on the front porch with his hands up shading his eyes, scanning the countryside. Beth sat very still, confident that her choice of hiding places and the dull khaki color of the anorak were good enough to conceal her from Connor's eyes. In a while Connor went down to his car, got in and drove out through the gate.

Beth stood up, dusted off her trousers and headed down to the house. She had at least half an hour, she guessed, before Connor returned. Thisby greeted her happily, trotting at her side and poking her nose into Beth's hand for a caress. She gave the dog a pat and went up the porch steps.

The door was unlocked, and the house silent. Beth found the coffeepot still turned on, and poured herself a cup. It was very strong and bitter, but she drank it. Then, though she wasn't hungry, Beth made herself another sandwich and took some apples from the refrigerator. Leaving them on the counter, she headed to the bedroom to find some warmer clothes. She did not intend to spend the night here again.

A car! From the bedroom, she heard engine noises out on the drive and froze. Connor already?

She considered going out through the sun porch before he discovered her. She could slip around the side of the house and into the barn. Sam's bike was there. She could take it and get away while he was looking for her inside. If the dog didn't bark and give her away, she'd be safe.

But as Beth crept out into the sitting room, some intuition made her wait.

It was Sam who came into the kitchen. He heard her, or knew instinctively where she was and strode straight through to the sitting room. It *was* Sam, dressed in his tweed jacket but without a tie. He had left his suitcase outside, perhaps, and had rushed inside to look for her. He stopped in midstride when he saw Beth, meeting her eyes across the space and freezing as if she'd shot him with a laser.

They stared at each other.

It took him thirty seconds to find his voice, and even then it was barely a rasp. "My God, Beth, you scared us," he said in an awful whisper. "Connor thought—"

"That I had run away?"

Sam heard her tone and understood. He saw her face and heard the message in her voice and knew then that Beth had finally found him out. Unable to move, Sam laid his hand on the back of the chair and held it.

Carefully, Beth said, "I intended to run, yes."

He didn't go to her, but his need to do exactly that was apparent in his gaze. He looked as if the pain inside him was as real as a muscle cramp or twisting weapon. In the same terrible whisper, he said, "You have to understand, Beth. I never meant any of this to hurt you."

"Didn't you?" Beth asked, surprised by how strong she sounded. She kept her distance and retorted, "The truth hurts, so you kept it all from me?"

Sam shook his head, watching her with an agonized look. His eyes were vivid, yet his face had slowly gone white. He said, "Beth, it's such a long story and you've got to hear it all before you make your decision. Will you trust me a little longer? Listen to me, at least?"

Beth was silent, telling herself that she should run now before she changed her mind. She could have put the rage inside herself to good use by confronting Connor, she thought, but not Sam. For Sam she had too many emotions, and she must try to bottle those up.

Sam was going to make her weak again, if she wasn't careful. Beth realized that she'd been strong in the hospital, but she had allowed Sam to sap her strength somehow. She was going to have to ignore the yearning in her heart. He had been her lover, her only connection with the real world, it seemed, until this moment. She could not trust him, and yet she was compelled to do so. Summoning her hardest, coldest voice, Beth said, "I want to know about Elizabeth."

Sam closed his eyes and then passed his hand in front of his face to hide his momentary reaction. Dully, he said, "Elizabeth is dead."

"I know. I know the day she died, in fact," Beth said coldly, intending to hurt him. "But now I want to know *how,* Sam."

"She—she died from—" Sam caught himself, looked away to catch his breath and tried again. He said quietly, "She was murdered, Beth. She had gone to New York like you, and they found her body somewhere in Pennsylvania."

"Just like what happened to me."

"Yes," Sam agreed, sounding more composed. He straightened and looked at her across the room again. "She was killed by the same person who hurt you, Beth, we're sure of it. But it happened two years ago, and the FBI hasn't made the connection between what happened to you and those other women—and the circumstances of Elizabeth's death. Connor figured it out."

"Connor?"

Sam nodded, and some of the color began to return to his face. Trying his best, he explained, "He's a cop, you know. And he—he loved Elizabeth very much. He wants to work for the FBI, I guess, but he thinks he's been buried out here doing—oh, it doesn't matter. He thinks this would help him get a post somewhere else, and—well, Connor wanted to find Elizabeth's—the man who killed her. He's spent the last two years trying to find some evidence against *anybody,* and he hasn't found a thing. Then when you—you lived when the others hadn't, he thought it was a chance to find out something new."

"By kidnapping me? Making me believe I was your—that I was Elizabeth?"

Sam heard the crack in her voice and stepped out from behind the chair to come to her. He moved so swiftly that Beth gasped and bolted to find safety around the sofa.

Sam froze again, seeing the fear behind her pretense of bravery. That knowledge brought a new dullness to his eyes. He said painfully, "I'm sorry. I won't hurt you. You can believe that,

Beth. I never meant to be a party to anything that might have hurt you. I never meant to help them."

"Them?"

"Connor and—and his father."

"Dr. Westham."

Sam's eyes widened. "You know it all, don't you?"

"Not all," Beth snapped, glaring at him anew. She was finished with being weak and foolish, and the resolve must have shown in her face. For a moment she wanted to hurt Sam, to see him in as much pain as she was. Her eyes must have reflected the turmoil of emotions, for he simply stared at her for an instant in confusion.

Then, running his hand swiftly through his hair, Sam shook his head in frustration and burst out, "My God, Beth! I've got to know what's going on in your head before I can go on with this."

Furious, Beth cried out, "I'm deciding how much I should hate you, Sam! That's what's going on in my damnably empty head right now!"

"Your head isn't empty," Sam said immediately. Then, more softly, he added, "And you're not capable of hate."

"Perhaps I wasn't before, but I am now."

"No," Sam said, sure of himself. He took a cautious pace toward her and then another. "You can't hate anyone, Beth, not even me. You're too good."

"You mean I'm too stupid!"

"You've been anything but stupid. You've handled this better than I would have, I'm sure. Darling, I—"

"Don't call me that!"

Sam took another step. "I love you, Beth."

She clapped her hands over her ears, feeling herself weaken. Spinning away from him, she braced her body against the back of the sofa. "No more lies, Sam! I won't be lied to anymore! I won't believe anything you say, so don't—"

"I love you. I love you more than I ever loved Elizabeth, and there was a time I thought my life was over because she was dead. Beth," he pleaded, coming the last few feet to her side. "Beth, darling, I want to help now. I've finished with my part in this—this mess Connor got us into. I'm on your side, and I always have been."

"Stop it!"

"It's true," Sam insisted. He didn't touch her, though he nearly did. His hands hovered over her shoulders, then dropped prudently away. He explained in a rush of words. "I wasn't going to help them in the first place, Beth, but Dr. Westham begged me to come to the hospital to talk about what they had planned for you. I went, intending to tell them to forget it, that I wasn't going to help. And then—I met you. I met you completely by chance in the elevator, and when I realized—we talked, do you remember?"

"Y-yes."

"And you had so much fire in you, I knew. You were strong, but the pressure—the police and the doctors and everything was pressing in on you so much that the fire was going to be smothered. I could offer you a way out of that hospital, Beth. You wanted out so desperately, and I could at least give you the freedom to start your life all over again. I'd failed terribly with Elizabeth, and I still haven't forgiven myself for that. I had let her go away and be alone, and she'd been *murdered* when *I* should have been with her. Beth, I owed it to Elizabeth. It—I just decided then that I had to try to help you, to make you happy again, to go through with Connor's stupid scheme even if it meant—" He stopped, suddenly short of breath.

Coldly, Beth prodded, "Even if it meant what?"

Sam sighed. "That we'll probably all go to jail."

Beth turned on Sam and lifted her head to stare at him. *"What?"*

"Not you, of course," Sam corrected miserably. "But Connor, Westham and I have knowingly committed fraud. I didn't care at first. I've botched my life pretty thoroughly, and it didn't matter if I spent the rest of it here or in some—"

"Because Elizabeth was dead, you were prepared to end your own life?"

"Not literally, but I didn't care what happened to me." Sam said the words simply. "Until *you* became the most important part of my life, Beth. Until you started to fall in love with me, and until I realized my own feelings about you, I didn't care if I went to jail. But now..."

"Now?"

Sam didn't flinch from her penetrating, truth-seeking gaze. Slowly, he said. "Now I want to spend the rest of my life making you happy. I love you, Beth. You've given my life back to me."

Shaken, Beth put her hand to her eyes and whispered, "Oh, God."

Sam did not respond for a moment, perhaps trying to determine exactly what Beth's feelings were. Then, carefully, he put his hands out and touched her shoulders. Beth shuddered under his grasp, but did not wrench away and run. She stood still, shivering, and Sam's hands tightened firmly. He did not pull her against him, however. His own relief at touching her finally seemed to flow through his hands. He waited until her trembling abated.

Then, speaking almost normally, he began to explain. "Connor never believed we'd fail. He thought all along that we'd bring you here, give you some hope and help you regain your memory. He imagined he'd become a hero, I suppose, but then he's always been a bit dim when it comes to reality. And Dr. Westham . . . Beth, he's been so distraught over Elizabeth. His own daughter! He's been just as obsessed with finding her killer as Con has. The two of them were determined—I don't know, out of revenge, I guess, to find the man who—who did those things to Elizabeth. Dr. Westham was sure that you'd eventually regain your memory, and that they—we—would get some useful information out of you. At first I refused, but then I met you and decided I had nothing I wasn't afraid to lose, and you only had things to gain, so we went ahead. Westham convinced the FBI that I was your husband. That was his job—the convincing. I don't know what he did exactly to talk them into believing you were my wife. He may have even bribed someone, for all I know. We pretended Elizabeth had never died, and we never mentioned that my wife had been Westham's daughter. We had her birth certificate altered to match our story. The identity we prepared for you was that of Elizabeth West Sheridan. When the FBI showed signs of investigating further, Westham made a fuss about your health and how you could really walk out of the hospital any time you liked without their permission, so—"

"But the FBI followed us here."

"Yes," Sam said, cutting short his explanation. "I thought they had figured out what we had done. Maybe they have, but I'm not sure."

Beth still couldn't turn around, but to clarify her thoughts, she said, "They stopped you in town. Why? To accuse you of what you'd done?"

"No, not exactly. They were cagey, and so was I. I couldn't tell if they knew or not, yet. It—it unnerved me, I guess. I knew the end was coming. And suddenly it really started to matter to me how things were going to turn out."

Sam was silent for a time, and then added, "Because I've fallen in love with you, Beth."

"Don't," Beth warned stiffly.

"Don't what?" he asked, still behind her. "Don't love you? I can't help it now. You're a good, good woman with courage and humor and sweetness that—"

"Stop it."

"I never meant for this to happen, Beth."

"What *did* you mean to have happen?" Beth demanded, marshaling her wavering resolve enough to half turn and look at him. "What did you expect, Sam? That we'd all live happily ever after?"

He released her then and stepped back. "I don't know what I expected for you. I expect to be punished for what's gone on, but I always assumed that you'd come out of this experience without being hurt. I didn't think we'd find ourselves so attracted to each other."

Beth took a step away from him. "I am not going to—"

"Stop," Sam commanded suddenly, his voice gaining authority, growing sharp. "Don't deny what's true, Beth. You said you loved me, and I realize how deeply I care for you in return. But I never intended for that to happen."

"What *did* you intend to happen, Sam? To me, I mean? What did you think I would do when I finally put two and two together?"

"I—I don't know," Sam said inadequately.

"You don't know?" Beth demanded. "You planned to use me as a pawn, to milk my memory to serve your own purposes and you never once considered how I might feel about it all?"

"I admit we were stupid," Sam snapped. "We didn't think things through very carefully. For God's sake, Beth, we were all sick with grief over Elizabeth, and—and half crazy over the circumstances of her death, I'm sure. We just didn't think this far ahead! Believe me, we never intended for you to be harmed. Honestly, Beth, I didn't want any of this to happen. I especially didn't want to fall in love with you."

Beth stared at him and was silent.

Sam held her gaze uncertainly, unwillingly. He said, "I didn'
want to love you, Beth. I didn't want to complicate your life any
more."

"Complicate it? What a laugh!"

Sam reached tentatively. He grasped Beth's wrist and lifted he
left hand to the light that shafted down from the skylight. He
ring, her wedding ring that had for so long been a part of he
hand, sparkled suddenly in the brightness of the slanting sun
striking Beth into a wordless trance. Sam didn't want to say th
words, but he forced himself with a visible effort.

Quietly, he said, "Because you're married, Beth. To anothe
man."

Beth choked on an involuntary sob that caught immediately i
her throat. Her eyes widened and she felt them begin to burn wit
tears. She hadn't realized. For all the facts she had discovered, thi
was one she had completely forgotten. Or perhaps denied. "Oh
my God."

Without hesitation, Sam gathered her into his embrace, then
a safe harbor when too much information stormed her. He hel
her head against his chest and wrapped his long arm around he
quivering body. It felt good, and Beth gave in instinctively to th
warmth he offered. He dropped his cheek against her hair. "Dar
ling, it's too much for you to handle now, I know. I wanted to hel
you, to offer you some friendship, perhaps. But I knew I shoul
not treat you as if you were really my wife. I stayed away from
you, though I was tempted right from the start to touch you an
hold you the way you wanted me to."

Beth swallowed. Her head was a kaleidoscope—too full o
dazzling, frightening colors, it seemed. There was suddenly to
much to assimilate.

Sam rocked her gently in his arms. He held her tightly an
spoke over her head. "Darling, there were so many reasons to kee
my distance, but I couldn't. You needed me, and pretty soon
needed you, too. I've fallen in love with you, when I knew from
the start I shouldn't."

Beth suddenly understood the troubled look she had seen con
stantly lurking in Sam's eyes. He'd been wrestling with muc
larger problems, while she had been trying hard to please him

He'd been in pain then—for Elizabeth and for her, too—and she had only made his decisions more complicated.

"I love you now," he said. "And heaven forgive me, I want you to stay with me. I don't want to face losing you, Beth. It would be worse than the way I lost Elizabeth."

Without thinking about her actions, Beth slipped her arms behind Sam's back to hold him. Even as she clasped him, she laid her right hand over her left and felt the rigid metal of her wedding ring under her fingertips. Another man's ring. Sam needed her now, she realized. He still hadn't overcome his grief for Elizabeth. He needed Beth, no matter who she was.

"I've been trying to find out who you are, Beth," Sam continued, his voice still harsh with pain. "I want you, but I can't suppress who you really are any longer. It was cruel to force Elizabeth's past on you. I've been racking my brain for ways to find something out about you. Connor's been doing the legwork. We hadn't a clue until you got that flash of memory about the bicycling. I started reading through old biking magazines. Finally there was—"

"Oh, no," Beth whispered, shutting her eyes against the words to come.

Sam heard her voice and held her fast. Determinedly, he said, "I found something, Beth. It took forever, it seemed, but I found it. And I went to San Francisco to confirm—"

Beth held her breath and waited.

Sam stopped explaining and sighed. Then, quietly, he said, "Your name is Bettina Foster. You lived in San Francisco, and your husband's name is Matthew."

CHAPTER THIRTEEN

BETH BURST INTO TEARS—weak, stupid, senseless tears that hurt her throat and burned her face. Her pride was in shambles, but the pain inside her was worse, wrenching and tearing at her with a force Beth couldn't have imagined.

She didn't want to know. She didn't *want* her name and her identity. Finally, here it was, and she didn't want it.

Sam held her so hard that it seemed his was the only power that held Beth together for those first terrible minutes. Here was Sam, the man who was her strength and her weakness, the man who had caused her pain and who would now try to ease it. He had said he loved her. She had a choice. She could have Sam or—what was his name? Matthew? Did she want either of them?

No, no, she couldn't go through it all again, not knowing herself, not knowing the people who loved her. She couldn't do it, couldn't summon the energy. And yet she couldn't trust Sam now, not after discovering all his lies. She was back in limbo.

"It's all right," Sam was murmuring, stroking her hair very gently. "It's not so bad. Your name is Bett, not Beth. It's so close, don't you see? You must have remembered part of yourself if you nearly chose the right name at the hospital."

Beth's breath was so tight in her chest that she could hardly speak. Unconsciously, she grabbed her hands full of the fabric of Sam's shirt and held on, burying her face against him. Almost to herself, she moaned, "I don't want another new name. I don't want to hear more!"

"Yes, you do. It's all good, my love. Don't cry. Beth, there's a chance you'll regain all your memory, don't you see? You're getting close. But you'll *never forget* what we've had, Beth. You may get a new name and a new set of papers that tell you something about yourself, but you'll never lose this—what we have together."

"But him? This Matthew? What about him?"

"I didn't find him," Sam said quietly, still petting Beth to soothe her. "I couldn't make myself try, to tell the truth. I only found that he does exist, but I didn't see him. I found out about you, though."

Beth was glad to ignore Matthew for a while. She could still deny that a little longer. She loosened her grip on Sam's shirt a little and asked unevenly, "Well? Am I—is there anything I should—?"

"Yes," Sam said gently. "There's plenty. Come and sit down, all right? I don't want this to overwhelm you."

Beth moved stiffly, allowing Sam to draw her back to the kitchen. His suitcase was there, abandoned on the counter beside the sandwich and apples. He must have guessed immediately that she was going to leave him.

Sam ignored the evidence, though, and eased her onto the stool before turning away to fill a glass of water from the tap. Beth watched him dully, her brain almost numb. Should she trust Sam now? Or be afraid of him and what he could do to her with more deception? Her emotions jumbled together, too confusing to separate and make into sensible thoughts. Sam needed her, he said, and here he was, taking care of her once again as if she were an invalid. If he was acting a part, he was very convincing. He moved swiftly, his hand steady on the tap. He was calm, Beth realized. Oddly calm. Perhaps everything had been an act for him all along.

Sam turned away form the sink and pressed the glass into Beth's still-trembling grasp. He slipped his other hand naturally under her hair to touch her nape and tipped the glass to help her take a sip. The water was very cold and strangely cleansing. Beth thankfully felt her head clear a little, and was sudde ly grateful that she wasn't alone. Even if she couldn't trust him, she needed Sam a little longer. She would not tell him, though. She was going to have to be as clever as he. Beth was afraid of the weakness he seemed to inspire in her now. Just being with him made Beth feel dependent and female. She must be careful—use her head and stay in control. She held the glass with both hands then, taking it completely from Sam's hands. She did not look up at him but tried to collect herself.

He stood back a little, but kept his fingertips resting comfortingly on her back, just below her hair. "Can you listen now?"

"Yes," she said, with an effort to sound normal. "Tell me."

Sam hesitated, judging her tone of voice, before he decided it was safe to continue. He said, "You're called Bett by your friends, I think. I didn't speak to anyone who knew you well, since I wasn't sure what their reaction would be. You're a writer for a magazine. You were the fiction editor—that helps to explain why you're so literary. It's a San Francisco publication. Small, but well respected. I'd heard of it. In fact—" He stopped and began on another track. "You lived in an apartment complex near the Bay. The neighborhood was fashionable, I'd say."

Beth looked up finally, swiveling the stool so that she could see Sam's face. Somehow, she was interested in what kind of home might have appealed to her before. She asked, "Did you see the apartment?"

"No, I was afraid to ask too many questions and arouse suspicion." He said the words straight out, as if she was now an accomplice and could not be shocked by his methods. "I walked around, that's all. There wasn't time for much, to tell you the truth. I couldn't check at the magazine since it was Saturday, but I thought I could wander in there on Monday and ask for you, just to see what kind of reaction I'd get. But I came back here instead when Connor called me. I had started by checking bicycle shops, you see. They were the best source of information."

"Bicycle shops?" Beth demanded, startled anew.

Sam slid onto the opposite stool and took both her hands in his warm ones, holding her as though he could understand her responses better if he touched her this way. When Beth did not withdraw, he explained seriously, "It was the bicycle thing that got me started. It was obvious that some part of your brain recognized the bicycling experience. And you were a natural, Beth, it was obvious. I started going through back issues of the biking magazines, and I found your picture."

"Mine?" Beth cried, jerking unconsciously in his grip. "Why didn't you show it to me?"

"How could I know what your reaction would be?" Sam asked softly, sensibly. "Besides, I would have to concoct some other elaborate lie to explain things to you, and I was so sick of lying to you by then! The Bettina Foster name was in the caption."

Beth looked away, shaking her head a little. He could be so damned calm about this now, while inside, Beth was still reeling from the deluge of information. Hesitantly, and with a shade of wonder in her whispered voice, she repeated to herself, "Bettina Foster."

Sam smiled at Beth's first sign of acceptance of her new identity. "Not so bad, is it? Kind of pretty, in fact."

Beth did not respond to that. She was not ready to warm up to Sam just yet and refused to give him any encouragement. Instead, she pointedly withdrew her hands from his. She found that she wanted to know more about his trip to San Francisco, so she asked abruptly, "What did you do at the bicycle shops?"

Sam released her agreeably and nodded, ready to explain it all, it seemed. "The magazine picture is in my bag. I'll get it out later, if you like. It shows you after you'd won some kind of race out in California, and the caption gave the city where you lived. I went to San Francisco and started asking questions, showing your picture in the various bike shops around town. By the third shop, I knew I was on the right track. They'd all heard of Bett Foster, but they didn't know anything specific about you. It wasn't until I came to the shop where you apparently did all your business that I found out some hard information.

Beth looked at him uneasily in spite of her determination to maintain her poise. "And?"

"They told me where you worked. They even had your bike in the back room, up on a rack. They said you'd left it with them more than three months ago to be serviced, but you hadn't come back for it. You were planning on moving, they said, and you wanted the bike checked one more time before you left."

"Where was I going?"

"To New York."

Startled by that, Beth looked at Sam and found that he was watching her steadily. She said, "So I must have moved already, right? Otherwise, why was I in New York when I was attacked?"

"I went to the magazine offices, but they were closed. I hung around a while and ended up talking with the doorman of the building. He had remembered you and said you'd disappeared. He had heard you were going to New York—partly to find cover art for the magazine, I guess. He wasn't sure, but he thought maybe you'd decided to take a vacation, instead." Sam shook his head.

"I couldn't get anymore information out of him than that, but he didn't think you had moved. I don't believe you'd have left San Francisco without your bike, anyway. Maybe you went to New York on business as he said, or it was just a trip to find a place to live. There are lots of possibilities."

Beth considered the facts for a moment. She regarded Sam, wondering what was in his mind. He returned her look with a watchful, but cautious expression. He, too, was thinking of her husband, the man who stood between them now, though neither would recognize him if he appeared. There were many questions to ask Sam, but the ones that bothered Beth the most just then were the ones she could not ask him. At least, she could not ask him yet. What was going to happen to them? Would Beth be forced to return to the husband she wouldn't recognize? Did she want to? Could she trust Sam ever again or even now? Just thinking of those questions turned her heart cold. She composed her face, determined to be strong, and cupped her hands around the water glass.

Perhaps seeing her resolve to stay cool, Sam went on with his explanation smoothly. "Once I had your name and employer, I had lots of places to look for more information. Even the telephone book was helpful." He paused and added, "That's where I found your husband's name. I think he's an agent for actors, but I haven't confirmed that yet."

"You were afraid to see him."

"God, yes," Sam said on a sigh. "I should have done it, though, I know. You've been through hell, Beth, and I should have at least spared you some of this. But I needed more answers before I could—could go to another man and say I wanted his wife."

Beth looked away quickly and set the glass down on the counter before she dropped it. "Don't, Sam."

He said, "I won't talk about it now, if you need time to assimilate everything, Beth, but I won't drop the subject completely. I mean it. I won't let you go without a hell of a fight."

"You may not have a choice."

"If I'm a free man, I do have choices. I want you here with me."

"I think," Beth said coldly, looking up into his face then, "that the choices are mine, Sam."

"You're upset," Sam said, matching her quiet and holding her gaze with his own. "Don't give yourself any ultimatums right now, Beth. You need some time to think."

"I've had plenty of time to think," Beth returned, summoning a glare for Sam. "I just spent the whole day sitting at Elizabeth Sheridan's headstone. That's given me enough time to decide for myself."

"Beth—"

"Don't touch me," she commanded, even before his hand made contact with hers.

"All right," Sam said, trying hard, she could see, to stay calm. "Look, Beth, we've all been through our own kind of torment. You're within your rights to hurt me all you like. I deserve it. But don't misunderstand why all this has happened."

"I understand," Beth snapped. "It's very clear now. You're all using me to avenge Elizabeth's death. Simple."

"That's the way it started," Sam agreed seriously. "But motives have changed, Beth. At least for me. Maybe Connor wants to see his sister's murderer brought to justice like some kind of wild-West-movie lawman, but I just want to see the end of that part of my life so I can begin again. Elizabeth is gone, and I'm just starting to comprehend that I couldn't have prevented her death. But I can prevent yours."

"Mine?" Beth asked, fear running cold inside her suddenly.

"Beth's," Sam corrected. "You can leave this place and go out into the world now and become Bettina Foster, don't you see? But I don't want Beth Sheridan to disappear in the process. You're too good, my love. You're too sweet and gentle. It would be a tragedy for you to lose those qualities."

"A tragedy for whom? You or me?"

Sam might have winced, but he controlled it. Instead, he said, "For both of us. Beth, we belong together now."

"The law says otherwise," Beth replied, flattening her left hand on the counter so they could both see her wedding ring. "We don't belong together except in some kind of complicated deception that you've created, Sam."

"That's not true," Sam said, urgent now. He leaned forward and covered her wrist with his hand, holding her fast. "Maybe the scheme started out with the wrong intentions, Beth, but as soon as I saw you, I knew we had something between us. You felt it, too, I know you did."

"There must have been something left over in my memory about you," Beth said swiftly, wanting to hurt him suddenly. "I remembered about bicycling. If I was an editor for a magazine, I must have known about you—Sam Sheridan, the famous playwright!" She saw his expression change and demanded, "That's it, isn't it?"

"Look—"

"Don't lie again, please!"

Sam blew a sigh, this time in exasperation. "Yes, as a matter of fact. I was interviewed by that magazine several years ago. Budding playwright and all that garbage. There were pictures, too, I remember. But I *don't* remember talking to you, Beth. Somebody else must have done the interview.

"But I could have worked on it," Beth said remotely, as the last iota of magic seemed to evaporate from their relationship. She had held on to the memory of their first meeting as though it was her lifeline. There had been an electricity between them from the first moment, but here was the logical explanation. Something died inside Beth as she asked emptily, "I could have written the piece, couldn't I? That's why I recognized you, I'm sure now. If there was anything else between us, Sam, it must have been purely sex."

"Sex isn't so bad," Sam argued at once, hearing her tone. Without letting her go, he insisted, "Besides, you know the attraction between us has been more than sex all along. At least for me."

"For you?" Beth demanded, trying to laugh with sarcasm. She turned her gaze on him, full of fire and anger once more, and then struck out at him, saying cruelly, "You wanted to protect this poor little waif who had no hopes except to get out of a stifling hospital! Sure, there was more in this for you, Sam. You were taking care of me like you were doing penance, weren't you? You did everything for me that you wanted to do for Elizabeth."

"For a while, yes," Sam agreed, his brows snapping down in anger that equalled hers. "For a while you took Elizabeth's place."

"Even in her bed!" Beth gasped, scalded anew by her own foolish actions. "I really pushed myself into that, didn't I?"

"You didn't force me to do anything," Sam said sharply. "After a two-year dormant period, I was surprised that I wanted you sexually the same way I wanted Elizabeth—the only woman I thought I'd ever make love to. But you attracted me, Beth, long before you started asking me about our—about a physical relationship. You attracted me differently than Elizabeth did, but with just as much—oh, hell—you're different, Beth, and you've never let me forget that. You're sensual, where she was only sexual. You take pleasure differently—more deeply, somehow. You have more determination than Elizabeth ever did. Yet you're kinder, too. You're thinking of everyone else around you before you think of yourself."

"I guess it's high time I started thinking about myself, isn't it?"

"Yes," Sam retorted, ignoring her bitterness. "But you'll figure yourself out pretty quickly, if I know you, and you'll start thinking about everyone else who's involved, Beth. Once you calm down, you're going to take more than yourself into consideration."

"What do you mean?" Then she guessed. "About the future?"

Sam nodded, watching her face unswervingly. "What comes next, Beth? You were running away, I can see. Even without knowing who you were. Where were you going?"

"It doesn't matter now. I was just going to put as much distance between myself and—and all this mess you and Connor have started. Now—" Beth pulled away from Sam's grasp again and slid off the stool. "Now I've got places to go, haven't I?"

"Not alone," Sam said, full of authority.

Beth tried to laugh derisively again. "You're coming with me? To confront my husband? My real husband?"

"No matter where you go, I'm coming with you."

"Sure, come along if you like! It's bound to be a scene full of high comedy, Sam. You might be able to use it in a play if you ever start writing again."

There was a crunching of gravel outside them, signifying the arrival of a car in the driveway. Sam turned away, nonplussed by her insults, and glanced out the window.

"Well?" Beth asked acidly, watching his profile. "Is it the cops coming to arrest you? Or maybe just your sidekick accomplice returning to the scene of the crime?"

"It's Connor," Sam answered, turning back to her. "Are you going to tell him?"

"That I know what's going on? Of course. I'm no good at lying, Sam. Not like the rest of you, anyway. I don't intend to stand around and argue with Connor, though. I'm leaving as soon as I can."

"I'm coming, too, wherever you decide to go. You're not strong enough to go anywhere by yourself."

Beth heard Connor's door slam and his rapid footsteps on the driveway. She met Sam's eyes, though, and shut out the rest of the world for a moment. Most of the life she remembered had been spent with Sam. He'd brought her alive, and perhaps she'd done the same for him. For that, he wasn't going to stand aside and let her walk out of his world. Sam was too strong willed to let her go when he'd just decided he loved her. Still, he'd wounded Beth. He had lied and lied so thoroughly that now it was impossible to separate the truth from fiction. How much of what he'd told her was fact? Perhaps he'd lied about his feelings for her as well as everything else. Undoubtedly he had. He was a very good actor.

Who knew if he was lying now or not? His face, always unnaturally still, gave away nothing. Beth put out her hand and touched Sam's cheek, her fingertips tracing the sharp planes. He didn't flinch. She touched his mouth very lightly with her thumb and marveled at how motionless he remained. It had been nearly the first characteristic about him that she'd recognized. Only Sam's eyes gave any clues, and now their gray-green color was too smoky to show any fire within.

Sam took her wrist again, holding her hand to his cheek a moment longer, even as Connor's boots rang out on the porch steps.

But Beth pulled away. Quietly, she said, "I'm stronger than you think, Sam."

He didn't answer, but nodded, conceding.

Then Connor burst in, looking frightened and angry and startled all at the same time. The door slammed back and struck the wall with a crack, but Connor didn't notice. He froze inside the doorstep and stared at Beth as if he'd seen a ghost. His blond good looks were windblown and dirty, as if he'd been searching the roughest countryside all day. He licked his lips and asked, "Wh-where have you been?"

Distinctly, Beth said, "To hell, Connor. And back again."

She turned and started to leave the kitchen without waiting for his reply. She had packing to do.

"Beth—" Connor objected with a gasp, convulsively moving to follow her. Perhaps he meant to stop her, explain or ask questions. Too distraught to see what had happened in his absence, he tried to go after her.

But Sam was there, interceding. He stopped Connor and said, "Don't, Con. She knows."

"Knows?" Con's voice cracked. "Knows what?"

"Everything. Probably more than we do ourselves."

"*What?* You idiot, why'd you tell her?"

Beth turned in the doorway, feeling calmer than ever. Whether it was Con's verging on hysteria or her own returning wits, she couldn't be sure, but she was suddenly quite in command of herself. "He didn't have to tell me, Con. You've all been dropping hints like crazy, I suppose, and I was just too afraid to put them all together to make the puzzle fit. You've all lied very nicely, very thoroughly. But you, Con, you make me the angriest. You took such *pleasure* in it, didn't you?"

"Beth—" Sam warned.

"At least you suffered a little, Sam," she swept on in a voice that trembled, but not with fear this time. She was shaking with rage once again, glaring at Connor. "But Con loved this! He played with my life like it was some kind of game, and he had every intention of throwing away the pieces when he had finished!"

"Don't guess," Sam interrupted, protecting Connor suddenly. "Beth, he—"

"I'm capable of seeing the future without benefit of a crystal ball! My dear, loving brother was going to wring as much as he could out of me, purely for his own gain. Making me feel nice and secure with all his talk about his sister, our past, our childhoods—"

"I didn't lie," Connor said, sounding odd and rather childlike. His face, usually taut and alert, had somehow crumpled and turned gray. His plans were ruined, his hopes in ashes, and Con knew it. Inadequately, he tried to explain. "I told you everything about Elizabeth. She was—" He struggled a moment, and then said simply, "She was my sister and I loved her."

Beth took a big breath and held it. She had been full of fiery anger a moment ago, but seeing Connor's cockiness slowly being demolished before her eyes was too much. Why she had ever imagined that Connor could do her harm, she didn't know. Sam didn't have to stop her. Beth checked herself, holding back more accusations. She was silent, staring.

Connor's face twisted even more, and suddenly Beth knew he was holding back tears. He stretched out his hand in a parody of melodrama, then balled it into a fist and—slowly—touched it to his forehead to contain something awful that threatened him inside. Connor had his own demons, too, it seemed. Choked, he tried to explain, saying, "She didn't deserve what happened to her. I want—I wanted—"

"Con," Sam said gently, stopping him. He touched Connor's shoulder.

Beth turned around and left. Unable to stand seeing any more, she walked quickly through the sitting room, shaking her head to rid herself of the image of two men comforting each other. It was too much. She shouldn't have to cope with their troubles as well as her own. Stupid Connor! He'd been just as naive as she had! She stormed into the bedroom and slammed the door behind her. Leaning on the door, she put her hands to her face.

Con's voice rose in the kitchen, sounding querulous and out of control.

Beth shut her eyes, hoping to block out the sound. Connor had loved his sister. He'd been doing only what he felt he needed to do. He had used every means possible on behalf of his sister. He probably hadn't meant Beth any harm.

And Sam? Yes, Beth could understand why he'd been moved to help. He might have been first lured by the idea of coming to Elizabeth's defense. Then kindhearted Sam had seen a way to help someone who needed him. That he had fallen in love with her had only made things more difficult.

Beth sighed. Sam had been right. Here she was, thinking of others. She had brushed aside her own problems and was thinking of Sam and Connor. And Dr. Westham, too, she supposed. In the hospital Dr. Westham had taken Beth under his wing. He, no doubt, had many reasons, but Beth believed that somehow she had touched his heart, too.

There wasn't much choice, was there? Beth realized why Sam had been so calm. She was calm now, too, all because she recognized she had a goal. There was a job to be done, a direction in which to travel. She had a purpose.

Sam tapped on the door from outside, not daring to go into the bedroom without permission. Testing, he asked, "Beth?"

Turning around slowly, she opened the door. Then she looked at Sam's face, both grave and wary, and asked, "Is Connor all right?"

Sam shrugged. "As good as any of us."

Beth stood aside, allowing Sam into the bedroom. "Come in and tell me the rest," she said. "While I pack."

"You've decided already?" Sam asked.

"Yes. We're going to New York. I think there's a murder to solve before I leave you, isn't there?"

CHAPTER FOURTEEN

SAM WASN'T SURPRISED. He wasn't meek either, and he didn't apologize for what he'd done. He had declared his intention to stay by her side, and he didn't listen when Beth objected. They talked and Beth packed. Then Sam made some phone calls to prepare for their trip to New York. When the time came, he simply picked up his suitcase again and drove with Beth to the airport.

On the flight, Beth sat silently beside him, not willing to talk anymore after he'd explained everything to her satisfaction. She needed to consider all the information. She wasn't ready to dissect her own motives yet, but she needed to think and make decisions. Sam did not interfere. Undoubtedly he had his own life to ponder.

They landed at LaGuardia and Sam took charge again. Instead of fussing over Beth, he led her through the airport, found a cab and handed her into it as expeditiously as possible. By that time it was night, of course, and he directed the driver to a West Side address. Beth didn't listen very clearly. She was exhausted already, but she wasn't going to admit it. She held herself very still and watched the blurring rush of confusing New York scenery.

The address was apparently an apartment building. There was a doorman and an elevator, then a short, badly lighted hallway with five doors. Sam had a key in his pocket. He knew the trick of the lock and let Beth precede him into the dimness of the rooms. There was a musty smell of disuse inside. But before Sam had stashed their baggage and found all the light switches, Beth knew it was his place and probably dated from before his marriage to Elizabeth. Why he still kept it, she couldn't guess.

Sam unlocked some windows in the kitchen and created a breeze through the apartment, some much needed fresh air. Beth hung silently in the small living room, too tired to explore. In a moment Sam returned to collect her.

He took her arm, using some force for the first time all day. "Come on," he said, with a tone that tolerated no argument. "You are going to bed."

She was smart enough not to resist him, though some less mature part of herself wanted to wrench out of Sam's grip and tell him to leave her alone. Beth obeyed, though, for she was more than tired. She had her own facade to maintain now. She began to understand how much energy pretending could consume. How had Sam maintained the lies for so long without cracking?

He began undressing her. He helped her out of her sweater and unbuttoned her shirt. Beth relaxed as he did those little tasks, wondering almost distantly about Sam. Was he playacting? Was he using her to replace Elizabeth even now? Did he love her truly? Or was he just transferring the emotion he had felt for his wife to a new, needier, compassion-starved woman? Beth pushed aside his hands before he undressed her completely. She suddenly didn't like Sam's caretaking. Without speaking, she took her nightgown from her suitcase and went into the bathroom alone.

He turned down the bed for her and snapped off the light. When Beth came out of the bathroom and into the darkness, he took both her arms in his hands and held her still for a moment while he kissed her softly on her forehead. Beth didn't react, didn't want to. She closed her eyes, though, against the surge of emotion that threatened to weaken her once more. Tempted to respond to his gentle kiss, she moved out of Sam's half embrace and climbed into bed, hoping she could shut off her emotions a little longer. Perhaps understanding her need to reject him just then, Sam tucked the bedclothes around her and left the room.

Shortly, Beth heard his voice on the telephone. She felt safe and warm, tucked into his slightly dusty-smelling bed hearing his voice in the next room, quiet and deliberate as always, though with a weariness. But Beth had learned her lesson well. Feelings of contentment were misleading. Nothing was ever what it seemed.

She tried to sleep, and when the nightmare came again—the screeching cat with the horrible eyes—she managed to force her face into the pillow before she cried out. With her head full of frightening images, Beth fought the urge to scream and instead found herself sobbing into the muffling bed. She struggled to keep silent, praying that Sam didn't hear her. If he came to her bed just then, she'd surely give in. She loved him, after all. There was no denying that fact. She loved him, but she couldn't trust him.

In the morning she woke to find a note on the bathroom door. He had gone out for some food, it said. Alone and still in her short nightgown, Beth made a cautious tour of her surroundings.

It had been a writer's place, Beth could see. Sam had kept his typewriter at the Wyoming house, but this apartment *felt* like the home of a real writer. The living room was packed floor to ceiling with haphazardly constructed bookshelves that were crowded with books and papers and badly bound manuscripts. The second bedroom was even less attractive, with more bookshelves—planks set between concrete blocks—and a wide, long library-style table that must have served as a desk. There was a large empty space on it where the typewriter must have stood. Cartons of papers, a cupful of pencils and pens, a tattered Rolodex, were all signs that a prolific and businesslike writer had indeed worked here.

There were other signs too, clues about Sam's life in New York. On one wall was a poster advertising *Bitten*, autographed by an actor who wrote, "I've really been bitten on this one! When do I get a raise?" Some funny greeting cards were pinned on a corkboard, all wishing Sam a happy birthday. An empty champagne bottle, an opera program, ticket stubs, a coffee cup with a printed inscription: Grr. Another Monday Morning!

The living room furniture was minimal, but near the front window a comfortable leather armchair and matching footstool stood beside a once-expensive brass floor lamp. There was a pillow, too, faded with worn ruffles. It was a needlepoint and the stitching read, A Son is a Son is a Son is a Pain Sometimes! The initials must have been Sam's mother's. The chair itself was an ideal place to read, and Beth gravitated toward it, once she had explored the rest of the apartment.

She curled her legs under her and nestled into the chair, holding the pillow in her lap and looking with undeniable interest at her surroundings. Yes, she could see Sam here. Though he had seemed at home in Wyoming playing the gentleman rancher, she suddenly understood that Sam belonged in New York, near his theaters, near his work.

He had been tormented by Elizabeth's death, it was clear. He had needed to be with her—to be with her memory, Beth supposed. He had stayed at the ranch until he could forgive himself for allowing her to die. Sam was a deep and thoughtful man, one who shouldered burdens without complaint and without excuses. He had isolated himself and grieved.

Beth had been the first person Sam had allowed into his life, she knew, just as he had been the only one she had opened herself to. Perhaps there was no future between them, but Beth felt she owed Sam some peace of mind. He needed to return to the land of the living. For his sake, she had to put Elizabeth's memory to rest.

And for Connor, too, and Dr. Westham. Perhaps they had hurt her, but their motive had been love for Elizabeth. Beth couldn't dismiss their genuine love for the dead woman she had been forced to impersonate. She had to devote some time to finding the man who had murdered Elizabeth Sheridan.

Beth wasn't going to fool herself any longer, and she knew that working on the "case" was a way of postponing her own life. The longer she stayed in this safe limbo, the longer she could avoid the trauma of rediscovering her husband and family.

A key rasped in the lock, and the door opened with an accompanying rattle of shopping bags. Sam must have taken a peek into the bedroom and found her gone, for a moment later he poked his head into the living room to look for her.

Beth met his eyes without flinching, without moving. Inside, she felt her own body start to ache. Lord, yes, she loved him.

"Stronger today?" Sam asked pleasantly enough, but without a smile. He was nervous, though the signs would not have shown to anyone but Beth.

"Yes," Beth told him calmly and stayed in the chair, pillow on her lap. "I'm starting to get a grip on myself again."

Sam came into the room with two smallish grocery bags in his arms. With his deceptively casual rolling saunter, he crossed to the footstool, saying, "I don't think you ever lost your grip. Damn, it's embarrassing how tough you can be while the rest of us run around like chickens. Good morning."

He kissed the top of her head, which Beth bowed just in time to avoid the touch of his lips on her face. After putting the bags down on the floor, he made himself comfortable on the footstool, one leg stretched comfortably, the other knee bent. Then, rummaging through his purchases without looking at Beth, he said, "You're looking quite at home."

"Perhaps at peace with myself," Beth replied almost at once, and wondered what had made her say so. She wasn't sure it was true, but added, "I think I know where I'm going, at least."

Sam handed over a foam cup with a plastic lid. "Here. Try this. It's from a deli around the corner, and I remember it being the best coffee on earth. Watch, it's hot."

Beth accepted the cup from him, conscious that Sam was methodically ignoring the subject she introduced.

He groped into the other bag. "I'm surprised how little this neighborhood has changed in two years. I always think of the city as metamorphosing every few weeks, but things look just the same. Look. Bagels and cheese Danish. Marvelous stuff, and you can't buy them west of the George Washington bridge, I swear. You must be hungry. Paper napkins are the best I can do."

"Sam," Beth interrupted gently when he was about to thrust the food into her lap. "Sam, you're chattering."

He looked at her and blinked. "I'm what?"

"Chattering. I never thought I'd see the day. You're nervous."

He allowed a smile, one that was surprisingly full of charm while his eyes were so full of misgivings. "You're surprised? I'm about to win or lose the woman I love, and you're surprised to see me nervous?"

Beth's smile faded and she ducked her head. "Let's not talk about that, please."

"That," Sam repeated with an edge of anger flicking through his words, "is us. You and me and how much we love each other. We'll talk about it eventually, Beth."

"Eventually is not now," Beth said, trying to sound harsh and not daring to look at him. She pushed away the food and said with as much nastiness as she could muster, "I'm not Beth, anyway, am I? How long are you going to call me that?"

"Forever. To me, you'll never be anything else."

She withheld a sigh and wished they didn't have to be so direct so early in the morning. Tensely, she inquired, "Are you deliberately trying to make me break down?"

"God, no," Sam said at once, setting aside his cup. He reached for her hand swiftly and clasped it in his two. "Darling Beth, I'll do anything you want. I've brought you here, haven't I? Without questions? I'll support you no matter what you do today, but I won't break you. I don't think you can be broken, my love. Just don't expect me to walk away, all right?''

"Sam," Beth said steadily, ignoring the sting in her eyes. "Sam, if I ask you to do something for me, will you promise to do it?''

He was silent, knowing what she was going to say.

"If I ask you to leave me," she continued, her voice quavering suddenly as she looked up and found his gray-green eyes watchfully regarding her, "If I ask you to let me go on with my life, will you give me that much? When all this is over...?''

Sam did not answer. Perhaps he was going to lie again, or maybe he just couldn't respond at all. Beth didn't know, and he had once again shuttered his face so that no clues were revealed. He let the question go by as if she had never asked it. Holding her hand and looking down at it as though he were holding the most precious sculpture in the world, he said, "What are you going to do today?''

Beth stared at Sam's dark head for a moment. No, she couldn't expect him to turn off his emotions. Sam felt things too deeply, Beth knew. She was tempted in that long, quiet moment, to touch his hair, to smooth it back from his temple, perhaps, and press the softest of comforting kisses there. She did not, however, but nodded, accepting his question and explaining, "I'm going to start looking at galleries, I think. You said that I had come to New York looking for cover art for the magazine. The police have told me that undoubtedly I met the man who attacked me in a gallery, probably in Greenwich Village. He found all his victims in galleries. I'd like to just look around today. I have a feeling—I can't help suspecting that I might recognize something if I just look around.''

"All right," said Sam, turning her palm over in his hands as he spoke. "Marcus thought that would be the best way to start also. If we—''

"Marcus?" Beth asked sharply, jerking in surprise.

Sam held her hand and looked up into her face, his own expression guarded. With deceptive calm, he said, "Yes, you met him at the hospital. I called him last night and—''

"Marcus with the FBI?" Beth demanded, wanting clarification.

"Yes," said Sam. His eyes were steady. "I thought I'd better come clean entirely. Don't you agree? I called him after you'd gone to bed. I told him everything."

"Everything?"

"Well," Sam hedged, glancing away, "I told him that I had deceived them. I didn't implicate Westham or Connor. Not yet, at least. They'll be found out soon enough, but I thought I'd take the heat for a while first."

So he had delivered himself to the lions. Startled, Beth put down her coffee and couldn't stop herself from touching her hand to Sam's cheek. "Are they—? Will you be—?"

"Arrested? Not yet," he said grimly, turning to meet her gaze. "I—I offered them my services for a while—until this thing is over one way or the other. They can't seem to restart the murder investigation without me at this point, so they're stuck with me for now."

"And later?" Beth whispered, her heart thumping for him.

Sam shrugged and tried to smile. "Who can guess? We'll see what happens. They don't trust me any farther than they can throw me, of course. Marcus sent a man around last night—Byers. Remember him from the hospital? He's a New York cop. He's sitting outside in the hall like some kind of warden. He follows me everywhere like Thisby—even to the deli."

"Oh, Sam," Beth whispered, caressing his face with her fingertips.

He managed a smile then, not moving from her featherlight touch. "Don't worry. I've known exactly what I got myself into from the start. Beth—"

She realized what she had been doing and began to pull her hand away.

Sam caught her quickly though and turned toward her. He captured her wrist and held her. "Beth, everything I've done so far has been despicable. I'm trying to put things right, now, but it may not be enough, I know. Just please—you've got to understand that—"

"I know."

"I love you."

"I—I know."

"Do you? Do you believe me? I'm not lying to you now. I never have about my feelings for you. Darling Beth, I'm not confusing you with Elizabeth and I'm not trying to . . . to make you feel better about yourself by claiming feelings I—"

"I know," Beth said, closing her eyes. "And I've loved you, too, Sam. I can't say how I feel now except for being hurt."

"You don't know how I hate making you suffer like this."

"I think I do," Beth said steadily. "I think you're suffering more than I am. You're like that, Sam. Your depth is what made me love you most. But I—right now things are so bad between us that I can't—"

Sam gathered her up then, pulling Beth into his body so easily that they might have been lovers for years. He tucked her head into his chest and wrapped his arms around her. Over Beth's head, he said, "I understand, my love. Let's get through today, all right? I'm here for you today. Will you count on me? Trust me?"

Beth inhaled the scent of him, laid her ear against his chest and felt the steady rhythm of Sam's heart. She said, "Yes, I need your help today. Will you take me to these places?"

"Of course," said Sam, kissing her hair once, twice. There was relief in his voice and fresh strength in the way he held her. "I'm with you, darling. I intend to stay there."

Beth didn't argue, didn't challenge him. It felt too good to be in his arms. She reveled in his kisses but did not return them for fear he'd misinterpret her softening of heart. Relaxing in Sam's embrace, she found that she was smiling.

She could sense his passion, though, the kindling desire that happened each time they found themselves in each other's arms. No, she wasn't ready for that! Beth reluctantly pushed Sam away and got up. She made a light remark, which made Sam laugh a little, and she laughed with him. Suddenly they knew where they stood with each other. They were together and working, in a way. They were a team and had been lovers once.

Beth showered and dressed and felt strong. She finished her coffee and ate her breakfast while Sam got cleaned up and dressed again. Then, accepting Mr. Byers like the third of the Musketeers, they took a cab to Greenwich Village and began.

BETH WASN'T SURE what she was looking for. She only knew that three months ago a young woman named Bettina Foster had come to a gallery within just a few square blocks and had been abducted by a man who had done the same thing before.

Beth hoped that something would click in her head, just the way it had when she had tried bicycling the first time. Though her method seemed like pathetic shots in the dark, it couldn't hurt to try, she reasoned.

The New York City cop reported to Sam that the FBI had begun working on the case soon after Sam had talked with them the night before. They had begun tracing backward, apparently, trying to find out anything and everything about Bettina Foster and her buying trip to New York. It seemed that the whole investigation team had been mobilized again with fresh hope of finding the killer.

Sam was methodical. He had taken some pages from the phone book and photocopied them, and with that information in hand, they started looking into each gallery. First one street and then the next. Beth wandered into each shop and looked around, sometimes studying the pictures on the walls, sometimes just getting a feel for the rooms. Each time, she shook her head and led the way back to the street. She wasn't sure what she was looking for, but she'd know it if she saw it.

By lunchtime Byers was looking bored. He started allowing Sam to accompany Beth into the galleries alone, while he remained on the street outside, smoking cigarettes. Once he dashed off to make some phone calls.

"I guess I'm not one of the Ten Most Wanted men even yet," Sam had said to Beth, making an effort to demonstrate good spirits. "What does it take to get the FBI's attention?"

Beth had smiled at his attempt at relieving tension and said wryly, "Don't press your luck, all right?"

He had laughed and squeezed her elbow and pressed through the next door for her.

More galleries, more shops. More photographs, more paintings. Some good, some bad. Some compelling, others trite. Some prints, some original works. The search went on for hours. Beth's feet began to hurt, and finally Sam insisted they stop for some food.

"One great thing about Greenwich Village," he said, "is the variety of restaurants. What do you want? Thai? Japanese? Mexican?"

"Just a sandwich," Beth had said, distracted by her self-imposed task. "And some tea, maybe."

"A hamburger?" the cop suggested plaintively. "I'm starved."

"Tea? Hamburgers?" Sam demanded. "Do you know how much I've been longing for New York food in the last few—? Oh, all, right. The next thing I know you'll be asking for hot dogs from the street vendors." Catching Beth's eye, he said quickly, "Forget you heard that. Just come with me and we'll get you some rest, all right? We can take a break for an hour."

So sandwiches it was, in a bar on a busy corner. Beth sat at a table by the window and watched the throng on the sidewalk, the varied, sometimes bizarre, often startling crowd that pushed past the window before her. She didn't really see anything, though. She was too engrossed in searching the galleries. She knew she had something in her head that would help. She only had to dig deeply enough to uncover the information.

"Come on," she said, tugging Sam's jacket sleeve when it looked like Byers was going to light up his fifth cigarette. "Let's get going again."

More galleries. One would be posh and expensive, the next a crummy hole-in-the-wall operation with the pungent smell of nearby restaurant cooking hanging in the air. Then, oddly, they turned a corner, and started up a street and the daylight changed for Beth. Sam was looking down his photocopied list and Byers was once again groping into his pockets for his cigarettes.

"There's one up here," Sam said, making a note with his pencil. "Then we'll turn up ahead and go around the block."

The feeling came: eerie, yet exhilarating.

Beth put her hand out and opened the door to the next gallery before Sam could reach it.

"Beth?" Sam asked, seeing her face.

She walked in, feeling as if her feet were suddenly not on firm ground. Her head began to lighten, almost spinning.

It was a weird place, the walls crammed with pictures all done in the same style by the same artist, certainly. Some were huge, some tiny, but they were all the same.

It was the cat. The yellow cat with malevolent eyes and those long, very sharp little teeth. The cat from her nightmare. The force of seeing all those cat pictures blew Beth back two steps. She couldn't breathe.

"Beth," Sam said sharply this time, catching her as she backed into his body. His arm came around her from behind, holding her steady. "What is it?"

She really couldn't breathe then, for her chest was locked in fear. Her eyes, too, were fastened on the largest of the paintings, the cat with glaring eyes and that horrible yawning, yowling mouth. Though the gallery was probably quiet, the sound from Beth's dream began to reverberate in her head. It was the scream, the awful howl that had dragged her out of deepest sleep so many nights in the last few months.

"Beth!" Sam said, turning her away form the pictures. "Tell me! What is it?"

She was trembling, no, shuddering from the impact. Her voice wouldn't come, then squeaked and sounded silly. "It's my dream. Sam, it's—those cats. They're—"

Sam spun around, staring at the array of pictures on the walls. He held Beth so that she faced the doorway and couldn't see what terrified her so. He said, "You recognize these? They're all the same! You actually see these cats in your dreams? Is that what you mean?"

Beth nodded, jerking.

Byers was galvanized suddenly. "Really? She's getting something here?"

"I think so. Let's go outside and calm her down first, all right? She's—"

"I'm okay," Beth said hoarsely, fighting feebly out of Sam's grasp. "I was just—for a minute there I couldn't—"

"It's all right. Take it slow."

Beth couldn't help herself. She stared at the cat pictures in wonder, half of her recoiling in fear, the other half strangely fascinated. "My God," she said. "These are exactly what I see in my nightmares. Sam, it's got to mean something. I must—maybe Dr. Westham would know. I just—it's scary. I feel scared inside."

The owner of the gallery came out from behind the counterlike desk, then, clearly having seen Beth's reaction to the pictures. He was youngish, badly dressed with ragged sandals on his feet. His fair hair was long and hadn't been combed recently. He was small, probably weighing less than Beth. He had a cautiously inquiring look on his narrow face, not a hostile one. "Uh, can I help? Is there something wrong?"

"No," Sam said. Then, "Yes, actually. Maybe so. Are you—? Are these pictures—"

"They're my wife's," the young man informed them, pawing his hair back from his eyes. "She paints upstairs. Were you interested in buying a—"

"No, no," Sam said, still holding Beth loosely in his arm. He made an instant decision then, determining that this small, almost frail young man couldn't be the murderer they sought. "We're trying to retrace my—this woman's steps. She thinks she might have been in here once."

"About three months ago," Beth added, feeling stronger as long as she averted her eyes from the cat pictures. "Almost four, I guess."

The man's eyes narrowed as he studied Beth's face and tried to recollect. He said slowly, "We don't get a lot of traffic in here, you understand. We're a kind of specialty store. My wife does all her work in the same style, using the same subject, so we don't have people come in off the streets just to browse. We're mainly into greeting cards now—you know, the strange kind."

"Think," Sam urged, interrupting. "Could you have seen this woman before?"

"I was on a special trip," Beth added, holding still while the man looked her over with a frown of concentration. "I was looking for work to put in a magazine that—"

"A magazine?" the young man repeated, his eyes lighting up. He snapped his fingers. "You were from California!"

Beth gasped, half laughing in relief. "Yes! Do you remember me? I must have come in—"

"Sure. You were lost," he said with a grin. "You were looking for the place on the next block. It was raining, so you stood in here for a while and we talked about magazine covers. Yeah, I remember."

Sam blew an enormous sigh, as if bracing himself for more. "Thank God. Do you remember anything else about her?"

"Yes," Beth added quickly, almost pleading. "Was there anyone else around? Could I have met someone perhaps? Or—"

"Just the guy from Cleveland," the store owner said calmly, putting his hands into the deep pockets of his loose trousers. "He was here that night, too. He shows up every few months and buys a carload of pictures and takes 'em back to Ohio. Yeah, he was here, I guess. The three of us talked a while, and you two left. He was going to drop you off at the other gallery."

The cop with them stepped forward then, alert suddenly. "This man from Cleveland. He had a car?"

"Sure. A station wagon. He comes all the time."

"And you saw this young lady leave with him?"

"Yeah, sure. They went out into the rain together. It was really dark that night."

"You'd recognize him?"

"The Cleveland guy? Sure, I think so. He's a regular customer. Do you think I can do something to help you find him?"

The cop turned to Sam with a wickedly triumphant grin. He pulled his cigarette from between his lips and said simply, "Bingo."

CHAPTER FIFTEEN

BYERS IMMEDIATELY CALLED his superior. Two uniformed policemen arrived and took up positions on the sidewalk. Before the FBI arrived in the form of Marcus, Sam took Beth in hand and slipped outside with her.

"You don't need to hear any of this," he said to her. "It will take hours, and surely there's nothing else you can tell them now. They'll find us when they need us. Let's go home."

Beth agreed, for she was feeling shaky. She didn't want to break down and make a fool of herself, so she went with Sam. Within a few minutes they were in a cab and headed for the West Side again. Beth felt increasingly calm as the car took her farther from the scene of the crime. She tried to put the cat pictures out of her mind.

But the images persisted, and Beth began to think about her flashes of memory as well. What had once seemed to be only dreams to her were now becoming fact. What else was swimming around in the black pools in her brain? And Sam had said, perhaps there was a chance that she was going to remember more. The prospect was suddenly not unpleasant to Beth. She could cope with what she learned, she realized. No matter how bad the things were that she was going to learn about herself, she could handle it.

What made her sad, though, was knowing that her time with Sam was running out. He wasn't going to be with her as she learned about her past. Unconsciously Beth slipped her hand into his for him to hold. She turned her face to the window and tried to make some sense out of the muddle in her head. She really felt like two women now; one who wanted and needed Sam, another who would never trust him.

Sam stopped the cab a few blocks away from the apartment, and they got out and began to walk together. Though the side-

walk wasn't so crowded there, he took Beth's hand and held it
again, letting her keep her thoughts to herself as they walked. He
tugged her into a deli and then into a liquor store for some
already-chilled bottles of wine that he took his time choosing, and
finally into a bakery for some croissants and more bagels.
Whether he was laying in supplies for a long stay in New York or
postponing the time when the FBI would seek them out, Beth
couldn't say.

She did not object to Sam's dawdling, either. She helped him
carry the packages and walked with him. They didn't talk. Silence was becoming their best companion, Beth thought with a
twinge of regret. Once they had talked together nonstop for hours
about books and incidentals, and now they were afraid to say more
than a few words to each other. She stayed by his side, not paying
a whit of attention to the surroundings, but watching Sam and
each little gesture or expression that made up his personality. It
was as if she could learn about herself by watching him.

They rode the elevator up to Sam's apartment. The phone was
ringing as he unlocked the door. He pretended not to hear the
summons, though, and Beth did not call his attention to it. The
FBI was probably calling. They'd show up soon enough, Beth
thought ruefully. How much time was she going to have alone with
Sam before the rest of the world intruded?

They unpacked the parcels together, bumping elbows in the
galley-style kitchen. Sam plugged in the refrigerator; it had been
standing open and unused when they had arrived.

Beth peered cautiously inside the refrigerator and asked him,
"How long has it been since this was cleaned?"

Sam was refolding paper bags and filing them in a rack behind
the pantry door. "I was here for a few months about a year and a
half ago. The building super looks in from time to time, but I
don't suppose he does any cleaning."

Beth wrinkled her nose and began to search the drawers for a
dishcloth or a sponge. It seemed perfectly natural to forget what
had happened in the art gallery. She found a clean rag and ran it
under the tap. Then, kneeling in front of the refrigerator, she
started to wipe out the dust, thinking. Eighteen months ago would
have been several months after Elizabeth's death. Had Sam come
back here to collect his things? Had he intended to shut himself off
from the world and stay forever by Elizabeth's grave site? If so

why had he kept paying for an apartment? It was obvious to Beth that some part of Sam had wanted to return here some day. With manual tasks to keep them busy, she thought she was safe in asking. "Why did you keep this apartment, Sam? I thought you were completely settled in Wyoming."

He kept busy, too, sorting through the cans of food and bottles of cleaning products that were lined up inside the closet. "I thought I was settled there, too. I'm not sure what made me hold on to this place. The rent's certainly atrocious."

"It has a different atmosphere than the other house," Beth ventured, concentrating on her cleaning job. "Almost like a different person lived here. Maybe you've got two personalities, too."

He made an amused noise, not a laugh, exactly. "About the time you start melding into one personality, you think I'm splitting into two?"

"Have you?" Beth asked, sending an honest look of inquiry up at him. "I think you *were* different here."

"Different, yes," he agreed, his voice suddenly quiet. He looked away, avoiding her gaze.

"Happier, I think," Beth guessed.

Sam closed the pantry door and stood still, not looking at her. He seemed to be looking inward. "Yes," he said finally. "I suppose I was happier here."

"Will you move back to this apartment sometime?"

Sam seemed to pull himself out of deep thought and turned his head to regard her, his face composed in his best motionless expression. "I never considered it, Beth. I didn't think I wanted to."

But he was thinking of it now, Beth knew. It would be unwise to question him further, though. She could see that Sam was thinking of many things just then, and she didn't need much intuition to know that she was included in his thoughts. It was time to change the subject. She finished swabbing out the refrigerator, put the food they had bought on the second shelf and closed the door. Then she found some drinking glasses and rinsed them out as Sam watched in silence. Afraid of what he was contemplating, Beth suggested, "Let's have a drink, all right? I think we could both use one."

Sam obeyed her wishes and reached for the bottle of vermouth he'd just removed from the liquor-store bag. It was cold enough, so he poured each of them half a glass without ice. He handed one

to Beth and leaned his hip against the counter until she tried her
first sip. When Beth had swallowed and smiled a little at the dry,
yet searing taste, he asked, ''Are you all right now? Not scared?''

Beth smiled a little and shook her head, wrapping both hands
around her glass. ''I'm not scared. I'm wondering what comes
next, I suppose. Do we sit and wait for something to happen?''

Sam nodded and glanced at the clear liquid in his glass. ''Marcus will find us when he wants us. I'm sure you've done enough,
Beth. I'm glad, to tell you the truth. I hope you're finished.''

''Finished looking for that man?''

''Yes. It gave me the creeps today, watching you remember bits
and pieces of what must have happened to you in that gallery.''

Beth was thankful that the vermouth was already warming her
inside. She smiled nervously. ''I felt creepy, too. Like it was a ghost
story. Do you really think we found the right place? The right
man?''

Hearing her voice shake, Sam moved toward her cautiously,
before the impact of what had happened that afternoon really hit
her. As he put his arm around Beth's shoulders and turned her
naturally toward the living room, his voice turned light again, as
it had sounded when he was trying to keep her spirits up. ''I think
the expression is 'fingered.' You've given the FBI all they need to
know to make a real John Dillinger arrest. I bet they'll have the
guy in custody soon—probably today.''

''In Cleveland,'' Beth said, trembling a little as she walked
through the kitchen doorway. Sam put his arm around her, and
she felt stronger just having him so close to her again. No matter
what had happened, her body seemed ready to trust Sam once
more, to seek his warmth when she needed it. Beth was still unnerved, she knew, but she was finding it easier to cope with those
feelings of anxiety. Honestly, she admitted, ''I'm glad the arrest
will take place far away. I didn't want to have to—to actually see
him. Did you?''

Sam guided Beth toward the leather armchair in the corner of
the living room. ''There was a time when I wanted to do more than
just see him. Now I'm not so sure. It scares me to discover I'm
capable of that kind of hate and anger. I thought I was past that
point, after the real pain of Elizabeth's death was over, but today—'' Sam sighed and touched Beth's hair absently as they
paused by the chair. ''Today I felt that rage all over again, Beth.

I don't want to think of you and—and what happened to you that night."

Turning to face him, Beth caught his hand and held it in her own. "That's the good part about having amnesia. I can forget the horrible things, Sam. I think you ought to try forgetting, too."

"Some of it," he said slowly, watching her eyes, "I don't want to forget."

"About Elizabeth?" Beth asked, knowing she was wrong.

Sam shook his head. "What happened to Elizabeth doesn't matter much now. I'm thinking of you, Beth."

She pretended to sip from her glass, but Beth knew nothing could have gone down her throat just then. She asked bluntly, "Will you ever think of me and not think of Elizabeth at the same time?"

The question goaded him. Instinctively, Sam put his glass down and ran both his hands into her hair very quickly, tipping Beth's face up to his and holding her firmly. A kind of violence came and went in Sam's face, but he controlled it before he said quietly, "I've never confused the two of you, Beth, believe me. You're not even a little like her."

"You loved her once," Beth said, challenging him.

"Very much," Sam agreed. "But I don't remember loving anyone as much as I love you right now."

"Sam—" Beth protested, though her self-control was as fragile as spun glass at that moment.

"It's true that I married Elizabeth and loved her for several years. We had a fire-and-ice relationship, she and I. One of us was always running hot or cold, and the other managed to maintain the balance somehow. It didn't last, Beth. We—we burned each other out, I suppose, or we just got too tired of fighting the opposites in each other. After a while, it was sex that kept our marriage together, that's all. Neither of us wanted to put an end to those erotic games Connor told you about, but—"

Beth closed her eyes. "Don't—"

"But even sex doesn't last," Sam went on roughly. "We had split up long before Elizabeth died, Beth. I told you that. Even if Elizabeth was alive right now, I know I'd feel the same way about you that I do this very minute. You're warm all the time. Making love with you means more. And we're compatible! You said so yourself when you first came to the ranch."

Beth opened her eyes and tried to glare at him. "What happened between us at the ranch was a lie, pure and simple, Sam."

"The circumstances were a lie, yes," Sam agreed. "But—"

"The circumstances are still the same," Beth interrupted quickly, afraid to touch Sam, yet feeling the swiftness of his pulse through his wrist as he held her head. "I'm married, Sam. To somebody else. We can't change that, can we?"

"Beth," Sam pleaded with a desperate kind of sigh. He bent quickly and kissed her forehead. "Beth, darling, we can't change it, but we could ignore it. At least for a while longer, please. I—"

"Sam!" Beth objected, frightened now by what he was suggesting.

"Just give me tonight," Sam said, kissing her cheek, her temple. "Pretend with me for one night, Beth. Let me say goodbye. Forgive me for what I've done to you—at least for one night. Don't leave me so suddenly. I couldn't face it."

He kissed her face and the corners of her mouth, not taking her lips fully until she agreed to let him. Sam's heart was tearing along; Beth could feel it beneath the palm of her hand. If her composure was fragile just then, Sam's was even more so. He was tightly strung, barely in control. Hadn't Sam suffered enough? If she objected now and refused him . . .

"Beth," he pleaded again, his breath warm against her ear.

She didn't have to answer him.

There were heavy footsteps in the hall outside. A moment later the bell on the door buzzed twice, and someone rapped on the door.

Sam's grip loosened, but did not lose its power. Trying to smile, Beth automatically reached and touched his face. "I think we've got business to attend to."

He dropped his eyes away and let her go, his disappointment in check.

Beth caught Sam's arm, holding him against her body for another moment. Softly, she said, "Sam, I wish a lot of things were different right now."

The door buzzed again, and Beth finally felt compelled to answer it. She left Sam standing silently in the living room and went to the door. After a steadying breath, she opened it.

It was the burly cop Byers, the unhappy teddy bear, and with him, standing closest to the door and looking official as ever, was Marcus, the chief FBI investigator for the case.

Beth managed a smile somehow. "Hello, Mr. Marcus. It's nice to see you again." She put her hand out to shake his.

The big man's expression didn't change much, except to show just a glimmer of surprise. He had expected her to be the same woman he'd seen in the hospital, but she was pleased that the changes she felt in herself were so apparent to others. He accepted her handshake. "It's good to see you looking so well," he said. "And under better circumstances this time, Mrs. Foster."

Beth didn't fail to notice how he underlined her new name. She kept up her smile to show him that she didn't mind what he called her and stepped aside. "Won't you come in? I suppose we have lots to talk about. You too, Mr. Byers. He isn't going to make you sit outside again, is he?"

The two raincoat-clad lawmen came into the apartment, standing awkwardly in the entrance hall until Beth showed them the way to the living room. Sam was there, composed and blank-faced, ready to receive the worst, it seemed.

"Hello, Sheridan," Marcus said, all cool politeness. Apparently, he still resented Sam. "I thought we'd better pay a visit. I tried calling ahead."

"We've been out," Sam said, eyeing the FBI agent with barely disguised dislike.

"Yes, the cupboard was bare," Beth put in, trying to smooth things as much as possible. "Would you like a drink, Mr. Marcus? I'm sure *you* need one, Mr. Byers. There's no ice yet, but—"

"We're on duty at the moment," Marcus said kindly. "We'll just talk for a while, if you don't mind. Sit down, Mrs. Foster. I hear you've had a rough day."

"A busy one," Beth agreed. She moved to Sam's side and took his arm, as if holding on to Sam might protect him, somehow. It was foolish, she knew, but Beth didn't want Marcus to arrest Sam and haul him away like some kind of criminal. To her way of thinking, Sam had suffered enough.

She tugged Sam toward the leather chair while the two FBI agents sat on the nearby sofa. Byers relaxed in comfort, sinking into the pillows as if he was quite at home. But Marcus remained

perched on the edge of the seat and said seriously, "We appreciate what you did today, Mrs. Foster. I know it must have been
tough on you."

"Not as tough as I thought it was going to be," Beth admitted,
facing her questioner. She had summarily pushed Sam into the
leather chair while she herself sat on the edge of the arm, with
Sam's shoulder riding comfortably against her lower back. "Was
I helpful? Or did I send you off to Cleveland on a wild-goose
chase?"

Marcus smiled, studying her as if from a fresh perspective. "No,
it wasn't a wild-goose chase at all. In fact, I'm very pleased to say
that we've made an arrest, Mrs. Foster. Our people in Cleveland
picked up a man just half an hour ago. They're going over his car
now for evidence, and he's being questioned."

"Ohh," Beth said, letting her breath out in a whispered sigh as
she groped for Sam's support. "Oh, my."

Sam took Beth's hand in his and held her tightly. "You were
quick, Marcus. Are you sure he's the right man?"

Marcus did not fail to see the gestures that passed between
them. He nodded and said, "I'm quite confident, as a matter of
fact. He fits the profile. I think we can finally relax. We owe you
a lot, Mrs. Foster."

"I—I only wish it could have been done sooner."

"Hmm," Marcus agreed, looking at her from under his eyebrows. "We all wish the case could have been closed a long time
ago, but sometimes things just have to cook awhile, you know. We
can all be relieved that no one else was hurt after his attack on
you."

"Yes," Beth said softly. "If someone else had been murdered
because I couldn't remember—"

Sam squeezed Beth's hand, stopping her. "It's over now."

"Yes," Marcus said slowly. "Almost over."

Beth heard his tone and lifted her head quickly, composing
herself. "I don't—look can you tell me something. About what
happened to me, perhaps? I'm interested, you see."

If Marcus understood her ploy to postpone talking about Sam's
deception, he gave no notice. He linked his hands together and
looked thoughtful, frowning. "We've put together some ideas
already. It's guesswork so far, of course. From what the gallery
owner told us, you left his place that night with this man from

Cleveland who was a regular customer of his. So the owner felt no concern for you, even though the other murders had been well publicized. He offered to take you to the gallery you really wanted to see."

Beth nodded, "One that was close by, I understood."

"Yes. It was just a block and a half away, but there was a rainstorm that night. The gallery owner confirmed that it was pouring."

"So it didn't seem odd," Sam interjected, "that Beth chose to ride that short distance?"

"Right. She'd have been soaked if she'd walked. And we presume that she had talked with this man for several minutes and established, at least in her own mind, that he was safe. Once outside, though, we can only guess what happened."

"What do you suppose?" Sam asked, truly interested. He sat forward in his chair.

Marcus continued, as if speaking only to Sam by this time. "If it were me, I wouldn't risk taking the young woman in the car with me even from the start. She would quickly see that something was wrong and protest, or jump out of the car. I'm betting that he overpowered her right away. It would have been easy to catch her off guard in the rain, perhaps running toward the car. He probably kept some twine in his pocket. He could have caught her hand—"

"Pretending to help her into the car," Sam suggested.

"Right. Tied her wrists like a calf-roper and dumped her quickly into the back of the station wagon. He probably bound her legs, too. We know that he later used a knife to threaten the women, but I suppose he could have struck her with something else, hoping he'd rendered his victim unconscious. On a dark night in that alley, it's unlikely that there'd be any witnesses."

"The pictures he'd bought must have been in the car already," Beth said dazedly. "I must have been tied up in the back of the car, with nothing to look at but those cat pictures."

Sam slid his arm around her body. "That's why the nightmares have been bothering you. You must have ridden like that for hours."

Marcus nodded. "It would have taken probably four hours minimum for him to have driven to the place in Pennsylvania where you were later found. Perhaps during the drive you struggled against the twine he had used to bind you. Your wrists and lower legs were badly bruised, I remember. He drove to the same secluded kind of place he'd used in the past."

Beth swallowed hard. The story still seemed unreal, as though it had happened to someone else, not herself, but the reality seemed closer now, like a telescope focusing. She found herself asking, "Why was I able to get away, Mr. Marcus? Why didn't he kill me?"

Marcus was matter-of-fact. "You're taller than the other women he killed. You're in good physical condition, too. And I think the place he chose that time was not as private as the other strip-mine sites he had used before. I suspect he got you out of the car and fastened your wrists to the luggage rack on the top of the station wagon—giving you just enough play in the rope so he could touch you and make you do what he wanted. He probably started to undress you and put your clothes into the car. We found the place later and picked up some other clues. There were marks on the ground indicating that you fought, all right."

"And probably screamed your lungs out," Sam suggested, with a glimmer of a smile up at Beth. "If I know you, you didn't shrink away."

"Right," Marcus said, smiling a little. "From what we pieced together about the personalities of the other victims, they were quiet women, shy and easily frightened. He was probably able to control them better, or perhaps they fainted in the face of the knife-threatening. But you—I think you fought him every inch of the way. You shouted for help, and some of the nearby residents heard you. They discovered you later, but they must have come out of their homes with lights and startled your attacker. I think he was afraid of being discovered, and panicked. He probably jumped into the car and started to drive."

Sam swore softly. "With Beth still tied to the roof rack."

"Exactly," Marcus said, looking at Beth for signs of distress. "He probably dragged you for several hundred yards. The twine unwound little by little, until your head began to strike the road as you were dragged. It's a wonder you weren't killed."

Sam said, "He probably intended for her to die that way."

"Probably," Marcus agreed blandly. "He stopped the car and checked after half a mile. We saw the tire marks and footprints. He probably assumed you were dead but was too frightened t take the time to make absolutely sure. We believe that he wasn't interested in killing his victims as much as he wanted to—'' Marcus stopped himself, apparently assuming that the FBI's theories on the man's sexual eccentricities did not need to be aired at this time. He said, ''Well, let's assume he cut the twine and left behind what he thought was a dead body. Forgive me, Mrs. Foster, but you looked pretty terrible the first time I saw you, so I could believe this man assumed you were—uh—lifeless. Then he went home to Cleveland where he has a kind of gallery of his own. He sells the pictures that he buys in large quantity in New York.''

''And in a few months,'' Sam continued, ''when his supply of pictures ran out, he was going to make another trip to New York, abduct another woman on his way home and . . . ?''

Marcus nodded again. ''That's the pattern all right.''

Sam sighed and shook his head. ''It sounds so damn easy, doesn't it? He could have been doing it for years.''

''If he varied the sites he used to dump the bodies,'' Marcus said, watching Sam exclusively now. ''Yes, he could have gone on for years. In fact, we don't know how many times he could have done the same thing before we caught up with his system. Maybe he buried the bodies. Maybe other victims were found years ago, but were never connected with this case until lately.''

Sam met Marcus's gaze and said nothing.

''Other victims?'' Beth asked, starting to feel the rise of panic inside her. Marcus was trying to trap Sam now, she knew, but she couldn't think of a way to intervene. ''How—how many do you suppose he killed?''

''I don't know, Mrs. Foster,'' Marcus said, his eyes on Sam. ''What do you think, Sheridan?''

Sam didn't play games or try to pretend anything. He said, ''All right, so you know now about my wife?''

Marcus nodded and reached for the pocket of his raincoat. He came up with a small notebook and began to flip through the pages. ''Elizabeth Westham Sheridan. It took us over a week to collect all the facts, but we did find that she had been—''

''Over a week?'' Beth interrupted. ''So you knew a long time ago about what . . . ? You didn't arrest us?''

Marcus leveled a look at Beth. ''Why should we arrest you? Sheridan was the criminal, the one who was committing a felony. You were just a victim, Mrs. Foster. In more ways than one.''

"In many more ways," Sam said quietly, letting a new implication hang in the air.

Marcus asked sharply. "What does that mean?"

Sam made a wide gesture with his free hand. "We all know what I did. Let's get that out in the open."

"What you and Dr. Westham and his son did," Marcus corrected.

So they knew, Beth realized. The FBI had figured everything out a long time ago and had let them all go on playing their parts without interfering.

"All right," Sam said. "What we did was wrong. We had a lot of reasons for pretending to be Beth's family, but none of them were good enough to justify our actions. I know that, and I'm prepared to be punished for it. We used a woman when we shouldn't have. Does it sound familiar, Marcus?"

The FBI man didn't move for an instant. "Are you suggesting . . . ?"

"That you were using Beth even before I showed up? Of course," Sam said calmly. "You made sure there was a lot of national publicity, didn't you? You made sure every newspaper in the country knew that you'd found a living victim of this particular murderer. You hoped that he'd read about Beth and come get her, didn't you? You never said a word to the press about her amnesia, so that man knew Beth was alive and thought she could identify him. You hoped that he'd be brave enough to come to the hospital and try to kill her."

"She was under constant protection."

"Even when you let her go jogging in public? No, Marcus, you used her as *bait*. She shouldn't have been allowed out of the hospital that way—and not just because of possible injuries. You never released Beth's picture to the press. Dr. Westham begged you to find her family, but you didn't want her to be identified, did you? Not yet, anyway. You knew Beth's family would take her home and protect her—not just from this man, but from you. You dangled her life like a carrot and you wanted to keep on doing that until your murderer showed up. What I did was wrong, yes, but wasn't gambling with her life. What's the FBI policy on that kind of thing, anyway, Marcus? Is that a method you use a lot?"

The FBI agent didn't look up for a long time. He snapped his notebook closed and considered the facts. The silence stretched and finally he said, "Mrs. Foster, I think I'll take you up on that drink after all. I'm starting to think I could use one."

Beth hesitated, not sure she had heard correctly.

Sam gave her a push off the arm of the chair and said, "Go ahead, Beth. I'd like a refill, too."

He handed his glass up to her, though it was still nearly full. Beth looked down at him questioningly, and Sam looked up and winked at her. There was a smile lingering on the corners of his usually very straight mouth.

And when Beth went past him on her way to the kitchen, Byers gave her a wink, too.

All, it seemed, would be resolved.

and finally yielded. "Here, Sam, let me help you get out of that crazy chair." But even on the couch I could see one—

[faded lines]

CHAPTER SIXTEEN

"THE FBI DOESN'T make deals," Marcus was saying when Beth returned.

Beth put the tray down on the coffee table, too frightened by those ominous words to interrupt for an explanation.

Sitting forward in his chair, Sam reached for the glasses and began pouring vermouth into one. "I'm not asking for a deal, am I? I'm just pointing out a few facts that the newspapers are going to find very interesting."

"Are you making a threat?"

"I'm not exactly in the best position for threatening, am I? Here."

Marcus accepted the glass from Sam without thanks. "I'm beginning to feel I'm not in the best position either."

Beth sat on the footstool near Sam and held her breath. It looked as though they were working out some kind of deal, all right. Maybe Sam was going to get out of this mess, after all.

Sam passed the next glass to Byers and began to pour the third glass for himself. "Actually, the FBI's done a very good job on this case. This kind of investigation is tricky, I know. Sometimes you need outside help, though, right?"

"Sometimes," Marcus agreed. He waited until Sam had his own drink poured, and then lifted his in a toast. "I think we all had the best help possible. May I be the first to say thank-you, Mrs. Foster? Without you, we'd all be in terrible shape!"

Sam smiled at her, and then all the men lifted their glasses in an appreciative toast. Beth found herself blushing at the praise like a kid. She expelled a long, relieved breath and managed to grin. "I think you're going to be in even worse shape if you drink that stuff! It tastes like gasoline, don't you think?"

The men laughed at her and didn't seem to agree, for they all drained their glasses pretty quickly after that. Marcus didn't look inclined to leave just yet and studied Beth from the sofa for a moment.

"You look very good these days, Mrs. Foster," he said. "Much better than when I first saw you. I think that country air did you some good."

"The air had little to do with it."

"Perhaps not." Marcus glanced at Sam briefly. "I—uh, I'd like to extend the Bureau's services to you, though, considering everything that's happened. You have some relatives to look up, don't you? Would you like us to give you some help? We could make some contacts for you. Your husband, for instance."

"Not today," Beth said hurriedly. "It's—well, so much has gone on today. I don't think I'm ready to start looking up my family tonight. You understand."

"Of course. But you must realize that we can't keep this information out of the newspapers. By morning, your name will be—"

"Yes," she said, understanding that her moments of privacy were now numbered. "By morning I'll be ready, though. Tonight I'd like to just—well, forget a few things."

Sam glanced at her, but Beth couldn't meet his gaze.

Marcus nodded. He leaned forward and set his glass on the table. "I understand. Maybe we'd better clear out and let you rest, then. Mr. Byers will leave some phone numbers for you to use. Maybe by morning you'll decide you'd like us to give you a hand. Feel free to call me, all right?"

They were all getting to their feet, and Beth stood up also. "I bet I'll hear from you again soon, anyway, right? This investigation can't be over yet."

"No," Marcus agreed with a rueful smile. "We'll be in touch with you a lot, I'm afraid; you'll be the prosecution's leading witness. You'd better be prepared for a long trial when it finally comes up. It'll be here in New York, I'm sure." He hesitated, and with all sincerity added, "I'm glad that you've improved so much lately, Mrs. Foster. You really seem to be a new woman. Dr. Westham was right to get you out of the hospital, I guess. I thank you for your willingness to help us. If you'd been a different kind of lady, you'd have minded your own business, and this man might still be free."

Beth took the hand that Marcus extended to her. She was grateful for his speech, but more thankful that he had decided not to arrest Sam. Perhaps that emotion showed in her face. She tried to smile and didn't quite manage, so she said earnestly, "Thank *you,* Mr. Marcus. I'm very grateful to you."

Then he, too, winked at her. Marcus turned to Sam after that and shook his hand solemnly, like a man who respected another. He said gruffly, "Good night, Sheridan. Take the phone off the hook, all right? The papers will be out in a few hours."

"I will," Sam promised.

"We'll leave a man in the street to keep an eye on things for you," Marcus added as he led Byers out into the hallway. He turned and glanced at Sam and Beth, framed together in the doorway. "You ought to have a quiet night."

"Thanks," Beth called, waving.

"Yes," said Sam. "Thanks, Marcus."

The FBI men were gone, then, and Sam closed the door very gently.

BETH FELT AS NERVOUS as a bride on her wedding night. She didn't know what to say to Sam.

Obviously he was going to play the scenes to come without guilt, without second thoughts. He latched the door and asked quite blithely, "Are you hungry?"

Beth wasn't brave enough to look up at him just then. He'd asked her for one night, that was all, and that night had apparently begun as soon as their guests departed. Beth's voice shook with the smallest of quivers as she tried to sound normal. "I'm starved. Unless I have to do the cooking, of course, and then I'd rather just have a—a bagel or something."

Sam laughed and tugged fondly at the back of her hair as if nothing was wrong. He turned away and started for the living room. "This is the land of plenty. We'll send out, all right? Pizza? Chinese? There's a Hungarian place—if it's still open—that makes the most—"

"You've been dieting in Wyoming, haven't you?" Beth asked as she trailed him into the living room. "There must be a—a fat man inside you, Sam. You've thought of nothing but food, I think, since we got here."

He didn't argue with her teasing, but found a phone book in a drawer and pulled it out. "Chinese, I think. No dishes that way. What do you like? Fish? Pork?"

He was denying reality completely, Beth saw. Just as Beth had pretended in the past few weeks that nothing was wrong, Sam was now acting as if they were an old married couple back in their nest for the first time in a long while. He was flipping through the phone book pages, apparently concerned only about his stomach. He did not want to discuss the man who remained between them. If Beth brought up the subject of her husband, she suspected that Sam would streamroll over her and order Hungarian food in addition to the Chinese meal he was so set on.

After all, she had agreed to spend the night with him. He had asked for one night, and Beth had essentially said yes.

For one night more she could pretend she was Sam's wife.

Well, she could playact as well as he could. Beth blew a sigh, ruffled her hair and said, "Oh, you decide. I think I'll go take a bath and unwind. Can we have a bottle of wine?"

Sam spotted the correct entry in the phone book and dove triumphantly for the telephone. He waved at her. "Coming right up!"

So the mood changed yet again. Beth ran the bathwater and undressed while Sam telephoned. She donned her terry bathrobe and hugged it to her waist just as Sam arrived in the bedroom with her glass of wine.

She accepted the glass, trying not to feel shy. It was ridiculous, after all. She had lived with the man for weeks! Why did there have to be tension between them tonight? Couldn't she pretend as well as he could? Before he could exit, Beth caught Sam by the collar of his shirt and pulled him close, her heart crashing in her chest as she did it. It was now or never. She wasn't going to make it through this night with Sam if she couldn't be brazen, so she covered her nervousness by nuzzling her nose seductively along Sam's throat. In a bedroom murmur, she asked, "Care to join me?"

Sam's arms went around her naturally, as if there was nothing wrong, and he pulled her more snugly against his body. It wasn't a sexual embrace. He murmured, "Beth, you don't have to go through with this if—"

"I want to," she interrupted in a whisper.

"But if it makes things worse?"

She smiled and hugged him. "How much worse can things get?"

Sounding amused, he said, "One of your best qualities has always been optimism."

She smiled against his chest. "Does that mean you'll come into the bathtub with me?"

"No," he answered, and gave her a gentle shove toward the bathroom. "Let's take it slow, all right? Go relax for a while. You deserve it. I'll putter around out here, and get the place organized. I feel like we're camping."

Beth agreed and climbed into the tub in a few minutes, listening to Sam move around in the apartment. She let the warm water work on her tired muscles, but soon discovered that she didn't want to be alone with her thoughts. This evening with Sam was going to be emotional enough without any more soul-searching in the beginning.

She let the water out of the tub and dried herself roughly with a towel from the cupboard. Feeling clean and renewed, Beth wondered what she ought to put on. It was barely seven o'clock in the evening, but she decided upon her nightgown and terry robe. What she'd have given for one of those sexy nighties Sam had once suggested! She brushed her hair and went looking for Sam with her now-empty wineglass in hand.

He was just hanging up the phone when she arrived in the room, but when he glanced up at her he took the telephone receiver off the hook again. He seemed struck by her appearance as she stood bathed in lamplight. It took him a moment to absorb her nightclothes and long, bare legs, but then he collected himself and said, "That was Connor. He's—"

"How is the farm?" Beth interrupted breezily, coming to set her glass on the coffee table where Sam had put the bottle and his own empty glass. She didn't want to talk about Connor and his involvement in the deception, so she changed the subject quickly. "Has it been raining again?"

"No," said Sam, watching her with his head down. "The weather's been warm."

The buzzer on the door intervened, then, and Sam immediately went along to answer it.

The food had arrived. While Sam paid the delivery boy and collected the packages, Beth pushed the coffee table over and pulled the pillows from the couch, laying them on the floor to suit herself. She snapped off one of the two lamps, and when Sam came back, she was sitting on the floor pouring wine for both of them.

With a smile—partly relief, Beth supposed—Sam joined her on the floor, and together they set about opening the white cartons of Chinese food.

As soon as Sam sat down, Beth wriggled over until her thigh was pressed warmly to his, and they remained that way as they ate. If Beth had hoped for romance, soft laughter and stimulating conversation, she was to be disappointed. There was nothing to talk about that would not eventually lead back to the subject they both intended to avoid. Therefore, in the quiet apartment with street noises barely audible, they were quiet also, making a pretense of enjoying the food, but in reality enjoying nothing more than being side by side and alone together.

In time, when it seemed ridiculous to keep their silence any longer, Sam gestured tentatively at Beth and remarked, "It's an art to use chopsticks, you know. You're a real expert, did you notice?"

Beth hadn't questioned the use of the chopsticks, having accepted them from Sam at the outset of their meal. She looked at the sticks in her hand, clasped easily between her fingers as if she'd done it all her life. She clapped the sticks together. "I guess I am."

"It still amazes me," Sam said. "I never know what you're going to remember. You recognize some things very naturally, and other times it's as if you just landed from Mars. Beth, you've coped with your—with the amnesia very well. I've often marveled at your mental health."

Beth didn't smile, though she probably should have. The tension of the day and the evening to come were weighing heavily upon her. She answered him, though, for this subject seemed safe. "I don't know how well I've coped," she said, toying with her chopsticks, having lost interest in the spicy food. "Sometimes I thought I'd go crazy, you know. The frustration is the worst. I— once in a while I just wanted to scream."

"Or throw a bottle," Sam murmured with a wry smile. He relaxed back against the couch for comfort. "Tell me about it."

Perhaps he only wanted to hear her voice that night, or maybe he really did want to hear about the things that had gone on in her head. In any case, talking about her amnesia was one way of communicating with Sam while avoiding talk of their life together. Haltingly at first, then with growing fervor, Beth began to talk. She told him about the hospital, and the doctors. She explained how after a while the nurses had become her real friends, for they had gradually stopped treating her like a freak.

"I often felt like a—like a bug on a pin," Beth said slowly. She put her uneaten food on the coffee table and added, "The doctors and the police were always looking at me and poking around, asking questions, testing me all the time. But the nurses eventually started acting like I was one of them. That's what I wanted, you see. I didn't want to be different. I wanted to be like other people."

"How are other people?" Sam asked quietly. It was Sam the playwright inquiring now, a man who had often looked into the human psyche, Beth thought.

Perhaps he might understand. She said, "Other people *have* things—no, not things, I mean they have other people. Nobody is alone. Everybody has somebody, you see. Except me. The longer I stayed in the hospital, Sam, the more I wanted to have someone and belong to that someone. The nurses all had boyfriends or husbands, and that's mostly what they talked about when we all sat around drinking coffee on their breaks. People need to have connections, I think, and I didn't have any at all. I felt more alone because I was so different from everybody else, too. Then, when you . . . you came . . ."

Sam heard her voice tremble and touched her arm. He laid his hand on her to quell the rising anxiety.

Thus steadied, Beth spoke calmly again. "When you came along, I had someone, you see. You were perfect for me. You accepted me right from the start and you didn't get frustrated with me. Everyone else got annoyed from time to time, but not you. You didn't make judgments, and you—well, you *listened* to me instead of giving me a bunch of questions to respond to. I hadn't had any real conversation with anyone before that. You were very patient." She smiled a little and peeped sideways at him. "Maybe that's why you went off by yourself so much—to get away from me once in a while."

"No," Sam said, and he didn't smile. "You know why I left you alone so much."

Beth ducked her head and nodded. "Because you were afraid you'd give yourself away. I understand that now, but at the time I just felt it was natural, I guess. You were good to me, Sam. You gave me room to be myself. I know, I know—even if I was supposed to be Elizabeth, you didn't force her on me the way Connor did. You—you just let me get to know myself, but I could depend on you when I needed someone—that other person that everyone else seemed to have."

Sam began, "I wish..." He stopped himself. Beth thought that Sam undoubtedly wished for many things just then. She knew that he loved her. He hadn't lied about that. And it wasn't the kind of love that he might have felt for a helpless sparrow he'd nursed back to health. Beth decided that Sam loved with an intensity other men rarely experienced. He had kept his emotions tightly bottled while he mourned Elizabeth, and now his full potential for giving was apparent. For Sam, love meant the deepest kind of caring that any human could experience.

He touched her then, smoothing his fingertips up along the ridge of her arm until he encountered the sleeve of her terry robe. Sam seemed to be absorbing the heat that her skin radiated, while he felt the slender curve of muscle there. He was perhaps remembering a time when he'd seen her arm completely bare. Every sensual nuance of her flesh seemed to recall memories that another man might dismiss as being insignificant. Sam was extraordinary. Yes, Beth thought, he would wish many things right now.

Impulsively, Beth reached. It was an inadequate gesture, but she touched Sam's sleeve and said softly, "In the hospital I felt analyzed all the time, Sam. But with you—even from the start—I felt loved."

Sam slipped his hands into her hair, too eagerly, almost, until he checked himself. Gently, then, he tipped her face until he could see her expression, and the contours of her lips and cheeks and eyes. It was as if Sam was trying to memorize every minute detail of her, to remember in distant years. His own gray-green gaze was full of torment, but the shadows began to give way to warmer emotions. He said nothing.

He had asked for tonight already, and Beth knew he would get it. She linked her hands behind his neck, feathering her fingers in the darkness of his hair. Then, pulling him closer, she drew Sam down to kiss her.

He obeyed, kissing Beth's mouth so softly that it might have been the wisp of butterfly wings touching her lips. The caress lasted only an instant, but in that tiny space of time, Beth felt every ounce of logic within her melt away to nothing. Of course she loved him just as completely as he loved her.

Sam lingered, not kissing her again, but clearly longing to do just that.

Beth eased closer and slipped her arms around his neck. Memories of lying in Sam's arms came rolling over her like weightless clouds, memories of days and nights in their bed at home, of warm afternoons snoozing together in the shade, of electric moments when passion sparked and Sam snatched her up in his arms. He hesitated now, though. He was not going to insist.

The initiative was Beth's. Hesitantly, she lifted her mouth to kiss him. But hesitancy evaporated, for instinct soon overcame her. She pressed her body into Sam's hard frame and kissed him deeply, opening her pliant mouth to his. His lips were warm, but more and more heat began to build as the moments passed. He was her Sam, the man who felt passion and desire as if they were fires within his body and soul. He could make love to her so beautifully that Beth might laugh or cry spontaneously. Now he held her so tightly that their hearts seemed to beat together.

It was no time to be passive. One night might pass very quickly if she allowed it. Beth savored the kiss as if it was nectar and when it broke finally, she gazed into Sam's eyes but couldn't muster a smile. Instead, she eased herself away from him and got to her feet. She extended her hand and helped Sam get up also. Without words, she turned to lead him to the bedroom and the bed she would share with him this one last night.

But Sam held her back. He gripped her hand and forced her to stay within the golden circle of lamplight. He was very tall, and for an instant his size was threatening. Then he touched one fingertip to Beth's chin and lifted her face to his.

He was solemn. "Beth, what I asked you before—I have no right to make you stay with me tonight."

Beth was silent, trying to hold herself together.

He said, "But I love you. I do want you with me tonight, if it's all I can have of you. I respect you, though, and if you've decided to—"

"I want to stay," Beth whispered.

Sam hesitated, but he traced her lips with his thumb, a caress that seemed firm and without reservation. He said, "If this is all we're going to have together, I want it all, all right?"

She tried to smile in spite of the sudden trembling that nearly sapped every bit of strength from her legs. Warm liquid rushed inside, the first signs of sexual excitement. "All the erotic games?"

He didn't smile. "I can't promise that I'll be gentle."

Beth's courage quavered. "No?"

"A part of me is furious that you're leaving, Beth. A part of me wants to hurt you."

She did smile then, and walked straight into his arms. "We've talked about that before, haven't we? You can't hurt me, Sam."

But, in the end, he tried. He took her to the bed and undressed her and didn't hold still while she stripped him of his clothing, too. Kissing her hard, he laid her back on the bed without preamble. He took pleasure in her body, first with savoring slowness, and then with a powerful kind of ferocity that was exquisitely satisfying. Sam's anger boiled out from inside him, driving Beth to the brink of ecstasy so many times she was exhausted before her final climax shuddered inside her. Along with the physical explosion came the emotional release of all her pent-up tensions. Beth heard herself apologizing, vowing the love she felt would last forever, begging Sam not to be angry with her.

Finally, locked for a time in an ethereal consummation, they lay together and let the tempest subside. Sam's rage dissipated, and tenderness returned. He kissed Beth gently again, but no less desperately. He wanted to savor every inch of her, committing her to sweet memory.

The hours passed in a honeyed haze of pain and pleasure. Few words were spoken, for fear the spell of a single night might be broken. Before the break of dawn they had only silent solace to give each other, and then exhaustion—or perhaps relief—brought on the welcome blackness of deep sleep.

CHAPTER SEVENTEEN

IN THE MORNING Beth woke first, and found herself nestled in the curve of Sam's long, warm body. For a long time, an hour perhaps, she stayed beside him without moving. Her body ached, but deliciously so. In one night she had known the rapture of mindless eroticism combined with soul-shaking emotion. Now she imagined that the night had been a dream, too beautiful for reality.

Unwilling to rouse herself completely and dispel the memory of Sam's fierce lovemaking, Beth let her mind wander over the events of the past few weeks, hoping to find the clue that would explain her feelings for Sam—the deep love and the despair over his deception. Why did she love him after all he'd done?

She avoided thinking about the upsetting things—her abduction and probable beating at the hands of her now-arrested assailant. But she tried purposefully to remember the happiest moments with Sam: bicycling with him, making popcorn after she'd botched yet another meal, working on the tractor, the evenings alone when they had talked and talked until a delicious languor overcame them and they would make love.

Beth loved Sam very much, she knew. With his body locked next to hers in bed and his unconscious breathing matching the tempo of her own, Beth realized that she couldn't allow circumstances to come between them. She could not allow her life to be separated from Sam's now. No one, not even a husband, could force Beth to deny her love for Sam. She couldn't separate herself from Sam Sheridan any more than she could cut off a part of her own body.

It was wrong, but she was going to have Sam. She would find her husband and break the marriage, no matter what the costs.

She slipped out of bed and grabbed her robe. Belting it, she rounded the bed and found Sam's wristwatch. It was nearly noon

Quietly, she laid the watch back down on the night table, thinking that perhaps she had awakened Sam with her quiet movements. His breathing changed, and Beth suppressed the impulse to bend over him and kiss him lightly. She needed to be alone for a while first.

Trying to be soundless, Beth went out to the living room and found the telephone. Sam had taken it off the hook the night before, so she cradled it gently and took a moment to organize her thoughts. If it was noon in New York, what time was it in California? She thought she would take the chance and picked up the receiver.

With the help of long-distance operators, Beth got the telephone number of one Matthew Foster in San Francisco, California. She dialed, and realized that her hands were not even shaking. She knew exactly what she was doing.

The line rang four times before it was picked up. A woman's voice with a foreign accent responded, "Hello, Foster residence."

Beth swallowed hard. "Is Matthew there, please?"

"No," said the woman, sounding businesslike in spite of her thick Hispanic accent. "Mr. Foster not here."

"Can you tell me where I can reach him?"

"He not here."

"Yes, I understand that. Could you tell me where he is?"

"Mr. Foster out of town for some days," said the voice, insisting. "He *not* here."

"*Where* is he?" Beth demanded, feeling foolish as well as frustrated.

"You wish to speak with him? He a long way away." Then, as an afterthought, the voice added, "Waldoor Hotel in New York."

"In New York?" Beth repeated, startled by the news. "He's in New York City?"

"At Waldoor Hotel."

"The Waldoor Hotel?" Beth asked, puzzled.

Behind her, Sam said, "The Waldorf."

Beth jumped, surprised that Sam had come into the room. She whirled around and almost cowered. He had pulled on his jeans, and he held his shirt in his free hand. When Beth sought his gaze, she found that his eyes were dark. Gone was the warmth and tenderness from the night before. As if it was the first time they had ever met, Sam's face was blank and controlled.

Distinctly, he said, "It's probably the Waldorf-Astoria. Ask."

Trembling at the look she'd seen on Sam's face, Beth returned to the telephone. The voice on the other end was squawking by that time, so Beth had to interrupt. "Do you mean the Waldorf-Astoria Hotel in New York City?"

"Yes, yes," said the woman. "Who is calling, please?"

"Thank you very much," Beth said breathlessly, and hung up the phone as quickly as possible. She kept her back to Sam this time.

"You didn't waste any time this morning, did you?" Sam asked.

"No, I didn't," Beth said steadily. "I want to get my life settled as soon as possible. You can understand that, can't you?"

Sam let out a tense breath. Then, coldly, he said, "I'll go take a shower. You can call him now, since you're in such a rush."

"That's not fair," Beth snapped, glancing over her shoulder at him.

But Sam had already started back toward the bathroom. "Is anything fair, Beth?"

"Sam!"

He turned, looking stubborn.

Beth held his eyes and said bluntly, "I can't make any promises, Sam, but I do love you. I want to be with you. I'd like to promise that I'll break my marriage and spend the rest of my life with you, but like you I can't make promises without being sure I can keep them." She paused and added, "But I want to try."

Sam's gaze sharpened, clearing abruptly.

Beth continued, "Let me find out what kind of situation I'm in, Sam. Then...then, I guess we'll have to see what becomes of you and me."

Sam's face lost some of its hardness. His body was suddenly less tense with the relief that swept over him. For a moment it looked as if he couldn't summon his voice, but then he said, "All right. Neither of us can promise anything at this point, can we?"

"No, Sam."

"All right," he murmured again, after a moment. "You've given me some hope, Beth. I can't let myself be happy yet, though. Do you understand?"

"Of course I do. I won't expect you to be cheerful, Sam." She tried to smile but failed miserably, so she said, "I hate this whole affair as much as you do."

Sam nodded curtly. He nearly said something more, but checked himself, then turned and left her alone in the room.

Beth did not chase after him. Her heart was thumping in her chest so hard she couldn't quite catch her breath for a moment. There was too much to get settled before she could draw an easy breath, that was all. She plunked down on the footstool and reached for the Yellow Pages. She was going to get this day over with as soon as possible.

The Waldorf answered promptly, and Beth heard her voice sounding queerly childish as she asked to be connected with Matthew Foster's room.

"Just a moment, please."

It was the longest moment of Beth's life.

Then the line clicked, and he answered, "Yes?"

For an instant Beth couldn't speak. She strained her ears, trying to discern some ring of familiarity in the single syllable she heard. Clutching the receiver with both hands, she asked, "Matthew Foster?"

There was a silence that matched hers before he queried oddly, "Bett?"

She gasped and closed her eyes, then said in a strangled voice, "Y-yes."

"God," he said. "We thought you had—I couldn't believe it. Are you—Bett, are you okay?"

"Yes, I'm fine." Foolishly, she said, "How are you?"

He laughed, sounding just as breathless as she. "Me? I guess I'm okay. I—the newspapers, though. Last night when I read about what happened—Bett, we had no idea what you'd been going through. I caught the first plane here this morning."

Beth opened her eyes and felt her pang of dismay turn into a real lump of fear. "You came to get me?"

"Well, somebody had to come. Your mother's a basket case, as usual, and your father thought he'd better stay with her until we found out how—"

"My mother?" Beth repeated, stunned by the prospect. Good heavens, she hadn't imagined that she'd have a real family!

The male voice paused and said curiously, "Oh, brother. It's true, isn't it? You don't remember anything?"

Beth's laugh was nervous. "Not a thing, I'm afraid. You're going to have to start from the very beginning with me."

"The very beginning?"

"From the start," Beth said, trying to manufacture some cheer. "I've only known my name for a couple of days, I think."

Hesitantly, as though he hadn't bargained for such an enormous task, Matthew Foster said, "Uh, well. I suppose—I guess we'd better get together, hadn't we? Have you had lunch yet?"

A lunch date with her husband. Somehow that seemed impossibly incongruous, and Beth was at a complete loss. "N-no, I haven't eaten yet."

"Well, uh, where are you? Near here?"

"I'm staying with a friend," Beth said composedly. "I could get a cab, though."

"A friend? Oh, the fellow who took you out of the hospital?"

"Yes, that's him," Beth said quickly. "Look, uh, Matthew, I'll come down there as soon as I can, all right? There are some things I guess we ought to talk about."

"Of course," said her husband. "I suppose you'll want some answers, won't you?"

"If I can think up some questions, yes."

He laughed at that, sounding surprised by her wry attempt at humor. "Yes, well, as soon as you can, then? I'll make a lunch reservation."

Beth hung up the phone, not sure how to say goodbye. She sat for a few minutes, listening to the shower run. It was going to be a very odd day.

Sam let Beth have the bathroom, but they didn't speak in passing. In a short while they were both dressed, and Beth went looking for Sam in the living room.

"I have to go his hotel," she explained to Sam without preamble. "Will you take me, please?"

Sam nodded curtly, and in a few minutes they were out on the street together. Sam waved once at the FBI agent who was stationed outside and then flagged down a passing cab. They climbed in together and didn't speak again for several minutes.

Finally, when they were close to their destination, Sam asked "Do you want me to come along?"

"No," Beth said quietly. "I can do it by myself. He wanted—we're going to have lunch."

"Lunch," Sam repeated, sounding derisive. "He's sounding very civilized, isn't he?"

"If you were in his shoes," Beth asked, trying to be tart, "what would you do, Sam?"

He glanced down at her and didn't blink. "As a matter of fact, I'd probably want to make love to you all afternoon."

That remark shut Beth up completely, and she hastily turned her face to the window. Sam was right, of course. That's exactly what he'd do. And what about this Matthew? The man had sounded almost perplexed on the phone. How was Matthew Foster going to react to the new Beth? Was she going to be very different from the woman he'd married? He had sounded almost afraid to see her. Did the prospect of leading an amnesia victim through the simplest steps of her life frighten him? Sam hadn't been daunted by the task, she remembered. He had enjoyed each of her small triumphs along the way to recovery. Would Matthew be so patient with her?

One thing Beth was sure of: she had better keep Sam as far away from Matthew Foster as possible. There was no telling what Sam might say, considering his mood. He was positively surly.

Of course, Beth reasoned, he didn't know that she was determined to return to him. He ought to at least have faith in her, she thought indignantly. Could he really believe she was so fickle?

The cab stopped, and Beth reached for the door handle at once.

"Wait," Sam exclaimed, thrusting some bills over the seat to the driver. "Beth—"

"I'll be finished in an hour," Beth told him, speaking over her shoulder. "I'd appreciate it if you'd meet me here then."

She had a fleeting impression of Sam staring after her. He asked, "Shall I come in after you if you're late?"

"I won't be late," Beth promised, as she walked toward the entrance of the hotel.

She'd come a long way, she thought as she entered the Waldorf's opulent lobby. She had been terrified of being left alone in the Baltimore airport, and now here she was marching into a fray of proportions that she couldn't imagine. And she wasn't even scared!

Well, perhaps a little.

In five minutes she was standing in front of room 605. She didn't have to raise her hand to knock. Matthew Foster was expecting her. He opened the door from within.

He was not as tall as Sam, but trim and feisty in appearance. His golden-boy hair was perfectly blow-dried, and he had a mustache that looked almost dapper. He was handsome, dressed in a three-piece suit that was undoubtedly Italian, with an immaculate red-striped tie that had a little gold pin thrust through its knot.

Beth felt a pang of hope, a sudden wish that she was going to look into his face and remember what this man had been to her. But no rush of pleasure overtook her. She sensed no recognition, and part of Beth felt suddenly very sad. She could not remember her own husband.

Matthew looked startled, and his watery blue eyes widened. "Bett? Good grief, it *is* you!"

"Hello," she said, trying to smile. She noted abruptly that he was appraising her clothing, an almost nondescript skirt and her heather-blue sweater—the outfit Beth thought her most flattering and certainly most comfortable. She knew Sam liked the color of the sweater, but this man seemed only startled by her dress. She suddenly wondered how out of style she might be. Such details hadn't mattered much to Sam, and certainly not to her.

"You look lovely," Matthew Foster breathed, correcting his faux pas promptly as he stepped back to allow her into the room. "Gorgeous, in fact. So different! You're wearing your hair differently. It's very nice. You look years younger."

Beth entered the room, keeping a generous distance between herself and this stranger without actually being conscious of her actions. "How did I used to wear my hair?"

"Up," he said, closing the door behind her. "Pulled back very tightly, in fact, but it showed those lovely cheekbones of yours to perfection. You're a classy lady, you know."

Beth took a quick cursory glance around the hotel room and then turned to study the man, looking serious. "I don't always feel like a classy lady any more. I'm pretty confused most of the time, in fact. Think you can stand me?"

He clasped his hands nervously in front of himself, and then behind, looking uneasy and not so sure he understood whether she was trying to be humorous or not. "Sure," he said with an atempt at cheerfulness. "I can stand it. Uh, would you like to sit own for a minute? Or should we just go to lunch?"

"I'd like to talk first, if you don't mind, um ..."

"Matt," he supplied when she hesitated over his name. "You alled me Matt. I'm Matthew to everyone else, of course, but ou ... Gosh, this is weird for me! Don't you remember a thing, eally?"

Beth smiled ruefully as she sat on the edge of the bed. "Imagine how weird it is for me. No, I don't remember a thing. Would ou mind if I asked just a few questions?"

"Ask away," he encouraged, again with a fervor that was just shade overzealous. He pulled out a Louis XIV-styled chair and at down. "I'm ready for anything."

Beth should probably have been puzzled by then, for her husband had made no overtures of affection, no warm expressions of elief. He was nervous, perhaps. Beth smiled again, trying to put im at ease. "Thank you. I'm curious about my family first, I hink. Could you ... ?"

"Of course," Matt said, and without more prompting he leasantly began to explain her family history.

Bettina Foster, nee Bettina Van Nuys, had been born and raised a California. She had two sisters, both younger, and her parents were still alive and presently living in the community of Brentwood. "Your father's in real estate," Matt said, as if that should xplain a great deal. "He was an Olympic athlete and now—"

"An athlete?"

"Yes, a bicyclist. You are too. Did you know?"

"Y-yes."

Matt continued. Bettina had held a job with the San Francisco magazine that Sam had already investigated, and Matt explained he circumstances of her disappearance.

"It was very odd," he allowed, eyeing her sideways, as if wary f her reaction. "I suppose we should have realized that something was wrong, Bett. You were planning on moving to New York to take a new job. Did you know?"

Beth jumped. "I was? *I* was? Alone, you mean?"

"Of course," Matt said, perhaps not noticing her perplexed uestion. He went on with his tale, saying, "You've always been plucky thing when it comes to your work. You took your two weeks of vacation time to come to the city to look for an apartment for yourself, and—"

"For myself?" Beth asked. What did he mean? Had they planned to commute between the coasts to keep up both their jobs?

"Yes," Matt said impatiently, trying to head off further questions before he got the whole story laid out. "You came apartment hunting and to look for some pictures, I gathered, for an upcoming piece in the magazine as a favor to the art director.

"That's why you were looking in galleries, I suppose. When you didn't come back to San Francisco on schedule, no one panicked. You are—were your own kind of woman, you see. You frequently acted as you saw fit, without consulting anyone. Your co-workers assumed you were doing something about your new job here, and didn't begin to get concerned until a week later which was almost three weeks after you'd been found in Pennsylvania. By then the publicity of the—of what happened to you had blown over, and none of us ever made the connection between you and this—this serial murder thing. We just assumed you'd gone ahead and taken the job here in New York and had decided not to return to San Francisco."

"You mean nobody thought to look for me?"

"Not for almost a month after you'd been—uh—attacked. By the time the company realized you hadn't cashed your paycheck and your landlord realized that no arrangements had been made about your apartment—why, it was just too late, I guess. Your parents started looking for you, but that was mostly in California, you see. You'd been—well, there was a man you'd been dating for a while and—"

"What?"

Matthew Foster looked at Beth, surprised, it seemed, by the vehemence in her tone. He said, "I beg your pardon?"

"I'd been *dating* someone?"

"Yes, should I have mentioned that? Your parents thought you might have gone sailing with him or something, even though you'd never seemed very serious about him. No one really thought you'd ever made it to New York, you see. We had no confirmation that you'd arrived here. It was a mixup, you understand. Your friends and family were looking for you, Beth. We were just looking in the

rong place. Then this whole thing blew up in the papers and—
ell! You can imagine how stunned we all were.''

"I can imagine, all right,'' Beth said, feeling more than a little
tunned herself. What kind of marriage did they have, anyway?

"And we were all horrified, of course,'' Matt said solicitously.
Bett, you and I have certainly had our differences, but I can't tell
ou how shocked I was by all this. You must have been—well, it
ust have been a terrible ordeal.''

"Yes,'' Beth said dryly. There was that word again. "An or-
eal, all right.''

"Well, it's over now, right? At least the worst part. Your fam-
y is dying to see you. Your mother sends her love—through me,
you can believe the irony of that! She wants you to call as soon
s you can. She'd like you to come home immediately, of course.''

Beth was silent, struggling with the questions still to be asked.
he wasn't sure exactly how to ask them yet.

"And your father is determined to make up and be friends, he
ays. He doesn't want to feud with you anymore, but you know
im! He'll say anything to please your mother. Margo is just as
lieved as your mother—''

"Margo?''

"Your sister. And Katie had her baby, so you're officially an
unt. And Abby sends her love, too, even though you've never
et.''

"Abby?'' Beth asked.

"My wife,'' said Matthew, very simply.

Beth stared.

"What's wrong?'' Matt asked, startled by her expression. "Are
ou—? Bett, good grief, don't faint!''

She nearly did, she realized later. She must have swayed and
oked deathly pale, and the next thing she remembered was Matt
rcing some water down her throat and patting her back rather
ntatively. He began to chatter like a nervous blue jay. "I never
alized! Good grief, of course! You imagined all this time that
ou and I—? That we still—? That our divorce was never—?''

Beth choked and stared up at Matthew Foster in amazement.

"My dear, I'm very sorry to shock you so badly. Didn't you
now, really? Bett, heavens, you and I have been divorced for two
ears.''

Beth held up her left hand, indicating her ring. "Then wh[?] this?"

"Good Lord," said Matt, still looking stricken. "You must b[?] still doing that old trick! You used to wear the ring when yo[?] traveled, my dear. You said it kept the riffraff away! You hated t[?] be bothered by single men on the prowl. Bett, I'm very sorry t[?] disappoint you!"

Beth couldn't stop herself. She threw her arms around Mat[?] thew Foster's neck and began to laugh and cry at the same time[?] "Oh, Matt, you've just made me the happiest woman in th[?] world!"

CHAPTER EIGHTEEN

"Now LOOK," said Matt when he had escorted her back down to the lobby of the hotel, lunch forgotten, "you've got my number, right?"

"Yes."

"And when you've got yourself settled, you'll call, okay? I've got a fabulous idea for you."

Beth linked her arm with Matt's, feeling comfortable enough with him to smile upward at him. "What idea?"

"A book. What do you think? I bet you'll have publishers eating down your door by nightfall. It'll be great—the story of what happened to you. When you've got the property ready, give me a buzz. We'll see if Hollywood's interested."

"Oh, Matt—"

"Don't reject the idea," he cautioned quickly. "After all, what are you going to do with your life now? You can't very well go back to your old job right away, can you? You've always been a good writer. You've got to think of the future, Beth."

She laughed and turned toward him. "I haven't thought any further ahead than this afternoon."

Matt grinned. "I'm sure this Sam character of yours will take the news of our divorce very well indeed. Say hello to him for me. Tell him he's certainly got my blessing."

"I'll tell him."

They hugged then, and it felt natural and good to Beth. She liked Matt Foster, all right. He wasn't her cup of tea anymore, but she could see why a woman might want to marry him. He was kind.

Beth met Matt's gaze one last time, smiling with him. Then, oddly, something stirred in her mind, like lacy curtains shifted by the merest spring breeze. It was her memory, Beth realized.

Somewhere inside her head, she could feel herself recognize Matt once her husband, once her lover, once her companion.

Almost instantly, though, the impression was gone, and Beth found herself smiling with a stranger.

They parted without any more words. Matt waved, watching her almost benevolently as Beth let herself out onto the street. Beth had a feeling that Matt liked her, too, though he hadn't expected to, she could tell. She wondered if perhaps Bettina Foster had not been a very nice person. Matt had been surprised by how nice she was now.

Well, she thought, all she wanted to be was Beth from now on, Beth Sheridan, in fact. Impulsively, Beth began to tug at the ring on her left hand. She started to walk.

There was Sam, standing half a block away, with his back to her. He wasn't moving, but he stood watching the street, the people, the busy lives that flowed around him like unchecked waters. He was at home here, breathing in the life that the city had to offer. Sam was thinking, Beth realized, as she walked toward him. He stood with his hands thrust deep in the pockets of his jeans watching the shoppers and the street people, the beggars and the hustling executives. He watched and absorbed and searched for his own place among these many souls.

She took three more steps and touched his back. Her palm slid familiarly downward until she'd caught her thumb on the back of his belt. Sam turned, almost in surprise, and looked down at her, his face not quite controlled.

"Hi," she said, though her voice was shaking so badly the syllable was hardly audible. She had a smile, though, one so big that her face was hurting. And her eyes sparkled with pleasure, too.

"Beth," was all he said. He caught her shoulders in his hands, turning her body to face his.

The sidewalk traffic pushed past them in a never-ending stream, but Beth didn't notice. She put out her hand, palm up to offer the gold wedding band. "Here," she said. "This is for you."

"What?" Sam took the ring automatically, his puzzlement giving way to barely checked excitement, she could see. His body tensed expectantly.

"I don't need it anymore. I haven't needed it for two years." Beth slipped her hands around Sam's waist and hugged him, her face tipped mischievously upward. It was going to be fun to tease

im a little. The tension was over. There was only wonderful
appiness to come. "Let's go get something to eat, Sam. Can you
nd that Hungarian place?"

"Beth—"

"Maybe they've got take-out. You did say, you know."

Sam put all the clues together, watching Beth's gaze as the flow
f triumphant delight dawned in his own eyes. He cupped her face
a his hand, as if it was the most beautiful treasure he'd ever seen.
n a voice that was indulgent, but half-choked with emotion, he
sked, "What did I say?"

"That you'd make love to me all afternoon," she answered
ghtly. "Remember? If a husband had been given back his wife,
e ought to make love to her all afternoon."

"Beth, darling Beth, is it true?"

"Will you have me?" she asked, hardly aware that her face was
urning with tears.

"I couldn't live without you. Trite, but true." Sam smoothed
er tears away gently and said, "I was ready to storm the Waldorf-
storia, damn the costs. Beth, I couldn't have let you go."

"I wouldn't have left you, Sam. I spent the morning rehears-
ag how I was going to tell my husband that I wasn't going to be
is wife anymore. Sam, I love you."

"Enough to marry me? For real this time? Forever?"

" 'Come live with me and be my love . . .' "

He laughed at once, delighted with her. "Yes, my love. I'll live
ith you. Starting now, with an afternoon we'll not forget."

Remembering Shakespeare, she teased him, " 'Tis a consum-
ation devoutly to be wished.' "

Still laughing, Sam turned her and they began to walk along the
dewalk, bumped by some passersby, but neither noticed. Sam
ut his arm across Beth's shoulders and looked at the ring in his
ther hand. "Do you know how much I hated this thing? A little
it of metal that stood between us, Beth."

"Not anymore, Sam. I'm yours."

Sam tossed the ring up, and caught it deftly once again. Then,
assing by a blind man who stood on the street corner, Sam
ropped the ring into the tin cup. He clasped Beth's hand, and
gether they stepped off the curb and started across the street. It
as crowded with people, just like in her dream. The throng
oved around them, and Beth felt the odd exhilaration of seeing

her dream come true again. Just like the cats, this intersection ha
been a vision in her mind time and again. But this time she ha
Sam by her side, her hand in his. She smiled to herself and walke
with him across the street. Across to a new life.

**American Romance invites you to celebrate
a decade of success....**

It's a year of celebration for American Romance, as we
commemorate a milestone achievement—10 years of
bringing you the kinds of romance novels you want to read,
by the authors you've come to love.

And we're not stopping now! In the months ahead, we'll be
bringing you more of the adventures of a lifetime... and
some superspecial anniversary surprises.

We've got lots in store, so mark your calendars to
join us, beginning in August, for all the fun of our
10th Anniversary year....

AMERICAN ROMANCE
We'll rouse your lust for adventure!

10-AN

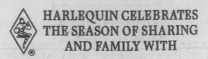

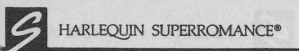

HARLEQUIN SUPERROMANCE®

HARLEQUIN SUPERROMANCE WANTS TO INTRODUCE YOU TO A DARING NEW CONCEPT IN ROMANCE...

WOMEN WHO DARE!
Bright, bold, beautiful ...
Brave and caring, strong and passionate ...
They're women who know their own minds
and will dare anything ... for love!

One title per month in 1993, written by popular Superromance authors, will highlight our special heroines as they face unusual, challenging and sometimes dangerous situations.

Dive into a whirlwind of passion and excitement next month with:
#562 WINDSTORM by Connie Bennett
Available in September wherever Harlequin Superromance novels are sold.

HARLEQUIN SUPERROMANCE®

THE MONTH OF LIVING DANGEROUSLY

LIVE ON THE EDGE WITH SUPERROMANCE AS OUR HEROINES BATTLE THE ELEMENTS AND THE ENEMY

Windstorm by Connie Bennett pits woman against nature as Teddi O'Brian sets her sights on a tornado chaser.

In Sara Orwig's *The Mad, the Bad & the Dangerous*, Jennifer Ruark outruns a flood in the San Saba Valley.

Wildfire by Lynn Erickson is a real trial by fire as Piper Hillyard learns to tell the good guys from the bad.

In Marisa Carroll's *Hawk's Lair*, Sara Riley tracks subterranean treasure—and a pirate—in the Costa Rican rain forest.

Learn why Superromance heroines are more than just the women next door, and join us for some adventurous reading this September!

HSML

Harlequin is proud to present our
best authors and their best books.
Always the best for your
reading pleasure!

Throughout 1993, Harlequin will bring you
exciting books by some of the top names in
contemporary romance!

In August,
look for
Heat Wave by

A heat wave hangs over the city....

Caroline Cooper is hot. And after dealing with crises all
day, she is frustrated. But throwing open her windows to
catch the night breeze does little to solve her problems.
Directly across the courtyard she catches sight of a man
who inspires steamy and unsettling thoughts....

Driven onto his fire
escape by the sweltering heat, lawyer Brendan Carr
is weaving fantasies, too—around gorgeous Caroline.
Fantasies that build as the days and nights go by.

Will Caroline and Brendan dare cross the dangerous
line between fantasy and reality?

Find out in HEAT WAVE by Barbara Delinsky...
wherever Harlequin books are sold.

Calloway Corners

In September, Harlequin is proud to bring readers four
involving, romantic stories about the Calloway sisters,
set in Calloway Corners, Louisiana. Written by four of
Harlequin's most popular and award-winning authors,
you'll be enchanted by these sisters and the men
they love!

MARIAH by Sandra Canfield
JO by Tracy Hughes
TESS by Katherine Burton
EDEN by Penny Richards

As an added bonus, you can enter a sweepstakes contest
to win a trip to Calloway Corners, and meet all four
authors. Watch for details in all Calloway Corners books
in September.

CAL93

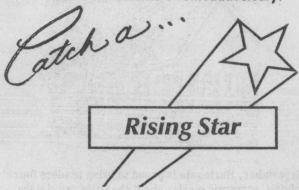